D1465834

READER'S DIGEST

CONDENSED BOOKS

FIRST EDITION

THE READER'S DIGEST ASSOCIATION LIMITED
25 Berkeley Square, London W1X 6AB

THE READER'S DIGEST ASSOCIATION
SOUTH AFRICA (PTY) LTD
Reader's Digest House, 130 Strand Street, Cape Town

Printed in Great Britain by Petty & Sons Ltd, Leeds
Members of the BPCC Group

Original cover design by Jeffery Matthews FSIAD

For information as to ownership
of copyright in the material in this book see last page.

Reader's Digest
CONDENSED BOOKS

GOLDENROD
Herbert Harker

SURPRISE PARTY
William Katz

THIS TIME NEXT WEEK
Leslie Thomas

AT THE GOING DOWN OF THE SUN
Elizabeth Darrell

COLLECTOR'S LIBRARY EDITION

In this Volume:

GOLDENROD
by Herbert Harker (p.9)

Jesse Gifford had once been a champion bronco rider, admired by all and with a wife who loved him. Now, his career ended by a broken pelvis, his wife living with another man, he goes from one menial job to another, desperately trying to earn enough to keep his two small sons. But when self-respect has gone the spirit is weak, and it seems as if all the fight has gone out of Jesse. Only a memory of the love he once had keeps him going, and the hope that somehow he might win that love again. His struggle to survive makes a moving story of heroism rediscovered and love reaffirmed.

SURPRISE PARTY
by William Katz (p.85)

Samantha's eight months of marriage to Marty Shaw have been pure bliss. Now, for his fortieth birthday party, she's planning a special surprise, seeking out teachers and old friends to send birthday reminiscences. But as she digs into his past, amazingly she finds nothing: no records, no memories of a man named Marty Shaw. The more she probes, the more questions remain unanswered. Just who *is* her husband? And why has he covered his tracks so thoroughly? What secret is he trying to hide? A taut thriller of almost unbearable suspense.

THIS TIME NEXT WEEK

by Leslie Thomas (p.203)

Their father dead, their mother gravely ill, Leslie Thomas and his little brother knew only that their train would be met "by a man from Dr. Barnardo's". So began a journey into the unknown that separated the two and brought Leslie to a London orphanage during the last years of the war. And as the bombs fell the young boy faced his lot with courage and humour, discovering fun and companionship in his new life, and learning that joy can be found almost anywhere. . . . A touching, true story from a bestselling author.

AT THE GOING DOWN OF THE SUN

by Elizabeth Darrell (p.291)

For the Sheridan brothers, born to wealth and privilege, the coming of World War I irrevocably changes their lives. Roland, the devoted country squire, is forced to leave his beloved Dorset estate for the horrors of the trenches. Rex, carefree and cavalier, joins the Royal Flying Corps, where his heroic exploits soon become legendary. And Chris, the young scholar, is faced by terrors that could break his mind. This memorable saga of three men and the women who love and wait for them is a stirring novel written in the very grandest tradition.

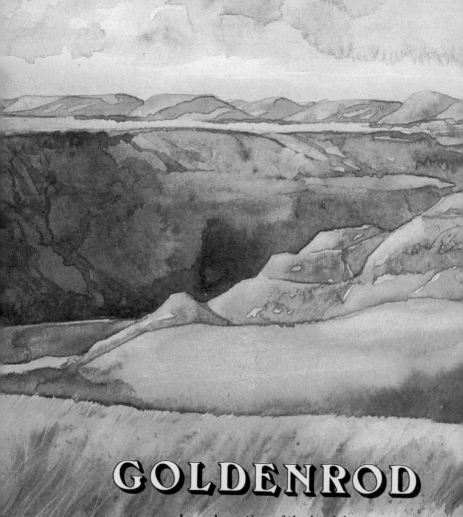

GOLDENROD

A condensation of the book by
HERBERT HARKER

Illustrated by Alain Massicotte

Published by Random House, New York

Jesse Gifford, once a champion bronco rider and king of rodeo, is now a loser.

Tormented by the lingering agony of a broken pelvis, his spirit defeated by the loss of his wife to another, more successful rider, he drifts in a world of small humiliations and increasing despair. But he has two young sons who love him more than he can love himself—and who long to admire him again. It is through their faith and courage that Jesse finds the strength to go on and, ultimately, to triumph.

Set in the wide open spaces of western Canada, this is a story of bravery and human frailty . . . and of a love that will not let go.

Chapter 1

Jesse and his boys had travelled for three days. Now it was evening again, and as he looked back across the distance they had come, Jesse saw their long-legged shadows ripple over the uneven prairie behind them. He was weary beyond feeling. The numbness of his body was intensified by the ache that hung inside him, swinging with the motion of the saddle. Sometimes that ache seemed suspended from his heart and sometimes from his broken pelvis.

"Boys," he said, "we should be there soon."

The piebald Shetland that jogged beside his horse carried his two sons. The one who rode behind was half as old, and looked about half as big, as the one in the saddle. "Are we going to sleep in a bed tonight?" the older boy asked.

"Tonight we sleep in style," Jesse replied. "John Tyler Jones'll probably bed us down on feather mattresses."

The wind had stopped and a hush came over the prairie with the going down of the sun. The saddles creaked in cadence, the bridles clinked, the horses' hooves fell in jagged syncopation on the sod. Beneath them lay the river valley, broad and shadowed, with the white skein of water tangled among the trees. An owl swept out of the darkness, directly at them, arced, and with an almost processional beat of wings, faded swiftly into the prairie. To the east, the distant hills still held the light.

As the riders forded the river and came up on the flat, they saw a few buildings set among the trees and the dim outline of a corral. A dog barked.

"Shut up, Spider!" a man's voice said. The barking paused, and then began again, moving closer. When they had passed him, the dog fell in behind them, silent.

The man was standing beside the corral gate. As they stopped in front of him, the big horse lowered its head with a weary snort.

"I'm looking for the Jones ranch," Jesse said. "John Tyler Jones."

The man replied, "Who do you think you're talking to?"

Jesse leaned forward in his saddle, squinting at the man. "I didn't recognize you there against the light." He got off his horse, and extended his hand to J.T. Jones. "Your directions brought us out right on the nail." He motioned to the boys. "Climb down, fellows. This is the place, all right. J.T., I'd like you to meet my boys." As they came to stand beside him, he said, "This is Ethan. And the little fellow is George."

J.T. Jones said, "What do you mean, this is the place?"

"I mean this is the place we've been travelling three days to reach. I told you I'd be here Wednesday but I had some business to straighten out."

"I ever seen you before?" J.T. Jones asked.

Jesse took off his hat. "It's Jesse Gifford," he said.

"Jesse Gifford?"

"Saturday night," Jesse explained. "In the Alexander Hotel in Lethbridge. You gave me a job bronc-bustin'."

"Saturday night?" J.T. Jones repeated.

"You were my long-lost brother on Saturday night. You had just the spot for a man like me."

"Bronc-bustin'," J.T. said. "What would I want with a bronc-buster?"

The words were as cruel as bullets. "You really don't remember?" Jesse asked.

"Mister," J.T. said, "if I was in Lethbridge on Saturday night, I was drunk. And if I was drunk, who knows what I said?"

"Then you don't have a job?"

"I start haying in a week or two. I can use a man then."

"When I bust broncs, that's all I do," Jesse said. "And I get fifty bucks a month."

J.T. laughed. "And when was the last time you busted broncs?"

It had been five years ago—on a windblown camp way out on the Milk River Ridge. "There's not too much call for my kind of work any more," Jesse admitted. "Why else do you think I'd leave a good job wrangling and ride three days to get here?"

10

"You quit your job?" J.T. exclaimed. "If you take my advice, you'll turn right around and go get it back."

Jesse could hear San Soucie laugh if he ever showed up there again. And that pompous Frenchman would probably hire him back, just so he could dig his spurs in Jesse's flanks some more. "You need a man for haying?" Jesse said.

"That's right," J.T. replied. "I'll need a man, but that doesn't start for a week or so."

"Is there some place hereabouts we could live till then? All we need is a stove and a roof."

"You claim you rode out here on my say-so," J.T. said. "Maybe you did. I've done some fool things when I was drunk. Move into the old Hazlett place, and when haying starts, I'll give you a job."

Jesse and the boys ate supper with John Tyler Jones—except that George fell asleep on his chair before he'd taken three bites—and then J.T. directed them to the old Hazlett place, half a mile down the river. When they got there, they found a two-room shack with the door partly open. As they clumped inside, Ethan with the lantern and Jesse carrying George, they heard mice skitter for the corners. In the second room were two board beds fastened to the walls, and Jesse laid George on one of them. Then, while Ethan tended the horses, Jesse untied the ungainly bedroll from behind his saddle and carried it into the kitchen. There, by lantern light, he dismembered it—kettles, winter coats, clothing, and a variety of ragged quilts and blankets. Within a few minutes they were lying in bed, Jesse on one side of the narrow room and the boys on the other.

Presently Ethan said, "Do you think Mama will come back, Jesse?"

"No. I don't think so."

"It was sure fun to live with her, wasn't it? I mean, when we were all together?"

"It sure was."

"Dammit, I miss her."

"She wouldn't want you talking that way."

"Then why doesn't she come home and stop me?"

"She's not coming home."

"She might. You don't know what she's going to do, Jesse."

That had been proved well enough. "No, I don't."

"So. She might come back."

Jesse looked across the room. "Goodnight, Ethan," he said.

The boy did not reply. Perhaps he was asleep already. Jesse raised his arm across his eyes and turned his face to the wall. It had been years now—two years—since he had seen Shirley, and still the hollow of his body felt as tender as a wound where some part has been torn away. "Oh, God," he breathed. He himself could not have said if it was a curse or a prayer.

Chapter 2

The next day Jesse was awake shortly after daylight. He did not get up at once, but lay looking at the spot the sun made on the wall above the boys' bed. The interior of the house was not bad—cobwebs and dust of course, but saved from gloom by the skim of whitewash that someone had brushed on it, perhaps years before. It was home now anyway—for how long, he could not even guess.

He had been at San Soucie's for four years. Each day for four years he had felt a small diminishment, as if another drop of vital force had seeped away. And he had seen clearly the husk that would be left after the force was gone. He had seen it in Lars, the chore boy at San Soucie's, sixty, dry and bent as an old pea pod, grey-coloured, muttering. Lars now, but in ten years his name would be Jesse.

He couldn't have survived at San Soucie's. Even now he wondered if he had got away in time, for he felt a great weariness in every limb. But he wasn't old yet. All he needed was a little rest, a chance to get his head up.

He left the boys asleep, saddled his horse, Czar, and headed towards Lone Rock, his hat slanted over his eyes. Besides the need for some groceries, he felt a hankering for adult companionship. In his heyday he had had more friends than he could count—cowboys, ranchers, newspapermen. Then had come the ride on Sundown—the ride that would win him another championship. The ride, and the lost stirrup, and Sundown's hoof in the small of his back, and for months afterwards nothing but misery and the slow erosion of people he had called friends.

When he got to the prim green town with its grain store standing over it, the shop was not yet open. He squatted on the step, or walked up and down the board sidewalk, as the cool air of early morning was slowly dispersed by the wind from the mountains. Finally, a tall humped man unlocked the door from the inside, then walked behind the counter. Jesse bought flour, sugar, coffee, bologna sausage, potatoes, canned vegetables, butter, bacon, evaporated milk, eggs, and a loaf of bread as a treat for the boys.

For some reason Jesse always felt good when he was spending money. He'd managed to save almost two hundred dollars while he was at San Soucie's, but a bank account never gave him any satisfaction. Only now, as he peeled a ten-dollar bill off the roll in his pocket, did money seem to have any relation to his life. It seemed now, in the act of parting with it, to purify him somehow as if, along with the money, he was sloughing off unhappy memories and fears for the future.

He whistled as he rode out of town. The warm wind blew out of the mountains behind him and seemed to push him along, so that almost before he knew it he was headed down the river hill towards his home. The shack was long and narrow, with a low-pitched roof. Chop out the jungle of weeds which surrounded it, put in a couple of lilac bushes, give it a coat of paint and a little furniture, and it would make a home good enough for any man.

J.T. Jones's car was parked in front. At the gate, Jesse got off Czar, took down his box of groceries from the back of the saddle, and started towards the house. George came running down the path. "Did you get some bologna?" he asked.

"Yes. I got some bologna."

"Can we have breakfast now?"

"Yes, sir. Right now. I'm hungry as a bear."

"*Rowr!* Me too," George said.

When Jesse walked into the house, Ethan and J.T. Jones were sitting opposite each other on the beds in the back room. "Howdy, J.T.," he said, putting the grocery box on the table.

J.T. came to the kitchen doorway. "Hello, Jesse," he said.

"Have you had breakfast?"

"Long ago," J.T. replied. "Did you ever drive a tractor?"

Jesse loathed tractors. He never knew what to expect from them, or what to do if they stopped. They were noisy and smelly. "Sure," he said. "San Soucie had three tractors." He set the frying pan and the coffeepot on the stove, and took bacon, eggs and coffee from his box.

"I've got summer fallow needs working," J.T. went on. "Take about three days. I'll pay you two dollars a day, seven till seven."

"You want me to start this morning?" Jesse asked.

"No," J.T. replied. "My cultivator's broke. I've got to go to

Macleod tomorrow and get it welded. You can start the next day—no, that's Sunday. Start Monday morning."

"I'll be there. How's chances to go to Macleod with you?"

"Sure. I'll pick you up."

George had been unloading the grocery box. "Oh boy," he cried. "Baker's bread."

The bacon and eggs were frying now, all scrambled together in the frying pan. J.T. walked towards the front door. "See you tomorrow."

"This coffee's about ready," Jesse said. "Might as well stop and have a cup."

J.T. paused. "Maybe I will. That bacon sure smells good, too. Truth is, didn't eat much breakfast. Too early."

"There's plenty," Jesse said. "Get some plates down, Ethan. We'll have to go in the bedroom to sit down, though. There isn't room in here for all of us." He scooped the eggs onto a tin plate, then returned the pan to the stove and fried four slices of bread. Within moments they were sitting on the beds, tin plates of hot food in their hands and cups of coffee at their feet.

"Tastes good." J.T. sat chewing, and looking around the room. Jesse followed his gaze. Cobwebs still clustered in the ceiling corners. Clumps of overalls and jackets hung from nails on the wall.

"We haven't cleaned house yet," Jesse said. "That's the first thing on the list this morning."

"It's hard for a man alone," J.T. agreed. "Nine years since I buried the missus. It's been hard."

Between the beds was a wooden table which held a red bandanna, a hunting knife, the stump of a pencil, some horseshoe nails and a Bible. In the midst of it all stood a small oval picture frame with a photograph of Shirley, her eyes deeply shadowed by lashes, her hair falling across her cheek.

"She looks pretty young," J.T. Jones said at last.

"She was when that was taken," Jesse said.

"What did she die of?"

"She isn't dead."

After a minute Ethan said, "She ran off with another man."

J.T.'s eyes darted to meet Jesse's, and then away again quickly. "Oh," he said.

Jesse knew what he was thinking. Something like: My wife died. The Lord took her. I couldn't help that. But let some mortal man fool around with her, and he would have been dead. And she with him. It was the way they all thought—the hands at San Soucie's, the boys in town. They all said something like, "Gee, Jesse. That's tough." But what they thought was: What kind of man are you?

J.T. wiped his plate with a piece of toast and put it in his mouth. Then he drank the rest of his coffee. "Thanks," he said. He set his cup carefully in the middle of his plate, as though it were the least he could do to bring order into the world, then spoke with calm deliberation. "I always figured a man can make his choice between a beautiful woman and a faithful one." He stood, holding the cup firmly in place. "Mine were faithful," he said. "Both of 'em." He walked out through the kitchen. They heard the door close, heard the car start, and saw it drive by the window, back up the hill.

"Let's go hunting," Ethan said. "Get some meat for dinner."

"Maybe, after a while," Jesse said. "You fellows go outside and play. I want to clean up the house."

Jesse sat on the bed, alone: I'd have killed 'em both, if it was me. That was what they all thought and that's the first thing Jesse had thought, too. He had taken his hunting knife and gone after them.

There'd been no warning, or at least he hadn't read the signs. He came home after work one night and found the fire out in the kitchen stove, and the boys playing alone in the living room. The house held an emptiness as heavy as death. He knew she'd gone.

"I'm hungry," Ethan had said. "Where's Mama?"

"Didn't she tell you where she was going?" Jesse asked.

"She just told us to go down and play in the gully. When we came back she was gone."

She didn't leave a note. He looked for one, offhandedly at first, as if it didn't matter, then more earnestly. And all night, as he searched, he seemed to remember little remarks she'd made that might have warned him if he had listened.

Before the sun was up he woke Ethan, and told him to stay out of school and look after George until he got back. And he'd gone after them, the scabbard strapped to his belt, his hand touching the knife. For a while he tried to pretend that she had gone alone, that she had only wanted to get away for a day or two. But she couldn't have gone alone.

It took him all day on the train to get to Calgary. And when, wandering the city' streets in the early morning, he came across Keno's Buick parked in front of the Empress Hotel, he knew he'd found them.

Bile. Bile in his throat. Choked by it. Up the hotel steps and in through the big glass doors. The sleepy-looking clerk. The room number. The clerk awake now. The room number. Three fifty-one. The stairs, two at a time. The long hall. The doors, like mileposts. Three hundred and forty-nine miles. Three hundred and fifty miles. Three hundred and fifty-one miles. The feel of the knife on his hip. The quiet tap on the door. Keno's voice. The tap again. Waiting. The hard handle of the knife in his palm, but the blade still in its sheath. The boots crossing the floor. Boots! Boots at eight in the morning? Did he sleep in his boots? The door open a crack. Keno's eye. The door swinging wide. Keno naked to the waist. Keno's striped trousers and black boots, a duster in his hand.

"Well," Keno said. "We sure didn't expect to see you." He turned back into the room. "Look who's here."

He followed Keno into the room. Shirley was lying in bed, her shoulders bare. She turned her face away, and slipped deeper under the covers. Keno put his right boot on a chair and rubbed the cloth across the toe, back and forth. "What brings you to town?"

Jesse could see the muscles moving along the broad white back as Keno rubbed. He wondered just where the knife blade should enter to strike the heart. He knew he should act quickly, but he glanced towards Shirley.

"Get out of here," she said, and pulled the blankets over her head. He'd known where her heart was; even under the covers, he'd be able to find it. But as he stood looking at the bed, his anger all drained out through the soles of his feet.

Keno gave a final wipe with his cloth and stood up. Jesse didn't look at his face again. In the first glance he had memorized it. He would never forget that face, the face of the champ.

Chapter 3

That afternoon, when Jesse had finished sweeping the house, he untied one of the bundles that lay in a corner and took out three shotgun shells. "How about fresh meat for supper?" he said.

George came running in his bare feet. "You bet!"

Shotgun in hand, Jesse walked with George down the path through a forest of sunflowers to the log stable that stood against the fence. Jesse looked around him. The homestead rested between the river and the hill, screened by a cottonwood grove from a view of the water, but still permeated by the gentle sound of it. Far up the valley he could see the pale blue tops of the mountains, still with a few remnants of snow.

Ethan came up. "We're going hunting," George said.

"Hunting for what?" Ethan asked.

"Whatever strikes your fancy," Jesse said.

"Partridge pie, rabbit stew . . ."

They started towards the river. Above the gravel bar, they stopped to skip rocks on a quiet pool. Then they began to hunt seriously, walking a few feet apart through the trees and bushes, parallel to the river. "Quiet," Jesse cautioned them.

"Here," George cried, and clapped his hand over his mouth. Then he whispered, loudly, "Quick, Jesse. Here. Quick."

But when Jesse got there, he could see nothing. "What is it?"

George pointed. "A rabbit. He went right into those bushes."

"You fellows stay behind me," Jesse said. He moved forward, bending low between the bushes, shotgun ready. There was a flurry in the grass to his right. As he turned, a rabbit hopped into sight then stopped, head high, ears alert. Jesse raised his shotgun and squeezed the trigger. Nothing. The rabbit still sat there.

"Shoot him," Ethan hissed. "Why don't you shoot him?"

Jesse lowered his gun. "Shh," he said. He had forgotten to load. "He's not very big. Maybe he'll lead us to another one."

"Shoot him," Ethan cried, and at the sharp sound of his voice, the rabbit darted away. "Why didn't you shoot him?"

But George was tugging on Jesse's sleeve, pulling him back the way they had come. Jesse looked where George pointed. In the brown, tangled grass and dead branches, Jesse saw the crouched body of a baby rabbit, its ears pressed flat against its furry back—absolutely motionless. "Please don't shoot him," George whispered.

"He's not big enough to be any good, anyway," Jesse replied.

"He's so cute," George said. "I wish I could take him home. He'll die if we leave him here."

"That was his mother that hopped away," Jesse said. "She'll come back as soon as we're gone."

George crouched, staring at the tiny creature. Its fur was so soft that it seemed to riffle even in the motionless air beneath the bush. But its eyes did not move, nor any part of its body. George bent over it. "Poor little fella." He reached with his hand, closer and closer, repeatedly stopping, then moving it yet closer. At last he touched the rabbit and began to stroke its fur. "See! He likes me."

"Can you feel his heart beating?" Jesse asked.

"Yeh. It's going so fast!"

"That's 'cause he's so scared. Come on now, let's leave him alone."

They started away, but George stopped. "Can I wait until his mother comes? To guard him?"

"She won't come as long as we're here," Ethan said.

Reluctantly George went on and, as they walked, Jesse loaded his gun. They were out of the trees by the river when a flock of partridge flew up almost at their feet. The sudden trill and whirr of wings startled them but, almost as a reflex, Jesse brought up his gun and fired twice. One bird, then another, fell to the ground. "Well, boys," Jesse said. "Roast partridge for supper." They picked the birds up and set off towards the house.

As Jesse walked round a clump of purple birch, he saw a cow among the shadows, her tail switching intermittently, her face bland, her eyes on Jesse.

"I bet I can ride her," Ethan said. The cow lowered her head.

"Ride her?"

"Sure. I've got to get practised up for the stampede, haven't I?"

The idea took Jesse by surprise. Years ago he and Ethan had talked of little except the stampede, but for a long time now they hadn't mentioned it. Jesse said, "You're too young."

"Not any more, I'm not. This year I'm twelve."

Jesse had raised his son to be a cowboy, but now he wasn't sure. "I tell you what," Jesse said. "If you can ride that old blister, I'll let you enter the stampede. But if she throws you, we all stay home and put up hay for J.T. Jones."

"All right," Ethan said. "As long as I get a surcingle, I'll ride that rooster till the sun goes down."

"Go and get your surcingle, then." Ethan started off at a run, back towards the house. "Bring the lariat, too," Jesse called after him. He put his partridges down on the grass and sat beside them with his back against a tree.

George came and sat near him. "Aren't we going to eat?"

"After the stampede. Ethan's putting on a stampede for us."

Ethan came back wearing spurs and gauntlets, a coiled lariat over his shoulder and a soft halter rope in his hand. Several cattle had drifted close, surrounding them with the sounds of crunching grass and snapping twigs. "Where is she?" he asked.

"Over behind that tree," Jesse said. "With blood in her eye."

Ethan dropped the halter rope beside Jesse. As he walked

towards the cow he shook out his lariat loop. The cow looked at him suspiciously. Then she swung away, and the boy threw the rope in one swift motion. As the cow plunged to escape, she ran into the loop, pulling the rope tight and yanking Ethan almost out of his boots. Running, he swung as wide as he could round a tree. The rope whirred round the tree trunk, pulling the boy back in a straight course behind the running cow. But the brush with the tree cost him so much rope that he was getting dangerously close to the end of it. The trotting cow changed direction just enough to give Ethan a little slack. He raced to one side again, round another tree, playing out what rope he had left as he went until the rope was a full turn around the rough tree trunk. The cow hung back at the other end, eyes rolling. Jesse ambled up with George running behind.

While George drove the cow closer with a stick, Jesse and Ethan pulled in the rope until the cow's jaw was neatly fitted round the trunk of the tree. While Ethan held her, Jesse tied the surcingle behind her front legs. "Well," Jesse said, "now you've got her, what you going to do with her?"

Ethan was puffing. "I'm going to ride her," he said.

"You sure picked a dandy," Jesse said.

The cow was becoming more uneasy. Jesse held the lariat and Ethan walked quietly to her side. Surcingle in his left hand, he stood back, stepped and jumped, swinging his right leg high, and landed on her back. He clasped the rope firmly with both hands, knuckles down. "Let 'er buck," he said.

Jesse loosened the rope from the tree and from the cow's neck, snatching the loop over her horns. Then Ethan's spurs landed in her ribs, and he cried, "Hee—yi!"

The cow's first jump was a reflex; but then, finding herself free from the rope, she lowered her head and plunged upwards. Jesse had a glimpse of Ethan's face, both frightened and bemused. Off flew his hat, and the boy's dark hair flipped back and forth. The cow bucked in an irregular circle, her head towards the centre. With every jump she threw her hindquarters high, at the same time twisting them first to one side and then the other. The boy's body flowed with the movement of the cow, as though his legs were fused so close to her sides that he could feel through the hide each signal of her intention.

Jesse felt a peculiar blend of exultation and dismay. He remembered the thrill—so old that he had almost forgotten it—of his own first ride on a full-grown steer. That thrill had been the initial infection. The disease which followed brought alternating attacks of gaiety, and despair so profound that he would not wish it on anybody, least of all his own son. But he knew that now it was too late to alter the direction Ethan had taken.

At last Jesse shouted, "OK! OK!" Ethan closed his legs above the cow's shoulders and jumped clear, jerking the knot so that the rope would loosen and drop off. He landed on his feet, but the thrust of the cow's lunge was too great, and he pitched to the ground.

George ran to his brother. Jesse walked over to pick up the halter rope where it had slipped to the ground. The cow stood a short distance away, looking back at him with her head held slightly high. "Well!" Ethan cried, "I guess we go to the stampede, eh?"

"I guess we do," Jesse agreed.

"Why don't you enter again, Jesse?"

"Me?" Jesse laughed. "I'm too old for that stuff. Let's go eat now."

WHEN J.T. CALLED at the shack on Saturday morning, Jesse was ready to go. He got into the new Dodge and pulled the door; it closed with a solid *chunk*. The car moved away as if drawn by a silent, invisible hand. Jesse looked down at his boots, grey against the shiny rubber floor mat. The toes were worn through completely, and from each hole sprouted a little tuft of fuzzy lining. He glanced at J.T. The little man's eyes barely cleared the rim of the steering wheel. He didn't look at Jesse and he didn't speak. For all a person could tell, he was alone.

As they drove up in front of the Queen's Hotel in Macleod, Jesse said, "Let me buy you a beer."

J.T. looked at him. "If you got any money, you spend it on somethin' for your kids," he said.

"Listen, I've got some money, and I'm no sponger. You give me a trip to town, I buy you a beer. Anything wrong with that?"

"I guess not," J.T. said, and he went with Jesse into the beer parlour.

"Any idea what time you'll be going home?" Jesse asked.

"An hour or so. As soon as I get this tow bar welded." J.T. added, "I can't wait, though."

As soon as his beer came, he drank it. Then for the first time he looked at Jesse, deliberately, his eyes travelling slowly from feature to feature, as though Jesse were some kind of exhibit. "Stand up," he said. Jesse stood up. J.T. bent over and looked at his stomach. "Where'd you get the belt buckle?"

Jesse liked his belt. It was the only decent piece of clothing he owned—hand-tooled leather two and a half inches wide, with a silver-mounted buckle as big as a postcard. The buckle was embossed with the head of a longhorn steer, and engraved to Jesse Gifford, Saddle Bronc Champ.

J.T. was still bent over, studying the buckle. "How come I never seen it before?"

"I don't wear it every day," Jesse explained.

J.T. straightened up and looked Jesse in the eye. "Well, I'll be damned," he said. "You're Jesse Gifford."

"I told you I was, the first time I saw you."

"I knew I'd heard the name," J.T. said, "but I couldn't place it. It's been a while, you know."

"Yes, it has."

"I was on the board of the Southern Alberta Co-op the year they gave that trophy. I helped pick it out." He sat down and filled his glass from Jesse's bottle. "How come you quit riding?"

"I broke my pelvis," Jesse said. "It never knit properly."

J.T. said, "There's money in that game. Did you ever think of going back to it?"

"Sure."

"Well, why don't you?"

It was a fair question. Jesse couldn't answer it, even to himself. In his day he had broken arms, legs, ribs, ankles—even his jaw—but he had always managed to come back and ride again. The pelvis had been different. He was able to walk again, but his spirit never seemed to recover. "It's hard, with the boys," he explained. "I can't leave them and I can't take them with me. And it keeps me scratching just to put food on the table. I can't go stampeding."

"I got an idea," J.T. said, after another pause. "Let's you and me be partners. I'll pay you wages, starting today. Good wages. Thirty dollars a month. When there's a stampede on, we'll go stampedin'. When there ain't, you work for me."

Jesse tried not to get excited. This was John Tyler Jones talking— the same man who gave him a job as bronc-buster. "You don't have to worry about the boys," J.T. went on. "We'll make arrangements to take care of them."

Jesse asked, "Are you drunk?"

"You're worried about that thing in Lethbridge? I was drunk then. Right now I'm sober as a prophet. I put up the money and you put up the know-how, and we split the winnings. Of course, we might never make a dime. But I'm willing to do it, as a sort of favour, you see."

"Don't do me any favours. I'll give you twenty-five per cent."

J.T. snorted. "You'll give me! You won't give me a thing—'cause you haven't a thing to give. You're stranded, mister."

J.T. was right. He didn't have to negotiate. He had his thousand acres and his cattle, and if he never saw Jesse again, he wouldn't be hurt. Jesse wasn't so lucky. "I don't know," Jesse said. "I'm not sure my back could take it."

"I tell you what," J.T. said. "It's the Stavely Stampede today. Let's take a run up there. You try it out, and then we'll decide."

The idea appealed to Jesse. There wouldn't be anybody at the Stavely show—all the name cowboys and best bucking stock were in Cheyenne this week. Jesse could slip in quietly and try his spurs on some old range horse against a bunch of novices. Who could tell—they might even win a couple of bucks.

"OK," Jesse said. "And then we'll decide."

BY THE TIME they came out of the beer parlour, Jesse felt that there wasn't a man he couldn't lick; there wasn't a horse he couldn't ride.

They got in the Dodge and started off for Stavely, forty miles north. "You're a lucky man, John Tyler Jones," Jesse said. "You just made the best deal of your life. I got a special gift. When I was just a kid I could watch a horse's ears and tell what he'd be like to ride, and when I straddled him my bones knew what to do, like they were born to it.

To the west he could see the Porcupine Hills, with the tops of the distant mountains just showing above them. Under the wheels of the Dodge the ground rushed by. "Yes sir, J.T., there's not an animal dressed in horsehide that I can't fan till his tail drops off. Next week is the Macleod Stampede. Then Raymond, and Calgary. You're in for a summer, J.T., I tell you that. You can hire Indians to put up your hay. With what you'll be making, you could hire the Prince of Wales and still be money ahead, eh, pardner?"

"We're not partners yet," J.T. reminded him. "Not till you fan that first bronc."

The road ran straight, leading them north where the distant prairie was blurred by the wind and blowing dust. The sun gave the dust an amber tinge, so the earth seemed wrapped in clouds of powdered gold. While they were still miles away, the grain stores at Stavely rose out of the mist, three great square-shouldered sentinels, sounding the alarm: "Jesse Gifford's coming! Sixteen feet high, with eyes like furnace doors. Iron skin and granite bones. Run, you cowboys! Jesse Gifford's coming!"

Stavely was a thin Y of dirt roads set against the railway track, with stunted trees and houses as grey as the road. Today, the town was filled with people. People walking, people in cars, people on horseback, drifting up and down, waving banners, honking their horns.

"I need a drink," Jesse said.

"Getting nervous?" J.T. asked. "You don't have to worry. Nobody'll remember you."

The car pulled up on the grass behind the grandstand. Jesse climbed out and stretched on his toes, hands above his head. Twenty feet high, with arms like bear traps. J.T. walked like a two-legged puppy dog, and Jesse strode after him, the people swirling around his knees like water.

Sound and colour, dust and turmoil; cowboys swinging small looped lariats against the wind; bucking bulls with bells a-clanging; names called through a megaphone—names nobody had heard of. Moaning horses wrapped in yellow chaps, horses made with stiff front legs for stamping hoofprints in the earth; other cowboys, old and broken, the scars of their bodies showing in their eyes. "Hello, Jesse. What you doin' here?" "Hungry for a bit of gravel?"

More painful to be remembered than forgotten. Jesse Gifford shrinks. Hands in pockets, he pulls up to hold himself tall, but still he shrinks. A kid in yellow chaps drops down into the chute. The man with the megaphone says, "Jack Tatum on Blue Angel!" The clang of the chute, and Blue Angel floats out like a dancer, lands with a jolt that breaks the kid loose from his saddle, his hat loose from his head; still he clings, riding her neck it seems, first on one side, then the other; the kid is clear, spread-eagled, floating, shirt a flutter in the wind; Blue Angel goes her way alone, still faintly bucking; the pickup men, not needed now, follow her to the gate; the horn sounds and men in white coats pick the kid out of the dust; he pushes them away, legs in yellow chaps grope for the ground, shift to try to make the world hold still; he walks towards the chutes, the crowd stands up to cheer.

Breathe that air: the stampede air, thick with the dread of blood, but hungry for it; the same air used for cheers by people in the stands, but wasted on them; thick air that turns to solid grit when cowboys breathe it.

24

Jesse smaller now, shrinking from inside where he can't reach it. He's scareder than a kid. Not scared to die, but scared of pain and months in bed; scared of young men's laughing eyes if he gets piled; scared most of all that he's finished—that he'll never ride again. But then, the shrinking stops. He grows a bit again. He'll show those young yahoos what riding is.

"Jesse Gifford riding Calico! Chute number two!" Down in chute number two they're tightening the cinch around old Calico— jugheaded, long as a noodle; no doubt pulled a hay rake yesterday. Down in the saddle, boots in stirrups. Calico's long neck raised, head turned slightly, one eye looking back; Jesse's hand as short on the rope as it can get, right hand pulling down his hat. "Let 'er go!" The chute slams open, Calico stands still. Jesse suddenly hot, wild, insane, raises his spurs beside old Calico's neck, rakes him from neck to belly. Calico plunges, slams against the chute, turns, pivots and comes apart, legs and neck in all directions; grandstand turns dizzily past; chutes, horses, ground spin by in jagged blurs, Jesse showing daylight, riding loose, raking Calico all the while. "Wa-hoo!" He'd ride old Calico right over the mountains.

The saddle came up against him hard, jarring his bones like a sack of rocks. Suddenly he'd lost his rhythm. Before he could recover, Calico rolled out and left him alone with only a halter rope in his hand. The rope slammed him down to the ground, and he could see Calico's underparts stretched above him. He rolled, and the earth beneath his head shook when the great hooves landed. If he'd lain still, it would all be over now. He wouldn't have to get up, and wave at the cheering crowd, and smile, and walk back to the chutes.

J.T., standing beside him, cursed. "Let's go home," he said.

Chapter 4

Monday was another long day, and that night Jesse couldn't sleep. Towards midnight the pain in his back almost subsided and still he lay, turning over the day's events like carcasses in his mind. The morning had begun for him on the iron seat of J.T.'s tractor, with a cultivator lurching after him. A west wind blew from the mountains. The tractor exhaust pipe was in front of him and dust rose in a cloud from the cultivator behind him, so that he seemed to ride in a pall of fumes and dust. Sometimes the tractor lugs broke through the crust of the earth, and sometimes they were held up by it, so that the machine seemed to progress by intermittent jolts, thrusts and hesitations. Almost from the beginning, his back began to hurt.

Presently remnants of stubble began to pack so tightly beneath the cultivator's frame that they lifted the blades out of the ground. He stopped the outfit and spent half an hour hacking at the impacted stalks with his pocketknife until he could continue. Almost at once the straws began to catch on the cultivator again. Jesse watched closely. This time he would not let them get so solidly embedded. In fact, he watched the cultivator so closely that he didn't see the big rock until it was too late, and the outfit jerked to a shuddering stop, a wheel and one cultivator blade neatly straddling the boulder. What he needed was a jack.

He walked across the field and over to J.T.'s farmyard. J.T. was not around, but in the shop Jesse found a lumber jack that must have weighed thirty pounds. Holding it in one hand, he started to walk back, stopping frequently to rest. The jack prised against his innards when he lifted it until he thought the old pelvis was coming right apart. When he reached the tractor, he set the jack down and lay back on the hard, lumpy ground. Gradually the pain in his back subsided.

He raised himself. So far he had completed two and a half rounds of the field. J.T. wouldn't think much of that for a morning's work. He set the jack under the cultivator frame beside the rock and slipped it into place. As he pumped the jack, the end of the cultivator rose by slow degrees until the wheel was perhaps eight inches clear of the ground. Jesse knelt down and tried to judge whether the machine would clear the rock now. It looked as if it would.

At the front of the tractor a crank hung out like the tongue of a dog. Jesse primed the machine, seized the crank and gave it a quick turn. There was a *pop*, a ball of blue smoke shot into the air, and then everything was quiet. Jesse turned the crank again; and again. The machine had started with one turn for J.T. that morning. At last, in desperation, Jesse seized the crank in both hands and spun it as fast as he could. Just when pain and anger had driven any awareness of hazard from his mind, the tractor backfired. The crank reversed direction, snapping back with such sudden force that Jesse was thrown to the ground. His left thumb and wrist felt as though they were broken.

Jesse glanced up to see John Tyler Jones surveying the situation. "Did you set the magneto?" J.T. asked. He pulled, or pushed, something on the tractor and turned the crank. There was an eruption of noise and smoke. J.T. throttled it down, and the machine stood there idling. J.T. swung up on the seat, put the machine in low, and slowly let out the clutch. The cultivator moved an inch, and stopped. The jack had begun to tilt. "Is it going to make it?" J.T. shouted.

Jesse bent down to look. "I think so," he said. J.T. moved forward another inch; another; another. The jack tipped, thrusting the cultivator forward; the blade rang against the rock and the jack fell.

J.T. jumped down, picked up the jack, and set it in the well between the shuddering fenders of the machine. He walked over to Jesse. "You hurt yourself?" he asked.

"I'll be all right," Jesse said. "Just sprained my wrist."

"You'd better go home and soak it," J.T. said.

"I've never run a tractor very much," Jesse said.

"No wonder!" J.T. exclaimed. He climbed on the tractor again. Then he glanced back at Jesse. "I'll work late to catch up!" he shouted. "You milk my cow, will you?" He opened the throttle wide, the noise rose up like the dust from the cultivator, and the outfit moved slowly away, its roar punctuated by a chorus of shrieks as the steel-pointed shoes struck against the stones of the field.

That night, lying in the dark, wide awake, Jesse tried to think where it was that he had gone wrong. J.T. had treated him like a fool, and made him milk the cow for punishment. He wished he hadn't milked her. All afternoon he'd lain on his bed thinking about that cow, nursing his sprained wrist and giving his back a chance to recuperate. He lay there thinking about J.T. and the cow, and San Soucie and old Lars, and the fact that though he wasn't yet thirty-five, everybody looked at him as if he were already another Lars—not a man, but someone who used to be one.

The boys walked in and out of the room as if it contained a corpse. At suppertime Ethan cut some bread and fixed syrup sandwiches. Jesse wasn't hungry. He had gone to J.T.'s to milk the cow. It took him a long time because he could milk with only one hand.

Later on, Ethan came in and sat on the bed across from him. "How are you going to work with a bad back?"

"I'll be all right, come haying time."

"What happens after haying's finished?" Ethan's face had little smears of syrup on each cheek, like an inspector's stamp certifying its youth. His eyes, though, were old, with weariness in them.

"Haven't we always gotten along somehow?" Jesse said.

27

"I guess we have," the boy agreed. "Somehow." He paused. "I'm scared, Jesse. What's going to happen to us?" For a long time Ethan looked at the floor. When he looked at Jesse again, he said, "I always wondered why Mama left us." He stood up. Then he blurted, "I think I know now," and ran out of the house; each pounding footstep seemed to land square in the middle of Jesse's back.

Again pain gushed up in him, crushing his spirit against the walls of his body until he knew he could not endure it. This was not a physical pain; it was the pain of disappointment, old and unremitting, but in the days with Shirley, so softened by the sweet smoke of love that he had never really noticed it.

Shirley coming home late at night, cool and black and unafraid— black dress, black hair, black eyes, black heart. Shirley walking down the road from God knew where, softly singing to the whole countryside with a voice so rich and low it seemed to come out of her belly. Jesse in the cottage, still slumped in his old wicker chair, staring straight ahead as he had been when the sun went down. Shirley opening the screen door at one o'clock in the morning, standing against the light of the doorway. Shirley, faceless, black against the moonlight through the door. "You didn't have to wait up."

"I wondered what happened to you."

"I went for a walk."

In high-heeled shoes, she went for a walk. "George was home alone. I thought something must have happened."

"George wasn't alone. Ethan was here."

"Ethan got home from school late tonight. When I came in, George was alone."

Shirley striking a match, lighting a cigarette; Shirley, who never smoked. In the flare of the match he had seen her eyes—cool, black and unafraid. "Blame Ethan, then. Don't blame me."

"I'm not blaming you." But he had. George, four years old, alone in the cottage. Why hadn't she lied to him, at least? That was the terrible part—she didn't even care enough to lie. No doubt if he asked her where she'd been, she'd have told him that, too. "I was worried about you," he said.

"Very touching." Shirley going to the bedroom, kicking off her shoes, stripping, her body white and curved and slender in the moonlight. Jesse in the doorway, watching her—watching her white skin, as white as the first snow of winter. He longed to touch that cool, soft snow. He walked towards her. She slipped her nightgown over her head. When he came close he saw her eyes, black as the snow was white.

"Shirley," he said.

"Don't touch me!"

Chapter 5

The morning air clung around Jesse, hot and motionless. When he thought of fifty more years of life on the earth, he shuddered. This morning he couldn't face it alone. He needed people around him, people who didn't know Jesse Gifford. He might find them in Lethbridge. The question was—how would he get there? It was an all-day ride on horseback. J.T. wouldn't take him, that was certain. He was marooned.

Then, in the morning stillness, he heard a train whistle. Tuesday morning. Train day! That was the warning whistle. Lone Rock to Lethbridge. He ran into the house, and pulled on his socks and boots. It was possible that he might never come back. The boys would go to Shirley. He'd never stop missing them—as he still missed Shirley—but there was nothing else here that he couldn't either carry with him or leave behind and never feel a twinge.

A half hour. That was all the time he had. Old Czar would have to run for it. He did pause when he thought of Czar. He could take his saddle and bridle on the train, but it would be goodbye to Czar. He'd probably end up in Keno's horse pasture.

Fully dressed, Jesse slipped on his denim jacket and took his sheepskin coat from a nail. He put his picture of Shirley in one pocket, shotgun shells in the other, took the gun in his hand, and ran out through the door. He dropped his coat beside the stable door, grabbed the bridle, and hurried to the pasture to catch Czar.

He was halfway across the field before he realized he still had the shotgun in his hand. But he couldn't put it down in the wet grass. He hurried to where his two horses grazed. As he approached, Buster, the piebald, raised his head. Then Czar whinnied softly. At the very last, Czar was the only friend he had in the world.

As he ran up to the horse, he spoke to him softly. "Czar old boy, we've got a race to run this morning." He raised the bridle. Czar snorted and moved out of reach. "Whoa, boy! We've got no time for games." He never had any trouble catching Czar, but he'd never run up to him before, either. He walked forward, his hand stretched out. Czar broke into a trot. "Whoa, boy!" Leaning the shotgun against a gopher hole, Jesse ran after him.

Czar was standing against the fence. Time was getting short, but Jesse forced himself to slow down. He knew he ought to stop completely and let them both settle down a little. Czar's tail was raised like a flag, and when he looked back at Jesse, the white showed in the corner of his eye. Crazy horse. Jesse extended his hand. "Whoa, Czar. Whoa, old fella." He stepped closer. His hand was inches from Czar's head. Czar backed off a step, then another. Jesse's chance was slipping away. He lunged, and slipped the bridle rein around the horse's neck, but his sudden movement startled Czar, who threw up his head and reared. The bridle rein pulled free. The big bay turned, galloped to the far end of the pasture, and stopped close beside the stable door. Jesse ran after him, picking up the shotgun. If old Czar felt like a run, he could get his fill of it taking Jesse to catch the train.

He had no watch, but he didn't need one to know he was running out of time. From now on if he missed a single movement, he was finished. It would cost him his ticket on the last train out of purgatory. He was breathing hard, whether from running or frustration he wasn't sure. Czar stood by the stable, head and tail high. He seemed to be looking down his nose at him. Puny man. What do you think you're going to do?

This was the final betrayal—Jesse's horse had joined the rest of the world against him. At that moment the second whistle blew— the departure whistle. They'd missed the train. Czar reared slightly, with neck bowed, then galloped straight at Jesse, as if he were playing a game. But Jesse was not playing games. He dropped the bridle, took a shotgun shell from his pocket, loaded, and fired at the horse. Czar squealed. His front legs went from under him, and he rolled on the grass, where he lay kicking convulsively. The almost human cries of pain penetrated so deeply inside Jesse that he felt he would carry them with him for ever, that on earth or in hell he would never escape them. His vision of Czar blurred as his eyes filled with tears.

There was one more necessary act. Walking towards Czar, he wiped his shirt sleeve across his eyes, so for a moment he could see more clearly. Down the long scrolled barrel of the shotgun he saw Czar's face, only inches beyond. Jesse pulled the trigger. The head fell back. Jesse looked away.

He sank to his knees on the cold grass. Then, as he looked down, he saw, still in his hands, the barrel of the shotgun, strangely warped and rippled through his tears. He rose to his feet, and taking the end of the barrel in his hands, he spun himself around and around, and let the shotgun go in a twisting arc that raised it in the sky, then let it fall back to earth, hidden for ever among the grass.

Again he sank to the ground, his palms pressed against his wet cheeks. At last he lay full length in the cold, damp grass. The warmth of the sun gradually penetrated the back of his shirt. He shrank from the sun. It seemed to extend a forgiveness of which he was not worthy. He waited for his punishment. He longed for it. Far off, he heard the train whistle again. Then the silence returned. At last he realized that his punishment was simply to go on without absolution—to carry the weight of what he had done to the end of whatever road he was cursed to travel.

AS HE LAY THERE, the sun moved higher, drying the field around him. He knew he would soon have to rise. The hardest thing to accept would be the body of Czar, stretched out beside him.

He heard running footsteps. A short way from him the running stopped, and he could hear quick, youthful puffing. More footsteps. They stopped beside the first. Jesse waited. At last he heard George speak. "Is he dead?"

"I don't know," Ethan said. "Czar sure is."

When George spoke again, he had moved to one side; he must have gone to inspect Czar. "Ooh, yah," he said, with a shiver in his voice. Looking through his fingers, Jesse saw the little boy squat on his heels, looking at his father.

"He ain't moving!" George thrust both fists into his eyes and began to cry. "He's dead."

Ethan came round then and stood beside his brother. Jesse tried to hold his breath. If they thought he was dead and went for help, he could slip away.

Ethan said, "Maybe Czar kicked him in the head. Maybe he's just knocked out." Through the crack in his fingers, Jesse could see Ethan's boots approach him. Jesse closed his eyes and stopped breathing. Ethan's fingers touched the back of his hand. Then Ethan said, "He's cold. That means he's dead."

Still sobbing, George said angrily, "What did he have to go and die for, anyway? I'm too small to be an orphan . . ."

"You're not an orphan. Not while Mama's still alive."

"Will we go to live with Mama now?"

"Not as long as she stays with Keno. But we can take care of ourselves. You stay here with him while I dig a grave."

"You going to bury him?"

"If I don't, we'll have to tell the neighbours. Then Mama will come for us and take us to live with Keno."

"I'm scared, Ethan."

"I'll be right back." Ethan walked away.

George still sat on his haunches. He had quit crying. Jesse had better do something fast or these gravediggers would have him six feet under. He stirred slightly and groaned.

George sprang to his feet and began to back away. "Oooo," he sobbed. Then he yelled, "Ethan!"

Jesse raised himself slightly. "I'm all right, George," he said.

"Ethan!" George screamed. He turned to run, glanced back at Jesse once, then ran after his brother, skimming over the meadow like a low-flying bird. "Eth-a-a-a-n!"

Jesse sat up as Ethan turned round. The two boys met in the pasture, and then came back to Jesse, George walking behind, peeking round Ethan's legs. They stopped in front of Jesse.

"We were afraid you were dead," Ethan said. "What happened?"

"Old Czar went crazy and I had to shoot him."

"You're not dead!" George cried. He came from behind Ethan and ran to Jesse, his arms closing tight around his neck.

"No, I'm not dead." Jesse hugged the little boy against him.

Ethan stood looking down; then he suddenly plunged forward, stumbling to his knees, and threw his arms round both of them. "Oh, Jesse," he sobbed. "I was so scared."

Chapter 6

It was then, in that moment when he felt closer to his boys than he ever had, that Jesse realized he must send them away. He had failed them. He had tried—the good Lord knew he had tried—but nothing seemed to work. Their situation only seemed to get worse, and he had neither the strength nor will nor understanding to make it better. It was not fair to endanger the boys' future by persisting.

He stood up. "Boys," he said. "There's something I want to tell you. You're going to live with your mama."

Ethan flinched as though Jesse had struck him. "We can't," he said. "She doesn't even want us."

"She wants you. It wasn't you she ran away from, it was me. And she did right, too. Only, she should have taken you with her."

"You've been kicked in the head," Ethan told him.

"No, I haven't. I'll write her that you're coming on the train."

"I'll get off the first time the train stops. I won't live with Keno."

"You do as you please, so long as I don't know about it." Jesse started walking towards the house, conscious of his sons watching him. He raised his head, squared his shoulders, and marched across the meadow away from his boys.

They were going, whether they liked it or not. They'd be a lot better off with Shirley, and Jesse could somehow make his adjustment to life if he didn't have these kids for ever on his mind, wondering what they'd eat, and what they'd wear, and what they must think of their father. If they caught the train next week, he'd have time to contact Shirley so she could meet them.

In the house, Jesse picked up a pencil and sharpened it with his pocketknife. He realized that he didn't have any paper in the house. The only book he owned was a Bible he had carried since his wedding day. Now he opened it and read again the inscription he had made on the ornamental title page: "Jesse and Shirley Gifford." What had become of the man who had written those words?

At the back of the Bible there were two or three blank pages. Jesse carefully tore one out. He cleared the kitchen table and sat down with the paper in front of him, pencil in hand.

Dear Shirley,

That must be the right way to begin. It was important to keep this letter businesslike.

The boys are coming on the train and they should get in Calgary about a week from Wednesday. Maybe you can check at the station and see what time the Lethbridge train gets in.

Should he give some explanation? No. Ethan could explain when he got there. He wrote his name at the bottom: "Jesse."

He knew it wouldn't do. Somewhere he had to put in something with an edge to it. Deep under her scars, Shirley still had soft, living tissue that would flinch if he could touch it. He rubbed out the word "Jesse." But what would he say? "I hope you are happy?" He hoped she was miserable.

He shouldn't blame Keno. If everything had been reversed, he'd have done the same thing. He didn't know how much she had been running to Keno, and how much she had been running away from Jesse.

He looked again at the piece of paper in front of him. Wasn't there something in her life so personal that she wouldn't explain it to Keno? Something that only she and Jesse shared? Looking at the picture of his wife, he remembered the day he married her. Then he wrote the single word *Goldenrod*, and signed his name at the bottom.

GEORGE WANDERED BACK to the house about noon.

"Where's Ethan?" Jesse asked.

"Gone. Run away. He says he's not coming back." George sat solemnly on a kitchen chair, while Jesse fixed some lunch for them. Through the afternoon he did not speak or look at his father, and when Jesse spoke to him he pretended not to hear. The sun went down, and they got in their beds, and presently Jesse could hear George crying.

"Ethan'll be all right," Jesse said. "He can take care of himself. If it was some kids, you'd worry, but not Ethan. He may be out there all alone, but he's not worried—not for a minute. Like as not he figured out a way to cook some supper, and right now he's fast asleep in a haystack somewhere."

The sound of crying subsided. George sniffled, and wiped his eyes with the blanket. Jesse could see his small pale face staring at the ceiling.

Several times during the day Jesse had almost started after Ethan, to bring him back. For all his brave words, he was sick at the thought of the boy spending the night alone on the prairie. But there was something indefinable, yet very real, involved. His son's dignity required that his decision to leave them be honoured. Jesse could not risk wounding that boyish pride.

Outside in the darkness he heard quick, short hoofbeats coming down the hill, passing his window. A few minutes later, he heard boots coming up the path and into the kitchen. Jesse raised himself on his elbow. "Ethan?"

"You awake, Jesse?" The boy appeared in the doorway.

Ethan sat on the bunk opposite. "You'll never guess what I found." He scarcely paused. "A ranch. The prettiest little ranch you ever did see. Right in the foothills. Those old mountains lean right over on top of it, like it was in a closet of sunshine. A creek running through it. There's a house, and a barn, and a hay shed. Some machinery, but I don't know whether that goes or not. And there's a sign nailed to the fence post. *Ranch for Sale.*"

"How many acres?"

"Well, it can't be too big, 'cause there's just an old log house, set down under the trees by the creek, no more'n three or four rooms. The sign didn't say the price and I didn't talk to anybody. Just rode in and looked at it from on top of the hill. There was a woman and a couple of girls out in the yard sometimes, but I didn't see anybody else. I just sat there on the hill all afternoon, and the longer I sat, the more at home I felt. Jesse, could we buy that ranch?"

"I couldn't buy the sweat off a sick bull, and you know it."

"You could if you went back to riding."

Jesse sighed. How simple the world is when you are twelve years old. You wanted a ranch, you entered the saddle-bronc contest, and with your winnings you bought a ranch . . . Huh! Jesse had carried that dream until he was almost thirty. "It's late," he said. "You'd better get to sleep."

"I can't sleep," Ethan replied. "You can do it, Jesse. I know you can. Just say it has two hundred acres. There wasn't any crop land, only hay and pasture—and trees. And a creek. Say five dollars an acre. That's a thousand dollars. You could win that much easy."

Jesse had let this go on for too long. "Listen to me. Suppose it's five hundred acres instead of two. Suppose it's ten dollars an acre instead of five. That's five thousand dollars. Where're you going to win that kind of money? And what good's the land if you don't have any cattle to run on it? And how're you going to run cattle without a few head of horses? What about machinery to cut your hay? But what are we talking for? I can't ride broncs any more."

"I'll bet you can ride 'em good as ever."

"No, I can't. I tried. When I went to Macleod with J.T., we were sitting in the beer parlour, and decided to go to the Stavely Stampede. And I tried to ride a bronc. A dirty old plough horse. He flung me thirty feet high."

"You were drunk. You can't ride a rocking horse when you're drunk. That's what Mama used to say." Ethan pulled off his boots and threw them into a corner.

"You might as well forget about it," Jesse went on. "In the first place, I'm not riding any bucking horses. And if I won a pot of money, do you think I want to spend the rest of my days grubbing on some two-bit spread?"

"Yes," Ethan said, "yes, I do." The words fell across Jesse's mind like a gate, suddenly he could think of nothing more to say. Ethan pulled off his shirt and overalls, and slipped into bed beside his brother. After a while he said, "I wish I hadn't come back."

Chapter 7

Next morning, Jesse sent the boys to borrow a horse from J.T. so he could ride up to Lone Rock and mail his letter. He was straightening up the house when he heard Ethan call from down by the barn. He put the letter to Shirley in his shirt pocket as he walked down the path and found the boys, Ethan holding the bridle of a big brown gelding, all saddled and ready to go.

"J.T. says you can borrow Zigzag for a day or two," Ethan said. "Says maybe you can wear down that hump in his backbone."

It looked as if J.T. had figured out a way to get Jesse to break his broncs without having to pay for it. He took the bridle reins from Ethan. "I'll be back this afternoon," he said. "I'm just going to mail a letter to your mama. You fellows will be catching the train next week, so you might as well settle yourselves to it."

He raised himself to the horse's back, feeling muscles under the saddle as hard and square as a stack of lumber. He touched his spurs to the gelding's sides. Zigzag arched his back and bucked. As he lowered his head, Jesse pulled on the bridle reins. They came loose in his hand. He saw that one cheekstrap on the bridle was unfastened, and the throat strap was not buckled. When Zigzag's head went down, the bit slipped out and the whole bridle came off, back over his ears.

Jesse glanced at Ethan, who had a broad grin on his face. "Ride 'im, cowboy!" Ethan yelled. The little devil. He had set this up. Zigzag came up under him, and Jesse tossed the bridle away.

"Ride 'im, Jesse!" George's shrill young voice shouted.

Ride 'im. Hah! He made a grab for the saddle horn, but stopped his hand just short of it. He felt just enough in his guts for one more challenge. He took the jolt of landing with both hands free, and as they started up again, his spurs were sunk in Zigzag's shoulders.

"Wa-hoo!" he yelled. Might as well give the boys their money's worth. He leaned back in the saddle, trying to make his body flow to the motion of the horse's plunging leaps.

There was no horn, no pickup men or catch pen. He and Zigzag were cut loose in time and space, with no restrictions on either. But he felt good. To stay aboard the old blister, Jesse would have to know how to ride. Zigzag bucked straight across the pasture, then lunged against the fence, making the wires screech. Jesse bent his leg, and the barbs tore Zigzag's side instead of his rider's calf. With a groan of pain, or perhaps rage, the horse turned back towards the middle of the pasture, seeming to leap higher and harder with every jump. The two boys ran behind and mingled their cheers with Zigzag's snorts. Jesse had to admit that Ethan was right—he could ride a lot better when he was sober.

It did not last long. Each lunge required greater effort. Zigzag bucked a few more times and stopped, head down, breathing heavily. He knew he had been licked.

Ethan ran up. "See, Jesse? You can ride as good as ever."

George came cavorting behind, mimicking Zigzag's efforts. "Wahoo!" George cried. "Ride 'im, cowboy."

Jesse swung down from the saddle. "Where's that bridle? Maybe now Zigzag is ready for a jog up to town."

"You don't have to mail that letter now," Ethan said. "George and I can stay here."

"What do you mean?" Jesse asked him.

"I asked J.T. if he had a horse that liked to buck, and he said he sure did. That was to show you that you can still ride broncos."

"So I can ride that spavined old plough horse. What does that prove?"

"It proves that you're still a champ."

J.T. came across the pasture to him. "You're some rider after all, Jesse. Ain't many cowboys can stick old Zigzag when he gets going. What say you and me be partners after all?"

"No, sir. I'm not breaking my neck for anybody."

"What's the matter? Is it the fifty-per-cent split? I'll give you seventy-five."

"If there *is* any prize money, I'll give you ten per cent."

They finally settled on a twenty-eighty split. Jesse took the letter out of his pocket and tore it in little pieces, letting them flutter from his hands onto the grass.

On the day of the Macleod Stampede, he found himself with the other cowboys waiting to register for the saddle-bronc event. Keno was there, standing in front of the chutes. "Hello, Jesse," he said.

"Hello." Jesse's whole rib cage seemed to collapse inside him. If Keno was there, Shirley would not be far away.

"That's Keno," Ethan muttered beside him. And George, coming along behind, cried, "Where? Where?"

Jessie hurried the boys away from the chutes. "Yes. That's Keno," he said. What had possessed him? By what obscure reasoning had he convinced himself that he could compete again? Here he was, old and broken, going up against Keno and a flock of young cowboys eager to win their spurs.

But he had changed after the ride on Zigzag. He had felt a new man grow inside him—a man perhaps even capable of achieving the old dream. Jesse scanned the distant faces in the stands until he saw Shirley. She had a yellow ribbon in her hair.

Ethan saw him staring at the crowd. "Is Mama here?" he asked.

"She's here," Jesse replied. "Right over there in the stands."

"Let's go see her."

"The show's about ready to start. You boys go ahead. Just tell her hello for me, will you?" He watched the boys hurry away.

Tell her hello for Jesse. And when she says, "Who's Jesse?" tell her he's that spavined old cowboy she used to love, back when she was just a girl. She'll remember. No matter what has happened since, she still gave her first pure love to that cowboy. And for years after, that love had grown. It wasn't what he'd done, but what he hadn't been able to do, that killed it. And now he realized that the circumstances had not changed her until they changed him. As long as he worked for something, she stayed. But when he gave up, when he accepted his defeat and began pushing a broom in rhythm with old Lars, she got desperate. Now he understood what she had been trying to say when she pleaded with him to leave San Soucie's.

They were lying in bed. Their lovemaking had become a ritual, its meaning lost. And Jesse felt a sort of terror grip him. Was this what happened after you had been married for only nine years?

"Jesse," Shirley said. In the moonlight he could see her face on the pillow, her dark hair in disarray where his hands had entangled it. She turned towards him and touched his cheek. "Jesse."

He waited for her to say more, but she didn't speak again, and as he watched, her eyes filled with tears. Was this the way love dies? "It'll be all right," he said.

"It won't be all right. Not as long as we stay here."

"San Soucie took me on when I was just out of the hospital. Our money was gone—I had to have a job, didn't I?"

"It's been a year and a half."

"My back still isn't better. I've got to wait."

"Then let's go somewhere else to wait."

"I can't walk out on San Soucie just when I'm getting well enough to be some use to him."

She took her hand away and pressed the back of it against her mouth. He could see the sobs move up her throat, only to be stifled by that firm, determined hand. Presently she said, "Can't you see what's happening? San Soucie hopes you never do get better. He likes to have a champion for a chore boy."

And now, at last, Jesse understood. Three years too late he saw that she had been trying to save the old Jesse—the one she loved.

The afternoon events began. And though Jesse competed, though he was caught in the dust and whirl and noise of the stampede, he moved through the day like a tin soldier, head erect, eyes straight ahead, expression never changing. Finally, his ordeal was over, and they were in the Dodge driving home. George's cheeks were still flushed from the touch of his mother's lips as he told about how Shirley bought him popcorn, and hot dogs, and ice cream and sodas. Ethan said she had asked about Jesse, and wanted to see him. Ethan had taken first prize—ten dollars—in the boys' steer riding.

J.T. smiled and talked about the future of their partnership. Jesse, too, had winnings in his pocket, but he wasn't even sure how much. The central truth of the day's events was that Shirley had watched him win. For all the money in his pocket, he knew that Shirley was the prize. Though Keno took her home with him tonight, the competition had only just begun.

NEXT MORNING, Jesse heard a tractor coming down the road outside his window, and sat up. It was J.T. Jones. He stopped outside the door and, leaving the tractor to idle, came up the path. Jesse grabbed his overalls and pulled them on. He felt the roll of bills in his pocket. This called for some sort of celebration. Tomorrow, the first of July, they'd be off to Raymond for the next stampede, so they would celebrate today by going fishing. He hurried out to meet J.T., his finger across his lips. "The kids are still asleep."

"Well, get 'em up," J.T. said. "We've got work to do. My old shepherd's half crazy with pain. I got to get him to a dentist, so I reckon you and the boys will have to mind the sheep."

Sheep! Mind the sheep? Was J.T. crazy? Jesse restrained himself. "I'm not a shepherd, J.T., I'm a cowboy."

"Today you're a shepherd. Besides, you know a cowboy is only a shepherd with his brains knocked out. If I only get twenty per cent of your winnings, you'll have to work like a Tartar between stampedes to pay your way."

Jessie sighed. J.T. was just a carbon copy of San Soucie—a little fainter, but he said the same thing. I've got you where I want you, Jesse Gifford. "We'll be over after breakfast," Jesse said.

When breakfast was ready, Jesse called the boys. They ate in silence. At last Jesse said, "J.T. wants us to herd his sheep today. He has to take his old herder to the dentist."

"Not me," Ethan said. He drew himself up to indicate an attitude suitable to a future world champion bronc-buster.

"Yes, you," Jesse said. "That is, if you want to go to the stampede tomorrow. You can bring Buster if you want to."

Jesse walked over to J.T.'s, with the boys riding beside him on the piebald. When they got there the old herder was already in the car, his face framed by the red bandanna tied around his jaw.

J.T. hurried out of the house. "Oh, there you are. I turned the sheep out half an hour ago. Just keep them out of the summer fallow or they'll trample it all into the mud." He got into his car and shut the door. "And keep them a mile away from the alfalfa."

The shepherd dog ran to the car, whining. "You can't use the bitch. She only pays attention to Carl." The Dodge drove away, the dog running behind.

"Well, boys," Jesse said, "let's go find these sheep."

When they caught up with the herd, Jesse realized that he had worried unnecessarily. He hadn't the faintest notion what shepherding consisted of, but as they came through the trees and he saw the quiet tableau of the sheep grazing on the hillside, he felt a sort of peace come over him. The three of them climbed to the top of the hill, where they had a good view of the pasture beneath them and, stretching off to the north, the field of summer fallow, green with stinkweeds, thistles and wild oats. To the east, Jesse could see the emerald alfalfa patch, tinged with pale violet blossoms.

"Well," he said, as he sat down with his back against a fence post, "looks like it'll be a tough day. How about a game of mumblepig?" He reached into his pocket for his knife, opened the blade, and flipped the knife a couple of times so it sank point-first into the turf.

"Can I be first?" George asked.

"Front hand," Jesse said. "Then backhand, breaks, picks . . ." He played left-handed to give George encouragement.

As they played, a few of the sheep grazed up the hillside towards them. Before long they were surrounded by grazing sheep. They worked at their morning meal with a lofty seriousness. Occasionally one of them, raising her head to chew, would look down her nose at the man and boys with steady indifference.

"They make me nervous," Ethan said at last.

"Chase them away, then," Jesse told him. "They're pretty close to the summer fallow, anyway." Almost instinctively, Ethan seized a big ewe by the wool on her shoulders and, straddling her, took a wild ride down the hill, starting an avalanche of sheep. He came back waving his arm, "That was fun!"

As the morning progressed, they moved up and down the brow of the hill, wherever the sheep grazed. At noon, while they were eating their sandwiches, a black-faced ewe led a small band across the road into the summer fallow. Etham jumped on Buster and galloped away to drive them out. But by the time he returned to finish his sandwich, they were back in again, in greater numbers than before, eager to reach the green young stinkweeds. Ethan galloped back but where earlier the sheep had turned and run when Buster came, now they scarcely noticed. Ethan got off his horse and, shouting furiously, began to pelt the sheep with clods of dirt.

"You stay here," Jesse said to George. "Don't let any sheep across the road. I've got to go and help Ethan."

Together, with Jesse throwing clods of dirt and Ethan galloping up and down on Buster, they finally drove the reluctant sheep back across the road and chased them·down the hill towards the river. Jesse climbed up to the crest of the hill again, but the sheep were preparing another assault on the summer fallow. He and the boys had to hurry to turn them back as they spread over the fallow like locusts in the land of promise. It took a little longer, but at last they were able to get all the sheep back over the hill.

At least Jesse thought it was all of them, until he saw a single line hurrying over the hill and disappearing through a hole in the fence around the alfalfa patch. Jesse ran towards the fence. "Stop 'em!" he shouted to Ethan, riding ahead. The grass was high along the fence, and it wasn't until he got there that Jesse could see inside the field where twenty or thirty sheep now grazed, only their woolly backs visible in the thick hay.

He vaulted the fence. "Come on, boys," he cried. "We've got to get them out of here quick." If they gorged on green alfalfa, the gas would blow them up like balloons. He ran around the sheep, shouting. They moved back towards the fence, but the hole in the wire operated like a valve that let them in but not out. Jesse looked up and down the fence. As far as he could see, there was no gate. He rushed two or three of the sheep against the fence, caught one by the wool on its shoulders, lifted, and thrust it over the fence. "Catch 'em!" he cried to the boys. "Don't let 'em eat." Already the sheep were starting to swell. Before Jesse finished lifting them over the fence, the last few sheep were down, their bellies huge, the skin on the inside of their flanks stretched tight, their mouths open and bubbles of froth building outside their lips.

Jesse looked helplessly about. It was possible to save bloated sheep by puncturing them, but you had to know the right place or you could stab the poor brutes to death. On the other hand, they were going to die, anyway. He took out his pocketknife and knelt beside one of them. He picked a spot on her swollen belly high on her side near the hipbone. Then he raised his arm, and brought the knife down with all his strength. The rush of air from her body seemed to lift his hand away. He must have got it right.

Ethan said, "J.T. Jones is here."

Jesse glanced up. The Dodge had stopped just outside the fence, and J.T. was running from one sick animal to the next, swinging his knife with swift assurance. The swollen woolly bodies slowly deflated. Behind him the old herder came along, lifting the sheep to their feet and pausing occasionally to give a signal to his dog, who was over a quarter of a mile away, quietly driving the main herd out of the summer fallow. They finally got most of the sheep out of the field, but six lay dead in the alfalfa.

"Six dead," J.T. said. "Your back bothering you?"

"I had to lift the sheep over the fence," Jesse said.

"You take care of that back," J.T. told him. "You're on deck for tomorrow, you know."

"I know," Jesse said.

They skinned the dead sheep, threw the hides in the Dodge trunk, and drove away.

Chapter 8

The morning of July the first was bright and hot. Jesse rose with mixed feelings of excitement and despair. The day before yesterday he had won and with winning came the pressure to win again. But it was worth it. It was worth the risk of humiliation, and being a cripple for life, because when you did win, there was nothing like that sweet taste of triumph. He'd go if it killed him, and by the way his back felt, perhaps it would.

Shortly after breakfast, J.T. called to pick them up. As they drove along, J.T. asked him, "How's the back?"

"Cracked glass," Jesse replied. He was a silly old fool, galloping after trophies that would make suitable goals for a twenty-year-old. The five thousand or so people gathered at Raymond today would probably have a good laugh to see Father Time himself out there on a bucking horse.

He didn't mind the laughs. A stampede crowd spent its time on the edge between groans and laughter. In his time, he had inspired both—he could still hear the moan from the grandstand, even above Sundown's thumping fury, when the big bay horse came down on him—and of the two, he preferred the laughter. It wasn't the crowd he cared about today. It was a one-hundred-and-five-pound woman. Would she be laughing? As he thought about her, he found himself growing tense as a green kid going into the arena for the first time.

As soon as they got to the stampede grounds, the boys hurried away to find their mother. J.T. went with Jesse to register for the saddle-bronc competition.

The afternoon dribbled away. The great climax for which Jesse had tried to prepare himself never came off. He got through the ride, but the pain in his back held him from spurring as he should have and, when it was over, his greatest feeling was one of relief. First prize money went to Keno. Jesse was happy to have been placed fourth. At least that should keep them from laughing at him.

As Jesse and J.T. walked back to the car, the boys ran up to them. Ethan had taken the boys' steer-riding event again; the kid had a gift. If he kept his bones intact, he'd be in the big time some day.

Ethan walked up close to Jesse and whispered, "Mama wants to see you."

Why would Shirley want to see him? "You go ahead," Jesse said to J.T. and George. "We'll see you at the car." He followed Ethan back through the crowd to the front of the grandstand, and began mounting the broad stairway of empty seats that reached up into the shadows of the gabled canopy. In the middle of the seats sat a solitary figure. Jesse was amazed to think that anything so small could leave so great a cave of longing when it was gone.

Ethan ran ahead of him and reached her first. As Jesse approached them, they sat side by side looking at him. "Hello," Jesse said.

"Hello, Jesse." For a moment she looked directly into his eyes. "Your back hurts, doesn't it?" she asked.

"A little."

"I could tell, the way you rode this afternoon." She turned to Ethan and roughed his hair. "Let me talk to your daddy," she said.

"About what I said?" he asked.

She hesitated. "No. Not that."

Ethan looked at Jesse, then turned to his mother. "OK," he said. "I'll see you in Calgary." He went down the stairs away from them. Jesse sat on the bench at Shirley's feet.

"Ethan wants me to come back," she said.

"That's the thing you told Ethan you wouldn't talk about?" He felt defensive.

"Yes."

"Then why talk about it?" He couldn't stand the pain of an open wound again. He stared out at the infield, where three cowboys were driving the last of the stampede stock out to the fields.

"It's about Ethan," Shirley said.

"You want him back, is that it?" Though Jesse was looking away from her, he was very conscious of her knee beside his arm.

"I'm not asking to take Ethan away from you," she said. "Or George either. I know what you must think of me. But they are still my sons. What I have done doesn't change that. Jesse, please don't let Ethan be a cowboy."

After everything that had happened, was that all she had on her mind? She hadn't changed. Sometimes, when Jesse got hurt, she used to try to talk him out of stampeding. They could get a little ranch, she said. It never concerned her what they'd use for money to get the ranch. "I don't see how you can even think about it," she went on. "Look what it's done to you."

What had it done to him? Broken his back. Lost him his woman. On the other hand, look what it had done for Keno. Who could say that Ethan wouldn't be lucky?

She said, "I wanted to cry when I saw him out on that bucking steer today. What if he'd been trampled like you were?"

But he hadn't. Ethan had a gift. How could Jesse explain that when you accept a gift from God, you take the whole parcel? "You don't understand," he said.

"That's what you used to tell me," she replied. "As if there was some great secret to it. Keno doesn't . . ." She stopped abruptly.

Keno doesn't pretend it's a secret? Of course he doesn't. He's not a bronc-buster; he's a businessman who happens to ride bucking horses better than anybody else who is around just now. But wait till a real rider comes along—one who can change the whole bucking contest into an acrobatic dance, and Keno won't last five minutes. "Then talk to Keno," Jesse said. "Don't talk to me."

For a while neither of them spoke. For two years he had dreamed of a time when he might see Shirley again. He'd planned over and over in his mind the things he'd tell her. But what he said was, "Ethan has a gift. We think gifts from God are free, but sometimes, for them, we pay the most."

She said, "I suppose you have a gift, too? Is it God's fault you broke your back?"

"You still don't understand, do you? The greatest thing in this world is to find out that you can do one thing better than any other man. It's worth anything it costs."

"Anything?" she asked.

"We don't know the cost beforehand. But it's worth the risk."

Shirley stood up. Jesse heard footsteps on the stairs, and turned to see Keno ascending towards them. "I have to go," Shirley said. As she stepped past Jesse, her fingers rested for a moment on his shoulder. It was the only time she had touched him.

Keno came up to her. "Has old Jellybones Jesse been moaning to you? Come on, Shirl. We're late."

Unable to speak, Jesse watched them go down the stairs, like a man and a little girl. But just before they turned the corner, the girl glanced back at him. She had the face of a woman. His woman.

BY THE TIME JESSE got to the Dodge, most of the other cars were gone from the meadow behind the grandstand. The boys jumped out of the back seat and ran towards him.

"Is Mama coming back to live with us?"

"Not that I know of. Why?"

"That's what she wanted to tell you, wasn't it? That she was coming back?"

"We'll talk about it at home." They walked towards the car, Ethan holding one of Jesse's hands, George the other. J.T. sat slumped low behind the wheel, his hat tipped forward over his eyes.

As they opened the car doors, J.T. pulled himself up in his seat. He set his hat square as he drove away. "Where you been?"

"Somebody I had to see," Jesse said.

"Yeh. Ethan said you were talkin' to your wife." J.T. looked across at Jesse. "Get rid of her," he said. "In court, so she can't demand something she calls her rights."

"Let's not talk about it now," Jesse said.

"She's got you in a sweat. You still in love with her?"

"I said let's drop it."

They drove the rest of the way home in silence.

That night in the shack, though, the boys were full of thoughts about their mother. "She's so nice," George said.

"She wishes we could be together again," Ethan told him.

"Well," Jesse replied. "I tried to send you, you know."

"I mean all of us," Ethan said. "All together. You and Mama and George and I."

"That's what you mean," Jesse agreed. "But did *she* say so? The four of us back together again?"

Ethan faltered. "Not just that way. No."

"She can come back, as far as I'm concerned. But it was her decided to go. She'll have to decide if she comes back."

George had crawled into bed, and Ethan got in beside him. Jesse blew out the lamp and sat down on the side of the bed. Ethan's face showed dimly in the darkness. "You're like your mama. You always think you know just how things should be. And right now you're figuring out that when you see her in Calgary you'll tell her how we want her to come back. Well, that's not for you to say. She's *my* wife. Now, will you talk to her without making any slips?"

The boy hesitated. "Yes," he said at last.

George was asleep, and his quiet breathing seemed to be the only sound in the house.

"We'll have to get a bigger bed for you and Mama," Ethan said. "It'll sure be crowded in here."

Jesse saw that Ethan understood their conversation as a sort of pact. Without realizing it, Jesse had committed himself to a plot to bring Shirley home. Perhaps it was just as well.

MONDAY MORNING the sun came up like a gong, and just as bright and brassy. Jesse and his boys jumped out of bed, put on their clothes, ate some porridge, and then whisked through the dishes, Ethan talking continually. As soon as they were in the car and on their way, J.T. asked, "How's your back?"

"It feels good this morning," Jesse said. "I've been doing some exercises for it, and that week of rest really helped. Today, I swear there's not a horse living I can't ride."

"Stay humble," J.T. told him. "I remember the last time you could ride any horse in creation." He had taken the road to the west, instead of the north. "We'll go the long way round. I seen a feller from Pincher Creek on Saturday—says he can't use his stampede tickets so we can have 'em for half-price."

They were getting close to Pincher Creek when Ethan suddenly cried, "Jesse. This is where that ranch is. The one that's for sale. Drive slow, Mr. Jones. Please."

When J.T. slowed the car at the top of the hill, they could see the sign, RANCH FOR SALE. J.T. stopped the car. "What do you want a place like that for?" he said. "You'd starve to death."

The hills were green, and above them rose the mountains. "I've always wanted a cattle ranch in the foothills," Jesse said.

J.T. shrugged. "Are we goin' stampedin'? Or are we shopping for cattle ranches?" He put the car in gear and drove on.

Chapter 9

When they got to Calgary, Jesse and Ethan registered for their events, then Jesse gave each of the boys fifty cents and sent them on their way for rides and refreshments.

Stampede week got off to a good start for Jesse. During that first afternoon, he gave a winning ride in the saddle-bronc event. That'd rot old Keno's gizzard.

But in the saddle-bronc contest on Tuesday, he drew a stupid old mare that plopped herself in the middle of the infield and humped her head to the east, and north, and south—as hard to ride as a fence rail. He got a reride, and the second horse was better—just enough to put his back through double torture without changing the outcome. Keno took the day.

Wednesday, Jesse drew a horse called Hardtack that had a bad reputation all over the circuit. Riders liked a horse that would buck, but they didn't like them too tough. The judges scored partly on the difficulty of the horse and partly on the cowboy's performance, so it was nice to get a horse that kicked high, but in a predictable pattern, so you could ride loose and still make it look good. That horse wouldn't be Hardtack, but Jesse got on his back with calm determination. Either he'd ride him and win, or fall off and lose. He rode him. When it was over and the pickup man had plucked him from Hardtack's saddle, his skin was still dry and tight from the rush of fear he'd felt when the big horse erupted under him. But he'd stuck; and at the end of the day they announced he'd won.

Thursday, Keno won. On Friday, a new kid from Rosebud took day money in the saddle-bronc event: Jesse and Keno were both out in the cold. Jesse hadn't seen Shirley anywhere.

On Saturday morning, the doctor encased Jesse's back in wide strips of adhesive tape. It seemed to help, but his back was still hurting like crazy. Why put himself through all this misery? He tried to rouse himself for another effort by remembering his hatred for Keno. His mind could remember, but his belly did not respond.

When the afternoon's events began, Jesse took a seat on the top rail of the corral and tried to compose himself. If he were able to win today, his purse would be a thousand dollars. That was almost enough to buy a ranch. Four years ago, he and Shirley had had one all picked out. Shirley had started to plan what she would do with the house. And then came Sundown; Sundown, and darkness blacker than he had ever imagined the dark could be. This was his last chance. From here on, either he would sit on his own front porch watching his cattle feed on his hillside, or he would finally give up.

Keno rode first that afternoon. He had drawn a good horse, and he gave a ride to match it—riding loose in the saddle, with one arm trailing and his spurs arcing rhythmically across the horse's shoulders. When the horn blew to end the ride, the audience came to their feet, cheering.

Ethan came running up to him. "Hi," he said, smiling. Ethan had won the boys' steer-riding almost every day this week.

"Hello, cowboy," Jesse replied.

"Mama sent you something," Ethan said, and handed him a folded slip of paper. Jesse opened the paper and saw written there, in Shirley's looping scrawl, the single word *Goldenrod*. Jesse felt a surge rush up through his body, and for a moment all his defences were down. "What shall I tell her?" Ethan said.

Tell her? Tell her to come back. Tell her I'm going to win today, and we can buy the ranch. Tell her there are people on this earth who love her, and she should live with them. "Tell her thanks, will you?" Jesse said.

"Does it say she's coming home?"

"No. It's personal. You wouldn't understand."

When Ethan had gone, Jesse climbed to the top rail again, to wait for his turn. *Goldenrod*. She'd turned all his muscles to string, just at the time he needed them. *Goldenrod*. Neither of them had mentioned it for fourteen years. Now, within a week or so, they had both written it as a message to the other. And he had received her message while his lay torn in pieces, scattered by the wind in J.T. Jones's pasture.

One September day the two of them had ridden into Lethbridge for a dance. They stopped on the crest of a hill. The prairie rolled away from them in all directions, and there in the field of goldenrod he'd made love to her for the first time. He could feel again the soft stalks bending under them, and smell the powdered gold dust in the air. He could see Shirley's frightened eyes, and feel her body bend to him. That same afternoon, in the cold grey chambers of the Lethbridge City Hall, they'd been married. Through the ceremony Shirley stood like a beautiful child, clutching a spray of goldenrod beneath her throat. *Goldenrod*.

"Out of chute number five!" the announcer called. "Jesse Gifford riding Polka Dot."

Polka Dot had Appaloosa blood in him; he was mottled with splotches of black and muddy grey. He was new to the circuit and Jesse didn't know what his bucking style was. As Jesse lowered himself into the saddle, he reared and struck at the boards. The crowd cheered. They liked a wild horse. But Jesse knew he needed more than action in the chute. He needed a horse that would buck. He didn't care if he fell off and the horse did a tap dance up his spine; if he lost today, he wanted it to be because he wasn't good enough. He wanted the whole business settled, once and for all.

Polka Dot was down on all fours again, and Jesse thrust his boots deep into the stirrups, took a firm hold on the halter rope, pulled his hat close over his eyes, and said, "Let's go." He smelled goldenrod. The gold dust of it drifted around him.

The chute clanged open. Polka Dot stood for a moment, uncertain. Then he spun on his heels and leaped into the arena. Jesse felt blue sky under him, but when the horse came down hard on all four feet, he chucked back into the saddle like a rifle bolt going home. He felt as if his pelvis had been smashed with the shock, but he could still swing his legs, so he knew nothing was broken. He raised his spurs high, brought them down full force into Polka Dot's shoulder, and raked them across his front quarters to behind his cinch.

Polka Dot rose in the air again. Jesse could see he was in for a high-flying, stiff-legged, jarring ride—the hardest kind for him to

take. Every time Polka Dot landed, it felt as though his spine were telescoping. He clenched his teeth and swung his legs back and forth, spurring the horse. Polka Dot lunged more and more desperately, squealing with fury. The forty thousand people were gone. There were only the two of them—Polka Dot and Jesse, struggling alone in a cloud of goldenrod dust. When the horn blew to mark the end of the ride, Jesse's whole body collapsed. He rolled from the saddle and fell face-first in the dust, and the earth beneath him shook again and again, each time more faintly, as Polka Dot's thumping hooves retreated.

THAT EVENING there were chuck-wagon races, and then a stage show—musicians, acrobats and comedians on an open-air stage in front of the grandstand. The long twilight ended and darkness gathered round the stage, heightening the effect of light and swirling colour. Ethan and George were enthralled by the dancing bear, and even J.T. forgot his impatience during the high-wire act.

After the orchestra screamed out the finale and the dancing girls kicked their last, came the awards ceremony. Jesse joined the rest of the cowboys gathering on the stage. They nudged one another, hobbling like bowlegged penguins, ten-gallon hats sitting over their eyes or held in fumbling hands in front of their shirts. All the power and grace they had displayed in the arena seemed to have been left in the barn with their horses.

One by one they were called out of their wide semicircle to come front and centre and receive their trophies. And for Jesse, the hell he had felt during his ride on Polka Dot had paid off. He had beaten Keno, to be the winner that day. With his presentation, the president of the Stampede Board gave a little sermon on courage and the thrill of watching a real comeback, until Jesse was so embarrassed he almost wished he'd gone home five hours ago. Still, the applause that welled out of the stands and flowed down over him was good to hear. He accepted the silver-mounted saddle and the cheque, and returned to stand with the other cowboys, the trophy on his shoulder.

One thousand dollars. That brought his winnings for the week to fourteen hundred; for the summer to seventeen or eighteen hundred dollars. For a moment he felt tall again—so tall he could see right over the grandstand, over the miles of dark hills to a valley still green in the sunlight, a place where darkness never came. He'd buy that valley now, and bask in its sun for the rest of his life.

The awards had scarcely been completed when the sky flared white and crackled with the opening burst of fireworks. Jesse had wanted to be with George for the fireworks display—it would be the first he'd ever seen—but the crowd was filing down from the grandstand, jamming the area round the stage with people, their upturned faces illuminated by the coloured flashes. Wes Monahan, one of the cowboys, was shouting to him. "At the Wales!" Jesse heard him say. "Room 403. Stop by for a drink."

"Sure!" Jesse called back. "Thanks." When the fireworks ended, he crossed the car park to find J.T. and the boys waiting for him beside the car. George immediately crawled onto the back seat and went to sleep.

"Wes Monahan would like us to stop by for a drink," Jesse said.

"I don't know any Wes Monahan," J.T. replied, "but I can tell right off he's my kind of man."

"The Wales Hotel," Jesse said. As they moved off, Jesse glanced back and saw Ethan's face, white in the glare, signal weariness and disappointment. "We'll only be a minute," Jesse assured him.

Ethan shrugged. "It's all right," he said. He slumped back across his brother's legs and turned his face to the side window.

In the lobby of the Wales Hotel a sign said NO VISITORS AFTER 11 P.M. and a large pendulum clock told them it was forty-five minutes to midnight. But there were people milling in the lobby, running up and down the stairs, ringing for the lift. When he and J.T. got to room 403, the door was open, spilling some of the occupants into the hall—mostly cowboys and their wives, people Jesse had known in days gone by. Inside, people were sitting on the bed, the chairs, the desk and the windowsill, while Wes dispensed drinks from the top of the dressing table. There were many voices and frequent bursts of laughter, but when he saw Jesse, Wes made himself heard. "Here's the champ!" he cried. "Quiet, everybody!" Within a moment or two, the uproar subsided.

"You know this ain't a formal occasion," Wes said. "But I reckon a host has privileges. Tonight it's my privilege to propose a toast to my old friend—a fella with more guts than a slaughterhouse—you may bust his back, but you'll never dint his spirit—and still the best bronc rider I ever did see—Jesse Gifford!"

The assembly drank; there was a short cheer, a couple of cries for a speech. But Wes shouted, "Come on, Jesse. I got a drink for you here that would raise hair on a brass saddle horn." Jesse passed through the crowd. The conversation began again.

He left Wes talking to J.T., and began to greet old friends from the rodeo circuit. It felt good to be a kind of celebrity among these people he respected. As he stood listening and talking, he saw Shirley only a few steps away. She came towards him, hand extended, her lips saying the word "Congratulations." In the hubbub the sound was lost.

"Thanks," he said.

The warm pressure of her hand continued. In a quiet voice she said, "You looked good out there today. I never saw you give a better ride."

"Well, thanks," he said. "That's good to hear." He wanted to say something intensely personal to her, but no words would come. At last he blurted, "I got your note."

"You understood. I didn't know what to put. I mean . . ." In the midst of the din, they had achieved a sudden intimacy. Shirley went on, "I know I'm supposed to be wicked, but I don't feel wicked. I only feel mixed up, and sometimes lonely. But I wonder what you think of me, and I never know what to say to you any more. It all seems to come out twisted. Even 'Goldenrod'."

"I understood. It was the best medicine I've had in years." She still looked so young, as though the years had left her untouched. "Come home with us," he said.

"Not yet. I can't come yet."

"We need you. Not only me. The boys need you, too."

"I know. I feel so miserable."

"I'm going to buy a ranch. Ethan found it really. He ran away from home one night, and came back all excited about this ranch he'd seen."

"Ran away?" she cried. "Why did he run away?"

"It wasn't anything," he said quickly, knowing he'd blundered. "He just went for a ride to cool off. He gets mad at me sometimes."

"The crazy little kid." She looked up, then leaned towards him, even closer than before.

"It's in the foothills," he went on. "With a creek, a log house."

"It's all my fault, isn't it? I've ruined it for all of us—you and Ethan and George . . . and me, too. For me as much as anyone."

"It's all right. You can come home with us tonight."

"If only I could. I've made such terrible mistakes, it seems I'm afraid to do anything any more."

"I think about you every night. I never go to sleep without thinking of you."

"Oh, Jesse . . ." Her voice stopped abruptly, and Jesse looked up to find Keno standing beside them.

"I hope I'm not interrupting anything," Keno said, so loudly that his voice seemed to ride above all the other sounds in the room, until they faded to a murmur, and then stopped completely. Keno seemed uncomfortably aware that he was causing a scene. At first he looked as though he might continue to play it out, but then he hesitated. When he spoke again, his voice was almost a whisper. "It's time to go home," he said. His big hand closed on Shirley's arm and turned her towards the door. Jesse stood flat-footed and watched them leave.

The party seemed to shudder and die. People turned to one another as if in search of a spark that could give life to the room again, but the silence only deepened. Jesse found J.T. Jones. "Ready to go?" he asked quietly. Wes was full of apologies—he shouldn't have invited Keno, but he just didn't think. . . . It was all right, Jesse told him. In fact, it was the best thing that had happened to him all day.

Outside the hotel, there was an old man by the door. "*Albertan,*" he said. "Morning *Albertan.*" Jesse bought a copy and opened it under the light from the hotel window. There on the front was a picture of Jesse Gifford receiving his silver-mounted saddle. He folded the paper, and followed J.T. to the Dodge.

On the long drive home, Jesse tried to stretch out in his half of the front seat. No matter which way he turned he could not relieve the pain, but even as he writhed, he whistled to himself. In his pocket was a cheque for a thousand dollars, and in the boot of the car, wrapped in sacking, was a silver-mounted saddle engraved to Jesse Gifford, Saddle Bronc Champion. Tomorrow he would tack the front page of the *Albertan* to the wall and try to imagine how Keno felt when he opened the paper that morning.

The car finally stopped. They were home. J.T. wakened the boys, and they walked unsteadily into the house. Jesse hobbled in and flung himself on the bed. He heard J.T. clump his trophy down in the kitchen, and soon the sound of the Dodge faded off into the night.

The boys were asleep again, in bed with their clothes on. Jesse roused himself enough to take off their shoes and pull the covers over their shoulders. He lay back on his own bed, and felt his pain beginning to ease.

He was the Champ. There was nobody else as good at his business on this globe.

Chapter 10

For the next few days, while Jesse nursed his back, it seemed as if the only topic of conversation was "the ranch". J.T. tried to talk Jesse into buying irrigated land where, as he put it, a man could make a living. But Jesse didn't want to spend his springtime sloshing through an irrigated field, or his summer hoeing in a potato patch, or milking a half dozen cows night and morning for the sake of a creamery cheque once a week. He pictured hills covered with buffalo grass and cattle. Ethan campaigned for the ranch he had discovered, and one morning J.T. came over to ask Jesse if he'd like a ride to Pincher Creek. "I got to take a part in to the blacksmith's."

"You mean, and look at the ranch?"

"That's what I was thinking of."

"Let's go, Jesse," Ethan exclaimed.

"Oh, I don't think you kids would want to go," J.T. said. "What would you do in town all afternoon?"

It was clear that J.T.'s invitation had not been meant to include the boys. "They wouldn't be any trouble," Jesse said.

"I don't care what you do," J.T. replied. "Bring your horses and dogs, too, if you want. I'll pick you up about noon." He walked out of the house and drove away.

Shortly after lunch the four of them headed west towards the mountains. They travelled several miles, crossed the Waterton River, drove up a long hill past the Yarrow Church from which, it was said, you could see for fifty miles in any direction. To the south and west, the view was cut short by the mountains, but the blue hump of the Porcupine Hills was visible far to the north, and east of them the prairie faded across an immense distance, until only a shadow of the Milk River Ridge could be seen at the horizon.

Soon after they turned north on the Waterton-Pincher road, they came to the sign nailed to a fence post. "It's still there," Ethan cried.

"I'm running late," J.T. said. "I'll let you off here, and pick you up on my way home." No doubt he had planned a day spent wandering from pool hall to beer parlour. The boys would cramp his style, so he was ditching Jesse, too. Jesse got out of the car, the boys behind him, and J.T. drove swiftly on his way.

When the sound of the Dodge had faded over the hill, the quiet came down like a curtain—a quiet deepened by the gradual awareness of insect noises and an awesome rushing sound that seemed to flow out of the mountains. Near at hand a grove of aspens rustled, like the sound of a man turning over in a straw bed.

"Come on," Ethan said. He started up the road. Jesse looked at his younger son, whose face was tipped towards the mountains as if he were caught in a spell.

"Shall we go?" Jesse said. George put his hand out to his father, and hand in hand they followed Ethan deeper into the hills.

The road ended with a gate across it, and from there the two dirt tracks in the grass wound through and over creeks and hills. Finally, the track dipped sharply towards a creek and then flattened onto a clearing which held a squat log cabin and a few outbuildings. Further back among the trees, Jesse could see the roof of a hay barn. "There she is," Ethan said.

As they drew near the cabin, the door opened and a woman stepped out. Three girls slipped round her and lined up against the log wall, staring at them. Jesse walked closer, then stopped and took off his hat. "Howdy, ma'am," he said. "You got a ranch for sale?" The woman nodded and Jesse turned his head, viewing the creek, the barn, the log house. "How much land?" he asked.

"They's a half section. Hay and pastureland."

"We'll look around," Jesse said.

She pressed her thin lips together twice before she spoke. "They's a harse in the barn if you want to ride."

"Is the place fenced?" Jesse asked.

"They's a fence hall the way round the south half, and a cross-fence down the middle. Hall the cattle yer see belong—'bout sevenny-five head or so. Half a dozen harses."

"We'll see you in a while," Jesse said. "After we have a look."

They got the horse out of the barn. Jesse and George rode, while Ethan ran beside them, along the creek and over the hills. "It's perfect," Ethan said, puffing.

The buildings were half-falling down. The fences needed repair and the hay should have been cut two weeks ago. "Pretty near," Jesse replied.

After they returned the horse to the stable, they strolled round the barnyard. In the grass on a high creek bank, a few pieces of machinery stood in various stages of decay. On a hay rake, Jesse could see remnants of red paint. An old mower stood at one side, cutter bar raised. Its tongue had been broken and spliced with boards wired like splints on either side.

They passed under some trees and came to the log barn. It had been built into a hillside, so that one end of the roof butted directly against the steeply sloping grass, and the other soared thirty feet above the ground. On the floor of the barn lay sunken heaps of last year's bleached and musty hay crop.

"What do you think?" Jesse asked.

"Perfect," Ethan said.

"It's too far away from anywhere," George said.

"Let's go see what she wants for it," Jesse said.

The cabin door opened as they approached, and the woman invited them in. The interior, though larger than their place at J.T. Jones's, seemed smaller because of the furniture, boxes and trunks in it. The log walls were almost black, the mortar in the cracks grey with age.

"Set down," the woman said. She tucked a loose strand of hair into the bun at the back of her head.

Jesse and Ethan sat on straight-backed chairs, and George sidled between his father's legs. "Your husband home?" Jesse asked. The woman sat down at the table. Her girls stood against the wall.

"My husband's daid," the woman replied. "He died in the winter. I'se glad, Lord forgive me. He died, and I'm goin' to heaven—back home to Manitoba." She sighed. "They was a blizzard. We couldn't get him to town." She looked at Jesse, her lips working. Her eyes kept sliding off him. "I'se scared of that man alive, and I'se scareder of him daid." She hesitated. "We stuffed him through a hole in the ice. I ain't been down the creek all summer. I jest been settin' here prayin'. Ain't planted no garden. Ain't cut no hay. Jest milk the cow and pray. You buy this ranch, you're an angel, mister."

"How much are you asking?" Jesse said.

"Two thousand, five hundred dollars. Lock stock and barrel. We won't take nothin' with us but the clothes on our backs."

"I haven't got that much money," Jesse said.

"How much money you got?"

"Fifteen hundred dollars. Cash." Counting what Ethan had won, he had a little more than that, but he didn't want to start ranching flat broke.

"Thank the Lord. I'll take it." She opened the drawer of the kitchen table, took out a large piece of paper, and unfolded it carefully. "This is the Duplicate·Certificate of Title." She handed it to Jesse. "Everythin' free and clear."

The title granted to Mabel Gunderson an estate in fee simple, and described the section, township and range west of the fifth meridian, containing three hundred and twenty acres, more or less. It was dated May 27, 1919.

It was a bargain—a bailing-wire bargain. They might take a while to get it in shape, but Jesse had lots of time. "How come it's in your name?" he said.

"I bought it with my own money that my pa left me. Gunder never had nothin'. He come home from the war all dressed up in his uniform, full of big talk and plans fer his cattle empire, as he called it. I'se just a silly girl in them days, and I believed him." She shook her head. "He wanted it in his name, but I never done that, thank the Lord."

Jesse looked at Ethan. "It'll be a big job," he said.

The boy's eyes were bright with excitement. "We can do it!"

The woman had even got a printed bill of sale from the store. As Jesse filled out the form, he wondered if she was really as simple as she pretended. When he had finished, she didn't even read it—just took the pen and laboriously signed her name.

"We need a witness," Jesse said.

"We'll stop at the lawyer's office when you take me to Pincher. We'll catch the six-thirty train. Can you drive us in the democrat?"

"Today?" Jesse asked.

"Right now. We been packed for months." She rose and dragged a trunk out of the corner. "Get your things," she said to the girls. They disappeared into a bedroom. "They's a democrat behint the barn," she said to Jesse. "Time you get it hitched, we'll be ready."

"Don't you want your money?"

She looked at him. "I forgot." She sat down again.

Jesse reached inside his shirt and pulled the money belt from round his body. He emptied the pockets and counted the notes on the table in front of her. "Fifteen hundred dollars," he said at last.

The woman placed her hand over the untidy stack of notes as if they might blow away. "The Lord's hand is in it!" She tucked the money into her pocket.

"You better let the Mounties know about your husband."

"I'll tell 'em when I get to town," she said.

They brought round the rubber-tyred democrat and loaded the trunk and boxes into it. Ethan prepared to drive the women to Pincher Station, while Jesse and George stayed behind in case J.T. should call for them. "Be sure you stop at the lawyer's," Jesse told Ethan. "Leave the papers with him and ask him to register the title." As soon as the women were seated, Ethan flipped the reins and clicked his tongue, and the democrat rolled silently away.

The woman looked back over her shoulder, her face turned down, but her eyes raised as if the mountain were about to fall and she was escaping just in time. "Thank the Lord," she said.

JESSE WATCHED the democrat pull over the hill and out of sight. He felt stunned. For the first time in his life the ground beneath his boots belonged to him, and somehow the whole earth had changed. He was no longer a gladiator struggling in the dust of the arena for other people's amusement; he owned a three-hundred-and-twenty-acre corner of God's creation.

"Come on," he said to George. "Let's see if we can get that old mower ready to go." Hand in hand, they walked across the barnyard. Hay to cut, fences to fix, calves to brand—he'd have to register his brand now—harness to mend. A body down the creek.

The grass had grown up so thick beneath the mower that when he let down the cutter bar, released the connecting rod and tried to pull out the blade, the rusty sections wouldn't move. Pushing the knife back and forth, he finally mangled the grass enough to pull the blade out. Then he saw that along its four-foot length, at least three sections were broken. If there were new sections somewhere, the gentleman down the creek wouldn't have tried to mow with this snaggletoothed blade. The best he could hope for was to find a whetstone. He started towards the old log shed. Rings and wheels and bits of chain hung from its sides: Gunderson had apparently never thrown anything away. Jesse saw a wheel grinder beside the shed. He sat down on the narrow wooden saddle and pressed the treadle with his foot. The grinder did a slow quarter turn.

George put his hands over his ears. "Ooh," he said. "It squeaks."

"It squeaks," Jesse agreed, "but it turns." He held the mower blade like a balancing pole, pressed the treadle down, let it up, pressed it down. . . . The grinder turned, screeching on two melancholy notes. He brought one rusty blade section down against the whirling stone. There was a sharp, grating noise and a spray of sparks. "Wow!" George cried.

Jesse had found one thing on the ranch that worked. Inside the shop was a grimy oilcan, and with it he toned down the squeaks of the grinder. Then he settled himself comfortably to sharpen the sections and grind a cutting edge on the broken ones. Sparks flew out like the tail of a comet. A few followed the stone all the way round, so it appeared to be circled with a slender rim of fire.

Jesse still felt stunned. Two hours ago he had been a bum; now he was a landowner, a taxpayer, a solid citizen with a half section of land and a wheel grinder. It was salvation, pure and simple. He had promised Shirley a ranch. But it had taken longer than he expected—too long.

Still, Shirley had never asked for any promises. He was a green cowhand and she was the boss's niece, come from Wyoming to spend the summer. She helped her aunt fix meals for the cowboys and take care of the house. After supper one night he'd begged off from a horseshoe game and strolled down the lane where he knew she sometimes walked in the evening. He'd missed quite a few horseshoe games after that . . . "You ain't careful, Jesse, the next ring you get'll be on her finger, and in your nose." It pleased Jesse to be teased about Shirley. It was an acknowledgment that she was his girl.

And one summer night under a tree down the slope from the ranch house, he'd lain with his head in her lap and talked about the ranch they'd have: not big, a couple of sections maybe, but good land, with lots of white-faced cattle. There'd be a red barn by the river, with an iron horse weather vane swinging from the peak. The upstairs windows of the house would look over the roof of the veranda that went all round the front. In the summer the organdie curtains would blow back and forth in the open windows.

"It sounds beautiful," Shirley said. "But I don't care whether the barn's red, or the house has a porch, if I can live there with you."

Well, there was only a half section of land here, the cattle were either brockle-faced or spotted and the barn was weathered old logs with a thatched roof that needed replacing. But it was where he lived. If Shirley knew about it, wouldn't she live here too?

He turned the mower blade over. The cutting edges gleamed in a silver zigzag against the ugly rust. He took the oilcan with him back to the mower and oiled the machine. As he slid the blade into place, it smoothly clipped the grass which had grown between the guards. "George," he said, "as soon as Ethan gets back with the team, we're ready to cut hay."

It was almost dark when Ethan drove into the yard, the team walking with heads down and tails hanging straight. He pulled the horses to a stop in front of the barn. Then he and Jesse unhitched them. "Did you go to the lawyer's?" Jesse asked.

"Yup. He'll take care of everything. And she caught her train all right. You'd have thought someone was after her."

"Maybe she pulled a fast one," Jesse said. "But she couldn't fake the title. As long as she *is* Mabel Gunderson, and as long as they didn't mortgage the place after this title was made, I can't see how she could have fleeced us."

"She sure seemed to keep looking over her shoulder."

They led the horses into the barn and unharnessed them.

"Mama's coming home now, isn't she?" George asked.

"I think she is," Ethan said.

"What do you tell him stuff like that for?" Jesse said. "You only make him unhappy."

"She didn't ask you when she went," Ethan said. "Does she have to let you know when she's coming back?"

The team, turned loose now, walked slowly out of the stable. The sun was down. In the strange, unreal light of evening, the heavy beasts lowered themselves to the ground and, groaning wearily, rolled in the dust of the barnyard.

Jesse heard a car horn sounding impatiently at the top of the hill—it was probably J.T. As he started walking up the road, Jesse called back over his shoulder, "You boys better go see where they put the lamp or we'll be eating our supper in the dark."

He returned in a few minutes. "That was J.T. all right. He thought I was crazy to buy a place like this, and maybe he's right. Anyhow, he went off in a huff. I told him we'd fetch our things later, but for now, the first thing we have to do is mow some hay." Jesse thought about the outline of the hay barn, high and black against the sky. "Think we can fill that old barn with hay before the snow flies?"

"Sure we can," Ethan said.

Chapter 11

Jesse had never known a morning like the one that followed. The sunlight on the hills looked as yellow as if it had been taken from a palette; as if, should you touch it with your fingers, they'd come away yellow. Jesse left the boys still sleeping while he went to milk the cow and harness the team. As he crossed the yard, milk bucket on his arm, he felt a peace that he had never known before. While he milked, he thought of the things he must do. The first was to fill that barn with hay to be sure of getting their cattle through the winter. And, later that day, they'd get their things from J.T. Jones; they couldn't wear the same pair of socks for ever.

Something else bothered him. When he went to the pasture to catch the horses, he remembered the man who was buried in the creek. Where was that man now? Hooked on a branch somewhere? There seemed to be a blemish in the air—a hint of decay he hadn't noticed before.

The haying went well. The mower worked. They found the remnants of a set of harness, and by stringing together every scrap of leather on the place with copper rivets they found in the shed, they fitted out another team of horses. While Jesse mowed, Ethan raked the hay into rows to dry and, later, tossed it. Within a few days they were ready to start stacking. The weather held, and the machinery didn't break down, and Jesse could bear the pain in his back. And here they were into August already. But periodically Jesse seemed to catch again that faint, revolting stench of death. Had Mrs. Gunderson told the Mounties?

It was a hot day, almost without a breeze. Each forkful of hay that Jesse and Ethan lifted onto the wagon gave off a trail of chaff and dust that seemed to glitter in the sunlight. George drove the team along the row, and when he drew abreast of a haycock, Jesse shouted, "Whoa!" George was delighted. He stood on the floor of the hay wagon, scarcely tall enough to reach his arms over the top board and hold the reins. When the hay got as high as they could reach, Ethan climbed on top of it and made his way round the outside edge, stamping. The high, fluffy load quickly flattened and spread against the sides of the hay wagon.

Forking up the hay from the ground, Jesse felt the fires of hell in his back: he was not sure how long he could continue. At last he shouted, "OK!" and tossed his fork on top of the load. Then he followed, climbing over the rear of the wagon, and lay down on the soft hay. George started the team, and they turned back towards the barn, half a mile away.

As they approached the barn, George stopped the team. Inside, the results of their effort were beginning to show. The hay was stacked under the roof to a height of ten or twelve feet. In fact, they'd soon have to start a stack out in the field.

Jesse took the lines from George. "Giddap!" he shouted, leaning back, his arms flexed against the rhythmic pull of the reins as the horses marched close beside the huge logs of the barn. "Whoa!" Jesse shouted. The team stopped abruptly. He tied the reins to the hay wagon's middle upright, and turned to take up his fork.

"Who's that?" Ethan asked.

Jesse looked up the track that led into the yard. A man on horseback was approaching. Even on this hot day he wore a fringed buckskin coat. Horse and saddle and man all seemed caked with the same grime and sweat. The man was tall, perhaps fifty years old. Beneath his chin a bush of grey, matted hair sprouted from his open shirt. He rode close to the hay wagon and stopped, facing Jesse.

"Who are you?" he said.

"Jesse Gifford."

The man gestured towards the hay wagon. "How much she givin' you fer puttin' up the hay? She ain't got no money to pay ya, so you must be doin' it for a cut. How big a cut is she givin' ya?"

"Who are you?" Jesse asked.

"Who am I? This is my hay yer puttin' up." The smell of death came on the wind, stronger than ever.

"You're not Gunderson?" Jesse asked him.

"Who'd ya think I was?" He looked around. "Why ain't she out here? She some kind of lady now—too good to work in the hay?"

"She told me you were dead."

"She told you what?"

"She said you died last winter. She sold the ranch to me."

Gunderson laughed. "That sly old dog sold the ranch to you?"

That sly old dog? Could a simple-minded woman put on an act like that? Jesse had the bill of sale, and the title had been in her name. She might have lied about her husband, but the land transfer was legal.

"How much did you pay her?" Gunderson asked, still laughing.

"Fifteen hundred dollars."

He looked at Jesse. "You poor son-of-a-gun!" He laughed so hard he doubled over his saddle horn. Then he straightened, looked at the hay barn, and shouted, "Then you ain't got no cut at all. I got my hay put up for free." He laughed again. "Where is she now?"

"I don't know," Jesse said. "She caught the train for somewhere."

Gunderson sobered again. "Manitoba! She went back to her brothers." Suddenly he shouted at Jesse, "Get off my ranch."

"You don't have a ranch," Jesse said. "You never had one."

The man sat on his horse, glaring at Jesse. His cheeks showed a pallor through the brown skin, like milk in an amber glass. "Mister. When we first come out here my wife thought just 'cause she paid for the ranch it give her a little say. It took a while, but I learned her different. I ain't got time to work with you like that. Now git down off'n that hay and all of you git up the road."

"You're trespassing," Jesse said. "I have a bill of sale to prove it."

The man whooped. "Bill of sale! You're like my wife. She had a Duplicate Certificate of Title she told me a thousand times. A piece of paper ain't nothin' up in these hills, mister. I broke my back workin' this place for seventeen years, and no piece of paper can take it away from me."

Jesse didn't know what to say.

"Why d'ya think she told you I'se daid?" Gunderson went on. "'Cause she know'd the ranch was mine, that's why. Yer a stranger here, mister, but you ask any man in forty mile whose ranch this is, and he'll tell you Asa Gunderson's. Just 'cause I rid away fer a little peace and fresh air ain't the same as if I'se daid. So you can walk out of here or git carried out, and either way it don't matter to me."

Jesse couldn't think of any way to answer Gunderson. He pulled a forkful of hay free from the load and tossed it high into the barn.

"Look out!" Ethan cried.

Jesse spun round as Gunderson threw his lariat and his horse turned, dancing sideways to the hay wagon. Jesse flung up his arms and ducked—too late. The rope whipped round his body as Gunderson's horse lunged away. Jesse felt himself yanked over the edge of the load with stupefying force. As he crashed against the ground, his leg buckled under him and he was dragged forward, bouncing on his stomach through the dust behind the galloping horse. He heard Ethan shout behind him. He glimpsed flashing hooves through the dust and felt the barnyard rocks smashing against his sides. Then he closed his eyes and wondered how long it took to drag a man to death.

When he hit the creek, he felt the cold water splash in his face. His body planed onto the water and began to sink to the boulders on the bottom, as he floundered and choked. But then strong arms dragged him to the side of the creek, and laid him down on his back. The lariat was taken off over his head. Through a blur of water running down his face, he saw Gunderson laughing.

"You poor son-of-a-gun," he said. "Thought I'se goin' to drag you to death, didn't ya? I'm a kindly feller. 'Tain't yer fault my old lady lied to ya. But if I ever catch yer face on my land again, I'll strangle ya. Savvy?"

Jesse saw Gunderson get on his horse and ride away, and a moment later the faces of his boys appeared above him. "He was going to kill you, wasn't he, Jesse?" Ethan said.

"No. He only wanted to scare us a little." And that proved the

64

ranch belonged to Jesse. If Gunderson had a legal claim, he wouldn't have to use such tactics.

Slowly the pain which at first diffused through Jesse's body began to concentrate in certain areas. Then, as he tried to move his leg, the entire weight of pain rushed there, so massive and pervading that he collapsed completely, breathing as though from a long run. "What's the matter, Jesse?" Ethan asked.

"My right leg." He couldn't even raise his head to look at it.

"It's all funny," George said. "It must be broken."

That was all he needed now: a broken leg. Six weeks in traction, and Gunderson would have his hooks so deep in this ranch that Jesse could never break him loose. As the pain in his leg began to mount, he raised gingerly on his elbows to peek down and see the toe of his boot canted unnaturally to one side. "Take your pocketknife," he told Ethan. "Cut off my boot, 'fore it gets any tighter. And be careful."

The boy was careful, Jesse could tell. Still, when he got to the swollen ankle, the boot was so tight that it was difficult to cut, and at times Jesse felt as though the knife went deep into his swollen flesh.

"Where'd Gunderson go?" Jesse asked.

"Over the hill, like he was headed for town."

Gunderson knew his wife had fifteen hundred dollars, so he might head for Manitoba. Or he might simply have ridden over the hill and be hiding somewhere watching and laughing.

"I've got to get to a doctor," Jesse said. "Ethan, you hitch the team to the democrat, load the box with hay, and bring it over here. George, see if you can find two straight boards about three feet long. And bring that binder twine that's in the shed."

While the boys were gone, Jesse dragged himself painfully onto a level patch of grass nearby. George returned with some boards, and then Ethan came with the democrat. Under Jesse's direction, he placed a board on each side of the injured leg, from the knee down past the heel, and began to wrap it with binder twine.

"Now," Jesse said. He wiped his palm across his cold face. "Fetch a couple of blankets from the house," he said. He had in mind to climb in the democrat while they were gone, so he could moan a little if he had to. Halfway over the wheel, he changed his mind, moaning, and decided to wait for Ethan to help him, but he could neither lower himself nor pull himself over. The muscles in his arms began to tremble with the weight and stress, and he knew he'd have to do something. With one blinding effort, he hitched his good leg beneath him, heaved with his hands, and pushed upwards with all his might. Just as the world went dark, he felt himself roll onto the hay in the box of the democrat.

Consciousness came slowly. He was aware first of the sun in his eyes, then the gentle, rhythmic movement of the hay beneath him. His leg seemed numb now. He heard George's voice from the front of the democrat. "Giddap." Gently tipping his head up, and raising his eyes as high as he could, he made out the crown of the boy's hair, the colour of a halo, bouncing across the sky.

"Where's Ethan?" Jesse asked.

"Whoa!" George cried, and pulled on the reins so hard that he sat down, almost on top of his father's head. "You all right, Jesse? Gee. I'se scared you was dead."

"You always think I'm dead. Where's Ethan?"

"He stayed home."

"Stayed home! That crazy guy will kill him!"

"He's guarding the ranch," George said. "I'm s'posed to take you to the hospital."

"Not without Ethan, you're not. Turn this outfit round, George, 'fore I trounce you good."

George scrambled to his feet again, and moved out of reach. "Giddap," he said, and they started to move again. "Ethan said you might not like it, but we got to keep that bad old guy off the ranch."

It took them hours to get there. The sun was far down in the sky as George drove the team up in the shadow of the hospital, and Jesse was so exhausted that the moment they touched him, he blacked out again. This time, when he came to, he was in a hospital room with a scaffolding above him, and his right leg stretched upwards like a whitewashed log. He remembered the boys, and fumbled for a buzzer. Presently a nurse appeared.

"Did you see the boy who brought me here?" Jesse asked.

"No. I wasn't on then."

"Could you find out what happened to him? He's only six years old. And could you ask the Mounties to send somebody over?"

The nurse left, and in a minute returned. "Nobody saw where your boy went," she said. "He's gone now."

Crazy little George. Did he start back to the ranch alone—back through the evening foothills into the dark mountains?

The nurse said, "The constable will be right over."

When the Mountie came, the officer's wide shoulders seemed almost to fill the room. "Mr. Gifford?" he said.

"Hello, officer." Jesse felt the words tumbling up into his mouth faster than he could speak. "Please hurry."

"First you'll have to tell me what you want me to do."

"Save my boys," Jesse said. His face was still cold and damp as he rubbed his palm across it. He couldn't be sure whether the dampness was from tears. "The crazy little beggars. Save my boys."

Chapter 12

As the light of morning slowly rose in the hospital window, Jesse tried to think how, lying there, he could control the delicate world he had scarcely started to build outside.

First, the boys. They couldn't stay on the ranch alone. But what would happen to the ranch with nobody there? The hay crop would be lost. And if the cattle found a hole in the fence, they might wander back into the mountains and become food for the bears. Well, he could ask Shirley to come and take the boys. But if she did, he might lose them for ever.

About midmorning, the Mountie returned and stood above him, smiling under the hard, flat brim of his hat. "Those are some boys you've got, Mr. Gifford," he said.

"You brought them to town?" Jesse asked.

"No. I'm afraid this time the Mounties didn't get their man. They're all right. They just don't want to leave the ranch."

"But they've got to. There's no telling what Gunderson will do."

"Gunderson won't do anything for a while," the Mountie said. "Yesterday he turned his horse in to the community pasture outside town and caught the train for Manitoba. Mr. Burns sold him the ticket and saw him get on the train."

"Thank heaven for that."

"But the boys aren't taking any chances. I drove out there this morning, but when I got out of the car, they shouted for me to leave. One had a rifle pointing at me."

"Ethan!" There had been a Winchester carbine hanging on the wall of the Gunderson cabin. Jesse turned his face away for a moment. It seemed like a serious offence to threaten a Mountie, and he didn't want the officer to guess that he was proud.

"I could have forced his hand, I guess, and brought them here," the man said. "But to tell you the truth, I liked the boy's spirit. I thought I'd come and discuss it with you."

"It's probably best to leave them alone," Jesse said.

"Well, they should be all right for a week or so. In the meantime, I'll try to slip out there once in a while to see how they're doing."

"I'd appreciate it," Jesse said.

The days inched away. The doctor had projected four weeks in traction, followed by several months in a walking cast. That became his goal—the walking cast. With that, at least he could go home.

One day, the nurse announced visitors and Ethan and George came in right behind her. Their faces and hands were clean, and their shirts and overalls had apparently just been washed, but not ironed. Ethan was unsure what to do, but George flung himself up onto the high bed and threw both arms round Jesse's neck.

"Careful, sonny," the nurse said. "You mustn't get up there."

Jesse clasped his arm round the little body. "He's all right."

When the nurse left, Ethan bent over him and Jesse extended his embrace to include both of them. For several minutes they just lay there, so close they could feel the thump of each other's hearts. Finally Ethan raised himself up, but George still remained, his arms round his father's neck.

"How's it going out there?" Jesse said.

"Fine. We finished the hay," Ethan replied. "Just what you had cut. We got it all in the barn."

"How did you get it up there? It was so high I could hardly reach."

"We got a rope and an old basket. George fills the basket with hay, and I pull it up into the barn."

How had a waster like him fathered boys such as these?

"It takes us all day to unload," Ethan continued, "but we finished today. We had to celebrate, so we decided to come and see you. When can you come home?"

"Not for three more weeks. When I get my walking cast. Listen, if I can find a place for you fellows to stay, will you come into town? I don't want you out there alone."

"We're all right. Aren't we, George?"

George didn't look at Jesse. "Sure," he said, but his voice was very soft. He nodded his head. "We're all right."

"Besides, we got to be there when old Gunderson comes back," Ethan said. "We won't let him take our ranch away."

"Well, that's something else I want to talk to you about," Jesse said. "Gunderson is crazy. The only way to treat him is to stay a long ways away. I've got word from the lawyer that our title has been registered, so it doesn't matter how wild he acts, he can't have the ranch. If he's sitting on it when I get out, we'll just take a Mountie home with us and put him off. If you see any sign of Gunderson, get out the back door, and come in here and tell me. You hear?"

"You said yourself he's crazy. How do you know he won't steal the cattle, and bust up the machinery, and burn down the house? We're ready for him. Aren't we, George?" George nodded.

"He could kill the both of you!" Jesse exclaimed. "Do you think that lousy ranch means anything to me without you fellows?"

"He won't kill us," Ethan said solemnly. "We'd better get back."

"Do we have to go already?" George cried.

"Ethan," Jesse said. "You've got to listen to me."

"I have to take care of the ranch," the boy replied.

George sat up and gave Jesse a squeeze goodbye, but Ethan stood back, away from him. "Don't go yet," Jesse said. "Let's talk a while."

"We'd better go," Ethan said. "I don't like to be away too long."

"Goodbye, Daddy," George said. And the boys were gone.

Gunderson might get back any time now. There was only one thing to do, and that was get the boys off the ranch. And he could think of only one way to do that. He asked the nurse to phone Shirley for him and see if she would come.

HE HAD BEEN DOZING when she walked in, and she approached the bed so quietly that he didn't know she was there until he heard the chair scrape. He opened his eyes just as she sat down. At first it seemed like a dream.

"Hello," she said. "What *have* you been up to?"

"I got yanked off a haystack by a dead man, if you can believe that."

"You sound like you're still coming out of the ether," she said. "Where are the boys?"

"That's why I wanted you to come." He told her the whole story.

"So you really bought a ranch," she said, when he was through.

"Oh, it's not much. Just prairie wool and dandelion. But it's good enough for us. We can live on it."

"What do you want me to do?"

"The boys are out there waiting for Gunderson to show up. Before he comes, I want them off the place, and you're the only person I know that can talk to them."

She smiled. "You want me to get shot at?"

"They won't shoot at you and you know it."

69

"Come on, don't be so serious."

"But this is serious, Shirley. Ethan won't want to leave. If you have to hog-tie him, do it."

"How do I get to the place?"

"It's only fifteen miles by car."

When he had given her directions, she rose and walked out of the room. He could see her body beneath the red cotton dress, curved and soft as it had always been.

Two days went by. Every moment Jesse expected to see them come through the door. First he wondered what took them so long. Then he began to worry for fear there'd been trouble. Finally he realized that she must have taken the boys and returned directly to Keno's. They hadn't even stopped to see him.

But on the second afternoon Shirley and George came in, hand in hand, laughing. George climbed up and hugged his father. Shirley let her cool palm rest on his arm for just a moment. Her lips were smiling. "How are you?" she asked. "Did you think we were never coming? We had work to do, didn't we, George?"

"Sure did. We washed the windows. Mama scrubbed the outside and I scrubbed the inside, and we pulled faces at each other."

"I've never seen such a place," Shirley said. "Well, you know some of the places we moved into. But the house really had a board floor under all that dirt. We washed all the bedding, and Ethan made three trips to the junk pile with the wheelbarrow full of stuff."

"Where is Ethan?"

"He wouldn't come. He had to stay and guard the ranch."

"I told you to get him off that place."

"Jesse, I tried. But he's just as stubborn as you are."

"Knock him over the head. Kidnap him."

"No," she said coolly, and sat down. "You'll be in here another couple of weeks. I've decided I'll stay with them that long."

"You're as bad as Ethan. Do you think Gunderson would hesitate to break your neck?"

"I don't know. But I think Ethan is right. It's important to stay on the place. I don't think anybody should walk in and take over just because it's unoccupied. Especially after we've just cleaned it up."

"And stacked the hay," George said.

Jesse groaned. "So here I have you come down to help, and all you do is join the enemy. What about Keno?"

"I'll phone him and tell him not to expect me for a week or two."

"I just can't let you do it," Jesse said. "It's too risky."

"Oh? And how are you going to stop us?" She reached into her handbag. "We brought the cribbage board," she said. She smoothed a place for the board on the side of the bed and handed the pack to him to shuffle. "Come on. We haven't played crib for a long time." Her slender fingers pressed the pegs into place. Jesse began to shuffle the cards. To him, it seemed that perhaps in a previous life he might have played cribbage with Shirley.

After that, Shirley and George came to see him every afternoon with reports on progress at the ranch. The house was clean. Their clothes were mended. The fence was fixed. The hens were laying more eggs. One of the mares had a new colt. Somehow, even the dark shadow of Gunderson began to grow hazy in Jesse's mind.

Then one day they were late. His first thought was Gunderson. He'd had time to go to Manitoba and get that money from his wife, and now he was back to claim the ranch. Jesse pictured his wife and boys pitted against Gunderson. How could he have been so foolish? They were his responsibility and, once more, he had failed them.

Towards evening, Shirley and George came in. They were walking slowly, but they smiled. "Did Gunderson come back?" Jesse asked.

"Quit worrying about Gunderson," Shirley replied. "If he comes, we'll just give him a piece of pie full of broken glass."

"That guy would think it was peanuts," Jesse said.

"Forget about Gunderson," Shirley replied. "We've had a big day. We went to J.T. Jones's and got your things. The dishes and shotgun and bedding. Your trophy saddle is beautiful." Then she added, "The little photograph was still on the table."

"I kept it for the boys. So they wouldn't forget you," he said.

Why did he say things like that? He kept it for himself—to torture him every night before he went to sleep, and every morning when he woke up, because even the misery of remembering was better than trying to pretend she didn't exist.

"I'm tired," she said. "It was cold today. No sun, and a cold wind blowing. I guess our summer is over. Do you know when you'll be able to come home?"

So she was anxious to get back to Keno. "About a week, I guess."

"Maybe I'll stay an extra day or two. Help you get settled."

"That would be great, if you could," he said. "I'll probably be pretty awkward when they turn me loose."

"Of course, if you don't think it would be right . . . I mean, proper . . ." She was almost blushing.

71

Look who was talking about proper! She was still his wife, wasn't she? It would be a lot more proper than for her to go back to Keno. "You'll be safe," he said. "I couldn't catch Hungry Dog's grandmother with this fence post of a leg."

"What if I didn't run?" Shirley asked.

He had something in mind to say, but at her words it seemed his senses dissolved. All he wanted to do was put his arm round her, to heal the wound that had lain open for so long. He couldn't speak, for fear he'd reveal his confusion. She sat, not speaking either, while the colour rose in her cheeks. "We'd better go," she said. For a moment she rested her hands on his. "Hurry home."

Chapter 13

The next day they didn't come at all. Jesse had begun to watch for them in the early morning. Over and over in his mind, he brought back the words she'd spoken yesterday. If she was trying to tell him something, why didn't she just come out and say it? Then, when the day passed and she didn't come at all, he felt that she'd been deliberately playing with him.

Darkness came. Slowly the activity of the hospital subsided. The nurse prepared him for sleep and turned out his light, but Jesse didn't want to sleep. Still, in time, he began to drowse.

He became aware of someone near him, and opened his eyes. There was a shadowy figure crouched on the side of his bed away from the door. It spoke in a whisper: "Jesse."

"Ethan. What are you doing here?"

"Shh. I sneaked in."

"What's the matter? Did Gunderson come?"

"No. Keno came to take Mama. He says she's going back with him. But she says she won't leave George and me alone. So he says they'll take us too. I'm not going to live with that guy."

"Did he chase you?"

"I ran out the door and George started after me, but he grabbed George and held him. So I got on a horse and headed up in the hills. Then after a while he got out the other horse and came looking for me. I kept ahead of him, but I was scared, Jesse. I decided the best thing was to come and talk to you. He had me cut off from the road, so I had to go 'way back through the hills."

"Shirley's still home?"

"She and George are at the house, and Keno's beating the bushes for me."

It was one thing for a man to take your wife away from you, if she went of her own accord. It was something else to kidnap your whole family. "Can you tell if Shirley wants to go or stay?" Jesse said.

"She wants to stay. I can tell. We've had so much fun since she came." Then he added, "'Cept we needed you, of course."

"Well, I'm coming home with you right now."

Ethan looked at the overhead bars and ropes and weights. "You can't," he said. "Not till they take this stuff off you."

"Then we've got to be quiet," Jesse said. "We can't turn on the light and we can't shut the door. Now, untie that rope from the hook in my cast. Be sure you've got hold of the weight. If we drop one of those, we might as well blow a bugle to tell them we're going."

Ethan had a firm hold on the weight when the end of the rope slipped free, but Jesse's leg fell like a log to the bed. At first he felt as though he could not move it, but finally he raised himself and sat on the edge of the bed. "See if my clothes are in the closet," he said.

Ethan groped in the little cupboard. "Just a shirt and overalls. And your boots. It's cold tonight. You can't go without a coat."

Jesse motioned for the boy to bring the clothes. He put the shirt on over his hospital gown. "Where's your pocketknife?" He took it and slit the outside seam on the right side of his overalls from top to bottom. Then he pulled them on over his good leg, with the belt holding them together at the top and the right leg flapping free. Above the cast his thigh was partly bare. He slipped on his left sock and boot, then slid off the bed and balanced on one foot. The room seemed to turn and slant. He caught Ethan's shoulder.

"How do you feel?" the boy asked.

"Like I haven't been out of bed for three weeks," he said. He hopped over to the window. It slid up easily, and the cold wind rushed in. "Let's go this way," he said. "You first."

They were at the rear of the hospital. Ethan put both legs through the window and, hanging onto the sill with his hands, let himself down. There was a *chuck* when his boots struck the ground. He looked up at Jesse. "OK," he said. "Come on."

Jesse put the leg with the cast out of the window. The wind blew against his exposed thigh, and fluttered his shirt. He put his other leg through the window, letting himself slip downwards as he turned over. His hip joint ached with the sudden weight of the cast. He lowered himself, hesitated, dropped, trying to hold the cast up, staggered when he landed, and tipped dizzily against the building. Slowly he rolled round on his good leg until he was facing outwards.

"Bring your horse here," Jesse said.

While Ethan was gone, Jesse leaned against the wall. He felt as if he had no substance—as if the cold wind were blowing right through him, shaking his bones. Slowly, though, the ground came up firmly beneath his good foot. When the horse came he took the saddle horn in both hands, lifted his left foot in one swift motion to the stirrup, raised himself, and with the help of his hand, crossed his broken leg over the back of the saddle till it dropped like a stone on the other side of the horse. He put his hand down for Ethan, and the boy swung up behind him. Jesse slackened the reins, and the horse galloped onto the road, then turned south out of town.

They couldn't see any stars above them but the wind had almost stopped and now the night seemed sealed in an unearthly stillness. The only sound was the soft click of the horse's hooves on the road, and the creak of the saddle. Snow began to drift down out of the black sky, and the sound of the hooves became muffled. Jesse and Ethan moved silently through the flakes, Jesse's hands gripping the pommel in front of him. Ordinarily his saddle was like a second home, but tonight he felt that, without Ethan's arms round him, he would roll off onto the ground.

At the bottom of the hill, the boy spoke at last. "What are you going to do, Jesse?"

"I don't know." Then they could see the light in the cabin window. A truck and a car sat nearby—Keno's delivery truck and the Buick that Shirley had brought when she came.

The horse stopped. Ethan slid to the ground. When Jesse followed him, the cast pulled him down with a rush that almost broke his hands away from the saddle horn. He clung on, and managed to keep his good foot under him while he waited for his strength to return. Then he put his right arm over the boy's shoulder and, partly hopping, he covered the distance to the house and leaned against the wall. Ethan opened the door.

Shirley and George, sitting at the kitchen table, looked round.

"Jesse!" Shirley rose. "Jesse, what are you doing?"

George ran to him. "Jesse. You're home!"

The three of them clustered round him and helped him into the bedroom. "What did you do?" Shirley scolded. "Break out of the hospital?" She threw back the bed covers. "Let's take off those wet things. You boys wait in the kitchen."

Reluctantly, they backed out of the room. Shirley brought the lamp from the kitchen, set it down, then closed the bedroom door.

"Hey," Ethan called. "It's dark out here."

"I'll only be a few minutes." She started to unbutton Jesse's shirt.

Jesse fumbled at the buttons, but his fingers were too cold to do any good. "Where's Keno?" he asked.

"Maybe he's lost. He took a horse and went to look for Ethan. When I heard you come, I thought it was him. I was scared, Jesse."

She pulled off the shirt. Then, while he sat on the bed, she reached her arms round his neck to untie his hospital gown. He put his hands on her waist, and felt its slender softness and the firm swell of her hips. A chain of recollection was begun in him, as if with his whole body he remembered all of hers. "Shirley . . ."

She drew back. The hospital gown came off over his arms and she pulled off his left boot and the sock. He couldn't stop shivering. She slipped his trousers over his legs, then began to rub his body with a towel, drying and warming it.

"Shirley." He reached for her. "Stay home. Come back to us."

She had moved to arrange the covers round his feet. "You don't want me back," she said.

"It's all Ethan talks about. You coming back."

"Yes. Ethan would take me back. Ethan and George."

"I'll take you back."

She looked at him, her face solemn, then shook her head. "Keno will never let me stay."

"Well, I won't let you go."

They heard hoofbeats approach and stop outside. A moment later the door swung open. "Where's the light?" Keno shouted, and Shirley opened the bedroom door. "Did the kid get back? His horse is . . ." Keno must have seen the boys then, by the lamplight from the bedroom. "Well, thank the Lord. Now we can go."

"There's been a change of plan," Shirley said.

Keno came to the bedroom door and looked in, his coat still on, his hat pushed back on his forehead. "Well, damn me."

"I'll be staying a while, to take care of Jesse."

"Like hell you will. You and me are goin' home."

"She's already home," Jesse told him.

"Boloney! This ragtag and haywire outfit!" Keno laughed.

"I can't leave Jesse alone."

"He won't be alone. This just means we won't have to take those kids with us now."

"They're my children."

"Well, they're not mine. Come on. It's snowing hard."

"Go ahead."

Keno was tall, standing in the doorway. He looked the same as he always had—dark, smiling, erect. The champ. But as Shirley spoke, he turned, and for a second it was as if a beacon had crossed him, revealing a heavy grey face with dull eyes. And Jesse realized that Keno was vulnerable. It had come too easily to him—the championship, the money, the ranch, the girl. He'd got them all. Then he'd rested. For years now he'd rested, and he was soft. Jesse hadn't had a chance to rest. He had struggled. Now he was hard as a horn.

But Keno's eyes were bright and powerful again. "Stay, then," he said. "Stay your whole life, for all I care." He left the bedroom; they heard the sound of a chair overturning, and then the door slammed.

They waited for the sound of the truck, but the night was silent. Then they heard footsteps on the porch. Keno came back in and stamped snow off his boots. "First time I ever see snow in August," he called. They heard him fumble in a cupboard. Then he came into the bedroom, half a bottle of whisky in one hand and three glasses on the fingers of the other. "Bein' as how old Jessie just got out of the hospital, I think we should have a little drink before we go."

No one answered him.

Keno sat down by the foot of the bed and pulled the cork out of the bottle with his teeth. "Lucky I had this in the truck." He set the glasses on the floor and poured whisky into each of them. Shirley handed one to Jesse, and he raised himself on his elbow.

Keno lifted his arm. "Well, Jesse," he said. "This'll put spine in your busted leg." He tipped up his glass.

Jesse sipped his drink. The liquor made a warm path down his throat into the icy centre of his body.

Ethan and George stood in the bedroom door, watching them.

Keno poured himself another drink. "I got to admit it, Jesse. You're a bronc-bustin' son-of-a-gun." He took a gulp from his glass. "You got an eye for women, too. You take Shirl there. She is some woman, for all she cries a lot. And when she ain't cryin' . . . or sometimes even when she is. . . . I just can't leave go of her, Jesse, that's a fact."

Jesse threw back the covers and sat up on the edge of the bed. "Get out of here, Keno."

Keno drained his glass. "We're going. Come on, Shirl." He got Shirley's suitcase from the corner, flung it open on the floor, took her clothes from the hangers on the wall and snapped the suitcase shut. "Come on." He threw her coat at her. "Sooner or later you're goin' to need old Keno, and you know it."

Shirley stood up. She looked down at Jesse, where he sat on the bed. He could see her eyes glistening. "Oh, Jesse."

Keno swung his arm full across her face, so hard that she fell against the foot of the bed.

For a moment Jesse felt as though he were watching a silent film. There should have been a scream at least, and sobs, and there was nothing. And then the sudden weight of understanding came to Jesse. In the uneven war between Shirley and Keno, silence had become her defence. How she must have fought until she learned it. He longed to restore what Keno had destroyed in her, and he realized that he was not afraid of Keno any more.

Though he sat naked and disarmed, his right leg was still encased in hard white armour. Concentrating all his strength, Jesse stood up, headfirst into Keno's solar plexus. Keno went down, and Jesse swung his massive leg against the side of Keno's head. He was drawing it back for another swing when Keno, with a desperate sweep of his arm, knocked Jesse's good leg out from under him. He fell on his back, and Keno rose above him. He saw Keno's fist coming. It slammed against his face. He struck back but his punches had no impact. Another fist landed on his face, and another; solid, methodical blows that seemed to be hammering him down beneath the threshold of consciousness.

A terrible roar erupted in the room. Keno half-rose and turned, his face suddenly grey and the look of death on it, as if he could feel the buckshot already in his body. But splinters flew in the log wall above them, and Jesse knew the shot was high. The air was heavy with the smell of powder. Ethan still held the shotgun, but the recoil had flung him back against the wall. He pumped the action.

"Next time I'll aim lower," Ethan said.

Jesse rose on his hands and knees, and climbed unsteadily up to sit on the bed. "Give me the gun, Ethan."

"Let me shoot him, Jesse. If you do it, they'll hang you."

"Do as I say."

Ethan edged into the room, always careful that Keno was able to look straight down the shotgun. Keno still held the crouched position he had taken. Only his head moved, his eyes following the muzzle of the shotgun like a bird watching a snake.

As Jesse took the gun, Keno raised his eyes from it and rested

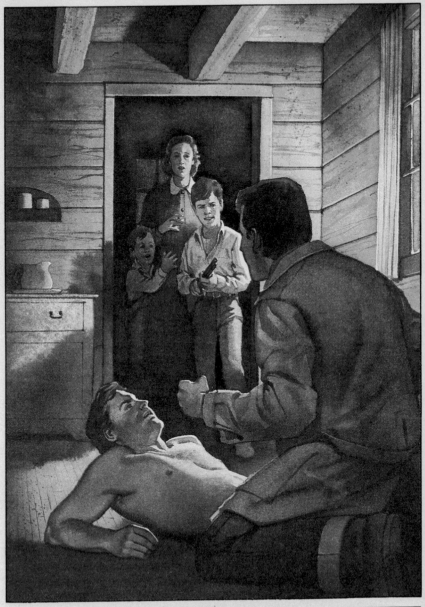

them on Jesse. Drops of sweat ran down his face. His voice seemed to drag over his throat like a chain. "They'll hang you, Jesse."

Jesse glanced towards Shirley. Her face was flushed and her eyes bright, as though she were ashamed of something. His nakedness? *They'll hang you, Jesse.*

Jesse almost smiled. He wasn't going to hang. And he wasn't going to wonder who was champ any more. Why, he could make old Keno crawl out of there on his knees if he wanted to. He had the words already in his mouth: "Get down on your knees, Keno." But before he could speak them, he realized that he, too, was ashamed.

Jesse drew the stock of the shotgun back tight against his shoulder, and pumped the action twice. Two shells flipped out onto the floor. He laid the shotgun down. "Keno's going home," he said to Shirley. "Do you want to go with him, or stay with us?"

"Stay with us!" George cried.

"No!" Jesse said. "We're not telling you what to do. George wants you to stay, and Ethan wants you to stay." He could not believe how coolly he spoke. "I want you to stay, if that's what you want."

Shirley took a step towards him.

"Whatever you decide is all right with Keno. Isn't it, Keno?"

Keno didn't reply. He stood as tall and square as ever, but he seemed to have been drained of substance, as if, should they open the door, the wind would blow him against the cabin wall.

"Ethan," Jesse said. "Will you and George show Mr. Ingram where that pile of rocks is down by the barn? He'll need some weight in his truck before he can get up the hill."

"Sure, Jesse." The boys went through the door.

Keno looked at Shirley. "You're coming?"

"You'll have to hurry," she told him. "The snow's getting deeper all the time."

"You can come if you want to. You heard what he said." He picked up the whisky bottle from the floor.

Shirley sat down beside Jesse.

Keno stared at her. "Good Lord! I only came down here out of the goodness of my heart, to get you away from this mess. And here you are, feelin' so sorry for old Jellybones. Well, it don't matter to me. Anything you got is waitin' on every street corner." He tipped his head back and drained the bottle. "So when you get sick of this hole, don't call for Keno. I'll be busy."

When he turned, his manoeuvre seemed to take up half the room. The bottle still in his hand, he walked through the door, across the kitchen, and outside. They heard the truck door slam, the engine start with a roar. Headlights scanned the room as the truck circled towards the barn, and moved away into the storm.

Shirley sat so still that she might have been carved from wood. Then a tear slipped down over the curve of her cheek. "Oh, Jesse. I've been such a fool."

Jesse thought, Was it possible that anything good could come from so much pain? "Suppose we could start over."

"Suppose," she mused. "If supposes were roses, I'd make a bouquet. If wishes were fishes, I'd catch some today." She almost smiled. "You used to wish for a ranch."

The path of the tear down her cheek was still visible, like the scar of an ancient wound. He wiped it away with his finger. "Tonight I wish for you."

"Just because you already have your ranch."

She was teasing him. He tried to think of something to say, but his mind was in a kind of jubilant confusion, and his throat so choked with wonder that for a moment he couldn't have spoken anyway.

Abruptly she sobbed and turned her head onto his shoulder. "I don't know how you could want me now."

Because my arms are shaped to you, like the twisted root of a tree when the stone it grew around has washed away. "I love you, Shirl. I've never stopped loving you."

He felt her hand against his body, drawing him to her. "Jesse."

She raised her face, and he could see in her eyes the reflection of the lamp, as soft and bronze as swaying fields of goldenrod.

Herbert Harker

As a young boy growing up during the thirties on a farm in southern Alberta, Herbert Harker dreamed of writing professionally. But it would be more than three decades before he realized his lifelong ambition.

After completing his high school education and a short stint in the Canadian armed forces, Harker moved from his family's farm to Calgary for on-the-job training as a geological draughtsman with an oil company. Then wanderlust struck, and Harker made his way to California where, for twenty years, he supported himself as a draughtsman while submitting a constant stream of short stories to publishers across Canada and the US. "I had a perfect record," he recalls wryly. "They were all returned."

But, unlike his hero Jesse Gifford, Harker never lost sight of his dream, and when he was forty-six years old his first novel, *Goldenrod*, was published to glowing critical acclaim. The prestigious New York Times Review called it "one of the most enchanting novels ever written about the West."

Although *Goldenrod* grew out of Harker's empathy with a childhood friend whose mother abandoned her family for another man, the book's characters are purely products of Harker's imagination. "There may be a bit of Jesse in me," he admits. "But then I feel there's a bit of Jesse in every man." So vividly does Harker recreate the physical sensations of bronco-busting, it is hard to believe he has never actually pitted himself against the likes of a Polka Dot. He credits the novel's authenticity to the fact that he is a keen rodeo fan and knows many of the top riders well. According to Harker, "Many of the fellows dream of owning their own ranch. Unfortunately, all too often, their earnings are eaten up by the expenses of following the rodeo circuit."

Harker, now in his late fifties, lives in Santa Barbara, California, where he is currently working on a new novel which deals with "the confrontation between pioneer values and those of the modern world." He has also written a lighthearted murder mystery and a novel about a Mormon community in Canada. "There are so many things waiting to be written," he says. "I only hope I get a chance to try my hand at some of them."

SURPRISE
PARTY

A condensation of the book by
WILLIAM KATZ
Illustrated by Dennis Lyall
Published by Robert Hale

Beautiful, red-haired Samantha is happily married
to Marty Shaw. She loves everything about her
new husband, and to celebrate his fortieth birthday
she is planning a special party for him—a party full
of surprises.

But when she tries to contact people from Marty's
past, it is she who is surprised: his old college has
no record of his attendance, and no one has heard
of him in the home town he claims to love. Who,
she begins to wonder, really *is* this man she's
married to?

Slowly, as the date of the party approaches, a
terrible suspicion begins to take shape, and with it
a perilous plan to unearth the truth. Its success
could destroy Samantha's marriage. Its failure
could destroy her life . . .

Prologue

He looked down at his sixth victim, proud of his work. She lay there, as the others had, utterly still, life taken from her by a combination of two weapons. Her hair, in that bright, wonderful colour, was spread out over the grass. She'd be discovered soon, he realized, and the authorities would know that he'd succeeded again. And they would prepare for his next insult.

He had to do it one more time. That was the compact. That was the act of faith. He knew who his victim would be, he knew everything about her. She wouldn't suspect, any more than the others had suspected, nor would she resist. She too would play her role as if rehearsed by some gifted director. It would happen on schedule. All his victims died on schedule.

And it would be very easy.

SPENCER CROSS-WADE looked down at the picture of the sixth victim, baffled. What was the key? What was the motive? Why had this monster eluded him and every other detective on the case? He knew the killer would strike again, and once more Cross-Wade would have to walk up two flights to his superiors and report another dead woman and another fruitless day for the New York City Police Department. He was determined that this would not happen. It was becoming a passion, an obsession in a career marked by a cool reserve.

He *had* to find him.

1

Each of them had a secret.

They sat opposite each other at breakfast in their enormously spacious apartment overlooking New York's Central Park. Samantha was thirty-five, with blue eyes and auburn hair that she wore long and loose, and she was incredibly happy. Her eight-month-old marriage to Marty was sublime, and the thought that anything could shatter it was inconceivable. Some marriages were made to last, and she believed passionately that this was one of them.

"I'm still bowled over," Marty said to her.

Samantha smiled, knowing what he meant. "By the party?"

"Yeah."

"Marty, honey, it's weeks away."

"Hey, I've never had my wife throw me a fortieth-birthday party before. Let me enjoy it. You making up the list?"

"Sure. I want everyone who means anything to you."

"That's a pretty big bunch."

"I'll get to them early," Samantha said. "I'll bet you don't have a single refusal." She leaned forward across the white tablecloth, closer to Marty's eyes, which, as usual, remained fixed intently on her. "Marty," she asked, "are you absolutely sure about that date for the party? December fifth?"

"That's my birthday, isn't it?"

"A Thursday? A weekday?"

Marty sighed. "Sam, we went over this. It means a lot to me to have the party right on my birthday. Thursday, December fifth." Then he lowered his eyes and fell silent.

Maybe he was thinking of the little speech he'd make as guest of honour, she thought, or of friends from the past he wished to invite. Samantha gazed at him, momentarily contemplated how her life had changed, and realized once again how lucky she was.

Little more than a year before, Samantha Reardon had been a second-string copywriter in a small advertising agency, barely keeping up with the rent on what she liked to describe as a "junior studio" in a crumbling section of Manhattan. The men she'd met were mostly combat veterans of broken marriages—dazed, weary males with war stories to tell of crabby wives, conniving divorce lawyers or dive-bombing in-laws. Samantha had desperately wanted to find a man to love her, one she could love in return. But she wasn't going to settle for any of the walking wounded. She'd wait, she told herself, for the right man.

Then, at a publicity party launching a diet product, she'd met Martin Everett Shaw. Marty.

Samantha had grown up on Long Island, her mother a high school English teacher, her father a lawyer for an airline. She had an instinct for elegance and style, and Marty Shaw had both, as well as something more basic. It wasn't simply his imposing height—he had the build of a fullback—or his unerring talent for matching the right shirt with the right suit. It was also his indefinable air of being in charge. Marty could walk across a room, rattle the floorboards, and make it clear that he was getting to the other side, no matter what or who was in the way. His voice was firm and resonant, but he never raised it. He radiated power. Samantha felt it, revelled in it.

"Got a big lunch today?" she asked him now, as he was finishing his breakfast.

"I don't think so," he replied. "But something usually comes up at the last minute."

"Home on time?"

"You jest. I tell you, sweet, when you run your own public relations business, you own everything but your time. You ought to see the stack of paperwork."

"Can't someone else . . ?"

"No. I've got to be my own man."

It was the kind of thing Samantha's father might have said. In fact, Marty reminded her of her father, which might have been the magic ingredient.

And yet Marty filled a need that Samantha had felt since childhood. Her home had been cold. Her parents had led independent lives, with little to say to each other and even less to her. She'd been an only child, without the special attention such children often receive. She'd idolized her father from a distance, and when he died while she was a teenager, she felt she'd never known him.

Marty gave her the attention and recognition she craved. He focused on *her*, on what she was saying. He made her feel wanted, for just being Samantha. He had lost his parents in his teens, and their similar experiences seemed to create an even deeper bond between them. Still, it was hard for her to believe that this strong, achieving man had no family at all. She recalled the shock of sympathy she'd felt when he told her how he'd lost both parents, how he'd worked his way through Northwestern University, how relatives had abandoned and ignored him. Samantha could imagine him going from town to town, getting jobs with small newspapers, finally putting some cash together to come to New York and launch his own public relations firm.

Now he had a family—a wife. Someone who cared.

To Samantha there was only one thing that seemed curious about him: those eyes, which sometimes appeared to shift defensively. They were guarded, watchful eyes, and Samantha often wondered why. Maybe it was the reality of business competition. Maybe it was Marty's tough early life, his sense of aloneness. But something made Samantha want to take care of him.

Her energies now were directed towards his party. Samantha had to tell Marty about it because he often went out of town, and she wanted to be sure that the guest of honour would actually be present. But she had kept one great secret. She was certain he'd never suspect. It would highlight the evening, give him an occasion he'd always remember, and make the event what she really wanted it to be—a *true* surprise party.

Marty glanced at his watch, got up, and kissed Samantha with a concentrated affection rare for a successful and harassed executive. "I'm off," he said. She watched him disappear out of the door, and soon she heard the lift open, then descend.

Samantha walked across the deep white carpet to the living-room window and looked down at Central Park, where the late autumn leaves were falling. The view of the park and the city skyline was magnificent, but Samantha knew it wasn't the scenery that gave her, for the first time in her life, such complete peace. She saw Marty rush out at the front of the building, turn, and wave up at her. That was the factor. That was the cake and the icing as well.

She gazed around her apartment. They'd used contemporary design—indirect track lighting, lots of whites, some metal. It was a contrast to the brooding presence of the sixty-year-old building, formal with its grey stone facade, more suited to an era when doormen wore white gloves and the upper crust arrived in open cars. Samantha grabbed a phone, tapping out a familiar number.

"Lynne? Sam. Marty just left. Want to come over?"

Lynne would be here right away. She'd been entrusted with Sam's secret, and they'd have a productive day. By this time, Samantha knew, Marty was in a taxi and halfway downtown, heading for his office.

He had entrusted *his* secret to no one.

LYNNE GOULD WAS a woman of endless energy who seemed to get twenty-six hours into every day. She worked for a legion of charities, ran an art gallery, and took care of two young children, all the while keeping her pretty, blonde hair absolutely in place. Lynne and her family occupied the apartment across the hall, and she had become Samantha's best friend since the Shaws moved in. Samantha was five feet three, so Lynne, at five seven, seemed to tower over her. It would have been intimidating, except that Lynne exuded a simple warmth that put the world at ease.

A few minutes after Samantha called, Lynne charged in, pencil and pad in hand. "I'm ready," she announced. "I expect to spend the rest of the morning delving into Marty's sordid past."

But Samantha served some coffee first. "You have no idea how much Marty is looking forward to his birthday," she said. "He keeps mentioning it. Even this morning . . . " Then a slightly troubled look came across Samantha's face. "But you're sure *this* is a good idea?" she asked, wanting encouragement.

"Are you kidding?" Lynne shot back. "It's sterling. I mean, going back to the beginning of Marty's life, contacting his friends and teachers and having them send messages for his birthday. Boy, if anyone did that for me, I'd kiss 'em."

"I just hope it doesn't bring back any bad memories."

"Come on, Sam. You know the way Marty talks about his early days. Tough, sure. But he's nostalgic, like all of us. Look, you're right on target. You're doing *This Is Your Life* for Martin Everett Shaw."

Lynne had volunteered to track down the numbers, while Samantha would actually place the calls. Lynne had saved her considerable time, but more important, she'd be moral support, a buddy to be with during the party planning.

It wasn't long before Samantha was seated at a small black writing table in the hallway, phone in hand, pressing the 312 area code and a phone number in Evanston, Illinois, then waiting as the clicks brought her closer to her first encounter with Marty's past, the roots he talked about so much.

Her heart began to beat faster. Yes, Lynne was right. This *was* a super scheme, a spectacular love feast. Inevitably her mind flashed back to Marty's tales of his pranks at Northwestern University's Medill School of Journalism, where, he never tired of telling her, he learned the craft that eventually made him a public relations wizard. She remembered him describing how he and a friend had fanned out through Evanston, going door to door, soliciting orders for gift-

89

wrapped cans of elbow grease. They had got, so Marty claimed, twenty-three orders when the dean found out and demanded that they apologize. Their apologies had been so touching, Marty related, that six people reordered.

Samantha's phone connection was completed. "Alumni office," said a high-pitched female voice.

"Yes," Samantha answered. "I wonder if someone could help me with a special request about a former student."

"Are you an employer?"

"No, a wife. Well, what I mean is, I'm married to someone from your class of '66. I'm having a birthday party for him, and I want to collect old stories, remembrances by professors, that sort of thing."

"This *is* an unusual request."

"I know," Samantha replied with an embarrassed little laugh. "Look, if it's a bother . . ."

"Not at all. Give me his name and I'll get out the yearbook. I assume you don't have a copy?"

"No. Marty misplaced it before we were married. His name is Martin Everett Shaw, and he graduated from the Medill School of Journalism with honours." Samantha spelled the name.

"I'll check."

There was a long pause. Samantha and Lynne smiled at each other now that the delightful plot was under way. Oh, Marty was going to love hearing from those Medill people, Samantha thought. She could already see the glow on his face.

The voice came back on. "Ma'am, are you sure of the class?"

"Yes. Why?"

"There's no Martin Shaw listed."

"That's impossible. Marty always talks about the class of '66."

"Wait a second. Did he get a master's or a bachelor's degree?"

"Bachelor's."

"Sorry. I had it wrong. One moment please."

Samantha waited, winking at Lynne over the delay and tapping a ballpoint pen with her right hand.

"Ma'am?"

"Yes."

"He's not on the baccalaureate list either."

"There's obviously some mistake," Samantha said.

"Well, I've checked the yearbook and our own official list of graduates. No Martin Shaw. Is it possible you're confusing us with some other journalism school, like Columbia?"

Samantha felt a little irritated. "I know where my husband went to school," she replied. Then she realized she was being rude to someone who was trying to help. "I'm sorry. Maybe you've got him listed in the wrong year."

"I've checked the master list of alumni on our computer," the voice replied stoically. "I don't know what more we can do."

Samantha searched her mind for a way out of the confusion. "Marty was feature editor of the newspaper," she recalled. "His byline would be there."

"I'll check the bound volumes." The voice was getting annoyed.

"I know I'm asking a lot," Samantha said.

"It's all right. By the way, does your husband get alumni mail?"

Samantha thought for a moment. "I haven't seen any. But he's moved quite a bit and—"

"Our graduates are journalists. They often move, and we follow them." Now the voice was abrupt, delivering a message. Samantha heard the woman leafing through pages ... many pages. "No," the answer finally came. "I've checked six issues of the paper from '66. Someone else was feature editor."

"Impossible."

The voice let out an impatient breath. "May I speak frankly?"

Samantha was startled by the question. "Of course."

"This kind of thing happens all the time, Mrs. Shaw. It's obvious that your husband never attended this school, and I *hope* he isn't using our name to secure employment. If we found out, we would instantly notify—"

"Thank you very much." Samantha hung up, actually growled at the phone, then pushed her pen aside. "Would you believe that?" she asked Lynne. "Would you believe they can't find Marty's name? An honours graduate? Some journalism school! Can you believe the incompetence?"

"Yes," Lynne replied. "It's the computers. They probably lost his name from one of those little discs. I bet all she did was punch some button. No name, no deal."

"But she looked through books."

"That's what she said. Sam, it's an old story with these college computers. We'll straighten it out."

"I know that," Samantha answered, trying to shrug off the incident. But inside she was going through a mixture of anger and denial. Not for a second did she believe that Marty had lied about his background. That wasn't her Marty, and she knew him inside out.

She also knew what she'd do next. She'd talk to the dean, not just some flunkey in the office. She'd get the information she wanted.

But when she called, she was told the dean was at a meeting. She'd have to try later.

"Do you want to make some other calls?" Lynne asked. "I've got the number for the Elkhart city hall."

"I want to nail down the college stuff first," Samantha replied. "In the meantime, let's talk war plans."

"Sure."

Samantha opened a copy of *New York* magazine and turned to an ad near the back. "There's a guy here who videotapes birthday parties."

"That's a great idea."

"You think anyone would mind?"

"If they mind, they can turn away from the camera. This is better than home movies. It's got sound and everything."

"I'll give him a call," Samantha said, jotting down a note. "If Marty knew what this cost, he'd lynch me."

"Sam," Lynne rebutted, "men never lynch when the cash is spent on *them*."

They talked on, getting to the menu. Marty was a meat-and-potatoes man, so the menu would be simple, but served elegantly and romantically. Samantha made a few additions to a guest list that was already too large, a tribute to the many friends Marty had made in New York. She wanted a live band too, so she phoned a little group from the Juilliard School that entertained at parties, playing anything from classical to pop.

"Why not try that dean again?" Lynne asked after an hour.

Samantha reached for the phone, then stopped. She wanted to call the dean. Of course she did. She wanted to get the whole Medill business taken care of. But somehow, Samantha was a little uneasy. She almost wished that Lynne weren't there for the call. Sure, it was a gigantic mix-up, but it was an *embarrassing* mix-up as well, and even between friends these things could get awkward. After all, what if the dean couldn't find Marty's name either? What would Lynne think?

"I don't feel like calling now," Samantha said abruptly. "I'll do it later."

She needed some ammunition for that second call, and she knew where to get it: from Marty himself.

She was sure there was no problem.

2

The only thing Marty worried about was seeing someone he knew. Why was he getting off a subway in Queens at lunchtime on a business day? Of course, Marty would have a quick explanation. Marty Shaw *always* came up with the right words. But this was one day he didn't want to be noticed.

He walked down the packed street, the cold wind hitting him in the face. He hated days like this. His mind became a blur of images, memories erupting inside him to fuel a growing rage. He tried to clear his mind, but knew from experience that he couldn't, that this episode would have to run its course.

He saw Granville's Hardware Store, one of the larger shops on the boulevard, and assumed a store its size would carry what he wanted. There were things he had to have. Urgently. Automatically he straightened his tie and ran his hand through his hair. Look right. Look normal. Don't seem anxious. Pay cash. No credit cards. No name on the receipt.

Marty moved slowly down one of Granville's aisles. He feigned a look of confusion, drawing a tired salesman with a narrow moustache. "Lookin' for something?"

"Uh, yes," Marty replied. "I need one of those sockets that screw in, the kind that takes a bulb."

"You want one with a pull chain?"

"Yes, that's the kind."

The salesman was slightly hunched and emitted a strong scent of low-grade tobacco. Marty followed him down the aisle to the electrical-supply section. The salesman pulled a socket from its hook. "That is what you want. Anything else?"

"Uh, let me think," Marty answered. The light socket was a ploy. Marty sometimes bought extra items to hide the ones he really wanted. "I need a Roberts tack hammer," he finally said, fearful that he might have sounded too anxious.

"A what?"

"A Roberts tack hammer."

The salesman grunted and shook his head. "I never seen a guy who wanted a brand of hammer. A hammer's a hammer. Look, I got Stanley, I got Estwing. But I ain't seen Roberts in—"

"But you've heard of it." There was an unintended intensity in Marty's large green eyes.

"Sure, I heard of it."

"Where could I get one?"

"Try Becker. He's two blocks down. Somethin' else?"

"A bicycle chain. For locking up a bike."

"That I got."

"I want one with a red coating over the links."

The salesman took a deep breath. "Gotta be red?"

Marty thought back. Yes, it had to be red. "Red," he answered, his voice now its usual assertive self.

"I think I got one."

The salesman led Marty to the toy and game department and picked out a bicycle chain covered in red. Marty took it from him, curling his strong fingers over the links as if caressing it. It was heavy. It *had* to be heavy. He wound it around his right hand like a snake, then quickly realized he was focusing too much attention on it. "I'll take this," he said. "That's all."

He left the store with the light socket and bicycle chain in a brown paper bag, and walked towards Becker's. He slipped the bag into his leather attaché case. "This is for you," he whispered, hardly moving his lips, as if talking to someone close by. But nothing of the turmoil showed on the outside. Marty Shaw was just another businessman walking down the street.

He glanced at his gold watch. It was one forty-six. He was due at his office for an appointment at three. It was important to be on time, important to avoid questions. He walked faster. He found Becker's and went in. Hiram Becker, tall and elderly, came over to him.

"Need help?"

"Yes," Marty replied. "I need a tack hammer, a Roberts. It has a light handle and the head is painted black."

"Insist on that model?"

"It's a gift for my son. It matches his other tools."

"I'll look. I'm a franchised dealer. Authorized." Becker went to his storeroom, then came back carrying the hammer, which was sealed in plastic and cardboard. "Here, I got it. Last one."

Marty followed Becker to a cash register, paid the eight dollars and ninety-eight cents plus tax, and quickly left the store.

As Marty walked down Queens Boulevard, heading for a subway that would take him back to Manhattan, he knew there were other things to do before December 5, but they could wait. The electric trains were no problem. The right set could be picked up easily enough. Samantha would accept the explanations about new items

94

being brought into the apartment. Samantha was always so understanding. She was perfect.

Marty boarded the subway, sitting in an overheated carriage next to an old woman reeking of alcohol for most of the ride. He gripped his attaché case tightly, his knuckles turning white. As the train rattled towards his stop, his eyes shifted around, exhibiting the wary defensiveness that Samantha so often noticed. He didn't want anyone making a try for his expensive-looking case. Too much had been invested in what was inside.

SHAW ENTERPRISES HAD sprawling rooms on the twelfth floor of a modern stone-and-metal building on the Avenue of the Americas. Marty's offices were the artistic reverse of the neat, functional styling of his apartment. Here everything was lavish, in curving French design, more like a museum than a place of business. The windows were outlined with heavy draperies, and the prints on the walls were mounted in ornate gold-leaf frames.

Marty smiled as he opened the heavy oak door. "Afternoon, everyone. Calls?"

Lois Carroll, his twenty-year-old secretary, instantly responded by handing Marty three pink sheets as he stopped at her desk. He gently put his case on the floor and flipped through the messages.

"What did CBS want?"

"They need an interview with the girl who's trying out for the new football team," Lois answered. "Since we represent—"

"Let's hold off on that," Marty said. "I'll call and offer them something else. I don't like that image for the team." He turned to the next call sheet. "*Newsweek*?"

"Just to say they don't want the story of Rohr-Tech's water-softening process."

Marty nodded. "And what'd Samantha want?"

"Just for you to call back. She seemed a little tense."

"Sick?"

"No, just not your usual laid-back Samantha."

"Call my home number, please."

Marty rushed into his spacious office, one of its light brown walls lined with framed copies of stories he'd placed in magazines and newspapers. Lois made the call quickly, feeling the pressure of Marty's concern. Everyone in the office knew how Marty protected Samantha, how he watched out for her. It was an old-style devotion, rare for those in the crazed media world.

"I have Samantha," Lois said finally over the intercom.

Marty picked up. "Sam? Is something wrong?"

"Oh, no. Not at all, sweet."

"You sure? You sound a little shaky."

Samantha couldn't hide her continued annoyance over the Northwestern flap. "No, really. I'm just tired. I called because I was getting things together for the great gala. There's a guy who videotapes these things, and I think it would be terrific, unless you're against it."

"Why should I be against that? Forge on."

"I wouldn't bother you at work, but I have to arrange it early."

"Sam, you never bother me."

"Oh, that's so, so good to hear. Say, Martin Everett Shaw, I had another bright idea: framing your college diploma and having it up for the party. You've never had it done, and—"

"Sam, you know I don't believe in that stuff."

"But I do, Marty. I'm proud of you."

"Can I exercise my veto?" Marty asked, a slight touch of embarrassed laughter in his voice.

Samantha hesitated. "Well, as president of Shaw Enterprises, you have the power, I guess. But Marty, you should at least preserve the diploma. I'll take care of it. Where is it?"

There was a long, painful pause. "You know," Marty answered, "I don't even remember."

A chill shot through Samantha's body. "Think, genius," she told him, trying to hide her heightened concern.

"Gee, I . . ."

"Try." Samantha was almost begging.

Marty snapped his fingers. "Sure," he recalled. "You know that pile of papers in the file drawer of my desk?"

"It's not stuffed in there, is it?" Samantha asked scoldingly.

"Guilty. My sincere apologies to the Medill School of Journalism, Lawrence S. Krieger, dean and general bore."

"I'll rescue it. Look, you're busy. I'll let you go."

"I'm home by seven."

"Bye, love."

They hung up. Marty was a bit baffled. Why had Samantha called him about the videotape instead of waiting until he got home? And who cared about a diploma? Sam's manner was usually so casual, so much the opposite of urgent. Maybe it was the challenge of throwing a big party for the first time.

Marty decided to forget about it.

SAMANTHA RUSHED TO Marty's desk and rummaged through the papers. Soon she found the large blue folder with the seal of Northwestern University. Quickly but gently she opened the folder and slid out a piece of stiff paper protected by a sheet of tissue. She could feel the relief overcoming her. Of *course*, that lady at the school had been wrong. Here was undeniable proof. Samantha examined the diploma carefully, feeling closer to Marty's past simply by holding it.

MARTIN EVERETT SHAW
Bachelor of Science with Honors
June 16, 1966

She reverently slipped the diploma back into its folder and put it in a fireproof cabinet for safekeeping. Now she felt guilty for having asked Marty about the document. She'd never need such reassurance again, she told herself. Never again.

Samantha continued to put off her second call to Northwestern. Yes, she had the diploma, but she was offended by the response to her first call, and her reaction was to find other things to do. She sat down instead for some more party planning, then placed her right hand on her stomach. Samantha tried to restrain her hope that December 5 would bring not only a great party but an announcement of even greater joy. How Marty wanted it! There were some signs that it might happen. She'd made an appointment with her doctor for tomorrow. Now, she hoped and prayed.

MARTIN EVERETT SHAW slowly dialled the combination on his office wall safe and swung open the armoured door, which was at eye level. Aside from a brown envelope, the safe was empty. Marty carefully placed the tack hammer and bicycle chain inside, pushing both items towards the back. He recalled how he had put the last hammer and chain there the year before.

His eyes and body motionless, he gazed at the brown envelope as if it contained some holy artifact. He reached in and took it out, placing it on his desk. Then he walked to the office door and locked it, and closed the curtain on his large picture window. He was alone, completely at one with himself. He walked back to his desk, sat down, and opened the envelope. Inside were newspaper clippings—some yellowed, some more recent—from all over the country.

Marty snapped on his intercom. "No calls, please," he said. He selected one clipping near the top of the pack. He had read it many

97

times before, but he particularly liked its tone and style. He read the story again, savouring each word. "Connecticut State Police were baffled today by the discovery, in a patch of grass just off Interstate 95 near Greenwich, of a ..."

3

University Hospital, on First Avenue in the Thirties, is part of the New York University–Bellevue medical complex. Samantha's heart pounded as she saw the buildings that she knew would play a part in her life and Marty's. When the cab pulled into the driveway, Samantha paid the fare and walked into the medical centre.

Now her pounding heart was joined by a tension in her throat and stomach. Samantha took the lift up. She checked in with Dr. Fromer's nurse and waited more than forty-five minutes before being shown into the examining room.

Dr. Harold Fromer was approaching fifty, heavy and tired, with a drooping chin and thinning hair. And yet he was quiet and attentive, and a thoroughly reliable physician. He'd been Samantha's doctor for years.

After the examination and tests, he saw Samantha in his office.

"What do you want me to say?" Fromer asked as he sank into his chair. He said it with a smile.

"Tell me we'd better start saving for college," she replied.

"Start saving."

Samantha didn't jump up, or laugh, or cry. Rather, a kind of spiritual serenity came over her. Perhaps it was because she knew this would bring Marty and her even closer together.

"Well," she asked, her face finally breaking out in a glow, "what do I do?"

"You celebrate. Does your husband want a baby too?"

"Sure. He participated. He was a volunteer."

Fromer laughed. "I see no reason why you shouldn't have a normal pregnancy," he said. Then he carefully explained all that Samantha had to know, and gave her a booklet that told of the changes she would experience.

"I'm guessing I'm in my second month," she said.

"You're about right. When we use the ultrasound to examine you, I can be more precise. Would you want to know the sex of the baby beforehand?"

"No."

"Really?" Fromer's eyes widened. "You'd only have to choose one name. You could get ready . . ."

Samantha shrugged. "We're a little old-fashioned. My husband had an unhappy childhood. I think he'd like to do things the way people used to do them."

"I see." Fromer tapped a pencil on his desk. He seemed concerned. "Are you holding something back?" he asked her.

Samantha stiffened. "What do you mean?"

"You were more tense than usual during the examination. When you mentioned your husband, I could detect a little . . . unease. This is a time for you to be relaxed, not under stress. If there's a problem in the marriage . . ."

"Not at all." Samantha was slightly offended, but knew that Fromer meant well. "I'm planning a big party for Marty," she said. "It's on my mind. Maybe that's why I seem a little uneasy."

"Right," Fromer replied. "Just stay calm. The first three months are a bit touchy." Then he came from behind his desk and kissed Samantha on the cheek, something he saw as an obstetric prerogative. "Congratulations," he said. "You'll be fine."

"Thank you. When do you want to see me again?"

"One month. Go home and give your husband the news."

As Samantha rode down in the crowded lift, she felt unbridled joy. She started smiling, not even realizing it, drawing curious glances from doctors and patients. Instinctively she placed her hand in front of her stomach as other passengers boarded and the crush became greater. When she left the building and got into a cab, her first words were, "I'm pregnant. Drive slowly." The driver smiled, and actually followed her instructions.

LYNNE WAS ABOUT TO enter their apartment building on Central Park West when Samantha stepped out of the cab into a light, windy drizzle. Lynne's instinct gave her all the information she needed. "It's a go," she said.

"It's a go," Samantha confirmed.

"I knew it." Lynne let out a laugh, grabbed Samantha's arms, and steered her towards the building. The doorman let them in, oblivious to their excitement, and their heels clicked as they walked through the lobby, almost entirely marble and lit by a huge crystal chandelier. "You have to make a big dinner," Lynne said, insistently pushing the lift button.

"Why?"

"Why? When you get pregnant, you make a big dinner to tell your husband. Didn't you ever see it in the movies? It's the American way."

"I'm not telling Marty."

"You're not ... You're putting me on."

"I'll be announcing it at the party. I want everyone to see his reaction."

Lynne began warming to the idea. "And you'll have it video-taped. Boy, what a moment to remember."

"I just want to see Marty's face," Samantha said, more to herself than to Lynne. "Just that face."

They went up into Samantha's apartment. "Hey, I collected more numbers for you," Lynne said. She whipped a pad from her handbag. "Here's the number for George Braden Elementary School, Elkhart, Indiana. Marty's first alma mater."

Samantha beamed, feeling herself back in the rhythm of party planning. She sat down at her small table and dialled the number.

"Braden," answered a dry midwestern female voice.

"Yes, hello," Samantha said, a little nervous. "I'm calling from New York City. It's about my husband. He was a student at Braden in the 1950s. I'm having a fortieth-birthday party for him, and I ..."

"How nice."

"And I wanted to collect the remembrances of old friends and teachers. Can I get the names of his teachers, and his principal?"

"Well, I guess so. Some of the teachers might be deceased, but the principal is the same."

"Really?"

"Mr. Cotrell took over in his twenties, back then. He's in his office now. Would you like to speak with him?"

"Yes," Samantha said. "I'd love that."

"Your name, ma'am?"

"Samantha Shaw. My husband is Martin Everett Shaw."

Samantha heard clicks on the line, and cupped her hand over the receiver. "She's connecting me to the principal," she told Lynne. "He was there with Marty."

"Mrs. Shaw, Lou Cotrell," came a cheerful, singsong voice. "I remember your husband well."

"You do?" Samantha asked excitedly.

"Shaw was a hell-raiser. Always the devil."

"That's Marty."

"Thin little boy."

"No, heavy."

"Well, they change. You're feeding him too well."

"Probably."

"Surprised to hear Martin's in New York. He was one of those out-door types. Sorry he never came back to visit. I'd like to see him."

"I'll make a note of that," Samantha said. "I'll insist that he go back. Both of us, in fact."

"Grand. I understand you'd like some remembrances."

"Yes."

"I'll give you some myself. Tell you what, do you have one of those cassette machines?"

"Yes, we do."

"Then I'll make a little tape for you. You just give me the address. And you tell Martin that the old schoolyard is just waitin' for him to dig it up again."

"Thank you, Mr. Cotrell."

"Thank *you* for thinking of us, Mrs. Shaw."

Samantha gave Cotrell her address, and added the phone number in case he had some last-minute thoughts. She also cautioned him that this was a surprise and asked that the tape be sent on a Monday so it would arrive midweek when Marty wasn't home. Then, because of her deep feelings for Marty, she asked, "Do you remember anything about Marty's parents, Mr. Cotrell? Warm stories, anecdotes, that kind of thing?"

"I remember them as nice people."

"Well, unfortunately they died rather young. Both, while Marty was in his teens. It was tough for him, but he worked his way through Northwestern."

"That's Martin's spirit."

"Yes, it is. Thank you again, Mr. Cotrell."

They hung up. "Well, that was terrific!" Samantha told Lynne.

"I got the drift," Lynne replied. "Now you're cookin'." Then she looked at her watch. "Hey, gotta dash," she said. "Big art shindig downtown."

As was Lynne's style, she was gone in seconds, with no long goodbyes. Now Samantha was alone, feeling good about herself, about Marty, about life. She'd had a completely successful day.

She took out Dr. Fromer's pamphlet and became engrossed in the reading. It was straightforward, describing the techniques that would be used to check the pregnancy, pointing out that the mother would probably feel the baby move during the fifth month, and warning against smoking and drugs. She was reading the section on the hospital's nursery when the phone rang. Samantha picked it up.

"Mrs. Shaw?"

She knew the voice instantly. "Mr. Cotrell, how nice of you to call back so soon. Did you remember something about my husband?"

"Well, that's why I'm calling. Oh, this is *very* embarrassing."

"Embarrassing?"

"Well, let me put it this way. You know, it's awfully easy to get mixed up when you've known so many children. And my memory . . . When you called, I had a youngster in mind. But his name isn't Martin, it's Melvin. Mel Shaw."

"You don't remember my husband?"

"You said his parents were dead. This youngster's mother is alive, and still living here. That's what jolted my memory."

Samantha sensed how mortified Cotrell was, and felt for him. "Mr. Cotrell," she said, "it's OK. How could you possibly remember all your students? Look, we'll get the school records, and maybe some teachers will remember—"

"That's the other problem, Mrs. Shaw."

"I beg your pardon?"

"I sent for the records. They don't show a Martin Shaw."

"What?"

"Surprised me too. Now, occasionally a pupil's record for one year is lost. But *all* of his are missing."

The Northwestern call flashed violently through Samantha's mind, but she repressed the thought. The world was full of mistakes. She'd simply run into two in a row. "Martin went to Braden," she said, almost too firmly. "He talks about it."

"I understand. But without the records we're kind of lost, Mrs. Shaw. All I can think of is that they were requested before and were taken out and left somewhere."

"That must be it," Samantha replied, grasping for any straw.

"But that doesn't explain the pictures."

"Pictures?"

"Class pictures. Every class gets its picture taken every year. I had them check the pictures. No Martin."

"He could've been absent," Samantha retorted.

"Six years in a row!"

There was a long silence. Samantha finally broke it. "Mr. Cotrell, what does this mean?"

The principal laughed, an uneasy kind of laugh. "Well," he said, "maybe we've got a mistake here. You know, sometimes a kid comes from a poor family, and when he grows up, he's embarrassed about it. So he . . . improves on his background."

"I see," Samantha said quietly. A chill shot up her spine.

"It's hardly the worst thing, Mrs. Shaw. There are some outlying areas around Elkhart . . . modest areas . . . and maybe Martin thought Elkhart sounded better."

"I can't believe that," Samantha whispered.

"If there's anything more I can do, please call," Cotrell concluded. "Goodbye now."

Samantha was stunned. This couldn't be. Marty couldn't be hiding his past from her. He'd spoken in detail about Braden Elementary. Wouldn't someone with something to hide avoid it altogether? This was just another case of poor record keeping. The Medill thing had worked itself out when she found Marty's diploma. After a few minutes Samantha began feeling good again, convinced that this flap, like the first, would end happily.

She did feel, though, that some of the fun, the zip, was taken out of the party planning by these foul-ups. She hungered for the first call to someone who remembered Marty, knew a lot about him, and hadn't lost a chunk of his past.

FOR MARTY IT WAS ANOTHER lunch hour of shopping. This time he was in Brooklyn, on Thirteenth Avenue, which was crammed with mothers, prams, assorted pickpockets and pavement hawkers. It was an avenue of small shops, a throwback to the era of the little guy and the closely knit neighbourhood. There was a kind of organized chaos, and Marty felt like an alien. But, as in Queens, no one was likely to recognize him here.

He walked down the packed avenue, and again there were the cold winds. Again the bitter memories erupted inside him. Words shot through his mind, words that he associated with cold winds.

"You only care about him! I'm just garbage. I just clean up and wipe their mouths! You bring 'em toys! What am I doin' with you?"

"Come on, it's his birthday. It only comes once a year, Alice."

"You're a bum! Go play with your trains!"

"I'm not a bum. I need a break."

"Other men don't need no breaks!"

The words reverberated in his brain, and Marty knew they'd be there as long as he lived.

He looked around at the addresses now, trying to find Walson's, a well-known toy and hobby store. He finally found it between a luncheonette and dry cleaner, and was immediately impressed with the place. A good hobby shop had model planes and trains jammed end to end. It had kits that were almost impossible to find and back issues of such magazines as *Model Railroader*. It had concave-chested, thick-spectacled salesmen in their early twenties who could tell you every train engine that Lionel ever manufactured, and the year each came out. Walson's had it all.

"Need help?" asked a young salesman enthusiastically.

"I called," Marty replied. "I spoke to Steve."

"I'm Steve. You wanted the diesel switcher."

"Yes."

"Over here." Steve led Marty to a section at the back where used electric trains were sold. He pulled out an orange-and-blue Lionel box from the early '50s. Inside was an oblong-shaped black loco-motive with the Santa Fe insignia on its side. "Santa Fe," Steve said. "That's the one you wanted, right?"

"Yes, exactly," Marty replied, holding the engine in his hand and caressing it. "How much?"

"One hundred and twenty."

"I'll take it."

"You wanted a milk car too, I think," Steve said.

"That's right."

"I've got it, but only with five milk cans. It works, though."

"If it works, I want it."

"You have the operating track?"

"I'll need one," Marty replied. Now his mind came alive again with memories: how he pressed the little red button attached to the track, how the man shot out of the milk car and delivered the silver cans to the platform, how the mechanism buzzed. And he remem-bered the voice. *"Are you happy, Frankie? Is this what you wanted?"* It was such a kind voice, a good voice. *"Frankie, this is for you."* Marty seemed to be in another world.

"You OK, mister?" Steve asked.

"Oh, sure," Marty replied. "Just tired." He requested a few more items, and Steve wrapped the package. Marty paid in cash—$371.86. There were no signatures to trace.

Holding the trains, Marty felt a special thrill as he walked down Thirteenth Avenue, heading for a subway. He'd loved his trains, even though he'd only had them a little while.

104

"You're a bum! Go play with your trains!"

The words came back to Marty once more. He knew the trains would trigger them again. It happened the year before, and the year before that.

"Not in front of the children, Alice!"

Had it really all been because of the trains? No, Marty knew it had been much more. Again he fought to blot it out, especially as he walked down into the subway station, where three teenagers eyed him and his package. Marty looked away, felt his heart palpitate, and got to the token window as quickly as possible.

The chain, the hammer, the trains. Marty was getting closer; December 5 was getting closer. Soon, he knew, he would have that strange feeling, that compulsion, and he wouldn't be able to resist.

4

Methodically, Samantha continued tracing Marty's past. She still put off calling Northwestern back, but she pursued his early life in Elkhart. She called the junior high school, but the assistant principal refused to cooperate. Samantha would have to send a letter, notarized, explaining her request. So she called the high school. The atmosphere there was much warmer.

But there was no record of a Martin Shaw.

He was not among the list of graduates.

Samantha felt panic, but she quickly contained it. She recalled Cotrell's wondering whether records had been requested, then not returned. *All* of Marty's records might have been requested some time, then not put back. There could be many explanations.

So Samantha called the Elkhart City Municipal Building, requesting a birth record. "No, ma'am," came a gruff bureaucratic voice. "We don't show a Shaw, Martin, ever having been born here."

"Could his birth have been unregistered?" Samantha asked, a touch of desperation in her voice.

"Possible," came the reply. "But a thousand-to-one shot. I mean, that was modern times. *Everyone* got registered."

Now Samantha's incipient panic began to grow. No birth certificate. No school records. No trace of Marty in Elkhart. Planning for Marty's fortieth-birthday party was becoming a horrible excursion into a past that might not exist. Yet Samantha refused to believe that. There had to be *some* explanation.

She could turn to no one for help. Only Marty could provide the answers. And Samantha knew he would. But she wouldn't confront him directly. To reveal she'd been probing his past would blow the surprise. She would extract information subtly. He'd never know.

But first, Samantha realized, there was one call she had to make. Awkward or not, she had to call Northwestern again and get that issue nailed down. After all, Marty *did* have his diploma. That was solid proof.

She steeled herself. Every call was difficult now. She looked up the number, reached the school, and asked for the dean of students. She waited nervously.

He answered in a drab, uninterested voice.

"Hello, my name is Samantha Shaw."

"Yes, I know about you," he said, with no warmth at all. "The alumni office told me you called yesterday. What more can I do?"

"Well, first off, I have some good news," Samantha replied. "Marty does have his diploma. It's right here."

"Oh, really?" The coldness in his voice shook Samantha.

"Yes," she replied. "He had filed it away."

"Madam, it's a fake."

There was dead silence. What could Samantha say to that? What could anyone say?

"How do you know, all the way out there?" she asked, fighting to control her frustration.

"It's because I *am* out here that I know," he said. "Your husband never went to Northwestern. It's as simple as that."

"But how do you *know?*"

"Because people don't pass through here without a trace. You might have a little talk with your husband, if you care to risk it. Now if you'll excuse me . . ."

The conversation ended on that sour note. Instinctively Samantha rushed to examine Marty's diploma once more. It looked genuine enough. She was unaware how her hands were shaking until she tried to read the fine print under the words "Northwestern University". This was a full-blown crisis, the first in their marriage. Never had Samantha expected to confront Marty's past this way. Never had she expected to question him.

He'd be home in a few hours. Samantha had to plan her actions, plan each nuance of conversation. She felt the strain. She felt it in her head, and now even in her stomach. She feared for her baby on the very day she'd learned it existed.

MARTY CAME HOME hungry and tired, as usual. He noticed nothing different about Samantha when he walked in. She was dressed in the same grey skirt and blue top she'd worn this morning; her hair was combed back; she looked calm. She had the ability to hide worries and, on this remarkable day, to hide the news about the baby.

But when Marty's eyes were elsewhere, she stared at him more than she usually did. Those eyes, those suspicious eyes—were they hinting at something in his background? She wondered what the real story was, how the riddle would be solved.

"You look exhausted," she said.

"Exhausted, yes. Meetings all afternoon." He slipped off his coat and jacket and loosened his red-striped silk tie.

"How about sirloin steak for dinner?" Samantha said.

Instantly, Marty seemed to relax. "Now that's greatness," he answered. Then his eyes lit up. "By the way, I saw a note on your table. Didn't you have an appointment with Dr. Fromer today?"

Samantha thought fast. "Yes. Just the annual Pap smear."

"Is it OK?"

"It takes a few days for results. But I'm healthy."

"You sure are," Marty replied, putting his arms round her, and Samantha *knew* there was love in those words. "You'll live to be a hundred ... and I want to be there."

"You will," Samantha said softly.

"Why don't we eat?" He eased himself away and went to wash while Samantha finished cooking.

Dinner at the Shaws' was always by candlelight, at a table near the living-room window, and always with a white tablecloth. To Marty and Samantha this elegance symbolized that their marriage deserved the best, that it was extra special, that every evening was an event.

As they sat down, they gazed out of the window at the city lights fully aglow. They never tired of the sight. The skyline simply whispered romance. This was a dream, Samantha had always thought, one that she desperately wanted to continue.

And yet she had to get information out of Marty. "Something funny happened today," she said as they began to eat.

"Oh?"

"I was walking near Fromer's office, and a man stopped me for directions. He was about your age. Guess where he came from?"

"Mars."

"Close. Elkhart."

Marty brightened. "Maybe I know him."

"You might. We got to talking. His name is Fred Wilson." Samantha watched and listened carefully. How would Marty respond to a complete lie?

"Doesn't sound familiar," he said.

"He was a year behind you. He *thought* he knew your name."

"It was a long time ago. There were other Shaws in Elkhart. I don't know the guy."

"He went to high school there too. He said he played football. Did Elkhart have a good team?"

Marty shrugged. "Fair."

Samantha tightened but tried to hide it. She'd done her homework and called an Elkhart paper. For three of Marty's four high school years the team had been undefeated. "Only fair?"

Now, suddenly, Marty stared at Samantha intently. There was the familiar suspicion in his eyes. "Why?" he asked abruptly.

"Just wondering," Samantha replied, feeling her heart skip a beat. "The way this guy was talking, you'd think they were the New York Jets."

Marty started eating again. "I didn't follow football much," he said. "With all my family problems."

There was an awkward silence. Samantha felt a little ashamed.

"Come to think of it, though," Marty continued, now sounding more cheerful, "I remember they had an undefeated streak that went on for years."

For Samantha there was instant joy. He knew. He remembered. "That's what he told me," she said. "You two would probably enjoy talking."

At that moment Samantha saw a subtle fear in Marty's eyes. "You didn't give him our number, did you?"

"No."

Marty looked relieved. "Never give the number," he said. "I worry about something happening to you." Then he reached out and grasped Samantha's hand, as if wanting never to let go. "You've got to be careful," he implored. "You're my whole world."

"I'll watch out for both of us," Samantha replied. They were like that for almost a minute, just looking into each other's eyes, hardly moving, their emotions expressed through the grasp of hands. Marty needed her, Samantha knew. It was a very good feeling, even with the questions about his background.

Finally, slowly, they resumed eating, and Samantha changed the subject, still probing. "You know," she said, "I was watching the news today, and they had this reporter on who was blasting journalism schools. He mentioned yours, and Columbia. He said they produced mechanics. Kind of made me angry."

Marty shrugged. "That line's been around for a long time."

"He said you could learn the same things on the job."

"You could say that about any field," Marty declared.

He had no idea that she'd made up the TV interview. "What did you take at Medill?" she asked.

Marty leaned back on his chair. "Oh, let's see. There was newswriting, reporting, copy editing, photography."

"I'm surprised they never send you anything. They must have an alumni group."

"Yeah, but I didn't keep them up to date on my address." Then Marty looked directly into Samantha's eyes. "Boy, you're really going into my past tonight."

Samantha felt the ice, but feigned nonchalance. "Hey, I love you. Your past interests me."

"Well, I don't think it's so hot."

Samantha knew not to press too far, fearing to arouse suspicion. They finished dinner and discussed the party. Marty approved some new guests but was clearly preoccupied. He was fighting memories again, memories of an electric train going round on tracks laid temporarily on the living-room floor.

For Samantha, Marty's being preoccupied was a rarity, but she was less concerned about that now than with the results of her discreet probes. She suddenly realized that she had learned very little. So Marty knew about Elkhart High's football record. So what? Any man faking his past could have familiarized himself with local sports news. The same held true for his knowledge of Medill's curriculum.

She cooked up one more scheme that night. It was a go-for-broke shot, something that might crack the logjam and expose at least part of the truth. As Marty was getting ready for bed, Samantha intentionally looked apprehensive.

"What's wrong?" Marty asked.

"You really want to know?"

"Yes." He was all curiosity.

"All right, here goes," Samantha said. "You were a little touchy about your past tonight."

Marty stiffened slightly, then laughed. "Not really."

"Oh, yes," Samantha insisted. "You got quite testy. Maybe I should've understood. At any rate, I wanted to get you this really great birthday gift."

"Sam, the party's my gift."

"Besides that. Something for you. For us. I thought it would be super if I got you ... got us ... some plane tickets."

"A vacation?"

"Kind of." She shrugged innocently. "I thought we could go to the Midwest. You could return to Elkhart, visit your old home, then hop over to Northwestern in Evanston. I know how tough it was, love, but every man wants to go home again." She turned away, playing it to the hilt. "Maybe it's not such a hot idea."

He paused. "When would you like to go?" he asked quietly.

"After the party. Christmastime. It's cold, but festive."

"Let's do it!"

"You mean it? Elkhart? Northwestern?"

"Absolutely. It's a great time to go. I'd love to."

A thrill began forming in Samantha's heart.

"I'll show you my room at Northwestern," Marty went on. "It had a view of Lake Michigan that ... Well, I'll just show you."

"I want to see the house where you lived in Elkhart."

"Little white place, clapboard, with two chimneys. Everyone knew the Shaw house by those two chimneys."

A new optimism was beginning to come over Samantha. By agreeing to the trip, Marty was hardly evading the past. He seemed, in fact, to be enthusiastic about it. "I'll get the tickets," she said.

"Why don't we fly to Chicago and start with Northwestern? Then we can rent a car and drive over to Elkhart. I used to do it all the time."

"Any good restaurants in Evanston?"

"Sure. And they'll remember me. There was a guy at the journalism school who wanted to be a food critic. He changed later and opened his own restaurant. I'd get a kick seeing him again."

Samantha was in heaven. *This* was what she'd wanted to hear.

Then Marty did what he'd done only once before, just after she'd agreed to marry him: danced an Irish jig around the room. He stopped. His eyes widened, like those of a little boy.

"I'm sending out for ice cream," he announced. "That new place delivers twenty-four hours. Chocolate chip OK?"

Samantha laughed at him, but she really loved the scene.

"OK," she replied.

Marty made the call.

He was sanguine.

He knew that the trip to the Midwest would never happen.

5

"So it's still there, with the two chimneys. That's wonderful. And look, thank you for the name of the family that lives there now. We'll be contacting them."

Samantha put down the phone, thoroughly pleased, and turned to Lynne. "That's the kind of phone call I like. Makes my day."

"The house is still the way Marty described it?" Lynne asked.

"Exactly. That's what the police captain said." Samantha was rolling now. The call to the police precinct in Marty's old neighbourhood in Elkhart had been reassuring. The captain confirmed every description Marty had ever given her of the area. And Samantha had made another successful call too. Remembering that Marty had a passport, she phoned the State Department and learned he had used his birth certificate as proof of citizenship. It had been issued in Elkhart. Elkhart City Municipal Building, Samantha reasoned, had given her the wrong information.

Her full confidence in Marty restored, Samantha still had to tackle her main objective: getting people who'd known Marty to share their recollections.

"He talks so much about the army," Samantha said to Lynne. "You know, he enlisted."

"I can believe it," Lynne replied, taking an apple from a basket of fruit on a glass table. "Marty's so gung ho."

"They wanted him to be an officer, but he refused. He liked the enlisted guys. So there he was in some office, a private with a journalism degree."

"He ever tell you the names of his army buddies?"

Samantha reflected for a moment. "There was a Corporal Bose. That was his best friend. Richard Bose."

Lynne bit into her apple and got up. "Call Washington and find out where Bose lives now," she said. "Maybe they'll know."

Samantha got the number for the Defence Department and called. Within seconds she was phone to phone with the military bureaucracy, and by her own count she was transferred nine times before reaching the personnel people.

"Sergeant Mulligan."

"Sergeant," Samantha replied, "my name is Samantha Shaw."

"Yes, ma'am. How can I help you, ma'am?" Mulligan's voice gave the impression that he was sitting at attention.

"My husband, Martin Shaw, was in the army back in the '60s, after college."

"Was he in Vietnam, Mrs. Shaw?"

"Only for a short time. He was mostly at Fort Polk. He had some close friends there, and I'm trying to find one of them."

"And you want us to give an address if we have it?"

"That's right."

"No big hassle. We get requests like that all the time. If you'd give me the name of the serviceman, ma'am."

"Bose. Richard Bose."

"I'll see if he's in the computer bank."

"Thank you."

Samantha could hear Mulligan tapping out something on a computer keyboard. She waved to Lynne, who was going out of the door, gesturing that she'd be back soon. Everything fell silent.

"Ma'am?"

"Yes?"

"I don't get a Richard Bose on my terminal, but that's not unusual. I could cross-reference it by punching up your husband. Do you know his unit designations?"

"No, I'm afraid not."

"I guess you wouldn't know his service number either."

Samantha's eyes lit up as she swung round in her chair. "Now *that* I know. I once memorized it as a joke. It's RA38567194."

"I'll punch it up."

Again Samantha waited, going down her list of people to contact after she'd located Bose. Marty had worked for a paper in California before he got into public relations. They'd be next.

Mulligan came back on the line. "That number came up, ma'am. Shaw, Martin." Then there was a pause. "His service history," Mulligan went on, but there was a distinct change in his tone. He was quieter, less flamboyant. "It's in front of me, ma'am."

Samantha noticed the change. "Is something wrong?"

"I'm . . . I'm sorry about your husband, ma'am."

"What about my husband?"

"I'm sorry he was killed in Vietnam, Mrs. Shaw."

It was as if someone had hit Samantha between the eyes. For a few moments she almost blacked out. She said nothing, but simply removed the receiver from her ear and stared into it, almost believing she could see Mulligan's face. It had all been so wonderful just hours before, when Marty had agreed to the trip west. Now everything was in ruins once again. She had heard words she would not believe. They were too bizarre, too sick. Marty was alive. He was flesh and blood. But who was dead?

THE CONFERENCE ROOM was filling with smoke. Marty sat at the head of a long teak table, presiding over a strategy session with an important new client—an airline whose passenger business was falling off rapidly. The company was represented by eight executives, including two lawyers, an accountant and a psychologist. Marty, with a bunch of loose-leaf presentation books in front of him and his tie pulled slightly down, looked like a man ready for combat. It was an act. It was the image of an image maker, and Marty knew how to turn it on.

"Your problem," he told the gathering, "is that no one sees your airline as having an outstanding trait. You're Mr. Average."

The airline president was a trim man of forty-eight, suntanned and healthy, a former pilot. "What is your solution?" he asked.

"We've got to identify things that make you different," Marty replied. "You're too modest. Now, I want you to tell me what you're proud of in your operation."

He leaned back in his chair and gestured towards the president, who began to speak, first haltingly, then rapidly, about the technical talent he'd been able to attract. But as the client spoke, Marty's thoughts started to drift. As December 5 approached, his mind simply couldn't stick to business. Now he heard the voices again.

"Afraid the kids'll find out about you? The way you lose jobs?"

"Maybe they'll find out about you! *Where'd you spend the night, Alice?"*

Marty barely heard the executives drone on. He felt the sweat oozing from his forehead. It was a horror show, an internal storm that contradicted the picture of his being in complete control.

"Frankie, maybe you'd better go to your room."

And then Marty heard a question darting across the table. "Wouldn't *that* be something for the airline to emphasize? What do you think, Marty?"

Lucky he'd heard the question, he thought. But he hadn't heard the sentences that had gone before. Fake it. Fake it good.

Marty cleared his throat. "I think it has to be weighed against other factors," he said. "Not all things can be treated equally."

"But we *could* emphasize it," said an airline vice-president.

"I don't think we should commit to it now," Marty replied. "I'd like to do some testing."

"I'll buy that," the president said.

They all nodded. They knew Marty was sharp.

"I'd like to hear more," Marty said.

The accountant started rambling on, and Marty's mind again began to travel. An image formed in his brain: the trains set up and running, their clickety-clack filling the house. As the accountant rattled off a list of figures, Marty took out a pen. The executives thought he was making notes. But he was composing a letter.

Dear Dad,

It's that time again. Just like last year and all the years before. I'll remember you the right way. I hope you'll be proud of me on the fifth.

Your loving son,
Frankie

The accountant stopped. "Did you get all that?" he asked.

"Oh, sure," Marty replied. "I jotted down everything I had to." He slipped the letter into a folder.

"I SEE," SAMANTHA ANSWERED as she looked down at her trembling hands. "I'm sorry I took up so much of your time." She hung up.

So, Marty hadn't worked at the San Diego *Union*, although he'd told her stories of how he'd covered the police and the courts. The newspaper had never heard of him. Now Samantha was no longer able to believe that all the people she'd contacted were incompetents with faulty records.

She was thunderstruck by the fact that there'd been a Martin Shaw in the army and that her husband had used his service number. But why? And why was he so willing to travel back and retrace a past that, it was becoming clear, was in the shadows? Samantha was beginning to feel overwhelmed by the questions, frightened by the possibilities. Maybe there was something mentally wrong with Marty, something that made him lie. Maybe he'd had an accident and injured his brain. Maybe he just imagined things.

But if he was normal and there was something unusual in his past, why had he not confided it to the woman he'd married?

115

Samantha couldn't handle this herself. She decided there was only one person to call for counsel. Yes, he was a friend of Marty's, but a friend so special, so loyal, that in Samantha's mind no damage would be done. Tom Edwards was, after all, Marty's best pal.

Tom was a real-estate agent for one of the major brokers in Manhattan. He was a few years younger than Marty, but with prematurely grey hair. Like Marty, Tom was well built, but he had a quieter, softer personality, with none of Marty's commanding flair. They understood each other, Samantha thought, on an emotional, subliminal level. She dialled his number.

"Tom Edwards," he answered in his matter-of-fact, I'm-just-a-nice-guy style.

"Tom, Samantha."

"Hey, Sam. What an honour. You never call me. You looking for a new place or something?"

Samantha laughed. "No, Thomas, I'm looking for *you*."

"For me? What'd I do?"

"Nothing illegal. I just need some help. I'm not getting you at a rough time, am I?"

"No, it's a slow day. In fact, I'm gonna call old Mart later just to chat. So shoot. How can I help you?"

"You know the bash I'm having for Marty?"

"Of course."

"Keep this under your hat." Then Samantha stopped, frozen for a moment. She couldn't do what she had planned—she couldn't reveal everything that had happened, even to Tom. She wasn't as emotionally ready for that as she'd thought. No, she'd ease into it. She'd start by probing. "Tommy," she finally continued, "I'm adding a surprise. I'm trying to find Marty's old friends and teachers and have them give remembrances."

"Fantastic."

"So ... do you know any?"

"Let's see." Tom pondered for a moment. "Harold Tyler."

"Marty knows Harold now. I want people he's lost touch with."

"Oh, I get the picture. Well, let me think. There's ... Sam, I just don't know any," Tom finally admitted. "Marty and I have only been buddies about five years. It may sound strange, but we never talk about old times. His only friends I know are the ones you know, with maybe a couple of exceptions."

"Tom, you're not telling me that Marty never *mentioned* anyone, are you?"

Tom laughed, a bit nervously. "Well, maybe some old girlfriends. But all I have there are first names."

"So I'm batting zero," Samantha said.

"There's no other way you can get names?"

"How? I don't want to tip Marty. And he doesn't have many ... links to his past."

"Well, it wasn't the hottest upbringing. Going back into his past may not be that fantastic after all. Memories have strange effects. And it's his present friends who really matter."

"You think so?"

"Well, who knows? But think it over."

"I will," Samantha promised. "Hey, you're working. I'd better be going."

"If you need help on the party, just whistle."

They hung up. Samantha had learned nothing. But Tom's lack of information did confirm one idea—that Marty's past was no open book. How, after all, does a man not discuss his early years with his best friend? That was unnatural, abnormal. The conversation with Tom simply increased Samantha's anxieties.

AFTER DINNER THAT NIGHT Samantha and Marty relaxed, watching an old Humphrey Bogart movie on television. In the middle of the film Marty got up and started walking out of the room. "Are you interested in the movie?" he asked.

"Not really," Samantha replied.

"Come with me."

Samantha followed Marty into their bedroom. He stood at one end for a few moments and surveyed the room, his eyes moving gradually from left to right, then back again.

"What's this about?" Samantha asked.

"I want to rearrange the room," Marty replied.

"Why? It's fine the way it is."

"Fine isn't great." There was a mildly contemptuous tone to Marty's voice that Samantha had not heard before. It bothered her, but she tried not to show it.

"What'd you have in mind?" she asked.

"Something I saw in a decorating magazine. I liked it. And let me show you something." He took a package out of his attaché case next to the bed and unwrapped it, revealing a gold-coloured picture frame, gaudy and cheap-looking, made for a five-by-seven picture. "I bought this," he went on. "I think it should go over the bed."

117

"Well . . ." Samantha began, utterly repelled by the frame.

"What's wrong? You disagree?"

Samantha was becoming increasingly exasperated. "Marty," she said, "we've always bought things together. If we're redecorating, I have some ideas."

Marty rushed over to Samantha and embraced her. "Hey," he said, suddenly the old Marty. "This is a partnership. I want you in on *everything*. But Sam, this will be a great layout. It means a lot to me. Let's at least try it."

"Sure," Samantha agreed. How could she resist when Marty spoke so reasonably? Without a word he started rearranging the room, refusing help from Samantha. He had a determined, almost passionate look on his face, as if his deepest feelings were involved. She couldn't understand it.

Marty moved the bed round so the headboard was against the radiator—something Samantha knew was absolutely wrong—then nailed the picture frame to the wall above it. And surely he knew that the bureau shouldn't block a window. But when he was finished, it did. It was beyond her that any decorating magazine would feature such an arrangement.

"There," he said after the job was done, beads of sweat running down his brow. "I happen to like that."

Samantha said nothing.

"I know it's unusual," Marty went on, "but let's give it a chance. If you decide you don't like it, I'll change it back."

"Fine," Samantha agreed. It was curious . . . very, very curious. She walked out of the room to make some notes for the party.

Marty Shaw slowly approached the bed, then lay down. He clutched Samantha's pillow to his chest, as a child would a stuffed animal. "Frankie wants a kiss," he whispered.

6

The shop was on West Fifteenth Street, near the Hudson River. The area was crammed with warehouses and importing firms, and trailer trucks filled the street, picking up and delivering. Samantha's ears were assaulted by what seemed like one long honking of horns. It was the symphony of West Fifteenth.

The sign outside the store said SIMON'S FRAMING AND LAMINATING, and when she walked in, Samantha could feel the sawdust in the air. The front of the shop was divided from the rear by a simple partition, next to which were a metal desk and chair. It wasn't regal, but if Simon had the answer to one critical question, nothing else mattered.

Howard Simon was a man in miniature—very short, well into his eighties, with a narrow face that made him look elfin. He had virtually no hair on his head. When he saw Samantha he immediately smiled, almost deferentially. "May I help you?"

"Yes," Samantha replied. "I have a diploma."

"And you want it framed?"

"I don't know. It's for a ... business associate. But I have a question about it. I don't know if it's genuine. It might be a mistake."

Simon could see right through Samantha's awkwardness. The problem had come up before. "May I look?" he asked.

Samantha had the diploma in an oversize handbag. She took it out and handed it to Simon.

"Northwestern," he said. "A fine university." He turned the diploma over and examined the back, running his hand along its surface. "Too bad this person didn't go there."

Samantha's whole body tightened. "What do you mean?"

"The document is a fake. I've seen many, many genuine diplomas from this school. They're all engraved. You can feel the letters through the back. This is printed. A very cheap job."

"You're ... sure?" Samantha asked.

"Sixty years in the business, madam."

"Thank you," Samantha whispered. Her eyes welled up with tears. There was something about the physical evidence that was so definitive, so final. Now there could be no doubt about Marty's Northwestern years. They had never happened.

Without another word, she left the shop and took a cab back home. It was the saddest ride she'd ever had. Marty had lied to her about Northwestern and, she was beginning to understand, about many other things. He *wasn't* the Marty Shaw she thought she knew; he was someone else. And the marriage wasn't the dream she'd assumed it to be; it was becoming a nightmare.

She fought to remain in control, not to panic, not to go to pieces. She began thinking that she must have overlooked the one logical, honourable explanation for all she'd discovered, the solution that would let her retain her love and respect for Marty.

As she reentered her apartment, she made a firm decision: she needed professional help. If there was something wrong with Marty, she couldn't diagnose it herself. A psychiatrist would be her best bet, and she knew exactly whom she wanted. She'd heard him lecture once. He seemed articulate and learned, yet warm. His subject had been the stresses in men's lives. Samantha grabbed the phone and made an urgent appointment with Kenneth S. Levine, MD.

DR. LEVINE HAD a small private office in a town house on East Sixty-sixth Street. Samantha had the taxi drop her at the end of the block. She had an uneasy feeling about psychiatrists and was even a bit embarrassed. Slipping on a pair of dark glasses, she climbed the white steps to Levine's office.

Up close, he seemed older than Samantha had remembered. He was in his late fifties, with totally grey hair and deep-set eyes. He *looked* like a psychiatrist, Samantha thought. His office was done in reddish wood panelling, with indirect lighting. It was easy on the eyes, designed to help anxious people relax. Levine sat in an orthopaedic chair behind his cluttered desk as he talked with Samantha.

"I don't understand it," she told him. "Marty's an honest man. People in business respect him. So many things he told me weren't true. Yet he wants to make that trip back to the Midwest."

"Does he have a tendency to exaggerate?" Levine asked.

"No."

"Does he seem to feel the need to impress you?"

"He doesn't brag. He doesn't claim abilities he doesn't have."

"I see." Levine made notes on a yellow pad as he went along. "Has he changed since you married him?"

"Not really."

"Any medical problems?"

"No."

"Brushes with the law?"

"None that he's told me about," Samantha answered.

"It's important that I know," Levine explained. "What I'm trying to get at is anything that might be disturbing Marty, something that may be warping his judgment. Sometimes people lie—about their past, for example—out of desperation. They may need to invent a second identity."

"I understand," Samantha replied. "But I can't think of anything that could be disturbing him. He seems quite content."

"Have you discussed the fake diploma with him?"

"No."

120

"Well, don't. People can react to a challenge like that in very strange ways."

At the end of the interview Samantha was exhausted, and Levine had filled many pages with notes. "Mrs. Shaw," he said, "you've described a perfectly normal man—except for his false past and this odd redecorating of the room. It will be impossible for me to assess this without seeing Marty."

"But Dr. Levine, you asked me not to challenge him."

"That's right. You couldn't confront him with your real concerns. We'd have to find another way to get him in here."

"Like what?"

"Perhaps you could say that he seems under stress from work. You could urge him to see a doctor for *your* sake."

Samantha shook her head. "He wouldn't buy it," she said. "Marty's one of those I-can-handle-it types."

"Well, Mrs. Shaw, the bottom line is, no Marty, no answers."

It was a dead end. Samantha couldn't devise a way to get Marty to a psychiatrist, and now wondered whether Levine could have helped anyway. What if Marty were just a deceitful man with no mental problems? What could Levine do with that?

A discouraged Samantha left the office, trying to collect her thoughts, to figure a way out of her dilemma. Now she almost wished she'd never thought of the party or of finding people from Marty's past. Ignorance *is* sometimes bliss, she thought.

AS THE DAYS PASSED, there was one question Levine had asked that kept going through Samantha's mind. It frightened her, but it wouldn't go away. He'd asked whether Marty had had brushes with the law. It was a possibility, Samantha knew, one that could explain why he'd falsified his past.

She decided to see a lawyer, perhaps a criminal lawyer, someone who might have handled problems like the one she now faced. So she left her apartment one Thursday, in the middle of a November snowfall, and took a cab to the New York Public Library. There she went through back issues of newspapers, seeking the name of a lawyer with a winning record. If Marty was in trouble, she'd want him to win. No matter what he'd done, no matter what he'd told her, she'd still want him to win.

What she needed was a modern-day Clarence Darrow. And she thought she'd found him in L. Douglas Grimes.

Grimes had two offices, an opulent set-up on Wall Street and a stylishly shabby affair in a West Side brownstone. He saw Samantha, a lady with a personal problem, in the brownstone. The tiny office was the perfect setting for the downtrodden and those who imagined they were. Behind the desk were sixteen awards from civic groups, citing Grimes as certifiably wonderful. That was clout.

Common looks, rolled-up sleeves, mussed hair, worn shoes, and creased, wide-braced trousers all worked to Grimes's advantage. He was always one of "us" rather than one of "them".

He listened to what Samantha said, his practised eyes staring her down, and she did spill out everything. When she finished he waited a full minute before commenting. He removed his rimless glasses, leaned back, and placed his hands flat on his head, signalling that he was thinking carefully. He tried to detect, from twenty years' experience, whether she was lying. He guessed she wasn't.

"You have one of the most difficult problems I've ever encountered," he said. "I don't know how you take it."

"I love him," Samantha replied. "That's how."

Grimes laughed. "You'd make a good defence witness. Very sympathetic. But I'm amazed you haven't confronted him."

"I can't. What if he has good reasons for all this? Sometimes I think I'd be better off if I'd never known."

"I understand." Grimes eased out of his chair and stood leaning on the edge of the desk. "But you don't mean that. You want the truth precisely *because* you love him. You sense he may be in danger. After all, you did come to see me."

Samantha conceded that Grimes was right. She would forgive almost anything, even a past littered with shame, but she had to know.

"Do you think he may have a legal problem?" she asked.

"Impossible to say," Grimes replied. "You'd need a private investigator to trace his roots. That's expensive, and he might come up empty-handed. But don't jump to conclusions. There are other possibilities. Maybe he did something heroic, like turning in a criminal, and the government established a new identity for him."

"What if I went to the police?"

Grimes shrugged. "Chances are it wouldn't have any effect. They've got hotter cases to worry about."

Samantha felt herself coming to an obvious conclusion—one she would fight—that Marty had to be confronted directly.

"Do you have any legal advice?" she finally asked Grimes.

"Sure. If your husband does something suspicious, don't get

involved. You could be charged as an accomplice, even if you claimed you didn't know. If he does something odd, call me."

"What's odd?"

"Anything that smacks of sudden material gain. If he wants a vacation that he can't afford, don't go. He may be using dirty money. If he brings you a gift that busts the budget, tell him you'd be embarrassed to accept it, and buzz me." Grimes approached Samantha, gazing directly into her fearful eyes. "If you discover a weapon in the house, call me *instantly*. You'll sense if something's wrong. Wives always do. You're the best private eyes."

On that note they parted. Samantha returned by cab to her apartment building. She had no idea what to do next.

FOUR DAYS AFTER Samantha saw Grimes, Marty brought home the electric trains. Samantha was nonplussed. A grown man with choochoo trains? In a city apartment? Without kids? But Marty explained it. "I never had trains," he said boyishly. "They're great. A lot of men have them."

She wasn't convinced.

"Look, I'll build a small layout that can be taken apart and put in the cupboard. You'll love it."

"I guess it'll be all right," she said.

"It will be relaxing for me," Marty went on, as if appealing to Samantha's devotion. Then he explained he had bought only used trains because he preferred the older models. "You have to understand the hobby. The old Lionel stuff—it's terrific."

It was odd, perhaps, but not odd enough to trigger a phone call to L. Douglas Grimes. And Samantha saw nothing to link the trains to the mystery of Marty's past. She was prepared to let the trains chug by as an eccentricity of a hardworking man.

Marty's friend Tom Edwards came over and helped him set up the trains in the living room. They ran them for a time, then Tom went home, allowing Marty to run them alone. Samantha studied him from the hallway—watching the intensity in his face, the fascination in his eyes. "I've never seen you happier," she said, walking into the living room.

He didn't answer. He didn't even acknowledge her presence. All right, men got wrapped up in things. It happened. She forced herself not to take offence.

As Marty was pressing the button that sounded the diesel horn, Samantha noticed that some locomotive grease had smeared on the white rug. It upset her. Marty was always so careful about what he owned. What was so important about these trains that would allow him to sacrifice a good rug, without so much as a comment? Maybe the trains were more than a hobby. Maybe they meant something to Marty that he just didn't want to reveal.

For the next few days she tried to organize some strategy for dealing with the mystery of Marty. "Police" kept going through her mind. Instinct told her that it might be her only way.

ONE MAN WAS WAITING for Samantha Shaw to decide to come to the police, but neither he nor she knew it.

At Manhattan's main police headquarters, Spencer Cross-Wade glanced up at his calendar and felt a surge of disgust, coupled with the intense frustration he had felt since taking on the case. Only three weeks remained until December 5. Three weeks to piece together a horrendous puzzle. Three weeks to prevent another tragedy. Three weeks to cap a career approaching its end. He had circled the date with a black marking pen, and the blackness itself seemed to capture the moment.

Small, balding, pushing sixty, Spencer Cross-Wade was more Scotland Yard than New York City Police Department. His father had been with the Yard, and *his* father before him. But Spencer had visited America while in the Royal Navy during World War II, married an American, and returned to stay. His wife died in 1955. They had had no children. He never remarried. He lived alone in a small Brooklyn apartment overlooking the East River, seemingly content with his memories, with his recollections of England, and with plans to travel when he retired in a few months.

His detective's office was simple—a steel desk, grey walls and, for cheerfulness, an assortment of flowers that he kept replacing. "A man should have a garden," he was fond of saying to his associates, with a twinkle in his eye. It was very British, very much a part of his campaign to bring a bit of gentility to the New York department.

His intercom buzzed. He reached over, pressed the red button, and heard Sally, the receptionist.

"Sir, Detective Loggins to see you."

"Ah," Cross-Wade replied, "I've been expecting him. Let me come fetch him."

Arthur Loggins was seated on a metal visitor's chair, reading over the sports pages of the New York *Post*.

"Arthur!" Cross-Wade exclaimed. "Come in. I need you."

Loggins, forty-two, heavy-set, plodding, but with a detective's eye for subtlety, followed Cross-Wade back to his office.

"Sorry I'm late, sir," Loggins said in a maddening monotone, "but I had to finish a case."

"A policeman must always finish," Cross-Wade admonished. "I admire that."

"Yes, sir," Loggins replied, not having expected a homily on police wisdom. They entered the office and sat down.

"Now," Cross-Wade said, "you've been transferred to my command for a single case, because you're a dogged investigator, a detail man. This is not to be discussed outside this office, and not with the press. Am I clear?"

"Yes, sir," Loggins replied, impressed that he should be called for something so hush-hush.

Cross-Wade got up from his desk chair and tapped the circled December 5 on his calendar. "That date is our target and our nightmare," he told Loggins. "If it arrives without an arrest, a woman will die. I hope you regard that as serious."

"Very serious, sir. I just got off a murder case."

"This is multiple murder," Cross-Wade continued. "It seems that each December fifth for the last six years, a woman has been murdered in the same way, somewhere in North America. All have been struck on the head with a blunt instrument, then choked with a chainlike device."

"Did the victims have anything in common?" Loggins asked.

"Yes," Cross-Wade replied. "Each had long, auburn hair."

"Nothing else?"

"Nothing that we can tell. There were some scattered witnesses from a few of the killings. They saw a large man in the vicinity of the murders, but no one could give a clear physical description."

"You said North America, sir. I wonder ..."

"I was getting to that, Arthur. The last three killings occurred in or near New York, which is why we've been brought in on the case."

"No suspects?"

"Not one. But we do know something about the killer. The date itself seems to be the key to the puzzle, so I've had my men check crime records for each December fifth for the last fifty years." Cross-Wade reached into his desk drawer and pulled out a green folder. "The results are quite remarkable." He handed the file to Loggins. "I also had our psychologists look at the case. A question, Arthur. Have you ever heard of the term 'anniversary excitement schizophrenia'?"

"No, sir."

"Well, you'll be hearing it a lot. I call it calendar schizophrenia. It's all in the folder. Read what's there, then report back to me."

Loggins left the office. Cross-Wade stared ahead, knowing that the assignment of still another man, no matter how capable, would probably bring him no closer to his target. To know the probable motive, to know the date of the next killing, to know the physical characteristics of the victim, yet not to know the identity of the killer—that was the greatest frustration of his police career.

7

Samantha had blundered. She'd forgotten that all the calls she'd made checking Marty's past would appear on the phone bill. And as luck would have it, the bill came on a Saturday, Marty was at home, and it was he who went down to the lobby to get the mail.

He noticed immediately. The calls to Evanston, to Elkhart, to Washington. *What* was Samantha doing? Why was she calling these places? Marty stood against a marble wall in the mail room, just staring at the bill as if it were some Chinese puzzle. Did she suspect something? Had she been tipped?

He couldn't ask her about those calls. The question itself would be suspect. He would simply pay the bill without showing it to her, hoping she'd never notice that she'd not received that bill.

He was apprehensive, and he wasn't used to it. He'd always been in exquisite control, never felt any real risk of detection. But Samantha's making these calls was something he *couldn't* control. This was the most important year of all, the final year of the compact, and now things might be messed up.

MARTY WENT ON ANOTHER SECRET mission the next Monday, to 116th Street and Broadway—Columbia University. None of his midtown crowd had reason to be up there, and he melted well into the diverse neighbourhood. He crossed Broadway to Radius, a travel agency. It was on the second floor of an old sandstone building, and had airline posters in the window, advertising cut-rate fares.

He walked up the short flight of wooden stairs. Inside, Radius was the traditional agency—rows of desks piled with papers, timetables, and phone messages. A woman employee spotted Marty. "Help you?" she asked, gesturing for him to sit.

"Yeah," Marty answered. "I'd like to buy a ticket to Rome."

"Sure." The woman reached for a thick blue book of international airline schedules. "Is this a round trip?" she asked.

"Yes." It wasn't, but a one-way ticket to Rome might raise suspicions.

"For yourself?"

"Yes. One person."

"OK, and when would you like to go?"

"December sixth." The date sent an unaccustomed chill up Marty's spine.

"And you'll be returning . . ?"

"December eighteenth."

"Too bad you can't stay for Christmas," she said.

"I know," Marty answered, "but I just can't do it this year."

"You want nonstop, of course."

"Sure."

"Alitalia leaves at six o'clock in the evening and arrives in Rome about eight the next morning."

"That's fine."

"Will you be needing a hotel?"

"No, I'm staying with friends."

"OK. Let's check your return." She found an acceptable flight and started taking ticket information. "Your name, sir?"

"Steele," Marty replied. "Elliot Steele." And he had a fake passport to prove it. Indeed, in his safe he now had a complete set of Elliot Steele ID papers, acquired from the same San Francisco counterfeiter who, years earlier, had made up all the documents he needed to become Martin Everett Shaw.

He was now one step closer to December 5.

THE TENSION WAS TOO MUCH for Samantha.

She was pacing the living room, pondering her next move in penetrating Marty's past, when she suddenly felt dizzy. Nothing much, she thought. Maybe morning sickness. But then something seemed to squeeze her nostrils together. She gasped for breath, felt on the verge of panic. She stumbled to the phone and called Lynne.

"Lynne . . . I'm choking," she said, and collapsed.

It took six precious minutes for a handyman to let Lynne in. Samantha was unconscious but breathing. An ambulance lurched up to the building's entrance twelve minutes later, and two paramedics charged into the apartment with medical bags and an oxygen tank.

"What happened?" one snapped at Lynne.

"I don't know," she answered. "She said she was choking."

Samantha's colour was good, her breathing relatively normal. There were no signs of choking. The second paramedic whipped out his stethoscope and checked her heart. Normal.

"History of heart disease?" he asked Lynne.

"None that I know of. I'm just a friend."

They brought Samantha round with smelling salts and massage. She opened her eyes, looked about fearfully, finally focusing on Lynne. "I'm sorry," she said. "I guess I just lost my breath." Instinctively she felt her stomach. "I just hope . . ."

"Let's go to the hospital," Lynne said.

"No," Samantha answered. She wanted no hospital, and she *didn't* want Marty told. "I'll just rest," she said. "It was only a fainting spell. Maybe something I ate."

But she did agree to have Lynne take her to Dr. Fromer, who saw her immediately. He examined her, then sat her down in a tiny office adjoining his examining room.

"Look," Fromer said, "I don't see any medical problem. There's no complication with the pregnancy." He could see the relief cross Samantha's face. "But be honest with me. Did you do anything to bring on this fainting?"

"No," Samantha insisted.

"Drinking? Other substances? You know what I mean."

"I wouldn't *touch* that stuff!"

"Of course," Fromer said with a warm smile. "Not in normal times. But times change. When you were here before, I said you seemed under stress. That appears to be worse now."

Samantha shrugged. "Maybe it's having the baby," she said.

"I don't think so." Fromer had seen too many women with personal problems to be fooled. "If there are . . . emotional difficulties . . . perhaps you should consider counselling. Another episode like this *could* affect the baby."

Samantha looked at him. Suddenly she realized that the crisis might affect the health—the life—of someone other than herself. It was something she hadn't confronted before.

"Thank you," she said softly. "I really want this baby."

"HORRIBLE," LOGGINS SAID as he walked into Cross-Wade's office carrying the folder of background material on the calendar schizophrenic case. "This is just horrible."

"Yes," Cross-Wade replied. "And nothing new has come in since we last talked. Have you any theories, Arthur?"

"No, sir. Any clues would come from the past murders."

"Precisely."

"And there's not much."

"I've been weighing a change in strategy," Cross-Wade revealed. "If we issued a public alert to women with long auburn hair—there're thousands of them—maybe we could frighten the killer. Or maybe one of these women would see something suspicious in a man she knows."

Loggins frowned. He didn't think much of the idea.

"On the other hand," Cross-Wade went on, "it might encourage him, maybe even others. A public alert is a dare." Cross-Wade was beginning to agree. "No," he concluded, "I think I'll hold off."

December 5 was seventeen days away.

SAMANTHA RESTED FOR A FEW days after her fainting spell. She'd come to a crushing conclusion: she had to reach out to close friends to solve the mystery of Marty's past. Nothing else was likely to work. Thoughts of the baby spurred her on.

Inevitably her mind turned to Tom Edwards. She'd called him before, of course, but she'd hedged, not revealing how serious her problem was. If there was one person who could help, it was Tom. No one knew more about what made Marty tick, what he thought. Samantha called him and asked him to lunch. It was about Marty, she said, and it was important.

"Is he sick?" Tom asked urgently.

"Possibly," Samantha replied. Be as dramatic as you can, she told herself. Jolt Tom.

"When do you need me?" he responded.

They agreed to meet at noon at a small Chinese restaurant near Tom's office. When he arrived, he took one look at Samantha and saw trouble. There was a vacant look in her eyes that made Tom sense the worst. "Sam, what's wrong?" he asked. "I want it straight."

"I'm not sure," she answered, still zipped into her winter coat, thawing out from the cold.

"Is Marty dying?"

"No, nothing like that."

"You said he might be sick."

Samantha hesitated. "Another kind of sick," she said. "Tom, is there anything about Marty's past that you know directly?"

129

"Directly?"

"Firsthand. Without his telling you."

"No."

"I see."

"Sam, what is this about? You've got to tell me."

Samantha looked around the dimly lit restaurant. She leaned forward, making sure that he would hear every word over the clatter and din. "Tom," she said, "I went back to find people for the party. I called Northwestern, Elkhart, the army."

"That's great."

"No, it isn't. None of it is true, Tom. Marty never went to Northwestern, or the Elkhart schools."

Tom was flabbergasted. "Come on," he said.

"I checked and double-checked. There *was* a Martin Shaw in the army . . . but he was killed."

Tom simply stared at Samantha. "I don't believe it."

"Neither did I," Samantha replied. "Tom, I took Marty's diploma to be checked. It's a fake."

Tom took a deep, troubled breath, showing tension rare for him. "Let's order," he said, buying time to think. They chose some simple dishes, the talk with the waiter reducing the electricity by a few volts. Then Tom got to the core of the matter.

"Now," he asked, "is it possible you're overlooking something? Maybe Marty's diploma is a duplicate. People lose their originals and get copies."

"Tom, there's no *record* of Marty at Northwestern . . . or anywhere else. Marty doesn't seem to have a past."

Tom leaned back, finally accepting what Samantha was telling him. "Now I know why you thought Marty might be sick. You meant mentally sick."

"Yes," Samantha replied softly.

There was a long, almost ominous pause. Then Tom smiled with the special warmth that was his. "Sam, Marty's a straight guy," he said. "If he had to tell you some tales about his past, he must've had a reason. If I know Marty, it was a *good* reason."

"Tom, I've tried everything." There was a rare pleading look in Samantha's eyes. "I've even seen a lawyer."

"But you haven't talked to Marty."

"Oh, no."

Now Tom looked sternly at Samantha, ready to give her a dose of common sense. "You love him, Sam?"

130

"Of course."

"Would you still love him with something sour in his past?"

"I really think I would."

"Then you've got two choices—either forget the whole thing or confront him directly."

The first course came, and they fell silent. Samantha was learning nothing from Marty's closest friend. She felt, in a way, that Tom was protecting Marty. Maybe he thought that probing Marty's past was an improper intrusion for a wife. And maybe it was.

Samantha was starting to feel a bit foolish. The lunch would result in nothing.

December 5 was thirteen days away.

MARTY WAS STILL CONCERNED. Yes, the plans were made. Almost everything was set. But what about those phone calls on the bill? What was this woman up to?

It was four in the afternoon when a bonded messenger arrived at Marty's office with a sealed note. He knew whom it was from by the envelope, and was surprised. He immediately closed the door and carefully tore open the envelope. He read a handwritten note that he'd feared might some day come. "She knows," it said. "She knows you have no past."

He shredded the letter.

"I'VE NEVER TASTED such chicken," Marty raved to Samantha as he was eating dinner that night. "My lady, you have that special touch."

Samantha hadn't seen Marty this buoyant since the night he set up the electric trains. He was smiling with that large, rugged face that had magnetized Samantha from the first moment. Yet it couldn't be the same for her now. The questions were racing through her mind. How do I find out? When do I confront him?

Marty looked at his watch. "Say, how about a movie?"

"Tonight?"

"Unless I have to book you months ahead."

Samantha wasn't up to it. Her head was in too much turmoil. "Could I beg off?" she asked softly.

"You're not feeling well," Marty said. Samantha thought she saw worry crossing his face.

"No, I'm just tired."

"OK. Can't blame a fellow for trying." He finished the last bit of dinner, got up, and crossed behind her. He started stroking her hair, something he hadn't done lately and that she rather liked. "You know how special you are?" he asked.

"Yes," she replied, "but I don't mind a refresher course."

"OK, where do I begin?" He kept up the stroking. What could *possibly* be going on in her mind? he thought. And how did she manage to conceal her suspicions so well? In an odd way, Marty was more impressed with Samantha than he'd ever been before.

But he had a scene to play out. He'd do it with style. He'd always done it with style. "Well," he said, "you're special because you're thoroughly loving."

"Good," Samantha responded. "And?"

"And beautiful."

"Go on."

"I think I'll reserve the rest."

"OK, I'm satisfied," Samantha said. Then a question just poured out, as if she couldn't control it. "Marty, what did you do at Fort Polk?"

Marty tightened imperceptibly. "I was a hero," he replied. "I was given a special commendation for using extreme caution under cover."

"Marty . . ."

"All right. I'll come clean." He stopped stroking her hair. "Clerk-typist. I typed accident reports for jeeps." He laughed. "Does that lower me in your estimation?"

"No. I wasn't expecting a general."

They talked for a few minutes about the big party; then Marty glanced at his watch again. "Hey, if we're not going to the movies, I think I'll get some work done."

"Sure." Now Samantha sensed the tautness inside Marty. It was there in his voice, in the quick rhythm of his speech. He went directly to the bedroom and pretended to examine a pile of reports. Then those words, permanently etched in his memory, came back to him.

"Frankie's a good boy. He's waited a long time."

"Don't gimme that. He's a kid. How long can a kid wait?"

"I want him to be happy."

"Him happy? What about me happy?"

"You know I've tried."

"When have you tried? Yesterday or this morning?"

Marty remembered that day, the picture never losing its clarity! Now he'd almost arrived at another special day, when remembrance turned to noble deeds. He felt his hand quiver. The memory

132

wouldn't leave him. It was reinforced as he looked round the room, with its odd arrangement, its bizarrely placed picture frame. Did other men have this thing inside? Did *anyone* else have it? He found himself staring at the furniture.

"Frankie likes it," he whispered to himself.

8

The next Monday Samantha made the decision to go to the police. She'd exhausted everything else, and she began to fear that whatever was wrong about Marty might some day explode in her face. She could be hurting him by going, but she could also be protecting him. To limit her embarrassment, she decided against going to Twentieth Precinct headquarters, near home, where friends might see her go in or out. Even so, afraid of being recognized, she disguised her appearance a bit with a scarf and took a bumpy, rattling cab ride to main police headquarters, a modern high rise in lower Manhattan, where Missing Persons had its principal office.

Police Plaza was teeming with cops. As Samantha got out of her cab, she saw a veritable sea of blue. It felt vaguely military, as if she were in a fortress, surrounded by a hostile landscape.

A helpful officer directed Samantha to the Missing Persons office. She reached its door, which was emblazoned with gold letters that were beginning to chip. Once inside, she filled out a little pink card, and had to wait more than an hour. There were other cases ahead, and Samantha was struck by the fact that virtually all were women. Why? she wondered. Were they there to report missing children? Or were there many Martys, many more than she realized? Occasionally she heard sobs from the room beyond the closed door.

Finally a sergeant stuck his head out of the interviewing room. He read from Samantha's card. "Mrs. Shaw?"

"Yes?" She froze in her seat. Now that her time had come, needles of fright shot through her.

"This way, ma'am," the sergeant said, a slight smile on his face. Samantha looked up at him, only then realizing that he was Oriental. She rose and followed him through the door into a large room divided into cubicles. She saw his indentification plate on his desk: SERGEANT YANG. He gestured for her to sit down.

"Now," he said, "I see you live over in Twentieth Precinct country. You didn't see anyone over there?"

133

"No, I was . . ."

"A little embarrassed?"

"Yes."

"I understand." He noticed Samantha staring at him. "My mother was American," he explained, as he did to virtually every visitor. "My father gave me the eyes. He comes from Taiwan." He smiled broadly. Samantha liked him. For a few minutes he studied the card Samantha had filled out earlier. "A phantom past," he said finally.

"Yes," Samantha replied.

"And you've sought help elsewhere—professional people?"

"Yes. I tried everything before coming here."

Yang leaned back, his chair groaning with age. He flipped the pink card onto his desk. "I want you to be aware of some things," he said. "First off, we don't find many missing people, because most people who are missing *want* to be."

"*Want* to be?"

"Yes. They just decide to change their lives. They drop out, go away. Especially married men. They reach a certain point, the pressure builds up, a lot of bills, and they chuck it all."

"Marty isn't that type," Samantha told Yang.

He smiled. "No husband ever is," he said. "But look, your husband hasn't disappeared from *you*. Your concern is that he may be missing from somewhere else."

"Yes. Sure."

"All right," Yang went on. "Let's list the possibilities. He could be missing voluntarily or involuntarily. If involuntarily, it could be the result of mental illness, or some injury that produced a mental reaction. If voluntarily, he could have been fed up with his old life, or he could be running from something. It doesn't have to be crime. It could be a personal scandal, a professional failure, even a misunderstanding."

"I just don't know," Samantha responded.

"Of course. But let's think hard. Has Marty ever let slip a name that you haven't recognized?"

"Only business names. And he always tells me who they are."

"Has he ever seemed confused about his past? You know, saying one thing, then correcting it?"

"No, not at all. Marty talks about his past—or what he *says* is his past—all the time. We've even agreed to take a trip to Elkhart, Indiana, where he says he grew up."

"Oh? That's interesting." Yang jotted down a note about the trip.

134

"Most people who are running wouldn't do that. But I wouldn't put much stock in it."

"Why?"

"Because Marty might genuinely know the areas you're visiting, yet could still be lying to you about having lived there. It may reassure him to see that you believe his story."

Samantha gazed down. "This is all theory," she said.

"Sure," Yang answered. "But you've heard the old proverb—it's from my father's part of the world—that a journey of a thousand miles begins with a single step?"

"I've heard that," Samantha answered.

"Well, we can take that first step here. We might not discover who Marty is, or where he's from, but we can narrow things down." Again he smiled at her.

Samantha suddenly felt close to him. Of all those she'd spoken to, Yang was, to her, the most human. An invisible shield had separated her from the psychiatrist Levine, from the lawyer Grimes, even from Tom Edwards, but it just wasn't there with him. I can talk to this man, she thought. I *want* to talk to him.

"Look, can I say something?" she blurted out.

"Sure."

"I'm pregnant."

"Congratulations."

"Thanks, but that's not the point. I want the baby. It's my baby. It's *ours*." She paused. "Sergeant Yang, it's Marty's baby, but strangely, I don't know who the father really is."

And then Samantha did what she didn't want to do. She started to cry. Yang knew it was the best purgative and he said nothing, waiting for Samantha to compose herself.

"I'm sorry," she finally said, taking a tissue that Yang offered and dabbing her eyes. "This is hell. It never came out like that before."

"I'm glad it came out here," Yang said.

"I waited for Marty all my life," she continued, trying to hold back the sobs. "I kid myself that he's this great knight I thought he was. And I've got his baby coming."

Yang did not interrupt.

Samantha stared at him, stared deeply into his eyes. "You see a lot of women like me, don't you?" she asked.

"All the time," he replied. "And I want you to avoid the usual pattern. Many women start feeling that *they're* at fault if their husband disappears or has Marty's kind of problem. I see this

136

beginning in you. The problem is *his*, not yours. If he's done something wrong, you share no blame."

"Thank you," Samantha said quietly.

As the conversation continued, Yang was pessimistic about solving the case; Samantha's verbal portrait of Marty told him that this was a shrewd, calculating man, the kind who'd cover his tracks well.

"We have access to a nationwide computer bank," he told Samantha. "It has pictures of thousands of missing persons. It's a long shot, but I'd like you to look at some of them. They're catalogued. I'll only show you men about Marty's age. Are you willing to take a look?"

"I'll try anything."

Yang escorted Samantha to a photographic library down the hall. It contained long metal files filled with pictures of missing persons. Yang selected the right batch and sat Samantha down at a table to start her search.

"Remember," Yang told her, "your husband could have changed his appearance. Try to study facial contours and skin markings. Anything that looks familiar. Watch the hairlines also, and the size of the ears."

"OK," Samantha said. She felt good about looking through the pictures. At least she was taking *action*. She was amazed at the sheer number of photos—thousands of them. Some were pathetic, others heartbreaking. Most showed men with their wives and children, in happier times. Almost all the men seemed ordinary, not the kind to melt away or get into trouble.

"Many probably have new wives and kids," Yang explained. "Sometimes they disappear again and again. We had one case of a man who'd left three different families."

"But aren't there *legitimate* missing persons?"

"Oh, of course. A lot of children. That's a national scandal. Sometimes grown-ups disappear involuntarily too, particularly after they're robbed. They're disposed of so they can't testify."

Yang stayed with Samantha, going over each picture. After a time they all began to blur. None of those men even remotely resembled Marty. Samantha didn't know whether to be happy or depressed. Some clue, however grim, would be better than this mystery, this wondering. Or would it? She went through pile after pile, one minute hoping to recognize Marty, another minute hoping not to.

And then . . . A picture came up. A man in jeans and a sports shirt, two little boys beside him, in front of a large ranch house.

Samantha held the picture, studied it. The facial features were so familiar. She blinked her searching eyes a few times to clear them, to fight the fatigue and double vision.

Marty liked ranch houses. He'd said so. A ranch house in the country. That's what he wanted for summers.

Maybe he'd *always* liked them. Maybe he'd lived in one.

There was a companion picture. The same man, this time with an attractive young woman. Samantha felt the tears well up. Could it be? The pictures weren't that clear. They were taken in 1972. But that face, and the build, and the shape of the shoulders, and the ranch house....

Yang caught Samantha's reaction. With a slow, gentle motion he reached out to a shelf and took down a loupe, a small magnifier. He slid it across to her. She placed it over the face in the second picture and bent her head down, centring her eye above the glass. She clenched her fists, then bit her lip. Her body seemed to stiffen, as if receiving a sudden, stabbing wound.

"Marty," she whispered, "I found you."

"Wait one moment," Yang advised. He showed no jubilation at her discovery. He knew she was going through agony. In missing-person cases the familiar picture usually confirms the darkest fears. He went to another file and found a brief report whose serial number linked it to the pictures Samantha had just identified. As he pulled it out, she sat motionless, staring at the pictures, her face blank except for the moist eyes.

Samantha felt more numb than angry, but questions gnawed at her: Was that woman, were those children, still alive?

What should she hope for? What was right?

Yang brought her the report, contained in a yellow folder marked BRANNEN, KENNETH. "Your husband know anything about banking?" Yang asked.

"He knows about money. We've never talked about banks."

"The man in the pictures was a banker. He had this wife and two kids. They were living in Green Bay, Wisconsin. He disappeared in 1973 on his way home from an army reserve meeting."

Samantha's heart suddenly sank. "You mean ... the family was alive when he disappeared?"

"Yes, I suppose so. There's nothing to contradict that."

"I see," Samantha said quietly.

"Please look at the pictures again. Are you sure it's Marty?"

Samantha studied the photos through the loupe. "It sure looks like him," she said, ice in her voice now. "Yes, that's Marty." The reality was building, grasping her, overpowering her.

"There's very little in this man's folder," Yang told her softly. "It's incomplete, but we do know that he's probably committed a felony."

"He has?"

"Abandonment. He abandoned his family. If this is your Marty, there might be charges in Wisconsin. I've got to get more data. I need an ironclad identification, even with your testimony."

Yang took Samantha, with photos, back to his office. Using his desktop computer terminal, he tried to search out more information on Kenneth Brannen in national crime files. He drew a blank. Yang decided to call the police department in Green Bay, Wisconsin.

The sergeant in charge there located the old missing-person file on Kenneth Brannen, but it was incomplete. However, there was one thing that Yang could use.

"The subject had an interest in railroads," the sergeant said in a raspy, cigarette-ruined voice.

Yang turned to Samantha. "Your husband like railroads?"

She almost jumped. The trains. Those silly trains. "Yes. Definitely yes!" She knew this was the right man.

The data from Green Bay also included one piece of information that Yang had to pass on to Samantha, no matter how much pain it might cause, no matter how much bitterness. A 1982 memo inserted to update the Green Bay file read:

Mrs. Kenneth Brannen (Kathleen) has not remarried, although she had her husband declared legally dead after the usual seven-year period. Mrs. Brannen still seeks information about the whereabouts of her husband.

Yang repeated the memo to Samantha. "Unless you object, I'm going to check with her. By putting everything together, I hope to get positive identification ... if this is Marty."

"It's him. Believe me. But do you think she'll cooperate?"

"She still seeks information," Yang said. He was about to talk to Green Bay again when Samantha suddenly reached forward and touched his arm.

"Wait," she said, and took a deep breath. "I want to talk to her."

"You *what?*"

"I want to talk with Mrs. Kenneth Brannen, the first wife of my husband ... his only legal wife."

"Are you sure?"

"Yes," Samantha said firmly, amazed at her own control. If life was shattered, she told herself, pick up the pieces gracefully.

"It could be difficult," Yang cautioned.

"I'm ready. That woman and I have a lot in common."

Yang nodded, sensing Samantha's resolve. He got back on the line to Green Bay. "My subject wants to talk with Mrs. Brannen," he said. "Can it be arranged?"

"I can try," came the reply. "I'll get back to you."

"Thank you, Green Bay."

Yang hung up. "Now we wait," he said.

ONE FLOOR BELOW, Spencer Cross-Wade checked off another day on his calendar. Ten days to December 5, and still he had absolutely nothing new. Arthur Loggins sat heavily in a visitor's chair, equally stumped. Cross-Wade began to pace, his shoulders rounded, his head down.

"I am humiliated," he announced. "Even my flowers look sad."

"Yes, sir," Loggins answered with his usual dullness.

"You have reinterviewed all the witnesses, and only the whistle shows up?"

"Not exactly a whistle, sir."

"You know what I'm talking about, Arthur."

"Yes, sir. The lady who was near last year's murder site said she heard a person sounding like a train horn."

"It could have been anyone," Cross-Wade said.

"Yes, sir. But this was right off Interstate 95 in Greenwich, Connecticut. And it was around the time of the murder."

"So? Do we put out an all-points bulletin for anyone who impersonates trains?"

Loggins didn't answer. Like Cross-Wade, he was humiliated.

"Look, Arthur, there must be a picture of this man as a boy. We *know* where he lived. I can't believe that every one has disappeared."

"They have, sir, except for that grainy newspaper picture, and even that negative is gone. The photo is very blurry."

"Yes. Well, I have nothing else. This is a man who makes no mistakes, who leaves no real clues. He could even strike in Alaska this year, for all we know."

"Sir," Loggins said, "this may be one of those cases where the killings just go on until the guy messes up."

Cross-Wade stopped pacing and slumped down in his desk chair, fatigued by the ordeal. "You're right, of course," he said. "A life might be saved, or lost, by luck."

They fell silent, each man deep in his own thoughts—thoughts of failure, of another victim.

SAMANTHA WAITED.

Yang did paperwork while the sergeant in Green Bay tried to reach Kathleen Brannen. But Yang's mind was on Samantha and her emotional condition. He saw the delayed reaction setting in, as it does when the reality hits home. He could see her hands trembling slightly and her skin losing its colour. Then he saw her reach down to her stomach. "What's wrong?" he asked.

"A little pain," she replied, her voice quivering. She thought back to Dr. Fromer's warnings. The stress could cost her the baby. "I'll be all right."

"We have paramedics," Yang said with a touch of alarm. "Do you want me to call?"

"No." Samantha feared they'd take her to a hospital and she'd miss Kathleen Brannen. "It'll go away. I'm just nervous."

"I can understand," Yang said.

His phone rang. He picked it up. "Yang."

There was a pause. Yang was expressionless. "I see," he replied to the caller. "I appreciate this." And then he hung up. "She's calling here," he told Samantha. "Any time."

Then the phone rang again.

Yang reached out, but Samantha reached first. She picked up the receiver. "Hello?"

There was static at the other end, but the voice came through clearly. It was a lazy voice, common, not what Samantha had expected of Marty's first wife. "Can I talk to Sergeant Yan'?" Kathleen Brannen asked.

"Is this . . . Mrs. Brannen?" Samantha replied.

"Yeah."

"This is . . ." Samantha hesitated. How should she introduce herself? I'm the other woman, she thought. "This is Mrs. Martin Shaw," she finally blurted out.

"Oh," Kathleen answered, subdued but not angry. "I guess maybe we . . . know the same fella."

"I think we do," Samantha replied. She felt a sudden kinship with Kathleen, something she hadn't expected.

"Look," Kathleen said, "I'm not angry or anythin' like that. I'm not

141

interested in him any more. But why'd you go to the cops?"

"A long story," Samantha answered.

"With Kenny everything's a long story. The booze is a long story. The other women. The gambling. Even the eye."

"The eye?"

"Yeah. He loved to tell how he got it."

"It?"

"Miss, you readin' me?" Kathleen asked. "The glass eye."

"What! What are you talking about?" Samantha's heart pounded like a repeating cannon. She suddenly gasped for breath.

"His left eye," Kathleen replied. "Hey, lady, are we talking about the same guy?"

Samantha didn't immediately reply. This was impossible. It couldn't happen. Again she looked at the pictures. That *was* Marty. Was it Marty? Maybe this Kathleen was making something up. "There was nothing in your husband's file about a glass eye."

"I know," Kathleen said. "I didn't tell the cops. I thought if Kenny came back, he'd be steamed. *He* talked about the eye, but he got crazy if I did. Look, I'll give you his doctor's name. He'll tell you."

The pictures *weren't* Marty. It was a mistake, a terrible wrenching mistake. The camera had lied. Or Samantha's eyes had lied. Or maybe something inside had been wishing too hard.

"The doctor won't be necessary," Samantha said. "It was my mistake. I'm sorry if I upset you.

"Upset me? I'm beyond upset," Kathleen said. "I get calls like this every couple of years. It's life."

"Thank you. I wish you luck."

"Yeah," Kathleen replied. "You too."

The conversation was concluded. "I'm sorry," Samantha said to Yang. "I thought it was Marty." The tears came again.

"Don't apologize," Yang told her. "It happens all the time. *I'm* sorry we put you through this."

"I'd better be going," she said. She was humbled.

Yang felt for her. "All right," he replied. "You need some rest now anyway. But I want to stay in touch. OK?"

"OK." Finally Samantha smiled. She knew she had a friend. Yang helped her up and held on to her as they walked slowly back to the hallway. "I'm OK," she said to him. "I really am."

As a gesture of confidence, Yang let go of her. She walked alone, more quickly and evenly. But Yang was still concerned. "I can have a squad car take you home," he told her.

142

"Oh, no," Samantha insisted. "I'd be mortified if someone saw. I mean, nothing against the police."

Yang laughed. "I understand. Can I at least get you a cab?"

"Sure. Thanks."

They walked down the hall and rounded a corner. Samantha accidently brushed against a man walking in the other direction. "Sorry," she said.

"Perfectly all right," Spencer Cross-Wade replied, and strode on.

"It has to be a Model 630," Marty snapped into the phone, in the sweaty booth under Rockefeller Center. It was the kind of call he'd *never* make from his office—not when a secretary could be listening in. "I'm not interested in a substitute."

He surprised himself. He was rarely this short-tempered. Control it, he told himself. It's less than two weeks away. Don't fail Dad now. He never failed *you*.

"And it has to work?" asked the voice on the other end.

"Yes. I only buy sets that work," Marty replied. He was trying to buy a thirty-four-year-old ten-inch RCA Model 630 television set, now one of the classics of the television age. It was the model he'd been watching the night of December 5, 1952. You didn't buy this kind of thing from a TV shop, or even an antique shop. You went to a collector.

"All right," said the man on the other end. "I can locate one. I know somebody. But it'll cost you."

"How much?"

"I gotta see three thou."

"Three thousand dollars!"

"Look, fella, you're talkin' Model 630. You're talkin' classic."

"I know, I know," Marty shot back. "How soon can you get it?"

"How soon you got three thou?"

"Tonight, in cash."

"Then you got it. You want delivery?"

"No, I'll pick it up."

"Sold," the man said. They made arrangements to meet, and then hung up.

It was all coming together. Marty already had the videotape machine. And he already had the tape, made up by a company doing a history of television: Douglas Edwards presenting the news, sponsored by Oldsmobile. That's what they'd been watching the night of December 5, 1952.

Dad had always liked Doug Edwards. *"Frankie, this is about winter in Korea,"* he'd said that night as Edwards came on. *"You ought to watch it."*

Frankie had watched, and now would watch again.

9

"Frankie Nelson," Cross-Wade said, speaking on his office phone. "That was his name, although we assume he might have changed it. We've checked every Frank Nelson *inside* the United States, without result. The incident occurred just outside Omaha, Nebraska, on December fifth, 1952."

He waited as the person on the other end asked a question.

"There are *no* available legible pictures," Cross-Wade replied. "What I'm going on is simply a hunch that my target may live *outside* the United States part of the time. I thought that if the passport office could keep watch, we might come up with something." He paused again. "Thanks."

The conversation ended. Of all the shots in the dark, this was the darkest. The passport office of the US State Department was hardly a criminal investigation agency, but everything had to be tried. Cross-Wade knew that thousands of interviews over a period of months, or years, would probably lead to some useful clues. But he didn't have months, or years, or even weeks. He had days.

And another day had passed. Another day without progress.

He checked off the date on his calendar. Murder minus nine.

A batch of memos appeared on his desk. Routinely Cross-Wade studied missing-person reports, not in search of the calendar schizophrenic but in search of his victim—some woman with auburn hair who might be missing, lured by her potential murderer. He went through the reports quickly yet thoroughly. It was just after three pm, a sunny, unusually warm winter day. Cross-Wade felt a bead of perspiration on his brow, and the increasing dampness of his wilting collar. And then . . .

He almost went past it. It was a memo, impeccably written by Sergeant Yang, whom he knew and respected. The subject: one Samantha Shaw. It wasn't the physical description of Samantha that grabbed Cross-Wade. In fact, her hair colour wasn't even mentioned. It was something else, something far more intriguing. He reached for his phone and was connected immediately.

"Yang, this is Cross-Wade."

"Yes, sir." Yang responded in a clipped military style.

"Yang, my dear boy, do you recall a Samantha Shaw?"

"Do I?" Yang replied. "One of my toughest, sir."

"A question: this December fifth reference—did she elaborate?"

"No, sir. Just what's in the report."

"Tell me, do you recall her hair colour?"

Yang thought for a moment. "Uh, no. She wore a scarf. We're more interested in the missing person's description."

"Of course," Cross-Wade commented. "Did the lady feel she was in any danger?"

"No. She was just concerned about her husband's past."

"Yes. A fine report. Look, I'm working on a case where this date is significant. I may ask the lady a few questions."

"Sure," Yang said. "But could I request that you go easy, sir? There's a lot of pain there."

"Gentleness is my middle name," Cross-Wade answered. He hung up and flipped on his intercom. "Fetch Loggins, please!"

Moments later Arthur Loggins lumbered in. He could see the glint in Cross-Wade's eyes. "Something new, sir?" he asked.

"Possibly, Arthur, and possibly important. A missing-person dispatch. A woman came in yesterday with a curious complaint. She was scheduling a party for her husband's fortieth birthday. She wanted to find friends and teachers from his past. But she couldn't. The gentleman's past simply doesn't exist."

"Interesting, sir. But how does it apply to us?"

"The husband's birthday is December fifth."

"Wow."

"Yes ... wow. We know our killer's birthday is that day."

"Could be a coincidence, sir."

"I'm aware of that, Arthur. It probably *is*. But it's the only strand I have—a man with a birthday on our significant date, with no detectable past, the right age."

"Anything about auburn hair?"

"I don't know yet. Look, Arthur, be a sport. Go visit this lady, this Mrs. Shaw, and ask her the usual questions. Today!"

"I will, sir." Loggins left, and Cross-Wade was once again alone with his thoughts. The new thread was so tenuous, the lead so vague, and yet he felt a certain excitement. Instinctively he braced himself for disappointment. No matter how much he wished it, he didn't expect much from Samantha Shaw.

LOGGINS TOOK THE SUBWAY to Seventy-second and Central Park West, stopping to pick up a copy of the New York *Post*. He also bought a pack of Bazooka bubble gum, to which he was mildly addicted. Loggins knew Samantha's neighbourhood. Lots of gold chains, babies with nurses, boutiques all over the place—wealth.

He'd phoned ahead to make sure that Samantha was in the apartment and that her husband wasn't. Now he was directed by a doorman to Samantha's floor. He pressed her buzzer.

"Who is it?" Samantha asked automatically, although she already knew.

"Detective Loggins, ma'am." He pulled out his identification, ready to flash it. He saw the peephole open and soon heard the clicking of a lock. The door opened, and Arthur Loggins saw.

"Good God."

"What?" Samantha asked.

Loggins quickly regained his official poise. "Uh, sorry, ma'am. I was just thinkin' of something. May I come in?"

"Yes, of course."

Loggins couldn't take his eyes off Samantha's long auburn hair. He walked in awkwardly, realizing that any questions he might ask were probably unnecessary. The auburn hair—that was the whole thing, the complete pizza, as he liked to say. It changed everything, made everything possible.

"Please sit down," Samantha said.

"Thank you, Mrs. Shaw. I'm awfully sorry to be subjecting you to questions."

"You're not at fault," Samantha assured him. "He is." She gestured towards a picture of Marty on a glass table.

Samantha was remarkably composed, emotionally recovered from her ordeal with Yang, plunging back into planning the party, even toying with the fantasy that everything would be resolved happily.

"Ma'am, I came over to clear up a few things," Loggins said. "But, well, I wonder if I could make a phone call. Privately. Official business." He stared at her hair.

"Yes, of course," Samantha told him. "There's a phone in the kitchen. I'll go into the bedroom."

"Sorry to inconvenience you."

"It's all right."

Loggins went into the kitchen and dialled Cross-Wade's direct number. The man himself answered.

"Sir, Loggins here. And you won't believe this."

146

"What won't I believe?"

"The lady I came to—she's got long auburn hair."

There was a brief silence, then, "Arthur, we just might be on to something. Wait for me. I'll be there as soon as possible."

"That's what I'd hoped, sir."

They both hung up. Cross-Wade restrained his emotions as he sped towards Central Park West in a commandeered squad car. Was her hair auburn or red? Loggins might have made a mistake. Anything was possible, Cross-Wade knew, and it would be foolish to get his hopes up.

He arrived at the building and took the lift. Instinctively he made a visual sweep of the hallway outside Samantha's apartment. There was nothing of interest. He pressed the buzzer.

Samantha, alerted by the doorman and with the protection of Loggins in the apartment, simply opened the door.

"Cross-Wade," he said. He looked at Samantha's hair.

"Come in," she told him.

They went to the living room and joined Loggins. "Mrs. Shaw, I know it may seem unusual for me to rush over here," Cross-Wade explained, removing his coat and placing it neatly on a chair. "I apologize for the inconvenience. But Detective Loggins called with a most important point, and I wanted to speak to you myself."

Samantha had no idea yet what Cross-Wade was talking about. "I appreciate your coming," she said.

They sat down. "Mrs. Shaw," Cross-Wade began, looking at Samantha grimly, "Detective Loggins and I have a problem. It *may* be related to your situation. But I must caution you—it's a very disturbing story. You must brace yourself."

"I'm ready," Samantha replied, almost in a whisper.

"Madam, have you ever heard of the work of a man named Bleuler?" Cross-Wade asked gently.

"No."

"He was an early experimenter in psychiatry. Brilliant chap. I am mentioning him because he devised a number of categories of the mental illness known as schizophrenia. Are you familiar with that?"

"I've heard of it, of course," Samantha answered. "But I really don't know much about it."

"Neither do I. But there's a subcategory known as anniversary excitement schizophrenia. It's a rare thing. It's when people have a disturbance on a particular calendar day. It's usually related to something that's happened on that day in their past."

147

"I see," Samantha said. "Like feeling sad on the anniversary of someone's death."

"Precisely. But it sometimes goes beyond feeling sad. These people can do strange things."

"Like?"

"Some of them can kill."

Samantha didn't react. The idea of murder was outside her frame of reference. Murder happened in other families, other worlds.

"I know that may be frightening," Cross-Wade told her.

"To put it mildly."

"Well, one cannot hide from the truth. Our police psychologists believe that someone with this condition is loose. Let's call him a calendar schizophrenic, for short. His crimes occur on one calendar day of the year. And that day, Mrs. Shaw, is December fifth."

"Marty!" Samantha blurted. She felt the blood rush from her head. "My husband's birthday."

"That's what alerted us in Sergeant Yang's report," Cross-Wade answered in a soft, healing voice. "That and your husband's ... unusual past. And now, something else."

"What's that?"

"Mrs. Shaw, this individual we seek is a murderer. His victims are all women with the same colour hair. That colour is auburn."

"Oh, no, no, no," Samantha cried. "I can believe almost anything, but not that my Marty ... Marty ... is out to *kill* me."

"I know how you feel," Cross-Wade said gently. "I'd feel the same way." He saw the denial fade from Samantha's face, replaced by a valiant attempt to stay calm. "It's best that you know the whole story, that you understand." Cross-Wade slowly got up and walked over to the part of the sectional couch where Samantha was sitting. He sat down next to her, trying to show his concern, his feeling. "There have been six of these murders," he revealed to her. "One in each of the last six years. All have been carried out with a blunt instrument and a chain."

Samantha winced.

"These murders have occurred in North America, the last three in or near New York. We expect another woman to die on December fifth."

"That's the night of Marty's party," Samantha said. "He insisted on that date, even though it is a weeknight."

Cross-Wade thought that odd. *All* the murders had occurred at night. Why would Marty, if he was the murderer, fill his night with a party? But Cross-Wade pushed ahead. "I deduced that the December fifth date had some special significance," he said, "so I had my people check back in criminal history. It seems that there was a murder just outside Omaha, Nebraska, on December fifth, 1952. The victim was an unemployed labourer. He'd bought his older son a set of electric trains—"

Samantha gasped.

"What's wrong?"

"Marty bought trains." She was almost frantic now. "Just recently. He set them up on the rug. He stained it. There, you can see the stain." She pointed to a grease spot on the carpet.

"Did he say *why* he wanted the trains?" Cross-Wade asked.

"Just that he'd always wanted them. That it was a big hobby."

"I'll wish to see them," Cross-Wade said, "but let me continue with the background."

"Please." Samantha was breathing heavily. The news about the trains made even Cross-Wade feel a sense of lunging anticipation.

"This unemployed labourer came home with the trains and gave them to the boy. His wife resented the gift. With all their money worries, she couldn't understand his spending on trains. They argued. It got violent. The wife struck her husband on the head with a hammer. He fell, but apparently was still alive. So she choked him with her younger son's chain-style bicycle lock."

"Dear God," Samantha whispered.

"The older boy witnessed the whole thing," Cross-Wade said.

"What happened to those kids?" Samantha asked.

"They were separated and taken in by relatives. The mother died in prison a few years later. We haven't been able to track down even one member of the family. They simply melted into the landscape. The whereabouts of the boys are unknown."

"What was their name?"

"Nelson. The older boy was Frankie Nelson. Of course, it could be different now."

"And how does this—"

"I'm getting to that. The mother had auburn hair... like yours." Samantha squirmed at those words. "We believe that the older son is the calendar schizophrenic, that the date December fifth triggers an uncontrollable frenzy in his mind. He seeks out auburn-haired women because they represent his mother. In his mind, they *become* his mother."

"And you believe," Samantha said, "that Marty is this man."

149

"I didn't say that," Cross-Wade replied. "It's just something worth looking into."

"Why can't you check it?" Samantha asked.

"I'm not sure what you mean, madam."

"A picture of this Frankie Nelson should tell you if Marty resembles him. And aren't there medical and dental records—"

"There are no pictures. The family albums disappeared. All we have is a newspaper photo from the day of the father's funeral. It shows Frankie and his younger brother in the distance. Much too blurry to be of use. And the medical and dental people are gone, and with them their records. So you see, we have no practical way of checking your husband by going into the past."

"Yes, I see."

"We'd pieced together the information we do have through routine police work. What was missing was a real suspect. We now have that because you were wise enough to come to us."

Samantha felt strangely revolted. She had got Marty into trouble. Well, he deserved it ... maybe. *Maybe.* She suddenly resented Cross-Wade, loathed the little man. This cop had come to tell her she might be murdered by her own husband, by the man she'd waited for, loved, revered, whose baby she carried. Who was he to come in with his chunky assistant and say these filthy things? She didn't realize it, but her face was expressing hostility and contempt. Loggins spotted it. So did Cross-Wade.

"I understand your reaction," Cross-Wade said quietly, sounding like a grandfather. "You resent what I've said, but I can only tell you what we know. This is just an inquiry. No one is being charged. It is important that you know the background. My main concern now is *you* and your safety."

He'd said the right things. He was on his way to winning back her trust.

"What should I do?" Samantha asked.

"Very little. We're going to follow your husband and study his movements. Something he does might tell us what he's planning, if anything. I do hope he's innocent."

Cross-Wade really didn't. In fact, he fervently hoped he'd found his man. His feelings were a spinning mix of genuine concern for Samantha and sparkling visions of glory, of last-minute capture. But he had to say the right things.

"And," he continued, "I'd like your permission to search the apartment—to get a feel for the way your husband lives, and to see if

150

anything reminds us of young Frankie Nelson's life in Omaha. We might find something even *you* don't know is here."

"Like what?"

"Like a hammer and chain."

"Go ahead," Samantha said.

"Please accompany me," Cross-Wade requested. "I may have some questions."

Samantha started leading Cross-Wade and Loggins round the apartment. Her resentment receded. She knew her own life might be at stake.

"The trains," Cross-Wade suggested. Samantha led the detectives to the cupboard where Marty had stored the electric trains. Cross-Wade examined them, handling every piece, determining small details. "Remarkable," he finally said, turning to Loggins. "Arthur, what do you make of these?"

Loggins studied the trains. "Old Lionel," he replied. "This stuff comes from the '50s."

"Arthur, is there any record of the trains that caused the fatal dispute in the Nelson household?"

"No, sir. There was no description at the trial."

"Damn," Cross-Wade said quietly. Then a thought struck him. "Mrs. Shaw, are you sure your husband bought these recently?"

"Of course. They weren't here."

"No, you misunderstand. I know they weren't *here*. But are you sure he didn't own them? He could've kept them elsewhere."

"What are you suggesting?"

"That these may be the very trains Frank Nelson owned as a child, the very trains that led to his father's death."

Samantha stepped back as if the trains were contaminated. "Why would he bring these things home?" she asked.

"I don't know." He turned again to Loggins. "Arthur, there couldn't be that many used-train stores in New York. Make a list of these trains. Check to see if anyone bought them recently."

"Yes, sir," Loggins replied.

Cross-Wade entered the bedroom. He was startled by the bizarre arrangement, especially the headboard against the radiator and the bureau blocking a window. His eyes focused on the gaudy picture frame. "Interesting," he commented.

"I know what you're thinking," Samantha said. "It's awful. This is Marty's taste."

"Beg pardon?"

"He insisted on redoing the room this way. Recently. He said he wanted to try it, that he saw this in a magazine."

"Has he done anything else . . . unusual?"

"Nothing that I can think of. I mean, nothing obvious like that."

Cross-Wade went through the rest of the apartment. "Only the trains give real cause for suspicion," he finally pronounced. "But there's certainly nothing decisive. It needs more investigation. Madam, I must ask for your cooperation."

"Of course."

"Change nothing in your schedule. That might just tip Mr. Shaw that he's being watched. Try to show happiness. Oh, by the way, have you told anyone that you've been to see us?"

"No."

"Good. Naturally the doormen downstairs know. Before I leave, I'll instruct them. Your husband must not find out we were here. Now, on December fifth—"

"It's so close," Samantha moaned.

"Yes, a bit more than a week. We'll have men in the building that day and night to ensure your safety. There'll be listening devices here. Is there a vacant apartment on this floor?"

"No . . . but someone down the hall is away for a month."

"We'll contact the building manager for permission to use that place. We'll be able to hear everything going on between you and your husband. If anything unusual occurs, we'll be in here in a matter of seconds."

Then Cross-Wade did something no other detective on the New York force would do. He took Samantha's hand and kissed it. "You are a lady," he said. "It pains me to see this happening to you."

"Thank you. Thank you so much." She was genuinely touched.

"Help us so we can help you," Cross-Wade concluded. It was his standard exit line, perfected over the years.

And he was gone. With one visit to Sergeant Yang, Samantha Shaw had stepped to the centre of a massive criminal investigation. A mistake could destroy her life. A victory would destroy her marriage.

10

"I don't believe it," Samantha said.

"Isn't it beautiful?"

"Well . . . it's nice. But what goes, Martin Everett Shaw? You becoming an antique dealer? First the old electric trains, then this old TV. I don't understand."

They stood in the living room, the old Model 630 on the carpet, its brown wood cabinet gleaming with a new coat of polish, its ten-inch screen yellowed with age, the ancient tubes visible through the air holes in its back.

"It's a collector's item," Marty explained. "This was one of the very first commercial sets in regular use. It practically built the TV industry. This was the set Uncle Miltie was on."

"I'm moved," Samantha replied. In ordinary times she would have burst out laughing at Marty's sales pitch, his boyish enthusiasm. But these weren't ordinary times, and her first thought was of reporting the purchase to Cross-Wade.

"It works," Marty assured her. "I tested it myself."

"Wonderful." She delivered her lines, but she was far away. I love him, she thought, but he may be planning to kill me. *Kill* me! "What are you going to do with it?" she asked.

"Set it up. Look, it cost fifty bucks. It's a conversation piece. People will be interested. You'll see at the party."

The word "party" sent an electric jolt through Samantha, and suddenly she felt the heat of fear. She hadn't fully realized it until this moment. She was afraid of Marty. Afraid of her husband. Afraid of a date on the calendar.

"I like it," she finally told him, hoping to close the subject. "It's . . . quaint. Put it anywhere you like." She played along, precisely what Cross-Wade would have wanted her to do.

THE NEXT MORNING Samantha called Cross-Wade to report on the television set. He told her that an RCA Model 630 had been found in the Nelson home after the murder.

Another link.

Another blow for Samantha.

But another word of caution from Cross-Wade: the Model 630 had been common. It had been in thousands of homes. A coincidence, maybe. Some cases had many coincidences.

Cross-Wade also reported to Samantha that Loggins had checked the used-train stores around New York. Marty had indeed bought his set recently. "But again, we must be cautious about drawing conclusions." He told her that he was showing pictures of Marty to friends and relatives of the calendar murderer's victims. It turned Samantha's stomach. *Her* husband's picture, like some common mug shot, would be circulated among those who lived in grief. She had to remember it was only an inquiry. She had to try to stay calm. But how much restraint was any human being supposed to be capable of?

Samantha took Cross-Wade's advice and once more plunged into the party planning. But her ambivalence was tearing at her like a ragged blade. It seemed so strange to prepare a gala that could turn into a night of terror. It was unfair, so horribly unfair.

Tom Edwards volunteered to help. He had some vacation days with nothing special to do, so he came over. He'd been upset since their lunch, he told Samantha, but could think of no real way to help her. At least he could work on the party with her.

Samantha appreciated that. Tom knew Marty's business friends better than she did, and he was a godsend in working out table arrangements. Samantha made final choices of menu and trimmings. Inevitably, though, the talk got around to "the problem", as Samantha referred to it.

"Anything, uh, turn up?" Tom delicately asked, in that naive manner Samantha found so affecting.

"Nothing," Samantha replied. "I'm sweeping it under the rug."

"Wise move. You didn't confront him, did you?"

"No."

"I'm glad. You've got a great marriage. Don't ruin it."

"I've thought of that, believe me. Tom, do you think chocolate-chip ice cream is good enough for dessert?"

He thought for a moment. "Yes, that's great, but have an alternative. If it's a cold, wet night, no one goes for ice cream."

"Chocolate mousse?"

"Overdone, my dear Samantha."

"Yeah, overdone. You're right. Too fancy." Samantha crossed off the choice. "Hey, you know, you're a doll." You were right, Samantha told herself. Tom had exquisite taste in virtually everything. In a way, she was attracted to him, especially since her marriage to Marty had turned so bizarre.

Samantha felt the urge to tell about the baby. After all, she'd told the New York City Police Department. Why not Tom? She still planned, despite everything, to make the announcement at the bash, and couldn't bring herself to tell Tom before Marty.

Yet she couldn't resist a little gentle probing. "Tom," she asked after a long silence, "is Marty happy?"

Tom turned to Samantha, a curious look on his face. "Hey," he said, "I thought we were putting all the agony to sleep."

154

"This isn't agony. It's just a question. All wives want to know."

"Doesn't he tell you?"

"Sure. But maybe he has a concern, a worry, that he talks to you about. I mean, I don't want to pry."

"Sam, Marty is a happy man. And you're making him even happier with the party. It's all he talks about. I'm bored stiff with it. Get the whole thing over with, will you?" He laughed.

So did she.

There was no more agony talk.

IT TOOK TWO DAYS for Cross-Wade to interview the friends and relatives of the victims he wanted to cover. But he came up with nothing. Sure, some of those who were interviewed said Marty looked familiar, but a lot of people look familiar. Indeed, Cross-Wade knew, the murderer might not even have known his victims. He might simply have followed them and trapped them on December 5 because of the colour of their flowing hair.

It was November 28. Thanksgiving.

Cross-Wade was so completely focused on the case that he hardly noticed. He still had nothing on Martin Shaw—nothing but suspicion and coincidence.

Meanwhile, it was Marty's and Samantha's first Thanksgiving together. But with Marty having no family at all and Samantha having no one close, they spent the holiday quietly, watching a bit of Macy's parade as it passed along Central Park West and having a modest turkey dinner. The peace inside their apartment was in stark contrast to the storms going on inside their minds.

NOVEMBER 30.

Loggins came into Cross-Wade's office at midday. "Surveillance report," he told the boss. Loggins himself had tailed Marty during the morning shifts, relieved by another detective for the afternoon and evening.

"Anything?" Cross-Wade asked.

"No, sir. He's a regular person."

"A regular person," Cross-Wade echoed.

"Yes, sir. Of course, because of the Thanksgiving holiday we haven't been able to determine much. He gets up at a normal hour and proceeds by taxi to his office in midtown. He works until twelve thirty, when he proceeds to lunch."

"Nothing else?"

"He has proceeded to business appointments at corporations where his company has work. It is a very normal pattern, sir."

"And our night reports show the same, I believe."

"He returns home. That's it."

"So far, we haven't advanced beyond the interview with Mrs. Shaw," Cross-Wade said.

"I regret that, sir."

"Arthur, people with compulsions usually have definite rituals. This killer seems to have murdered women he hardly knew, or didn't know at all. Now we theorize that his new target is his wife. This is entirely out of character, for him to focus attention on himself. It doesn't fit. Why would he do that?"

Loggins shrugged. The question couldn't be answered.

"And yet, Arthur," Cross-Wade continued, "I've never seen anything quite like this. The trains. The December fifth date. The auburn-haired wife. Might all be coincidence. You know, this is a shrewd killer. Look at the way he manages to remove his fingerprints from every murder scene. Intelligent. Thoughtful. He may just be too good for us."

"Too good for *you*, sir?" Loggins asked.

Cross-Wade needed that compliment. "We'll see," he replied. "We have five days to go. Five days to save a life."

IT WAS ON THE MORNING of December 2 that the investigation took a new turn. It was one Cross-Wade had feared, one he loathed, yet one that finally answered the fundamental question that had haunted him since he first spoke with Samantha: Was Martin Shaw really Frankie Nelson?

As he had told Samantha, he assumed that little Frankie Nelson's medical records had been lost for ever. But on December 2 a large brown envelope arrived at police headquarters by express mail. An accompanying letter from the Omaha police explained that Frankie Nelson's medical records had been found. They'd been misfiled, kept in the storage of the criminal court. They were enclosed.

Rapidly the New York police experts compared them with the records obtained from Marty's doctor. They compared eye colour, skin markings and surgical scars.

The records didn't match. That was it. Proof positive.

For Cross-Wade the question had been answered. His investigation collapsed. He fought being overcome by despair, and reached for the phone, dialling Samantha Shaw.

156

When the call came, Samantha was asleep, feeling the fatigue of pregnancy, of a party, of a marriage in crisis. She reached over to the night table and brought the phone to her ear. "Hello?"

The detective sensed her grogginess. "Mrs Shaw? This is Cross-Wade here."

Samantha sat up sharply. "Yes?"

"Mrs. Shaw, I have some news for you."

Samantha's face froze with tension. "Please tell me," she said, putting up a brave front.

"Martin Shaw is *not* the man."

It was a thunderbolt, totally unexpected. "He's not . . . please say that again."

"I say, Mrs. Shaw, your husband is not the man. We have absolute proof. There's been some coincidence here, but there's nothing to worry about."

A sea of relief washed over Samantha. Marty wasn't a killer. But another truth prevented the moment from erupting into joy. All right, he wasn't that horrible thing Cross-Wade was searching for. Then, who was he? That question hadn't been touched. *Who was he?*

"I'm relieved, of course," Samantha said to Cross-Wade. "But now can you tell me who my husband is?"

"I'm afraid not," Cross-Wade replied "We learned who he *wasn't* by medical records that finally turned up. We actually have nothing new on him. From your point of view, you're back to square one."

"Yes, I guess I am," Samantha agreed.

"But Mrs. Shaw, think of it this way. You are safe. I feel for your other problem, but your safety is of paramount importance."

"Yes."

"I am at your disposal, madam. If there is anything I can do to help, please call me. Even though I'm in Homicide, I might have suggestions. Good luck. I hope you find your answers very soon."

"Thank you for your help," Samantha responded. They hung up. She might have been back to square one, but at least she didn't have to worry about her husband's killing her.

Spencer Cross-Wade sealed the investigation of Martin Everett Shaw. He cancelled the surveillance and started looking for another suspect. He all but wrote off the chance for success.

MARTY KEPT WORRYING about those calls Samantha had made. Was she still making them? Was she still probing? He'd know with the phone bill that would come after December 5. And since it was already December 2, he kept telling himself to hold out. This is for *Dad*. You can hold out for Dad, can't you, Frankie?

During his lunch break he walked into a jewellery store near Rockefeller Center. A woman with a thick yet charming accent greeted him from behind a counter. Her cold, watchful eyes followed Marty as he walked to a display case where gold necklaces were laid out, each one snaking over blue velvet. He studied each necklace.

The woman approached Marty. "Are you looking for something in particular?" she asked, rolling her *r*'s in the Slavic manner.

For a moment Marty didn't answer, so intently was he staring into the case. "Uh, yes," he finally said. "I need a thin gold chain with a pendant. A red stone with gold round it. You know."

"Of course," the woman said. "We have a very nice selection. Let me show you." She reached into a drawer under the case and slid out a tray. "Here are some fine pieces."

Marty studied the selection carefully. His mind drifted back. Dad had saved so long to buy that pendant for Mom. She'd hardly said thank you. Wasn't as big as her sister's, she'd muttered. But she'd worn it. She'd worn it that night, that December 5. How it swung as she'd raised the hammer over her head. How it swung back and forth, wildly, on its thin chain.

Marty's eyes focused on a necklace. "There's a nice one," he said, "Uh, what is the price?"

The woman picked up the piece, slinking it over her hand. "This would be one hundred twenty-five dollars, plus tax."

"That's fine," Marty said. He paid cash again, and at his request the necklace was carefully gift-wrapped in a white box and tied with a blue ribbon. He'd give it to Samantha, and she'd wear it at the party. Everything was falling into place.

Marty returned to his office and, as he had often done during this season of rituals, locked the door and ordered that all calls be held. Then he took out pen and paper and wrote another letter to the person whose presence he felt wherever he walked.

Dear Dad,

 The day approaches. Isn't that wonderful? There's been some trouble with Sam, though. She may know that I've made up a lot of what I've told her, but she's no real threat. I'm doing the best I can for you. Some day we'll be together.

Your loving son

Frankie

P.S. I got the trains.

ANOTHER DAY PASSED, and Martin Shaw prepared to carry out the final part of the ritual before the fateful day. First step: the phone call to Samantha from his office on the morning of December 3. The urgent voice. The tinge of regret.

"Sam," Marty said.

Samantha was sitting amid caterer's tables that had already arrived, their metal tops not yet covered with linen. She'd heard that tone in Marty's voice before. It portended bad news, disruption. "What's wrong?" she asked.

"A little problem in St. Louis," Marty replied. "One of our clients out there got involved in a lawsuit, and it's a public relations mess. I've got to go. Today."

"Marty!"

"Hey, don't worry about the party. I'll be back in twenty-four hours. No client could keep me from that."

"Well, that's a relief. For a minute ..."

"Sam, *you* before business." For an instant it was the old Marty, smooth and sentimental, affectionate and caring. "I don't know where I'm staying yet, but I'll contact you as soon as I can. And Sam, the staff here doesn't know the real reason I'm going out. We want to keep this under control. I told them just that I'm going for a fast confab."

"OK," Samantha said. "Sweet, I'm sorry you have to go like this, right before the party."

"Yeah, so am I. You know, I wanted to be home tonight to help out. I really looked forward to that."

He sounded so genuine, so filled with emotion, his voice trembling. "It's OK," Samantha told him. "You'll be back tomorrow, love. I'll take care of everything. You know I will."

"That I know," Marty said. "Look, don't strain yourself. Hear me? It doesn't have to be the inaugural ball."

"I won't," Samantha agreed. "Not with the—" She stopped.

"Not with the what?" Marty asked.

"Not with the caterer doing all the real work."

Great save, Samantha thought. She'd almost tipped him off about the baby.

Marty blew a kiss into the phone. It was something he rarely did. It was affecting, moving, so right for the moment. Again Samantha's lingering optimism surfaced. Maybe his secrets were *good* secrets, for a good cause, something to be proud of. Maybe. It was always maybe. But Samantha blew the kiss back.

THE UNITED FLIGHT glided in over St. Louis in early afternoon, giving Marty a glistening view of the great arch that symbolized the city. He was on the ground a few minutes later. He entered the terminal, but he would not be going into town.

Of course, his secretary had booked the flight to St. Louis under the name Martin Shaw. But when Marty had arrived at La Guardia Airport, he bought an additional ticket for a flight from St. Louis to Omaha, paying in cash, under the name Frank Nelson. It was his tribute, his homage to his name, his deference to Dad. Now, in St. Louis, he glanced at his watch, already set to Omaha time. It was one fifty-five. The flight to Omaha would leave at two thirty. He was Frank Nelson now. Frank Nelson again. It felt wonderful. He checked to make sure his sunglasses were in his jacket pocket. He would need them for security. Someone in Omaha might recognize his face, even though a generation had passed since he'd lived there.

He walked to the TWA terminal section and boarded the Boeing 727 for "home". Marty felt his heart pound as the plane lifted, heading northwest to Omaha. He glanced out of the window as the city grey slowly turned into muted country browns and greens, the colour of the Midwest where he grew up, where he had been scarred for life. He felt a sharp chill race through him.

IT WAS A BUMPY LANDING in Omaha. Marty stepped out of the plane, walking briskly. He did not head for the baggage area. He'd always kept a small overnight case in the office, with a two-day supply of basic needs. He'd taken it straight onto the plane.

Marty rented a car at the Hertz counter. It was a late-model two-door blue Chrysler LeBaron. He knew the way, as he had learned the routes into places like Elkhart, Indiana—places that he used to construct his falsified past. He drove slowly and carefully through Omaha as a few drops of rain began to splatter the windscreen. Soon he arrived in his old neighbourhood.

The old neighbourhood.

Clapboard houses. Some close together, some on isolated lots. A rural feel, though it was only eleven miles from the centre of Omaha. One main street and a few side roads, none with street lights. There was a row of stores, including a supermarket and a hardware store and the inevitable bar. It was one of those desolate sections that never seem to change. Nowhere, USA.

Marty saw the house—that strange green clapboard with the pink

160

trim Mom had demanded, set apart from the others, on a small hill with no trees.

Abandoned. Partially boarded up.

Home.

"I'M HERE. I'M HERE, Frankie."

Marty remembered the voice. He now stood on the same spot, at the side of the house. Dad had taken the bus home—the car had been broken and there was no money to fix it.

"Frankie, where are you?"

The voice had been cheerful. It had always been cheerful, no matter how hard times were. Now Marty ran to the front of the house, as he had that December 5.

"Hi, Dad." He remembered saying it.

Dad had the big box cradled in both arms. *"Happy birthday, Frankie."* Frankie'd known instantly what was in the box. All he had been talking about was trains, trains, trains. And Dad had promised. *"For your next birthday, if we can afford it."* Dad had gone ahead and got the trains anyway, even though he'd known he couldn't afford it. *"Come on inside, Frankie,"* he said, his voice so clear, so alive.

Now Marty walked up the front steps. The house was locked, as it had been for years, known as a murder site, unsalable. He couldn't go in, but he could look through the windows. It was all the same.

Marty remembered the good times—Dad pillow-fighting with him and his brother; Dad playing his old banjo; Dad making those phone calls, those endless phone calls, trying to get work. The phone wire was still connected to the wall in the living room, Marty saw, although the phone had been ripped out. And there was still an old dusty pillow on the floor, where it had lain the night of December 5. Yes, everything *was* the same.

Then Marty heard a staccato voice behind him. "Hey, you looking for something, mister?"

He spun round. He hadn't heard the engine as the car pulled up. A police cruiser was idling, its driver looking right at him from behind mirrored sunglasses.

"Just curious," Marty replied, trying to smile, his own sunglasses his only disguise. "I like this neighbourhood," he went on. "This old house for sale?"

The cop shrugged. "There's a real-estate broker about a mile down that road—Calman Brothers—if you want to ask about it."

161

"Thanks," Marty said. "I appreciate that."

"OK," the cop concluded, and drove off.

Relieved, Marty decided to walk through the neighbourhood, past his elementary school, its playground filled with kids learning the rudiments of football; past the Avery house, where he'd spent some of his happiest hours playing; and past Doc Marsh's house. Suddenly he felt a lump form in his throat. The old cemetery was just around the corner.

Marty walked through the rusted, broken gate and stood for a moment, looking over the depressing place. It was poorly kept. The grass hadn't been cared for, some stones were overturned, the obscenities scribbled on one monument went unscrubbed. Marty was angry. Dad shouldn't have to lie in a place like this. He deserved better. Marty gritted his teeth. He had the money to move Dad, but couldn't. To move a body required a court order. He'd have to reveal himself, and ruin everything.

He started walking again, the dry grass rustling under his feet. None of it was trampled, for rarely did anyone come to this cemetery, especially in the cold. Marty felt the wind as he approached Dad's grave.

Dad. Squeezed amid a group of others was a small, thin headstone, the cheapest available at the time. Now it was tilted forward at a fifteen-degree angle. The inscription was partly filled in with dirt but was still clear: JOHN ALBERT NELSON, 1916–1952. He didn't live nearly long enough, Marty told himself.

He looked around. If anyone saw him now, there might be suspicion. But no one did. It was pure emptiness. So Marty knelt reverently beside the grave.

"Dad, I may be away a long while," he whispered, staring at the tilted gravestone. "But I'll be back, you know. We're showing that Mom hasn't got away with this, aren't we? We're sure showing it."

He edged over and tried to straighten the stone, but his strength wasn't enough. All he could do was clean the dirt off the front. "I want you to rest easy, Dad. I've got things under control. I'm playing with the trains. And I got that RCA Model 630 TV this time. We have things called videocassette recorders now. They play tapes of television programmes. I got this old tape of Doug Edwards. Remember how you watched him? I'll play it the night of December fifth ... for you, Dad."

Suddenly a vision of Samantha flashed through Marty's mind, but all he could see beneath her auburn hair was the face of his mother, and all he could hear was his mother's screaming voice. Samantha's transformation in the twisted depths of his psyche was intensifying.

"I failed you once, Dad," he said. "I failed you on December fifth, 1952. I should have saved you. But I'll never fail you again."

He got up and stepped back.

"Goodbye, Dad. Next time I see you it'll be all over." He left the cemetery.

II

The clatter of metal against metal rang through the Shaw apartment as the caterer's men brought in the last of the chairs and tables for the December 5 gala. Samantha and Lynne watched, occasionally directing the placement of a particular piece.

Samantha didn't know what to feel. A great party coming up, a husband cleared of a ghastly crime, that same husband about to be a father, that husband shrouded in mystery. As cloths started appearing on tabletops, Samantha slowly felt restraint slipping away and anticipation overtaking her. Lynne knew nothing of the trauma over Marty's past. Samantha had simply told her that inviting Marty's old friends had not worked out—that it had been too hard to find them and too expensive to bring them in.

A removal man brought another round table to the front of the living room. "It looks so ... commercial," Samantha commented.

"You just watch," Lynne said. "When they start getting it together, you'll have the Waldorf right in your living room."

"Think Marty'll like it?" Samantha asked.

"He'll love it. *Everyone* loves a party in his honour."

Samantha knew that Marty was flying back to New York that very moment, only a day before the party. She'd spoken with him the previous night, when he'd called from a St. Louis hotel. She didn't know he'd checked in only to maintain absolute credibility to the last possible moment. Marty Shaw overlooked nothing.

Of course he'd love the party, Samantha mused, just as Lynne said he would. But maybe—just maybe—he'd choose the special night, December 5, to reveal his great secrets. It would be wonderful if he ended the mystery on the night of the party.

And that was precisely what Marty had planned, but his interpretation was rather different.

"Mrs. Shaw?"

Samantha heard the voice and turned. A young, smallish man, about twenty, was at the door, which had been wedged open by the caterers. "Yes?"

"Nick Auerbach, Dimension Video. The doorman thought I was with the caterer and sent me up."

"Oh, yes," Samantha said with her ever gracious smile. Auerbach would be making the videotape of the party, and was here to scout the apartment for shots. "Please come in," she said.

Samantha showed him round, and Auerbach made sketches on a pad, noting measurements, table locations and the colours of walls. After finishing, he sat with Samantha at one of the tables. "I'll need some information from you," he told her.

"Like what?"

"Like whether there'll be any ceremonies or presentations."

"Oh, no, nothing like that," Samantha replied.

"I beg your little pardon!" Lynne interrupted. "Aren't we forgetting something?" She pointed to her own stomach. Samantha felt like a fool for not remembering.

"Oh—yes!" she told Auerbach. "I'm going to make an announcement from the head table. A special thing. Shall I signal you when?"

"I'd appreciate that," Auerbach said. He asked a question or two more, and left a few minutes later.

The workmen finished putting the white tablecloths on the tables, and Samantha saw the elegance Lynne had talked about. The apartment had taken on a formal quality, a brightness combined with high style. Samantha could imagine the rest—the place settings, the centrepieces, the silver service, the small band off to the side. It would be a party to remember.

It *would* work out.

It had to.

THE POLICE CRUISER sped uptown through Manhattan streets, its lights flashing and siren blaring. Traffic ahead squeezed to the right to let it pass. Inside the cruiser, a young patrolman sat at the wheel. Spencer Cross-Wade sat in the back with Arthur Loggins.

Cross-Wade gripped a large brown envelope in his right hand, gripped it tightly, as if it contained some state secret. Neither man spoke. They sat motionless, expressionless, contemplating what had just happened, how they would explain it, what it might lead to. Cross-Wade felt an embarrassment, a humiliation, that he had never experienced before, even during the darkest days of the calendar killer probe. He dreaded what was about to happen. He phrased his words in his mind and rehearsed every point. He felt for Samantha, for she would bear the brunt of the latest bulletin he had received.

When they arrived, he had the doorman announce him by intercom. Samantha, alone now, was startled to hear that he wanted to see her. He and Loggins rushed to the apartment, and she opened the door.

To Samantha, Cross-Wade looked grim, ashen, obviously agitated; she knew his visit was about Marty. That had to be it.

"Come in," she said nervously.

The detectives entered. "I'm sorry we had to disturb you," Cross-Wade said.

"I understand," Samantha replied. "Please sit down."

They all sat, Cross-Wade still clutching the brown envelope in his hand. "Mrs. Shaw," he said urgently, "as you know, I cancelled the investigation of your husband after we received those medical records. It was the proper move."

"Of course."

"But the way the bureaucracy works, some actions just went forward automatically. I had asked the Omaha authorities to send me pictures of Frankie Nelson's house, inside and out. They supplied the outside pictures, but neglected the interiors. So last week I asked again for pictures of the inside. They finally arrived today. I have them here." He showed her the brown envelope he'd been clutching.

"So?" Samantha asked.

Slowly, gravely, Cross-Wade opened the envelope. Inside was a set of eight-by-ten glossies. He gently handed them to Samantha.

She gazed down.

Her eyes widened.

"Oh, please, no!" she whispered in sudden panic. "Oh, no!"

She studied the pictures, holding one up. It showed a bedroom in the old Nelson house—arranged precisely as Marty had arranged the bedroom in the apartment. On one wall was a gaudy picture frame, identical to the one Marty had put up. There was even the same bizarre obstructing of the window and radiator.

And there, in another picture, was the old RCA Model 630 TV, clearly recognizable.

Samantha shook her head. "I don't understand," she said.

"It's self-evident," Cross-Wade replied.

"But ... you have his medical records."

"We thought so." Cross-Wade had a forlorn look on his face. "Mrs. Shaw," he said, "I've been in police work long enough to know that not everyone in our profession is completely reliable. Yes, we received a set of records with the name of Frankie Nelson on them. We compared them with Marty's, and they didn't match. Why? I suspect that someone simply made a mistake. But when we looked at these pictures of the Nelson house and remembered your bedroom, the truth was clear. Mrs. Shaw, your husband *is* Frankie Nelson."

Samantha got up slowly and walked over to the bedroom. Cross-Wade and Loggins followed her, not saying a word. Samantha gazed around the room, then down at the photos, which she still held. "Why would Marty do this?" she asked.

"I would surmise it's part of some ritual," Cross-Wade answered. "Perhaps it reflects an attachment to his youth, the youth that existed before ..."

"Before he saw his mother murder his father," Samantha said.

"I'm afraid that is it."

Samantha lowered her head. "A murderer," she whispered bitterly. "I thought we'd jumped that hurdle." She felt slightly faint and went to sit down on the bed. "I can't believe it."

Cross-Wade knew he'd taken Samantha on a roller coaster, first suspecting Marty, then exonerating him, now accusing him again. It had been savage, if unintended. "I realize this is very difficult for you," he said, his voice filled with genuine sympathy. "You've been brave. You'll have to be brave for a little longer."

Samantha knew what Cross-Wade was saying. It was December 4. "I guess I'm a target," she said. "*His* target."

"We must assume that. It's all in his mind. You're not simply his wife any longer. Now ..." Cross-Wade hesitated. He was entering the vague recesses of Marty Shaw's abnormal psyche. "Now," he added, "you've become his mother."

Samantha stared. "His mother," she repeated. "Isn't that just fine? I've got two babies ... and one carries a hammer and a chain."

Cross-Wade and Loggins glanced at each other briefly, each almost wishing he could take Samantha's hurt on himself.

"Well," Samantha asked, "what do you want me to do?"

"I want you to help us stop your husband," Cross-Wade answered. "We still don't have a single shred of hard evidence linking him to those other murders. The evidence is all circumstantial. We need something solid."

"And I'm to help you get it."

166

"Yes," Cross-Wade said. Again, as on earlier occasions, the tears started filling Samantha's eyes. "We can't confront your husband before the party and charge him. He'd never admit anything, and we might lose the whole case."

"How do you do it, then?"

"By asking you to go through with the party as if nothing had happened, and to let him reveal himself tomorrow, his crucial day, December fifth. I know it's hard, but we must make an airtight case. It's for your future safety. We'll have the apartment entirely covered," Cross-Wade continued. "It'll be wired with our advanced sound equipment. We'll be down the hall in the unoccupied apartment and in here within twenty-five seconds of alert. Everything will be on tape. Marty will be caught."

"Trying to *kill* me?" Samantha asked, visualizing the scene.

"It wouldn't go that far. We're very good at what we do."

"I can't believe he'd do it during the party," Samantha said.

"Neither can I," Cross-Wade agreed. "He'll undoubtedly make his move after the guests leave, but before midnight. However, we'll have him under surveillance the entire day. Indeed, we'll have one additional form of protection. In the morning, before Marty leaves for work, a telephone repairman will be in your apartment, supposedly to fix a circuit. Of course, he'll actually be one of our men."

Samantha glanced at her watch, her hand shaking, her arm coated with the first glisten of a cold sweat. "Marty was called out of town yesterday. He'll be back tonight. It'll all be over in a little more than thirty-two hours," she said. She buried her head in her trembling hands. "I'll help."

"You're a great lady," Cross-Wade said. He called headquarters to have the sound equipment installed in Samantha's apartment. He also ordered visual surveillance of Marty to be resumed upon Shaw's return, and ordered a squad of men to spend all of the next day in the unoccupied apartment on Samantha's floor, prepared to protect her in an instant. Then he returned to Samantha, who had drifted back to the living room with Loggins. She was sitting on the couch, staring at the party preparations, now all useless, meaningless gaiety.

"I think I should take the photographs back," Cross-Wade told her. "We wouldn't want your husband to discover them."

Samantha hardly realized she was still holding the pictures. She handed them over, the side of the envelope crumpled, almost punctured, from her tight, horrified grip.

"Do you have to leave?" she asked.

"We must. We have procedures to prepare."

"Yes, procedures," Samantha lamented. "Always procedures."

"You know, Mrs. Shaw," he said gently, "it has been my lot to visit many women who've suddenly found themselves without partners, often as a result of murder. I've seen their despair and their emptiness. But there is a tomorrow. Believe me. The wound will never heal completely, but there will be an easing. Even now, you must think about tomorrow. For the baby."

Samantha barely comprehended the words, so completely was she absorbed by shock. For the present, the only tomorrow that mattered was December 5. "I appreciate your thoughts," she told him. "It's hard for me to think at the moment."

Cross-Wade nodded his sympathy. "We must have our equipment in here before your husband comes home. Once the clock strikes December fifth, everything has to be heard by our men ... even when you're sleeping."

"I understand."

"We wish you the best, Mrs. Shaw."

After Cross-Wade and Loggins left, Samantha heard only silence.

Everything had changed once more. In the course of a few minutes her hope that Marty's secrets were good secrets had been dashed. Now she'd have to give up the life she had dreamed of. And she'd have to face loneliness again.

This can't be happening, she said to herself over and over, as she had before. There has to be a way out.

Somewhere there was a glimmer of light. Maybe Cross-Wade had made another mistake.

Her rational side didn't believe that in the least, but part of her had to believe it, to survive. Exhausted, she fell asleep.

12

The day came. December 5. That date would appear, if Marty Shaw had his way, on Samantha's tombstone.

It would appear, if Spencer Cross-Wade had his way, on a departmental commendation marking the date that he solved a major serial-murder case.

It would appear, if Samantha had her way, on nothing out of the ordinary—for she wished the whole nightmare would go away.

The day was cold, with occasional driving rain that pelted against the windows of the Shaw apartment as Marty and Samantha awakened. Marty staggered to the window and looked out, gazing at a sea of grey that blocked out every building on the New York skyline. "Great day!" he exclaimed, and smiled back at Samantha. She looked sceptically at him. "No, I mean it!" Marty said. "This is a great day for both of us!"

Samantha smiled, forcing it, determined to play the part Cross-Wade had asked her to. "You're right. Happy birthday, love!" She rushed out of bed to kiss him, and gave him an embrace that any man would remember.

As they kissed, the buzzer sounded.

Marty frowned. "At this hour? Don't the doormen announce people any more?" He started for the door.

"I think I know who that might be," Samantha said. "The phone company traced a problem to our line. They said they expected to be here early."

Marty continued walking. "Who is it?" he called out.

"Phone company," a voice answered.

When Marty opened the door, a tall, muscular telephone service-man stood before him, holding a company ID card. "Repair," he said. "We called."

"Sure," Marty replied. The man entered and went to work in the hall. Samantha felt temporarily safe.

Marty walked back to the bedroom, determined to resume the spirit of the morning. "You know," he said to Samantha, "I don't feel forty. I feel fifteen, tops." A devilish grin came over his face. "I even have my electric trains."

"Marty," Samantha kidded. "Please, not at the party."

"Why not? I thought I'd give everyone a chance."

"Marty . . . no."

"OK, no. Birthday boy doesn't get what he wants. Birthday boy might cry."

"Before you cry, what do you want for breakfast?"

"Steak," Marty replied.

"You want *steak* for breakfast?"

"Why not? Hey, I'll take you out. I know where we can get steak."

"Forget it. I've been teasing you. I've got it here. You once told me you thought a birthday would be perfect with steak for breakfast. And I remembered, love."

Now it was Marty's turn to go through the motions of rushing over to kiss Samantha. They were both such magnificent fakes.

Unconsciously Samantha kept glancing at an air vent high on the wall, where Cross-Wade's men had planted one of their microphones. "I'll start cooking," she told Marty.

"Wait a second," he said.

"Something wrong?" she inquired.

Marty walked briskly to the bureau. He opened a drawer and took out the gift box he'd got at the jeweller's.

"Here," he said, handing the box to Samantha.

"Marty . . . thank you," she said, genuinely surprised. "You didn't have to do this."

"I wanted to. You deserve it. Go ahead and open it."

For a flash Samantha almost forgot the horror she faced. This was so old-fashioned, so romantic, so typical of the Marty she knew. A present on his birthday . . . for *her*. But why?

She untied the ribbon, opened the box, and gazed at the pendant at the end of its slim gold chain. "Marty, this is beautiful."

"I thought you'd like it."

"Like it? I *love* it!"

"Put it on," Marty requested.

Samantha walked to a mirror and slipped the chain round her neck, letting the pendant hang gently over her nightgown. Neither she nor Marty spoke for a few moments, the slapping of the rain the only sound. "It's perfect," Samantha finally said.

Marty still said nothing. He just stood there behind Samantha and smiled, staring at her image in the mirror. Yeah, he thought, that was Mom. Sure it was. The long auburn hair. That pendant hanging from her neck. Too bad about Mom. Too bad about the kind of person she was. Too bad Mom had to be punished—and punished for good.

"I'll wear it tonight," Samantha promised.

"I'd like that," Marty replied. "It looks great on you."

Samantha turned round to Marty. "How about that steak?"

"Sure," Marty replied.

Samantha gently removed the pendant and returned it to its box. Then she put on her robe and went into the kitchen to prepare Marty's special breakfast, something she'd planned since she conceived the idea of the party.

In the vacant apartment down the hall, four of Cross-Wade's men listened on surveillance equipment. All wore shoulder holsters. All had keys to the Shaws' apartment. Two of them carried plumber's wrenches and the other two, carpenter's tools. As far as the tenants in the building knew, they were doing repair work.

MARTY BEGAN TO DRESS and inevitably went over the day's details. Hammer, chain, Doug Edwards tape, tomorrow's ticket to Rome. Everything was in order. The demon had taken over. The "5" in his calendar watch was enough to trigger the passionate lust for revenge that he felt every year on this date. This was the anniversary that counted, the only important date in his life.

"Now *that's* the way to begin a day," he said, walking into the kitchen and smelling the grilled steak. "I should be forty more often." It was all so normal, a typical domestic scene.

Marty and Samantha had breakfast, marred by one incident only—Samantha suddenly knocked over a cup of coffee, sending it splattering to the floor. "Nerves," she explained. "The party."

It was a half lie. It was nerves, but it wasn't the party. It was the vision of Marty wielding a hammer and a chain.

After breakfast Marty put on a brown wool coat and left for the office. Outside, in unmarked parked cars, and across the street on the rim of Central Park, were plainclothesmen, a few of whom trailed Marty's cab downtown. Other plainclothesmen, posted outside his office building, watched him enter. Marty took the lift upstairs, walked down the hall, and opened the door with a flourish. Then the normality of the morning evaporated.

"Surprise!"

The office staff had wanted to throw Marty a party before the party, just for the people in the firm. The offices were alive with streamers, crepe paper, balloons, food tables, and a large ice sculpture of the head of Martin Everett Shaw. Before Marty could even get inside, he was smothered with the kisses of secretaries and the backslaps of more restrained employees.

"Wow!" he exclaimed, beaming. "What have you people been doing?"

"A warm-up for tonight," someone said, and that set the tone for the rest of the day. Not much work would get done, but everyone was sure Marty wouldn't mind. And he didn't. Once December 5 was over, he'd never see these people again.

Leonard Ross, Marty's vice-president for media relations, a whiz kid of thirty with a well-trimmed beard and an abnormally deep voice, called for silence. "Folks," Ross called out, "I'm as anxious as you to get the party going, but I need a minute of your time." He gestured for Marty to stay close by. The staff of ten women and eight men turned to them.

"Marty," Ross began, "our people wanted to show you their

172

respect, loyalty and love. You may be the boss, but to us you've always been a good friend." Marty smiled modestly as the room burst out in strong applause.

"We wanted to show you a permanent token of our affection and esteem," Ross continued. "We thought that if you could choose anything to hang in your office to remind you of this occasion, it would be this. We hope you like it." He handed Marty a large, flat package, wrapped in decorative paper and a blue ribbon, with the number 40 drawn on the side in bright red.

"Well, thank you," Marty said, unwrapping the gift. It was a portrait of Samantha, her auburn hair flowing gently over her graceful, innocent neck. Her face glowed with the soft smile of one looking forward to a lifetime of happiness and love.

"Magnificent!" Marty exclaimed, shaking his head from side to side, as if he were filled with emotion.

"It's an oil," Ross explained. "We had it copied from that little picture of Sam in your office."

"Beautiful," Marty said "I want to hang it today. Then I want to bring Sam in to see it. Tomorrow. She'll love it."

"We hope so," Ross said.

"I'm taking it to my office right now," Marty announced. "Thank you all, from the bottom of my heart."

Marty raised the picture so everyone could see, then he marched into his office as the staff raced to the food tables to fill up. Once inside, he closed the door behind him. He removed a small mosaic from his north wall and replaced it with the portrait. Then he stepped back and surveyed it. "Dad," he whispered, "this is a great omen. It's as if some force made those fools out there realize Samantha wouldn't be long for this world. What a scene, Dad. What a great scene."

Marty rejoined the party. "You know," he told Ross as they sipped coffee, "I think I'll take that portrait home tonight. It's so gorgeous I want everyone at our party to see it."

"That's a very nice gesture," Ross said. "Everyone on the team will get a charge out of knowing that."

"Right," Marty said. "A charge."

As festivities were winding down, Marty returned to his office to prepare the items he would need to carry out the ultimate ritual. He opened his safe, took out the hammer and chain and put them in his attaché case, under some business papers. He also took out the videotape of the old Doug Edwards news show, placing it with the hammer and chain. Finally, he took out the ticket to Rome and his forged passport and place them in a side pocket of the case. He snapped the case shut and locked it.

He'd remove the picture, he decided, just before leaving the office. Bringing it home would be one of the last things he'd ever do to make Samantha happy.

The clock was counting down. Nothing could stop him now. It was ten forty-five am when he placed his attaché case in a corner of his office and walked to the reception area, where a few staff members lingered. "Great day," he told them.

"Right," one of them said. "And a great night ahead."

"Oh, yes," Marty replied. "It'll be all I've ever dreamed of."

Samantha's time had almost run out.

THE APARTMENT WAS HUMMING. The caterer was there, the video-tape man, the florist, the advance man for the musicians. Samantha was moved out of her own kitchen by cooks who began preparing for the feast.

Spencer Cross-Wade appeared just after one pm to survey the Shaws' apartment. Dressed in plain clothes, he was indistinguishable from the others who came in and out, and only Samantha knew he was a detective. They went into the bedroom to talk privately. Cross-Wade thought she looked remarkably calm, considering the circumstances. She was dressed in a pink silk housecoat, and her hair was perfectly combed.

"Beautiful arrangements," Cross-Wade said.

"Thanks," Samantha replied. "Too bad it's all going to waste."

"Let's hope something good comes of it, if only to bring one man to justice."

She lowered her eyes. Why did the "one man" have to be Marty?

"There are some last-minute instructions," Cross-Wade explained. "You've been told where all the microphones are?"

"Yes."

"We'll also have video people in a Fifth Avenue apartment across the park. It's a long distance and their image might be clouded. Make sure your curtains stay open."

"They'll be open," she said. "Everyone likes the view."

"Good. The video people are in instant communication with our men here. If we hear *or* see something, we can act."

"That's very reassuring," Samantha said. She was trying her best to accommodate Cross-Wade, but she felt numb.

174

"Who locks up at night?" Cross-Wade asked.

"Usually me."

"Fine. After the party, at some point go and *pretend* to lock up— and we'll hear you. Do you follow my logic?"

"I think so," Samantha replied. "You don't want Marty to suspect that I'm doing anything unusual."

"Precisely. Now, if you're in this bedroom after the party, the curtains would logically be closed, and your husband might be very silent about his actions."

"In what way?"

"He'll have a hammer and chain. They may not make a noise when he takes them out."

Samantha was chilled. "Then what can you do?"

"We'll depend on you. As soon as you see the first sign of a weapon, even a suspicious gesture on Marty's part, I want you to say the words, 'I think I'm getting a headache.' It'll only take us a few seconds to get in. We'll shout, 'Police! Freeze!' That'll stop him. He'll turn his attention to us."

"I hope so," Samantha said.

"Madam, I assure you," Cross-Wade told her, "if I thought there was any real risk, I wouldn't let you do this. But to increase your safety even further, I've brought you something." Cross-Wade reached into his pocket and took out a slim, palm-sized cylinder with a small red valve on top. "This is Mace. It has the combined effect of tear gas and nerve gas. I will ask you to clip it inside your clothing. If a desperate moment should occur, simply spray it in your husband's face. It will stop him, believe me."

"I believe you," Samantha replied, horrified that she might have to use such a weapon.

"Also," Cross-Wade continued, "you must observe your husband at all times. Am I clear?"

"Yes. Very clear."

"And I will tell you this: if we do rush in, please dive to the floor. It's for your own protection."

Samantha shook her head, utterly dismayed. "I still can't believe this is happening," she said.

"Tomorrow at this time, I trust you'll be free of this horror. And madam, I wish you a happy life after that."

"Thank you," Samantha replied.

And then Cross-Wade kissed her hand.

They started to leave the bedroom, Cross-Wade amazed at

Samantha's stamina. But then, as if it were inevitable, he saw her hands turning white and her body starting to tremble. The numbness she'd felt gave way before the starkness of her predicament. Cross-Wade took her arm gently. "I know," he said softly, no other words being necessary.

Then she drew close to him and he could hear her soft sobbing. "Sit down," he told her. "Don't go out there like this."

She sat down on the bed, trying to stop the sobs, to restrain the anger. "Why?" she asked, almost in a whisper. "Why *me?*"

"Why anyone?" Cross-Wade replied. "Why anyone?"

13

Marty came home at six thirty.

Samantha had pulled herself together and regained her strength in time to greet him at the door. She was a vision—the long blue velvet gown a magnificent contrast to her equally magnificent auburn hair, the pendant Marty had given her glistening at her neckline. She had never looked better. Yes, this was a performance—a superb, spirited once-in-a-lifetime performance.

"You're gorgeous," Marty said, standing in the doorway.

Samantha just smiled. She stepped aside so Marty could see how their apartment had been transformed into a magical arena for the great affair. She glanced down at a section of bunched fabric on her gown. The Mace was beneath it.

"Hey," Marty said, not yet stepping in. "I'm in some wonderland. Oh ..." He rushed forward to embrace Samantha as never before. For Marty too, this was a performance.

"I'm glad you're happy," Samantha said.

"There's not a word in the language to describe it," Marty answered. She suspected nothing, he assured himself. "I've got something for you," he said.

Samantha looked down at the pendant, surprised. "Again?"

"It's not exactly from me," Marty explained. He stepped back into the hallway, brought the portrait inside, and closed the door. "The people at the office gave me this."

Samantha gazed excitedly at it as he unwrapped it. "Marty, they gave you *that?*"

"Sure did. It's a wonderful job. Do you like it?"

"Of course I do! Isn't that nice of them. Where do we put it?"

"In my office. I just wanted it home tonight so you and all the others could see it. But tomorrow it goes up behind my desk."

Was she hearing it right? Were Cross-Wade, Loggins, and the others down the hall hearing it right? Did Marty really say he was taking it back tomorrow? Samantha felt nauseated. "Let's put it over there, in the corner, so people can see it," she suggested.

"Great." Marty placed the painting exactly where Samantha wanted it. Then he picked up his attaché case, ready to take it to the bedroom. Samantha watched, just as Cross-Wade had asked her to. She saw how tightly he clutched the case. Of *course*, she thought. That's why Cross-Wade hadn't been able to find the murder weapons anywhere in the apartment. They were with Marty, in the case. They had to be.

"Want me to take your attaché case for you?" she asked, hoping Cross-Wade, listening, would catch on.

"Hey, what are you, my valet?" Marty asked. "Of course not."

"Just trying to help the birthday boy. That looks heavy."

"Just business papers, Sam." Marty stopped to look round once more. He turned to Samantha. "I can't wait. Can you?"

"No." She giggled.

"Let me wash up and change." Marty took the case into the bedroom and closed the door.

The catering staff, the musicians and the bartenders started filtering in. Marty was getting ready. Guests were due at seven forty-five. Samantha rushed around seeing to last-minute preparations and replacing a few wilting flowers with an extra supply she'd kept in the kitchen. The food was already cooked and only had to be reheated.

The first real sign of action was the musicians tuning up. Samantha felt a sudden thrill, as if this really *were* a celebration. She felt almost like dreaming, like pretending, like trying to make the reality as painless as possible. In the bedroom, she knew, was a murderer, and out here, she was—a victim.

The buzzer sounded at seven ten. She walked to the door and opened it. There was Tom Edwards, with a beaming smile. "I thought I could help," he said.

The guy was terrific. If there was one person who could ease Samantha through this, it was Tom and his almost naive, old-fashioned earnestness.

"You're great," Samantha told him as she ushered him inside. "But I don't want you helping. You just relax."

"Me? Impossible." He was awed, as Marty had been, by the party

177

setup. "Now we're talking class," he said. "When the queen comes, nudge me, will you?"

"I'll do that," Samantha replied.

Despite her admonition, Tom walked around straightening the place settings and cards, arranging flowers, and generally getting things right. Samantha glanced at him from the kitchen, watching him work. She'd developed such a strong fondness for him.

Meanwhile, filled with anticipation, Marty washed and shaved. He'd slipped the attaché case under the bed, assuming that Samantha would never notice. He changed to a blue suit, his only real compromise of the evening. He'd wanted to wear khakis and a lumberjack shirt, as he had on the other murder nights. It was the outfit Dad had worn that day in 1952. But tonight, at the party, he'd never get away with it.

He left the bedroom and saw Tom. "Hey," he shouted, "what are you doing here?"

"Just acting as advance man," Tom replied.

"Stop. Have a drink." Marty rushed over and slapped his back.

Samantha came out of the kitchen. "He's been a gem," she said. "Without Thomas I would've fallen apart."

The last of the catering staff came in. Auerbach, without announcing a thing, started his videotape system and did some close-ups of Samantha and Marty preparing for the party.

Seven twenty-eight. A few guests arrived early. The band commenced with a medley from *A Chorus Line*, and the buzz level of the small crowd increased.

Seven forty-five. The hour. The party began to jump as friends streamed in. Marty was beaming. Samantha was radiant. No one could have guessed what they were thinking, or that every word was being recorded down the hall. No one could have known that each movement, each gesture, was being watched through telescopic lenses across Central Park.

The counters in the kitchen were spread with food and wine, and waiters were ready to dispense the delicacies. The small band hit a rapid beat, taking requests and giving the evening a thoroughly festive feeling. The presents were piled up in one corner of the living room. Marty made sure to take each guest to see the portrait of Samantha. One woman, the wife of one of Marty's most important clients, was especially taken by the richness of Samantha's hair in the picture. "Lovely!" she exclaimed. "I didn't realize Samantha's hair was so reddish."

"Auburn," Marty replied. On this night, that had to be right. Eight thirty-six.

By now there were more than seventy people in the apartment. "Dinner is served," the waiter announced, and people began sitting down, bringing their drinks, mugging for Auerbach's ever-present video camera. It might have been a great party in Marty's honour, but to many in the living room it was a business event—a chance to rub shoulders with media people, public relations types, and others who might advance careers. Ordinarily Marty would have studied the political manoeuvrings, but now he could only rehearse in his mind how he would attack Samantha. He would do it while she was in bed, he knew. That would be easiest, quickest, and least likely to make a noise.

Marty suddenly felt a thud on his back. He spun round and looked into the smiling face of Leonard Ross. "Spectacular party," Ross said. "Utterly spectacular. And thanks for bringing the portrait home. Does Sam like it?"

"Loves it. Everyone does. It's really made the day, Len."

Ross slapped Marty on the back again. He felt he had made the correct career move with the boss. Then he sat down at his table and Marty sat at the head table on a small dais.

Samantha was seated beside Marty, and Tom Edwards beside Samantha. Lynne and her husband completed the party on the dais. Samantha had insisted that Lynne share the honours, considering the work she'd put in. After everyone was seated, Tom Edwards started clinking a spoon against his wineglass. "May I have your attention, please?" he asked.

The room quieted. Tom rose, then lifted his glass. "I'd like to propose a toast," he said. Everyone else stood up. "To Marty, on his fortieth birthday." He drank. Everyone drank. "And to Samantha, without whom Marty would be—just a guy." Laughter. More drinking, then applause.

"May I respond?" Marty asked.

"No," someone shouted.

The banter had begun. Everyone sensed it would be a fun evening. "Speech!" someone else shouted.

"That's more like it," Marty said. "I, too, would like to propose a toast. To all of you, my good friends, who have made this night so wonderful." He drank, then everyone followed, somewhat awkward about toasting themselves.

"And there's one more toast that I must make," Marty said.

The room fell silent as the smile melted from Marty's face. He turned slowly towards Samantha and raised his glass. "Not much more than a year ago there was an emptiness in my life," he said. "And then this lady came in and filllled it. Without her, this fortieth birthday would be very lonely, completely meaningless. *With* her, I couldn't be happier. To you, Sam."

He raised his glass. There were misty eyes in the room, including Samantha's. She was doing a good job of acting again.

Down the hall, Spencer Cross-Wade, Arthur Loggins, Sergeant Yang from Missing Persons, and two other officers listened. "Disgraceful," Cross-Wade said. "The man is treating her like rubbish."

"I wonder what *she's* thinking," Loggins said.

"What could she be thinking? Her husband will try to kill her within hours. This toasting her is a little diversion. I suppose, Arthur, that even murderers like to have fun."

"Yes, sir."

But Samantha wasn't really concerned with the twisted irony of Marty's toast. By now she'd written off that side of him. She thought only of the time. It was eight fifty-nine. In a little more than three hours it would all be over.

Someone started singing "For He's a Jolly Good Fellow!" and everyone joined in. The apartment shook with happy sound. The little band followed the tune. Spirits rose even more as the aroma of roast beef floated through the apartment.

But there was something else before dinner.

"May *I* have your attention please?"

The voice was weaker than the others, and though Samantha tried to control it, it had a nervous shake. Her friends would assume this was from the excitement of the evening. People shushed each other, and the room quieted once again.

"This is Marty's night," Samantha announced. "He's a terrific guy and, as you just heard, a very special husband—more special than you can ever know." Applause. "He's so special, in fact, I kind of thought it was time to do something about that. And I did, with Marty's help." She quickly lifted her glass, broke out in a broad smile, and turned to Marty. "Here's to you . . . Daddy."

For a moment, utter silence. Samantha bit her lip as if overcome with feeling, forcing herself to act to the hilt. Marty was expressionless, stunned. The whole room gazed at him as Auerbach, video camera in hand, caught the frozen look on his face.

And then the reaction. "Ah!" and "Wonderful!" and "Congratulations!" Marty's face finally dissolved to a winning, delighted grin. Then he reached over to kiss Samantha.

"Kiss her again!" Leonard Ross yelled. And he did. And the band played "Rock-a-bye baby."

It was a glittering moment, warm and touching. But Samantha felt hollow. The moment meant only a baby without a father.

Marty's insides exploded in chaos. This was a thunderbolt, a curse, the worst possible news. This was something *Mom* would do. A baby? *His* baby? Inside *this* woman?

Everything had changed. *Everything*. It wasn't only Samantha who would die. It was the baby as well. But was that something he should even worry about?

Yes. For it was a direct descendant, Dad's first grandchild. It would have Dad's blood, possibly his features. Maybe its eyes would be Dad's warm eyes, its voice Dad's voice. Maybe it would even move like Dad or laugh like Dad.

Maybe, when Marty looked into its face, he would see Dad.

For the first time since the madness had gripped him, Marty was torn. He *had* to kill Samantha. Samantha was Mom. He'd married her *because* she triggered the image of Mom in his mind, *because* she was so ideal for the role he'd envisaged for her—the role of his final victim. It would be a violation of all he'd promised Dad in his letters, in his visit to the cemetery, to let Samantha get away on this December 5. But the baby...

He remained on the dais wearing that put-on smile, shaking the outstretched hands, getting kisses from well-wishing women, accepting a few cigars. "Thank you," he kept saying to the chorus of congratulations. "Thank you, it's really great." Inside he continued to boil. "Thank you. Yes, it was a complete surprise. No, I haven't got any favourite names. Not yet."

Auerbach stuck the camera in his face, and Marty broadened his smile. "This is the happiest night of my life," he said to Auerbach's microphone, his insincerity recorded for all time.

14

Only time mattered to Marty now. Get the party over with, get these people out of here, get to the end of December 5. But he was still in shock over Samantha's announcement and wasn't sure what he would do.

It was ten pm.

"Sweetheart, isn't it wonderful?" Samantha asked, still playing her role, and playing it to Cross-Wade's hidden microphones.

"More than wonderful. I want to start making financial plans in the morning." He and Samantha were now squeezed into a corner of the living room. "This kid isn't going to have to worry."

He meant it. If he decided against killing Samantha, making financial plans was precisely what he'd do. No kid of his would have to struggle. His kid would have some security, a business to enter . . . and a father who'd take care of him.

Ten thirty.

He began to sweat. It wasn't much at first, just a glisten on his forehead, but then his face seemed to ooze perspiration from every pore. Samantha, by now talking to friends, glanced over and noticed. She broke off and went to Marty, who sat down in a vacant chair to rest. "Marty, what's wrong?" she asked.

"The excitement," he answered. "You know, these things can get to you. I just overdid it, that's all." He smiled. "I should be asking how *you* feel."

"Just great," Samantha answered.

"Good. Won't you sit? You're breathing for two, you know."

She smiled and sat down beside Marty. He put his arm round her. "You still going to pay attention to me when the baby is born?" he asked.

"Not really," Samantha teased.

"That's what I thought. The father always gets the raw end."

"But Marty," someone said, "think of the bills you'll have the privilege of paying."

"I know. If it's a girl, I'll need a second job." He winked.

And the laughs continued, but so did Marty's sweating. It was the sweat of indecision, of disruption of a ritual that had become holy to him.

Ten fifty-three.

"Maybe we ought to wrap it up," he told Samantha. The next day was a business day. Some of the guests who lived in the suburbs had already left, and others appeared tired. But the time was the greatest reason. December 5 would soon be over.

Samantha didn't really want to wrap it up. She wished that time would stand still, for she knew what was coming when the guests left. She barely responded to Marty's comment and pretended to be distracted by a somewhat pushy guest. So Marty walked over to Tom

Edwards, who was deep in conversation with one of the bartenders on the subject of French wines.

"Tom," he said, "we'd better wind it down. Could you possibly drop some loud hints?"

"Sure," Tom answered, always obliging. But then he glanced across the room and saw a look on Samantha's face that he'd never seen before. It was more than tiredness, certainly not the fatigue of a pregnant woman. Her eyes seemed wider than normal, glazed, only partially focused. He decided that she'd just been overtaken by the excitement.

But Samantha was terrified.

Now *she* became obsessed with time.

"Wonderful party," Tom said loudly to a friend. "But it's getting awfully late. Work in the morning." Everyone knew the party was nearing its end.

As the exodus began, Marty glanced over to the corner where the gifts were piled. Oh, no, he said to himself. I didn't open the gifts! The party had gone by too quickly. No one had objected. Not yet. But he worried, and sweated. What if someone demanded that he open them?

He stood near the door with Samantha as the guests filed out. "Thank you," Marty kept saying. "I'll always remember this." His act continued.

"I'll remember it too," Samantha told everyone. So did hers.

Eleven ten.

By now the band members were gone, and so was the catering staff. Only Tom Edwards remained, still holding a Manhattan in his hand, sprawled out in an armchair that had been shoved to the side of the living room. Samantha understood why he wanted to be the last to leave: he felt a proprietary interest in Marty and in the party. He'd been present at the start of the evening, and he was more like family than friend. Samantha felt no awkwardness about Tom's lingering. In fact, she walked over and sprawled out in a chair next to his.

"When does the fun start?" Tom asked.

"Ha-ha," Samantha replied. Marty came over and joined them. "Tom wants more circuses," Samantha told him.

Marty smiled playfully. "Well, if I weren't married ..."

He's keeping it up, Samantha thought. A thespian to the last.

"It *was* a great party," Tom said. "Marty, I've never seen people have such a terrific time."

"Makes me feel good," Marty answered. "Of course, the prime

183

architect here deserves the credit." He gestured towards Samantha as if presenting her.

"Well, Tom and Lynne pulled their weight," Samantha reminded Marty. "I couldn't have done it alone, not this well."

"Sure you could, and did," Tom countered. "You were a hit, Sam." He saw Marty glance nervously at his watch. "And I'd better get going," Tom said, "or I'll be a flop tomorrow."

"Oh, no," Marty told him. "I was just checking the time. The evening's young. Stay a while."

He must be joking, Samantha thought.

It was eleven twenty-four.

"No, I'm really tired," Tom said, letting out a large yawn. "I just felt I wanted to be the last man. Gives me a sense of inflated importance." With some difficulty he lifted himself out of his chair and kissed Samantha. "I don't care if I make him jealous," he said. "The hostess always gets a kiss from me."

"Tom, take care getting home," Samantha said.

"Maybe some tennis this weekend?" Marty added.

"Yeah, why not?" Tom said as Marty opened the front door. "How about Saturday?"

"Fine," Marty replied.

Tom walked to the lift, which came almost immediately, and he was gone.

NOW SAMANTHA was alone with the man she loved, the man she feared. In the apartment down the hall, Cross-Wade and his men gathered tensely around a small black speaker that was transmitting the sounds from the Shaw apartment.

For a few moments after closing the door behind Tom, neither Marty nor Samantha said a thing. Marty just gazed around the apartment. Samantha watched his every move, his every glance, searching for some sign, some gesture, that the moment of hell had come. There was none.

He still hadn't decided. It was eleven thirty-one, and he still hadn't chosen between the roles of father and executioner.

Suddenly he rushed towards Samantha. For an instant she felt scared, but then she realized there was a warm, mellow smile on his face, and tears in his eyes. He embraced her, then stepped away, looking at her as he had on the day they were married.

"What can I say?" he asked. "How can I thank you?"

"Marty, you don't have to thank me."

184

"Oh, yes, I do. Sam, I never had anything like this. I never had anyone to give me anything like this."

"Now you do," Samantha answered.

"I sure do. And I'm gonna hang on to you too," Marty said. "There aren't many people in this world who have happy marriages, and I happen to be one of them."

It was never ending, Samantha thought. He'd play it to the last.

"I hope it's a girl," Marty went on.

"Why?"

"Because she'll be like you."

"And if it's a boy—like you—is that so bad?"

"Not as good as the first choice," Marty replied. He still had that moisture in his eyes. "What a surprise! What a night!" Then he turned suddenly melancholy. "I wish I had a family to share this with," he said. "That's the one thing I miss."

Samantha walked slowly to him and put her arms round his neck. "I understand," she whispered. "But we'll build a close family right here." She couldn't believe she was mouthing the words.

"That's right," he answered. "We'll build our own family. Maybe Saturday, after I play tennis with Tom, we can shop for prams and pushchairs and stuff like that."

"A little early."

"For *my* kid?"

"We'll shop," Samantha agreed.

Eleven thirty-five.

"I think Daddy better get some sleep," Marty said, once again glancing at his watch. "A big day in the office tomorrow."

"I'll just put away a few things," Samantha said.

Marty walked into the bedroom, his mind still in turmoil. He liked talking about the baby, but he liked vengeance as well. Decide, he ordered himself. *Decide.*

Eleven thirty-eight. Automatically he started getting undressed, laying his clothes neatly on a chair. Then he got into his pyjamas and waited for Samantha to come in.

She entered a minute later, startled to see Marty ready for bed. Was this part of the ritual?

Suddenly he walked over to the bed and bent down. It was then that she noticed the attaché case. It was under the bed. Her heart began to pound as she saw Marty going for it. Slowly he slid it out and undid the lock.

He reached inside.

185

Samantha was ready to say the words that would bring Cross-Wade crashing into the apartment. If this was the moment, she'd grab the brass lamp on top of the bureau and hold it out to protect herself, or reach for the Mace.

Marty felt around inside the case. Samantha heard the rustling of papers and clips.

Then his hand started coming out slowly.

Samantha saw a flash of black.

Marty took out his comb.

"I can't find the comb I keep in the bathroom," he explained. "I've looked everywhere."

Samantha let out a deep, agonized breath of relief.

"What's wrong?" Marty asked.

"Oh, nothing. I'm just feeling the effects of all the excitement."

"Sam, sit down. Please. You're in a delicate condition."

And Samantha did walk over to the bed and sit. It was eleven forty-four. What was he waiting for?

He slid the case back under the bed, then stood before the mirror and combed a few stray hairs. He turned round. "My birthday will be over soon," he said, almost like a little boy.

"I know," Samantha answered.

"I really don't want it to end. It's so important to me."

Here it comes, Samantha thought. Instinctively she got up from the bed and walked nonchalantly over to the table lamp.

"Why are you walking over there?" Marty asked. There was a nervous edge to his voice.

He was going over the line. She felt it. What do I say? she thought. Think fast. "Marty, my leg fell asleep. I just want to shake it."

"Your leg never fell asleep before."

"Maybe it's the baby. This condition does funny things."

"All right," he said, but there was a strangely hostile look coming over him. Now the fear welled up in Samantha again. She glanced up at the air vent where a microphone was. Cross-Wade was listening. *He* would know that Marty's tone was beginning to change!

Eleven forty-six.

"ALL RIGHT," Cross-Wade said to his crew. "Let's get ready to charge." One of his men walked to the door of the vacant apartment and opened it slightly. Cross-Wade and Loggins felt for their shoulder holsters and loosened their guns, which they prayed they wouldn't have to use.

186

"I can't believe it," Cross-Wade muttered. "She hasn't gone to unlock their apartment yet." He had the key, but knew that precious seconds might be lost unless he could burst in. He was worried, even panicked. He'd made a solemn pledge to protect Samantha, and something had already gone wrong. Now *he* had to decide—wait until Marty struck, or get in now and prevent a crime, but miss the incriminating caught-in-the-act evidence he needed. For a few more moments he listened to the speaker.

"I FEEL MUCH BETTER NOW," Samantha said, still wondering how close to the end Marty would stretch this.

"I want you to take care of yourself," Marty replied. "You're carrying some valuable cargo. Come and sit down."

Eleven forty-seven.

She walked slowly towards the bed. And then remembered. "Wait a second. I didn't lock the door."

"I locked it," Marty said. "After Tom left."

"I'd better check."

"Sam, I *told* you, I locked it. But I'll check if you want."

"Marty, don't treat me like an invalid!" It was the perfect line, and Marty was startled enough for Samantha to begin walking out of the room before he could respond. She looked back with a warm smile, to soothe him. "I'm only pregnant," she said softly.

He did nothing. Samantha went to the front door, jiggled the lock as Cross-Wade had instructed, so that he and his colleagues would hear it, and left it unlocked. To Cross-Wade, listening intently, she'd just become something of an angel.

Eleven forty-eight.

Samantha walked back to the bedroom and sat next to Marty. It was a risk, but she felt a sense of control. With the door unlocked, Cross-Wade was only seconds away. Marty seemed lost in thought, as in fact he was. The decision had still not been made.

"Penny for your thoughts," Samantha said.

"I'm thinking of names," Marty lied.

"Well, if it's a boy, I insist on Martin Everett junior."

"I'd like that," Marty replied. "I could start a family tradition."

"And if it's a girl?"

"I don't know."

"What about your mother's name?" Samantha suggested.

Marty seemed to tighten. "No," he said. "Not my mother's name. I never liked her name."

187

It was another sign, Samantha thought. Marty's hatred of his mother had slipped out. It was coming. He *was* over the line. It was a matter of minutes, or seconds.

Cross-Wade thought the same thing. At eleven forty-nine he, Loggins, and a third man stood ready at the Shaws' door. They listened to the conversation on small earphone receivers.

"How about Ruth Lenore?" Marty suggested.

"That's very nice," Samantha said. "Did you just think of it?"

"My father liked the name. He once told me that if I had a sister, Ruth Lenore would be her name. I like that."

"So do I. If it's a girl, Marty, that'll be her name."

"Dad would have been happy." It was the truth. Dad *would* have been happy. He had wanted a little girl. "It's unfair," Marty went on. "Dad should have had his little girl."

For Samantha it was still one more sign; Marty was the little boy who'd adored his father.

Eleven fifty-one.

"It's too bad he died so young," Samantha said.

"He would have been very good to that little girl," Marty said. He seemed to stare into space, to slip into a different world. "I'll bet she would've been the best-behaved little girl in town," he continued. "Dad would've made sure of that."

Samantha became increasingly frightened by the stare on Marty's face, by his morbid monologue. She felt for the Mace. Then she eased herself up and walked once again to the table lamp. This time he hardly noticed. It was eleven fifty-two.

In the hallway, Cross-Wade was sure the moment had arrived. "Get ready," he whispered to Loggins and the other officer.

"He would've bought her dresses and ribbons," Marty intoned. "Dad was always so good to me. Did I ever tell you about the time I carried me piggyback through a kiddie park?"

"No."

"He did. And he had a bad back too. But he wanted to give me a good time. Mom wasn't along. She never went to kiddie parks. Dad liked all those things. Like electric trains. It was tough to afford them. Y'know, times weren't great."

"You told me."

Eleven fifty-three.

"He got me the trains, though. Just like the ones I bought. The very best. Dad always liked the best things for me." He stopped. He glanced at his watch. "Come here," he said.

188

Samantha didn't move.

"Come on over here."

Cross-Wade heard, and placed his hands on the doorknob.

Still Samantha didn't move.

"You afraid of me?" Marty asked. Without waiting for an answer, he got up slowly and started walking towards Samantha.

She glanced back at the table lamp.

Marty approached her. He put his arms round her.

Eleven fifty-six.

He held her for a full minute, not saying a word.

Eleven fifty-seven.

"Dad would want to see our baby," he finally said. "No doubt about it." He turned round and walked over to the bed. Samantha could see that he was looking downwards, towards his attaché case. She was ready to utter the words that would bring Cross-Wade.

Eleven fifty-eight.

Marty smiled at Samantha and blew her a kiss. "Thanks for a wonderful evening," he said, "and a wonderful baby."

Eleven fifty-nine.

Without a word he got into bed. He closed his eyes.

Samantha couldn't believe what she was seeing.

December 5 passed into history.

15

Samantha kept staring at Marty.

Then she looked at the clock on the bureau. It was a minute after twelve. It was over. It *was* over.

She felt her muscles fall into repose. She felt as if half the weight had evaporated from her bones. And she felt complete again. The vague hopes that had sustained her during the horror she had lived through had been answered. Marty was no murderer. She still didn't know who he was, but he wasn't the grown-up version of that pathetic little boy from Omaha. Cross-Wade had been wrong. There Marty lay, on the morning of December 6, an innocent man.

Cross-Wade still stood outside the front door with Loggins and another detective. Now Sergeant Yang, who'd been waiting in the other apartment, joined them. They were all baffled.

"I don't understand," Cross-Wade whispered to Loggins and Yang. "Everything pointed to him."

"Everything we suspected was wrong," Yang lamented.

"Maybe," Cross-Wade replied. "Maybe not. He might just have decided to stop killing, or to skip a year or whatever."

"Or maybe it isn't him," Loggins said.

"In that case," Cross-Wade said, "somewhere else a woman has died tonight. And *I* am responsible."

"Not true," Yang said.

"It is true," Cross-Wade insisted. "Accountability, sergeant. And tomorrow we must start all over. Back to square one."

Cross-Wade was interrupted by the clicking of the doorknob. The door opened and Samantha stood there. She was not surprised to see that the officers were huddled right outside her door. She *was* surprised to see Yang.

"I didn't know ..." she began to say, looking at Yang.

"I wanted to be here," he replied.

Then Samantha shifted her eyes to Cross-Wade.

"I have no answers," Cross-Wade told her, still whispering so as not to wake Marty.

"Neither do I," Samantha whispered back. Then she went to throw her arms round Cross-Wade, an embrace that reflected her relief after the ordeal they'd just been through. She just stayed there, her head resting on his shoulder, as he placed his arms gently about her.

"I feel I've served you poorly," Cross-Wade said. "You have my profound apologies."

"I know you did your best," Samantha replied.

"How do you feel?" Cross-Wade asked.

"I don't know," Samantha told him. "I'm relieved, enormously relieved. Obviously. But I still don't know who my husband is."

"I have a feeling all the answers will be disclosed," Cross-Wade said. "I hope they make you happy."

"Thank you."

"We'll be leaving now. We are, as I've told you, at your service. I still have this case to solve. I'll be working on that."

"Good luck," Samantha said. She removed the Mace from her gown and handed it to Cross-Wade without comment.

"And good luck to you, madam. I'll be watching for the birth announcement."

Samantha said her farewells to the other policemen. She felt a tug towards them, an emotional connection. She lingered in the hallway a few seconds, then slipped back inside.

190

SAMANTHA GAZED AROUND the darkened apartment, wishing she'd known at the start of the party what she knew now. She would have had a much better time. She would have felt the original fullness of her bond with Marty, the sense of completeness in being with him. Even with his mysterious past, the knowledge that he was not about to kill her would have been the greatest relief.

Now she walked into the bedroom. Marty's breathing was regular, his body still. Was he dreaming? Probably, Samantha thought. Marty had always been a heavy dreamer. And if he *was* dreaming, it was probably about the baby. Samantha easily reverted to the belief that Marty's past was noble, if secret, and that it would all be made clear in some grand moment, with his child on his knee.

She got undressed and put on a light blue nightgown, Marty's favourite. Then she slipped into bed. Instantly she felt Marty's warmth beside her. She knew she'd have trouble falling asleep, her mind still filled with the rushing events of the evening, but that warmth comforted her, gave her security.

"Goodnight," she whispered to him, expecting no reply but feeling the need to say it nonetheless.

She could hear the city quieting down outside, the traffic thinning, the pedestrians retiring. It was twelve sixteen.

Samantha rolled over and rested.

AT TWELVE THIRTY-FIVE AM Martin Shaw opened his eyes.

He hadn't been asleep. He'd been fully awake.

Waiting.

Waiting for the precise moment.

He had decided. And now he would act. Slowly, deliberately, he got up from the bed. He started walking out of the room.

Samantha, unable to sleep, opened one eye. She watched him, assuming he was going to the kitchen for a snack. She heard him walk on down the hall and enter the living room.

Marty walked to the closet where the electric trains had been stored. He started taking them out. Quickly he set up a simple layout on the living-room floor, an oval about five feet long. He placed the trains on the track and turned on the power.

Samantha heard the trains. What was going on?

As the trains were running, Marty stared at them intently. "Do you like my trains, Dad?" he whispered, too low for Samantha to hear. "Am I doing a good job for you?"

He returned to the bedroom and looked at Samantha to see if she was asleep. Samantha didn't move. She didn't want Marty to know she was awake. Marty reached under the bed and took out the attaché case. He withdrew the videotape of the Douglas Edwards news show. Samantha opened one eye and saw him do it.

Marty walked back to the living room. Samantha heard him moving furniture. She could not see that he was moving the old Model 630 out of the corner where it had been pushed. The set was mounted on a cabinet that also held the Shaws' videotape machine. Samantha recognized the sound of the machine's tape door clicking open. Then she heard it close. There were more clicks as Marty turned on the power for the video machine and the television set itself. The old tube set began to warm, and the sound started droning in about thirty seconds later.

Samantha heard a man's voice. He was delivering the news. She recognized the voice but couldn't quite place it, although it sounded like one she'd heard long ago.

Douglas Edwards. That was it. She remembered. But why was Marty watching an old Douglas Edwards tape? And why was he watching it while the trains were running?

Marty focused on the tape, mesmerized. He remembered how Doug Edwards sounded that horrible night. He remembered the calm, even tones, the undramatic, straightforward delivery.

Everything was set.

The trains were running.

Doug Edwards was on the Model 630 TV.

Marty was ready for the last great ritual before the act. It was twelve forty-eight am.

He slowly walked back into the bedroom. Again Samantha pretended to be asleep. Marty went to her side of the bed. He reached down and grasped a small alarm clock on her night table.

Samantha sensed his presence and barely opened an eye to see what he was doing.

He picked up the alarm clock and started turning the clock back.

Back exactly one hour.

Back to eleven forty-eight.

Back to December 5.

Now a spike of fear so sharp it seemed to slice her in half shot up Samantha's spine.

Marty walked to the clock on his night table. He turned it back. The clock had a calendar. Samantha watched with one eye as the 6 became 5.

Why? What was going through his mind?

Frozen with fear, Samantha listened as Marty left the room and walked round the apartment. She heard him stop several times. The direction of the sound told the story.

He was stopping at wall clocks. He was turning back the time. He was turning back the date.

December 5 . . . again.

No, Samantha thought, it isn't true. He isn't actually going to do anything. That's foolish. Stupid. She remained in bed, still paralysed with fright.

Marty stood in the living room, observing what he'd done and finding it good. It was so much like that night in 1952. It was more like it than the nights of the other murders. This was ideal. This was the way it should be.

"I hope you're proud of me, Dad," he said. He did not whisper. Samantha heard him. What was *this*? "I've done everything I could, Dad. You hear the Doug Edwards programme, don't you? And listen to those trains. The same ones you got me, Dad."

Samantha could stand the suspense no longer. She lurched out of bed and started walking slowly towards the living room to see for herself. She reached the door and gazed in. "What's going on?" she asked.

He did not answer. He just stared at her, then glanced at a wall clock. It was eleven fifty-three. After staring at Samantha a few more seconds, he started moving his lips, but no words came out. A quaint, questioning look appeared on his face. Then the sound of his voice came—soft, kind, almost reverent.

"I'll get a job," he said.

"Marty, you *have* a job," Samantha answered. "You run a company." What's happened to him? What's gone wrong?

"I just wanted him to have these trains," Marty went on. "He's always wanted them."

"Who, Marty? What are you talking about?"

"Frankie loves the trains."

"Frankie?" And then Samantha remembered. Frankie Nelson was the name of the boy in Omaha, the boy who, Cross-Wade had said, grew up to be the calendar killer.

God, it's true! Samantha realized it. Marty *was* Frankie. *This* was Frankie, his mind a prisoner of December 5, 1952.

He'd turned back the clocks and the date.

It *was* December 5.

He was going to kill. And there were no police. There was no protection. There was nothing. Samantha was alone with him.

"I'm not a bum," Marty said. "I need a break."

"Of course you're not a bum," Samantha answered. What could she say? Humour him. Maybe he'd stop.

"Not in front of the children, Alice!"

Maybe she should scream. But that could panic Marty, and by the time someone responded, it could all be over. Run for the door? He'd surely catch her. No, the only chance was pure, agonized self-defence. Samantha was trapped, and she knew it.

"Maybe they'll find out about you!" Marty blurted out. "Where'd you spend the night, Alice?"

"Marty, what are you saying?"

"Where'd you spend the *night?*"

"Here, Marty, here."

"Not in front of the children, Alice!" Suddenly he started back towards the bedroom. He stopped. "Come with me!" he ordered.

"Why?"

"Come with me!"

Samantha eyed the front door. Marty stood in her way. He'd never let her by. She walked with him into the bedroom, thinking of appeasing him. "I'll find the money for the trains somewhere," he said.

"Of course you will."

Marty lunged for the attaché case. In a flash he pulled out the hammer and the chain.

"Oh, my God!" Samantha screamed.

The sight of the weapons was the ultimate confirmation of her deepest fears. She saw a clear path to the front door. She bolted.

Marty was faster.

He stopped her, tripped her. "Don't do that!" he ordered. "I want you here, Mom!"

Samantha sprang to her feet. "I'm not Mom!" she shrieked. "I'm Samantha, Marty! I'm not your mother!"

Marty didn't answer. He charged at her.

He raised the hammer.

Samantha screamed, then grabbed a lamp, hurling it at Marty. It hit him, a metal point puncturing his arm. He stared at the blood. "You're not nice, Mom. A nice mom doesn't hurt her Frankie. You were never nice."

He came at her again. She snaked around furniture, finally grabbing an alarm clock and trying desperately to turn the hour hand

195

ahead once more. "December sixth, Marty. It's December sixth."

But Marty swung the hammer at her, knocking the clock from her hands. It smashed to the floor before she could change it.

She saw another opening. She shot past Marty. He caught up with her. She broke away. He blocked her path to the front door. She bolted for the kitchen. There were knives there. *Knives.*

He trapped her in the kitchen. "Not in front of the children, Alice!" He said it over and over.

"It's too late, Marty," Samantha pleaded. "It's December sixth. Nothing will change that, Marty. You're too late. You can't kill me. It's not part of the game." She went for the knife drawer, throwing it open. She thrust out her hand to grab a knife.

She was stunned.

There were no knives.

They had all been used for the dinner preparations and were in the dishwasher ... right next to where Marty was standing.

Samantha had nothing. She had given back the Mace.

It was all over. She was sure of that.

Marty walked slowly towards her. She backed against the counter, too frightened to scream.

Marty's face broke into a strange, mystical grin. "Dad," he said, "this is for you." He lifted the hammer above his head.

Suddenly there was an enormous thud behind him.

The apartment door swung open.

Samantha saw only a blur, then a flash. Her ears rang from the sharp report.

She heard a horrid, choking groan.

Marty's grin turned to shocked surprise.

He collapsed to the floor.

"It's finished," Spencer Cross-Wade said, holding his service revolver and looking compassionately at Samantha. "I'm sorry it ended this way."

Samantha hardly heard. Her ears were still deafened from the sound of the gunfire. Shock overwhelmed her. She barely saw Cross-Wade standing before her. But in a few moments she felt his supporting arm as he led her out of this room of horrors.

"Sit down," Cross-Wade said to her as they reached a couch in the living room. "Try to be calm. You're safe now."

Samantha closed her eyes, trying to rebound from the convulsion that had struck her world. Cross-Wade looked around and saw the electric trains still running, the tape of Douglas Edwards still beaming forth, in its 1950s grainy glory, from the old Model 630. He stopped the trains. He snapped off the tape machine and the TV. The remnants of Marty's past were suddenly quiet.

"How did you know?" Samantha softly asked the man who had just saved her life.

"One might call it a detective's hunch," Cross-Wade answered. "I was riding home in one of our unmarked cars, and I looked at my watch. It suddenly occurred to me: it had turned December sixth here, but it was still December fifth in the one place that mattered—Omaha, Nebraska. They are an hour behind us. Marty may have lived here, but on this one day his mind slipped back to Omaha time."

"He turned back the clocks," Samantha whispered.

"Yes . . . to Omaha time. Your husband wanted perfect vengeance. He tried to duplicate, as exactly as he could, his night of nightmares in 1952."

"It wasn't Marty who tried to kill me tonight," Samantha insisted, still speaking in a whisper. "It was Frankie."

"Precisely."

"I will always love Marty," Samantha said.

"I hope you will," Cross-Wade replied. He got up, walked to the phone, and put through a call to the coroner's office.

It *was* over. The terror of the calendar schizophrenic had come to an end.

Epilogue

Marty was buried four days later. Now that Samantha knew who he really was, she had his body flown back to Omaha and buried in the little cemetery—beside Dad. His real name, Frank Nelson, would appear on the headstone.

In the months following Marty's death, some of Samantha's friends drifted away, believing Samantha somehow tainted by the calendar schizophrenic saga, which was reported in detail in all the papers. Even Lynne was correct but not close. But Tom Edwards was thoroughly devoted, caring, giving of himself. He started visiting Samantha every day, taking her to dinner, sometimes to a movie or a play. He even drove her to the doctor's surgery as the baby grew nearer to term.

Tom and Samantha became close, and Samantha developed a deep feeling for him. He was becoming so much like Marty,

Marty before Frankie took over. Samantha liked that, for she still clung to the side of Marty she always wanted to remember.

The baby, a boy, was born on schedule. Samantha asked Tom for his advice on a name. He had only one answer: Martin Everett Shaw, Jr. And so, Marty junior came into the world.

Tom and Samantha grew even closer after the birth, with Tom coming over to take Samantha and the baby out for strolls three or four times a week. It was inevitable: fourteen months after Marty's death, Tom and Samantha were engaged.

Just before the small wedding, Tom told Samantha he wanted to visit Marty's grave. He wanted to go alone, he said, to pay his respects to his closest friend, perhaps to say a few words silently.

Samantha was moved. It made her love Tom more. She respected his privacy, and so he flew alone to Omaha. It was an icy, miserable day as he entered the cemetery's gate.

He approached Marty's grave and stood over it.

And he did say a few words.

"I think of you every single day. No one knows what we were to each other. No one suspects. I know now what you were doing, and I'll carry on for you. I'll do what you wanted to do . . . for you and for Dad. This I solemnly pledge to you. December fifth will come again. Rest well, my brother."

Two weeks later Samantha Shaw joined Thomas Edwards in a chapel and became his lawful wedded wife.

William Katz

It is no surprise that this taut suspense novel holds readers spellbound, for *Surprise Party* exposes two familiar nerves, according to author William Katz.

"First," he says, "we are all affected by calendar dates. So many are important to us—holidays, birthdays, anniversaries. I was fascinated by the idea of a character so obsessed with one particular date that he would take things to the extreme." This idea, he says, is based on a real condition which he read about several years ago—acute symptoms of schizophrenia described as "anniversary excitements" in Oxford University Press's *Psychiatric Dictionary*.

"Second, a growing number of people are making up their pasts for criminal reasons," Katz continues. "It's a chronic problem, and widows are often the victims. They are the perfect targets of men who seek to marry them for financial gain—falsifying their own pasts in the process. Fraudulent documentation is, unfortunately, easily available."

Born in New York City, the author brings a wide experience to his writing. After taking a BA from the University of Chicago, he went on to obtain a postgraduate degree in journalism from Columbia University in New York, and then served in the Central Intelligence Agency. There followed a brief stint in the army before Katz eventually became an editor for The New York Times Magazine.

In 1969 his life changed direction again when he began writing comedy scripts for television, but by 1972 he was writing on his own, full-time. Four years later his first novel, *North Star Crusade*, was published, and he has been, as he puts it, "primarily a storyteller" ever since.

William Katz lives in Scarsdale, New York, with his wife, Jane, and two daughters. When not writing, he enjoys interests as varied as politics and photography.

THIS
TIME
NEXT
WEEK

A CONDENSATION OF THE BOOK BY
Leslie Thomas

ILLUSTRATED BY EMMA HUGHES

PUBLISHED BY CONSTABLE

There was a song the Barnardo's boys used to sing:

This time next week,
Where shall I be?
Sitting by the fireside
Scoffing my tea . . .

For many of these abandoned children, home was still a place they dreamed of finding again. But Leslie Thomas knew that, for him, there was no going back. Orphaned at thirteen, separated from his younger brother, his only home was now the gaunt, forbidding London orphanage miles away from his native Wales.

Yet within those walls there was laughter and fun. There were larks, fights and friendships—the thrilling terrors of the Blitz, and later on evacuation to the countryside. And for the young Leslie there was beauty, too, as his eyes opened to the wonders of his new world.

Conveying the fresh, uncomplicated vision of a child, yet told with an adult's wisdom and maturity, this touching memoir from a bestselling novelist is a very special story.

Chapter One

One thing about living on a hill, there was always lots of sky to see and when you weren't busy you could study it. Sometimes the clouds would race along like lean, white lions; like heraldic lions on the shields of knights, I used to think. Sometimes they were grey and fat and slow. Old elephants pushing each other.

I used to watch that sky a lot when I was a kid, watch it in winter midnights, through the long pane of glass behind my bed, the only bit of glass in the whole of the window.

Boz, in the next bed, had cardboard and squares of black curtain stuck over his window because it had never been put in after the bombing. Some nights he used to creak over in bed and whisper, "What the 'ell are you looking up out there for? You're always doin' it."

I never had an answer. It was no good me saying about the lions, or the elephants, or the reassuring stars. Boz would have thought I had gone mad.

Boz was the first boy I knew in Dickies. Sometimes he was called Cherry or Shinybright, because he had a red nose. He was an enterprising character, a great pincher of bread, a raider of orchards in season. He had once run away from the home and had been at large for sixteen days, which was a record.

When I think about it all now, it is often Sunday that I remember. On Sundays the Gaffer would wear his green, hairy suit, perching like a patriarch on his chair at the top of the dining hall, while we slurped our mud cocoa and the cracking of Sunday eggs was as sharp as shooting.

Some things you could be completely certain about on Sundays. There would be a hundred and fifty eggs boiled in a pillowcase and you each got one at breakfast; you also got an individual egg on your birthday, unless the cook forgot, in which case you had to wait until next year. Another Sunday thing was butter beans and pale cold meat for lunch, and potatoes steamed in their froggy skins. In the afternoon Matron—the Gaffer's wife—would waddle into the chapel and talk about Jesus and thieving, and keeping clean in mind and body, and how her old boys used to write and say how much they had enjoyed it at Dickies. With normal luck that was the last we saw of Matron until the following Sunday.

The Gaffer was different. He was always there. His Sunday speciality used to be to warn us of swift and terrible vengeance if anyone was caught reading the *News of the World*. This retribution was presumably to come from him, although he intimated that it might easily arrive from God. Anyone found smoking would be struck by lightning. Then, on Sunday afternoon, the Gaffer would pick two or three of us at a time to be allowed out for walks in Richmond Park. We used to run there, buy the *News of the World*, and share it out amongst us.

He was not a man you could love, the Gaffer. But, after these years, I think of him with a deal of affection and some reverence because he was a good man in his narrow way. He was growling and grey, thin and with a slight stoop, although he would never surrender to the passing years, pushing his shoulders back and tautening his backbone whenever he felt them creeping up on him.

If the stoop was slight, his cynicism was large. He was entitled to it. Forty of his sixty-odd years he had occupied with boys. Thieves and angels; dull, brilliant, trustworthy; skulkers and workers, happy and sad, helpless and horribly capable. But all boys. The Gaffer had, by the time I became one of them, an all-embracing distrust of anything in short trousers.

I remember the first day I saw the Gaffer and Dickies. It was in March, and I had been thirteen a few days before. It was an empty day with rain on the pavements and in the trees and in the sky. Wind blew the rain into my face as I shuffled along from Kingston station beside the man who had brought me.

The man did not talk. I was carrying a blue sack like a pillowcase over my shoulder, and it contained very nearly all I had in the world. Big houses stood vaguely behind misty trees.

Towards the end of the road there shot up a high wooden fence, and I knew we had arrived. There was the gate. The man turned in and I followed.

Then I stopped. It may only have been for seconds, because the man was walking on, but I know I stopped and looked up. A quick loneliness came over me like a pain. No boy has ever felt so much by himself as I did in that moment, afraid and wondering what was going to happen to me from then on.

THE PLACE FILLED THE HORIZON. Yellow bricks and blank windows; a tower at the centre capped with a pointed roof, a horror built from some architect's nightmare. Across the front of the building were the words "The Dalziel of Wooler Memorial Home", blazoned in golden letters. In the middle of the tower, in more modest gold, was "Dr. Barnardo's Homes".

The man who had brought me went up some stairs at the foot of the tower and I went in through the door after him.

We were in an entrance hall reeking of floor polish. There was a boy standing there picking his nose. The man told him to go and fetch Mr. Gardner, the superintendent, and he went. Drippings from our wet coats made liquid explosions on the red floor and settled like small rubies at our feet.

Down the corridor echoed the Gaffer. He turned the corner with military stride and granite expression, shook hands with my escort, and led him into the office.

I remained, damp with rain and unhappiness, resting my blue bundle on the floor and crooking a parcel of books in my other arm. With two fingers of this hand I hooked onto a small package holding a tin half full of toffees. The full tin had been sent to me by an elder brother, just after my mother died, with instructions that half of the sweets were for me and the other half for my younger brother. I never heard any more from the elder brother, and I did not see the younger brother for another year and a half. But I kept the sweets for him.

A few yards from where I stood there was a pedestal, topped by a marble bust wearing a layer of dust. There was quite a lot of dust clogging the inside of the eyes and I attempted to cheer my miserable self by trying to imagine what would happen if the head came to life and found all that muck in its eyes. I don't know who the head was — or if I did, I have forgotten—but the gentleman in the picture on the wall, the one with the watch-chain and the lion-tamer moustache, was Dr. Barnardo, the Father of Nobody's Children.

UNDER THE PICTURE now stood the boy who had been sent to fetch the superintendent. His mission accomplished, he had returned to busily exploring his nose. I did not know it then, but he was Boz.

"'Ow old are you then?" he inquired solicitously.

"Thirteen last week," I said. "Wednesday."

He appeared to make some mental calculation. "You'll be gettin' fourpence, then," he said eventually.

"Fourpence? When?"

"Saturdays. That's when we get the dush."

"What's dush?" I asked stupidly.

"Wot I've just said," he repeated patiently. "Dush is money. Pocket money, see? You'll get fourpence. Some kids here get a tanner. And them that's in the band get more than that."

"There's a band?" I said, brightening.

"Yeah," he grinned. "But you can't get in it till you're fourteen and you've got to learn the bagpipes or the bells. But they get more dush."

Then I put the big question. "What's it like?" I asked.

He knew I meant the place. "Dickies?" he said. "'Orrible. Bloody 'orrible. Worse 'ome I've ever bin in."

Having given this assurance, Boz then welcomed the tortoise arrival of another boy. A boy wearing a foully greased blue jersey and with three teeth missing, all in the front; a boy with hair thickly plastered down with a substance I later learned was stolen lard. The boy's name was Breadcrumb George. He had gained this unusual appellation through his habit of gathering all the breadcrumbs from the table, piling them up and sweeping this harvest into his mouth with a deft movement.

Breadcrumb George was carrying a large tin of red floor polish, with a stick projecting from the middle of it. "Got the splosh," he said briefly, and dragged on down the corridor. Boz turned with him, saying to me, "We're on chapel."

Off they went, presently followed by a smaller, mild-looking lad wearing steel-rimmed glasses and bearing two large pieces of folded blanket. This boy was called Bosky because he was cross-eyed.

They went into a big room at the end of the corridor. At the far end I could see a wooden cross which stood out against a bright blue cloth draped across the wall. Boz took the stick, dipped it deep into the polish and, moving backwards along a broad strip of brown lino, banged dollops of red at frequent intervals. When he had accomplished this he stood at the far end of the lino strip, under the cross, and Breadcrumb George stood at the end nearest me. Bosky himself sat solemnly cross-legged on the pieces of folded blanket.

Breadcrumb gave him a push and he slid on his blanket-sledge along the lino, spreading out the polish by his journey. At the other end Boz swung him expertly round and propelled him back. Back he went, and back again. As they went thus lightly about their task, so the trio sang. I have never forgotten that song. It was simple, but sad in a way, although they would never have thought it so. Nevertheless it was a song of hope and of remembering. It went:

> *This time next week,*
> *Where shall I be?*
> *Sitting by the fireside*
> *Scoffing my tea.*
> *Plenty of comics,*
> *Lots of books,*
> *No more matron's dirty looks ...*

It was a lusty thing: a song of hope, unconscious perhaps, because each of us grew with a small and usually diminishing dream that one day we would find our own home again and be restored to it. And a song of remembering for those of us who had known such a home—once, anyway.

Chapter Two

Every now and then my father would blow home from the sea and break a few windows. He used to smash the windows, generally at the front of the house, because my mother wouldn't let him in. She said they were legally separated and nothing was going to change it.

One day the mistress of the cub pack to which I belonged came past on her bike. At the next cub meeting she asked me how the windows came to be broken.

"It was a bomb, miss," I said desperately. There had been a smattering of air raids that week, so I thought this was plausible. "A small German bomb. Right in the garden."

"Oh dear," she said. "Your poor mother! We must all go round and see if we can help her."

"No," I cried. "Mum's in hospital. The bomb blew her arms off."

My old man was stoking boilers in ships' stomachs for most of his life, journeying the world over, searching for whatever sailors search

207

Leslie Thomas's parents, David and (right, below) Dorothy Thomas, photographed about ten years before their deaths.

for. He had a funny, agile face with a habit of looking round corners with his mouth and his eyes. We hardly ever saw him, but what time he was at home my mother decided was too much. He had a weakness for getting drunk and for giving his money away. Sometimes, for variety, he would take up a lost cause in a dockside pub and challenge someone twice his size to a fight. He frequently arrived home plastered (in both senses) and bandaged from his waist to his spreading ears.

But I think he loved us dearly in his way. When he sauntered home from his far wanderings he would bring strange toys for me and my brother, Roy, and fragile china, as light as paper, for my mother. This was before their legal separation. My mother would accept with reserved gratefulness the Japanese coffee set, or the tea set from Macao, wash it tenderly and set it with her collection on the Welsh dresser. Then three nights later the old man would come home raving from the Dock Hotel, and be turfed out once more.

My father had been a sailor almost from the time he left school. His two elder sons had gone to sea in their teens and had risen, by study and endeavour, to the bridge, while Dad doggedly shovelled on in the boiler room. I have heard it said that nothing was too heavy nor too hot for him. My only prayer for him has been that he was not down there when the torpedo hit his ship.

In his young days he once jumped ship in Australia and went to the goldfields to strike his fortune. Months later he was in a seamen's hostel in Sydney, broke as a beggar, and a sea captain said he wanted a sailor for a voyage back to England. Jim Thomas willingly put his name on the line, and the next morning found the ship.

"Jesu," he used to say when he was telling the story, "I couldn't

208

believe what I saw. There's me been a stoker ever since I could lift a shovel of coal and this thing was all masts and rigging, like a spider's web."

The schooner took six months of horror and hurricane to get home. My old man, hanging tightly somewhere high in the rigging, reckoned he wept most of the way.

Looking back over the valley of these years I remember my mother as a small woman, pretty even in her late forties. Her unreliable husband, and the fact that her two eldest sons frequently vanished to distant seas for years and never bothered to write or send money, had led her to expect nothing from them. This was all she normally received. Her life was a tired serial of house-cleaning jobs, with a spell as a school cleaner and another as a factory sweeper thrown in for variety. One thing was constant: there was never any money to spare.

The first and last time I ever remember my parents embracing was in 1938. I recall the year exactly because of the reason for the kiss.

In Spain the civil war was rolling. My father and my elder brother were involved (on opposite sides, I believe), but strictly in the cause of cash. They were on gunrunning ships. The old man's vessel was in Barcelona harbour when a dive bomber appeared over the housetops and dropped a high explosive bomb right down the funnel.

Coldly, the BBC announcer said that all the crew were dead. It was a Newport ship and the curtains were drawn in many streets. My mother hardly said anything all day. Then came further news. Some men had been picked up. The announcer read the names and my father's was last on the list.

He came home, all bandaged up as usual, but at least honourably this time. My mother and he crushed together, and he let out a yell because she pressed on one of his fractured ribs.

About this time, he travelled to Barry to his father's funeral and came back maudlin drunk. He was arrested at Newport station and, not having any money, was kept in custody overnight. My mother grumbled all the way to pay the fine on that occasion, and I think it was from then on that their relationship began to wither drastically. In the early days of the war, when he came home from sea there were the window-smashing episodes and bitter, black rows, while we children cried and tried to pull them apart. From the spring of 1939 to the late summer of 1943 we lived in a district of Newport called Maesglas, which in Welsh means green fields. All reasons for the name had diminished to a joke as the docks spread along the black coast, and as the railways and the mean terraced houses followed them.

There *were* green fields, but in the distance, lying on their sides up a ridge of hills. My mother used to do cleaning at a house on top of the ridge. Sometimes she wore a red coat and when I came home from school I used to stand on the air-raid shelter and pick her out, bright as a ladybird, coming over the fields, and I would put the kettle on.

She did her best for us. Every summer we used to get new plimsolls—dappers, we called them—and go pounding down the pavements like young horses with white hooves. Every winter there were new wellington boots and we would go to school warmly wrapped in woollen balaclavas, scarves and mittens, knitted by earnest ladies for our brave merchant seamen. My father would bring them home, and my mother accepted them on the basis that they were gifts for the children and not her.

In the autumn of 1942 my mother became ill, and one evening she was taken to hospital. I remember it like a sequence in one of those shadow theatres where the shapes flicker round the sides of a drum.

All sorts of people came round. Mum was upstairs and she sent down a message about where Roy and I could find our clean pyjamas, because we were going to the hospital with her.

All the people sat like conspirators against the walls downstairs, and although we must have had the light on, I can only think of them as shapes and shadows. They crouched and gossiped, as people do, of other occasions when people had been taken ill, and death and hospitals and operations enthralled them until the ambulance came. But for some reason not one of those shadows ever offered to take myself and my brother in. Later, nearly a year later, when the time came for Roy and me to go away for ever, they were still of the same sympathy and the same reluctance.

The first time, Roy and I were allowed to stay in the children's ward at the hospital for a few days. Then we had to gather our things and journey down to the women's ward to see woolly-coated Mum, before being taken to our first brief experience of a home.

A strange word, home. Say it one way—just "home"—and it is the warmest syllable in the language; deep as a hearthrug, satisfying as dinner, assured as love. But add one letter, call it *"a* home", and immediately all the depth and warmth are gone, as though a big door has been opened and a wind has howled in.

I recall little of the home we went to that autumn day. The pictures that do come back are of a great, scrubbed table, white as whalebone, standing on the flagged floor of the kitchen; there was a black, open range, and a girl with a leg-iron who jolted around and shouted a lot. The home was on the road from Newport, up towards the valleys. One good thing about the place was that I was able to attend my usual school.

Our mother was out of hospital and home again after about three weeks. We went home. For a few weeks, or perhaps it was months, she was well again, and we began making plans for the holiday we were going to have in the country next summer.

In February my father turned up. There was a hopeful sort of half reconciliation between them. It was a streaming day, gutters gushing, and I came home from school and found him sitting by the fire with a cup of tea, talking about the war. He had seen men die in the acid sea, a rope's length away. He had seen ships suddenly blossom red and orange in the awful darkness and then watched the flower of flame sucked into the water. Men, he had seen, covered in oil and burning.

He leaned towards my mother, gave her his cup and, I remember this so well, he said, "Dolly, let me come back. I've got to have somewhere to go when I come home."

She did not answer right away. She took the cups into the kitchen, washed them and let their one chance of a last brief happiness slide down the drain with the water. "Let me think it over," she said when she came back. "Wait till you come home next time."

He went back to his lodgings. Then, the day before he sailed again, he came to the house. He did not stay long. But those few minutes are still bold and black and white in my mind. So clear are they that I might have known that this was to be the last time.

Just before he went, Roy was sitting on one side of the small bay window and I was the other. Mum was on the couch.

Dad came across and kissed Roy and me. He had a hard, bristly chin, and he was clumsy when it came to affectionate gestures. He went over to Mother and gave her a jerky kiss and a pat on the cheek and said something like, "Next time, then."

Then he did one of his round-the-corner grins or grimaces, I don't know which they were, and walked out into the street. A month or so later his ship, the SS *Empire Whale*, split by a torpedo, went down in the South Atlantic. All its men went too.

Five months after he had gone, my mother was deeply ill. Early in September I woke up one morning to hear her crying. I went in to her and she said that Roy and I would be going away that day—so that she could go into hospital.

"It's a school," she said. "Down in Devon. The masters play soldiers in the woods and the fields with the boys. I've heard they have a very good time. But you will write, won't you?"

Just like that. One minute—or one hour anyway—we were ordinary kids at home, and then we were packed and leaving, having kissed her and wept by her bed.

And that was the last we ever saw of her.

Chapter Three

A deep-throated creek comes in from the sea at Hope Cove, turns through the red and green fields of the South Hams, and finally collides, head-on, with a stone wall at Kingsbridge.

A mountainous high street, called Fore Street in the West Country manner, has its base at the stone wall which stops the creek. It climbs between the shops, past the church, and eventually to the crown, where there is a house that was once painted white and green.

It was to this house that I and my brother went the day after we left our mother. From home, we had first gone into Cardiff, taken there by a woman from some welfare office. We had to meet a man at the station.

"How will we know the man we have to meet at Cardiff station?" I asked.

"Oh," said the lady, "we'll know him because he will have a blue Dr. Barnardo's Homes badge in his lapel."

This was the first moment that we knew where we were bound.

Our mother had told us the encouraging lie of the "school" and no mention of Barnardo's had been made until then. Now, it came like a cold hand on the neck, the realization that we were destined for another "home", and this time a distant place, with the prospect of a much longer stay. How long, we did not realize then.

It is easy enough to blame a woman for sending her children away in this manner. But she knew, even if everyone else thoughtfully denied it, that she had cancer and was surely dying. There was virtually no one to whom she could look for help. In the years before the war she had alienated herself, after a long series of quarrels, from both her own and her husband's families. She distrusted a good many people, and did not want to "put upon" others. In the end she took the brave step of sending us to an institution. It was brave, for it must have broken her heart after the long struggle she had put up. Who can blame her? Not I.

The man who met us was wearing the blue badge. He took us to the Barnardo home in Cardiff and we spent the night there. My brother cried and I wondered whether we ought to make a run for it now, while we were still comparatively near Newport. I told myself that somehow my mother had been tricked into sending us to the home; that she had really *thought* we were going to a boys' school where they played soldiers in the woods and fields. But then I remembered her tears that morning and I realized that she had not been tricked into anything.

On the following day, as though fate were trying to torment us, we saw our house again. Taking us to Cardiff had merely been some organizational device and we travelled by train back through Newport to Bristol, and down to the West Country. As we crossed the Ebbw again we picked out the roof of our house behind the engine sheds. It was a chilly day. All the chimneys in the street were smoking except ours.

New arrivals at the Kingsbridge home. Leslie Thomas is pictured third from right; his brother Roy eighth from left.

But we were only boys, and once the train began to reach new and unknown places our sadness was pushed away by the eagerness of exploration. We had never travelled far. These dipping fields, these amiable towns, these rivers and copper trees were all part of a strange new country.

At Newton Abbot—the peculiar foreign names!—we changed, and a homely push-and-pull engine took us down a gentle canyon to Kingsbridge, in the South Hams district. Someone—a young woman this time, I think—had escorted us on the journey, and with her we walked from the station up the steep slope of Fore Street.

So this was the first real stop, the first resting place on a nomadic wandering that we would both experience until we were grown up. It was a solid, country house, the sort that sits contentedly by the side of many a road throughout England. This was a "reception home" and it only had twenty or so children.

On the first day they did not send us to school. Instead, we were told we could go for a walk. So we bought some apples and then went down to the head of the creek and made boats out of wood we found in the mud. It was very quiet down there; there were some swans and ducks on the far side, and Roy went paddling in the water up to his knees.

When I thought it was time to go, Roy turned and waded out. He

214

dried his legs on my handkerchief. Then he said, "We ought to be able to get 'ome for Christmas, din' we?"

"Yes," I said, "I 'spect so."

THERE WAS MORE SUN left in that summer. It browned the crops, and baked the ground. After we had been at Kingsbridge two weeks we had another three weeks off from school, the usual thing in Devon, for many of the children came from farms and were required to help with the harvest.

We wandered the fields, watching the men at the threshing, getting in the way, trying to help, hypnotized by the death-chase of dog and rabbit in the gold. The pale boys from overcast city streets ran in the stubble and drank rough cider from the mugs of the labourers. Breathless, every day, we went back to the house and had tea. We used to write every night and tell our mother what we were doing. And the letters were piling up on the doormat of our empty house many miles away.

There was a paddock at the bottom of the garden, and a barren orchard and three pigsties. They had not been used for a long time, and we went down there one Saturday, several of us, and made bows and arrows from the trees, and built a small fire to fry the sour, dried apples. All day the orchard was Sherwood Forest and we the snug outlaws in our settlement.

We went back to tea and it was peanut butter. I remember I had just started to eat when the door from the garden opened and the superintendent stood framed there, beckoning to me. At first I thought he was going to tell me off about playing in the pigsties. But he smiled as I reached the door and asked me to go out into the garden. Then I knew what it was about.

We walked towards a place where a lot of autumn flowers were out. So far he had not said anything. But I knew what he was going to say because I had dreamed about her in the night.

"Your mother," he started. "She was very ill and in a lot of pain. But she's out of pain now. She's dead."

The crimson and yellow flowers fused for a moment in my tears. I can never see a flower lying in the shallows of a stream, or blossoms behind a wet windowpane, without remembering it.

"I dreamed she was," I said. "Last night."

I don't think he knew how to go on from there. "I think I will leave you here," he said kindly. "Go in for your tea when you feel like it."

I walked down the garden and into the orchard. There were the pigsties where we had been so happy that day. I stirred the place where we had lit the fire to see if it was still alight. It wasn't. In all, I think I only cried for about five minutes.

THEY HAD THREE DOGS, Patch, Brutus and Judy, at this house.

They were a comedy team. Patch was a yapping terrier, small and short on temper and wind; Brutus was medium and brown and guileless; Judy was a huge Great Dane, with slobbering chops but a gentle nature. Taking all three for a walk at the same time was attempting the impossible. Judy would leap ahead with poetic strides that carried her clear and clean from the ground, Brutus would be somewhere about your feet doing his best to keep up, and Patch would be half strangled by his collar as you pulled him along behind, yelping and snarling at Judy to cut the pace.

One night towards the close of the year I took the dogs out in the moonlight with John, who was the oldest boy in the home. My brother had gone into hospital with appendicitis the day after I had been told of my mother's death. While he was in hospital he got diphtheria and then something else, so he was there for months, and all the time he thought that his mother still lived.

John and I had become good friends, and on this night we took the dogs up the climbing fields towards the night and its rising moon. I had the two smaller dogs and John was being towed along by Judy. They all ran hard in the cold air and eventually, at the crest of the fields, we stood with the panting animals looking out over the pale earth.

Then the dogs began to cry and pull. I looked round, and standing full under the moon was a giant of a horse, a white stallion, snorting the air. We ran, the dogs ran, and after us came the thundering stallion. I stumbled in the grass and then John tripped and wobbled.

"Let the dogs go!" I hollered as we plunged in panic.

"And run!" he called back, going like mad himself. "Run or the big sod will 'ave us."

The dogs flew off over the field. We reached the gate not long after them, and seconds in front of the stallion. The sky and its stars raced beneath us as we flung ourselves head first over the bars.

Behind us the drumming had reached a crescendo and then rolled to a stop as the stallion reached the gate. He stood there, his white nostrils up, snorting and steaming. We kept running, because you couldn't be really sure.

The dogs were waiting for us at the next gate, wagging their tails and looking a bit embarrassed at their fright. We caught up the trailing leads and laughed all the way home along the silver road.

There are not many moments you can choose from your life when you have known utter happiness. But that was one.

BY SOME IRONY it was while I was in the home at Kingsbridge that I discovered that I had a rich uncle. If not a rolling millionaire, Uncle Chris was comfortably off by most standards, with a car and a house in Barry, South Wales, and a business repairing and renovating ships that limped back from the war into the Bristol Channel ports.

He was my father's younger brother, and until he wrote to me after my mother's death I did not know he existed. The protracted cold war which my mother had chosen to carry on with both her own and my father's family had kept him a stranger. But when she knew that her life had only a little to go, she had reached out from her hospital bed and called for Chris Thomas and his wife Nance, the only people in the family who had any means or influence.

I can only believe that she wanted them to give us a home. But it never happened. There were legal difficulties, she died before she could sign a paper, and anyway they were both committed to a business which occupied them fully and was essential to the war. But at least they wrote often and gave me some outside anchor.

In the woodwork class at school I had sawn and chiselled and glued together a tugboat with barges, and a steamroller which I painted red. These were my Christmas presents for Roy, my brother. He had to wait until February until he got them, by which time it was near his ninth birthday. Then he came back from the hospital where he had been since the day after I knew that our mother had died.

He came into the big room, thin and white as a stick. He sat down and opened the presents, and then said, "How's Mum? I wrote but I didn't get any letters back. Is she better now?"

If I had been older and braver I might have told him then. But instead I just said, "She's still ill. She's in hospital."

"P'raps she'll be better soon," he said. "Then we can go 'ome. I didn't think we'd be away this long, did you?"

I felt hopeless and I said, "We'll go soon," and left it at that.

No one from the homes ever got around to telling him. It was an accidental silence, I have no doubt, but it was bad for all that. As it was, he didn't find out until after we had moved to London, and he and I were separated. It was a year or more since she had died.

Now and again, at Kingsbridge and in the following years, I used to have dreams about her. I would dream that she was sitting in the chair on the other side of the fireplace. I had our old cat on my lap and I was resting a book on him. And Mother was knitting and looking into the fire. I felt happy, and told myself what a fool I had been all this time. Of course she was alive. But then I would open my eyes and see the moon lying quietly across the beds of the other boys. And then I would know what was true.

In March Roy and I went down the steep street for the last time, in our new suits and with the rest of our clothes in blue bundles on our shoulders. We went to London on the train, and they met us at Paddington with an ambulance, presumably because Roy had been so recently ill.

As we skirted the streets I got my first view of the big city through the slit window of the ambulance, and I kept up an inadequate running commentary for Roy, who was lying on the bed. A woman sat there with us but, like so many of these travelling companions, she was neither communicative nor friendly.

Then, having seen the famous brick-wall poster with the painted "We want Watney's" legend, I asked what it was. I thought it was a real wall; after all, this was London, the place where the cry for Watney, whoever he was, might mean revolution, or anything.

"It's a beer," said the woman tonelessly. "You won't want to know anything about it."

We reached the Barnardo's "Garden City" at Woodford Bridge, Essex. The ambulance stopped. I was told to get out. My brother was going to spend the night at the hospital and I was going to one of the small houses. "Come on," said the woman. "You'll be together tomorrow. Hurry up."

I climbed out of the ambulance and I did not see my brother again for eighteen months.

Chapter Four

Porky, Chesty, Ear'ole, Israel, Darkie, Grandpa, Pongo, Rubberneck, Tiptoe, Ding-dong, Bug, Freddie the Fly, Professor, Snotty, Baggy and Scratcher Dan.

Depending on his habits, his proper name, his infirmities, his disposition or his physical attributes, so each boy was nicknamed. Porky was fat, Chesty a wheezer. Ear'ole had a mangled ear and Grandpa a hairy face. Israel was no anti-Semitic tag—the boy's surname was Hands and we had all read *Treasure Island*. Professor was studious, Pongo insanitary; Rubberneck moved like a tortoise, and Scratcher Dan just scratched. Breadcrumb, Bosky and Boz I have already listed.

The staff had names too. There were Korky, Chuck, Jessie and Rumbletum—and they were all women. Successive and oft-changing assistant masters were in the gallery as Marlow, Little Affie and Walrus.

The day after I arrived at the Kingston home from Woodford I was nicknamed. They called me Monkey. I went into the dormitory and there was a reception committee sitting on the beds. They wouldn't let me go past so I stood, trembling inside, looking at them.

As boys go they looked villainous enough. Jerseys, blue and grey, patched all over, trousers embroidered in the same way, socks around ankles and bursting shoes.

"'lo Monkey," said one kid, standing in my way.

"Trying to be funny?" I said.

"Yeah, Monkey," he grinned. "Let's see you swing on the beams."

The others all laughed, and I knew I was going to have to have a fight. "What do they call you, then?" I said to the spokesman. "Is it Ape? Or Chimp?"

He hit me on the side of the head with a sharp, stony fist, and I went straight over the iron bedrail and landed in the valley between two beds. My head was screaming and I could hear them all roaring around and above me. I heard someone shrieking, "A fight! The new kid's 'aving a fight!" From the next dormitory came a deluge of booted onlookers.

I knew I'd have to get up and I knew just as certainly that he would put me on my back again. At that moment I couldn't focus too well, but I thought he was no bigger than me. It was just that he'd hit me first.

"Come on out, Monkey," he yelled. "Let's see your monkey face."

My leg must have been sticking out because the fighter got hold of my foot. My shoe came off and he staggered back against one of the beds. When he came back I was up to meet him. I never could fight, but I was bristling with tears and temper. I ran at him and felt the top of my head crunch his nose. Then I hit him with fists and bony elbows, and caught him a cruel thrust with my pointed knee.

He was on the ground and I was on him, banging his head against the ground. His nose was discharging like a red river. In the end they pulled me off and in the true manner of boys carried me away in noisy glory while they left him to bleed.

I might have won my fight but I had not gained my point. Even in the flush of victory they were calling, "He's won! Monkey's won! Good old Monkey! Good old Monkey!"

OUR DORMITORY was on the first floor. Underneath, down a cold back staircase, was a dark corridor, stone, with doors leading off on each side. We called this Death Row. The most important rooms here were the larder and the breadroom. No one I ever knew, not even among that talented and adventurous crew, had ever broken into the fastness of food, but the breadroom locks—plural, because they kept changing them—could be frequently picked. And were.

In the breadroom, for an hour each day, was performed a sticky ritual called Spreading. Four boys, under the eye of a master who operated the cutting machine, spread margarine on inch-thick slabs of bread. It was established tradition that within reason the spreading boys could eat while they worked with their knives. Thus it was a favourite job, because you got only two slices for breakfast and another two—jam one day, margarine the next—for tea.

When someone had got the hang of the lock on the breadroom, a raid would be mounted. While the thieves were down there, working on the door in the tunnel of darkness, there was a tense expectancy in the dormitory. Those left behind eyed the closed doors of the matrons' rooms, which were on the landing outside. Then the slipping shadows of the raiders would filter back and they and their friends ate slices below the blankets.

A swing door away from the stone corridor was a cauldron of steam, spitting gas burners and smells, that was the kitchen. Beyond the kitchen was a dining hall, a big tank of a room. Wooden tables and forms went down each side, there was sad linoleum on the floor, and green gloss paint climbed halfway up the walls, where it met its inevitable brother, yellow.

Meals were never elaborate affairs. Breakfast varied only between a sparse plate of cereal one day, plus a slice of bread and marge and a cup of cocoa, and two slices of bread and dripping the next, with cocoa. On Sundays we had the boiled eggs. Occasionally at weekends there was a slice of bacon, or ham known as "walking ham" because it was rumoured to be high, active enough to escape if you failed to spear it quickly.

Lunches in the week we had at school, and it was just as well.

Every day we returned to the certainty that tea would be either two slices of bread and margarine or two slices of bread and jam, and a mug of tea, with a rocky bun on Sundays. Tea was the final meal of the day.

I recall this with no particular vindictiveness, or any memory of having actually felt starving. And after all, we weren't paying.

One morning I do remember, however. I recall it because the windows were starred with frost and fingers of wind were feeling around all the corridors as we went in to the same old breakfast. The cocoa was watery and hot, but with so little sugar that it was to all intents unsweetened. And as we sat warming our hands round the cups the kid next to me scratched a seeing-hole in the windowpane and peered through the space.

" 'Ave a dekko out," he said.

Coming cautiously across the icy yard was a thin boy called Thorn, who waited on Matron in her house across the way. His hands were round a large glass confectioners' jar, which was full of white sugar. He was walking from the stores to where tubby little Matron was doubtless cosily awaiting her breakfast. She had a very sweet tooth.

The house where she and the Gaffer lived was a straight, modern affair of red brick, standing in its own lawned garden. We saw little of Matron in the main building. Every one of the staff held her in the deepest reverence and always stood when she came into the room, as we boys had to do. But she spent most of her time tucked in her sitting room writing letters by the dozen. I did not like her very much, but in fairness she was becoming elderly, just as the Gaffer was, and both he and she would have probably retired long before had it not been for the war.

They had a son, a handsome army padre whom we saw occasionally, and who was married to a beautiful fair-headed woman. She was tall and completely dazzling. I remember I was digging in the garden one Saturday when she walked up the path. Her high heels tapped and she walked gracefully and her hair was smooth. She smiled like an angel at me as I leaned for a moment on the spade. Never had I known a moment like that.

ONE OF THE IRONIES of Dickies was that although its shabbiness was without question, it had within it something grand and brave and displayable—the band.

The band boys were the elite. They were older, they had different clothes, they got more pocket money, they journeyed to strange cities

221

in a big van. They had meals in *cafes!* They played in halls and people applauded them. When they returned from a tour, they were expected to do no work about the place but to conserve themselves for the practice sessions held three times a week.

It was a two-purpose outfit, this band. Arrayed stridently in kilts and jackets with flashing buttons, it sounded the fine and beautiful sounds of the pipe marches. Then came a quick-change act into page boy suits for every variation of ringing and chiming in "Bells Across the Meadow".

Certain boys, who looked as if they might be able to blow the pipes or ring bells, were occasionally selected from the rest of us and ordered to attend the practices. In the frantic hope that I might be one of the chosen I used to wander whistling Scots airs through my teeth so that the Gaffer might hear. But he never took the hint.

In my first month at Dickies it was decided to hold a church parade, with everybody marching down to Kingston in their Sunday best and the band wailing at the front. They gave the band a trial march up and down the mudpatch we used for football and cricket. We all stood round the edge bursting with admiration and envy, and a boy called Brice, who arrived about the same time as me, came and stood at my side. "That'll be me soon," he said confidently.

"You—in the band?" I said, feeling the dark lump of jealousy and disappointment in my stomach.

"Going to start on the chanter next week," he said. "You've got to learn that first. Then you get on the pipes."

"That'll be good," I said, watching the band wheeling. "Wish it was me." As it turned out I was not even permitted to march behind the band in the parade.

Now, at this distance, I can think of it and know with certainty that nothing ever hurt me so much in my entire life as that refusal. The Gaffer had us all on the benches in the chapel, picking us out in fours for the marching column. He pointed to boys of matching sizes and each quartet went out into the playground to form up.

I was fairly tall, and I had reasonable expectations of being chosen for the first few ranks. But the Gaffer's thin finger stabbed around: "You, you, you, you," and "You, you, you, you," and the icy realization came that he had gone past my height group and was now picking the shorter boys. Gradually, the room thinned and emptied, until I sat there with three or four other kids. Outside we could hear the pipes whining and warming up and the drums shuddering. The Gaffer said briefly, "Right, you go and get changed."

I could hardly see my way out for tears. I went to the dormitory and got my working clothes on and looked out of the window at the splendid column curving round the playground, with the pipes and drums setting the pace and the tune. The Gaffer, like an old soldier, marched beside them with a stick.

Off they went, out of the main gate, and down Kingston Hill. I sat on my bed and wondered what I had done to be left out. I did not know then, and I still don't. Unless it was that the Gaffer thought I was too skinny to be a good advertisement.

THROUGH GENERATIONS of boys a slang had been evolved at Dickies, an insular language that left strangers mystified, and which you had to learn from the start. Yet, strangely, the very word "Dickies" had grown without anyone being able to recall or even guess its origin. It was just called Dickies and nobody knew why.

A boy was a kid or, more generally, a guy. Thus a boy from the home was a Dickie guy. We used the verb "to dig" meaning to appreciate, all-unknowing that it was a pet phrase of the jazz world. But there was a shade of difference: to us it meant to appreciate and acknowledge the presence of danger. "Digs! The Boss!" meant the Gaffer was on the prowl.

A scoffer was a kid who ate everything he could get; a freezer was a shiverer in corners. A wildly cross-eyed kid was bosky, so was anything else that wasn't straight. A crook was just a crook, and a pot was a favourite with a member of the staff. Plonk was porridge, toppers were crusts, dush was money and tucks were sweets.

Saturday was dush and tuck day. There was a simple ritual. The Gaffer paid out the pocket money with one hand, then received it back with the other in return for sweets. It might seem harsh now, but it was logic to him, and to us too.

Adventure was always bubbling at Dickies. There was an accepted tradition that, at least once during your term, you should try and reach your former home. It was a sort of journey to Mecca, a tradition glorified by a thousand unlikely stories and adventures.

Running away was called "doing a bunk", and when your energy and ideas were exhausted it was a calculated policy to surrender to the police at about midnight. In this way you ensured a sympathetic supper before going to sleep in the police station, and a beneficial breakfast the next morning before being returned for retribution. Some boys were veteran bunkers, working around the police stations on a circuit, and receiving thus a variety of suppers and breakfasts, without raising the suspicions of the coppers. The more resourceful were at large for many days.

If you were not plotting an escape, there were other things. One red twilight in summer, a stroller in the road was shaken by the sight of a boy in pyjamas climbing along the top of the high golden letters across the front of the home. He tore in to report what he had seen.

The Gaffer politely thanked the informant and strode up the stone stairs. His timing was magnificent. He reached the top dormitory window just as the boy was going past outside, and without fuss he grabbed him and pulled him in. The boy forcefully denied he was trying to die, and added that he was just on the point of winning a tanner bet.

Boys there were in infinite variety. We had boys who were a bit simple and some with the flashing spark of genius. There were kids who wouldn't wash; kids capable of lifting anything from anybody anywhere; kids who could sit at the piano and play Chopin. Some used to swear and some pray, with equal fervour; some were crazy about railway engines, and some had an advanced preoccupation with women. We had one boy who used to sit like a monk, unspeaking and unspoken to, reading, reading, reading. We had another who had all the makings of a master crook, but who lay in the dark dormitory at night and spun a web of breathless adventure as lyrical as a young Stevenson.

Amid all this, in those first weeks at Dickies, there came on me a feeling that I can only remember and describe as a sort of settled happiness. Desolate though the place was, with little enough for comfort and less for love, I realized that this was now my home, and

would be until I was grown enough to go out and find myself some other place. Down at Kingsbridge I had felt no real contentment, because I knew our stay could not last; also, during those months, there had been talk and hope that Roy and I would eventually go back to South Wales to live with our uncle and aunt. But it did not come about. Now, there was no more uncertainty.

This odd contentment at Dickies was not even a matter of making the best of things. After that very first pang of apprehension outside the gate, I never again felt afraid, nor continuously unhappy. There grew from this ugly old place, with its dripping rooms, its hollow dormitories, its riotous boys, a sense of warmth, of familiarity, of fun, of fellowship, that was strong and real. There was a dramatic, unceasing stream of life flowing; a feeling of belonging that grew up all unconsciously.

It was the boys who made it so. Being there was hard or, perhaps a better word, robust. Outside, at school, the Dickie guys were the ruling tribe, defiant, warlike, rollicking, united by their bond and ready for anything. Inside, there was the constant adventure of keeping one move ahead of the Gaffer, and all authority.

Dickies could never be dull. Difficult, but not dull.

Chapter Five

It was a shaded evening in the early summer, and the Gaffer was sitting before us in the chapel. We always had five minutes there after tea, to thank God for all the good things that had happened to us in the day. Quite often, after we had said the prayers and belted out "Build on the Rock", the Gaffer would sit saying nothing.

There would be silence, we fretting to get out and play dusty cricket, he inclined to have a peep at his paper first. He would flicker his hooded eyelids at it, and occasionally say "huh". Sometimes some item would hook his attention, some deserter getting his deserts, some thief with his liberty taken, some drunk banished to the jug, and he would read it aloud to us, as a sort of extra lesson for the evening. He would lick his lips round the words of the prison term and say with more conviction than any prosecutor, "And serve him right too."

On this particular May evening the Gaffer suddenly pecked at his paper like a bird spotting a morsel, and said, "Thirty bob each. That's not bad, is it?"

There was a mumble of agreement that whatever they were, at thirty bob each they weren't bad.

It turned out that the bargain he had perceived was a pair of goats. It was the first act in the introduction to Dickies of the nastiest, most conniving, vicious, stealthy, sly, sinful and stinking inmates it had ever known.

Three of us he sent, to collect his goats. There was Grandpa, a melancholy youth with spinneys of hair growing out of his face, Frank Knights and myself.

We claimed the goats from a piggery somewhere beyond the river at Kingston Bridge, and we knew we were buying trouble. One was fawn and white and the other white. They were both billies. Both had pink, sleazy eyes and sniggering expressions. I have never looked upon two more debauched creatures.

"We oughta brought the cart," said Grandpa, dolefully regarding the animals. "We'll never get 'em back."

The cart referred to was a sturdy hand-barrow which nominally belonged to the Kingston cleansing department and was supposed to be used by road sweepers. The Gaffer had borrowed it years before and had never got round to giving it back.

"We'll walk 'em—like dogs," said Frank, who was one of the brainy kids in the home. "Let's get some string."

The crook who had sold us the goats grudgingly gave us some string, and we tied it round their necks. The putrid pair trotted along willingly.

"It's going to be simple as anything," I said.

"Yerse," muttered Grandpa. "They're too shagged out to cause any bovver. Look at 'em."

The bother came immediately they saw a trolleybus. It was going at a spanking pace and the white goat tried to get underneath it, pulling Frank with a swift decisive tug. Frank gallantly held on to the string, but the goat was going to do battle with the trolley, and nothing was going to stop him.

Fortunately, the bus driver had good reflexes. He hit his brakes ferociously; the ungainly vehicle skidded and stopped. When it stopped the goat, horns down, vile glint in its eye, was three inches from death. Frank was a fraction further away. The conductor of the bus had fallen from the platform onto the road.

There was huge confusion. Traffic squealing, bus driver in a near faint, conductor rubbing his backside, passersby giving advice and trying to tug the goat away from the trolleybus. In the middle of it all the goat I was holding, which had remained placid, had a hearty pee all over my boots. So interested was I in the animated scene that my first awareness of this disgusting act was when the warm water trickled through the lace-holes and soaked my socks.

Grandpa, tugging the string of the other goat with Frank, turned and shouted, "Wot you standing there for? Come and 'elp us."

"I can't," I bellowed, "the thing's just pissed all over my boots."

Everybody started laughing and Frank's goat, with two little frisky jerks, escaped and galloped away in the direction of Kingston Bridge. A whooping posse followed. At the bridge the goat stopped, and looked round mildly as if wondering who was causing all the confusion. Frank regained the string, Grandpa held it with him, and I splashed up with my goat which until that time had been more insanitary than violent.

But there was time. At the centre of the bridge my goat tried to jump the parapet, ending up straddling the coping, with its forelegs over the river and its hind legs on the pavement. In a red panic I released the string and grabbed two handfuls of the scrubby, stiff hairs on its back.

Frank and Grandpa, who were a few paces ahead, turned. "It's trying to get into the river!" I cried.

"Let it," said Grandpa stonily. "Best place for the soddin' thing."

Frank came to my aid, along with half a dozen passersby, and we eventually dragged the goat back; having had its moment of glory it seemed satiated, and content to be led along. So did the other one, and we triumphantly led them into Dickies.

The advent of this pair began a reign of terror. The Gaffer put them first in the fenced-off, grassy area beyond the mudpatch. But he knew more about boys than goats. The following day one was discovered challenging the traffic in the middle of Kingston Hill and was returned by a policeman, who said it could have caused a messy accident and should be tethered.

So the Gaffer had the goats tethered. They apparently liked their tethers because they ate them to the last strand. Chains were the next deterrent, but by industrious and secret tugging both animals were able to remove the stakes from the ground. Then they broke through the fence and flew in fury across the mudpatch, over the playground and through the rooms and corridors, scattering boys and staff.

"The goats are out!" the cry would ring, and we would flee with shrieks and shouts and tumblings. Once the goats plunged down the Death Row passage, with half a dozen boys just in front of their seeking horns and a hundred more shouting encouragement from behind. The pursued boys rushed through the kitchen, and the twin terrors charged round and round the big centre table like tribal devils.

One of them—the white one—found a cloth in which some Dickies pudding had been steamed. It gobbled up the cloth, and within the hour it was dead. Boz, who had been on kitchen duties and had witnessed the entire drama, related it in the dormitory that night.

"After it et the puddin' cloth," he said with relish, "it laid down and sort of swelled up. We thought it was going to go off bang. Then it just conked out."

"Fancy being killed by a Dickies pudding cloth," I remarked.

"It weren't the cloth," Boz said scornfully. "It was the bits of pudding that was sticking on it."

The other goat lived for years. Its escapades continued after its partner's departure, although it steered clear of the kitchen.

THE MUDPATCH, as hard and arid as a moon-desert in summer, and veined with muddy rivers in winter, was our Wembley and our Lord's. There was a boarded fence at the top, cutting us off from the customers on Coombe Hill Golf Course, and at that same end some knobbly trees that had dug their fingers underground and brought them up to bend near the muddy surface like beartraps. They were a potent danger to visiting football teams who did not know them, and we nearly always forgot to mention them. Partly because of this, partly because our goalposts were home-made to our own specifications, and partly because we could play soccer supremely well, we hardly ever lost a match.

We wore the red and white shirts of Arsenal—it was falsely rumoured that Arsenal had given them to us and this gave us added terror—and we thought nothing of hammering in eight or ten goals in a game.

Nearly everybody played. After school, in summer, there would be pockets of rushing, darting footballers all over the mudpatch, and unperturbed in the middle of them a hefty game of cricket.

It was scampering around after a tennis ball on the way to school, during the first few weeks that I was at Dickies, that resulted in my first experience of the comparative comfort of the sickroom. I tripped, the pavement met me halfway, and a few seconds later I was regarding with a somewhat sick interest a forearm that had taken on the shape of an inverted U.

They took me down to the hospital. I had fractured my arm, but they soon had it in plaster, and back I went into the sickbay at Dickies. Korky Leigh, the sick-matron, a fussy, kindly little woman like a mother cat, thought it best I should be there for a while, "to get over the shock", and I didn't mind.

228

The Dickies' football team in later years, captained by Leslie Thomas (centre front). "D.B.H." stands for Dr. Barnardo's Homes.

The sickroom was warm, enclosed and homely. And there was a radio. Not for eight months had I heard the radio, and I saw it like an old friend. In the old days, when the winter was heavy outside and the sky was full of wind, and the pavements were cold and shiny underfoot, we used to cosset ourselves by the fire, Mum and Roy and me, and listen to the radio from Children's Hour until bedtime.

The radio in the sickroom was on a shelf. In the afternoons Korky would switch it on and I would lie happily back against the pillows and listen to the music and the talks about Genghis Khan and Chaucer and windmills and boats and fine deeds and battles and inventions.

Once, in the evening, the Gaffer walked in. He went to the window and gazed sternly over the playground. After some minutes of silence he turned to me. "Fooling about," he said. "No wonder you break your arms."

I restrained myself from pointing out that it was only one arm.

"It's costing me a lot of money," he lied. "Two pounds every time they give you an X-ray. There's a fine thing. It'll take a lot of your pocket money to pay that."

With that he stalked out. He never stopped my dush. He just liked to talk like that.

THERE CAME A DAY in that first summer when at last there was some fullness in the sun. It was a Sunday, and even the early morning had the feel of velvet about it.

In the washhouse Boz came up to me, his mouth frothing pink with the toothpowder that came from the tin plate at the door. "Swimming," he whispered.

"When?" I asked.

"'s afternoon. When she's finished. 'Ampton Court. In the Mole. Pass it on to Bricey and Breadcrumb."

I passed it on. After breakfast the sun swelled out and hung like a challenge in the bursting sky. Stiff in our Sunday suits we marched to church. Marching back, we saw boys heading for the river with their towels and swimming trunks. They were outsiders. Our swim would have to be an adventure in the art of not getting caught.

In the chapel that afternoon Matron bumbled and mumbled, and I could see a bee in a flower by the windowsill. The sun was willing us to come out now. Would she never quit? Now she was on about nicknames. "They are so wrong. We have our Christian names as Christians and we should guard them because God gave them to . . ."

"Monkey."

"Yeah, Breadcrumb?"

"'ow long is she goin' on?"

"Don't ask me."

At last, the Gaffer came in and picked groups of us to go out for a walk. The finger lit on me, and Boz, and Breadcrumb, then Bricey and a couple of others. We strolled as sedately as monks to the front gate, and turned behind the fence. Then we went off down the road like the Sioux after Custer.

It was about four miles to Hampton Court. We ran a hot mile, then plunged sweating and breathless aboard a trolleybus. We whooped over Hampton Court Bridge, across the green on the other side, then slid down the bank to the little River Mole which there slips quiet and unnoticed to the side of the big Thames.

Our swimming trunks were hidden under our shirts. We changed like madmen and flung ourselves into the sweetness of the river. We splashed the water silver, and called to each other with our chins

230

on the silken surface, the breath of our shouts minutely ruffling it.

High up, the big trees looked down like tall men. In some places they bent over the river as though peering at the fastnesses and the fish. And the sun made petals where it touched.

"Monkey," said Boz, swimming up close, "did you know nicknames ain't Christian?"

I gurgled in the river. "Well, what d'you reckon the Gaffer is?" I said.

Chapter Six

Even when you are only a boy, scraping your feet to school or guiding a tennis ball between the cracks and squares of a pavement on the way home, for an unexpected moment you can get mixed up with history.

There was a spring afternoon when the sun meekly shone on the clean brick walls of the gardens on Kingston Hill, and at the kerb was a car, as jet and shiny as a rounded beetle. Bosky and Israel and some of the other boys were bunched at the side of the car, all chewing industriously, and talking and laughing with someone sitting in the back seat.

Many times I had seen this car, and others like it, gliding out of the deep lane between the rhododendrons higher up the hill. Their passengers were always service officers, usually Americans, splendidly uniformed and wearing grim expressions. I did not know then what was going on, but the pink and white cottage under the tunnelled lane had a name that was to become part of a famous story. It was called Telegraph Cottage. Its quiet walls saw the planning of D-day.

The cars that rolled down Kingston Hill from Telegraph Cottage often stopped when their occupants spotted us. They knew us by our blue jerseys and I suppose talking to kids was a change for them. But the car that waited on that pale afternoon seemed to be special. In front, three motorcyclists sat across their machines. Israel and Bosky asked if they could have a look at their guns. The motorcyclists glanced round and a man sitting in the back of the big car waved his hand. Out came the revolvers.

I got to the long flank of the car and saw there were two men in the rear seat, one in smooth khaki with fingers of medal ribbons over his pocket. His hair was sparse and when he grinned it was like a

231

banana. I had seen him in the newspapers. He was a general called Eisenhower.

He was saying, "OK, this is the last pack. Who wants it?"

I had poked my head down to look in at the window. He said, "Here, son. You have the last one." He gave me a packet of chewing gum, and I thanked him. Then he said something to the driver, and the car slid away down the hill with its roaring escort.

In the evening I was sitting on the hot water pipes at the end of the dining hall. I was reading, and I absently took the packet of gum from my pocket. The Gaffer walked in, saw the gum and pounced. He snapped questions at me, as usual giving me no time to answer. He stopped my pocket money for a week and sent me to bed.

"I've told you boys time and again," he snorted, "that I won't have you talking to men—and especially American soldiers."

IN THE EMPTY HOURS of one night I lay sleepless in my bed in the corner of the dormitory, and listened to the slow grind of an aeroplane high above, a pinpoint of sound in the huge and silent sky. The voice of the plane stopped. Silence. Then, far away, but clear, came an explosion.

Flashes like wings of big white birds flew across the dormitory. Guns bit into the dark outside and behind their barrage the air-raid siren sounded.

The kids were tumbling out of their blankets, pulling on their boots and overcoats. Boz, who once he was asleep was well asleep, half rolled over and then shouted irritably, "Shut the bleeding row, will you! Can't anybody get any kip?"

I pulled him out onto the floor and he woke up. Then I clattered down the stone back stairs with the rest, out into the crashing night and down the hole in the ground to the air-raid shelters.

There had not been a serious air raid for months, and none since I had arrived at Dickies, so the shelter was new to me, long and ghostly and damp. But it was a good place to be. We heard another hoarse engine overhead, the same cut-out, the protracted, ominous silence, and then, much nearer this time, the explosion. All night the guns were thumping and we heard the strong, uninterrupted engines of our own hunting planes while we crouched in the damp and the dark.

The summer morning came early and the birds sang in the grey trees as we crawled out of our refuge. The first night of the flying bombs, the sinister doodlebugs, was over.

They returned quickly, however. It was a Saturday, I believe, and the Gaffer wouldn't let anyone out of the place, although we wanted to go swimming. About three in the afternoon a wicked shadow swooped out of the clear sun, swept across the tower, missing it by a wingtip, and exploded on the golf course a hundred yards away.

I was in the dining hall and Marlow, the Gaffer's assistant master, was walking through. He glanced out of the window and saw the falling shadow. "Down!" he cried out. "Everybody down!"

I was quick. I bounced onto the floor under a table, just as the impact of the explosion came. One of the floorboards came up and smacked me in the face. The shudder shattered the windows, flung the doors open, and resurrected the dust of ages in a choking cloud from the floor.

Every day the flying bombs fell. We lived like moles, rushing out to grab meals when we could. One evening there was a lull and the Gaffer trooped us into the chapel where we prayed, sang our hymns, and were nearly obliterated by yet another missile crunching down somewhere much too close.

When we had picked ourselves up, the Gaffer, looking shaken, ordered us to run for the shelters. Our route took us through Death Row, and we were running up the stone passage when Breadcrumb, who was a pace ahead of me, skidded suddenly to a stop and grabbed my arm.

"Blimey," he said. "Look."

The food store was gaping. We looked at each other, and discounting dangers immediately, flung ourselves through the door. We were in an Aladdin's cave of prunes, figs, eggs, sausages, condensed milk, sugar, butter and Lyons' fruit pies. We quickly loaded our pockets and our jerseys with good things, then fled up the passage and tumbled into the shelter just as another bomb shattered the air.

The bombs flew day and night. The Gaffer, ancient and brave, used to come tearing across, through the shrapnel and the hideous noises, his tin hat on the side of his head. He would fall down the entrance to the shelter and then, peering into the gloom, make sure we were all accounted for. Then he would growl, "If I catch anyone outside he'll be for it." Out he would go, back into danger, and run on his elderly legs to another of the four shelters dug around the grounds.

What a man this was. He was a hard old bastard, but he had his own ideas about duty and responsibility. At an age when he ought to have been down in Cornwall growing flowers, he had the lives of a hundred and fifty ragtag kids in his hands. He would have perished willingly, I know, rather than have had any harm come to the roughest, rowdiest young criminal under his care.

WITHIN THE NEXT FEW DAYS we became so exposed that there was nothing for it but to load us onto lorries and escape. Most of the boys found themselves living in two square and sturdy manor houses in Norfolk. But twenty of us had another adventure first.

We went, on a lorry, out of London and north through the small ways of Hertfordshire to a place called Goldings, where Barnardo's have a school.

For a month we were in its strange, military atmosphere, where everything was done to the blare of the bugle—everything, even praying.

On the first night, in the dormitory, with the last washy grey of evening pale at the windows, the bugle blared.

"What's that for?" I asked, as they all began to fall from their bunk beds.

"That's G," one boy said.

"What's G?"

"You 'ave to say your prayers," he explained, getting to his knees.

All around boys were crouching, heads bent, and a low mumbling filled the big room.

"Two queens and two aces ..."

"I've got a flush ..."

"So when this geezer gets to the door the dame is stark naked, see ..."

"I reckon he's better in goal, any day..."

Across on the opposite side of the bunk to me, a boy bent pop-eyed over a paperback book.

Prayers finished with the sounding of another bugle, and everyone got off their knees and resumed their activities. I never discovered why this nightly interlude was called "G". It may have been the initial for God. He must have been well pleased.

Early in the morning the bugle roused us: it summoned us to meals (which were better than at Dickies) and to a strict parade.

Each day the other boys would be marched away to their work. But there was nothing for us to do. Sometimes there was an hour or so of skivvying in the dining hall or kitchens, but for the rest of the day we were free, turned out to grass, as it were, into a large sloping field, and called in when it was feeding time.

There never seemed to be anything to read, so I used to lie back in the grass and think about things until I rolled off to sleep. I wondered sometimes, in those enclosed hours, where my brother had got to, and what my friends were doing in the dusty street back home.

The head at Goldings was a little button of a man who had strong religious feelings and a stronger arm with the cane.

"Gawd," I heard one boy say, "he cracked it down so 'ard I thought my arse was going to come off."

"What for did you get it?" said the boy on the opposite bunk.

"Caught smoking in the dyke. I got six."

"He prays before he canes you," said the other boy. "The last time I had it he told me to wait outside the door. I had a gander through the keyhole. And, d'you know what, he was down on 'is knees praying like mad. I reckon he was praying for strength."

Nevertheless the head's geniality stretched to reading out odd, interesting paragraphs from the newspapers at breakfast time, and to granting a half-day off when there was an especially grisly war film on in Hertford.

OUR EVACUATION TO GOLDINGS proved to be a dubious move, if its object was to avoid the danger of the flying bombs. Although there was no unremitting attack, as there had been at Kingston, the bombs did occasionally nose north above London. One of them brought a frozen five minutes of terror such as we had never experienced in all our time at Dickies.

The air-raid shelters at Goldings had been allowed to deteriorate until they were beyond use, so we were all instructed in the oddest sequence of air-raid precautions that anyone could have concocted in the entire war. When a flying bomb was sighted by a watchman who was stationed on the roof, he would warn everyone by setting off the fire alarms. Then, having been roused to face possible death, we were instructed to put our heads under our pillows.

This extraordinary drill was put into operation on the first night after its announcement. The shrill of the fire alarm—a frightening sound in itself—speared our sleep, and we all lay there, silent and afraid. We could clearly hear the bomb droning across the sky towards us, closer with every long-drawn second. Nobody moved in the dormitory darkness until one boy jumped from his bunk and ran to the window. He took one look, said "Christ Almighty", and dived back to the pillow which was supposed to be his shield.

The flying bomb was very low now, snarling nastily, and the light from its comet tail glowed on and off through the window. I put my head under the pillow and prayed strongly. The bomb went over and crashed somewhere in the country miles to the north.

Chapter Seven

Somewhere along the way, I suppose, there comes to everyone a time when they realize and mark the things that to them are beautiful and good. It can take all one's life, it is true. Or it can occur quite suddenly.

With me it took only a late summer, an autumn and part of a winter. In that time, when I was thirteen, I discovered the things, or the beginnings of them, that I have always loved.

A boy's mind is a circus of excitements. It is full of heroes and villains, deeds and misdeeds; dreams in which he scores goals, or finds fame or treasure, or beautiful and adoring girls. He does not look at a group of trees idling against the sky and find happiness in the way they are. Nor does he notice that some words have shape and colour, nor that music is more than sound, nor that stone and wood are eloquent and lovely. The trees are merely things to climb; words are solid, dull things in the pages of schoolbooks. Music is a jaunty tune to whistle through your teeth. Stones are to throw, and wood is something to cut with your pocketknife.

But the time comes. For me it was like a conversion. I still played football and had fights and threw stones, but I had a new awareness of things.

We had left Goldings after a month and gone to Narborough, a village in Norfolk. About half the boys from Kingston were already there in a large old house just outside the village, on the road to King's Lynn. It was there that I came to know the things I loved.

Afternoons in winter, when the light goes early; water in its wild state, and shadows on water; lanes and roads in summer, empty and dusty; voices calling across fields at night. And strong, sweet tea, and warm jerseys; wild animals who do not see you first; trees, any sort; old maps and books and letters, brown and full of secret things. Every clear morning; simple, beautiful words; seagulls, big blackbirds, and homecomings.

I used to list them. Not just in my head but in a book I kept. In it I would write too the things I had read which I wanted to remember, and anything which had happened to me which was strange, or happy. It was not a diary, although I dated the entries. I kept it secret and showed it to nobody, just in case they thought I was nuts.

Narborough House, where we lived, had a long lap of parkland stretching from the house, and the park had a collar of woods, thick and high, around it. Woods running with animals and flapping with birds, where you could build a tree-house and no one would ever find it. Woods which smelled like a warm oven in summer and crackled frostily in winter. The park enclosed by them was shaggy with rough grass and patched with heather.

Our first weeks there were full of hot days; days, it seems now, of an almost mythical boyhood summer: clean high mornings over the trees, big skies, sun all the time until we were tired, and then the misty evenings. There was not much work to do, so the Gaffer used to release us after breakfast and we would run out across the grass in front of the house. I recall long mornings, stripped to the waist, lying in the grass and reading. They were easy times, stretched out with old Bosky, who despite being wildly cross-eyed was a great reader too, captured by Sherlock Holmes, Biggles and Ballantyne.

About noon one day, Bosky, lank on the grass, threw down *The Gorilla Hunters* and sighed, "Blimey, that was a bleedin' good book." He looked up from behind his glasses to see the frowning form of the Gaffer. The Gaffer had his green suit on because he had been to King's Lynn, and his hands were forced into his jacket pockets.

"What did you say?" he asked Bosky.

"What, sir?" replied the trembling Bosky.

"About the book."

"The book? Oh, the book, sir. I just said it was a good book."

"You said another word."

Bosky thought. "Bleedin'?" he asked anxiously.

"Where did you learn that?" said the Gaffer.

"From the book," shivered Bosky. "It's in there."

"Show me."

Bosky panicked through the pages, but hopelessly. "It says that the bloke had a terrible bleedin' arm," he said lamely.

The Gaffer caught him full on the side of the ear and knocked his glasses somewhere round the back of his head. Then he looked at me. "What have you got?" he said. I showed him my book.

"What's it like?" he said.

"It's a jolly good book, sir," I said carefully.

IN THE AFTERNOONS we went swimming. A wide lake lay low behind the trees a couple of miles away, and in the buzzing warmth around two o'clock Marlow would take a string of boys across the fields. We went beside the river choked green with reeds, over stiles and through the scrub and woods. And then there was the lake, extending to the far distance, to where its shining tail curled round a headland and hid itself.

We swam there every day, stark naked, for no one ever walked that way, feeling the joy and the freedom of the gentle water, diving down through the liquid shadows, racing along the churned surface.

Someone had left a boat by the bank, cleverly made from a big aircraft fuel tank fitted with poles as outriggers. I think it had been left there by airmen who had been moved to another place.

Marlow ordered that only the boys who could swim a hundred yards or more should voyage out on the boat. I had taught myself a version of the crawl which began as a flurry of arms, legs and water, and ended twenty yards later at little short of panic. So I systematically set out to attain an unhurried breaststroke. Every afternoon I set myself a mark and a yard at a time I got to it. Within a week I eased my way along the measured hundred yards under Marlow's scrutiny, and qualified to go on the next trip in the outrigger.

Four of us went. I remember pulling the wooden paddle at the stern and feeling the tubby tank moving under me, across the broad midriff of the lake. We were coated with sun, the sky curved over us and the trees made a fringe around it. There was a heron sitting, still and splendid, on an out-thrust branch, and the water with its lumps of wood and floating leaves slid by without commotion.

MARLOW HAD BEEN INVALIDED out of the RAF and had returned to Dickies as the Gaffer's only assistant. He had achieved the near-impossible of being wholly popular with the boys and being strong enough to command respect at the same time. He could talk with you on equal terms, tell good yarns, and yet never be held in the contempt that familiarity so often induces. When he lost his temper it was best to clear out. Anywhere.

There came a morning when Breadcrumb George sat up in bed and announced that it was his birthday. He was one of those who had never received a letter or a parcel in all his life. But that day one of the kids stopped him and said, "Breadcrumb, there's a parcel for you in the Gaffer's office."

Breadcrumb whooped a foot into the air and tore around, shouting, "Guess what—I've got a parcel! I've got a parcel!"

He couldn't guess who had sent the gift. But it was there. Plenty of the boys had seen it. And about lunchtime the parcel appeared on his bed, beautifully tied, stamped and addressed.

Almost dumb with wonder and happiness he picked it up and examined it. Then he tugged and tore away the string and pulled the paper apart. Out onto his bed shot an avalanche of breadcrumbs.

With the infinite cruelty that only children can inflict the trick had been planned, the bait laid, and the trap sprung. Breadcrumb George sat there crying salt tears, with the crumbs all round.

Marlow walked in. Breadcrumb was a tough character and no great friend of Marlow's. But the master realized what had been done in the time it took him to stride from the door. Never had he been so angry. He howled around, blistering to get his hands on the guilty boys. No one told, so he cancelled the swimming for that day. Then he told Breadcrumb to get cleaned up and put on his best clothes. He collected money from everyone on the staff, bullying it out of half of them, and took Breadcrumb into King's Lynn.

Breadcrumb crept into the dormitory late that night. He put a parcel down on his locker, undressed and got into bed.

"What was it like, Breadcrumb?" came a muted voice from under a blanket.

"Went to the pictures," announced Breadcrumb. "Got a new pair of togger boots and my guts full of cream buns. It was all right."

THERE WAS ANOTHER KID, called Fatty Patterson, who was known as Patty Fatterson. He was a big, usually placid boy with a hare lip, who was pushed around by everyone. Sometimes someone would go too far and with a sudden tornado of temper he would lash out powerfully in various directions, smashing up a few chairs or some plates before his wrath was dissipated.

The explosions were always impressive. One day Marlow got in the path of one of them.

It was in the breadroom. Bread, margarine and knives flew as Patty flung himself into his fury. Marlow went after him, and Patty ran from the house and shinned up a tall poplar tree at the gate with unsuspected agility.

He stopped halfway up. Marlow and fifty boys were down below.

"Come on down," said Marlow.

"Not much," said Patty. "You'll fump me."

"No one is going to thump you," called Marlow. "Just come down. You'll break your neck."

"Leave me alone," hollered Patty. "I'm stayin' up."

He was left. The afternoon gathered itself in and at teatime boys appeared at the dining-room window with fruit pies in their hands, then apples and oranges. Patty, who was an enthusiastic eater, looked down from his tree.

"More fruit pies," someone called out of the window. There was a reluctant shuddering in the tree. Then down Patty came, walked fearfully into the house, like a gunman going to a duel, and joined the queue in the dining room. Marlow was giving out the fruit pies. He looked at Patty, Patty looked at him, the pie was handed over and nothing more was said.

Some of us lost a week's pocket money in bets that Marlow would thump him.

FRUIT PIES would have been a fine treat in former days, but now they, and other good things, appeared on the tables regularly. We also had sugar in our tea.

The place was better too. It had been built as a house, and that made all the difference. Dickies was built as a home, an institution, and all the luxuries in the world would never have made it a house. But at Narborough we had rooms measured in feet instead of yards, with two or three windows in each room instead of ten, with fireplaces, homely mantelshelves and doors that opened and closed.

Although we had less than half the boys from Kingston at Narborough, some had to sleep in Nissen huts that had been abandoned by one of the services and stood like black half moons beneath the cloudy trees in the park. At first I slept in the music room of the house, an elegant oak-panelled place, but before the cold weather arrived I was moved to one of the corrugated huts. This had its compensations, because we were allowed to have roaring fires in the bellies of the iron stoves, and in the dark and secret hours of the night we could cook things on their glowing tops.

After tea one evening the Gaffer told us that an entertainer was coming to amuse us. "He's going to give you a good evening," he growled, "so there's trouble for anyone who plays up. Trouble."

He said this because he had already seen Affie. An hour later we saw him too. He was a young man with a plodding Norfolk accent, large rural boots and dark hair plastered down over his scalp. He had a wart on his cheek, and when we first saw him we thought he was a clown, and the wart part of his make-up.

But Affie was a rustic evangelist. He had a glittering piano accordion, and a humping great book called *The Complete Home Entertainer*. He came to amuse and instruct us, he hoped, to sing songs, and to inject here and there a crafty word about God.

Affie would always end with a short prayer, but he cleverly concealed his true mission by beginning with a simple conjuring trick, which we always saw—and let him know we saw—before it was half through, or some innocently funny rhyme which he had culled from his bumper fun book.

From the opening night, audience appreciation was not high. Affie occasionally took from his book some entertaining problem which he should never have attempted, and he would struggle hopelessly with it on a blackboard until he stood there morose, withered and utterly defeated. Boz or someone would mutter, "Now he's had it," and everyone would laugh.

The Gaffer sometimes poked a suspicious snout round the door and simultaneously attentive silence, or polite laughter, would occur. Then he would go off to his dinner and Affie's purgatory would continue.

Sometimes this yeoman showman would run out completely of ideas, of puzzles, jokes, or songs to sing. He would stand there under the gaze of fifty or more hateful boys who were savouring every second of his discomfiture. Desperately he would cry, "Now who would loike to do a bit of a turn, eh?" Stubbornly we would squat there staring at him. Then he would flush red and say, "The lad that does us a bit of a turn—sixpence to him!"

There would be a savage charge to the front. Chairs would tumble and benches would spring on end into the air like the opening mouths of crocodiles. Affie would have a nightmare job trying to sort out the claims of who was first, and who had the best talent to offer anyway.

One day he picked on Israel. Had he known Israel at all he would have shrunk away, but he didn't. Instead, he asked him what he intended to do for his act. "Dunno yet," said Israel. "Can I 'ave the tanner first?"

Affie wasn't as rural as that. "When you've done," he said.

Israel glared at Affie and announced, "I'm going to sing."

No one had ever heard Israel give vent to any vocal efforts, and when he began he was very flat. But the song gained in interest as it went along, because we all knew what was coming, and waited with pounding anticipation to see how Israel was going to get over his trouble.

The song went:

> *My old man's a dustman,*
> *He wears a dustman's 'at*
> *He killed ten farsand Germans,*
> *And what d'yer fink o' that?*
> *One laid 'ere, one laid there,*
> *One laid round the corner,*
> *One poor soul, wiv a bullet up 'is 'ole,*
> *Was cryin' out for water.*

He was having a bad time. It was not so worrying that Affie was standing there, his face red and astonished. But the Gaffer was lurking by the door, wearing his grimmest look. Israel had to go on. With the inevitability of a pilot in a crashing plane, staring as his doom comes towards him, Israel sang:

> *Water, water, water came at last,*
> *I don't want your water,*
> *So stick it UP YOUR ARSE.*

Defiantly he flung out the last sentiment, knowing that it was too late to go back now. When he stopped there was wild ecstatic applause. The Old Man streaked down the gangway, making for Israel like a rugby three-quarter. One of the big sash windows was open and Israel went through it like a steeplechaser.

Off he ran into the moonless summer night and we could hear him singing afar off. He stayed away for a week, sleeping in barns and hayricks. When he came back the Gaffer gave him a good hiding.

IT WAS STRANGE how we never thought of the Gaffer and Matron as being married. Tall and white, he was still the boss to all of us, to be watched, to be feared, to be circumnavigated. She went on her normal tubby way, pottering about in her sitting room, with her cushions, her chocolates, her budgie, and her everlasting correspondence.

Then, when we were chewing the now monotonous fruit pies at tea one evening, Matron stumbled in bumbling with excitement. She couldn't speak. She had a telegram crushed in her podgy hand and she gave it to the Gaffer, nudging him frantically. He read the telegram and his face altered.

He was an upright-standing man and now he drew himself to attention. "Silence!" he ordered. We were quiet. "I've just had a wire to say that Mr. Desmond, my son, has won the Military Cross." He glared around. "For bravery," he added, somewhat unnecessarily.

Then everybody cheered madly and banged their mugs on the tables. Matron put her arm through the Old Man's, and he patted her wrist and grinned his wicked old grin while the tears ran touchingly down her Pickwickian face.

I was glad for them both.

Chapter Eight

By September the tractors and their sugarbeet wagons were creaking under the red trees, down the road through the village. We would tumble over the tailboards and sit on the lumpy cargoes, cutting chunks from the sweet vegetables and crunching them like apples. So long, and fine, and happy had the summer been that we had all but forgotten the possibility of having to go to school again. Now, we saw the village children trooping up the road to their one-roomed school, where they were instructed by a sweet, dumpty lady.

"We won't ever have to go to school," said Johnny Brice when we were seeking conkers one afternoon. "Stands to reason. There's no room, for one thing. And there's no teachers."

"P'raps they'll bring someone up from Kingston," I said. "I wouldn't put it past them."

I was right. The next Sunday evening, one of the Dickies boys who was in the church choir came flapping down the churchyard path as we reached the gate on our way in.

"She's 'ere," he said, looking, in his cassock, like an angel bringing news. "I got a dekko at 'er."

"Who?" I said.

"Maggie," he wailed. "She's in church. You see. Sod it, that means we'll have to go back to school."

Maggie was angular and earnest, a dedicated woman who could be persuaded into the most gloriously fighting tempers if you kept at it long enough. She had been a teacher at our school at Kingston and, knowing in full the risks she ran, she had sturdily volunteered to travel to Norfolk to educate the exiles.

She was there in church, and after the service she patted as many of our heads as could not escape, and announced that she would be starting school almost immediately. "Half will attend in the morning," she boomed brightly, "and half in the afternoon. We shall be taking over part of the village school—they've been most kind, truly Christian—and I know we will get lots and lots of work done."

As we walked towards home I said to Breadcrumb, who viewed the future with severe pessimism, "Well, it's only half a day. Better than all day."

"With 'er," he said rudely, "I'd just as soon 'ave no day at all."

"She's got one word—what is it?" recalled Boz. "She always uses it when she gets hairy."

"Despicable," said someone.

"That's right," confirmed Boz. "She called me it so many times that I looked it up in the end. It means 'orrible."

ON THE FIRST MORNING we discovered Maggie enraptured by a shaggy and vacant bird's nest which had been hanging out of the hedgerow near the school for weeks. Her bike, big as a bedstead, leaned against a bank of grass.

"It's beautiful," she was cooing, to no one in particular. "See how intricate the little creatures have made their home. I do hope they hatched their family successfully."

She beamed at us, and a new boy called Cabbagepants took the chain off her bicycle while we held her attention.

"We're going to have such fun, such wonderful fun," she laughed as we started off towards the school together. "Oh dear, the chain has come off. Never mind, I'll walk. We will really be able to study nature here," she burbled on. "The changing seasons, the birds and the flowers and the first frosts. Oh, it will be such a happy, happy time!"

The old dear really talked like that. And the sad thing was she meant it. On that sweet autumn morning all the meanness and the hopelessness of the crammed, outdated school at Kingston were no more, for her. She was ready for a new start, a clean fresh effort.

But the boys thought differently. Had she been a gorgeous young thing we would, no doubt, have followed her joyfully through the countryside glorying in nature, and listened to her, still and stunned, in the classroom. But she was not. So life quickly became hell for her.

The village school was one big room. For the purposes of our stay it had been divided down the middle with a thick curtain, the village children on one side and us on the other. This barrier may have kept the others from witnessing our appalling behaviour, but it could not stop them hearing. A lesson would begin placidly enough on our side until a low rumble, like the stirrings of a revolt, would roll; then came outbreaks of shouting and stamping of feet, then violent whistles, until poor Maggie was screaming to be heard over the riot.

The village teacher would cry to her class, "Out, children!" and they would rise from their desks and hurry from the place as though a time bomb had been discovered there. Every time we began the racket she would call for immediate evacuation on the other side of the curtain. It meant, in the end, that the village children were spending all their time in the playground. They used to tell us to keep it up.

Maggie tried so hard to be fair and kind. We usually came in loaded with sugarbeet off the carts, slipped them under our desks and munched them throughout the lessons. She was a bit short-sighted and she had not noticed this. But one day she spotted Boz chewing, and opened his desk. Her face cracked into one of her usual patient, boys-will-be-boys smiles.

"How interesting," she said. "Now, does anyone know what this is?"

"A marrow, Miss," we led her on.

"A turnip."

"A toadstool."

"No, you're quite wrong," she beamed, happy that she had at last caught our interest. "No. It's called a sugarbeet. Now, I'm going to cut this one up so you can each taste it. Just see how sweet it is."

Much to the chagrin of Boz, she patiently segmented the sugar-beet, handing out a small disc to each of us. We chewed with exaggerated delight and enthusiasm. "Yum, yum," we said, and "Ain't it smashing?" She probably never worked out how it was possible for us to go on chewing one small piece of sugarbeet throughout the whole day.

I was as bad as the rest. Once I was stood behind the blackboard as a punishment, and I poked the pegs holding the board out from behind, bit by bit, so that abruptly the blackboard descended on her foot. Everyone thought it was very funny.

Each morning she would bring one of us to the front of the class to read a passage from the Bible. She selected passages from each of the books, starting at Genesis, and one November day, with the rain washing the school's windows, Maggie called me out and gave me the open Bible to recite. I read it as we had always read it, gabbling fast, the quicker the better, to get it over with. But that day, suddenly, I knew what the words were; that put together they sang, like a song. I stumbled, then started again, but more slowly:

> For, lo, the winter is past,
> The rain is over and gone;
> The flowers appear on the earth;
> The time of the singing of birds is come,
> And the voice of the turtle is heard in our land;
> The fig tree putteth forth her green figs,
> And the vines with the tender grape
> Give a good smell.

When I got to the piece about "the rain is over and gone" they all howled because it was teeming outside. But I did not look up. The words of Solomon's song made me ache inside, and I was afraid it might show. I gave the Bible back to Maggie and, although she did not know it, she had taught me her first and only lesson at Narborough. I knew now about words, and I went on seeking them, discovering them, and wondering and delighting in their shape and beauty. For me, Maggie had made a miracle.

AT SEVEN EACH EVENING Miss Sauverin and the other matrons used to sit round their big oval table for the evening meal. They were waited on by the boys, and they would all turn expectantly towards the door as we came in bearing the laden trays and steaming tureens.

246

I got the job just after we settled at Narborough. It was good employment because you received double pocket money, and you could eat anything that the staff had left over from their meal: privileges not to be lightly scorned.

There were two of us: I and a powerful, quiet lad called Peter Lott who started the job on the same night as me. Curiously, I do not remember three sentences passing between us before that day.

Our duties were explained. We had to get up early, lay the staff breakfast table, serve them, get our own breakfast, and wash up before going to school. We did the same at lunchtime, and repeated the performance in the evening. We were also expected to keep the staff dining room swept, polished and dusted, and their cutlery and crockery in good order. At Christmas we got five shillings apiece, and we gave the matrons a two-bob calendar.

On the first night Peter and I served the meal, whispering to ourselves the instructions about which side to put what and how to avoid pouring soup down people's necks. Then we took the dishes to the scullery for washing up.

We were virtual strangers, and although we knew it was traditional for the staff boys to attack whatever was left over, we somehow hesitated. We were silent, dipping the plates in and out and wiping them vigorously.

Eventually, Peter said, "D'you reckon this is going to be all right?"

"Yes," I said. "I 'spect so. More dush, anyway."

We dealt with some more plates. Then he said, "That pie looks good, don't it?"

"Have a bit," I suggested cautiously.

"Might as well," he said, grabbing a lump of brown meat and pale crust. "Go on. You have some."

I had a taste. It was getting cold, but it was delicious. We looked at each other, then like two swimmers at the start of a race, plunged in with both hands. The whole lot went, pie, potatoes and beans. Then we waited for the leavings of the pudding and had that too.

We did the job for nearly a year after that; we became strong friends, and we never left a scrap in any dish.

These fringe benefits were well known to the other boys, and over in the Nissen huts where I went to sleep they suggested, then demanded, that I should smuggle something over for one of the midnight fry-ups on the stove. So one night I stored the leavings of a stew, thick and glutinous, in an empty cocoa tin. When I thought it would be a clear run, I took the tin from its hiding place and made for the door. Standing on the other side was the aproned Miss Sauverin, looking her most severe.

Sliding the tin behind my back I stuck it up my jersey, balancing it delicately on the rim of my trousers, where my belt pushed them out and made a little shelf.

"What's that?" she asked briskly.

"Where, miss?" I said, looking blankly around.

"The thing you have just slipped behind you."

"There's nothing, miss," I answered, turning round and with some deftness sliding the tin to the front of my jersey, so that it was still out of view.

"It seems that you are concealing something!" she exclaimed. "If you do not show me I shall get the superintendent."

Knowing when I was beaten, I took the cocoa tin from under my jersey. She took it, opened it, and peered in at the dead brown curd it contained.

"What is that?"

"Stew," I answered helpfully. "Just stew. Saved from dinner."

"What were you going to do with it?"

"Take it to the hut in case I came over hungry in the night. I often get peckish in the night, miss."

She carried it like a rat out to the waste bin and slopped it in. I watched morosely, thinking of the lads in the hut waiting to use it as a basis for their midnight feast. Finally she dropped the tin on top of the mess and said, "I can't imagine how you could think of eating such filth."

THERE WAS ONE HOUR of one afternoon of that winter at Narborough that I can almost touch, even now.

It was about four o'clock. There was a hard, stony cold in the air and clamped on the land, and I walked across the iron lawns not going anywhere in particular, just towards the distance.

The tufts had frozen solid in the morning and stayed petrified all day. I did not have a coat or gloves, just the blue woollen jersey that I always wore. I kicked at the white hedgehogs of grass as I went, and then stole into a run over the rutted ground.

I felt very good. The coldness on my face melted as I ran further and faster. There was no one around so I shouted, and some wood pigeons, which had been sitting cloaked and hunched like robbers in a tree, broke and curved away into the sky.

They were free and so was I. Free in a place filled with winter.

For a long time I ran, until my knees were red and aching and my breath smoked. At the end of the park there was a tree, a good big tree that I had often climbed in summer. Naked now, it stood alone on the grass.

I went up it easily, each handhold and each place to catch your foot returning to mind readily as I went. Higher up, some of the bark, brittle with frost, came away like a dead skin as I grasped the limb. But I scrambled and kicked and cut my shins on the trunk until, with no breath left in me, I reached the top of the fine tree.

I stood there on its head almost, looking out on the groping afternoon, to the house with its yellow lights, to the last red stain of the sun in the other direction.

Of things done, and things remembered, that is the brightest of them all. The best of all good things is to be happy. And I was happy.

Chapter Nine

On those days the evenings came early, but advanced gently, like old horses wandering home across the fields. The classroom lamp was lit by three o'clock and by the time Maggie let us out it was fully dark. We would gallop down into the village, where the lights from the cottage rooms fell out across the bumpy pavement. The blackout had been ended.

I used to love those glimpses of the warm, hollow rooms. Their fires and their lamps and wooden tables the colour of cheese, their collapsed armchairs and crippled sofas, their indeterminate pictures on the wall and their great square box radios in one corner. To me, on the outside, they seemed so cosy, so safe.

In one of the cottages lived the substantial Mrs. Wright, her daughter Mary, and their dog. Mary was a thin girl with big eyes and nearly black hair in ringlets. She had, like all the village girls, chosen herself a beau from the newly arrived Dickies boys, far back in the history of summer. Local consorts, faithful from early childhood, had been thrown over with typically female lack of ceremony once the new and robust Londoners came.

Mary's boyfriend was Freddie the Fly, a minor leader in the Dickies hierarchy. He would call at the cottage each day and walk with her to school, and we, who had arrived at Narborough late when all the girls had been claimed or allocated, had to be content to watch with some envy.

For me the envy was keen, because I liked the thin girl with the ringlets. I remember waiting at the gate of her house one morning while Freddie the Fly went in and called for her. Out she came with her dog and her mum, and I said to Peter Lott, who was with me, "I reckon old Freddie's got a real bargain there."

Now there was a sort of solid handsomeness about Peter, and as she came out of the gate that morning Mary took an interested look at him and turned shyly away, before turning back for a second look. We went to school with Peter walking next to her and me next to Peter, and Freddie the Fly on the other flank untalked to and wondering what he had done to deserve this.

The drama quickened on the next Sunday, in church, because Freddie was totally ignored and Peter received a tide of warm smiles from Mary. By Monday the transfer was accomplished. Peter had a girl and Freddie the Fly did not.

"But really, I don't want her," Peter said to me. "Straight, I don't. I reckon I'm too young to bother about women."

I was three months older. So I said, if it were all the same to him, I would have her.

"Right," he agreed. "You can have her. But you wash and I'll wipe for the rest of the week. All right?"

This was fair, I considered, so then Peter scribbled a note to Mary Wright saying, in effect, that he had decided that she was not for him, after all, and that his friend Les would be glad to deputize. Freddie the Fly was now out of the contest, and all that had to happen was for Mary to concur, which she did with no fuss, explaining that she liked the quiff which stood up in the front of my hair.

So I gained a girl, and not just a girl but her big bolstered mother, her idiot dog, a cottage, a chair, a radio and a fireplace.

There was no difficulty in escaping to all of them each night. When the matrons had dined, and the crocks were washed, I would slide to the back of the house, through the lurking woods, and out into the main road, where she was never late.

It was always the same. There was one self-conscious kiss, a cold little dab under the frowning wall. Then I would catch her hand, her dog would rustle from under some hedge, and we would run, all of us, to her cottage, where I would sit in the soft, broken armchair with the fire at my feet and the radio at my ear.

"Well, what you always listenin' to that ol' thing for?" my girl would say as she fidgeted and watched me.

Her mother would come puffing in, filling the room in one

movement. She gave me cake and tea and asked me if I would like the radio turned off, and I always said no.

This was something good. Something I had almost forgotten, and I felt it warmly around me again with happiness and sadness, like putting on a familiar coat after a long time.

"Well then, what is on your hair?" said Mary on one of the first nights. She had a voice small like her face, with the Norfolk slur sealing in the end of each sentence.

"Lard," I said, half listening to the wireless. "I swipe it from the matrons' store cupboard."

"It makes that bit in front stand up nice," she observed, studying me closely. "Have you got a middle name?"

"John," I said. "Just John."

"Ahhhh," she breathed. "I likes that name. John. I'll call you Johnny." Thereafter she did.

She was a good girl and asked little. Each night, rain or bright moon, she would walk back with me up the road, our small figures silently together, and the dog going mad somewhere across the fields. When we came to the stables we would stop and kiss again, warmer this time, but still only once. Then I would depart, I hoped mysteriously, through the trees, in truth keeping a fearful eye alert for escaped Italian prisoners of war who, according to the Gaffer, were all over the place.

The romance went on unchangingly for a long time and when it eventually ended she wrote to me an appealing letter which began: "Dear John, I've still got the same dog...."

EVERY DAY MAGGIE, upright as an Indian chief, pedalled her high bicycle to the schoolhouse, no doubt telling herself that today would be better than yesterday, and inwardly knowing that it would, if anything, be worse.

The village children of that year were scarcely educated at all, evacuated at every mumble of an imminent outbreak from the other side of the big curtain. But Maggie stood it superbly. It was a long time before she told the Gaffer what a pirate mob we were at school, and in the meantime she tried to inspire in us some interest in any legal activity.

Some of us she took to Norwich for a day, ushering us round the cathedral, the castle and the cattle market. It was a full day, and we ate our cheese sandwiches and apples and came home, well-behaved enough, on the train to Narborough in the middle of the evening.

The Gaffer made it known on the following day that there was to be an essay competition, judged by someone at head office, and with a grand first prize of five shillings. I wrote about the day at Norwich, called it "An Exertion to Norwich", and moved the Gaffer sufficiently for him to suggest that "Excursion" might be a better word unless the outing had proved particularly tiring. I changed the word. A week later I got the five-bob prize, my first-ever earnings from putting words on paper.

Maggie announced, two days later, that she couldn't take any more. Bedlam was an everyday condition, but water from the flower-pots had been spilled on her feet, someone had stolen her spectacles, and she had a suspicion that half the class had disappeared while she couldn't see. "Despicable, despicable!" she moaned, while the village kids clattered to the door. "Oh, despicable!"

She submitted a list of names to the Gaffer and said she refused to try and control these louts any longer. Gaffer lined us up and walked along with the list in his hand. Each boy's name he checked, and if it were on the paper he delivered that boy a resounding thump round the ear.

When he came to me, he hit me, and while I picked myself up, I clutched in my pocket my precious five shillings prize money, because I expected him to take it back there and then. But he didn't. Perhaps he had some hopes of me as a writer. But probably it just didn't occur to him at the time.

ONE SATURDAY MORNING I saw Boz by his bed, furtively shining his shoes on his counterpane. "This place drives you mad," he said with his everyday aggressiveness. "Stark mad. Nothin' to do. Every blinkin' day."

"Going to bunk?" I asked.

"Naw. But it's dead 'ere. Somewhere lively, I want, just for a bit. I'm goin' to Swaffham if he lets us out."

"Swaffham?" I said. Swaffham was all of five miles.

"Yeah," he said. "I've got two and ten. Want to come?"

"If he pays out," I said, "I'll come."

The Gaffer did pay out and let us out for the afternoon too. Boz and I went down the road to the bus stop, happy because we were free, we were running for a bus, we had four and six between us and we were going to the bright lights.

Swaffham was a small disappointment. It was almost like Narborough's elder brother, touched with the same tiredness, the same oldness, although it did have some shops and a cinema. In ten minutes we had explored its interests, bought some apples, and arrived outside the cinema.

Boz led the way into the foyer, but when we looked at the times of the films his rosy face dropped. "'s no good," he said. "Last bus back is at five, so we'll only see half the blinkin' picture."

"See if they'll let us in for half the money," I suggested. "We'll only see half the film."

Boz became businesslike and strutted to the paybox to put his cut-price proposition to the cashier. The discussion was depressingly short. He came back.

"Old cow," he commented. "Now what'll we do?"

Someone slipped from the darkness and, as they opened the door, we saw a cowboy on horseback wing a man with one shot of a rifle.

"Firing from 'is hip," said Boz expertly, his eyes and nostrils wide as though he had smelled gunsmoke. "Did you see?"

I had seen. "Come on," I said. "We don't get 'ere every day."

We marched to the paybox, thumped down our ninepences, and went in. Inside, in the dark, we became lost in the screen. Mistily, somewhere in the thick air at the side of the hall, there was a clock glowing eerily, like a Hallowe'en pumpkin. At the end of the cowboy picture we had to look at the time.

"Give it another ten minutes," I said. "Let's see the news."

Ten minutes were gone.

"Another five," said Boz. "We'll run for the bus."

The second picture started. We kept glancing at the clock. Then, when the hands had gone so far that we knew the bus was already coughing its way towards Narborough, Boz said, "We'll walk. Save some dush."

We lolled back, like criminals beyond the point of redemption or return. Now we could see the whole cowboy picture through again.

Five steady miles we tramped in the rain. There was no conceal-ment when we got back. We were sent to bed without tea, and the certainty of no pocket money for the next fortnight.

We lay in the shadowed dormitory, with the rain knocking on the window. "Good picture, Boz," I whispered.

"Smashing," he agreed.

Quiet for a long time. Then I heard him stretch out his legs and arms and yawn.

"There's no doubt about it," he said. "When you're in a place like this dump you've got to get out and see a bit of life now and again."

Chapter Ten

When the snow came that year, it came in a storm that blew for two days and one night. The storm was thrilling. Over the top of the woods the snow flew, sometimes horizontally, curving out and down like spume from a hurrying sea. I remember running face into it that night, away from the house, over the crackling park to the Nissen huts, now like igloos and looking much better for it.

It was usually good sleeping in the huts because there were no matrons and no rules, or none recognized, and there were the fires that rumbled, and reddened the iron stoves. But because of the presence of the stoves there were times when excitements became dangerous, and the night of the storm was one. The boys had been out snowballing in the dark and had run in late, soaked, some of them only in their pyjamas. They were shouting and scuffling when I got in after finishing laying the next day's breakfast for the matrons.

I was like a sober man walking late into a party. Spikey Thorn, a reedy lad, was bounding from bed to bed trailing a flaming piece of sacking behind him. The place was running with smoke and I stopped abruptly inside the door as Spikey leaped down the line of beds towards me.

"Good ol' Monkey!" he called, and swung the burning brand downwards towards me. It went like a red curtain across my eyes and I jumped away, running back out of the door into the snow. Outside, I realized it had not touched me. But I flew in through the door again in a temper hardly less burning than the thing which had caused it.

Spikey was circling the fire around his head now. The others were still screaming and laughing at him. Before he could know that I was not joining in the game, I had grabbed the sacking from his hands and stamped out its flames on the concrete floor.

"You blinkin' well burned my face with that, Thorn," I said.

"Didn't touch you," he answered from his stand on the bed.

"I ought to know. You're mad, you are."

Now the boys all began to jeer and shout "Monkey, Monkey, poor old Monkey. Got 'is fur burnt. Ol' Spikey burnt 'is Monkey's tail."

I reached up and gripped Thorn and pulled him down to me, using both fists in my temper until I had hit him down onto the ground. I was everybody's enemy then. They piled on me and levered me away. I blathered and screeched, but they held me down until I was exhausted.

Then they let me go. A kid called Painter, who hadn't been in the home long, came over to me and said, "'Ow about ' fightin' me then, Monkey?"

"Any time," I said.

"Tomorrer," he suggested.

"Any time," I repeated, noting that his eye was steady and feeling my outward sureness crumbling on the inside.

Everyone went to bed. Over the horizon of my blankets I could see the stove, still hot in the dark. I had a convincing feeling that Painter would be a good fighter. He was shorter than me but, I suspected, a great deal harder. I reflected, with no calmness at all, that in the morning we would know exactly where we stood or fell.

The snow stopped when the first daylight came. We went over to the wash-houses, and I washed well away from Painter, but nobody had forgotten, and afterwards he was waiting at the plank bridge that went from the lawn to the park.

Word of a fight travelled swiftly and the encouragers were standing there too. We faced each other silently, circling symmetrically so that our feet fashioned a rough arena in the snow. One's breath always felt tight like a drum when one started a fight, and I could feel my heart banging against the drum now.

Shouted on by the boys, who wanted to see blood on the snow, we closed, and jabbed in the first blows. Mine caught Painter on the upper arm and he hit me surely on the left cheek, with such a crunching force that I knew then who would be the winner. But the contest went on a good distance. Once I thrust a lucky one to the side of his chin and he slipped and slid. He got out of the snow and came at me like a small tiger. I flew to stem him, but his fists hit me everywhere at once, and abruptly I was looking up at him, and they were all proclaiming him the victor.

Suddenly, everyone became aware that the Gaffer was watching. He walked over to Painter. "That last one was a good one, son," he growled approvingly. "Right on the end of the chin. That's the way to do it." He didn't even look at me.

Everyone went away cheering and I rubbed my bruises and reflected on the lack of justice in the world. The Gaffer might be admiring old Painter's killer punch, but he would have changed his ruddy tune if he had known why I was fighting in the first place.

Muttering, I began to walk away. Then something made me look round. Yes, there it was: my shape in the snow, thin but perfect, with each arm spread out beautifully on either side of the body.

ONE EVENING I FOUND a letter on my bed from my uncle in Wales, with a folded pound note in it as a Christmas present. The Gaffer usually opened letters, and any money that was in them was kept for you and you could draw it half a crown at a time. But he must have overlooked this one.

I pocketed it secretly, and on the Saturday I went down to Narborough station and got on the afternoon train to King's Lynn. The streets there were narrow and hurrying with Christmas people. It was very cold and the wind sped round corners and whistled over the people's heads.

My intent, now I had money, was to buy Christmas presents; but I was standing looking in a bookshop window when it came to me that I couldn't think of anyone to buy them for. There was my brother, of course, but I did not know where he was. My letters to him at Woodford Bridge had brought no response, and somehow I could not bring myself to approach the Gaffer and demand to know where he was. For all I knew he was gone from me for ever. It was Christmas, though, and I would have liked to send him something. For that matter, I still had the half a tin of sweets which my elder brother had sent.

I bought a Christmas card for my uncle, and another for the Martin family, our neighbours in Newport. Then who? I remembered the superintendent of the home at Kingsbridge and his wife, and so I bought them a book in a little case. It had green binding and gold lettering, and looked rightly sober and solid. It was, I remember, *Vanity Fair*, and it set me back six shillings.

I bought myself some splendid banana gloves of imitation leather and then went for a walk down by the harbour. The salty gale was shrieking in from the Wash, and the Lynn fishing boats were leaping convulsively like nervous ladies sitting on a series of pins. The salt smelled good, and it got on your lips in keen crusts. It bit sharply and made my face sore, but I enjoyed the buffeting, the bending into the wind, and the thrill of seeing the bouncing boats. As far as I knew I was the first Dickies boy to come this far unescorted.

Back at the station, I found there was an hour to wait for the train. The lights were on now and I felt the cold getting through me, and eventually went down to the waiting room, where I discovered a big fire energetically jumping up the chimney. I sat and waited for the short hour to go. I examined my banana gloves and decided they were superb, and I read the first two pages of *Vanity Fair* and wondered what on earth it was all about.

IT WAS A FROSTY CHRISTMAS: set, icy weather, echoing and crunchy. We all went to an American Air Force base near Norwich on Christmas Day and ate turkey, sweet potatoes, candied carrots and blueberry pie for dinner.

On New Year's Eve we were in our beds when a throaty plane came in low over the house. It was very near the trees; we could tell that because we could hear it swishing, and we waited in the darkness to see what would happen. It exploded with a double bang, and the next day we saw it up by the lake, all shattered and charred and terrible, and with the body of the pilot still in a forked tree, hanging out clear against the sky.

It was a bitter morning, and the lake was grey, like a happy person grown old and sullen. Our little boat had gone from the landing place. Because we had been so carefree there in summer, and because of the aeroplane and the dead man, we went away sadly, knowing the place would never be the same again.

Chapter Eleven

Some time in January the Gaffer got news that a gang of Irish workmen had moved into his beloved Kingston home. I was in the staff room when he came in, seeking out Miss Sauverin.

"See what they've done!" he cried, waving the letter in the matron's face. "See what happens when you turn your back! They send in the Irish!"

The Gaffer was pounding round the room like an aged and angry wolf. "Irish, they've put there!" he repeated, as though someone was running a circus in St. Paul's Cathedral. " 'Repairing damage in the town!' Well, we'll soon have them hoisted out. Get the boys ready, Miss Sauverin. We're going back!"

"Now, sir?" she quavered.

"Now!" he shouted. "The quicker we strike the better."

It wasn't quite there and then, but within a couple of days the Dickies boys were leaving their exile. Down to the station came half the village. The village girls, including Mary who still had her dog, were all dripping tears, the village boys were grinning, and their schoolteacher, shocked with relief, stood like someone delivered from a dread illness.

At the other end of the journey, the Gaffer disembarked us and we formed up on the platform of Norbiton station. The trek cart was unloaded from the guard's van, and Grandpa and Frank trundled it to the front. Then we marched like a little army on Dickies, the cart our battle wagon, the Gaffer with that hoary old gleam in his eye, the inward light of every real warrior. We were wearing our navy jerseys and shorts and the Gaffer was in his green, hairy suit.

He halted us a hundred yards down the road from Dickies. The sight of the yellow brick tower brought a flush to the Old Man's gaunt cheeks. He was the general, about to rush the enemy.

"Straighten up," he said, cruising up and down his troops like Wellington before Waterloo. "Now—quick march."

We swung round the corner of the drive into the grounds of Dickies. Almost at once windows on the first floor were thrown up and two brick-faced, curly-haired Micks poked their heads out and regarded us with interest.

"Halt!" bellowed the Gaffer.

"'Tis a foine bunch o' lads you have there, mister," said one Irishman, leaning on his elbows.

"A stirrin' sight to see," agreed the other one.

The Gaffer, his face set like a pie, regarded them with distaste. "We've come back," he said. "And we are coming in to take over."

"That's good, mister," said the first Mick agreeably. "'Tis a long time since I've had such terrible digs. The quicker you're in, mister, the quicker we'll be out."

This rugged philosophy was ignored by the Gaffer, though it left most of us thrilled. He marched us into the building and we stamped through the old familiar green and cream, the echoing places, like campaigners come home. The Gaffer discovered that the workmen were occupying the front dormitories of Dickies, so he compromised and established us in the back dormitories, threatening terrible punishment to anyone caught fraternizing with the Irish.

ON THE FIRST MORNING after our return I woke up in the seven o'clock winter dark and knew that there was a different and delightful smell on the raw air. Everyone else seemed to be under their blankets, but Boz had left his bed. I slid out and flipped on cold feet along the linoleum, following the summoning aroma.

Boz was crouched on the landing. He looked up and grinned all over his ruby face. "Diggy that lot," he whispered. "Go on, 'ave a dekko."

Stretching round the stair rail, I craned down. The Irishmen were lining up before a steaming altar of sausages, bacon, eggs and fried

258

potatoes. We watched with awful wonder as they filled their plates and went off, apparently not noticing the riches they carried under their noses.

After a few minutes the queue came to an end and the two white-aproned women who were serving wiped their brows.

"Tea, luv?" asked one.

"Wouldn't mind," said the other.

Boz froze with joy as we realized they had gone into the kitchen, leaving their beautiful trays unattended. We slipped down the stairs like a pair of hunting panthers, grabbed something of everything, except eggs which were too slippery, then whirled round and shot up the stairs and onto the landing again, before anyone had caught so much as a shadow of us.

Boz was hopping about in a frenzy, which I took at first for excitement, until I realized that he had two scalding sausages dancing about inside his pyjama jacket. He hooked them out and rubbed his burned stomach, and then we padded back to the dormitory with our loot. There we hunched in the caves of our beds, while the light grew grey across the room, and devoured our sausages, bacon and fried potatoes, like winter squirrels gnawing into a secret feast of nuts.

We more or less finished at the same time, because I looked out and saw Boz's head emerge from his blankets in a small cloud of steam.

"What a scoff!" he grinned. "We'll do it again tomorrow."

Every morning we sneaked off down the empty stairs and made our flying foray while Lil and Mare went for their tea. One day we had to be caught. We were.

"What are you up to?" said Lil, grabbing me by the arm. A sausage slid like a live thing out of my pyjama jacket onto the floor. Boz stood red in the face and red-handed.

"'ere Mare," said Lil, still holding me. "Look at these two. Pinching all the stuff."

Mare emerged from the kitchen, her chin cupped in tea. "What've they got then?" she asked.

Lil made us empty our sizzling prizes onto the table.

"You won't 'alf get it," giggled Mare from her cup.

Boz did his Oliver Twist face and whimpered, "We was 'ungry miss. Starving. 'onest, miss. We don't get enough to eat in Dickies."

"If you tell on us," I said, taking his cue, "we'll be put on the slosh."

Lil became pool-eyed. "The slosh? What's that?"

"Bread and water," said Boz. "That's all we'll get. Don't leg on us, miss."

A sudden big tear slipped into Mare's teacup. "Bread and water," she said. "You poor kids. Give 'em some sausages, Lil. I don't see why those lazy Paddies should 'ave it all when our own kids are starving."

"Nor me," snuffled Lil, loading us up with food again. " 'ere, take these and Gawd bless you."

"Thank you, miss," we said together, making for the stairs.

"Come down again tomorrow," said Lil. "We'll see you get some."

And so we did, each cold dawn afterwards until the Irishmen went away. The other kids could never understand why we gave away our bread and dripping.

IN THE DAYS after our return, the boys who were new to Dickies, who had come to Barnardo's when we were at Narborough, went round hardly able to believe their ill-fortune. Neither the war nor the Irish had been able to change the place very much. Nothing, it seemed, would ever be able to transform it from a building of caves, tunnels, high echoes and cold comfort. The yellow tower frowned from under its pointed hat; square, bleak and strong, as though defying any power to remove it.

The mudpatch was immediately ploughed by football boots, after basking fallow for a whole summer and autumn. Some intrepid grass which had set out cautiously from the fringes towards the centre was soon routed. Everything was as it had always been. Mucky.

OUR SPORTS GEAR always neared the primitive. Footballs were patiently patched: the punctures sought, found and remedied. Togger boots were precious, personal things, gained from all manner of places, guarded and never given up. We repaired our goalposts almost every week, for they frequently collapsed and the goalkeeper was often seriously stunned by the descent of the crossbar.

So when, one evening, the Gaffer brought "Brother Bill" in to meet us, he was greeted as the greatest benefactor since Dr. Barnardo himself. He was going to buy new sports gear for Dickies.

"My name's Bill," he announced loudly, "and I'm from a place called Sydney, Australia. I think you kids have been real sports while the bombing's been on, and I want to do something for you. Think of me as a big brother, kids."

He laughed, and the Gaffer came fairly near to beaming. Brother Bill asked him to select three boys to go out with him to get all the new stuff. On the next afternoon, they all went down to Bentalls store in Kingston.

They rode back in a taxi, an unheard-of delight, loaded with footballs, boots, cricket bats, gloves and pads.

"He's rich as anything," said one of the three boys who had been shopping with Brother Bill. "He got all that sports stuff, and he bought himself a watch and a radio set and some other things. He's got millions, I bet."

The Gaffer summoned us all to the chapel for evening prayers, and we enthusiastically gave Brother Bill a special, extra mention, following the Gaffer's dictation. The Australian was red with embarrassment when we'd finished thanking God for him. He said he was only too glad to do something for such dinkum little sports.

The Gaffer ordered three cheers, and then we sang what we knew of Waltzing Matilda, and waved Brother Bill splendidly off in the second taxi to call at Dickies that day.

Three days later we got the bill. Not just the bill for the footballs and the cricket equipment, but for Brother Bill's expensive wrist-watch, his radio set, and the other oddments he had purchased.

Sadly we sent back the things we had not used. Bentalls told us quietly and kindly to keep the rest, and the Gaffer added Australians to the list of nationalities against which he was prejudiced.

But we did not think too badly of Brother Bill, because the thought of that night and the Gaffer praying for him was worth remembering.

Chapter Twelve

The well-remembered farmyard boots of Affie plodded into Dickies that spring. Affie was in them, and looking as lost as a country mole in a big city. He wore his brown jacket and his solid trousers, and his eye was as evangelical as ever.

Marlow had, sadly, gone away, transferred to another branch. Affie had written for a job and they took him. So he arrived from Norfolk, with his square suitcase and his ploughman's gait, to begin this new life.

It never suited his gentle nature, although he strove hard. Every day he stumped around, greasy hair flung flat across his head, trying to get some authority into his shout but failing miserably as it skidded upwards into a piping shriek. More bread was stolen when he was in charge of spreading than had been appropriated in the entire history of Dickies, and he was often found scouring the sinks that were supposed to have been cleaned by boys.

Affie stuck bravely to the task of identifying himself with our interests. He jogged out onto the mudpatch and brayed about like an old donkey while we played football. Armed with his metal-studded boots he charged the field from goal to goal, plunging about, kicking frantically and, when he connected with the ball, usually sending it vertically into the sky.

With the same crusading enthusiasm he joined in the games of British Bulldog which were battled out on some nights in the gym. There was nothing in the gym except floor. No equipment, no apparatus. It was merely called the gym to identify it.

British Bulldog was a sort of infantry charge by one brigade of boys against another. When Affie joined in there was a tacit arrangement that at some stage both sides would suddenly stop piling onto each other and combine to pile on Affie. He would be ground to the wooden floor beneath an erupting volcano of boys. Bums, arms, legs all stuck from the mountain as more boys piled on the top, Affie's spread-eagled boots and fragile lower legs protruding pathetically from the base.

Eventually the boys would roll off, stunned from effort and laughter, and stagger back and stand waiting to see how Affie would react. But he was bony and hard, and he would gradually get up into a sitting position and look round at us. Then he would smile his good smile and say gently, "Oi always seems to end up on the bottom, don' oi?"

After some time Affie decided to go away to a religious settlement where he could train to serve Jesus. We were sorry when he went, but he sent us a nice picture of himself and some other young men wheeling a handcart along a road. A big notice on the side of the cart said: "God is Love".

Affie was too, in a way.

NOT LONG AFTER Affie there came Walrus. He had a big, sad head and a tobacco moustache with damp ends, and a pipe through which he sucked and blew alternately.

He was a serious and mild man, and another one quite unsuited for the vocation he had taken. Apparently the Gaffer was one of a dying breed, for masters came and went with demoralizing frequency. They strode in straight from the war, with a steady light in their eye, and staggered out weeks, or sometimes days, later, defeated utterly.

262

Like most of them, Walrus tried his best. But for me he contributed something special. He was the first person who ever told me that I ought to be a writer.

This happened after I had caught chicken pox. There was no isolation room in the home, and so the billiard room at Dickies was at last usefully occupied: a bed was established for me in one corner. There, covered in scabs and boredom, I sat and wrote a story about an otter called Sleek.

Walrus came in to see how I was getting on. He read my story and said, "You ought to have a go at being a writer, you did. Wait a minute and I'll go and get some books for you."

I read them all, and wrote frantically while the pox receded. The inner thought, which had been lying there in the darkness from the day at Narborough school when I realized what words really were, had been given nourishment.

When I got back to school I told all the Dickies boys that I was going to be a writer. The trouble was I did not know whether Barnardo's could give any help to boys who wanted to be writers. Carpenters and plumbers were easily placed, and if you showed any erudition you generally got fixed up as a clerk when you left. Would they laugh at me and put me in a shipping office? Would I have the courage to tell them at all?

But so urgent was the desire to know what the reaction of authority would be, that I took a trembling chance and asked the Gaffer. He was warming up to one of his occasional bantering moods one Sunday while we were waiting for Matron to arrive. That weekend he had paid out the dush and distributed the sweets (which no longer had to be purchased out of pocket money) without a murmur. Now was obviously the time.

I got up, gulped, marched up to his chair, and announced bluntly, "Sir, I want to be a writer."

Slightly to my surprise he seemed undismayed by the information. "Right, son," he replied calmly, "head office will fix that. And they'll see that you're a waiter in a good restaurant."

Crushed and horrified I turned away. Now I not only had the problem of becoming a writer, but the considerably more difficult one of not becoming a waiter.

WALRUS, MY MENTOR, left shortly after this, following what became known as the Pudding Incident. Occasionally, when there was anything left over from the day's meals, it was produced in the evening as supper. There was never enough to go round and it was, as always, the fittest and the fleetest who acquired most.

There were some suet puddings, round and heavy, left over one day, and Walrus bore them on a tray to the dining room at about eight in the evening. He stood over them, like a master gunner presiding over a pile of cannonballs, and put up his hands to stem our charge. "Stop!" he bellowed. "First we will say grace."

Then Walrus clenched his eyes and ponderously thanked the Lord for arranging for the puddings to be left over from lunch. It was not a long thanksgiving, but he took his time about it, and when he opened his eyes he saw that not a single pudding, nor a single boy, was left. On tiptoe we had advanced and pinched the puddings from under the devout rising and falling of his wet moustache.

He went like a bull through the entire home trying to trace the puddings before they were devoured, but he never found a crumb.

Expressions like "godless villains", and stronger ones of obvious military origin, tumbled from him. In the end, he packed his bag and went off to where the living was easier and more rewarding.

IN SUMMER THE MUDPATCH would bake as hard as old wood, fissured and grained. We played cricket on it every evening until the light went, and on Saturdays there were proper matches.

One Saturday I was going in to bat when Mr. Pamelly, one of the ebb and flow of masters about that time, called me.

"What are you doing?" he asked. He was a fair, pink man, and he never played games.

"I'm going in to bat, sir," I said.

"How long will you be?"

"Don't know, sir," I said, shocked that he didn't even know the rudiments of the game. "Until they get me out."

"Well, hurry up," he said impatiently. "You're coming down to listen to the *Messiah*."

"Oh," I said. "What's that?"

"It's by Handel," he said. "It's about Christ."

"Christ!" I said.

"Yes," he replied evenly. "About Christ. So get a move on."

I limped in to bat, the top of my one ragged worn-out pad flapping like an old dog's tongue.

"What did Pam want?" asked the kid who was keeping wicket.

"I've got to go and listen to something about Christ," I said, taking guard.

"Smashin'," he said. "Saturday too. That's a ruddy liberty."

Normally I used to get some runs, but that day the second ball carted my off stump some yards, and I turned and walked back. Grumblingly I got into my Sunday suit and followed Mr. Pamelly and three or four other kids down into Kingston, where a local choral society were doing the *Messiah*.

We sat in the gallery of the small church. Even now I can feel my chin hard on the dark wood, smell the dust, and hear the gloriously rising sounds and feel the swelling of exultation within me as they sang. Perhaps I was too easily moved, for it was only a nondescript choir and a church organ, but I know that it swept me away with its splendour and its joy, and I came out into the cool evening street knowing that again I had found something precious.

After that I listened to all the music I could. I walked to Twickenham one Sunday afternoon to hear Moura Lympany play, and sat frozen with disgrace and shame because not only did I begin to applaud between movements, but I did so during a quiet piece in the middle of a movement. Then I walked to Wimbledon and sat in the highest "gods" to see, or hear, for that was the important thing, *Song of Norway* and the music of Grieg. I went to an amateur production of *Lilac Time*, and to see, again from the ninepenny gods, Rawicz and Landauer at the Kingston Empire. I did not know what I was looking for and I had no guide. All I knew was that it was music.

By this time I was getting half a crown pocket money and could afford these luxuries. I also got bus fares to my new school each day and, by running in the morning and walking in the evening, I saved that money too.

One evening I was returning from school when I saw a board nailed to the door of a house. It said simply "Piano Teacher".

I pulled at the string of a reluctant bell. Whoever was inside seemed to have a painful job opening the door, and when it eventually swung inwards she was left coughing and gasping against the far wall of liquorice-coloured wallpaper. She was a little woman, dusty, fragile and old.

"How much are the lessons?" I asked.

"One-and-six an hour," she said gummily. "And you buy your own music."

My surprise and joy at finding instruction so reasonable must have shown. "Have you got one-and-six now?" she said.

I had. "All right then, come on in. We'll start. There's no time like the present, is there?"

265

In her living room there were piles of sheet music all over the place and a huge piano which occupied most of the room. To call it a grand piano would be an overstatement, but a good many years before it would have answered to the name. Its keyboard looked like a mouthful of bad teeth, chipped, yellow, with some missing altogether. There was a Guinness bottle squatting on the bass notes, and a lemon-coloured cat curled up asleep on the middle octaves.

The lady laid hands on the cat. "That's my Moggy," she explained. "He loves having a kip there, don't you, Mog?" She pushed him and he flopped easily, lazily over the lip of the keyboard, like a pile of dough slipping from a pastry board. Then the lady removed the Guinness bottle, which was empty.

We sat down on the stool together and began on the scales. Her fingers met the keys and jolted back again like old people trying to dance. She was probably the worst piano player of her generation, and she would never have made a musician out of me if we had struggled together until I was as ancient as she was. But she was brave and conscientious and happy and we liked each other.

In later lessons we achieved simple tunes, one called "Merry Bells", and another Rubinstein's "Melody in F", but we never made any more ground. I listened with delight still at concerts, and paid diligent attention to my scales, but at the end of many months and many one-and-sixes I still had only "Merry Bells" and "Melody in F" in my repertoire.

Perhaps I did not have it in me. Or perhaps the old lady did not know any more either. It's possible.

THAT AUGUST OF 1945 I went to my uncle and aunt at Barry for a holiday, and I returned sentimentally to Newport to see our house again.

But there was no heartache in the meeting. I had been taken into a different life so far and so fully that returning was only strange, not sad. Nothing much had changed; the holes in the front path had widened and some more of the gate was missing. But the number 39 was still on the top bar of the gate, screwed in with the wrong screws that my mother had used after we had detached it once and taken it away. I looked up at the window of my mother's bedroom and remembered that last morning, when she had embraced us for the final time.

All our friends were still in the street, and they asked me about Roy, but I could not answer them. I was an outsider now, and glad of it in a way. It seemed that I had grown out of the place, I who had travelled and now lived in the great city of London. I had seen Waterloo Station and swum in the Thames.

Only once did I find the old feeling inside me, like it had been before. I was staying with the Martin family, our neighbours in Newport, and one night, at midnight, I jumped awake. Through the open window I could hear people shouting across the road and suddenly the air-raid siren at the bottom of the street began to whirl. The war with Japan, all that was left of the big war, was finished.

All the people were out in the warm night, standing at their gates and drinking beer, just as they used to do during the air raids. Under the lamppost a man was swishing an accordion, playing "The White Cliffs of Dover", and people began to dance. Then the young boys began to run wild, and suddenly I was with them again like we used to be in the old days. A terrifying fire was built in the middle of the road and we went foraging for anything that would burn upon it. We ran down the alleyway behind the shops on the Cardiff Road, in gangs, and began taking the big wooden gates and doors off their hinges for the celebration bonfire. I was with the boys now, completely with them in the thrill and the spirit of the thing, at one with their excitement and daring.

The shopkeepers on the Cardiff Road screamed at us from their windows and I recognized the greengrocer, nightshirted now, who used to say that my whistling through my teeth drove him mad. They were unhitching his gate and he was shouting at them, and it sounded funny because he hadn't put his teeth in.

I jumped in to help, laughing like an outlaw, and bore the gate up the alley to the pyre that was burning the tar off the road.

MY COUSIN WAS CALLED ADRIAN; he was two years and a bit older than me and could drive a car, and he had a girlfriend who wore a flower in her hair. I thought she was beautiful, but Adrian treated her casually and on the day I met her I heard him promise he would take her for a drive in the evening "if he could find the time".

I was aghast that he should treat her so idly. Fancy having her driving along with you in a car—at night! But he was a man of the world, and I could only watch a little segment of his life and feel a bit jealous that this could not have been my life too.

My uncle and aunt were busy most days, and my holiday was happy but full of gaps when I was by myself. Now that I was away from Dickies I felt drifting and often lonely, and I thought that this was how the Outside must be and that I would not fit into it. I went to the pictures a lot by myself, and down to the salt-water swimming pool to practise the crawl.

I used to wear two swimming costumes at the same time, both blue, the holes in one hiding the holes in the other. The town had a swimming gala and, adding a bit onto my age, I put my name down for the fifty yards race for over-fifteens.

On the day, a fine crowd was banked high alongside the pool, full of summer enthusiasm and summer colour. There were dozens of boys in the under-fifteen races, but only myself and one other youth in the over-fifteen event. He was eighteen, muscled, bronzed and lithe, and I stood beside him on the edge of the bath, skinny and with my swimming costumes hanging round my middle like a droopy loincloth.

We bent on the starting edge, the pistol cracked, we dived, and my trunks came down. It might seem funny now, but then it was a moment of horror and shame, with everyone screaming with laughter as though I were the clown of the show. I pulled the trunks up round my bum and, crying tears of anger and rage, I set out after my rival, who beat me by thirty yards. I staggered from the bath, glad that my face was wet anyway so they wouldn't see I was crying. A lot of them were still laughing when I went up to the rostrum to receive my prize for coming second.

The Tarzan youth had been presented with a pigskin hairbrush and comb. I got a hairbrush without a comb, which I bore proudly and happily to my uncle.

THEN AT LAST I went back to Dickies and told Frank and Boz and Johnny Brice all about it, and especially about my cousin's girl with the rose in her hair.

Things had been happening at Dickies too. There had been three bunks, the film had caught fire in the projector on a Saturday night, and two of the kids had been taken to hospital after eating deadly nightshade.

"Gawd, it was amazing," said Bricey. "In the middle of the night Wullie and Herbie suddenly get out of bed and start charging about and yelling out. They're in Little Audrey's dorm and she went to see what was happening and they tried to *do* her."

Little Audrey was a new dormitory matron, young, bespectacled, but an improvement on most, since she was shapely.

"They tried to *do* her?" I gasped. "What happened?"

"Well," gurgled Bricey, "these berries they'd been scoffing are like a ... sort of ..."

"Love potion," said the Professor knowledgeably. "They had belladonna poisoning."

"That's right," agreed Brice. "It made them go all mad and randy. They went straight for Little Audrey. It must 'ave been a scream!"

They rolled all over the beds with the laughter of telling it again, and I nearly choked and the Professor had to bang me on the back.

I was back again. This was Dickies and this was where I belonged.

Chapter Thirteen

Bathnight at Dickies was an hour of tumult and steam; two boys to a bath, and then another pair, and another, until the water became so filthy that a bather emerged dirtier than he entered, and then it was changed. There were four fat baths, water hot enough to be just bearable, and gushing steam. On the night my letter arrived I was sitting at one end of the bath scrubbing my neck, and Cabbagepants was at the other.

Cabbagepants did a bunk from Dickies at least once a fortnight. He was about seven or eight and he was nearly always caught the day after bunking and returned, issuing tears and pledges never to do it again, to the stern Gaffer. He was unhappy because the other kids used to knock him about and jeer at him when he cried, which was often.

That night in the bathroom his knees topped the thick water like mudflats and his face was preoccupied as ever. "Got bashed up twice today," he complained. "I'm bunking from this dump and they won't get me this time neither. When I get 'ome to my mum she'll not 'ave me coming back to Dickies, you watch."

He had said it all before. In fact he was always saying it in some form or another, and I would have forgotten it just as I had the other times had it not been for my own adventure. And his.

A boy came round with the letters, whizzing the envelopes across the room, through the steam. I got mine, a letter in an oval scrawl, hunchbacked across the envelope, but the stamp stuck on very carefully and straight.

First of all I dried my hands on somebody's towel which was on the floor. Then I opened it and sat in the dirty water and read what my brother Roy had written. It was a short note on a single page, which

269

was filled with his big letters falling against each other as though needing support. It was strange too, for it was written in an unsurprised way, as though he had been writing regularly for the whole of the year and a half we had been parted. He was living with foster-parents in a village called Long Crendon, in Buckinghamshire.

I knew I would have to see him again. All the time, I had thought about him and about our life when we were at home with our mother. I still had the half tin of sweets that our elder brother had sent. As I got out of the bath I was working out how to run away.

The next day I went to the public library and looked up Long Crendon on the map. It was about sixty miles from Dickies.

I selected Sunday for the start of my journey to visit my brother, because it was the day we wore our suits and I thought it would be a good idea to go looking presentable. My suit was dark blue, and we had just been given a consignment of eggy yellow ties, which I thought would go well with the banana-coloured gloves that I had bought in King's Lynn. It did not occur to me that either they or the tie might make me conspicuous.

At breakfast I managed to pick up two boiled eggs instead of one, and an extra slice of bread. I also had three apples and about two and eightpence. My original plan had been to bunk immediately after breakfast, but there was a chance that the Gaffer would miss me if I didn't go to church. You could never tell with the Gaffer when he would decide to make a check. So we marched to church like we did every Sunday, and returned to the regular Sunday lunch of jacket potatoes, cold meat and butter beans. After that I was away.

It was my plan to cut across Richmond Park and go from there to Ealing, which was the first of the towns on the map I had drawn of my route to Long Crendon. With me I had the retired music case in which I normally carried my school books, and inside it was the hard-boiled egg, the bread, the apples, a pencil and paper, and my brother's toffees in their tin. The map I had in my pocket.

It was nearly October. As I walked over the grass of the park and under the trees, the black clouds were crowding together and there was one especially big one with the sun shining at the back, the beams flung out as though God himself were behind it. I reached the road and turned towards Ealing.

THE JOURNEY TO MY BROTHER lasted about five days. I walked a good part of the way, resting away from the road every so often in a field or a lane. I got two lifts, one on a lorry and one in a van.

270

At night I slept twice under bridges, once under a railway bridge and once under a bridge across a river, with a small path where the arch and the water touched. There was a leaf-shaped boat pulled up on the path and a tarpaulin in the boat. I lay in the boat, and the rain poured off the bridge into the river making a noise like a waterfall. Even when the rain stopped I couldn't sleep because the bridge dripped into the river all night.

On the other nights I slept on the benches in country bus shelters, with my collar pulled right up and my face turned away from the road so that it would not show up white to anyone passing. But no one bothered me all the time I was on my way. You might have thought that a boy in a deformed blue suit, with a yellow tie, yellow gloves and a music case, would have attracted some curiosity, but I did not. I made sure that I did not look too vagabond by carefully washing in a stream or river as soon as I could each day, combing my hair, and trying to keep my shirt and tie straight.

Before I had set out the thought that worried me most was that I might get so hungry that I would have to give myself up. But on the road there were orchards still bushelled with fruit, and blackberries clustered in the hedgerows; I collected ears of wheat left lying in open fields after the harvesting, and munched them as I went. In Wendover I bought a loaf of bread in a baker's shop, and I bought a couple of buns the next day from another place.

It was a fine journey really. It did not rain very much in the day and although I got tired, I was never sad.

There was plenty to see and think about. As I walked through the strange countryside and the unknown towns, I wondered how Roy would look now. It was a year and half since I had stumbled from the ambulance, with the woman promising that I would see him again the next day, and left him sitting up puzzled on the stretcher, with his small bundle of belongings on the floor.

It was in the late afternoon that I saw the first signpost with "Long Crendon" on it. It was ten miles away, and I knew I would never get there that night. I was tired and there was an autumn wind throwing birds and clouds about in the sky, and singing a song of a cold night to come. It meant sleeping once more in some rough place, cold and aching and afraid again, listening for footsteps and watching for headlights on the road.

I walked for about half a mile further and came opposite a country police station, a house really, with a yard and a notice board. For a moment I had a thrilling feeling that my picture might be on the notice board with the word "Wanted" above it, and a full description, down to my banana gloves, beneath. But there was no notice and nobody seemed to be about either. Then, at the moment when I was about to walk on, I noticed an open shed at the side of the yard. Inside were half a dozen bicycles.

It was a few strides across the yard. I took the nearest bike and ran with it out into the road, where I mounted. It worked. Apart from a tendency for the saddle to slip from side to side with each movement of the legs, it went fine.

Joyously now I rode, my music case hanging from the handlebars, the old bike going along like a charger suddenly freed from its stable. The wind was pushing behind my ears, and pummelling my back, and the grey clouds raced along above me.

The figures on the signposts diminished. At last there was one which said "Long Crendon 1 mile". The road led straight into the village, and I remember a big field with a low wall skirting it, and the road running along by the wall.

My brother was walking across the field, diagonally towards the road, as I pedalled along by the wall. Even though there was dusk and a year and a half between us, I knew it was Roy.

"Roy! Roy! Roy! Roy!" I don't know how many times I called, or why I kept calling like that, because he heard me first time and he knew it was me because he cried back and raced towards the gate.

He was running and I was pedalling. I got there first, but the bike was going at such a pace that it slid beneath me and careered on as I jumped off. I fell over, then got up again, just as he was running to the gate. He was not much different really, a bit taller, but skinny still, and grinning with his broken tooth at the front and his hair straight down over his eyes. He climbed on the gate and dropped over.

We just stood, facing each other, neither of us knowing what to do next. My instinct was to put my arms round him because he was my brother and I loved him dearly, but boys don't do that sort of thing easily. And it seemed too formal, too grown-up, to shake hands. So I said, " 'lo Roy."

" 'ello Les," he said.

"Here," I said, fumbling in my music case, "I've got some toffees for you."

BECAUSE THEY HAD NOT liked his name, his foster-parents called him George. This made me angry at the time, and still does. It was hard that he, at nine years of age, should suddenly be taken from everything he knew and then, after going through the pipeline of the system, should find himself with a new name.

His foster-parents were kind country people with a small house where they made me a bed on the landing. They did not ask me how I had made my journey, and I did not tell them. But to them Roy was George, at school he was George, and it reeked of injustice to me. Roy, after all, had been good enough for his first mother.

I sat on the end of his bed for hours that night and we talked of all the days we had known together, and the days since, and all that had happened. He had been the most unhappy after we had been parted, and he kept writing letters to our mother and getting no reply. When some old neighbours of ours went to see him and told him that she had been dead for a year he had cried, but felt relieved in an odd way too, because he had thought that she did not want to have anything to do with him any more.

He was content now in this small place. It was strange to hear him call the woman in the house Mum, and to hear him say that his father was a thatcher. All the things we had known, the lamppost games on winter nights, the dusty street in August, the Ebbw coal we cut from the black river bank, our friends and foes, our parents and the big black and white cat, were all of a different time and a different place, and would never be ours again.

But he was no stranger to me, nor I to him. For this I was happy and thankful. I had often wondered if he would still be my brother when I found him again. And he was.

ON THE FOLLOWING DAY I took the bike from the front door and returned the way I had come. Roy walked down to the wall and the gate with me. We knew that we would never lose each other again.

273

He climbed on the wall and waved as I went away, and he was still waving as I turned the bend in the road and left the village behind.

Easily now I pedalled back to the police station, into the yard, and replaced the cycle in the little shed with the others. Then I went to the door of the police station to give myself up. A surprised-looking policeman, with no helmet and a cup of coffee in his hand, saw me standing there.

"I'm wanted by the police," I said dramatically.

"Oh, are you?" he said, taking a drink of coffee. "Well, it looks like we've found you, don't it?"

I had a fine lunch there, and a good tea in the afternoon, before they took me back to Dickies in a police car.

I was apprehensive as the journey ended. After all, I had been away nearly a week, and the Gaffer had been known to be tough about things like that. But at the door of Dickies one of the staff matrons accepted me, and sent me upstairs for a bath. She said hardly anything at all and after I had bathed I was told to go to bed.

When the kids came up to the dormitory old Boz sat on the side of the bed and said, "Did you 'ear about Cabbagepants?"

"Did he bunk?" I said, slightly hurt that he hadn't asked me about my adventure.

"That's right," he whispered. "He did a bunk all right. Got on the railway line somehow last night, and a train came along and killed him."

Chapter Fourteen

All the days spun on, full of the things of our life, so full that their passing went unnoticed until they had queued and crowded into weeks and months and then into years. Summer days, and rain on the windows. White winter moons and the oldness of November. Christmases and outings, books and music and fights, and Saturday night picture shows in the gym with the Gaffer looking on, ready to stop the film the moment it became too sexy.

And all the time, as I grew from being just a boy, I made plans for the time when I went through the gate for the last time and the Outside was waiting. Sometimes they were more fears than plans. Fears that life, on my own, would be too difficult.

There was a small builder, I remember, who came to do some work at Dickies, and watched us for a few weeks. Then he said,

"You're a lot of little bastards. If a kid from this place came to me for a job I'd close the cashbox quick and throw him out in the road."

When you thought about it, imagining what might happen in the end, you wondered how many other people there were who would throw you into the road.

Social contacts with outsiders were not encouraged unless they had offered and, after being vetted, had been allowed to take you on some outing on a Saturday or Sunday. Of course, you were on your best behaviour and they were frequently quite as nervous and unsure as you, like someone taking a new dog for a walk, so neither they nor you learned much.

But sometimes something came from one of these insubstantial people which was a blessing for every one of us. A kid called Seek returned one Saturday with a mouth full of chocolate and an old book which some benefactor had given him. Seek was a boy of moods and occasional ages of silence. On this evening he stayed a long time with the book, crouching and shifting on his bed. The person who had taken him out had also given him five shillings, and on the following Monday Seek appeared with a box of electrical bits. He emptied them on the floor in a corner, and proceeded to assemble, from a diagram in the book, a crystal radio set. Coil and condenser, crystal and catswhisker were put together. Then he bought a pair of earphones, promising to pay back the indulgent shopkeeper weekly.

We laughed at him while he was putting it together, but on the day he brought the earphones home we all stood round the bed while he fixed the wires on the terminals. His face was set and anxious. He had scratched some of the black paint off his iron bedrail and looped the aerial wire round it, so that the whole bed, ingeniously, became an aerial. The earth wire was hooked round some pipes at the back of the bed.

Seek clamped the earphones round his doubting face like a halo, winced his eyes up tight, and listened. Nothing. His expression told us that. Then he reached forward and moved the catswhisker wire across the small, silver rock of the crystal.

He had bent low like a worshipper. Swiftly he straightened, joy and wonder and astonishment all moving in his face and in his eyes.

"It's going! I can 'ear it!" he exclaimed with a triumphant exultation that Marconi might have remembered. "Listen! It's music!"

We were all bouncing around the bed now. "Come on, then, let's

275

'ear it," someone shouted. Seek struggled out of the earphones and as soon as he did we all heard the sound of music. The earphones were lying on the bed, in the middle of the grey blanket, and the tune was coming from them. Taa tum tum taa tum. . . .

Within a week there were coggie sets, as they became called, all over the home. Boys lay half suffocating under their blankets until midnight, in secret delight listening to dance music, to Tommy Handley, to the news. We whistled and sang the latest songs, and talked about the plays we had heard. Seek, the aptly named, had found a new world for us.

I shared a coggie set with Frank Knights, who slept on one side of me. It was a good one and we had two pairs of earphones—or eardogs as they were named—fixed to it. Every morning, if you had the eardogs under your pillow, you could hear Big Ben at six o'clock.

I could lie and listen to music while I looked up through the window and watched all the fullness of the night sky. "The Planets Suite" I loved, because I could imagine each one a god riding by on a prancing horse. And "Fingal's Cave", all loneliness and longing. And "Night on a Bare Mountain", "Peter and the Wolf" and "A Calm Sea and a Prosperous Voyage". I travelled with them all, taken by the music to enchanted places. In the morning I was always dead-beat.

But even the precious coggie set was not so prized that it could not be sacrificed when the occasion came about. And it did. It was because of a girl.

Boz and I, and some of the others, were invited to a social evening in Surbiton, and we arrived there stiff as sandwichmen in our best suits and plastered hair. We stood about, and some motherly ladies, heavy with bosoms and scent, gave us sandwiches, sausage rolls and cakes. Then a funny man got on the floor and picked out one of our boys and asked him to go out and join him.

"What's your name?" the funny man asked.

"Willie Dye," said the boy truthfully.

"Will He Die!" exploded the funny man. "Of course he will!"

He collapsed with the weight of his own wit. Everyone bent themselves all over the place with the laughing. Except us. Because it was a pun we'd finished with in Dickies years ago.

Boz simply stood and glared at the funny man. Then a lady gave Boz two doughnuts to pacify him, someone started some music, and we were driven into the middle of the floor to join the outer of two circles, each revolving round the other.

"When the music stops you dance with the person who is opposite you," cooed the lady.

The music stopped and I was standing opposite her. She was about fourteen, rounded and pretty, with a river of gentle hair falling over her neck and shoulders. She stepped forward and said, "We have got to dance."

"But I can't," I said miserably, putting my arms out to her nevertheless.

"Nor me, very much," she said. "Never mind, we'll sort of walk." She said her name was Helen and she had a friend called Kathleen and they often went to the pictures in Kingston. I took a plunge from a great and frightening height and said I'd like to take her to the pictures, and I could bring along a friend who could take her friend. She said that would be all right.

When we got back to Dickies that night, I woke up Frank Knights and said, "'ere, guess what? I've got a date."

He sprang up immediately, wide-eyed. "With a woman?"

"'course," I said proudly. "Met her tonight. She's cracking, Frank, honest she is."

"You didn't kiss 'er or anything like that?"

"Not yet. But I'm taking her to the pictures. And I've fixed you up with her friend."

"YOU HAVEN'T!" he cried out with great joy. "You've got one for me too! What's mine like?"

"I don't know," I admitted. "Only mine was there tonight. But yours is called Kathleen and she's fourteen like Helen, who is my one."

"When's the date?" he asked.

"Saturday," I whispered. "We're meeting them at six o'clock at the bus garage."

"That's smashing," he gurgled in the dark. Then he said, "All we need now is some money." He stretched out his tall, bony body on the mattress and stared up as though trying to see the ceiling through the dark. "There's only one thing to do," he said deliberately, having thought long about it. "We'll have to flog the coggie set."

I was considerably shocked at this. I thought of the late, quiet hours and the music. It was a lot to sacrifice. Then I imagined her again, with the small nose and the nice eyes, and the falling hair. And I thought about us in the dark pictures, me with my arm about her, perhaps touching her hair with my fingers.

"Right," I said. "We'll flog the coggie set."

ON THE FRIDAY we both had haircuts and on Saturday at ten to six we waited on the corner, just a little distance from the bus garage.

"We won't wait right on the spot," said Frank in a voice heavy with experience. "Let them get there first. We don't want them to see us hanging around waiting. It's better to treat women rough."

At six o'clock we decided to wait at the bus garage after all. The buses nosed in and out, the people went past. Two girls walked nearly up to us at quarter past and Frank went stumbling towards them, and I had to pull him back and tell him it wasn't them.

By seven o'clock we knew they weren't coming. Our dream of fair women died with the strokes of the clock. We began to walk slowly back towards Dickies.

"I fancied that Kathleen too," sighed Frank unhappily.

"How?" I said. "You never even saw 'er."

"Well, I just fancied her, that's all. What's it matter anyway?"

Just then we slouched by a cafe with the menu pinned up on the door. Frank stopped and examined it. "You hungry?" he asked.

I stared at him. I had never in all my life had a meal in a restaurant.

"Let's have a scoff," he said, and opened the door and marched in.

It was empty except for a waitress sitting in one corner, her nose an inch from the evening paper. Every table had a nice paper tablecloth on it, with a little island fortress of salt, pepper and bottles of tomato and H.P. sauce in the middle.

We had sausages, eggs and double chips, a piled plate of bread and margarine, and two cups of leather-coloured tea each. When we had finished we were full. I looked across at Frank. "There's always plenty of women about," I said philosophically.

"Bags of them," he grinned wickedly. "Good scoff wasn't it?"

"Cracking," I said. We got the bill for five and twopence, paid it splendidly and left a whole sixpence for the waitress. Then we walked up Kingston Hill and home.

PEOPLE WERE ALWAYS sending things to Dickies. Some of the gifts were sound and useful, but a lot of them were not. The Gaffer would sigh his profound, croaking sigh as yet another diseased bicycle was brightly handed in at the door by someone who thought the poor little boys might like to play with it. Sometimes they even wanted a letter of thanks.

Christmas always brought a mountain of rubbish. One Christmas Eve saw the Gaffer crouched in his office, picking away at his typewriter, accompanied by a stuffed and nasty-looking weasel, half

278

a ton of custard powder, and a Princess Margaret dolls house, the sort of things that are always useful in a home for a hundred and fifty boys.

But sometimes there was something of value. Once, someone brought to Dickies a gramophone which worked, and some records. Frank had just been given a room of his own because he was sixteen, and it was to this room, at the dark top of the Death Row corridor, that he bore the gramophone. For weeks there floated down the stone corridor the wailing of a song called "Isle of Dreams" and a crippled version of Offenbach's "*La Belle Hélène*". They were played twenty times a day, until the grooves had grown deep and the needle dimmed, and the gramophone itself, elderly though willing as it was, groaned to a stop one evening and died of overwork.

It was in this cell of a room with its pale, cold, brick walls, and the wire guard over the window to prevent cricket balls from the playground breaking through, that Frank and I produced Dickies's own newspaper.

It started life as a wall-newspaper, hanging in two big sheets in the chapel, retelling the week's news of the home and school. There were cartoons by Frank, who was going to be an artist, and a short story by me. There was also a rhyme by an erudite boy called Medhurst who was very good at poems, most often completely unprintable. We gave the programme for the Saturday night cinema show and divulged who had been selected for the next football game.

Such was the success of this that we decided to print individual copies and sell them at a penny a copy. There was a jelly substance which could be bought by the tin, boiled in the kitchen and spread over a tin tray. Then you wrote your page of the newspaper in special ink and, when the jelly was set, you laid it on the tray. The ink sank into the jelly and from then on you printed copies of the page by laying them across the inked surface for a few minutes each. Our circulation limit was forty because by that time the jelly was exhausted, and the print sprawled and splodged over the page.

"Sell the good copies to the big kids," said Frank, who was a good businessman, "and the rotten copies to the little 'uns because they won't ask for their money back if they can't read it."

The paper sold well. We began to serialize, without permission because we didn't know we needed it, *The Monkey's Paw*. One day we got to a sentence which said that one character had chased another round the room with an antimacassar.

279

"What's an antimacassar?" I asked Frank as I copied from the book onto our printing paper.

"Never heard of it," he said. "Change it to teapot."

So I did.

We initiated an essay competition with a sixpenny prize for the best effort each week. The first week we got an entry headed: "Why the Gaffer is a Bastard", written anonymously by someone who elaborated on the theme with considerable observation. Frank was all for printing it, but I said the Gaffer would close us down. So we awarded the prize to a kid who, with a sweet ignorance of both biology and history, had written an epic entitled: "My Dad Was Killed in the First War".

The literary side of the paper was blooming, but the technical problems of production were burdening us. Boil it as we might the jelly, once it became overworked, smelled like seaweed and refused to jell. It was expensive, about four shillings a tin, so that on the jelly alone we were eightpence in the red with every issue.

We could not increase the price of our paper because we did not think that the Dickies guys would buy it for twopence, not unless it was a better production. So, with this in mind, I went to a jobbing printer in Kingston. I told him that I was thinking of giving him the contract for printing our home's magazine and asked him to name his price. He said he would have to go into more detail, but he thought it would cost about fifty pounds a month to make a decent job of it.

I felt my knees give a twitch and I looked at him hard. But he had a straight face. So I said, "I'll have to put it to the editor. We'll let you know if we accept your estimate." Then I picked up my school satchel and staggered out, sad because I knew our newspaper was dead.

Chapter Fifteen

When the Gaffer finally went his way, it was like the sinking of an old lean, wooden ship. He had been eager for his retirement for years, but as it approached he grew silent and fidgety and no longer spoke of the hollyhocks he was going to nurture along his Cornish garden fence.

But his age was telling. Boys he pursued, when he chanced on them breaking the law, could now outdistance him, leaving him holding his ribs and giving small puffs into his thin cheeks. He still threatened a good bit, but he did not seem to have the energy or the will to carry out his threats.

If any proof were needed that he was growing soft, it came one morning when Spikey Thorn, who was one of the regular skivvies over at Matron's cottage, approached the Gaffer in the dining hall.

"I've been and gone and killed the budgie, sir," said Spikey, dissolving into plunging sobs at the awful words he uttered. "It's stone dead, sir, in the bottom of the cage."

The Gaffer sat paralysed. The budgie was Matron's verbal foil, her friend and her confessor, to whom she read bits from the letters she wrote to her dear old boys. Matron was away for a few days and her companion was lying slain.

"Are you sure he's dead?" said the Gaffer in a pale voice. "He's not just sleeping?"

"No, sir," trembled Thorn. "I shot 'im dead with my catapult."

We had all known times when Spikey would have been smitten with a single blow. Now, the Gaffer did nothing but utter an uncharacteristic "Blimey" and lean back on his hard chair.

Thorn, it appeared, had been shooting dried peas around Matron's sitting room with his catapult, and Joey, the budgie, had made an ill-timed jump onto his perch at the very moment when one of these small, stony missiles was approaching. It had executed him quickly and efficiently.

"We'll have to get another bird," said the Gaffer decisively. "Matron is a bit shortsighted and one budgie looks much like another." He looked at Spikey with something of the old glint in his eye and said, "And you're going to pay for it, son."

They bought another bird, but trying to pass it off as Joey was like trying to disguise a navvy as a prima donna. The new pet was a labourer-type budgie, whereas Joey had been all sweetness and light. It cawed like a rook where Joey had chirped, and while Matron's late pet had been master of an extensive and pure vocabulary, the new bird could say only one word and that was indecent. But the Gaffer, I like to remember, never revealed the full story of Joey's passing.

Just after this Matron suffered a stroke and when she was sufficiently well to be moved the Gaffer, as gentlemanly and loving to her as he had been his whole life through, took her away to the cottage by the sea in Cornwall.

There she died, and in no great time he followed her.

THINGS BEGAN TO CHANGE for us, our lives widened and we saw, as we grew older, the way we were going. The terrible doubt that we would not be able to accept the outside world, quite apart from it accepting us, the thought that I should never be able to write for a living, the other uncertainties, were settled for us.

Frank was sent to a school of art because he wanted to be a commercial artist. I left school, and Barnardo's with astonishing promptitude arranged for me to take a journalism course in a college on the other side of London. I would have to wait for a term, but I would go there.

In the empty four months of waiting I worked in the office at Dickies. Some evenings in the week I used to go to night school and sit among the girls, doing shorthand and thumping rhythmically at typewriters while a gramophone wheezed "Colonel Bogey". After the first embarrassment I did not mind being with girls; in fact I viewed them with consuming interest.

There was one girl, of about sixteen, who used to talk about music, and I asked her in a casual way if she would like to go to the Albert Hall. With horror I heard her say that she would love to come, and a date was swiftly made. She came from Surbiton and she had a little, pointed Surbiton voice that, to me then, sounded complete sophistication and cool poise.

Now I pondered the financial problem. I was getting five shillings a week pocket money then, but I calculated I would need at least fifteen shillings to cover the cost of this adventure. So I went to the new superintendent, who was a young man and understood a lot of things, and told him I was keen to go to a concert at the Albert Hall and I wondered if I could have three weeks' pocket money in advance.

He agreed, and I went joyfully to the concert.

My girl was waiting, a trifle impatiently because she was like that. But she looked nice with her dark hair and her red coat and her high-heeled shoes. As I went to buy the tickets I felt as big and confident as though I came from Surbiton too. She made a small pouting face when I bought two tickets for the remotest gods, and she grumbled all the way up the stairs, pointing out that at this rate we would never have time for a drink before the concert began.

Fool! Why hadn't I realized? You couldn't just take a woman to a concert and expect her to be satisfied with that. You had to think of other things and other expenses. Like drinks.

I dawdled every step up to the gallery, and to my wild relief, when we got to our seats by the rail, the orchestra was just beginning to tune.

"The last time I came, when I was with Paul," she said sweetly, "we sat down there." She leaned over and pointed to the distant stalls.

"You get a better view up here," I said, sadly but stubbornly.

I leaned on the rail and, as ever, became lost in the splendid and lovely sounds that sometimes drifted, sometimes roared, from below. She sat upright, emitting little sniffing noises, fanning herself irritably with the programme that I had purchased for a precious shilling. She did not read it, she just fanned her face with it.

At the interval, she suggested that we went and had a drink. "Gin and ton for me," she said firmly.

Gin and ton! Whatever it was, it sounded as though it cost quids! Never in my life had I been in a bar of any sort. I would have to tell her, I just would, that there was no going on with this.

But she smiled like sunshine before I could confess and she said, "We'd better hurry, darling."

Darling! This angel, with her high-heeled shoes and her gin and ton, had called me darling! Me with my yellow tie and my suit that not so long before I had worn for my bunk!

The endearment caught me up in a cloud and I staggered towards the bar. She must be in love with me—girls didn't call you darling unless they were in love. All the time she had been hiding it, and doing it very well too. Darling!

I wondered if the woman at the bar had heard her. "Gin and ton please, darling," I said.

"Not so much lip," she replied smartly, and I realized what I had said. "Gin and tonic, is it? That will be one and eight."

I returned to the girl bearing the drink as though it were a love potion. "Gin and ton," I said idly.

"Good," she sniffed. "Aren't you going to have something?"

"I'm on the wagon," I said, feeling immediately pleased that the phrase tripped off so blithely. "Football training, you know. We're not allowed to drink."

"How boring," she said, pouring my one and eightpence down her throat. "Let's get back to this awful concert. Really, when I came with Paul ..."

All the second half I crouched over the rail like a gargoyle, laden with despair now because I had realized that I did not have enough money to pay for both our return fares. The only way out of the mess,

I decided, short of telling her that I came from Dickies, was to take her to Waterloo Station, buy her ticket and remember a sudden appointment on the other side of London.

The picture became composed in my mind. I would take her to the platform and kiss her softly but quickly and, like some strange adventurer, vanish into the crowd. She would sit on the train to Surbiton wondering about this mysterious man with whom she had become involved—well, she did call me darling, didn't she?—and I would walk home.

But I did not even have the satisfaction of this gallantry. When we arrived at Waterloo she produced a season ticket and said I need not bother to pay her fare. At least it saved me the walk. We sat stiffly, politely, on the train all the way to Surbiton. She had not called me darling again and I was feeling wretched. At Surbiton station she fenced with the idea of getting a taxi, but like a glowing fat angel on wheels a trolleybus flew round the corner and we boarded that instead.

Presently she announced that this was her stop, and held out a white limp hand. "'Bye," she said. "Nice evening. See you."

Then she had gone, leaving me wrung out, disappointed, and cursing Dickies and the fate that made me belong to it. If I had taken her in the stalls like Paul, whoever he was, and given her plenty of gin and tons, and got a taxi from the station, it would have been different. We would have madly embraced in the taxi and then ... oh hell, wasn't it murder with women!

By the time I had reached the dormitory I had grown a new skin over the wound. "What was it like?" asked Boz, his red nose sniffing over the sheet. He meant "What was she like?" but there was a certain code of ethics even among Dickies boys.

"Some women," I said casually, taking off my boots, "some of them drive you crackers. You should have seen this one, Boz. Went to the Albert Hall, drinks and all that. She put away the gin and tons, I can tell you."

"The what?" he said.

"Gin and tonics," I said impatiently. "They cost one and eightpence."

"Gawd," said Boz. "One and eight! How much did it cost you altogether?"

"Quite a bit," I said. "Over a quid. But she was worth it."

"I'll bet," he grinned wickedly.

"Goodnight, Boz," I said, sliding down in bed.

" 'night, Monkey."

"Don't call me that."

"Why not?" he asked, genuinely surprised.

" 'cos I don't like it," I said. "It's embarrassing."

MANY YEARS LATER I went back to Dickies. To the satanic tower and the corridors jingling with memories. In one corner of the dining room, with generations of paint over them, I could still see dents on the wall—the scoreboard of how many times Breadcrumb George swept the crumbs from the table into his mouth in one week. There were eight little cuts there, made by Boz and me, showing it was a time of good gleaning for him.

Most things had changed, of course. The formidable shell was the same, nothing but an earthquake could transform that, but inside there was no bleakness now: the dormitories had been divided into small bedrooms and sitting rooms. There was a paddling pool, television all over the place, and a batch of sailing boats in which the boys adventured on the river. At the gate, the same old gate, I saw two boys returning from school with their heads cocked to music from a transistor set.

Long ago they took down the golden words from the front, so no one could climb on them any more. A plate on the front entrance simply informed the arriving stranger that this was Dr. Barnardo's. The mudpatch was all black asphalt, the churned battlefield of our days preserved like Pompeii beneath it.

But, standing at the centre, I saw myself there again, with the ball at my toe, waiting for the touch to Boz on my right to start the game. And again I saw him pound through the mud, stockings hanging over his boots, and with joy hitting the ball under, or over, or occasionally through, the goalkeeper.

Or the mangy goat charging with terror and destruction on his horns. Or one Sunday morning, with the pipe band crying and the Dickies boys marching, and me at the window crying too, and hardly able to see the grand parade through my bitter, wet eyes.

285

And steamy Saturday nights in the gym when Frank Knights was in the projection room working the film, and the hero was about to put the heroine down on a terrible bed of straw. Then the Gaffer, leaping up and waving his arms into the beam of light, and shouting "Stop it! Cut it off! No more of this filth!" And we would have to wait until the next Saturday and an uninterrupted showing of Abbot and Costello.

Every childhood is a meadow. Ours was stubbly and had weeds and stony places. But there was sweet grass too in patches, and days of sun and freedom and happiness. And, at its end, there was the gate to the Outside, and it opened for each one of us, opened only once. Its notice, hung on its top bar, said: "Shut The Gate Behind You", which was an instruction as final as any.

Return as you might, Dickies was never yours again. Yours was the real world, to live in, to make fortunes, or to remain in unremarkable sameness. To journey far and to work and find joy and probably sorrow too.

Boz and Bosky, Breadcrumb, Professor, Grandpa, Bug, Willie Dye, and Monkey too, as much as any of them, are shadows now. And the others too, with their thumping laughter, their dreams, whatever they might have been, and their joyous crimes of old. It was all a strange and wonderful misadventure.

Leslie Thomas

Leslie Thomas has come a long way since leaving "Dickies" in 1958: now one of this country's most successful authors, with sixteen novels, several travel books and two works of autobiography to his credit, he exudes charm and well-being and is plainly a happy man.

Success was not achieved without some hardship, however. His first job on leaving Dr. Barnardo's was with a group of local newspapers in Woodford, Essex, where he progressed from folding papers by hand to actual reporting, until National Service interrupted his new career and took him to Malaya. Throughout his stint in the army (where, as his *Who's Who* entry puts it, he "rose to lance corporal") he was still determined to become a writer, and in 1951 he returned to journalism, eventually joining the London Evening News after several years of local reporting. As the Evening News' special writer he travelled all over the world, covering two royal tours with HM the Queen and attending the trial of the Nazi war criminal Adolf Eichmann in Jerusalem.

Then, in 1964 his first book, *This Time Next Week*, was published to ecstatic reviews, followed in 1966 by the runaway bestseller *The Virgin Soldiers*. Thomas had been wary of writing "yet another war story", but this first novel, based on his National Service experiences in Malaya, became instantly popular and has remained so ever since, selling two and a half million copies to date and also reaching the cinema screens as a highly successful film. Similarly *This Time Next Week*, which Thomas feared would be "too much of an 'Oliver Twist'", has become a classic work, being required reading for social workers specializing in childcare, and also a set book for school examinations.

Now, twenty years on, Leslie Thomas is a contented full-time author. "People still ask me if I've got a 'proper' job," he says with a grin, "and I suppose I could work harder, but what's the point? I want to enjoy life. It's never worth doing anything just for the money." He lives in London with his wife Diana and their son Matthew, and writes in a "very cosy" summerhouse at the bottom of the garden. And we've just learned that his eldest child Lois has presented him with twin grandsons.

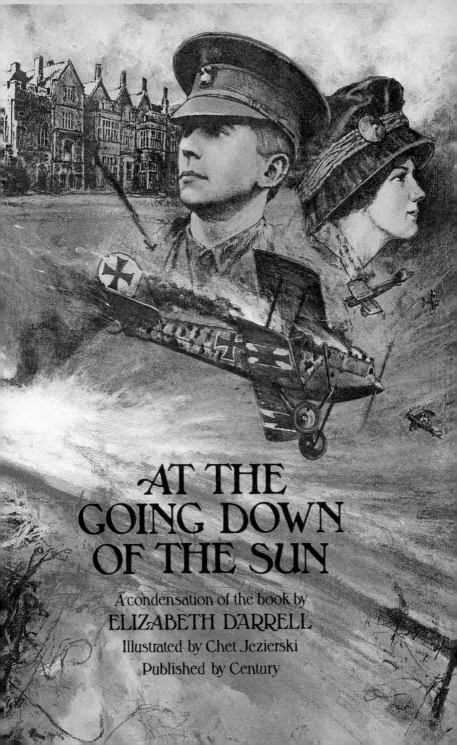

AT THE
GOING DOWN
OF THE SUN

A condensation of the book by
ELIZABETH DARRELL
Illustrated by Chet Jezierski
Published by Century

Summer in Edwardian England . . . and for the three Sheridan brothers, life at Tarrant Hall is carefree and glorious, filled with the joys of youth and the promise of adventure. Roland, the eldest, races his thoroughbreds over the lush Dorset countryside; Rex, the boisterous daredevil, takes to the skies in *Princess*, his beloved flying machine; and Chris, the brilliant scholar, looks forward to Cambridge.

But the month is June, the year 1914, and with an archduke's assassination the halcyon days are over. War is upon them, sending them into the carnage of Gallipoli, the mud-filled trenches and cratered battlefields of Europe. While the women who love them watch and wait, the Sheridans join the desperate fight for the England they hold dear.

A passionate, unforgettable story of love and war . . . and of a golden family facing a world in turmoil.

They shall grow not old, as we that are left grow old:
Age shall not weary them, nor the years condemn.
At the going down of the sun and in the morning
We will remember them.

                                        —*Laurence Binyon*

1

The Sheridans came home for the long holidays that summer of 1914 older, of course, certainly wiser, but basically the same as they had always been.

Rex was the first to arrive, as usual, roaring through the valley lanes that divided sloping meadows full of sheep, scattering those grazing nearest the hedges, setting lazy dogs onto their paws, barking, and drawing the glances of farming men out in their fields, who shook their fists at him. But it was done in a good-natured way, and the men still had broad smiles minutes after he had passed. The barking of the dogs was more joyful than aggressive, and the sheep soon returned to their juicy patches alongside the lanes. The Dorset village of Tarrant Royal had taken Rex Sheridan to its heart from the day of his first childish escapade, and there he was destined to stay.

It was as if the entire village had been listening for the sound of his motorcycle, for his progress along the winding, undulating way was acknowledged by waving, smiling people who had all come out into the June sunshine to see him go by. But, as he approached the centre of the village, his heady speed of more than thirty miles an hour was slowed until he could maintain no more than a walking pace, keeping himself upright by using his legs in scootering fashion on each side of the machine that came second only to one other in his pride of possession.

Plump matrons left their shopping baskets in the middle of the lane in order to crowd round him, questioning him, bringing him up to date with village news. Old yokels waved their walking sticks, and called out affectionate reprimands about noise and fumes, while secretly eyeing the fabulous machine with rheumy envy and longing for the youthful, clean-limbed strength of the second of Branwell Sheridan's sons. Small boys tumbled from doorways and the branches of spreading oaks, eyes glowing with hero worship, to beg a ride on the wonderful self-propelled bicycle. Each one was swung up, in turn, onto the fat petrol tank in front of the rider, and allowed to squeeze the rubber horn, whilst roaring, *"brrrrum, brrrrum,"* in imitation of the engine that was now only softly popping, with an occasional backfire that made matrons shriek with fright, then laugh at their own silliness.

But in the background were other observers, young, pink-cheeked farmers' daughters and buxom maidservants who hung from upstairs windows or stood shyly in doorways, peeping through rose-covered trellises or huge hanging wisteria blooms. They had waited since the Easter vacation for this day. Their hearts beat painfully fast at the manifestation of their dreams of this figure in boots, breeches, leather jacket and long flying scarf, as he sat astride his machine. The leather helmet hid his bright red hair, but he had pushed the goggles up to reveal those merry green eyes, and just one glance at that heartbreaking smile was enough to reaffirm their passion. Of the three Sheridan boys Rex was the least handsome, but he captured hearts along every path, and if he broke them, it was never deliberately.

Impatient though he was, Rex allowed himself to be waylaid by the women who had mothered himself and his brothers through most of their childhood and adolescence; the men who had substituted for a father rarely at home, and with whom he played skittles at the inn and cricket on the village green; the small boys who shared his passion for machines; and the young girls who willingly let him kiss and cuddle them during his vacations. As he finally escaped and drove off towards Tarrant Hall, he spotted the pretty faces among the wisteria and roses and winked his acknowledgment of their blushing greetings. The blushes deepened, and he laughed with the joy of youth and freedom as he turned into the uphill lane that led to his family home.

It was not to the house that he went, but to the flat meadow above it that ran for half a mile along the top of Longbarrow Hill. As he drove over the turf towards a large wooden barn, his heart began to thump at the thought of what stood inside that rough building.

Jake was expecting him. He waited by the open doors of the barn, grinning his pride in displaying his charge, unharmed and in spotless condition, for inspection. Rex shook Jake's hand warmly, then walked right round the aeroplane, worshipping it with eyes that had darkened to emerald with excitement.

"Oh yes, she's worthy of her name," he said. "A real princess."

But the eulogy was short-lived as he began a spar-by-spar, joint-by-joint examination of the biplane he had bought from an airman's widow and rebuilt from the wreck it had become in the crash that had killed the flier. One hour lengthened into two as he talked with Jake, the orphaned ward of the village curate, about the mutual love of their lives—the flying machine. It did not matter that one young man was wealthy, privileged and virile, the other a charity case, crippled in one leg. When they united in praise of aerial exploration, they were equals.

After every inch of *Princess* had been scrutinized, Jake made tea on the oilstove in his quarters above the barn. Rex sat beside him on a bale of straw, and while they drank the tea he told the lad that he had abandoned his studies at Cambridge and secured himself a job in a northern firm specializing in aircraft production. He was due to start in August.

Despite his middle son's aptitude and passion for things mechanical, Branwell Sheridan had insisted that Rex go from public school to university as befitted the son of a gentleman. But Rex had soon realized that he would never gain a degree in *anything*, much less the sciences. This last term had sealed his determination to follow his star. He was twenty years old, and life was full of adventure and promise.

June days were long, so there were maximum daylight minutes to seize with *Princess*. But when Rex finally roared up to the house, it was to hurry inside, swing Priddy, the nanny-cum-housekeeper, off her feet in a bear hug, practically crush the hand of Minks, the aged butler, and thump the three dogs in boisterous reunion before running upstairs with them at his heels.

"Don't bother about dinner," he called over the banister.

"But Mr. Rex, cook has skinned a hare and prepared your favourite asparagus," came Priddy's protest.

He flashed her a smile. "If I kiss her soundly on both cheeks, d'you think she'll give me some eggs and sausages, instead? I'm working on *Princess* tonight, and Jake'll cook them later."

"In the morning, more like," grumbled Priddy. "Once you get round that danged flying thing you forget everything else—even eating." She shook her head with pride and affection.

Laughing, Rex went to change his clothes in anticipation of spending the night in the barn with *Princess*.

The next day dawned blue and gold with a frolicking wind. Perfect flying weather! By eleven o'clock Rex and Jake were ready to go. They wheeled the aircraft from the barn, and the mere act of pushing it was enough to put a thrill of elation in Rex's breast. He could not wait for that lurch of the stomach as the machine left the ground, the dizzy sensation as it rose and banked in a turn, the surging sense of mastery as the patchwork landscape took on a distant enchantment.

Then it was reality, and he gazed over the edge of the cockpit as the whole of Tarrant Royal passed beneath the wings, several hundred feet below. Completely possessed by the effervescence of flying, he circled the village several times, waving to those who stood, faces upturned, in meadows and gardens. At the sight of old Mrs. Hart brandishing her husband's combinations, Rex laughed boisterously, waggled the wings in return salute, then headed off to follow the river towards Dorchester. If he turned north at the abbey and chased the railway for ten miles, he knew he would fly over Gunwater Lake, which was due northeast of Tarrant Royal. A good round trip.

ROLAND SHERIDAN'S PROGRESS through Tarrant Royal was more sedate than Rex's had been the previous day, because he was in the pony and trap Dawkins had taken to the station to meet his train. Branwell Sheridan's eldest son was destined to become a surgeon. There had hardly been a time in his memory when Roland had not been filled with this burning desire, and he had talked his father into allowing him to enter a teaching hospital on leaving school. At twenty-three he had one more year of general medicine before starting on his specialist subject. He had brought home a trunkful of books to study during the vacation.

Not that he intended spending more than an hour or two each week on his studies, because being at Tarrant Hall meant he could indulge his love of riding to his heart's content. Roland Sheridan was a very fine horseman and rider to hounds. His dashing style, his superb understanding of the relationship between horse and rider and his blond good looks ensured that he was greatly admired among the equestrian set. Yet it was into horses' ears that he spoke his innermost longings and emotions, never into those of his fellow men or women. His friends were not close friends, and girls found him no more than quietly polite.

Apart from horses, Roland also had deep feelings about his brothers and his country. He was unshakably convinced that England was the greatest nation in the world. He loved every wall and hedgerow, every meadowlark and spring lamb, every ancient oak and sleepy village, every awesome cathedral and country church. He would also claim the people of his homeland as the most honest, hardworking stock one could find. He was equally loyal to his brothers, and would defend them with his life, if need be. If he had one serious fault, it was that he was totally unforgiving if his trust and loyalty were betrayed.

Progress through the village was spasmodic, since he stopped to chat with the rector; with Ted Peach, the blacksmith; and with the landlord of the George and Dragon Inn. Then he told Dawkins to pull up again when they approached a house with a tiny office attached and a long rambling garden, where he saw the daughter of the village doctor by the gate, cutting honeysuckle. She glanced up, and colour touched her cheeks when she saw who it was. They had known each other all their lives, yet even with this girl Roland was very restrained.

"Hello, Marion," he greeted her, stepping down from the trap. "The garden looks even more splendid this year than last. After the prize again?"

She smiled up at him with a shake of her head. "Mrs. Hobley's wonderful delphiniums will take a lot of beating."

"How is your father?"

"Out delivering Mrs. Baines's fifth. But she doesn't really need him. She has them so easily she could almost do the job herself."

The discussion of a subject like childbirth caused Marion Deacon no embarrassment, because she helped her father in his medical practice. When her mother died two years previously, Marion had left her nearby school to comfort her father. It had seemed natural for her to act as nurse and dispenser under his tutelage, and her gentle nature seemed eminently suited for the cloistered life of the village she loved. Wearing a crisp buttercup-yellow blouse and long grey skirt, she made a beautiful picture, framed by the arch of creamy honeysuckle above the gate, and Roland smiled with pleasure.

At that moment three black labradors raced round the corner of the house to greet Roland with barks and flailing tails. Despite her order to them to get down, they bounced with excitement.

Laughing, Marion said, "They never heed me, as you know."

Looking up from fondling their sleek heads, Roland smiled. "You spoil them, that's why."

"That's not true," she protested. "Anyway, how many times have I seen you give your horses a sugarlump and a pat of encouragement even after balking at a hedge? Yes, and I once caught you kissing a horse, remember?"

"That was years ago," he said offhandedly. Then, to change a subject he felt was becoming too personal, he asked, "Shall you be riding with us in the morning?"

She shook her head. "Damsel has gone lame."

"I'll lend you Shuba," he offered immediately. "Be ready at seven and I'll bring her down for you."

"That's extremely nice of you, Roland."

"Not at all. That's what friends are for."

Silence fell for a moment or two, then she said, "Rex arrived in a cloud of exhaust yesterday. Daddy says he'll break his neck one of these days."

Roland laughed at that. "Not on your life! You know Rex. He has the luck of the devil. But give me horses any day. You know where you are with them."

"You certainly do." She bent to stroke one of the dogs. "I thought you might have travelled down today with Chris."

"He's gone to the Greek islands with a schoolfriend and his family, and won't be here for another month."

Marion looked up quickly. "Oh! Priddy didn't say anything about it when I saw her yesterday."

"She didn't know. Chris scribbled a postcard to me at the last minute, which I only got yesterday. The friend won't see much of him, I suspect. He'll probably wander off on his own to chatter to the Greeks, little thinking that the average peasant won't understand the language of Socrates."

"Poor Chris! It must be terrible to be so brainy. He must feel very lonely at times."

"Oh, I don't think so. Books are the only friends he needs."

"Some people might think that very sad."

Surprised, Roland shook his head. "He doesn't."

But the thought stayed with him as he continued on up to the house. What a strange thing for her to say! His brother had any number of friends. Yet, on reflection, he had to admit that although Chris drew people to him as a magnet attracts iron filings, he managed to remain complete without them. Was that what she had meant? If so, she had mistaken aloofness for loneliness.

Tarrant Hall looked symbolic of all Roland loved, as it came in sight at the end of a long curving uphill drive bordered by horse-chestnut trees. Square, crenellated, covered in ivy, the house was part of England's wild and colourful history. It had been built on the site of an old Norman castle by an eighteenth-century nobleman, and had been sold to Roland's now-deceased grandfather when the line ended, back in 1888. The air of past grandeur it exuded thrilled Roland and made him thankful he was the eldest son, who would inherit it by right. His brothers treated it as just a home; he loved it as part of a national heritage of which he was inordinately proud.

"Hello, Priddy," he said warmly to the woman who greeted him when he entered, "how are you?"

"Fancy asking that when here I am plumper than ever," she chided fondly as he kissed her. "But I'm never better than when you boys are home. The house wakes up during the holidays."

He smiled. "Even a house can't sleep when Rex is in it." Looking round to old Minks and shaking him firmly by the hand, he asked, "Where is he, by the way?"

"Out in that flying machine of his, sir," wheezed Minks.

"Well, better hold dinner until he gets back."

"Meantime, I'll send up a nice tray of tea and some rock cakes," said Priddy. "You must be parched after your journey."

297

"Mr. Roland is a fully grown gentleman, Mrs. Prideaux," reprimanded Minks in his haughtiest manner, "not a schoolboy like Mr. Christopher. I shall take up a decanter and glasses."

"At this early hour!" exclaimed the woman who had practically brought them all up. "You certainly will *not!*"

"I'd love a cup of tea . . . and perhaps you'd bring up the decanter later on," said Roland, the eternal peace lover.

"Very well," said Minks, slightly mollified. "Do you wish to see Mr. Jeffries tonight, sir?"

"No, no. Tomorrow will do. He's been managing the estate without my interference since I was last at home. I'm sure another day will make no difference."

With that, he went up to his room to take off the fawn formal suit in which he had made the journey from London.

Priddy's tea was soon drunk, and before dressing for dinner Roland made his way downstairs again and round to the stables—his home from home when at Tarrant Hall. The Sheridans' stables were extensive. All the Sheridans rode, of course, and each brother had been given two mounts by his father. But Roland had bought three thoroughbreds for himself, and they were housed in luxurious stalls designed to prevent any possible danger of the highly-strung stallions injuring themselves.

Ned Peabody, the head groom, greeted Roland with pleasure as he walked in. "Seen you arrive, sir. Now these varmints'll get some *real* exercise."

Immediately absorbed in inspecting the gleaming flanks of a roan, Roland murmured, "I'm sure you give them all the fuss and appreciation they deserve."

A whinny greeted him as he passed to the next, a grey with strong shoulders, and he stroked its nose while whispering endearments in the pricked ears. In the familiar warmth of the stables Roland lost all track of time as he walked round looking at the animals, discussing their health and diet, and outlining his plans for them during the holiday stretching ahead.

He was just telling Ned that Miss Deacon was going to ride Shuba for the next few mornings, when a growing roar overhead set all the horses fidgeting and snorting with unease.

Roland looked ruefully at the other man. "I suspect it's the volume of noise that provides the thrill for Rex," he said, walking towards the stable door.

THE BROTHERS DISCUSSED aeroplanes and horses and many other things dear to their hearts during dinner, but it was not until they were strolling in the garden afterwards that Rex said, "I take it Father doesn't intend paying us a visit while we're all at home."

Roland shook his head. "I called in at the office before I left London, and Peterson had just returned from Madeira. He told me Father was not too well again. You know what that means!"

Rex sighed. "Mother has been dead for fifteen years, and he is still suffering."

"Only because he indulges his grief," Roland said angrily.

"Oh, I don't know," Rex mused, as they turned down towards the sunken garden overlooking the village below. "Throughout history men have been known to love a woman to destruction."

"Don't you mean distraction?"

"No, I don't," Rex replied. "Incomprehensible though it seems to me, it happens. And men are ruined by it. I'm sure I'd rather not live at all if I had to live in darkness, as Father seems to do."

"But what about us?" protested Roland strongly.

"What about us? Be honest, we've seen him so seldom, it would have made no difference if we'd never seen him at all."

"All right, if honesty is what you want," came the angry response, "this house and estate could be going to rack and ruin and his three sons to the dogs while he sits in a Madeira château he's turned into a shrine. He has no sense of responsibility, no affection for anyone but a ghost. It's morbid, in my opinion. Do you truly think that's what Mother would have wanted?"

"I don't know," said Rex gently. "I was only five when she died. I can hardly judge what she would have wanted."

Roland turned away and walked on ahead. He could see the glow of lamps in the cottages down in the village, that dotted the haze-filled valley with welcome familiarity. Rising up was the damp, dewy scent of lush meadows full of buttercups and dandelions. Crickets were beginning to shrill from all over the darkening hills, and from the woods above the church came the bark of a dog fox. He felt anger almost as a pain in his throat. This village and its people were a monument to a way of life. Squires and yeomen for centuries had taken pride in this land, putting the sweat of their toil into it to make it what it was now. How dare his father turn his back on it to live on some primitive Portuguese island?

A hand fell on his shoulder, as Rex halted beside him to look down on Tarrant Royal. "What you feel for all this is probably what he felt for her. And you more than compensate for his neglect. They are all aware of that."

"I hope so," Roland said reflectively, turning to face his brother in the dusk. "But I can't compensate for his paternal neglect. Young Chris has just walked off with the classics prize, the senior languages award, the Fairley scholarship for Greek and Latin, and the highest marks for English and French medieval literature ever gained by a boy at Charterhouse, and Father was not there to see him receive them. I had important exams and couldn't deputize on that occasion," he finished bitterly.

"I was there."

Roland was surprised. "*You* went?" Warm affection banished his earlier anger. "Trust you not to let him down."

Rex grinned. "It gave all the ladies in flowered hats a shock when I roared into the quad on my machine. It was worth the day out just to see their faces."

Roland laughed as they began walking back to the house. "We'll have to get Chris out of doors as much as possible when he returns from Greece. Once he gets to Cambridge in September, he'll have as much studying as even he could wish. He ought to relax and enjoy himself."

"All right. I'll drag him out for a short spin now and again, if you'll tie him on a horse occasionally," agreed Rex good-humouredly. "But it won't make an atom of difference. I'll wager he's walking round the Greek islands thinking of Aristotle and not even noticing the sultry peasant maidens."

But Christopher Sheridan was not on the Greek islands.

2

Only as the train pulled into Greater Tarrant station, with its white-painted fence and beautifully tended rosebeds, did it occur to Chris that he had not told anyone he was coming. It was a nuisance, for he must now walk the six miles to the village.

"Afternoon, Mr. Christopher," greeted old Carter, waving his green flag and holding out the other hand for tickets. "Surprised to see you, I be. Mr. Roland come through day before lahst, and said you be off to forrin parts like till next month."

"No one knows I'm coming—I forgot to tell them." Chris lifted the suitcase he was carrying onto a rack alongside several milk churns. "I'll have to leave this here to be collected. My trunk is coming freight, so Dawkins can pick them both up when it arrives."

"What you could do with is for Mr. Rex to go pahst on that motorbicycle, or even that arioplane of 'is with no end of a danged racket. He could be up to the house before you could say mangel-wurzels, and send Dawkins down."

"You'll have to get used to aeroplanes, you know," Chris said patiently. "This is the mechanical age. Before long, everyone will be travelling about the country in their own motorcars and going abroad in aircraft. Locomotives will become obsolete."

Carter wagged his head. "Baint no use using them words to me, Mr. Christopher. If you takes my advice, a 'ansome lad like you ought ter be rolling maids in the 'ay, stead o' talking nonsense nobbut another brainbox would understand."

Chris laughed as he left the stationmaster and set out on his long walk. As the handsomest of the three Sheridans he would have had no difficulty finding maids to roll in the hay, had he wanted to. At eighteen, already six feet tall like his brothers, his muscular good looks were completed by fair hair, a fresh-complexioned sensitive face, and dark-lashed, almost violet blue eyes that were wickedly attractive in a man. But those striking eyes were more often than not covered by tortoiseshell-rimmed spectacles that enabled him to see the things in which he was intensely interested. Maids in haystacks did not come into that category.

Three miles along the road Chris came to the lower stretch of the river that ran through Tarrant Royal. He took the lane by the bridge and scrambled down to the water. He was dressed in grey flannels and a striped blazer, and with the temperature in the seventies the walk had made him uncomfortably hot and thirsty. But the river was always low in summer, and he had to go under the bridge and along the bank to find a pool of any depth. He took off his blazer, unknotted his tie and put it into a pocket. Then he knelt down, put his spectacles carefully on the ground beside him, and cupped the clear refreshing water in his hands to drink.

It was then that he heard splashing, and a small cry of surprise. Looking round too quickly, he overbalanced and fell sideways, half into the water and half on the grass of the riverbank. He pushed himself back onto his knees, groping automatically for his spectacles on the damp grass, while he tried to make out the features of what appeared to be a girl wearing a bluebell.

"Are my spectacles around?" he asked her. "I can't see much without them, I'm afraid."

A few small splashes, and she was holding them out to him.

"Thanks awfully," he said as he got to his feet. "You jolly well startled me, you know. I didn't expect anyone else to be here."

"Neither did I," said the girl breathlessly. "Least of all you."

It was not a bluebell that she wore, but a blue cotton dress she held bunched round her knees while she waded in the river. She still clutched it there as she gazed at him in the strangest way, as if she had seen something startling. He could not think why. They had known each other all their lives.

"Oh, it's you, Marion."

"You're wet through, Chris," she said, still breathless.

"I fell in the river, if you remember," he pointed out.

"What are you doing at home, Chris? Roland said you'd gone away with a friend to some Greek islands."

"I was going, but the trip fell through due to this Balkans scare."

"What's that?"

He looked at her in surprise. "Well, for years the Austrians have been hoping for expansion in the Balkans, but they've been hampered by the growing revolt of the enormous number of Slavs living unwillingly in Austria-Hungary. Many people suspect the Mayerling affair was not just a *crime passionnel* but a political murder. So, of course, with Hungary agitating for self-government and . . ." He broke off, realizing she was gazing at him in such a faraway manner she could not possibly be taking in what he was saying, and finished abruptly. "War in the Balkans now could prove calamitous."

Marion was quiet for a moment, then said in a strange voice, "You look awfully different without your spectacles, Chris."

He wondered what on earth had come over her, for she was usually quite sensible. He turned away up the bank and walked towards the bridge. "I'd better go," he said over his shoulder as he hurried off. "My clothes will probably dry during the walk home."

"Chris . . . wait," she cried, scrambling up the bank and running after him. "The pony and trap is on the far side of the bridge. I'm on my way back to the village."

"Good-oh," he said with relief. Together they sauntered back

302

to the road, where they found Dr. Deacon's pony and trap. Chris leaned against the little cart and was polishing his spectacles when Marion materialized mistily before him. She was looking at him in an almost trancelike manner. He climbed into the trap, and held out his hand to help her up.

THE INHABITANTS OF Tarrant Royal were not worrying about an Austrian emperor or his possible invasion of Serbia. It was the day of the twenty-fifth annual cricket match against Tarrant Maundle, their arch rivals. Tarrant Maundle was out for blood this year, having been soundly beaten three times running, mainly due to the inclusion in the Tarrant Royal team of Rex Sheridan, a star player with a reckless style.

Roland was to present the trophy. He was a ready, reliable player himself, but believed one Sheridan on the team was enough. He felt villagers should represent the village, not the sons of the squire en masse—Chris could also wield a bat when forced to.

Chris had been pressured to help erect the marquees. He had dutifully thumped wooden pegs for half an hour on the evening before the match, then felt he had earned his escape back to his books. But he would not have missed the match for anything, because Rex was playing in it. So he was there promptly at eleven that morning, sprawled in a deckchair, with a book of French poems for when his brother was not on the field.

It was not until well into the afternoon that he was able to delve into the book. Tarrant Maundle was all out, and the home team had just begun batting with Ted Peach, the team captain, and young Bill Bishop. Knowing Rex usually came in at number three, Chris abandoned his chair and flopped onto his stomach on the sun-warmed grass, opened the book, and rested his chin on his hands as he translated the beautiful stanzas.

"Hello, Chris. You know, you really can't do that."

He squinted sideways at the girl who had seated herself on the grass beside him. "Can't do what?"

"You can't read while the match is on."

"No one achieves anything with a negative attitude like that, Marion," he said, turning back to his book.

"What is it, anyway?"

"Take a look," he invited, settling his chin more comfortably on his hands as he frowned over two of the verses.

There was a waft of perfume as she leaned closer, and her smooth brown arm was suddenly warm against his own. The contact made him turn his face up to find that she was looking at him, not the book.

"Tell me what it's about," she prompted softly.

"You wouldn't understand it."

"Negative attitude, Chris?" Her teasing words were accompanied by a startling look in her eyes.

"They're French poems. About love," he admitted reluctantly.

"Read me one."

"I can't do that while the match is on," he retaliated, sitting up. "You just said so."

A burst of applause heralded the dismissal of Ted Peach, and Chris looked across to see his brother, in cream shirt and flannels, his red hair glowing, walk out of the tiny pavilion with pads strapped to his calves and a bat in his hand.

"There's Rex coming in now," he exclaimed with enthusiasm, all set to enjoy the game once more. "Just watch him show Maundle the stuff he's made of!"

"You think a lot of Rex, don't you?"

Chris turned in surprise. "Doesn't everyone? He's one of the best people I know."

He looked back just in time to see his brother's muscular arms swing the bat at the first ball and thump it way over the top of the George and Dragon. A great cheer went up from Tarrant Royal spectators, and it was the start of forty-five minutes of fun, excitement and thrills, as Rex cavaliered his way to a score of eighty-one, grinning with pleasure and winking at the girls who shrieked his name in worshipping encouragement.

Meanwhile, the sun had vanished behind ominous clouds, and the storm broke only moments after Rex had been caught, and walked from the field. The rain came suddenly and heavily, scattering everyone in all directions.

Chris got to his feet hurriedly, unbuttoning the front of his shirt to put the leather-bound book inside for protection. Then his arm was seized as Marion said, "Come on! Home's nearest for us."

They ran the few yards to the edge of the green, across the narrow road, and up the long front path to the doctor's house, heads bent against the beating rain. Marion flung open the door of the tiny waiting room, and they both tumbled in.

"Ooh," she gasped, laughing and shaking the skirt of her pretty green and white dress. "I'll fetch us some towels."

Chris carefully took the book from inside his shirt and wiped the leather lovingly with his handkerchief. Then she was back with a soft yellow towel for him.

"Thanks." He put the book on the window seat, then laid his spectacles beside it while he rubbed at his wet face and hair.

"I shouldn't think it'll clear in time for the match to continue," said Marion from a few feet away. She laughed in a high, unusual manner. "All that fuss for nothing!"

He looked up in her vague direction and said, "I should think they'll finish it some other time—tomorrow evening, perhaps. But it won't stop tonight's feast and concert from going ahead, as planned." He reached out to the window seat. Only the book was there. "I say, Marion, have you seen my spectacles?"

There was a curious silence; then she said, "Here they are." Her voice was soft and teasing. "Come and get them."

As sudden as a lightning strike outside that storm-battered house, a feeling of immense excitement rushed through Chris and was gone as quickly as it had come. But it left him intensely aware of the fact that, without those lenses, he could see no more of her than an indistinct pale shape.

"This isn't funny," he said angrily. "Everything is just a blur."

"You really ought to have them, in that case."

"Well, then!" He held out his hand.

"You come here!"

That suggestion of command, the strange breathless note in her voice, and the knowledge that all the time she withheld his aid to clear sight he was somehow in her power, sent the heady painful excitement rushing through him again, this time to stay. He began to move cautiously forwards. But she was either further away than he thought, or she was backing as he advanced.

Swallowing, he tried to control his now erratic breathing before moving off again towards the pale outline of her dress. He walked with his arms outstretched, feeling for her, impatient to catch and imprison her. When his hand finally came into contact with her arm, a gasp betrayed her own heightened excitement, and as he slid his trembling fingers along her smooth skin, she pressed against him to touch her mouth to his.

It was such a soft, moist, warm touch, he kissed her several times, his head pounding more with her every gasp. But then he broke away from her and stumbled towards the door and out into the garden, knowing his peace and isolation had been shattered by something he would be unable to ignore from that moment on.

WITH THE OUTCOME of the match in suspension, the atmosphere during the massive supper was high-spirited and relaxed, each side boasting unmaliciously of certain victory once the battle was rejoined. Outside the village hall the rain still pelted down, but nobody inside cared any longer. Everyone was tucking into meat pies, thick slices of pink juicy ham, crusty rolls, batches of golden scones spread with strawberry jam, apple pies, and great bowls of trifle with cream.

Rex was enjoying himself. He ate heartily, tickled the girls, and drank more than he really wanted in order to be sociable. He felt sorry for Roland, who would probably have no wish to abandon himself to such innocent fun. As the eldest son, Roland was often obliged to stand in for their father, although at twenty-three he was far too young to take on the duties of the leading gentlemen of the village. But the people of Tarrant Royal were yeomen, and demanded a substitute for the absent Branwell Sheridan. So Roland obliged.

As for Chris, he was nowhere in sight, which to Rex was strange. Although his younger brother invariably managed to remain aloof in the midst of any group, he was always hungry. After the tables were cleared away and chairs were placed in rows for the concert, Rex laughingly escaped some of the Tarrant Maundle team who were bent on making him drunk, and pushed his way through the confusion to the back of the stage. Together with three sons of another landowner in the district, Rex was due to perform a song-and-dance number in which saucy words had been put to well-known English folk songs.

The quartet opened and closed the concert with such success that they were mobbed the minute they left the stage. Abandoning all hope of remaining sober, Rex ruefully drank the concoctions mixed amid winks and nudges by the yokels. It was not surprising that he could hardly stand when a group of villagers finally dragged him up to Tarrant Hall on a haycart, tipped him onto his front doorstep, and rang the bell.

The door opened, and three old men stood there.

Rex smiled fatuously. "Hello, Minks. Hello, Minks. Hello, Minks," he recited.

"Can you walk, sir?" asked a dignified voice from one of them.

"Er . . . not very well."

"I'll fetch Frank to assist." Several people then appeared from nowhere, and they all set off towards the study where he was told gravely that Mr. Roland was awaiting him.

As Rex was lowered onto a cushion, Roland came to stand before him. He looked rather strange—almost doubled up. Rex leaned forward with unsteady caution, but still his head spun like a top. "S'matter, old chap?"

After what seemed a long while, Roland said, "There was a telegram here when I got in. Father's killed himself."

Rex felt himself slipping away, but managed to say before passing out, "I'm surprised he waited this long." He did not hear the full tragedy until the next day.

THE DRAMA OF Branwell Sheridan's suicide in far-off Madeira, after losing practically all he owned on the turn of one card, was of much more tragic significance to Tarrant Royal than the death of an Austrian archduke at the hands of a Serbian student in equally far-off Bosnia, although both had taken place on the same late-June day. The villagers had no access to the full details, of course, but rumours ran rife. They were somewhere near the truth.

The vineyards and wine-importing business had been inherited by Branwell's beautiful half-Portuguese wife, who had hated England's climate and was happiest in the sunny, blossom-filled island off the coast of Africa. Madly in love, Branwell had abandoned a political career for the wine trade. But when his wife died, tragically young, he could not bear to leave the island and the house where they had been so happy together. He sent his three sons to schools in England, with a motherly housekeeper and reliable staff to watch over them during their school holidays at the family home in Dorset.

Terrible destructive grief, plus his growing dependence on the heavy wine that had made his fortune, had led to compulsive gambling that lost him all his Madeiran property, the contents of the Sheridan cellars, and the wine-distributing company in London. Fortunately, he appeared to have forgotten Tarrant Hall and the estate surrounding it. He also appeared to have forgotten his three sons. The day after that fatal gamble, he had jumped into the sea that foamed over the rocks around the coast.

The Sheridan brothers were stunned. They all knew life would never be the same again. Rex accepted the sudden plunge into poverty with philosophical resignation. But he felt very sorry for Roland, who was shattered beyond belief; he had inherited a mansion set in a large estate, but no income with which to maintain it. It was a situation he could never have envisaged.

Three days after receipt of the telegram, Rex accompanied his brother to London for a series of painful interviews with the family solicitor who would put the full facts before them. Chris had no wish to go with them. He was trying to cope with a greater upheaval than either Roland or Rex faced. Being the youngest, he had seen even less of his parents than his brothers had, regarding Priddy and Minks as kindly bumbling chaperones, but Rex as his mentor. Chris was very fond of Roland, of course, but it was his middle brother who aroused immense devotion in his breast. Rex was always laughing. He was strong and athletic, recklessly daring, warm-hearted and versatile.

Yet Chris could not tell even Rex what ailed him now. It was like a fever that confused his thoughts and drove him from the house by day; had him sleepless and burning with fantasies by night. Desire had never touched him before. Now it would not leave him alone. He was ashamed that it even overrode the tragedy that had hit the family.

The day his brothers went to London was the first of July, the traditional date of the Tarrant Royal carnival, and Chris waited with growing restlessness for the evening to come. In view of the fact that the Sheridans were officially in mourning, there would be gossip if he was seen there. Yet he planned to go, in the hope of seeing Marion Deacon.

The staff were all leaving early, aside from Mrs. Prideaux and Minks, who felt attendance at the carnival would be a sign of disrespect to the dead, even though Branwell Sheridan had committed the sin of taking his own life. So it was easy enough for Chris to slip from the house after dinner when the old retainers believed he was reading in his room. In the mid-evening air the sound of shouting and music told him that the carnival was well under way. He loped down a wooded slope, then broke through the trees bordering the road. Following a milling crowd towards the fair in Lower Meadow, Chris passed unnoticed. He was looking for just one person. Yet she found him first.

"Chris!" came her voice, vibrant with excitement.

With heart thudding against his ribs, he swung round to see Marion in a tight, sophisticated costume, cheeks dark with a blush, and eyes luminous in the lamplight from the George and Dragon.

"I thought you'd gone to London," she said.

"The others went. I stayed at the house."

They stood looking at each other. Then she said, "I'm sorry about your father and . . . and everything."

He ran his hand through his springy hair. "My father was practically a stranger."

"Poor Chris," she said softly. Then, after a quick indrawn breath, she added, "I'm sorry you forgot your spectacles the other evening. I worried about them, but I didn't like to come up to the house when you had just received such bad news. Silly, I didn't realize you'd have another pair."

"I have to, in case I break them." The last stragglers appeared to have vanished towards the fair, and they found themselves alone in the lane. The stars were coming out in hundreds, and he felt he could not hold back from touching her much longer."

"Well . . . you'd better come indoors and collect them." She began edging away. "In case you break the ones you're wearing."

"Righto," he agreed quickly, striding along beside her to the gate beneath the trellis arch. The scent of honeysuckle was overwhelming as he followed her into the garden and round the side of the house to the attached waiting room where they had gone to shelter from the rain.

It was hot and dark inside that room, and she made no attempt to light the lamp. But the pale wash of the rising moon allowed him to see her outline quite well.

"I think I left them in here," she said, almost in a whisper. "Daddy's out. He was called to old Mr. Wiseman, who's dying."

Almost dizzy with his arousing desire for her, Chris stepped forward to catch her round the waist. With a gasp, she put her mouth up eagerly to meet his as he bent his head. Almost immediately, she gasped again and trembled with delight.

She did not try to stop him unbuttoning her costume and tugging it from her shoulders to bare the whole of her upper body. At first, she showed eager, sighing submissiveness. Then, when his hands slid the rest of her garments to the floor, she began to struggle. But the fight soon went out of her on the examination couch behind the floral curtain. When it was over, they both had tears on their faces—he because it was the most thrilling, elating thing he had ever done. He supposed she was crying for the same reason.

3

Roland felt as if he had been living through a nightmare for the past month. Every morning when he awoke, the weight of his problems had grown no lighter and the steps he was being forced to take were unavoidable. Outwardly competent, he was still inwardly stunned.

Due to the circumstances of his death, Branwell's body had been hastily buried in Madeira, and Roland arranged a memorial service in Tarrant Royal church for a few distant relatives and friends. But he was overcome to find the tiny church packed with villagers. He knew the gesture was really for the three sons of the man they were supposed to be mourning, and it brought the feeling of sadness the death of his father had failed to arouse.

His days were now burdened with the obligation to assume his new responsibility as head of the family. One thing seemed indisputable. Tarrant Hall had to be retained as the family home, a base for them all whatever else had to change. Since the estate now had to pay for itself, the income had to exceed expenditure and that could only be achieved by cutting staff and upkeep costs. With great regret he pared down the staff to a minimum, and listened to plans offered by Jeffries, the estate manager, to put more of the land under the plough, increase the milk yield, add to the number of sheep, and embark on timber production from the section of forest owned by the Sheridans.

Together with Rex, he agreed that Chris must still go to Cambridge, and on to become a don. To deny his intelligence fulfilment would be tantamount to destroying him, they both felt. Whereas they could adapt, Chris would find it impossible to do so.

Knowing he had no alternative, Roland had accepted the blow of having to abandon his medical studies and his dream of becoming a surgeon. He had also accepted another sacrifice that was almost akin to cutting off his right arm. But he could not bring himself to watch the valuable thoroughbreds that were almost a part of him being taken away to auction on a gorgeous July morning. He sat in his bedroom with his head down and shoulders heaving, as the sound of their hooves clattered on the gravel beneath his window. His brothers tactfully left him alone.

Similarly, Rex was left to himself on the day he returned from delivering *Princess* to her new owner. The narrow suntanned face, normally so alive, was distressingly bleak as he left the house in breeches and flying jacket for the last time, to return by train and pony trap. But if Chris was aware of what it had cost them both to ensure his academic future, they did not know.

Roland discussed their young brother with Rex as the latter packed for his departure to the northern town where he was due to take up his engineering job.

"Chris is going to miss you, Rex. With so many things to attend to, I find I've hardly seen him since Father died."

His brother looked up. "Neither have I, as it happens. Several times I've been up to his bedroom to drag him outside for some air, but he's been out in the grounds already, mooning around. Strange, isn't it?"

But Roland had no chance to comment, because the door burst open and Chris rushed in, brimming with urgency.

"Minks has just brought up the newspaper. Austria has gone to war with Serbia over the assassination of their archduke, and Russia is mobilizing! If Germany comes in, so will France. I don't see how we could stay out of it then. It's absolute madness!"

"You're theorizing, Chris. It'll never happen," Rex told him, stacking a pile of shirts into a suitcase.

"Besides," said Roland, "we've no intention of going to war with anyone."

But, a few days later, Britain mobilized her forces against the most formidable enemies she had ever faced. It was the fourth of August.

Rex departed for the north, and during the following six weeks Roland sank himself deeper and deeper into learning how to manage his estate. With only Mrs. Prideaux, Minks, Dawkins and the minimum of general staff left, he ran Tarrant Hall in a penny-pinching manner that distressed him. But he did not forget his obligations to Tarrant Royal, and attended meetings of the parish council, opened fetes, and generally showed that his personal disaster would not be allowed to affect the village. At church each

312

Sunday he was greeted with as much respect and pleasure as always, and the villagers chose to ignore the fact that their squire was now poorer than many of the area's gentleman farmers.

It was to this fact that Roland was forced to attribute Marion's attitude whenever they came face to face. He had been hurt to discover she was the only person in the village who was uncomfortable in his presence now. Their regular morning rides had ceased abruptly, and when he had tried to speak to her about it, she had stammered out a few sentences and moved away.

Then, on the day before Chris was due to depart for Cambridge, Minks came to him and said that Dr. and Miss Deacon had called on an urgent matter. Minks had shown them into the drawing room, and the moment Roland entered the large elegant room, he realized that both of them looked pale and strained—almost ill.

"You've brought bad news?" Roland asked with apprehension, looking from the stout balding man in baggy tweeds to the slender girl, so white-faced and red around the eyes.

"As a father, I can't think of any worse. As a doctor, I have to accept the results of my tests." Reginald Deacon stepped forward and gripped the back of the huge settee with shaking hands. "As God's my witness, Sheridan, I swear I'll thrash him raw when I get my hands on your brother."

Reeling with the implication of the cold words, Roland gazed at Marion with the pain of twin betrayals filling him.

"I . . . I admit Rex has a reputation for . . ." He hesitated, thinking of his brother's happy-go-lucky approach to girls. "But I can't believe he'd . . ."

"*Rex!*" cried the outraged father. "It isn't Rex, but young Christopher. My daughter's innocence has been outraged: she's eleven weeks advanced into pregnancy. This morning she told me who was responsible. When I get my hands on that lecher . . ."

"That's out of the question," cried Roland, now fully as angry as Dr. Deacon. "Chris is no more than a schoolboy!"

"He's eighteen, and capable of fertilizing female ova. So capable," the man went on in increased rage, "he did it in a mere five minutes under my own roof while I was attending a dying man. Well, he'll pay for his pleasure for the rest of his days!"

"Dr. Deacon," said Roland, in loud, icy tones, "you have just levelled a very serious charge against my brother. You can't expect me to accept it without hearing his defence. Just as you believe your daughter's veracity, so I believe in his integrity. I know there is some mistake."

Without another word Roland rang for Minks, and asked him to request Christopher to come down immediately. He was filled with contempt for the dark-haired pretty girl whom he had regarded with friendship and respect for so long. Not only had she been wantonly intimate with a man, she now attempted to blame someone else. And of all people, she had hit upon a schoolboy whose thoughts were so full of intellectual considerations that he never even looked at girls, much less bedded them. How could she use such a cheap trick against his family?

Chris came in warily, and his gaze flew straight to Marion. Reginald Deacon looked at the boy with near murder in his eyes, but stayed where he was on the hearthrug.

Roland went across to his brother and put a hand on his shoulder by way of support. "Sorry to disturb you, old fellow, but I'm afraid something rather disagreeable has arisen, and I can't avoid bringing you into it." He looked his brother in the eye. "I think we can settle the matter with just one question, Chris. Have you . . . have you ever been alone with Marion in her father's house in compromising circumstances?"

"Chris, I wouldn't have said anything," came Marion's broken voice for the first time. "But I had to."

The boy looked across at her like a trapped hare, then back at Roland. "What's all this about?"

"Don't try to lie your way out of it!" roared the doctor. "My girl is carrying your child, and it's going to have a legal father if I have to force you to the church at the end of a rifle!"

"That's enough!" shouted Roland, shaken.

But Chris was looking at them all with something approaching panic. "I can't *marry* her. I'm going up to Cambridge tomorrow."

Roland gripped his arm and swung him round sharply. "You're not . . . you're not saying that you *did* . . . that you could possibly be the father of a child—*her* child?"

Chris's expression said it all. A physical blow would have been easier to take. Roland's ideals, his deep belief in family bonds, mocked him as he stared at the handsome boyish face. "You little fool," he said to him with quiet savagery. "You threw away your whole life when you let your body rule your head."

"What do you mean?" cried Chris desperately.

314

"You can forget Cambridge and a brilliant scholastic career. They won't take married men at the university. Besides, I'm the head of this family now, and I won't have any bastards bearing our name. You'll do the decent thing and give your child the heritage it deserves . . ."

THE WEDDING WAS FIXED for the thirtieth of September, and the very haste to marry two youngsters under age gave rise to speculation that could not be avoided. However, the young couple were to live at Tarrant Hall after their marriage, so contact with the villagers would be minimal until Marion had passed the embarrassment of having her swelling figure scrutinized.

Chris lived in a vacuum of misery until his wedding day. He could not begin to accept that the payment for no more than a few minutes of exquisite pleasure could be so total. He could not begin to accept that the golden promise of academic laurels had vanished in an instant. And he did not see why he should pay so dearly, when it had been she who had deliberately awakened feelings in him.

No answer had been received from Rex to the letter Roland had written him explaining what had happened, and Chris's wretchedness increased further in the belief that his beloved brother was too disgusted with him to even write.

Roland's attitude towards him had softened slightly, but nothing would change his stand that Chris had no alternative than to do the honourable thing. The money set aside for his education now would pay for the things a husband was expected to provide, and Chris was to become estate manager, after working in harness with Jeffries for a year.

To minimize gossip, the wedding was to be as grand and conventional as if circumstances were normal. Roland and Dr. Deacon organized it together, but Chris realized that Roland had taken the whole business so hard that he would never be able to forgive the doctor or his daughter for taking away the hopes and dreams of a Sheridan.

The thirtieth of September dawned azure and russet, a perfect autumn day in which all of nature rejoiced. The bridegroom and his best man did not. The brothers were dressed in their grey morning suits and ready to set off for the church. They did not speak during the short drive down to the village. Chris wondered how Rex had managed never to land himself in such a position. At the thought of

315

Rex, his heart sank still further. Even a telegram about the wedding had remained unanswered. Roland's condemnation he could stand, but abandonment by someone he loved and admired so very much was almost more than he could take.

Yet, as the organ inside the packed church began the wedding march, a distant roar outside the church grew louder and louder until it rose to a crescendo. Chris swung his head round, and in a rush of relief he saw his red-haired brother walking down the aisle behind Marion and her father. Rex was attracting more attention than the bride, for he was dressed in a smart uniform of brown riding boots, khaki breeches, a khaki tunic in double-breasted style with a high collar, and a jaunty cap he whipped from his head as he came further into the church.

Realization rushed in. Rex had volunteered and was going to war! Pride and excitement vied with each other as his gaze met Rex's over Marion's head, and he smiled when he saw the warm understanding affection in those merry green eyes.

The marriage ceremony was tedious and lengthy, and throughout it all—the signing of the register, the walk back down the aisle with Marion's hand tucked through his arm, and the dash to the churchyard gate to avoid the hail of rice from laughing guests—Chris's mind raced with what he knew of the war situation. The Germans had followed their declaration of war on France by attacking through neutral Belgium, and British troops had been rushed across the Channel to aid the French army. Paris had been prevented from falling, and the Germans had been halted. With Russia attacking from the east, the Austro-Germanic hopes of a quick total conquest of Europe had gone. Why had Rex felt the need to volunteer?

When he heard the motorcycle coming up behind the carriage as they set out for the reception at Tarrant Hall, Chris said, "Trust Rex not to let me down, after all. Doesn't he look splendid in his uniform?"

He hardly noticed that the girl beside him made no reply, so busy was he waving as Rex passed, grinning, to ride ahead of the carriage like an advance guard. But when he came into the house where they stood greeting the arriving guests, he merely gripped Chris's arm and said, "I'll see you later, old fellow." Then he turned to Marion with his irresistible smile. "As your brother-in-law, I am perfectly entitled to kiss you."

The kiss was somewhat warmer than it should have been, but it brought colour into the bride's wan cheeks. He took her hands in his and squeezed them. "Welcome to the family, Marion. If you ever want help or advice, come to Uncle Rex."

The afternoon seemed to fly past, and it was not until Marion went upstairs to change into her going-away outfit that Chris was able to seek out his middle brother and step outside with him for a private talk.

Rex put a hand on his shoulder as they strolled down towards the sunken garden. "There's always something nostalgic about late autumn days like this, isn't there?" he said. "The smell of the sun on the fallen leaves makes me think of our childhood when we used to rush through them with the dogs, scattering them into the wind." They reached the low wall, and Rex put one booted foot up on it. "They were marvellous days, Chris, and we were marvellous companions. But we've grown up."

Chris nodded, looking out over the forested valley below.

"I suppose I should have had a word with you," Rex went on, "but you were always so uninterested in girls, I let it slide."

Chris turned to him angrily. "Oh Lord, Rex, it's so unfair! I just don't know how I'm going to face the next sixty years."

Rex gripped his shoulder and shook it gently. "You poor old chap! No one can take on sixty years in one go. Try taking them one at a time. Regrets never get a fellow anywhere. What you have to do now is turn what you have to good account."

Chris sat on the wall looking up into his brother's face, which was seldom as serious as it was now. "Got any ideas?"

His brother nodded. "Marion is a jolly nice girl from a good family. She's very pretty, and she'll be a credit to you. You're lucky. With a brain like yours, you can carry on studying and then obtain a post as a tutor somewhere after this child is born. Then, when the war ends, try for something similar abroad." He cocked an eyebrow. "Will that do to be getting on with?"

It sounded like a ray of hope; it was infinitely better than becoming an estate manager. Why was it things never seemed so bad when Rex was around? Chris said, "You're a bloody marvel!"

Rex cuffed him gently round the head. "That's just what the recruiting officer said when I told him what I could do."

Chris leaned forward eagerly, forgetting everything else. "When did you volunteer? What regiment are you in?"

"The Royal Flying Corps, muttonhead. What other regiment

would a pilot join? I went up to their headquarters a fortnight ago, which is why Roland's letter and telegram never reached me. Thank goodness I went back to my old lodgings to say goodbye to some friends and found them, or I'd never have come today."

"What made you do it, Rex? I thought the Germans had been stopped."

"Only temporarily, you can bet. But it had nothing to do with that. I wanted an aeroplane, and they wanted men." He cast Chris a rueful glance. "I was lost without *Princess*."

Chris sighed heavily, his problems returning. "If it hadn't been for the cost of my supposed university career, you needn't have sold *Princess*, and Roland needn't have sold his horses. Now I've chucked it all away. You must hate me."

Sitting down on the wall beside him Rex said, "Great Scott, you really are sunk into the depths of despondency to think that of me. That sort of thing is liable to make me fly off towards the sun and keep going. Where would the RFC be then?"

Unaccountably emotional, Chris forced a smile. "Idiot!"

"That makes two of us. Come on, that lovely girl of yours will soon be ready to leave. You'd better change out of that fancy outfit quickly, or you'll miss the train."

But Roland and Dr. Deacon made sure he did not.

THEY REACHED THEIR HONEYMOON hotel in Bournemouth too late for dinner, so they had a tray brought to their room. Conversation during the short train journey had been stilted and Chris had hardly looked at Marion, just being vaguely aware that his wife was dressed in a blue wool costume with a matching hat. *His wife!* Oh, how he hated her for what she had done to him!

He was still gloomy when Marion, who had disappeared into the small dressing room, emerged in a voluminous white nightgown with silly blue bows all over it. She climbed into the brocade-covered four-poster. "Aren't you coming to bed, Chris?" she asked in the same soft persuasive tones she had used in her father's waiting room.

It caught him on the raw, and sent him forward to clutch one of the oak posts. "You little hypocrite! For the past three weeks you've been going round like a wronged virgin, letting your father insult and vilify me, and wringing demands from my brother that I pay for my sin against you. They've never once been allowed to see what

318

you're really like, never once suspected that you are fast and completely shameless. And now you're at it again! You enjoyed every moment that night as much as I did!"

She looked shaken. "But I didn't ask you to give me a child."

Clutching the post tighter, he said hoarsely, "Do you think I wanted to? You've made my life a travesty and I'll never forgive you. *Never!* I hate you, Marion."

"Oh, *Chris!*" She was out of the bed and round to him before he guessed her intention. Her eyes slowly filling with tears, she said desperately, "I didn't want it this way, truly I didn't. But I didn't want to get out of it either. I love you, Chris."

"More fool you!" he said. Feeling sick, he went to sit on the chaise longue with his head in his hands. Then she was beside him, sinking onto the floor with her nightdress billowing round her, tears rolling down her cheeks.

"Chris, love is never foolish—it's just human. That's something you find it difficult to be. *Please* don't hate me. I know you are upset about Cambridge, but I'll be the perfect wife; I'll make you proud of your child. I'll follow you wherever you want to go, and I'll try to learn more so that you won't find me dull company. All I ask in return is that you accept me as your wife."

He looked at her in numb resignation. "I don't have much choice with that gold ring on your finger, do I? But I've given the child a name, and as far as I'm concerned my honourable duty is now done, I'll sleep in the dressing room tonight." He got up and walked into it, and locked the door behind him.

When they returned to Tarrant Hall at the end of their seven day honeymoon, Chris thankfully reclaimed his own bedroom. During the weeks that followed, he saw Marion only at mealtimes, and subdued her into silence by ignoring her.

4

The reputation that was destined to make Second Lieutenant Rex Sheridan's name familiar all over the world began at a flying school on Salisbury Plain on Christmas Eve, 1914.

Much to Rex's disgust, the fact that he was already an experienced pilot when he joined the Royal Flying Corps got him a home posting as an instructor. And he had to watch those he taught go off to France and the great adventure of war, while he buzzed round and round the airfield with one novice after another in the rear seat.

Because of the urgent need for pilots, training was very basic and done on a hit-and-miss basis. Unprepared for war, the corps had only a motley selection of aircraft, each with its own peculiarities of performance. Often a pupil would have two lessons in a Farman; then his instructor would find only a BE available the next day, or an Avro. This meant that flips, as they were called, could turn into a series of hair-raising stunts as the pupil copied what he had learned and found the machine responding in an unexpected way.

The RFC, having derived from the Royal Engineers, was very much an army corps. But it soon set about discarding the rigid military discipline practised by hidebound regiments dating back to Cromwell. This suited Rex admirably. Captain James Ashmore it did not.

On arrival at the shed, the morning before Christmas Day, Rex found this moustached gentleman looking at his watch with a frowning expression. The flying lesson had been scheduled for nine am. It was now five minutes past.

"Captain Ashmore?" Rex asked his pupil pleasantly.

"You're late!"

"Yes, I was late for breakfast."

"That's no excuse."

"It is when you've been practising night flying," Rex said in firm tones. "Are you all set to go?"

"*Sir.*"

Rex paused in the act of pulling on his flying helmet. "I beg your pardon?"

"Don't you respect rank?" snapped the captain.

"I respect the man with superior knowledge . . . which is me, at the moment." He jammed the soft leather helmet onto his red hair and fastened the strap under his chin. "If you'd like to climb in, Captain Ashmore, we'll waste no more time. I have six more men booked before lunch and I don't want to be late for *that.*"

Rex immediately forgot the exchange as he took the aircraft up to two hundred feet and began demonstrating the more advanced manoeuvring his pupil needed, after three earlier lessons with another instructor. Then he allowed his pupil to take over.

The lesson went well until Ashmore committed the cardinal sin of letting the nose drop while in the middle of a turn. Even as Rex bellowed the instructions that would correct the spin, he knew the man had frozen with fear at the controls. Taking over quickly, Rex did all that was necessary to pull out of the dive. For the moment, though, he had forgotten which aircraft he was flying and, rushing earthwards with the icy wind whistling past his face, he tried too late to come out of the situation cleanly.

Flattening out dangerously close to the ground, he banked to avoid a large shed. But the ancient machine could not cope with such treatment. It dropped heavily, bounded with a sickening jolt, then rose slightly to glide just above the ground until it reached a large haystack on the airfield's perimeter.

Rex spent Christmas and New Year's Day with a dislocated shoulder in the hospital bed next to Captain James Ashmore . . . and that was how he gained his wish to give up instructing and join a squadron in France.

THE QUARTERS REX was given, on a farm the RFC had taken over, turned out to be a bell tent he could pitch anywhere he liked, as long as it was not on the airfield. The mess was a wooden outbuilding that had belonged to the farm, and it still smelled of the beets and potatoes that had been stored in it. Even the commanding officer of 2F Squadron, a Major Crookhorn, occupied one stall in what everyone proclaimed had been the farm piggery. Apart from this collection of unsalubrious sheds, there was a tiny village called Grissons several miles down the road, and a canal two fields away along which barges passed regularly. In that early February of 1915 the surrounding countryside looked desolate, depressing and icy. Rex practically froze in his tent the first night.

In the morning, he met Lieutenant Mallory Haines—Mal would be his partner on patrols—and was introduced to the routine of patrolling the Allied lines in case stray Huns tried a bit of sharpshooting at the men in the trenches. Rain fell almost constantly for the next week, and it was a strange experience to fly over miles and miles of ditches running with mud and know that some poor devils were living in them day in and day out. The war had stopped in two lines of trenches facing each other across a few miles, apparently for no other gain than killing anyone who looked over the rim.

The death toll in the trenches seemed particularly poignant when a letter reached Rex. It was from Roland to say that Chris had a son,

David, born prematurely two days after the New Year, and that mother and child were doing well. The news made Rex unusually thoughtful as he and Mal Haines flew their usual patrol, under unusually clear skies, along the route Rex now knew by heart.

He was brought suddenly from his thoughts by a bang, as the observer behind him thumped the side of the aircraft—the usual method of attracting his attention. Some distance ahead, a plane was flying low along the line of French and British trenches. It looked like a bright yellow moth with the black markings of the Maltese Cross of Germany, as it glided along, a dark shadow cast by the watery sun moving along the earth with it. But it was a moth that spat death at those beneath it.

From his open seat, Rex gave a quick glance at Mal flying alongside, and encountered a broad smile beneath the goggles. He nodded agreement to Mal's signal to go down and sandwich the yellow-painted DFW while they peppered it from both sides.

As he dived on the unsuspecting Germans, Rex realized the troops below were being raked by bullets. So busy were the Germans with their gleeful sport, they only became aware of the pair diving on them a short while before Rex and Mal began to flatten out and draw alongside. The faces inside the yellow aircraft were full of alarm as they turned towards Rex.

For a moment or two, the three aeroplanes flew along in formation, firing at each other all the while. Rex thought only of handling his aircraft to the best possible advantage for his observer to use the light machinegun, and so that he could get in a few shots at the yellow plane with his own service revolver on the cord round his shoulder. Although he heard German bullets ripping through the fabric just ahead of where he sat, he kept doggedly on course.

Next minute it seemed the enemy's gun had jammed, for the German observer stopped firing as his pilot began to climb, leaving the yellow biplane completely at their mercy. But the grin left Rex's face very swiftly as he pulled up the nose of his own aircraft to look straight at three other machines with the black cross on their wings, which were now diving on himself and Mal. Caught in their own trap, Mal signalled Rex to break away in an inward turn so that they would cross each other's paths and reverse their direction, thus fooling the men diving in the expectation of following outward climbing turns.

Aircraft crisscrossed only a hundred feet above the ground in a desperate melee of machines that almost touched wing tips. Rex and Mal did not have time to signal to each other again; so, fastening onto the tail of one of the DFWs, Rex chased it determinedly as it lured him onto enemy territory. He knew he had to make his kill swiftly or lose all hope of advantage.

Dipping the nose, he took his aircraft down to a mere sixty feet, directly beneath the enemy machine, thus improving the chances of his gunner, who would now be firing upwards. The enemy pilot, who was unable to see where Rex was, flung his machine into some uneasy manoeuvres to remedy the problem. But Rex matched the DFW turn for turn, swing for swing, as he continued at his crazy height just above the ground. All the time, his observer was firing up into yellow fabric and tearing it apart. Suddenly, half a wing fell from the DFW and it turned onto its side, belching smoke, before dropping into some trees.

Flying over the spot a second later, Rex saw a whole crowd of French and English soldiers waving madly at him in jubilation. He grinned at his observer, who looked surprisingly pale, and waggled his wings at the cheering troops.

But joy was short-lived. Mal was hot in pursuit of an enemy aircraft, unaware that another was flying very low beneath him. Instantly Rex made a difficult right turn over a farm, frightening all the cows in the field, and put himself on a course that would take him head-on towards the yellow machine. The ruse worked. The German pilot's attention was taken by the new adversary, and he forgot about attacking Mal.

Rex kept straight on, nearer and nearer the other flier. The young German was smiling as he fired his revolver at Rex, until the moment his nerve broke. Apparently forgetting how low he was, he tried to dive beneath Rex but hit the ground at full speed, smashing his machine beyond recognition.

There was no sign of enemy aircraft now, so Mal and Rex headed off towards Grissons, where news of their arrival spread like wildfire. Later, in the mess, there began an evening of celebration that went on into the small hours.

Rex was the hero of the day, and everyone insisted on buying him a drink. It was while he was sitting there enjoying the camaraderie that he was approached by a stranger of around his own height, very dark-complexioned, with black hair and curiously pale, almost silvery, eyes. The stranger smiled and held out his hand. "You were away when I flew in to join the squadron. I'm Mike Manning, from Narraburra."

"Where?"

"Australia."

"How often did you refuel on the way over?" Rex asked him with a straight face.

"Oh, I've got a machine invented by the aborigines," came the straight-faced answer. "It doesn't need refuelling."

Mal Haines joined them and the three men sat in a corner with a whisky each, while Mike told a little about himself. His father had been sent to Australia to "make good" after he had been involved in a scandal concerning a lady in the Prince of Wales's circle. Joining the gold prospectors, he had struck lucky and made enough money to buy a large property and raise sheep. Mike and his sister, Tessa, loved the great stretches of land but felt that they cut people off from each other. At seventeen, Mike had begun building a flying machine to remedy this. It had been completed six months ago, on his nineteenth birthday.

"The only thing was, it didn't have an engine in it," he confessed disarmingly. "I couldn't afford that. So, when I heard there was a war going on over here, I got on the first ship leaving for England. I guess I'd outgrown the excitement of just sitting on the ground, and I hoped the RFC would have engines in theirs."

"Only just," warned Rex solemnly.

REX AND HIS OBSERVER were detailed to fly in a different machine the following morning. As usual Rex checked his control lever and engine and, as he opened the throttle, he glanced at Mal preparing to take off beside him. They grinned at each other as both machines began bumping forward over the field.

Rex's BE lifted into the air at the same instant as the other machine. He felt the usual tremendous elation as he rose like a bird alongside a man whose blood, he knew, would be tingling like his own. They were a good pair. They understood each other. Comradeship of the air was like no other.

They had just cleared the trees at the end of the field when Rex turned to check that Mal was about to make a right bank, as usual. At that moment, the engine of the other plane coughed, cut out, spluttered for a moment or two, then cut out again. The right bank turned into a complete loop only feet above the ground, and the machine plunged into a shallow quarry.

Stunned, Rex saw a lick of flame appear from beneath the body of the machine and start to spread. He returned to earth hastily, and leaped from his aircraft to run to the quarry and slither down the sides to where the BE was now blazing fiercely.

"Oh God!" he breathed. Throwing off his gauntlets, he rushed forward to where he spotted movement beneath the observer's position. Heat burned his skin as if the flames were already touching it. The observer had managed to release his restraining belt and drop to the ground, but he was bleeding from the head and seemed unable to think for himself.

Coughing painfully in the smoke, Rex pulled the man clear of the wreckage and handed him over to his own observer, just arriving on the scene. But his thoughts were fixed on Mal, up in the pilot's seat. Despite the flames that were now roaring along the fabric of the machine, Rex forced himself to go to the forward cockpit. Flaming debris lay on the ground to burn his hands and knees as he crawled slowly beneath the machine, and the pain of it grew so great he had to pause and consider giving up. Then through the smoke and flame he saw Mal dangling helplessly upside down, imprisoned by his belt.

"Oh Lord!" Rex rasped, feeling desperate and helpless.

But as he braced himself to a new attempt to penetrate the fire, the wreck shifted towards him. Instinct made him throw himself sideways and roll away before the whole flaming pile buried his first comrade-in-arms. In fact Rex only just escaped complete incineration himself.

In the small sick bay, he lay in physical and mental pain. It was the first time he had witnessed death, and he suddenly felt a lot older. His friendship with Mal Haines had lasted less than two weeks, but its very nature had made it special. Yet by the time the bandages were off his hands, a friendship had been cemented between himself and the young Australian named Mike Manning that was to totally change his life.

Two months later, Rex learned he was to be decorated for bringing down two enemy aircraft that had been machinegunning troops in the trenches, and for his rescue of Mal's observer from a burning wreck. 2F Squadron had acquired its hero, and the living legend of "Sherry" Sheridan had begun.

CHRIS STOOD ON the stone bridge three miles from Tarrant Hall and gazed down at the river, swollen now with the February rains. His overcoat collar was turned up against the biting wind and his tweed cap was pulled well onto his unruly fair hair. His shoulders were hunched as he leaned against the ancient stone of the bridge, and tears ran down his cheeks.

His forced marriage had become unendurable. He did not know which way to turn. As an estate manager he spent endless hours tramping round in mud and cow dung, standing in freezing forest to inspect trees and decide which should be cut for much-needed timber, squatting in smelly barns to look at grain and root vegetables. Or the days consisted of long, boring discussions on sheep pest and forestry, or even more boring study of pamphlets, farming publications and costing lists.

Rex's suggestion that he study at home and try for a post as a tutor once the child was born had not worked. At the end of the day he was too physically tired to study, and those few times he had gone to bed with a book had been spoiled by visits from Marion that ended in tearful quarrelling. Now, there was a baby crying night and day. For something so small, it had a wail that managed to reach whichever room of the house he was in.

Chris's sense of desperation had mounted until he felt like an animal in a cage. Then a letter had arrived from Rex, telling them that he was finally in France on active service, and that the war was turning into a long-term struggle in which men were desperately needed. That letter had shown Chris his escape route: there was a place where Marion could not possibly follow him, and where no one would condemn him for going.

Early that morning he had walked from the house and caught the first train to Dorchester, where there was a recruiting office. Now he was on his way back to Tarrant Hall. He took off his spectacles to wipe the tears from his eyes, then threw the things to the ground in despair. The army had turned him down the minute they had tested his sight!

Suddenly he remembered himself saying to Marion, "No one achieves anything with a negative attitude like that."

Bending with the swiftness of hope reborn, he groped for the spectacles and thought out a plan. All he needed to do was memorize the eye charts in Dr. Deacon's office. Then he would go to the Bournemouth recruiting office where they would not know him, and he would leave his spectacles off throughout the process. With all the information stored in his head, his only risk of failure would be if he fell over a doorstep as he entered.

ROLAND ALWAYS WENT through the post as soon as he could after Minks brought it in. On that mid-February morning he spotted a letter from Rex, with stamps of the army post office covering the envelope. But then he came across an envelope at the bottom of the pile that bore no stamp, just his name in Chris's thick scrawl. Frowning, he tore it open and read the simple message.

Rage filled him as he thought of the young dreamy boy who had arrived home for the holidays last June, and pictured that same boy stumbling through mud-filled trenches. But there was nothing he could do, except regret that he had not recognized the great despair that had finally driven Chris to do something for which he was so totally unsuited. He closed his eyes on the vision of the boy faced with the necessity to thrust a bayonet into someone, or waiting in knee-high mud for the enemy to appear through the smoke of heavy gunfire. Such experiences would surely break his spirit. Yet he must have felt his present life was doing worse—breaking his heart.

For a long time Roland sat cursing his failure to recognize his brother's state and help him. Then he forced himself to go to the nursery, where Marion spent most of her time, apparently devoted to her son. When he entered she managed a faint smile.

He looked her straight in the eye. "Chris has volunteered. He went into Bournemouth on the last train yesterday. He isn't coming back."

He thought she was going to faint, but she just stood there swaying as she clasped her stomach with both hands.

"How long have you known?" she whispered accusingly.

"I have just found the note in which he asks me to tell you."

"How cruel!" Her eyes filled with tears that ran unchecked down her cheeks. "How cruel he can be! Not a word to me." She sank onto a chair, totally distraught. "He hates me. But I thought the baby would . . . every man wants a son. How could he desert a helpless little creature who has done him no harm?"

"No harm?" Roland snapped, rage filling him now. "From the moment that child was conceived it harmed Chris. It robbed him of his rightful future, and nearly all the things in life he held dear. And what that child didn't do to him, you did."

"*Please*, Roland, don't say that to me," she implored tearfully. "I loved him. I have done everything in my power to make him happy."

"You've done everything except leave him alone. It wouldn't have made him happy, but it would have saved him from growing desperate enough to commit suicide like his father."

"Roland . . . *don't*," she cried, her hands to her temples.

"He's going to war to escape from something he regards as far worse here. He can't possibly survive, and he knows it." Suddenly the full force of his young brother's disastrous past few months took hold of him. "All you ever saw of Chris was an attractive body and a dreamy manner. Well, you've destroyed him now, and this family will never forgive you. I'd be glad if you'd move out of this house as soon as you can arrange it, and take the child. Chris has more than paid for those five minutes on your father's examination couch. Neither he nor I owe you anything more."

FOR THE FIRST TWO weeks Chris believed he had exchanged one form of total misery for another. When he was not jumping "arms out, feet astride" in the company of forty-nine others, he was running round a field with a full pack on his back or climbing over walls with a rifle. And the entire time he stumbled round in a world of blurs, having no idea whom he was speaking to, or where he was walking. His survival was due to his using his rest periods for solitary reconnaissance, wearing those lenses on which he depended so heavily, memorizing the layout of barracks and training areas, or making swift sketches, which he studied in the latrines or beneath his blankets with a torch after lights-out.

But his pretence was put to its severest test the day they were all sent to the rifle range for long-distance target practice. Sprawling on his stomach, he gazed miserably ahead at a few yards of fuzzy grass. The targets lay somewhere in the grey blank beyond that. He knew that if he fired he could very well kill one of the targetmen. Yet, if he did not, it would be the final grounds for throwing him out as unfit.

"Right then, Sheridan. Look lively, it's your turn!" bellowed a voice that made him jump. "Load and fire!"

With heart hammering. Chris felt for the breech, put the bullet in and closed it, ready to fire. Nothing happened when he pulled the trigger, and the sergeant's voice roared that he "had the bloody safety catch on". His hand ran along the barrel to find it and release it. Then, praying fervently, he fired.

The sergeant moved on, and Chris put his face down on the grass, feeling ready to vomit. A minute later he was told by a blur beside him that he was to report to his company commander. "You'll go with Corporal Meaker," said the voice, "and leave that rifle here where it's safe."

Chris's legs nearly buckled under him at that. He *must* have shot someone. As he followed a vague khaki shape, he felt more and more ill. He knew immediately, from the barracks plan he had memorized, that they were on a path leading towards the sick bay. He walked up the three steps he knew would be there, and the shape with him knocked on a door and opened it.

"Private Sheridan, sir," he announced. "In yer go," he added, giving Chris a small push.

There was a man standing behind what must be a desk. Shaking and giddy, Chris went forward and saluted him. "Good morning, sir. I was told you wished to see me."

"Just as I thought," came a voice behind him. "Blind as a bat!"

Chris turned round so swiftly he almost lost his balance, and a hand came out to steady him. "Take it easy, son. You'd better sit down while we get to the bottom of all this. That was my greatcoat on the tallboy you just saluted."

Chris was grateful for the chair. "I didn't kill anyone, did I?"

"The sergeant gave you a blank to be on the safe side. I think you had better tell me what you felt justified such a risk."

Since he now had nothing to lose, Chris told him how he had memorized the eye charts, to be accepted at Bournemouth, and then described how he had memorized the layout of the barracks.

"Incredible," said the voice. "Where are the spectacles now?"

"In the locker beside my bed."

"Right. I'll send someone to fetch them." The blur rose and continued. "How long has your sight been defective, Sheridan?"

"Most of my life, I suppose. Certainly since I went to school."

"Tell me about school."

He began hesitantly, but as he related the years at boarding school enthusiasm warmed his voice. The details of his awards, scholarships and prizes came out without any suggestion of bragging, but more as an eagerness to share his great passion with the faceless blur who offered to listen.

Someone arrived with the spectacles, and the gift of clear sight after so long doubled his sense of wellbeing. The man at the desk turned out to be a doctor, a colonel in his forties with a shrewd face and a clipped black moustache.

Chris smiled at him. "What's going to happen now, sir?"

The doctor grinned. "I want a few more answers first. With your academic propensity, why aren't you at university?"

Chris told his first lie. "There was no money. My father lost everything at cards."

"I see. But why were you so dangerously set on going to war?"

He told his second lie. "My middle brother is in the Royal Flying Corps in France. He's . . . well, he's something of a hero to me, and I suppose I wanted to show him I could match up." Then gloom returned as Chris remembered his situation. "Are you going to kick me out, sir?"

"No, not just yet. You're a very interesting case. I want to try some experiments with you."

For the next week Chris was excused from all other duties and asked to translate difficult passages of prose in Greek, Latin, French and Italian, which he did with ease. He was then given a long extract in German—a language he did not know—and a German grammar. It was faultlessly translated by the end of the day. Finally, he was given pages of meaningless English words and told to make sense of them. He did that even quicker than the German. It was the happiest week he had spent since leaving school, and at the end of it he was told he would be attached for intelligence work with the rank of second lieutenant.

It was a measure of his delight that he actually wrote to Rex to tell him of all that had happened. He did not write to Roland for fear of betraying to Marion where he was, but he asked Rex to pass on the news that he was happy and well.

THE PRIMROSES HAD BLOOMED and gone from the shady banks alongside the river that flowed through Tarrant Royal. Now the hedgerows were scattered with pinkish white brier roses, and filled with the nests of birds which sang as sweetly and joyously as they had last June.

But like every other village in England, Tarrant Royal had made sacrifices since then. Young Bill Bishop had fallen at Mons, Ted Peach had lost an eye and an arm at Picardy, and the only son of the

George and Dragon's landlord had been a victim of the terrible poison gas used so inhumanly only a month ago. Violent patriotism had flared up, and men were flocking to volunteer, leaving the land at a time when so much work had to be done. Even more violently patriotic were the women, who were rolling up their sleeves, taking their babies and children with them into the fields, and doing the jobs their menfolk usually did.

As Roland drove through the village on this late-June day, he reflected sadly on all that had happened in the last year. The village green and the ancient slumbering church looked the same, but the village seemed empty and unfriendly. Women no longer stood chatting at their doors, and those few who were about either took no notice of his passing or hurried indoors.

He could no longer ignore the truth. The villagers had turned against him. After the years of growing up with them, after becoming a generous and caring squire, the villagers, with the exception of the rector, treated him with disdain. From a few veiled comments at a committee meeting, it had mushroomed into open hostility from those families whose menfolk had already gone to war—some never to return. Then, at church today, the congregation had fallen silent when he had entered to walk to the family pew, and no one lingered afterwards to chat with him.

With his back stiff as a ramrod and his face set, he turned the small cart into the lane leading to Tarrant Hall, asking himself bitterly what more they wanted of him. Was it not enough that he daily expected to hear that Rex had challenged the devil once too often, that he faced the prospect of never seeing Chris again, that he must see an ill-conceived child grow up and claim his rightful heritage from the family whose name he bore? Was it not enough that he was struggling to produce food in the form of grain, sheep, and cattle, precious timber from his forest, and had just offered one wing of Tarrant Hall as a convalescent home for officers?

How could he go off to war? Who would run the estate? Who would produce the things so urgently needed by those who were fighting? Did the people down there in his village really not appreciate that it was important to make the land as productive as possible, to keep England running?

Yes, two out of three Sheridans in uniform *were* enough! His plain duty was to use the land they owned to produce food, and to do all he could here in England. Life had to go on. No medals would be handed to men like him, but he would give his all as much as any man.

Roland's back was still stiff and his face just as set when he walked indoors to greet Minks and go straight to his study. The day's post was on the desk. There was a long letter from the army, accepting his offer of a wing of Tarrant Hall for use as a convalescent home, and another letter from Rex, who appeared to be having a splendid time at Grissons. His promotion to full lieutenant had come through, and he had celebrated the fact with an Australian friend named Mike Manning. His sleeping quarters had been moved from a tent to a real bunk bed. But Rex also appeared to be still risking his life every time he took off, and his list of enemy "kills" was growing.

Whatever pleasure Rex's letter had given Roland disappeared when he saw the next familiar envelope on the tray. He swallowed painfully as he stared at it, then confronted the contents which fluttered out and lay on the carpet by his booted feet. A white duck feather!

It was a symbol that said more than words. A feather had been coming regularly each week and he felt the pain once again. Did the villagers have any idea what this did to him? Slowly he bent to pick it up and add it to the small pile in his drawer. He knew they would continue to come, but all the time he could face them and keep them near, his resolution to stay in England and work his land would remain.

THE STAFF AT the small department to which he was sent were a strange assortment of men, much older than Chris. But having found the perfect outlet for his brilliant mind, he forgot his misery, his married status, almost his identity, in the delight of what he was doing. He translated foreign dispatches with vital and dramatic contents, and invented codes. During his first two weeks he was given concentrated lessons in German and Russian. At the end of the fortnight German was like a native tongue to him, though Russian took a little longer to master. It was total release.

But that same release brought a breakdown in health that put him on his back with a fever for over three weeks. Doctors warned the head of the department that unless this healthy young boy of eighteen received a break from mental concentration, they would not answer for the consequences.

He was given leave, but stayed in his quarters, mooning around, sketching everything he could see from his window. In the end, it was this talent for drawing that brought a solution to the problem he had become. Two staff officers discussed their proposal with his department head.

"It meets most of the doctor's recommendations—plenty of fresh air, exercise, companionship with others his age . . ."

The man stared at them. "You're mad!"

"We have had an urgent request for someone who can read enemy messages, solve simple codes, and provide maps of the terrain. Young Sheridan is the very man they need. It's an incredible stroke of luck that he's also a first-class Greek scholar."

"But the enemy are *Turks*," said the department head sourly. "And Sheridan is classed as a noncombatant because he has very defective sight."

"There's no question of his *fighting*. He'll be drawing maps safely behind the lines at headquarters."

"Well, I don't know . . ." The man hesitated.

"There isn't anyone else," came the firm decision. "He sails with the rest at the end of the week."

When Chris heard he was to board a ship for the Aegean, his heart leaped with unbelievable excitement. He would be finally visiting the Greek islands he had missed a year ago. But no one told him his final destination was Gallipoli, where British and Commonwealth troops were dying by the thousand.

5

Chris saw the islands of Mílos, Páros and Naxos from the rail of a troopship as it steamed past at the start of August. He was wholly absorbed in and charmed by the emerald and gold islands in a sea of vivid cobalt blue, whose shores had witnessed scenes of greatness, disaster and romance.

He was fortunate in his absorption, because others with him on the ship could think only of what lay ahead, and tried to cover their fear by drinking, singing brave songs, and making friends so they would not feel so alone. They had heard what had happened to those who landed at Gallipoli earlier in the year. The drastic failure of the sea bombardment of the Dardanelles, and the present predicament of insufficient troops pinned down on sheer cliffs because of lack of cover and darkness to allow them to withdraw, had all caused a public outcry in England and helped to bring down a government.

The ingoing one had been left with little alternative. The situation on the western front was appalling, and growing worse. Casualty figures like sixty thousand in one day were being received too often. A glorious victory was needed somewhere—*anywhere*—to boost morale and silence critics.

The original reason for mounting a campaign against the Turks on the Gallipoli peninsula—that of drawing Turkish concentration from hard-pressed Russian troops in the north—no longer existed. However, since the British and Commonwealth troops could not be withdrawn without wholesale slaughter, the only thing left to do was to throw in enormous numbers of reinforcements to capture the heights and overrun the Turks, thus putting fresh heart into the Allies and changing the course of the war.

The fleet of ships steamed on between the islands. Chris, being a noncombatant on detachment to the headquarters already established on the peninsula, had no duties aboard ship and could spend as much time as he wanted on deck. He first saw the heights of Gallipoli in the sunset, which put a satanic red glow on the stony cliffs rising from the narrow beaches. He revelled in the formidable sight, the siren voices of ages past calling to him from over the sea.

Then he came from his thoughts as he realized that Rochford-Clarke, a subaltern of twenty, whom he had known slightly at Charterhouse, was shaking his arm.

"For heaven's sake, Sheridan, we're going ashore any minute. Where's your kit?"

"What?"

"Your kit, man! I thought we agreed you'd go ashore with me and my platoon."

"Oh . . . yes. It's in my cabin."

Rochford-Clarke looked out of patience with him. "Well, get a spurt on! I can't hang around for you once we're called."

Chris made for his cabin, trying frantically to push against a tide of men coming up the companionways onto the deck. Once there, he snatched up his heavy pack, clipped his Sam Browne on and slipped his arm through the retaining cord of his revolver, before jamming his pith helmet onto his head and grabbing the book on ancient ceramics he had been reading.

Rochford-Clarke greeted him with the news that his platoon had been detailed for the last boat.

"So there was no panic, after all!" Chris exclaimed. "I thought I had plenty of time."

"I . . . well, I feel responsible for you," admitted the young man, two years his senior, with slight embarrassment.

"Whatever for?" asked Chris, astonished.

"Someone has to be. You don't belong to a company or platoon. You don't have any defined duties. You don't even have a batman to sort out your kit. And . . . and your mind always seems to be elsewhere." He pointed shoreward. "Those are real enemies out there, firing real bullets. I don't think that fact has hit you yet."

"Yes, it has. But I shall be safely behind the lines at headquarters with my spectacles. It's you and the others I feel sorry for."

"Oh . . . we'll be all right," came the self-conscious answer.

It was a good thing the beach at Suvla Bay was wider than most in the area and within sight of only a few Turkish defence posts, because the men were exceedingly worked up by the time the last boats made their way from the fleet to the hostile shore. As a result, orders were changed, reaffirmed, then countermanded again. Those in command could not agree on the next step to take.

Dawn arrived, and the August sun blazed mercilessly down on pale-faced men in thick khaki serge as they lay on the sandy beach, unused to such heat. Each of them had come ashore with a full canteen of water, but further supplies lay in tankers offshore. Owing to regular shelling by the enemy, that was where they remained throughout that day and the following night.

Chris felt he would remember that nightmare of heat for the rest of his life. Sweat ran down his face like rain. His head throbbed with pain. His tongue felt chokingly swollen, his lips were dry and cracked, his throat tormented with thirst. As the day wore on, lack of water meant the troops did not eat, either. No man could swallow food, and the rations lay on the sand. Night brought relief from the sun, but that was all. Chris dragged himself from his torpor to go with Rochford-Clarke to immerse himself in the sea, and then lay in his heavy wet uniform beside his companion, to sleep heavily and feverishly until the short night ended with blinding sunlight again.

Although water now became available, the men were sluggish, demoralized and depressed. Then word arrived that the attack was on for the following dawn, and the pandemonium of conflicting orders and lack of organization began again. Chris asked those in command several times how he could get to headquarters, where he was needed. But he was told his problems were of no importance, so he spent yet another day on that sweltering beach. By evening, he was beset by an attack of dysentery that kept him awake all night.

Rochford-Clarke told Chris he had better stay with him and his platoon during the planned assault, since he could hardly stay on the beach alone. He agreed, although he knew little of the battle plan apart from what Rochford-Clarke had briefly told him.

They were among the last to leave the beach in the hour before dawn. An hour of strenuous and difficult climbing up the cliffs faced them, and the sky was already a luminous tinted blue before they were halfway to the top. The positions of the Turkish guns were known, and the plan was to put them out of action before breasting the ridge and forging inland to meet up with Anzac troops who were working their way north.

Chris was sweating profusely as he climbed, and battling against pains in his stomach. The cliff was steep and stony, and when he glanced over his shoulder the sea looked serene and a great distance below.

Suddenly, all hell was let loose. Guns at the top of the cliffs opened fire, and the air round Chris was filled with the scream of shells flying overhead, to explode several hundred feet below among the busy small boats bringing stores and supplies from the fleet anchored offshore. One carrying ammunition went up with a tremendous thunder of sound that rocked the earth. At the same time, the unmistakable chatter of rifle fire broke out ahead and just over the rim they were approaching. The sheer volume of it, plus the chorus of screams, shouts and whistle blasts, appalled Chris. The line of men ahead checked, surged forward again, then checked again when bodies began slithering from the crest to plunge down onto the beach. A red-faced captain came over the top at suicide speed and began scrambling past them all, yelling, "There's a whole army up there! Orders are to go forward in waves, and don't break ranks, whatever happens."

Reaching the crest, Chris scrambled over beside Rochford-Clarke, clutching his revolver. British troops were staggering across an open area ahead in anything but organized waves, and it was a scene of total confusion, fear, pain and death, all going on against a background of unnerving noise.

Then Rochford-Clarke was running forward and shouting to his men to follow, so Chris had no option but to run with him, ill though he felt. For as far as he could see, the ground ahead rose and fell in a series of shallow ravines, and the push forward was being accomplished by moving from the shelter of one and rushing across open ground to the shelter of another. The dead and wounded were left where they fell, for the stretcher-bearers to pick up later. As he ran, Chris vaguely registered the horror of the bloody wounds of war, but mercifully the need to run on made them fragments of a distant nightmare.

The nightmare lasted all day. At the end of it, he and a horde of other khaki-clad brutes guzzled the contents of their canteens, stuffing rations into their mouths with frantic speed, and went to sleep in total self-interest at still being alive.

But it all began again the minute there was a faint paling of the sky. Only this time it was even worse. The Turks came out of the greyness with such strength and ferocity, men soon formed a human carpet of broken bodies that heaved and moaned. Chris fired clumsily at those who ran at him with rifles—men with black moustaches and dark eyes flashing hatred. He killed some—he *must* have killed some. The noise was inhuman, deafening. Then there was a terrible scream beside him, and he turned. Rochford-Clarke had only half a face. Oh God! Chris pushed fresh bullets into his gun with trembling fingers and killed some more men.

Then they were coming with bayonets. "Retreat to the next ravine!" They all moved back and fired again. The heat pounded in his body, the blood pounded in his head, the breath pounded in his chest. "Retreat to the next ravine! Retreat! Retreat!" The ground shimmered and burned. Black moustaches and dark eyes flashing hatred. Where had they come from? There *was* a whole army of them. He ran, feeling desperately sick. Where had the other half of Rochford-Clarke's face gone? Falling into a hollow, he threw up. He did not think he could get to his feet again. But he had to when they rushed once more with bayonets. He fell, climbed to his feet to run with the others, and collapsed into the next hollow, doubled up with pains in his stomach. But there was no time to nurse pain. Up again with the vague shapes running with him. "Retreat! Retreat!"

Then it was night, and they were all back on the beach. They ate, drank, and went to sleep—those who were left.

337

THE GRAND AUGUST assault had failed. Massive Turkish reinforcements had been rushed in, unknown to the attackers. Gallipoli was now a bigger embarrassment than ever to the British government, and the problem it posed was shelved in the hope that it would solve itself.

Five days after landing, Chris finally joined the headquarters further down the peninsula. Headquarters consisted of a cave that housed half a dozen officers—including a British colonel and a New Zealand major—and a young lad who made tea, cocoa, snacks and bromides for them all.

Chris's arrival was unexpected and put the colonel, Petworth by name, in a temper. "I knew nothing about this. I never asked for any damned translator!"

"I understand it was a Colonel Partridge who put in the request," stammered Chris.

"Partridge died two months ago."

Conscious that the others in the cave were regarding him with curiosity, Chris listed his additional qualifications.

"I see; an expert at languages, are you?" countered the colonel. "Do they seriously think we have an espionage system at work on these confounded cliffs? A Greek scholar, you say? Do they think Gallipoli is a suburb of Athens? These intelligence wallahs are always the same. Too busy being damned geniuses." He turned to the tall, deeply tanned New Zealand major, who was around thirty-five and had prematurely silver hair. "Lord Almighty, Neil, save me from the intelligence branch!"

The major smiled faintly at Chris and said to his irate superior, "It's not young Sheridan's fault, sir. He had to obey orders. No doubt this was the last place on earth he wanted to visit."

"You're wrong, sir," said Chris, warming to a softer tone. "I should have visited Páros, Naxos and Mílos last year, but it was cancelled. When I was told I was coming out here, I couldn't wait to arrive. I . . . well, I wasn't told what the true situation was."

The major held out his hand. "I'm Neil Frencham, and I couldn't wait to get here, either. I'm a history teacher."

Chris shook his hand. "How do you do, sir. Ancient history?"

"Most emphatically." He smiled, his eyes crinkling at the corners. "Now you're here, I'll have someone to share my interest."

Colonel Petworth heaved a long sigh. "All right, Mr. Sheridan, I shall have to keep you since it's impossible to send you back."

Looking at Neil Frencham, he said, "But if he breaks those glasses he's wearing, he'll not only be useless, he'll be a liability."

After that dispiriting start, life for Chris became a meaningless routine of incredible heat, discomfort and idleness. His quarters were an embrasure off the main trench, about seven feet wide, ten feet long, and just high enough to allow his six-foot height to remain unstooped. As he endured the misery, he tried to forget Rochford-Clarke with only half a face. The young subaltern had gone off to one of the hospital ships on the start of his journey home, but Chris did not believe he would survive. How could a person live with one eye, one ear, half a jaw, and half a brain? Would a man want to live like that, even if it were possible?

Soon, however, Chris discovered that it was having nothing to do that was the most destructive element in his life. So he mastered basic Turkish from the book he had in his pack, and took to writing a diary of day-to-day life, which he then translated into every language he knew. He also wrote down every poem he could recollect, and translated those. When that palled, he took to inventing codes. When he was not writing, he was sketching. Occasionally he was sent by Colonel Petworth to climb through the scrub to a dangerous vantage point with binoculars, to sketch the inland terrain and mark in the present positions of the enemy, normally hidden from them.

Periodic assaults were made up the cliffs in an effort to establish a better foothold. But they were always beaten back with savage loss of life on both sides, and the mood of the men grew uglier.

All in all, during the four months leading up to Christmas there was only one element in Chris's life that kept him going. That was his friendship with the New Zealander, Neil Frencham. Together they discussed everything under the sun, escaped their present existence by entering those of centuries before. For all the knowledge Chris imparted on Greek and Roman beliefs and attitudes, Neil responded with a profound understanding of the Maori peoples and culture.

One day Neil told Chris he had found a place where it was possible to bathe, out of range of the Turkish guns. Seizing the right moment, they both slipped away to scramble down a trackless slope and arrive at the base of a narrow fault that ran up through a rock that overhung the sea in a convenient slab.

Chris was charmed with the peace and solitude. "How jolly clever of you to have found this without anyone knowing," he said, turning to Neil with a delighted smile. "Did you use Maori water-divining techniques?"

Neil laughed and ruffled Chris's hair with affection, much as Rex used to do. "Cheeky young devil! Get in there and wash away the lice!" As they took their shirts off, Neil added, "We can go in in the buff here. No dignity to lose in front of the troops."

"Good-oh," enthused Chris, longing for the cold cleansing salt water as he tugged off his uniform and carefully placed his spectacles on top of the pile. Then, naked, he looked at the blur of the other man. "Come on, I'll race you in."

Neil did not answer immediately, and when he did it was in a strange intent tone. "My God, you're only a boy, really, underneath all that wisdom."

They swam and dived for fifteen minutes or so, until they were both breathless. Then they climbed out onto the flat rock to dry themselves in the heat of the sun, Chris feeling unusually contented as he groped for his spectacles.

Suddenly, from close beside him, Neil said softly, "You know, you have the most wonderful eyes of any boy I've ever seen."

Something inside Chris began to curl up, and his feeling of wellbeing vanished instantly. He wished Neil had not said that. It brought back, out of the blue, something that the past four months had pushed to the far recesses of his mind. Now, like one of those murderous whistling shells, it zoomed out of nowhere to remind him that he had a wife and son at home—a baby that did nothing but wail, and a girl who had been seduced by his eyes.

"So wonderful they can't see a thing," he said with ferocity. Then, hooking the tortoiseshell frames round his ears, he snatched up his clothes and began pulling them on.

"What's the matter?" his companion asked sharply.

"Nothing. We ought to get back."

"Have I upset you? Please forgive me. I intended quite the reverse."

But Chris was scrambling up the rocky cliff face with scant care for safety, fighting a losing battle with the old feeling of hopelessness and despair. Suddenly he was halted by hands that gripped his shoulders from behind, and swung him round.

"Chris, *don't*. Don't run off like this," Neil panted. "I could bite my tongue out now. But I couldn't help it. You looked so beautiful standing there, and those eyes with the long lashes curling over them were more than I could stand."

"Wha . . . what?" Chris stammered, staring in horror at the intent suntanned face of the man whom he had looked upon as a fellow aesthete like himself, a loyal friend, a substitute for Rex.

"*Damn!*" he cried in sick anguish. "Is that all people ever see when they look at me—a beautiful body? You filthy devil! You've made a mockery of everything I care about." His voice began to break with fervour. "You've destroyed all I had left!"

Chris turned and clawed his way up the rugged slope, driven by a desperation that could no longer be contained. Up there, at the top of the cliffs, he could find freedom from it. He had seen others do it and shuddered. Now, he wanted it beyond reason.

He had crossed the line of trenches and was halfway towards the crest before he was seized from behind. Fighting desperately, he tried to shake off the older man who was clinging to his shirt.

"Chris, for heaven's sake come down!" panted Neil, his face wild and frightened. "This is no way out for you—you're worth far more than that. Suicide is for the unintelligent. If you go up there, you are admitting that there *is* no more to you than a body. Let that brain of yours work now. There's never been a greater need for it."

Chris scrambled a little further, more slowly, then stopped.

The voice went on, "I see now that I made a terrible misjudgment. Don't worry, it's all over."

Then Chris heard the sound of the other man walking away, and he could no longer hold back the sobs that racked his body. Sprawled there on the scree, he felt lost, degraded, and terrified by his own loneliness. But he did not climb to the top of the cliff. When it grew dark he dragged himself wearily down.

AN HOUR BEFORE DAWN the Turks made one of their fierce, frenzied attacks designed to shake the Allies from their tenacious hold and drive them into the sea for good. The battle followed the usual pattern. Waves of men were to be sent over the top to charge uphill with the object of capturing the machinegun that raked them all so continuously.

The whistles blew, and the first wave clambered from their trenches onto the exposed slopes. Chris watched through binoculars from the entrance to the headquarters cave. Within minutes, nothing moved on that cliff apart from the occasional inert body slowly sliding downwards on the loose shale. Another whistle blast; another wave of men, who fell alongside the others. Suddenly, the machinegun fell silent. The thing must have jammed. The mishap allowed the next wave of troops to continue climbing beyond the line of their comrades' bodies, and with only inaccurate rifle fire to face, they crept nearer and nearer the top. A new noise began. All round Chris men were cheering, shouting encouragement. Another whistle blast, and these same men were climbing from the trenches that were home to them.

The two lines of men were roughly a hundred yards apart—one only feet from the crest, the other advancing steadily behind—when Chris's attention was taken by the racing arrival of Neil. His face was worried and angry.

"My troops are going to take that gun," he panted to Colonel Petworth, "but I want better support from your men on that other cliff to cover them when they reach it. There may be a whole Turkish division up there."

Petworth swung round. "I've given you what support I can rustle up. All I can offer is covering fire from the trenches."

"That's no use," snapped Neil. "This is the nearest my men have ever come to taking one of their guns, sir. We can't let them down now, or they'll give up completely."

"I know. . . I know! Send one of your subalterns across there to persuade them that someone believes in their chances."

Neil swallowed. "I haven't got any subalterns left. They all went down in the first three waves. That's why we've got to have that gun."

"Then what about an officer?"

Neil's mouth tightened. "I've a captain with one leg in plaster, a lieutenant with dysentery, and myself. Take your choice. But if we lose that gun now we're so close to capturing it, I'll hold you responsible for the mutiny we'll have on our hands."

The colonel glared at him, red in the face. Then, as Chris shifted his feet noisily, the glare was fastened on him.

"Very well, Major Frencham, I'll give you support on the eastern flank. Young Sheridan can lead the attack."

"*No!*" came the desperate cry that betrayed much more than military protest. "You can't send him. I'll go myself."

Colonel Petworth flung him a contemptuous look. "Sheridan is a subaltern, and expendable. You are not. All we need is a figurehead, someone in officer's uniform out there in front to inspire confidence. Right, boy?" demanded the commander.

Chris felt weak with fright. "I don't know much about battle tactics, sir."

"You run like a mule with a bee under its tail and hope to hell they miss you." He drew his bushy brows together and almost smiled. "Scoot off, lad, and find Lance Corporal Green along the eastern transverse trench. He's got the whistle. When you get there, tell him to give two blasts to let us know. Then count to twenty and go."

Chris moved away, and as he passed Neil made an impulsive move towards him. But he did not even spare the man a glance, simply went out into the long winding trench, knowing he would never see any of them again. As he walked, he was not thinking of the glory of dying for his country, the honour of leading a vital charge, or any such uplifting but false idealism. He was filled with the anguish of knowing a man's mind and senses counted for nothing. For nineteen years he had revelled in the philosophies of wisdom, the refinements of culture, the language of beauty. Yet, in the end, it seemed all that was valued was his body.

6

The patient in bed nine lay for a long while gazing from the window, finding escape from pain in the scene outside. Snow lay everywhere, clean, dazzling, sharply beautiful in the pale cold sunlight. There was a large open stretch that must be lawn, then an extensive shrubbery behind which rose a row of dark cypresses, dappled green and white. Only yesterday his bed had been wheeled to this corner, where two windows gave him a panorama of the grounds. Up by the door he had felt on view to anyone who entered; down here he was in his own world.

But it was a world that could well be Hades for the torment he was in. The whole of his body burned, as if he were roasting over the fires of the devil. His stomach, neck and head thundered with pain, his throat was constantly parched, and his hands were two throbbing areas of anguish. What was more, he appeared to be blind until someone put a contraption across his face that made everything spring into focus.

He had been born ten days ago. When the torture grew too great, he cried out. Then they rushed at him, enclosed him with dark green screens, and stuck needles in him. He was trussed up in a manner that made movement impossible. From beneath his arms to the tops of his thighs he was tightly bound, and his arms looked like two wooden spoons with huge ovals of white gauze at the ends. One leg was immobilized and fixed to the bed with metal rings. Utterly helpless, he could only turn when they turned him, sit up when they decided he should sit.

He had not spoken a word to any of them. He did not trust them. They told him things he did not believe: said he was someone named Christopher Wesley Sheridan, nineteen years old, from a Dorset village called Tarrant Royal. There were two brothers called Roland and Rex, but no parents. There was a war in progress, and he had been seriously wounded by an exploding shell as he had led a charge on a machinegun post. He was now in a hospital for officers in Somerset.

They had tried to break his silence with slyness, bringing to the bed on three occasions a blond young man in tweeds with a dependable good-looking face, and saying he was the brother called Roland. The visits had not fooled him for a second. This Roland was one of their own number and would get no more from him than they did, however hard they tried.

But they held one trump card that threatened his resistance. His head was bandaged like an Egyptian mummy, with a slit for eyes, nose and mouth. Under those bandages, he knew, he had only half a head. When they spoke of taking off those bandages soon so that he could see what he looked like, he broke out in a sweat of real terror, and they put the needle in him. If they began unwinding the white cloth to reveal one eye, one ear and a bloody mess of brains, he would be totally lost.

Suddenly a dark blur appeared beside him, and he almost cried out in fright. But it was merely the pince-nez being slipped onto the bridge of his nose.

Everything leaped into sharp clarity and looked reassuringly normal. Then someone moved beside him again. She was wearing a starched cap and apron like those calling themselves nurses, but her long dress was pink instead of blue. He had not seen this girl before. Gazing warily at her, he found her gazing back, eyes full of some deep sadness, face very pale, body strangely stiff. Then she turned

344

away without saying a word, and he saw her run out through the swing doors. He was puzzled.

After a time the girl in the pink dress returned, looking paler than ever and red around the eyes. She had brought his dinner tray. He always made a point of eating meals because he needed to keep up his strength for the day he escaped from this place.

The broth was good, but the girl's hand was so unsteady as she spooned it into his mouth that a lot of it spilled on the sheet. She was not much better with the steamed fish, but they somehow got through it. There was the usual egg custard for dessert.

After dinner another nurse came. She whipped off the pince-nez, tipped some foul-smelling stuff into his mouth, lowered the backrest and went off. He grew drowsy very quickly.

Later on he saw his head in a mirror, with only half a face. He struggled to look away from the gruesome sight, screamed at them to cover it up again. They came and put a needle in his arm, and soon he was unable to see anything any more.

THE GIRL IN THE PINK DRESS came a lot during the next three days. She never said anything to him, just did the tasks she was given and went away again. Her pale sad face bothered him. She seemed so alone in her sadness, and he knew what isolation meant. Why did she stay?

Proof that she left the building and returned came on the fifth morning, when she arrived at his bedside, after being absent the day before, and put a small vase of snowdrops on the locker beside his bed, where he could see them. The small white hanging bells were so fragile and innocent, they were like a breath of the freedom that was waiting for him outside. He shifted his gaze to her face, and their glances interlocked for a long moment as he tried to understand why she had brought him the snowdrops.

She sat on the chair near his head to give him his breakfast, as she usually did. But she made a bad job of cutting the toast which was so crisp, it flew off the plate. Immediately the plump bossy woman who ran the room hurried towards them with an expression like thunder.

"Don't let her frighten you," he advised the girl swiftly. "Refuse to speak. They can't do anything about that."

She looked up at him, her face turning ashen. The plump woman stopped, then turned back, but the girl sat like a statue, seemingly

345

petrified. Then his spirits plummeted as he realized it was not them she was afraid of, but *him*.

When he could, he made himself ask, "It's my face, isn't it?"

"Your . . . your face?" she whispered.

"Only one eye, one ear, and . . . and . . ." He could not go on.

Her eyes were now shimmery with tears. "Chris, why . . ?"

"Don't call me that," he said sharply, afraid that she was one of them, after all.

"What shall I call you, then?" she asked, her voice now thick.

He gazed at her through the slit in his face bandages, suddenly as full of emotion as she.

"I don't know," he said helplessly. "I don't know who I am . . . or what I'm doing here. But I know I can never leave, because I've only got half a head."

They had to put the needle in his arm again that night.

REX WAS GIVEN a whole month's leave prior to the Easter of 1916. He could hardly believe it was over a year and a half since war had begun; that he had been out there flying for fifteen months and was still alive. The conviction that he would join Mal Haines and the others only when his time had come put a strange calmness inside him, and was responsible for his reputation as one of the top flying aces among the Allies.

The new single-seater biplane fighters had arrived in France in an attempt to break the German air superiority gained by the Fokker, and the pilots now had to navigate, reconnoitre, and operate the machinegun while they were flying.

Rex preferred being alone to having an observer. It meant only he held responsibility for his life. But it also meant he needed the greatest coordination of thought a man could attain, and so far he had been phenomenally successful, to the extent that his name was high on the list of prizes sought by the German squadrons in his area. Every young Hun pilot longed to claim he had shot down Lieutenant Sherry Sheridan.

Rex knew this, and had many times exchanged signals of respect and understanding with German fliers he constantly encountered, all of whom wore special symbols of identification in the spirit of deadly sportsmanship that governed air battles. Rex, himself, would never take off without wearing a cerise silk scarf around his throat, ends flying. The scarf was, in fact, the silk nightdress of a French countess whose contribution to the war effort was to keep the airmen in good spirits. The press decided to withhold that from the British public, and their hero's talisman had been dignified into a silk shawl owned by a noblewoman of a French branch of the Sheridan family.

Rex's request for leave to visit his brother, just returned from Gallipoli, broken in mind and limb, had immediately been approved. Permission had also been granted to his long-standing Australian partner and friend, Lieutenant Mike Manning, to go to England to see his sister, Tessa, who had come from Australia to do war work.

During the journey back to England Rex's spirits were subdued. The news of Chris had come as a terrible shock, all the more so because Roland's letter had been uncharacteristically emotional about the tragedy. Rex's intention to go straight to the hospital in Somerset was thwarted by trains and cross-channel services that were overcrowded, spasmodic and slow. He and Mike eventually reached London at six pm, so he decided to book into a hotel with his friend for that night, and go to the hospital the following day, which was Sunday.

While Mike went round to pick up his sister, who shared some rooms with an actress, Rex had a bath, dressed for dinner, and then stretched out on the bed to wait. He fell asleep.

A hand shook him awake and he frowned at Mike in bewilderment. Standing beside his friend was an attractive smiling girl in a yellow dress, with eyes that were the same curious silvery green as Mike's. That was the only similarity. Her slender shape was definitely more exciting than Mike's, her face was smooth and golden from the sunshine of Australia, and her long dark hair was put up in shining coils.

Rex studied her in appreciation, smiling back.

"The dreams they provide in this hotel are better than any I had at Grissons," he said.

She held out her hand. "Don't we get introduced?"

"Of course," he said. "But I only shake hands with men. I usually get a kiss from girls."

Merriment flared in her eyes, and she swooped quickly to kiss him. Straightening up, she told him, "Now I shall be known as the girl who has kissed Sherry Sheridan, and I shall receive proposals from dukes and earls."

"Make certain they're proposals of *marriage*, Sis," put in Mike earnestly. "Now, shall we go and eat? I'm famished."

It felt like Christmas as Rex worked his way through seven courses, the like of which he had long ago forgotten, and flirted with the lovely suntanned girl untouched by the tragedy of France, who spoke of her life on a vast farm in Australia. Between brother and sister there was obviously close affection, and Rex was immediately drawn in. The night was still young when they finished their meal, and Tessa suggested they all go to the theatre where her actress friend was performing.

Rex and Mike agreed, and the three of them jumped into a taxi and laughed over silly nonsense all the way there. They were shown to a box on the second tier, and sat on the red plush seats in semidarkness because the show had already started.

Rex hardly saw what happened on stage as a pair of dancing girls were followed by a comedian, then by a troupe of performing dogs. The large meal, the darkness, the long journey from Grissons and the months of flying now caught up with him, and he had to fight to keep awake. Finally Tessa leaned towards him and whispered, "This is her now. Watch—she's good."

Tessa's friend turned out to be a male impersonator, and Rex immediately lost interest. He much preferred girls in dresses. Laurie Pagett, as the girl was billed, wore top hat and tails while she sang a saucy ditty in a surprisingly deep voice, about a young man-about-town who could not distinguish champagne from lemonade and was always offending hostesses.

There was a sharp kick on his boot as Mike leaned across his sister to whisper, "What do you think of *that* for a bit of nerve?"

Rex straightened up in his chair and glanced in the direction of Mike's nod. The entertainer on stage had changed from top hat and tails, and was now prancing about dressed as a flier, with her arms outstretched like wings as she pretended to zoom up and down. But it was the chorus of her song that took Rex's attention.

When he flies, oh-so-high,
All the mam'selles cry
Chéri! Chéri!
He can't love them all,
But still they all call,
Chéri! Chéri!

There was another verse so blatantly, heroically patriotic it made him cringe, then back to the chorus which was repeated twice with the whole audience joining in. Rex then realized the figure on the stage had a cerise scarf round her neck. At the end, the girl walked to the front of the stage and treated her audience to an exaggerated saucy wink before "flying" off into the wings. "What cheek!" exclaimed Rex. She could only have been impersonating him with that scarf and the chorus of "Chéri" which sounded like Sherry. But how could he possibly have become the subject of a music-hall song?

Looking at Tessa, he said, "You had a hand in this, didn't you?"

She smiled with delight. "Mike always writes such a lot about you that doesn't appear in the newspapers, and I just passed it on to her when she said she wanted to do a number about Sherry Sheridan. You're not angry, are you?"

"Extremely," he told her, looking stern. "That song states I can't love them all . . . but I do," he concluded, with a copy of Laurie Pagett's broad wink.

After the show, they all went back to Tessa's rooms, which were in a boardinghouse. It meant tiptoeing up the stairs and past the landlady's door, because her rules forbade male guests to go beyond the downstairs parlour. Rex sank into one of the two chairs, and they were soon drinking tea, because alcohol in the rooms was also forbidden. Then Rex asked Tessa about the war work she did in London.

She made a face. "It's in a munitions factory. The work is most awfully boring, and I'd rather be in the open air."

Rex sipped his tea. "While I'm on leave, you must come down to my home in Dorset. Come for the weekend—you and Mike."

Her eyes sparkled silver. "Oh, I'd love that, I really would."

The door crashed open then, and a figure carrying a pile of boxes practically fell into the room. Boxes toppled onto the floor with resounding thumps, and a voice that was low and husky said, "That's torn it! If old Blisterbag doesn't rush up here thinking we're holding an orgy, I'll eat my hat." Then it paused and added, "Great Scott, we *are* holding an orgy!"

The girl just inside the doorway took the whole of Rex's attention, and it was as if his pulse had stopped beating. She was tall, voluptuously built, with a pointed face full of dynamic, vivid beauty, and hair as red as his own, cut very short in curls that covered her head. Her eyes, green, upturned and wicked, were fastened on him in a glance that seemed to still his blood.

"Do shut the door," begged Tessa. "She will be up if she hears you shouting about an orgy."

The newcomer kicked the door closed with a high-heeled scarlet shoe, then let her black fur-trimmed coat slip from her shoulders to reveal a scarlet dress that clung to her splendid body like a skin. Rex continued to stare at her, feeling punch-drunk.

"So introduce me," came the sultry voice.

"This is my brother, Mike," Tessa told her warmly. "He's on four weeks' leave."

"Hello, Mike," said the girl with enthusiasm, shaking his hand.

"And this is his friend, Lieutenant Sheridan!" Tessa grinned at Rex. "My roommate, Laura Pagett."

He got to his feet. This beautiful, vital, feminine creature was the male impersonator he had just seen? But she was staring back at him with her hand to her throat, eyes full of alarm.

"Lieutenant *Sheridan!* Oh no!"

"He doesn't shake hands with girls. He usually gets a kiss," advised Tessa. "And he saw your performance tonight."

"Oh no," said Laura again. "So that's the end of that!"

"Why a song about me?" Rex heard himself say.

"You give them all something to cheer. They get dreadfully depressed, you know, reading the casualty lists every morning. Sherry Sheridan has become a legend, a hero, and they go home feeling a little closer to their own sons and husbands because you are over there with them."

"Good Lord!" he said, astonished at her sensitivity.

"Aren't you furious with me?" she asked tentatively.

He shook his head. "I thought that wink was a bit much."

A smile touched her mouth and spread its brightness over her whole face. "Don't you really shake hands with girls?"

"No."

"Dare I kiss you, now you know who I am?"

His heart thudded ridiculously. "I think you owe me that much, don't you?"

She moved closer and reached up to touch her mouth gently against his, but his arms went round her, and the kiss turned into something that startled them both. They stood looking at each other in acute awareness of danger, the other pair in the room totally

350

forgotten. But he knew he was already lost. There had never been a girl like this before; there never would be again.

"Hey, this tea is getting cold," put in Mike. "Aren't you two going to avail yourselves of it?"

The spell was partially broken by Mike's intervention, and Rex offered a chair to Laura before sitting on a low stool beside her. They laughed a lot and drank gallons of tea. But the whole time, Rex was conscious of every movement, every word spoken in that husky voice, every expression on the mobile face of the girl beside him. He had four weeks in England. He wanted to spend every minute of every one of them with her.

At one point he asked her, "Why do you dress up in men's clothes when you're such a success as a girl?"

She looked at him frankly. "I suppose it's a form of defence. In the theatre a girl is very vulnerable, you know. She either has to be tough or pretend she is. I was brought up in a country vicarage. My father was horrified when I made it clear I wanted to go on the stage, and forbade me to do it. I left home and I haven't been back since." She smiled. "Besides, it's fun being Sherry Sheridan."

"I could see that," he said, then took the plunge. "I have to go to Somerset tomorrow to visit a hospital. My young brother was pretty well broken up at Gallipoli, and has no idea who he is now. Would you come with me?"

She looked at him steadily for a moment or two. "Poor little devil!" Then she nodded gently. "All right, if you'd really like me to."

He relaxed after that and let happiness engulf him. He would see her tomorrow; he would see her every day for a month! Soon the scarlet of her dress seemed too bright for his eyes, the mesmeric huskiness of her voice too much for his mind. Everything began to grow distant and unreal.

WHEN HE AWOKE, he was lying on the floor, covered with a white blanket. He got stiffly to his feet, almost falling over Mike, stretched out beside him.

There was a wonderful smell of eggs and bacon, and Rex followed it to its source in a tiny alcove where there was an oilstove. Tessa was there in a blue-and-white spotted dress with a wide blue silk sash round her tiny waist.

She turned, smiling widely. "Hello. So food has done what all

351

three of us failed to do last night. You were dead to the world. Sorry you missed your wonderful soft bed at the hotel."

"What shocking bad manners I have!"

She laughed, then indicated two plates. "I sneaked these up here for you and Mike. Luckily, Mrs. Beamish leaves breakfast on the sideboard on Sunday mornings."

He looked at her suntanned face, her neat tidy figure, and the shining dark hair in a chignon. "You're a very nice girl, Tessa." He kissed her on the cheek. "Now, where is Laura?"

"In bed, as she is every morning. You won't see her until noon."

"But she's coming to Somerset with me to visit my brother."

"Well, you won't start out until after lunch. Sunday's her one night off, and she likes to indulge in laziness for the whole day."

Rex was dismayed. They would not get down to Somerset and back if they started out in midafternoon. Then he had an idea.

"Suppose we all go! After visiting the hospital we could stay overnight at my home. I'll get Laura back in time on Monday."

"Oh, lovely!" cried Tessa. "I'll play truant from the factory tomorrow. After all, it's just as much help to the war effort to keep the boys of the RFC happy, isn't it?"

"Hello! That's settled," said Mike's voice through a yawn, as he appeared in the alcove. Then he and Rex ate breakfast, and after that crept down the iron fire escape and made their way back to the hotel. While Mike went off to buy a newspaper, Rex sent a telegram to Tarrant Hall so that they would be met by Dawkins at Greater Tarrant station. As he went upstairs to pack, he felt quite jaunty. The company of the others would help him face the dreaded meeting with Chris.

Mike looked remarkably long-faced when he walked into their room, holding out a Sunday paper open at an inner page. "I might as well draw your attention to this," he said quietly.

In curiosity Rex took the newspaper and read the headline: VILLAGE DISOWNS SUICIDE'S SON. Then, in smaller letters underneath: Brother of Flying Ace Branded as Coward.

With heartbeat slowing Rex read how the entire village of Tarrant Royal had turned their backs on a man who refused to volunteer to fight for his country. They had thrown him off committees and councils and rejected his assistance for community events. The article finished with a description of how the villagers had barred their former squire from entering the seventeenth-century church,

352

because they felt he did not deserve a place in the family pew, as his two gallant brothers did.

Rex was filled with painful sadness as he looked up at Mike. "Poor Roland. This will have completely broken him!"

7

"I'm afraid there is little chance your brother will know you," said the doctor gravely. "His amnesia would appear to be total."

Rex pounced on that. "Why do you say 'appear' in that somewhat sceptical manner?"

"Mr. Sheridan, this is a dangerously complex case. We have established, without doubt, that the boy's mind has shut out nineteen years of life so totally he has no recollection of anything before the ninth of January this year. We also know that your brother is exceptionally brilliant, but only in certain directions. This kind of brain crosses the fine line into eccentricity, and then insanity, far more quickly than the average . . . even without war and wounds to bring it about." The medical man paused, then went on, "Our main concern is to stop young Christopher crossing that line from whence he would never return. But the treatment is still experimental, and has to be backed up by a few prayers." He fiddled with a pencil he held between his fingers. "And your young brother is playing us at our own game, Mr. Sheridan."

Rex stared in complete confusion. "You mean, he's pretending?"

"No . . . not exactly. But he's one jump ahead of us all the time. He is full of suspicion, distrust and fear. For the first ten days we believed he found it impossible to communicate, until he suddenly confided to his nurse that he was remaining silent to hit back at us— *the enemy*. Even now, after two months, he will only speak to that one nurse. But most distressing is his total refusal to take part in our tests."

"Poor fellow!" exclaimed Rex, very upset.

"Until we can find the cause of his silence, we can do little for him. The danger is that he will withdraw too far before we get to the root of his hell—for that is where he must be."

Feeling choked, Rex got up to look out of the window, when a door opened near him and a girl in a pink dress and starched apron walked in.

353

"Marion!" he exclaimed in surprise. "*You* here?"

"I thought it was time I told you about the one nurse your brother appears to trust," said the doctor with a smile. "I'll leave you alone with Nurse Deacon. She'll fill you in on the other details before you go in to see Christopher."

He went out, and Rex took Marion's hands. They were cold despite the spring warmth of the day.

"My dear girl, whatever is all this? The uniform, and 'Nurse Deacon'? Roland said nothing about it in his letter."

"He wouldn't," she said quietly. "He tried to stop it, but didn't succeed. To his mind, I am to blame for Chris being here."

"No, that's nonsense," Rex protested.

She looked at him with sadness filling her dark eyes. "I *am* to blame—for everything." To his distress, she suddenly indulged in a fit of sobbing. He tried to calm her, then coaxed her to a settee where they sat down.

"Suppose you tell me everything. Remember I told you to come to Uncle Rex if you had problems."

She dabbed at her eyes with her handkerchief and smiled. Then she began by revealing that Chris had kept his married state a secret from the army authorities. "So the telegram went to Roland," she said. "But when I realized he had no intention of telling me what had happened, I came here and saw Dr. Stevens, whom you've just seen." She sighed. "I told him the full truth about our marriage and Chris's feelings towards me, and he suggested I become a probationer nurse here. That way, I would be with Chris in a way he would accept, and be helping them as well. We decided to use my maiden name."

Rex looked at her in compassion. "It must be a dreadful strain on you, seeing him like that day after day."

"It's better now than it was at the beginning." She almost broke down again. "But I don't give him confidence; he thinks he is giving it to me. That's the basis of our relationship."

"What really happened to him?" asked Rex anxiously.

"Chris was caught in a shell bombardment that blew off two of his fingers, smashed the bones in his left leg, and gave him wounds to the stomach and neck. He was left under a blistering sun for several hours, and machinegun fire wounded his shoulder and right thigh. He was given emergency dressings and assigned to one of the hospital ships, but a fire aboard the boat carrying the wounded to the vessel burned him badly and he was rushed home. No one realized that he had no idea who he was until he recovered enough to remain conscious. But, Rex, the most terrible thing is he thinks . . . he thinks he has only half a head under his bandages. He has nightmares about it. Isn't it hopelessly sad?"

Rex took her hands and gripped them tightly. "Yes, but Marion, you have the chance to start all over again with him, knowing he can't hold against you things he can't remember. This time I'm sure you'll make it work . . . if you want it to, that is."

"Of course I do," she cried. "I want little David to have a father."

"What's happening to my nephew while you're here?"

She smiled. "He's fine. I see him every five days. Young Nellie Marchant from next door takes care of him and Daddy is wonderful. Rex, you will come and see him while you're home, won't you?"

"Try and stop me!" He got to his feet. "Come on, let's go and see young David's father. Afterwards, I want you to meet my best friend, his pretty sister, and a rather special girl. They've been waiting outside for me all this time. Once I've seen Chris, we'll all have tea together."

Rex's lightheartedness was an act. As he and Marion walked towards the ward, his heart was hammering against his ribs. He could not describe how he felt when she stopped and smiled at the bandaged effigy everyone said was his beloved brother. One leg was in plaster, the hands lying on the coverlet were heavily bandaged. There was a kind of helmet on his head, padded at the back, low over his brow, and up to his nostrils, with a hole for the mouth. The large violet-blue eyes gazed ahead blankly.

Marion picked up a pince-nez from the locker to fix on the bridge of his nose, and he marvelled at her calmness.

"I told you your brother was coming to see you," she said quietly. "Why did you take these off?"

There was no response, although Rex could see intelligence in the eyes now that they could see properly. Chris stared at him as if at an unlikable stranger. It was more than Rex could take.

"Hello, old son," he managed eventually. "They've told you I'm your disreputable brother Rex, and they've told me you're my brainy brother Chris. With all those bandages over your face, I'll have to take their word for it . . . and so will you." He sat beside the bed knowing the meeting was a failure. "I've brought you something," he persevered, unbuttoning his pocket. "It's a book of

355

French poems that I would call risqué, and you would call aesthetic." He put the leatherbound book on the coverlet.

Marion smiled at Chris reassuringly. "It's all right. He isn't a doctor. I like him, and I think he wants to help."

Silence.

Rex felt he was achieving nothing and just putting unnecessary strain on Chris. He got to his feet again and smiled at the shell of his brother as best he could.

"I do want to help you," he said. "You trust Marion. Think it over about whether you want to trust me, and I'll come again soon. Don't give up, Chris."

With that he walked away, throat constricting painfully. But when he reached the end of the ward and looked back, the patient in bed nine was gazing at the window. The book of poems lay ignored on the coverlet.

THEY ALL HAD TEA in a cafe decorated with copper kettles and warming pans. They ate cucumber sandwiches, scones with honey, and madeleines. Marion made no attempt to hide her identity, and chatted about her small son with great animation to Mike, who had deliberately taken the seat beside her. Rex was grateful.

But the tea party had to be curtailed because four of them had to catch a train. Marion said she would be at home on the following Thursday, and hoped they would all come to admire her son. "He's really one of the most beautiful little boys you'll ever have seen," she told them with quiet pride.

It was dark by the time they reached Greater Tarrant, but the trap was waiting, and the family coachman was standing beside the pony, a broad welcoming smile across his weathered face.

"Hello, Dawkins," Rex greeted him warmly, shaking the old man's hand. "It's good to see you again."

"And you, sir," came the wheezy reply.

Dawkins then greeted the others courteously and gave rugs to the two ladies to put across their knees. Rex made certain he sat with Laura and put his arm along the back of the seat behind her.

On the six-mile drive home the past attacked him so strongly that it made the last eighteen months of his life fade into the background. Memories flooded through him. In that summer of 1914 he had had a motorcycle to dash around on, *Princess* to ride the sky with him, and a secure future as a wealthy landowner's son. He had

had a father in Madeira, and two good-looking successful brothers who were as happy as he.

It had all gone. Yet the lanes looked the same in the early moonlight, the primroses on the banks gave off the same damp fragrance as before, the dog fox still barked in the copse. A lump rose in his throat for the sadness of men, that did not touch the animals, the flowers, the bright moon.

A hand touched his, and he looked down at Laura's face in the moonlight. "You can't live your brothers' lives for them," she said softly. "There's enough danger in living your own."

"How did you know what I was thinking?" he said into her ear.

"I understand faces. I see hundreds of them in rows in front of me every evening. Yours is too sad, at the moment."

His arm tightened round her, and he said with fervour, "Not when I look at you."

THE GREAT CIRCULAR forecourt in front of Tarrant Hall's impressive front entrance was full of vehicles—a couple of motor ambulances, several motorcycle combinations, a staff car or two. Although Roland had written to warn him that half their home was now a hospital, Rex saw it all with dismay. The war was there in Tarrant Hall, after all.

As Dawkins pulled up at the side entrance, explaining that they could not go in through the wards, Roland came out to greet them. Rex vaulted eagerly over the side of the trap to greet his brother. It turned into an emotional moment, as they gripped each other's hands and found themselves lost for words. Rex realized with a shock that Roland looked ill and strained to the limit.

"It's good to be home," Rex said at last. He turned to draw Laura forward, and said, "I've brought some special friends I want you to meet." Smiling down at her, he made the first introduction. "This is my brother Roland, who is a great deal nicer and much more respectable than I am."

Laura's vivid face registered cautious appreciation. "He's also a lot handsomer! Hello, Roland. I'm Laura Pagett."

"Roland, Laura is a male impersonator and does a wicked song that just evades being eligible for a lawsuit by me."

Laura's wide inviting smile was turned on Roland, and her eyes danced with merriment. But Roland said stiffly, "How do you do, Miss Pagett. I think a lawsuit would be undesirable."

357

Hurriedly Rex introduced Tessa and Mike, then all four trooped into the small panelled hall.

"How's Priddy?" he asked, as they walked together into the side corridor.

"Older," came the uncompromising reply.

"And Minks?"

"I should have retired him, but he had nowhere else to go. Cook left six months ago, and the kitchens are now part of the convalescent home. My meals are cooked in the butler's pantry."

Rex halted incredulously as his brother opened the door that had once led into a morning room.

"Roland, just how much of this house has *not* been taken over by the army?"

With one hand on the door, Roland halted, too. "I have retained three bedrooms in the south wing, two servants' rooms, my study which I also use as a drawing room, this morning room where I now eat, and the outer hall which has been turned into the estate office. It's far more economical, and quite big enough for me." He smiled with the echo of former brotherhood. "But the place will come alive now you're here, Rex. A month, isn't it?"

"Er . . . yes. I want to talk about that later."

"About so many things," enthused Roland, leading the way to the study-turned-drawing room. "But there's plenty of time."

An hour or so later it was Tessa who broke up the evening after they had all been served sandwiches and coffee. "It must be the country air," she said, with a smile at Roland. "I'd forgotten how relaxing it can be. Will you please forgive me?"

"Of course," he said, smiling back with his reserved charm. "You'll be able to see the estate properly in the morning. You're in for a delightful surprise, Miss Manning."

"I can't wait . . . and I do wish you'd call me Tessa."

Laura rose to stand beside her, and said, "After so long, I'm sure you have been wanting to talk to Rex about family matters, yet you have welcomed us all into your home at very little notice, and I'm grateful." To Roland's complete surprise, she stood on tiptoe and kissed him, bringing a flush to his cheeks.

They all laughed, and after showing the guests to their rooms, the brothers went back downstairs. They sat for a few moments just looking at each other in the quiet contentment of being together again. Then Roland sighed. "You look older, Rex . . ."

"So do you."

"Tell me about your visit to Chris."

Rex leaned back in his chair and looked frankly at his brother.

"There isn't anything to tell. He's there. That's all I can say."

"No suggestion of recognition?"

Rex shook his head. "It's such an awful feeling." Then he decided to confront Roland right away. "Marion was there with him."

"She's always there with him."

"And she has every right to be. If anyone can help Chris, it will be her."

Roland got to his feet. "You must know that she is responsible for destroying him. Chris would never have volunteered if he had not been so desperate to get away from her and the baby."

"Now she needs the chance to build him up again."

"*She* needs!" cried Roland. "All I care about is what Chris needs . . . *and so should you!*"

Rex got to his feet knowing all this had to be said. "Whatever Marion has done in the past I would forgive ten times over, if she saved Chris's mind now." He took a deep breath. "Yes, she ruined Chris's chances at Cambridge and drove him to volunteer. But he ruined her life too, don't forget. The past eighteen months must have been terribly difficult for her. Pregnancy, husbandly neglect, hostility from you and sneers from the villagers. Chris desperately needs that girl now, and she just as desperately needs to do what she is doing. Please, Roland, try to be understanding towards her."

Roland made no further comment about Marion. Instead he walked over to the desk in the curtained window alcove. "Come here a minute," he said in a cold voice.

Rex joined him, puzzled. His puzzlement turned to horror when his brother opened a drawer filled with white feathers.

Picking one up and holding it between finger and thumb, Roland said, "The villagers have been sending me one of these every week. But there won't be many more. As soon as I appoint a bailiff, I'm going into the army."

"No," protested Rex immediately. "You're doing more than enough here. Don't let their lack of intelligence break you."

Roland stared at him. "Good Lord, it isn't because of the feathers. It's because of Chris. What has been done to him is so unacceptable, so tragic, I have to offer my limited knowledge to the Medical Corps so that I can try to help others, in his name. That's why I'm glad you're here just at the right time. I want to discuss the terms of our wills."

"Our wills?" repeated Rex, unable to think clearly by now.

"Once I don khaki, there's no doubt I'll be sent to France. If you and I are both killed, and Chris is declared insane, Marion will get this house and the estate in trust for that ill-begotten child of hers. I'd rather will Tarrant Hall and the estate to the army as a permanent hospital than let her and her father lord it up here. We've got to prevent that at all costs!"

8

Roland had lain awake for long troubled periods during the night. He had so looked forward to having Rex at Tarrant Hall for four weeks. However, his brother had breezed in with his friends, acting completely out of character over an actress he had known only twenty-four hours. Rex appeared infatuated beyond reason with this impossible girl. Although Laura Pagett apparently came from a respectable upper-middle-class family, she had abandoned her background to make a living in the sleazy world of the music hall— as a male impersonator, of all things!

In the morning Roland left the house and walked briskly across to the stables, intending to check some fencing that had been brought down by a recent storm. He breathed the fresh country air with its mixed scents of dewy grass, rich newly-turned earth, and wild violets. Deep regret sliced painfully through him. He did not want to leave all this; it was England, free and peaceful and productive. His heart would remain here when he went to war.

Entering the stable, he jumped at the sight of someone standing by his horse. She was just as startled, for she gasped.

"Good morning, Tessa," he said. "You're about very early."

"Yes, this heavenly morning woke me," she said enthusiastically. "Once outside, I just had to see your horses."

"They're only hacks," he said dismissively. "I've sold my thoroughbreds."

"They're in top condition," came her slightly reproachful response. "It's nice to find someone who really looks after his animals. At home, our lives depend on our horses."

"How many do you have?" he asked politely.

"About thirty or forty."

He stared at her, and she was amused at his astonishment. "With two hundred and fifty thousand head of sheep to control, we need quite a few stockmen, and each man needs a spare horse. They are mostly whalers—good sturdy beasts—but we have some thoroughbreds as well. Daddy races them."

He walked towards her, fascinated by what she was saying. It sounded quite incongruous coming from a tiny-waisted brunette with laughing silvery green eyes, who was dressed in a modest burnt-orange skirt and blouse. Yet she had the honest steadfast gaze of a girl from the country, he realized with sudden pleasure.

"You must forgive me, Tessa," he said with a smile. "Rex simply mentioned that your father had a farm."

She laughed. "And you thought it was similar to this? My word, no. We call them stations in Australia, and some of the big ones cover an area as large as Scotland and Wales. The only method of getting from place to place is to ride. You've no idea of the exhilaration of a dawn gallop after sleeping under the stars," she told him, with enthusiasm bubbling in her voice. "Now I must come clean, as the stockmen say, and confess that I would give anything to ride one of your horses."

"I'll give you ten minutes in which to change."

"No need." She laughed, and stood astride to reveal that she was wearing culottes. "May I ride without delay?"

Roland found himself laughing as he gazed down into her eager face. "Absolutely," he told her, unbolting the door of one of the stables. "And I'm letting you choose your mount."

They rode gently up to Longbarrow Hill and then began to canter across the sweet green hilltop. The sound of thundering hooves filled Roland's ears and the sight of Tessa's slender graceful figure delighted his senses. The canter turned into a gallop, and he had no hesitation in taking her across Middle Meadow, slashed by the river, past the old sawmill, and back through the long avenue of beeches that led to the west wing of Tarrant Hall. It was a gruelling route, but she took it with perfect ease and handled the horse with confidence.

A mile from the house Roland reined in. Unwilling to return yet, he explained about checking his fencing and asked if she would like to accompany him. They rode slowly, cooling their mounts and discussing sheep. It appeared she was an expert on the subject, and the idea came to him like a bolt from the blue. She knew about sheep, she rode like a man, and she understood how to run a farm. Tessa Manning would be the ideal bailiff for Tarrant Hall and the estate when he went into the army.

Sighing deeply, she said suddenly, "This is all so beautiful, after London."

"Why don't you stay for a while—you and your brother?" Roland said with careful persuasion.

"There's my job at the factory."

"I'm sure they'll understand if you take the rest of the week off. After all, who knows when Mike will get leave again?"

She turned to him with a disturbingly intent gaze. "You really want me to stay?"

"Yes . . . very much. Would you like to?"

"I . . . oh yes, of course I would!"

"That's settled, then," he declared, well satisfied. "Come on, let's have a final canter back to the house."

HAVING OVERCOME ONE OBSTACLE—that of coaxing Laura from her bed by mid-morning—Rex was faced with another. She stood beside him on the sun-washed gravel of the forecourt, looking totally stunning in a cream fine-wool dress trimmed with black velvet and jet beading, and regarded him with horror.

"Walk down to the village! You must be mad! I never walk further than the nearest tram stop. I'm a city girl."

He gazed at her in fascination, still unable to believe she was real and he had found her. Thinking quickly he said, "Wait here a moment. What's the use of being a hero if one doesn't take advantage of one's reputation once in a while?"

It took very little time to persuade the military to close their eyes while he borrowed one of their motorcycle combinations for an hour or two. After lifting Laura into the sidecar and making her comfortable with cushions Rex set off down the drive with a roar, and tried not to think of the old days when he had raced uphill to his home on his motorcycle. It seemed too many years ago to dwell on, so he concentrated on scaring the wits out of his passenger with his daredevil brand of driving, and enjoying every minute of her nearness.

They were catching the afternoon train to London so that she could be at the theatre in time. Roland was very disappointed, Rex knew, and had been reproachful towards Laura when she came downstairs, but it had made no difference to his plans. These four weeks were his alone, and he intended to spend them with this girl who made the world seem sane in the midst of madness. Having Laura beside him as he rattled through the familiar lanes eased the regret of noticing how many faces had gone.

But warmth of feeling for him was unchanged, he discovered. His progress was soon halted as the old stalwarts of the village spotted him, and clustered round the machine to shake his hand. Such lavish acclaim of his exploits and courage was unwelcome in the face of their treatment of Roland, but he responded with his usual good nature, sensing that he represented, to them, some sunshine in the gloom of lost village youth.

As they moved on, he gazed down into Laura's vivid face in the sidecar, and found himself longing for something that had never bothered him before—to keep this girl for himself alone.

"Do you know that I'm crazy to kiss you?" he said. "If I were not on this . . ."

"Rex," she cried swiftly, "look out!"

Too late, he turned to discover he had forgotten the bend in the lane. The motorcycle had gone straight into a field, and was just about to hit the soft remains of a haystack.

"*Oh no!*" he groaned, squeezing the brake hard.

They came to a halt surrounded by loose flying hay, and Laura dissolved into helpless laughter as she brushed wisps from her bright hair and the neck of her dress. The smell of the warm hay surrounding them, and the seduction of warm springtime England filled Rex with the urgency to live as fully as possible. Climbing from the saddle, he strode round to lift her from the sidecar, and the kiss she accepted in laughing understanding turned into something more as he surrendered the whole of his heart to a woman for the first time.

But she struggled free and gazed up at him, her eyes dilated with some kind of shock.

"That was a little more than I'm prepared to take from you," she said breathlessly.

He swallowed. "I've hardly begun."

"Then I suggest you stop right there." She turned away from him and looked out across the field, her body trembling with reaction. "I should have stayed in London. It was madness to allow you to persuade me to come away with you like this."

He moved up behind her and drew her back against his chest as he said against her curls, "Half my first week has gone already. I have to go back at the end of the month."

"Which is why this is so ridiculous," she told him in an unsteady voice. "Four weeks is nothing. When you get back there, all this will seem unreal."

He lowered his head until his mouth rested against the warm curve of her neck. "Don't treat me like an adolescent boy," he murmured.

She turned quickly in his arms, and it was plain she was under stress. "An adolescent boy would be easy to handle in this situation. But *you* . . . I don't want your kind of four weeks! I have a career to build. I love my work; I love the theatre and the excitement it creates, the thrills, the crowds. I love applause. I want to top the bill, become a household name, get myself announced in lights. Put me on that train this afternoon," she said emotionally, "then go home, Rex."

"I can't," he confessed quietly. "I love you, Laura."

"Oh no . . . *no*," she told him vehemently. "You mustn't."

"It's too late. I already do."

Her cheeks paled as she saw what was written on his face.

"How do you know you don't want my kind of four weeks?" he challenged gruffly. "You can't say you don't want something until you know what it is. And I haven't told you yet."

As she began to pull away, he seized her shoulders to prevent her. "I know you have to be at the theatre every evening. I just want you to spend the days with me."

"*Every* day . . . for four weeks?" she challenged uncertainly. "That sounds like a lot to ask."

"Compared with what I usually expect from a girl, it isn't," he retaliated, realizing she might respond more favourably to a light-hearted approach. "And think how much good it would do your career to be seen around with Sherry Sheridan."

The green glow in her eyes made a mockery of all she had said a moment ago, and he pulled her gently against him. "Now tell me, will you accept my kind of four weeks?"

"I suppose so," she conceded with a soft sigh against his tunic. "But I still worry over what they'll contain."

364

"Don't worry," he chided, with a touch of his old self. "You'll be far too busy to think."

But he dreaded to think how the time would end.

THE FIRST WEEK passed too quickly for him, and was a mixture of delight and impatience. Laura was a dedicated professional who would let nothing hamper her performance. She insisted on arriving at the theatre each evening an hour before her act was due to go on. This made afternoons very short. Furthermore, there were two shows, and although they slipped round to a little restaurant for some supper together between them, she was always nervy and keyed up for the second one. Rex understood, for he was the same before each patrol, but it did not help his growing desperation at time passing.

Away from the theatre Laura appeared to have forgotten her fears over their relationship. He found her a very passionate girl who allowed him more leeway than he had expected. But despite all his pleas and promises of good behaviour she stubbornly refused to go back to his hotel. As it was, he fell more and more helplessly in love with her, and watched the dates on the calendar advance with growing urgency.

Twice he forced himself to journey down to visit Chris, and returned dispirited and upset because the boy had again ignored him. His admiration for Marion grew each time, all the more since he had seen the child. David Sheridan was indeed a beautiful boy, so like his father it was almost heartbreaking. Rex knew it must cost Marion dearly to leave her baby during the week and also face the fact that his father might never know or see him.

Rex had been surprised to hear that Mike, still staying at Tarrant Hall with Tessa, had visited the hospital on several occasions, and had also gone to see young David with Marion. Feeling he should have a word with his friend on the subject of his brother's wife, and guessing Roland was forging ahead with his plan to join the Medical Corps, Rex asked Laura to come to Tarrant Royal for the third weekend of his leave.

"Your brother doesn't approve of me," she murmured, as she leaned against his shoulder on the park bench where they sat feeding the ducks.

"He doesn't know you the way I do. And I'd like to know you a lot better."

"Forbidden subject," she reminded crisply. Then, after a moment, she asked, "Are you going to call on Chris on the way?"

He shook his head. "It doesn't help either of us." Playing with the fingers of the hand he held, he confessed suddenly, "When my turn comes, I hope I'm killed outright. It's . . . well, it's degrading for the poor devil to sit there like that day after day."

She turned to him, full of surprising distress. "Rex, don't say things like that. Don't even think of them."

"I'm sorry, I didn't mean to upset you," he said quickly.

She got to her feet abruptly and walked to a tree at the water's edge. He went after her, and found her in tears.

"Laura . . . *darling* . . . what has brought this on?"

She faced him, full of wild accusation, and cried, "See what you've done? I knew what your kind of four weeks would be like, but you talked me into it, didn't you? Now I love you so much, I'm terrified. If you came back like . . . like Chris, I couldn't face it. I don't know how Marion stays there with him day after day. It's very brave of her and very wonderful." Her tear-bright eyes moved restlessly in their passionate search of his face. "But it would break me up."

He held her close in his arms while she cried, both of them oblivious of passersby, because he was going back to war and she had just told him she loved him.

Until it was time to go to the theatre they spent the rest of the day together, then Rex surrendered her at the stage door. Throughout the first performance he sat fighting the overwhelming desire to make her totally his before he went back to France and faced what lay awaiting him. The battle for the air was hotting up. Rex knew he would not get leave again for a very long time—if ever. It seemed that his whole life consisted of the next two weeks.

When the second show began, he went off to a place he had used during his Cambridge days, and reserved a private room with supper and champagne laid on. Returning in time to see Laura do her song about him with even more verve than usual, he felt heady with anticipation. She seemed perfectly happy with the supper arrangements when he told her, but when they entered the room he felt uneasy. He had not remembered the decor being so garishly crude. It was not what he had wanted for her at all. But the supper and champagne were very good, and she looked so beautiful in a dress of emerald-green shot silk with a coffee-coloured chiffon fichu at the neck, he lost his head the minute she finished eating and leaned back in her corner, smiling invitingly at him across her champagne glass.

Sliding along the velvet-covered seat to trap her in her corner, he said, "I thought that show would never end tonight."

"You shouldn't sit there night after night," she chided. "You must know all the acts by heart now."

"Oh yes," he agreed softly. "I know them all by heart—including this one."

She was taken completely by surprise as he went into action with the skill of a practised seducer. His mouth touched hers gently but lingeringly; his love words tumbled from him in desperate sentences; and his hands moved instinctively. But for the first time in his life he failed to charm his partner into submissiveness.

Struggling away from him, Laura stood up and smacked him hard across the face.

"I knew very well what you wanted when you suggested four weeks with me," she cried, shaking with anger, "but I fell for it hook, line and sinker, didn't I? Despite what I seem to be, I'm very soft inside. You worked hard on me, and nearly succeeded. But I'll tell you what I tell every other scoundrel like you." She backed into the middle of the room, her face white and shocked. "Just because I work the halls and live an independent life compared with most females, it doesn't mean I'm fair game for any man with a roving eye."

As he got to his feet she shouted, "Don't take one step towards me before I get out of this room!" Seconds later the door closed behind her with a crash.

Rex walked the streets of London for the rest of the night, and ended up at the flower market in Covent Garden. He bought a huge bunch of roses, then took an early taxi to Laura's lodgings. Mrs. Beamish answered the door only after he had been hammering for a full ten minutes. Strangely, her waspish words faded away when she saw his face and the great bunch of pink roses still with the dew on them.

Laura came down to the parlour in a Chinese-style wrap, and her arrival was far too quick for her to have been asleep. She looked red-eyed and miserable.

With Mrs. Beamish standing by to see fair play, he asked, "Will you marry me before I go back to France?"

"Yes," she said, as if in shock.

"All right. I'll go and see about a licence," he told her.

Out on the pavement he realized he still had the roses. But it did not matter now.

"Have you taken total leave of your senses?" stormed Roland. "This is utter madness!"

"We are living in a mad world," Rex told him quietly, having expected a reaction like this from his brother.

"But to *marry* the girl!" Roland's face expressed outrage. "A Sheridan marrying a cheap little music-hall performer!"

"I trust your adjective refers to the music hall and not the performer, so restrict your criticism to me and leave Laura out of it, or we are likely to come to blows," Rex said tersely.

Roland strode about Rex's hotel room and let his anger run riot. "Cancel this wedding before you sacrifice all you are and could be, and tumble her as you have all the other girls."

"She's not that kind of girl."

"*Ha!*" was his brother's contemptuous expression of disbelief.

Rex gripped his brother's arm impatiently. "I have a strong feeling of time running out. Statistics suggest it, even if you don't believe in presentiment. It's hell over there, and I want my week of heaven before returning to it."

Roland stared in disbelief. "So, for the sake of passionate fulfilment you are going to give this girl your name and all you own?"

"Which amounts to nothing," he reminded him coldly.

"Unless I'm killed before you when I get out there. Under the terms of my will, everything goes to you as next in line."

"Change your damned will," Rex said, in a rare burst of deep anger. "I don't want it—any of it. Leave the place to some charity— and leave me to lead my own life. One day you'll discover how little any of it matters, Roland, and grow more human. Integrity has been your god, but the time has come to acknowledge that you are more than liable to meet the real one sooner than you expected. He might give you a rough time of it if all you can claim to have done is worshipped a pile of bricks in the middle of some fields."

Roland's face had grown pale and set and they stood looking at each other for a long while, each trying to reach out to the brotherhood that had always been there. Finally, Rex said, "Even if there was no war, I'd marry Laura. I shall love her until I die, whenever that may be. It's something beyond my control." He held out his hand. "So come to my wedding this afternoon and let me pop champagne corks for one week with your blessing."

Roland gripped the hand. "You'll pop them for a lot longer than that, you rascal. You know you have a charmed life."

Greatly relieved, Rex gave him one of his broadest winks. "Tessa is counting on your being there today. She has really fallen for you."

"Good Lord, whatever makes you say that?" came the startled question.

"I haven't abandoned *all* my wicked ways. I still recognize a willing lady when I see one."

There was little time for further words, because just then the door opened and Mike walked in holding a newspaper, his expression brimming with amusement.

"Wow, are you in for a surprise, old mate!" he greeted Rex with a deliberately broad Australian accent. "Take a dekko at this!"

Rex took the newspaper in curiosity. The headlines were an inch high: FLYING ACE TO WED ACTRESS. Then half-inch-high words announced: RFC HERO SHERIDAN TODAY MARRIES GIRL WHO SANG HIS PRAISES.

Rex looked at Mike, filled with a mixture of disappointment and confusion. "She couldn't have done this, surely?"

"Oh yes, she could," his friend said vigorously. "It's the best publicity she could ever hope for."

"Good Lord!" swore Roland with vehemence, taking the paper. "This won't be a wedding, it'll be a theatrical performance."

THE TAXI TAKING REX, Roland and Mike to the venue inched its way through traffic until it rounded the final corner, when all three occupants stared in disbelief. A crowd of some hundreds surrounded the building they were heading for, blocking the road completely as people shifted and swayed, waving Union Jacks and bunches of flowers above their heads in celebration. Then, on the zephyr that blessed that mild March day, came the sound of voices in ragged unison singing Laura's song: "Ché-ri! Ché-ri!"

"Oh no!" groaned Rex as the implication of the scene hit him.

But Mike began laughing loudly, and expressed his enjoyment with a "Ya-hoo" in roustabout fashion, as he leaned from the window to shout, "Stand back! Here comes the bridegroom!"

"I can't get through this mob, guv'nor," complained the taxi driver, looking round at his passengers.

"I'll get you through," cried Mike, having the time of his life. "If I can sort out half a million sheep, I can control this lot."

Next minute, he was on the running board and heaving himself onto the roof, where he began to make a series of curious calls and shouts plainly intended to get animals on the move.

"He'll start a stampede," groaned Rex again.

"I don't think I can stomach this," said Roland, at his side.

"Stand back and let us through," called Mike's voice from the roof. "Here he is. The man of the moment, Sherry Sheridan."

As Mike's words got through to the people, the cry of "Here he comes!" began to ripple through the pressing throng. Next instant, those nearest to them spotted Rex inside and descended on the taxi, pulling open the doors to drag him out and hoist him up onto the roof beside Mike.

In a state of unreality Rex sat on the front of that taxi roof and witnessed the patriotic hysteria of a British public starved of hope or victory for too long. It was frightening, it was daunting, but it was irresistible. He caught himself smiling back at the fervent shining faces, and suddenly he remembered Laura saying, "I understand faces, I see hundreds of them in rows in front of me every evening." His bewildered disappointment in her began to evaporate. Whatever her reasons for sharing their love with the entire country, these people who had gathered here this afternoon were an audience longing to live a pretence for a while, to be young and in love again, to have a memory they could tell future generations about when the holocaust was over.

He laughed and waved his understanding of their hero worship in the same way he had done during the annual cricket matches against Tarrant Maundle. By the time the taxi was almost at the building, the euphoria had grown to proportions that would no longer allow him to remain out of the crowd's reach. The crush increased to halt the car, and Rex was pulled unceremoniously from his perch and, with Mike beside him, had to battle his way into the building through an almost solid wall of men and women before practically falling through the doors that were then shut firmly behind them by two uniformed officials.

"Oh lord!" exclaimed Rex in dismay, leaning against a wall and regarding his friend. "I hope I don't look the way you do."

"Worse . . . much worse," proclaimed Mike with a devilish grin.

Rex went to a large mirror fronted by a massed flower arrangement, so that he could comb his dishevelled hair and do what he could to his ravaged uniform. Roland, whom he had completely forgotten, then walked in looking immaculate in his dark grey suit and bowler hat.

"However did you manage to escape their clutches?" asked Rex in astonishment.

"They have all rushed off to wait for the bride," his brother said calmly. "And here she comes, by the sound of it."

He was right, and Rex forgot all else in concern for her treatment by an adoring public. But he had no need to worry. As a bride, Laura was hallowed by the onlookers, and she walked through the door, followed by Tessa, looking stunning in a blush-cream lace dress, large deep pink hat with a cream chiffon water lily on the dipping brim, and carrying a spray of pink roses with cream camellias. Rex gazed at her with all the emotion of knowing she was about to become his.

AFTER THE CEREMONY the party managed to slip away through a side entrance, and the taxis stopped at the hotel to allow the two fliers an opportunity to change into their spare uniforms before going on to the celebration meal at the Savoy Grill which Rex had planned.

Even Roland fell beneath the spell of Laura's gaiety as they sat round the flower-decked table, eating the best that money could buy in those days, and drinking pink champagne. More vividly beautiful than usual, she set Rex on fire with the promise of the night to come, and the minutes ticked past too slowly for him.

But first they had to go to the theatre, where Laura was committed to a Saturday night performance. Rex had protested strongly when told, but she had explained that her contract could not be broken, and had won him over with kisses and a bargain that, if he waited patiently while she did her ten-minute act after the wedding, she would do anything he wanted for the following week.

"Anything?" he had queried ardently. "That's a dangerous promise, I warn you."

She had laughed with husky seduction and kissed him on the tip of his nose.

With Roland, Tessa and Mike following in a taxi, Rex and his new wife set out for the theatre, he kissing her all the way, until she cried for a truce in order to get her breath back. But it was not her plea that stopped him, it was the sight of the mass of people outside the stage door.

"Oh no, I'm not going through all that again," he said firmly. "Laura, this is our wedding day, and it's being ruined by our sharing it with the whole of London. So far, I've taken your publicity stunt with good grace. Don't push me too far."

"It wasn't my idea to give all that information to the press," she said indignantly. "At least . . . not at first. It was while we were discussing the problem of getting next week off and adding it to the end of my run at this particular theatre, that Ben realized what an opportunity there was for a little publicity."

"A *little!*" he exclaimed, remembering the seething mass of hands reaching for him. "And who is Ben?"

"My agent—Ben Schumacher. He's very good."

"So I realize. But he'll have one less client after this."

She kissed him, stroked his cheek, implored him with her eyes until he agreed to sneak in by the loading doors. When they finally entered the backstage area, the stage manager came swiftly across to tell her, low-voiced, that her act had been rearranged to close the show for that one night.

Rex felt awkward and in the way there in the wings, and seeing Laura so near yet mentally so far from him, made the moment all seem unreal.

Then she was walking hesitantly into the limelight, still in the dress and hat she had worn to pledge her life and love to him, and still carrying the bridal bouquet. Something inside him cried a protest, but such thoughts were swept away as the whole theatre exploded into applause and cheers.

Gone was Laurie Pagett, the dapper man-about-town in top hat and tails. Instead, there was a breathtakingly lovely voluptuous girl, who glowed with life and vitality. She began to sing, not her usual programme but a sentimental song of the war. Her husky voice was full of emotion as she went through "Keep the Home Fires Burning". Rex found his throat constricting, but it was not the sentiment of the song that caused his reaction. She was superb, she was stunning . . . and she was his wife!

When the song ended, there was a moment of silence before the audience went wild again. With the sense of power plainly filling her more every minute, Laura had a quick word with the conductor, then suddenly threw off the hat, dropped the bouquet beside it, and went into a fast-paced song that turned into a sensation. She strutted back and forth, her gorgeous red curls flaming in the spotlights, winking and using her wicked eyes to emphasize the words to the greatest advantage. But, if she had not already captured every heart in the building by then, a daring high kick on the last line completed the mass capitulation. She knew it, everyone in the wings knew it, and so did Rex as his love for her plunged helplessly even deeper.

As the roar of acclaim slowly subsided, she nodded again at the conductor and began the song he would never forget.

> *When he flies, oh-so-high,*
> *All the mam'selles cry*
> *Chéri! Chéri!*

But the chorus got no further than that. Applause rose to a crescendo again, flowers began showering down onto the stage, and Laura had to stop, because she could no longer be heard. Then, as if she had had it all planned, she turned to the wings and began walking towards Rex, hands outstretched.

"Oh no," he muttered, backing away from her. "You won't get me out there!"

But those around him practically lifted him off his feet as they helped him make his stage debut. Laura seized his hands and dragged him to the centre of the narrow space left by a front cloth. Once there, afire with excitement, she stood on tiptoe and kissed him on the mouth. He was vaguely aware of lights flashing down in the auditorium, and row upon row of pale dim faces.

Then wild romantic fervour took hold of him too, and his old daredevil carelessness returned. He drew her into his arms for a kiss more lingering and expert than any she could give, before saying softly for her ears alone, "Try anything like this again and you'll get far more than you bargained for."

Laura now lifted her right hand to silence the crowd, and pulled Rex forward with her as the band struck up her song. But her voice was unsteady, and tears glistened on her lashes as a multitude of voices roared out the chorus.

When he flies, oh-so-high,
All the mam'selles cry
Chéri! Chéri!
He can't love them all
But still they all call
Chéri! Chéri!

Rex was not surprised when her voice broke completely during the second verse. Thinking quickly, he bent to pick up her wedding flowers and took the one step to the footlights before flinging the lucky bouquet out for some eager lovelorn girl to catch. Then, as the chorus was taken up again with gusto, he swept his wife up in his arms in a theatrical romantic gesture he knew she would love, and carried her through the wings and straight out to the street to the taxi he had paid to wait for them.

He put Laura onto the seat and sank down beside her, pulling the tearful exhausted girl into his arms so that his cheek rested against her bright hair.

"Now, my darling," he told her softly, "this is where you start doing anything I want for the next week."

FOR TWO DAYS they remained in their hotel room, so intense and all-consuming was their passion. In the atmosphere of time running out Rex forgot the world and everyone in it.

The idyll came to an end on the third day, when Rex said suddenly, "We'll have to go into the business of getting you an apartment. You can't stay with Mrs. Beamish any longer."

"Why ever not?" came her voice. "It's cheap, and I get on well with Tessa."

"The situation is different now. I don't want my wife living in cheap lodgings."

"You won't be there to see them."

"Stop that!" he cried. "What are you trying to do?"

"I'm trying to be practical. Besides, it's convenient for Ben's office. It's useful being close to one's agent."

"You won't need Ben once this present engagement ends," he pointed out.

"Of course I'll need him. How else am I to get work?"

He frowned. "You won't need to work now, with a husband to support you."

374

"What?" Laura stared at him in incomprehension. "You surely don't mean you expect me to give up the theatre."

"Naturally. You're my wife now."

"What difference does that make?"

"A hell of a lot," he cried.

After a moment or two she went into peals of laughter. "You are jealous! Oh, my darling darling."

She tried to push him with provocative playfulness, but he caught her wrists and held them. "I love you, Laura. Don't ever treat my love as a joke."

"I love you, too," she snapped. "How I wish I didn't."

It hit him like a slap across the face. "It's two days too late to make a statement like that. I thought you were happy."

"I am happy . . . and I'm terrified," she admitted, pleading with her eyes for his understanding. "Rex, I had ambitions for my career. The last thing I wanted was to get married. But you walked into my life and wrecked all my plans. In five days' time you're going to walk out again."

He pulled her against him swiftly and buried his face in her curls. "Don't you think the same thing happened to me, my darling? You walked into my life and took it away from me altogether. You *are* my life now. I'm not thinking of what comes later. We have five days yet."

She turned to reveal tears on her cheeks, and cried, wildly, "Five days! What are five days out of a lifetime?"

Collapsing into his arms, she poured out all her fears and doubts over the hasty marriage. He tried to soothe her, convince her that the war would be over soon, then ended up agreeing to her plea that continuing her theatrical work would occupy her days so that she would not worry herself into illness over him.

"And if I have a slack period, I'll get started on organizing a concert party for the patients in your brother's hospital," she told him.

But the prospect of her having a slack period vanished when they descended to the hotel lounge for the first time the following midday. The newspapers there were full of pictures of their kiss on stage, and of Laura's high kick that revealed very shapely legs. "Madame Sherry" was a phrase widely used, and there was no doubt at all that that was how Laura would now be known in theatrical circles.

THE NEXT FIVE DAYS were nothing like the first two they had so blissfully spent. Ben Schumacher pounced on Laura with details of offers that had poured in. And wherever they went they were recognized. Rex was forced to admit that it would be asking the impossible to expect her to give up the theatre now. He did insist, though, that she move to a reasonable apartment that he could regard as home, and this time she made no objections.

On the day before his last, he spirited her away down to Somerset and left her in a quiet little hotel while he visited Chris one more time. The outcome was heartbreakingly the same, but Rex gave his brother some fine pencils and a drawing block in the hope that he might soon recall his artistic skill and use them.

Saying goodbye to Marion was the overture to the terrible inevitability of the following day, and his farewell to Roland, who had arranged to visit the hospital at the same time, compounded a sadness he found impossible to contain. Tears blurred his vision as he walked alone on a dusk-filled hillside until he felt able to face Laura. This was how helpless she had rendered him! He had feared returning to France without making her his. Now he feared it because she *was* his.

When he finally strode back to the glow of the tiny hotel, he felt glad the day was finally over and night was offering solace. And it was a night he could take back to warm the coldness of separation. He and Laura loved and languished the hours away until she finally fell asleep in his arms. But he lay awake until dawn, just watching her. He might never see her again after that day. But he had loved her, and had lived through a champagne time that many men never knew.

Then they were there on the Victoria Station platform on a cold, wet and blustery afternoon, and their bleak expressions told each other that the champagne had run out, the corks had stopped popping. The station was full of men in khaki, and white-faced women. It looked grey and dismal in the gathering dusk.

Mike was facing the need to say farewell to a beloved sister, but Rex was oblivious of anyone but Laura as he held her in his arms and searched for things to say that were of great significance. But, as always on such occasions, the passing minutes were filled with inanities that would have been better left unsaid.

Soon the guard called for passengers to climb aboard. Rex swallowed hard. "Take care of yourself, darling."

377

She clung to his hand, pale and tearful. "You, too."

"You will write?"

"Of course."

There was a blast on a whistle to signify departure.

"Oh God, I can't bear it," she cried, looking at him like a frightened, trapped animal. "Why didn't you put me on a train and go home that very first day?"

Holding her still, although the train was starting to move, he studied her face for one last time. "I asked for a month, and you gave me the world. Don't have regrets, or you'll snatch it away from me again."

Kissing her fiercely, he let her go and ran for the door Mike was holding open for him. Behind him he heard running feet, and her husky voice crying, "I don't regret it. I don't . . . oh, I *don't*." But when he looked back through the open window in the door, smoke had swirled beneath the overhead canopy to obscure the platform and all those on it. She seemed to have gone from his life as dramatically as she had entered it.

9

They climbed stiffly from the back of a truck around midday. The airfield was quiet and deserted; the squadron was out on patrol. Despite the pale sunshine, Grissons was depressing. Rex raised his hand to the driver in a half-hearted salute of thanks as he and Mike began to trudge across to the building they now used as quarters. The old stone outbuilding echoed with the sound of their boots as Rex threw his bag onto his bed. He sat listlessly on the edge of it, still wearing his greatcoat.

"This is just like being the first boy back at school after the holidays. You've got to be there, yet there's nothing to do and no one to talk to."

Mike kicked moodily at the bed. "You could talk to me, for a start. You've hardly said a word since we left England."

Deep in depression he could not shake off, Rex took a moment before saying, "All right, I'll say something to you. What game are you playing with my brother's wife?"

Growing warily alert, Mike said, "Come again, old mate?"

"What are you up to with Marion? I know you saw her a lot."

Mike strolled to the open door, with hands in his breeches pockets, and leaned against the doorjamb.

"I've fallen for her. I think she's got a terrible life at the moment, and I don't think Chris deserves what she's doing for his sake. I know he's your brother and I do feel sorry for him—for any man in that state—but I just wonder if it wouldn't be better if the One Above finished what He began in Gallipoli."

Rex said, "That's brutally honest, Mike."

"We're living in a brutally honest age. Tell me, Rex, would you want to submit *your* wife to that?"

"Laura wouldn't do what Marion is doing. She'd throw herself into her career to try to forget, and end up breaking her own mind." He looked hard at his friend. "I either return from this war whole, or I don't return at all, Mike. If I ever crash and get trapped in a burning cockpit, don't rush over and drag me out."

The Australian returned his friend's look, then said laconically, "I preferred it when you weren't speaking to me." Then he straightened up, cocking his ear to the door. "Hello, that sounds like the squadron returning."

Only two thirds of them came back, and half the dead were boys Rex and Mike had never met. There were strange faces among the survivors, too—young, pale and shocked. And there was an air of desperation among them. The new Fokker was proving deadly against the antiquated machines owned by the Allies, and the Huns were systematically knocking them all from the skies. German morale was high, naturally, with heroes like Max Immelmann, known as the Eagle of Lille, and Oswald Boelcke, each receiving the Blue Max—Germany's most coveted medal for flying "kills" against their enemies. Correspondingly, the spirits of English and French fliers were low. They needed more pilots and, more importantly, a new type of aircraft to give them parity with their opponents.

Once in the mess that evening, though, it was flatteringly obvious to Rex that his return provided an injection of hope into flagging spirits. Drink flowed freely among the men in 2F Squadron, and the recent bridegroom was inevitably teased and ribbed over his marriage. One of the new flyers was Giles Otterbourne, an eighteen-year-old boy who had been at Charterhouse during Rex's last year there.

Ignoring the lad's obvious hero worship, Rex asked, "How long have you been with the squadron?"

"A week, sir."

"Mmm. I suppose they've sent you out all over the place."

The youngster nodded. "It's been a bit hectic, yes." Then he ventured, "Congratulations on your marriage. I saw the photographs in the newspapers. Your wife is a stunning girl."

"Yes, she is."

"Still, I expect you're glad to get back and have another crack at the Hun. You've got thirty-one already, haven't you, sir?"

"Are you counting aircraft or dead men?" Rex asked with sudden inexplicable venom.

Red flooded the boy's face. "I . . . well, I heard your score was thirty-one," he stammered. "I mean . . ."

"You must have known my brother Chris at school," Rex said, to put an end to the subject and soften his approach.

"Oh yes," came the relieved response. "He was a couple of years ahead of me, and streets ahead in brains. I heard he was most frightfully wounded after Gallipoli. There was another of our chaps at Gallipoli with your brother. Fellow called Rochford-Clarke. We heard he was most awfully knocked about, and died in a hospital in Cairo. None of us can imagine how he survived so long, for someone said he was left with only half a head."

"Half a head?" repeated Rex slowly, something Marion had told him coming back to him with those words.

"Pretty terrible though, isn't it? But it won him an MC."

"Yet that medal didn't win him Gallipoli, did it?" murmured Rex, still lost in the significance of coming across what he thought might be the key to one of Chris's problems. He walked away from Giles Otterbourne with only one object in view. To write immediately to Marion with the information.

THE DAWN PATROL was always the best of any for Rex. That first morning back at Grissons, while he was checking the guns, he was hailed by the commanding officer.

"You and Mike came back just at the right time. We've taken some terrible losses, and the men are all dog-tired. You inspire them because you've been here so long." He nodded at Rex's neck. "Why aren't you wearing your scarf?"

"It seemed inappropriate now," Rex murmured.

A slight frown creased the senior officer's brow. "From what I have heard of Madame Sherry she wouldn't object to something that has become your talisman. However, I want you and Mike to take some of the youngsters under your wings this morning. Take three each, and restore some of their earlier cockiness."

After a brief discussion with the rest of the squadron, they took off in formations of four, an experienced pilot leading three others, and headed for the front line. Rex felt strange, at first, to be back in the cockpit, checking the guns, watching for landmarks, and signalling to the three in formation with him, one of whom was Giles Otterbourne. In each pilot's pockets were two bombs, with another two tucked into the fronts of their flying jackets. Their objective was to bomb and machinegun a moving column of reinforcements reported by balloonists to be coming up just north of the Somme.

Rex preferred aerial attacks, where one flier matched his skill against another, but he found the old excitement returning as he climbed into the blue dawn and felt the cold air rushing past his face. He waved to Mike, some distance away, then made signals to his protégés and kept a lookout for Fokkers.

The column did not exist or, if it did, was not where reports had indicated. Signalling that they should split up into fours and go in search of the enemy until they reached the fuel limit, Rex took his own formation in a tight right-hand turn and began to fly towards the rising sun. As senior pilot he felt obliged to take the most difficult sector, and pushed his goggles up to avoid the dazzle on the lenses.

When they came, it was out of the sun, as he had feared: nine Fokkers in immaculate formation. Rex signalled his pilots to spread out and climb, but a youngster called Phipps had already been singled out and had three enemy aircraft on his tail. Rex made a tight turn to come up behind the Germans, firing his guns at the tail of the nearest one. But another dived on top of him, and he was forced to pull away to avoid the bullets ripping into his own tail. In that moment he saw flames leaping from Phipps's engine as the BE went out of control and spiralled to the ground.

Outmanoeuvring his attackers, Rex climbed up beneath a Fokker that was practically glued to Giles Otterbourne's tail, and kept on climbing, firing his guns until the German plane started to belch smoke and lose altitude. Then he turned to see Otterbourne chasing two of the enemy with fearless skill. Rex was impressed. As he turned his attention to two other Fokkers that were coming up after their destruction of Phipps, young Giles accounted for both his quarries by killing the pilots.

Now the odds were only two to one against them. Rex motioned Giles to circle and come alongside him so that they could make a dual attack on five of the enemy who were pursuing their other pilot, a lad called Brent. Indicating to his companion to attack from the rear, Rex made a fast climb, angled his machine in a turn until he was ahead of Brent, then went into a swallow dive that would take him headlong towards the group, using their own tactic of coming out of the sun. With a perfect sight of them, he emptied round after round into the enemy machines, forcing them to scatter from the sandwich they found themselves in.

Rex accounted for two that broke apart and fell in flaming pieces. Another he sent off with smoke pouring from it, plainly crippled. Giles accounted for a fourth, which was extremely creditable with the sun half blinding him. The fifth decided to cut his losses and was a speck in the distance when Rex remembered the last of them, who had carefully stayed out of the general melee.

It now curved into a climb and began to circle. Rex signalled Giles to escort young Brent, recovered but badly wounded, back to Grissons while he settled accounts with the remaining enemy.

Suddenly the Fokker climbed into the sun, then hurtled down, guns chattering, before Rex knew it. Bullets ripped into the fabric all around him. He felt a burning pain in his left temple, followed by a rush of blood that blinded that eye. He put up a gauntlet to wipe it clear and saw the Fokker had dived past him, flattened out, and was about to come up under him for the kill.

Quick as lightning, Rex pushed down the nose of his own machine and challenged his opponent in the manoeuvre for which he was famed. On a collision course, he dived as the other climbed, daring his opponent to keep coming. When it was almost too late, the German broke under the strain and they passed with wing tips practically touching. It should have been the end of the fight but, incredibly, Rex's gun jammed, leaving him to dive impotently on, knowing he was the one wide open for the kill now.

But acceptance of certain death lasted no more than a few seconds. As the Fokker turned and screamed down on him, another aircraft came in from the west, guns chattering loudly in deadly aim. It was flown by Giles Otterbourne, who should have been on his way back to Grissons. It was all over before Rex could really take it in. The German pilot, wily as they come, attacked the reckless inexperienced boy. Giles's body jerked as it was raked with bullets, then the bombs he was carrying in his coat were activated. The blast caught the German plane, and the two machines went down together. Then there was only Rex in his aircraft, and the whole empty sky.

HE BROUGHT IN the wounded Brent, coaxing him every mile of the way and every foot of his descent, until the lad had landed, taxied to a standstill, then practically fell from his machine. Rex landed a few minutes later, fighting a pull to starboard caused by damage, and unable to see through his left eye for blood.

The others were already back, apparently unsuccessful in their mission. Mike came up quickly as Rex began to climb from his cockpit.

"You've been hit!"

"Not as badly as the machine. Foxstead, get her patched up right away," he told the mechanic sharply. "Let me know the minute she's ready."

"You're not going out again!" exclaimed Mike. "That's a nasty wound on your temple."

Rex jumped to the ground and began striding towards the shed that housed the medical officer. "I'm going to find that bloody convoy . . . and you're coming with me," he told Mike, who had fallen in beside him.

"What happened to Phipps and Otterbourne?"

"They got Phipps, and Otterbourne disobeyed my order to return. In doing so he saved my life. I expect he'll get a posthumous medal for it. But what's the use of medals if they don't know which fragment of you to pin them on?" He walked into the shed unaware of the strange look Mike was giving him.

It was the start of a new phase in the career of Sherry Sheridan—a phase that was more daring, more spectacular, more ruthless than ever. The British public, the Royal Flying Corps, and 2F Squadron in particular, lionized him. But those who knew him well began to grow worried.

NO MATTER HOW MANY times Roland told himself he was doing it because it was his duty, he knew deep inside that that was a lie. Outwardly, it was easy to feel he had an obligation to check that his brother's bride was all right. But he felt a twinge of conscience when he collected Laura from her new apartment, and an uncomfortable stirring of guilt when glances strayed to their table or followed them when they got up to dance at the exclusive night spot he had chosen for the occasion.

He had thought to overwhelm the music-hall girl with the upper-class sophistication of the Sheridan family, but he had forgotten Laura was an actress. Wearing a chiffon dress in three layers of blue, shaded from indigo to hyacinth, with a daringly low back and trimmed with silver bugle beads, she looked so stunning that there was no doubt she stole the evening.

"I am glad I came, Roland," she confessed in her husky low voice as he sat opposite her. "I very nearly didn't."

"Oh . . . why?"

"I know you don't approve of me."

The truth of it threw him. "That's utter nonsense."

Her laugh was seductive and fascinating. "I tried very hard not to marry Rex, you know," she said, above the compulsive beat of the tango. "But he turned up at my digs at six o'clock in the morning with an armful of pink roses, looking as if his whole life was in my hands."

Roland frowned. "Marrying him only made it worse, surely."

She put her hand out across the table to touch his. "You know him better than I do. Have I made it worse?" When he did not reply, she said with a warm smile, "I'm very grateful for your kindness in asking me out in Rex's absence. You're a very nice person when you give yourself a chance to be human." She squeezed his hand. "But why did you ask me out, Roland?"

"To say goodbye. I'm joining the Medical Corps at the end of the week."

She was visibly upset. "Oh no! Roland, why? I know what has been happening in the village, but I thought you were strong enough to ride that out. Why are you doing this?"

The intimacy of the place, the strange feeling of closeness to this unusual girl, made him tell her his feelings. "Laura, I'm giving in because of Chris. Seeing him all in bandages makes me realize that standing by with ointment and a damp sponge for those who return is no longer enough."

She studied his face, her eyes grown deep green with feeling. "What is going to happen to your home, to the estate?"

384

"I've asked Tessa to be my bailiff and look after the place while I'm away. She's perfectly capable of doing so."

"Good Lord," she exclaimed, "what did she say to that?"

"Agreed with pleasure."

Laura looked at him consideringly. "You do realize she'd also jump at the chance of falling in love with you, don't you?"

It shook him. "Lord, no. Whatever makes you think that?"

The orchestra striking up the next dance brought an interruption to their conversation. Then, as dancers got to their feet, there was a minor scuffle round a table where three naval officers had been rowdily entertaining two young women. One of the girls was swaying on her feet as she loudly declared she would dance with all three.

As she half turned Roland saw with surprise that he knew her. Rosalind Tierney was an acquaintance from the county set, an avid horsewoman and racegoer. She was well bred and darkly beautiful. But just now she was behaving in a way she certainly never had on the few occasions Roland had been her escort.

He turned back to Laura with a frown, and suddenly their table jerked as Rosalind Tierney bumped into it. "Whoops!" she mumbled drunkenly, peering at them both. Then she bent forward to push her face almost against Roland's. "My lord, it's Roly Sheridan! You look different without a thoroughbred under you."

She straightened up and swayed dangerously. "Oh no," she corrected herself. "It isn't the horse that's missing—it's the uniform. I remember now," she proclaimed, turning to her companions. "He's a coward! Yes, he is." She began to cry, and the tears put dirty lines down her cheeks as her mascara ran. "They stuck a bayonet through Reggie. My darling Reggie. They killed him. He's gone," she whimpered. "And my brother went down with his ship, and I'll never find him again."

One of her companions tried to pull her away but she flung herself at Roland. "Throw him out!" she ordered wildly. "He's sitting there like a smug fat worm. Throw him out of here!" Then she picked up Roland's glass, and flung the contents right in his face.

He got to his feet as dark red wine ran down his chin and onto his immaculate starched shirtfront. Not the white feathers or the enmity of the villagers had affected him as this did. The villagers had acted out of spite and ignorance. But Rosalind Tierney was one of his set, someone who should have thought the way he did. She had done it because her menfolk had fought, and she vindicated him even as she accused him.

Her companions took her away sobbing.

Holding on to his self-control with difficulty, he looked down to find Laura ashen-faced with anger. "I'm very sorry about that," he said through a tight throat. "But I think we might as well go."

He took her arm as they crossed the floor, and Laura walked like an aristocrat going to the tumbrils. He found her composure helped him to ignore the disgrace.

"Don't take it to heart," Laura said, once they had found a taxi. "Rex wouldn't, but I have a feeling you will." Her hand took his. "The important thing is to make people feel *something*. It's when they walk past as if you're not there that you have to worry. No one will ever do that, because you are true to yourself, my dear."

Because he was going away with no one to wave him goodbye, because he knew he had been wrong about her, and because there would never be another girl like her, he leaned forward and kissed her briefly on the lips.

"That was for Rex," he told her. "Because he would want to thank you for just being you."

THE PRIMROSES WERE OUT all along the banks that lined the lanes of Tarrant Royal, and 1916 had produced some outsize flowers as if in defiance of the rows of vegetables that now filled the village gardens.

Up on Longbarrow Hill, Roland was saying goodbye. Like a courtesan tempting her lover to stay, Tarrant Royal had produced a soft enticing spring day that gave clear-cut outlines to the stone walls of the beautiful thatched cottages just below him. His heart ached as he thought of old friends within them who now turned their backs as he passed, and of others who had died.

Then Roland thought of his young nephew, David, and what might become of the estate in the event of his own death. During his leave Rex had declined the offer to inherit a country gentleman's life. So Roland had bypassed his middle brother and left the place to Chris in his new will, with the proviso that he must be declared mentally fit to handle his own affairs. If not, or if he died before that time, his son, David, was to inherit on reaching the age of twenty-one. Until then, the property would continue under the trusteeship of Rex and Tessa Manning. That clause ensured that Marion would never reign at Tarrant Hall or get a penny of Sheridan money without Chris at her side.

He had been to the recruiting office and signed the necessary papers. He was told that officers in the Medical Corps were qualified doctors, so he would not be eligible, since he had not completed his final year of medical studies. But Roland's strength of purpose could not be shaken, and he had enrolled as an orderly. He was due to report the following morning for his basic military training and his luggage was already in the trap when he returned to the house, to take leave of it and those who had served him well.

Poor Priddy found the occasion too much for her, and sobbed as she said goodbye to the third of "her boys" going to war. Minks was not a lot braver as he shook Roland's hand, but managed to say in a quaking voice, "Good luck, sir, and come back safely. I'll try to be here when you do."

"Of course you will, old fellow," Roland assured him, fighting emotion himself. "Look after each other, and Miss Manning."

Tessa walked with him to where Dawkins was waiting in the trap. She seemed wrought up, too. They stopped beside the vehicle and he held out his hand.

"Goodbye, Tessa. Thank you for being here. We'll keep in touch wherever I am."

She put her hand in his. "Goodbye, Roland. God watch over you." Then she reached up and kissed him on the cheek. "Courage comes in many forms, my dear," she whispered, "and I love you for yours."

Shaken, he climbed into the trap, and Dawkins told the pony to walk on. But the gentle progression down the hill between his beloved horse-chestnut trees seemed as painful as having a limb slowly torn off, and the drive through the village stabbed him with a myriad barbs of memories.

Once at the station Roland said farewell to his old retainer with hand outstretched. "Well, goodbye, Dawkins. Look after that cough of yours."

Unashamedly crying, Dawkins gripped the outstretched hand with both of his own. "Mr. Roland, sir, you don't have to do this terrible thing. We'll all stand by you."

"Yes, I know, old friend. But I'm doing it for Mr. Christopher.

387

People are giving up what they love in order to help him; I must give this up in order to help some other man's brother."

Then Roland was left alone on the small platform overlooking meadows and distant rolling hills, with the sound of carolling skylarks high above. There were tears in his own eyes now.

A FEW WEEKS LATER, the atrocious and appalling losses on the western front forced the British government to introduce conscription. Every able-bodied man within the age limits had to don uniform and leave everything to go to war.

10

The patient in bed nine trusted those around him no more now than he had at the beginning. They still tormented him by trying to take the bandages off his head. They still had to put a needle in his arm because he fought them. And he was still unable to move of his own accord; but his arms no longer looked like outsize wooden spoons. With the removal of the bandages from his hands, he discovered there were only two fingers and a thumb on his left one, and both were very red and painful to bend.

He could now feed himself, although he was humiliatingly clumsy. These days, Marion put the tray across the bed and left him in isolation until his plate was empty. It took him painful ages to accomplish this, but it was one small triumph that somehow kept him going in the midst of terror, despair, and the feeling of crossing an abyss on a tightrope. Without Marion he might have let himself fall. But he had to retain his precarious balance for her sake.

Today was Monday, he saw on the calendar hanging on the side of his locker, and she would not be here until two o'clock. Outside the window, on the oak, there was a jay, bright and perky, pleased with its courting plumage as it posed this way and that to catch the eye of any female in the grounds. How he would like to point out that bird to Marion so that she could also enjoy it.

His gaze strayed to the drawing block and pencils on the locker that the red-haired man called Rex had brought. Feeling that they had all been part of the plot against him, he had resisted the urge to use them for over a month. But all at once the desire to capture something for Marion overcame his distrust.

The instinct that had told him many times that he could draw proved to be right. Despite his stiff fingers, he forgot all else as he painstakingly concentrated on the bird. He was not happy with his efforts when the jay spread its wings and departed, but the clumsy sketch was sufficient to capture the bird's cocksure posture, and he put that page aside so that he could try the background on another. He decided on a hazy impression of the scene, as if it were early morning with mists blurring the outlines.

Slowly and carefully he covered the page, then looked at the finished drawing with a surprising sense of gratification. But he realized now that the jay had been real, full of confidence and strength. This scene was a fantasy; put one within the other and it would all fall apart. He reached across for the page containing the sketch of the jay, intending to destroy it, but it slipped to the floor as he moved, taunting him with his helplessness to reach it. He felt violently that he wanted no one else to see the bird he had drawn just for Marion. What was he to do? Swivelling his eyes to his locker, he noted a jug of water, a glass, and some flowers in a vase.

Despite the pain such movement brought, he slowly reached out and swept his right arm along the locker, sending everything to the floor with a tremendous crash. Nurses came hurrying towards him, but the piece of paper was sopping wet and ruined now.

He found the whole thing intensely amusing. He increased his victory by hiding the background picture beneath the sheet under his normal leg, and by taking off the pince-nez to put with it so that their angry looks and tight mouths would all be wasted. Then he closed his eyes and pretended to be asleep.

MARION WAS THERE when he opened his eyes. He knew it was her because she was always a pink blur instead of a blue one. Thankfulness welled up in him as her hand reached beneath the bedclothes for the pince-nez.

"Why are you hiding?" She placed the pince-nez on his nose, and her face leaped into perspective. "When you take this off it means you're hiding."

Marion looked nice, and he was extremely pleased that she was there at last. "Why didn't you come at two o'clock?" he asked.

She sat beside the bed. "I did. But I was speaking to the doctor for rather a long time. You were asleep until just now." Sighing, she stood up and began folding back the screens round the bed. "I've brought your tea."

"What is it?"

"Bread and butter with syrup, a piece of fruit cake, and strawberry blancmange."

"How do you know it's strawberry? Have you tasted it?"

"No, but it's pink."

"What has that got to do with it? Flavour is a taste, not a colour. Why can't strawberry blancmange be yellow?" he asked.

She smiled. He always liked it when he made her smile. "Yellow blancmange would be lemon flavoured," she said. "It couldn't be strawberry—strawberries are *pink.*"

"So is your dress, but I bet it doesn't taste of strawberries."

The smile developed into a laugh. "More like boiled linen, I should think." She sat down beside the bed again and asked, frowning, "Why did you push everything off your locker?"

The warmth inside him began to chill. "I had a reason—a very good reason," he said harshly, wishing they had not told her. "I had done something special just for you, but it dropped onto the floor. I didn't want them to see it, and I couldn't pick it up, so all I could do was knock everything onto it and spoil it."

"What was it?" she asked, in a funny voice.

"A bird. A jay." Now he reached beneath his normal leg for the other drawing. "This isn't really very good. That's why I decided to leave the jay out. It seemed much too positive a creature for the mood of this." He offered her the page.

She took it and sat looking at it for long anxious moments. Then she looked up, eyes shining with rapture.

"It's marvellous!"

Then he noticed with astonishment that there were tears on her cheeks. "What's the matter?" he asked.

"It's coming back! You've remembered how to draw, Chris."

"I thought you agreed not to call me that," he said sharply.

"It's your name."

"I don't know who I am."

"Yes, you do . . . or you wouldn't have put this on your drawing."

He stared at the paper she held out. There, in the right-hand corner, he had written C. W. Sheridan.

A dreadful coldness began to spread right up through his body, setting him shaking. He felt extremely ill—sick and giddy, as if he was falling into that abyss. She had forced him to be Christopher Wesley Sheridan, and he was terrified of that truth. Because of it, he began to retreat further into the comfort of oblivion.

OUT ON THE WESTERN FRONT, one of the most hideous battles ever known was being waged between the French and Germans for possession of Verdun. Begun towards the end of February 1916, as a desperate attempt by the Germans to break the deadlock of trench warfare and gain the strategic and morale-boosting victory that was so vitally needed, it turned into a massacre of seven hundred thousand soldiers. As the year advanced and the weather grew warmer, the decaying corpses spread disease like wildfire. Now the wounded were dying of gangrene, pollution and lack of medicines. Those left whole were going mad from the mental strain.

Yet the battle for Verdun could not be ended: no one could win it. The French, drowning in liquid mud, would not loosen their skeletal hold. The Germans, sick and demoralized, could not triumph, yet dared not lose face by withdrawing. The British were entreated to launch their offensive on the Somme as soon as possible, to tip the scales. Preparations that had already begun were stepped up, and as details of the grimness of Verdun trickled through to the British lines, the mood of the men grew tenser, and hatred of the Germans increased. Official military publications made no mention of bombing attacks on English towns by German bombers and the sinister zeppelins, but the men heard it all in letters from home, and vowed revenge.

All this while, the men who patrolled the skies over France were also being driven to the edge of endurance. By the start of June, the life expectancy for new British pilots was two weeks. They fell from the blue skies through inexperience, faulty aircraft, overwhelming opposition, or just sheer exhaustion. The boys straight from school never matured; the wily experienced aces were broken old men at twenty-two and twenty-three.

Rex and Mike were in that last category. By mid-June they were flying three missions a day, often taking the dangerous night patrol. Their faces had grown thin and taut, and their eyes contained a strange wildness, yet they were still a source of inspiration to those around them. Mike now had a score of thirty successes to his credit. Rex had forty-four. The renowned Sherry Sheridan, with his now restored cerise silk scarf flowing out in the slipstream, was a figure hunted desperately by all the German fliers in the Grissons sector.

Rex had been back at Grissons nearly three months, and there had been only two letters from Laura, the last six weeks ago. And while he fought back the pain of her neglect, he faced another and quite different problem. Since his return from leave, Rex had three times encountered a youthful, blond German ace flier, who had reputedly been sent to prove that Sherry Sheridan was not invincible. His name was Heinz von Heldermann, and he had notched up a reputation for daring against all odds in a very short time, distinguishing himself from the rest of his fellows by wearing into action a gaudy, gold-splashed cavalry jacket beneath his open flying coat.

The most recent encounter between the two aviators had lasted fifteen minutes, before von Heldermann had made a dash for home, signalling that he was out of ammunition. Then, last night, a lone Fokker had flown low over Grissons to drop a message weighted by a stone. It was an invitation for Lieutenant Sheridan to meet Count von Heldermann in single combat to finish what had proved inconclusive the previous day. It was, in effect, an old-fashioned challenge to a duel.

2F Squadron was roused by the urge to teach the arrogant German a lesson, and the challenge, in his present mood of savage frustration, was just what Rex wanted. Pride, too, was at stake. The colleagues of the man who did not return from the encounter would be demoralized. Rex was determined they would not be his own.

Despite an official ban from the commanding officer on accepting such a challenge, every member of 2F Squadron, including Mike Manning, was at a window or open door when, just before dawn, Rex walked out to his aircraft. He took off and calmly circled Grissons before heading for the rendezvous. Unashamedly he acknowledged that today was for Laura, first and foremost. If he were the victor, it would not be laurels he'd lay at her feet, but von Heldermann's life. In the first light of morning he began scanning the sky for his opponent.

The blond German was there, and they circled each other several times, smiling and nodding their agreement on the rules. Then, with a mutual salute that was a symbolic raising of swords, they acknowledged that the duel had begun.

They started making wider, more watchful circles in the silvery sky, like swordsmen walking round each other awaiting the right moment to lunge. Rex was content to watch the other aircraft's performance for a while. Like all Fokkers it was superior in nearly all respects to his own BE, but he had devised his own tactics based on its few weaknesses. And common sense and coolheadedness told him that the longer he could prolong the affair, the more rattled the arrogant von Heldermann would grow. With luck, the man would bring about his own downfall.

At first, they were evenly matched in guile and flying skill, each getting a lot of shots on target. Then Rex saw a chance to make one of his unorthodox climbing attacks, and achieved the first real blow by holing the other's fuel tank. Rolling over in a desperate turn, von Heldermann made a shallow dive on Rex, guns blazing as he passed dangerously close. Despite the great jagged tears in the wings caused by this, Rex felt a surge of triumph. His opponent was growing angry.

However, just as Rex was telling himself he must watch the other man like a hawk, there was a crack behind him. He glanced swiftly round, to see a gaping hole in the fuselage near the tail, where von Heldermann had put so many bullets that the fabric would no longer hold together. Cursing beneath his breath, Rex saw his opponent screaming in at him, using his own daring nose-to-nose challenge. But Rex had no intention of being caught with his own trick, and veered away well before the German could fill the nose of the BE with bullets. As Rex guessed, the other pilot took the veer as a sign of lost nerve, and a smile of contempt appeared on his face as he flashed past.

By now both aircraft were riddled with holes and hard to handle. Von Heldermann was losing fuel fast; Rex feared a violent movement would rip off his own tail altogether. But von Heldermann's expression showed clearly that he thought Sherry Sheridan's reputation had been grossly exaggerated, and as the sun began to rise Rex decided to abandon his cautious tactics. With a suddenness that took the German by surprise, Rex swooped in a dive, to come up under the Fokker, knowing that the sun was still low enough to blind the other man as he looked down. He put a long burst into the belly of the enemy machine, then found his climb slowing until the BE faltered and began to fall away in a spin, unable to take the strain put upon it.

Before he knew it, von Heldermann came up behind him fast,

showering the cockpit with bullets. There was a burst of agony in Rex's shoulder, and he gasped, bending forward instinctively with his hand over the wound. Then, as von Heldermann flashed past recklessly, Rex realized why. His gun was hanging from its mounting, completely useless, and the German knew the game was over for Sherry Sheridan.

But this was where an old fox was slyer than a brash cub. Still slumped forward in pain, Rex adopted a "falling leaf" dive, the air rushing past his face to clear the giddiness brought on by his injury. Von Heldermann followed him down, ready to fire a finishing burst at the first sign of recovery, but the avid German forgot to watch his own height. When Rex suddenly pulled out of his plunge with very few feet to spare, the Fokker hurtled into some trees and exploded in a mushroom of smoke and flame.

Rex hardly had time to feel a sense of triumph, for he realized his own aircraft had performed its last manoeuvre. The tail, after the strain of the spiralling dive, suddenly snapped and hung by just one tough piece of fabric. Weak from exhaustion and loss of blood, Rex just had time to unclip his restraining belt when the machine somersaulted, throwing him out some yards clear of it, and burst into flames behind him.

When Rex came to he was in a field, surrounded by men in mud-caked khaki. "Are you English?" he asked weakly.

"Not 'arf, mate . . . and bloody proud of it with blokes like you on our side," pronounced one with a grin. "There's only one flier 'oo wears a silk nightie rahnd 'is neck and I'm going to write 'ome that I've shaken the 'and of Sherry Sheridan."

He grabbed Rex's hand and pumped it up and down enthusiastically, but it was the one attached to the wounded shoulder, and Rex passed out again.

HIS RETURN TO GRISSONS was greeted with lunatic pride and excitement. But his greatest reward for what he had done was to find Mike waving a letter from Laura to him.

Darling, Darling, Darling, please, please, forgive me. How you must hate me for not answering your letters. I have been working till I drop into bed with exhaustion. But you have no idea how I long for you, how empty my life is without you here to share it. I love you, love you, love you.

The rest of the letter was as vivid as Laura herself, as she gave details of a concert she was organizing for the patients in Chris's hospital, and of how well she and Marion were getting on together over the arrangements. The long rambling letter ended with some marvellous intimate passages that made Rex's toes curl.

In consequence of that letter, he was in a daze of delight and longing for her throughout the party his colleagues held in his honour that night. Then, the following morning, the commanding officer called him into the office to pass on a communiqué just received. Rex had been promoted to captain and given command of a new squadron being readied for the great military offensive the following month. This squadron was to be equipped with the new Nieuport fighter plane.

"The aircraft are in England," the CO explained. "These orders are for you, Mike Manning, Cedric Meader and Gerry Keane to go over there and fly them back. Despite your injuries, you leave today." He held out his hand. "Good luck! I'm afraid there'll be no leave granted any of you. In five days you have to learn how to handle these Nieuports and teach the new boys how to survive in battle. No second honeymoon, old chap. Sorry!"

But Rex was not listening. In two days he would see Laura and hold her in his arms. Five whole days and five whole nights!

THE NEW AIRCRAFT were very exciting. Their greater manoeuvrability and more modern design filled the battle-weary pilots with the confidence of meeting the deadly Fokker on equal terms at last. That, together with the respite and pleasure of being in England, was like a tonic to them. The introduction to the Nieuports on Salisbury Plain took the whole of that first day, until late in the evening. Then, despite the fact that no leave had been granted, the men all mysteriously vanished into the lavender haze of the late-June dusk.

Rex did not exactly steal the motorcycle that was intended for dispatch riders, because he had used his new rank of captain to breezily assure the young lance-corporal guarding the vehicle compound that he had to visit his dying grandmother. But as soon as he rode off, his heart almost burst with elation within him. He pushed the powerful motorcycle to its limits as he raced towards London and his wife, who had no idea he was so close to her at the moment.

It was a long journey, and it was one am before he pulled up outside the apartment. Weariness fled as he mounted the stairs and knocked softly on the door. Then the door was opened, and Rex was stunned anew. He had forgotten how breathtakingly sensuous Laura looked in the middle of the night, when her wicked eyes were luminous with sudden awakening, and her red-gold curls flamed round her head in a tumbled mass. But it was her mouth, full and soft with deceptive innocence, that made restraint impossible. They stood looking at each other as if the past three months had been three years, before Rex pulled her against him in a long, lingering kiss.

He did not remember walking into their apartment and kicking the door shut behind him, because his arms were around Laura, and she was gazing up at him in rapturous disbelief, saying, "Is this another of your damned four weeks?"

He shook his head. "Five days, that's all."

"Oh my darling, my hopeless impossible darling!" She pulled his head down to hers, tormenting his lips with her kisses that were wet with her tears.

Her body was trembling as he picked her up in his arms and headed for the bedroom, saying thickly, "All the way from Grissons I've been thinking of this moment."

And then they lost themselves in a passion that could never ignore the running sands of time.

WHEN REX ROUSED it was to find the low sun blinding him, and then through one eye he saw a cloud of red curls on the pillow beside him. As it all rushed back, he hauled himself upright, looked at the clock, began frantically pulling on his clothes while he shook Laura awake.

"Darling," he said, "I should have left an hour ago. Get me a cup of tea and I'll tell you the plan."

The next minute she was out of bed and in the kitchen fixing the tea.

"Rex . . . oh darling," she murmured huskily when she returned. "Do you really have to leave?"

Between gulps of tea he told her that he could be court-martialled for taking a motorcycle without official permission and for driving to London with petrol reserved for carrying vital dispatches. "On top of that, I shall be back late. There's a formation-flying exercise at nine, and Mike won't know how to explain my absence. Darling, I'd give half my life to stay with you now." He kissed her fiercely. "But I can't. Do you understand?"

"Is that all there is, then?" she asked quietly. "A few hours in the middle of one night, then goodbye again?"

"No! No, of course not." He pulled her against him and held her. "I'm at the flying school until Monday, which means we have four more nights together. There's a nice quiet hotel near the airfield which will be ideal for us. After I've left, pack a small bag and catch the train to Salisbury." He gave her a swift kiss.

She stood there, the milky whiteness of her skin sharply contrasting with the red of her hair. "I can't come to Salisbury. I have a performance every evening at seven thirty."

"Not when I'm in England."

She waited a while before saying, "Darling, please try to understand. The show only opened last week. The whole thing has been planned round me. I'm the star . . . and still trying to prove myself as Madame Sherry. Besides, two men have risked a lot of money on this show, and they'd never agree to my having a week off at this stage."

".Then have it without their agreement."

"They'd kick me out and put an end to my career."

"I risked mine to come to you."

"They wouldn't court-martial a popular hero."

"They wouldn't kick out the star of the show," he retaliated angrily, as he headed for the door.

She ran to him then and clung to him with desperate arms. "Forgive me! Oh, darling, darling, please forgive me. I love you so much."

He stopped and turned round wearily, drawing her against his chest with all the helpless love she aroused. "I've been almost crazy without you over there. You're my life."

She arched back and studied his face with tear-stained unhappiness. "I've been almost crazy without you, too, and every time there's a knock on the door I think it's a telegram saying you . . . you . . . The only way I get through the days is by concentrating on this show. Understand, oh my darling, please understand."

Conscious of time flying past, loving her, he said with some difficulty, "All right, I'll come back here tonight. Somehow."

Then he left quickly for the long journey back.

FOR THE NEXT three days, Rex and the other three experienced fliers from Grissons worked at top speed getting the men into an efficient team that understood the Nieuport's potential, limitations and weaknesses. Knowing what they were returning to, most of them tried to relax at night. But Rex risked military discipline by helping himself to a motorcycle and speeding up to London the minute he was free.

Laura was there waiting for him with a meal on a tray and a bath ready. They would sit close together while he ate, talking of all that had happened to them both that day. Then, after their passion was fulfilled, they would sleep in each other's arms until the alarm clock told Rex he had to leave. They were wildly, madly happy.

On his fourth evening Rex found himself telling her about Heinz von Heldermann. Yet, in the normality of that room, the whole affair seemed unreal, bizarre, sickening. He could clearly remember coming out of his dive and seeing the other man's plane plummet into the earth, explode, and burn.

He pulled Laura close and laid his cheek against her bright head. "I took a man's life just to prove I was a better flier than he was," he said with emphasis. "When I'm here with you, I wonder how I can do such things day after day."

"You do them because it's them or you, darling. And you're a better flier than anyone. They all know that."

"But I've never been like that over things I can do—proving I can go one better. War turns men into beasts."

11

The windows beside Chris's bed at the end of that long room were pushed back, and the grounds outside slumbered beneath the heat as a blue jay flew by. Longing swept over him—longing for the sloping lawns, clustering trees, paths leading who-knew-where, longing for freedom! Helplessly weak, he found tears welling in his eyes. When would it end?

It was the sight of the jay, of course. That bird was a symbol of something, but he felt too tired to work out what it was. It was then he spotted a bed of deep red roses in the garden. He frowned. Deep red roses! There had been masses of rainbow lupins in that flower-bed. How could there be roses now? Still frowning, he turned to look at the calendar on the side of his locker. June 1916. Dear God, where had April and May gone?

Sweat beaded his forehead as he fought back terror. But that was only its beginning, for he realized there were no bandages over his face to soak up the running sweat. He began to scream as he thought of his half head, and with strength born of terror he clawed at the locker in an attempt to get off the bed and run. Then, his screams were born of an agony in his leg that became overwhelming, and with the onset of night, the sound of his own voice grew fainter and fainter.

When he opened his eyes everything was a blur, and the fuzzy pink outline of the girl called Marion was beside the bed. He felt incredibly weak—so weak and lifeless he sensed he would slip away altogether if he did not cling to something.

"Help me," he whispered through dry lips. "Don't let me go."

A hand clasped his, and the pink blur hung over him. "Chris, don't be afraid, I'm here," she told him. "You fell over the side of the bed. They had to give you an anaesthetic to reset your leg, and that's why you feel the way you do."

Next minute, spectacles were put on him, and he saw her face clearly, only a few feet away from his. Behind her stood a man in a white coat. Then he remembered, and felt the terror rise again.

"It's all right," she said quickly. "Everything's all right."

"My *face*," he croaked.

"There's nothing wrong with your face, Chris. *Think*," she urged. "Haven't I just hooked your spectacles over *both* ears? And aren't you looking through *both* lenses? I promise you, it's all right."

She started running her hands over his face with the lightest of touches, saying quietly, "You had severe burns and a deep wound in your neck, that's all. We had to keep it all covered until the new skin was ready to stand the light. Your face is complete . . . and it's a very nice face, Chris. Here, feel for yourself."

She lifted his hand to move it carefully over features that felt rough, but complete and normal.

"Now have a look in this mirror," she said gently.

He gazed into a face that was bright pink, very youthful, and topped with thick springy fair hair. It was not the horrific half head he had imagined, but it was the face of a complete stranger.

His gaze swung back to Marion's. "I did see it," he said weakly. "There was only half of it left."

She shook her head, putting the mirror away. "That was someone else. Rex wrote to me about it. He says it was a friend of yours who lost half his face in that terrible battle you were in, and that you saw it. That's why you couldn't forget it."

He lay thinking it all over, hardly noticing that the man in the white coat nodded at Marion, then departed. His face had merely been badly burned, not blown half away. Had he been wrong about those people all along? Could there really have been a war, and a battle in which he had been seriously wounded? Would he really be able to go out one day and walk along one of those garden paths into the cobwebby, mysterious beyond?

His eyelids began to close in exhaustion. It was all right. Soon he was so soundly asleep he knew nothing of Marion lifting his hand gently to her mouth before she placed it carefully back onto the white coverlet.

THE LAST SUNDAY in June was another lovely day, and that afternoon there was to be a concert in the shady garden for all the patients. As the weather was so perfect, the entertainers from London agreed to use the broad flagged terrace for their performance, and a piano had been carried out there. The wheelchair patients and those who could walk were seated on the lawn under an awning. Others considered well enough to see the concert had their beds wheeled into the ward off the terrace.

Chris did not really care about the concert, but he was glad to be thought well enough to see it. Enjoying the different view, he lay propped up against the backrest, lost in thought. Marion had told him that the girl who had organized the concert was married to his brother Rex. That was the red-haired man who had brought him the drawing block and pencils. Just then Chris looked up to see the subject of his thoughts walking towards him, with Marion. They wove their way through the beds, and she said gaily, "Here's a lovely surprise! Rex is in England to collect some new aircraft, and has been given permission to visit you."

The red-haired man appeared much older than Chris remembered. He sat on the chair beside the bed and looked at him critically. "They've done wonders with your face, Chris. And Marion tells me you've been drawing again." He smiled broadly. "It's about the only thing you *can* do, all bound and bandaged like that, isn't it, old son?"

Marion had moved away, and Chris could see her through the doors leading to the corridor, talking to a man with very dark hair in RFC uniform and a girl who looked like him. Something about the way Marion was gazing up at this man suggested there was a secret between them. He felt unbearably deserted as he watched her, and turned his face away from the sight.

"If you ever feel like writing—just as one chap to another—I'd enjoy hearing from you," Rex was saying. "Being on an airfield is very much like being here, you know. It's very restricting, and one soon loses touch with what's going on outside."

"How well do you know Marion?" Chris said suddenly.

"Oh . . . not quite as well as you do," came the easy answer.

"Yet you wrote her a letter."

"That's right. I'd heard about a chap who'd gone out to Gallipoli with you and received bad head injuries. I thought it might have something to do with your unfounded fears on those lines. It seemed a significant coincidence that I heard it from a lad who had been a pupil at our old school. Giles Otterbourne."

"Otterbourne. He was a frightful duffer."

"Was he?" came the slow comment. "How do you know that?"

Chris looked at the other man for a long time, frowning. "I just do." He felt stricken then. "Look, they're going to start," he said, nodding towards the terrace, where the pianist had taken his seat.

The concert was a tremendous success. Chris quite enjoyed it, after all, even though he had spotted the dark-haired man and girl being seated outside by Marion before she hurried in to sit beside Rex. Then a girl came on and something hit him so hard in the chest that he could barely breathe.

She was more beautiful than anyone he had ever seen. She was tall, with red-gold hair and an unbelievable shape. But it was her face, pale, pointed, with slanting dark eyes and a smile that made a person feel it was solely for him, that held him spellbound. In her beautiful white draped dress, with a garland around her curls, she stood incredibly still and intent to sing a song with a tune so haunting that Chris found the tears welling up and blurring his lenses. He realized she must be Diana the huntress. Vague visions of distant islands, deep blue sea, white cliffs and temples wavered in the blur caused by his tears.

The other men were all spellbound, too, gazing at the girl who seemed to be pouring her heart out with those sweet, low, husky

401

stanzas. Then his wandering gaze reached his brother, and he was startled at the naked pain of his expression as he watched the girl, who must be his wife.

There was a brief interval, then the girl returned to end the concert, and there was a gasp as she marched smartly onto the terrace dressed as a grenadier guard—at least, her top half. Below the tightly fitting jacket and tall bearskin she wore nothing but flesh coloured tights. Her legs were long, beautiful, and devastating to look at. She sang patriotic songs in that husky voice and marched sensuously back and forth.

The men loved it; their faces glowed as they cheered her. Next minute, she was tripping inside straight towards him, and Chris felt his heart bump. But she seized Rex's hands and dragged him unwillingly and rather set-faced, Chris thought, out onto the terrace, where his appearance was greeted with another rousing cheer and crutches waved in salute. It fell very quiet, however, when the girl signalled Rex to lift her onto the piano, where she sat to sing the lovely and sentimental "Every Little While". The pair looked at each other as if there would never be another time or place, and the sadness of those two figures so poignantly poised filled Chris with longing to draw the scene.

Soon the concert was over, and the nurses began to wheel everyone away for tea. A tray was brought to Chris, but he felt too confused by all that had happened that day to eat. Then Rex appeared with the girl, who was now wearing a dress of soft floating yellow material caught round the hips with satin ribbon.

"They've only allowed us a minute, because you must be tired," said Rex. "But I wanted you to meet Laura—your sister-in-law. And she very much wanted to meet you."

"Hello, Chris," she greeted. "I'm so glad they've taken off your head bandages. It must be so much more comfortable for you." She smiled up at her husband. "My, you Sheridans are a handsome breed! I thought Roland was splendid enough, but young Chris goes one better still. Those eyes!" She turned back and winked at him.

"Did you enjoy the concert?"

He nodded, unable to speak.

Rex squeezed her arm. "I think we'd better leave the lad alone now. He looks rather tired." A hand dropped on Chris's shoulder, and his brother's voice sounded rather thick as he said, "I'll come and see you on my next leave, old son. Keep up the good work. You're winning, you know."

"Goodbye, Chris," said Laura softly, her deep green eyes glowing. "Don't worry. Everything is going to work out fine."

They walked away. Behind them he could see Marion talking to the dark-haired man again. He pushed aside the tea tray, then took off his spectacles. He did not want to see them any more.

Marion came eventually and grumbled about his unfinished tea while she straightened the bed. Then, struck by his silence, she asked, "Chris, why are you hiding?"

It always annoyed him when she accused him of that, so he retaliated by asking, "Why do you do everything for me? The others don't always have the same person. Why do I?"

A small pause. "You're angry with me, for some reason. What have I done?"

"I don't need you here all the time."

"All right, Chris. I'll ask to be put on general duties, if you'd rather."

"Yes."

The pink blur moved away, and he closed his eyes as he turned his face into the pillow.

THEY FLEW BACK to France on a stormy morning that put an end to the summer idyll of the past few days. The new airfield, at a place called Saint-Brioche, could have been Grissons, for there were the same old farm buildings and tents. But it was nearer the front line and guns could be heard constantly, like thunder rumbling in the distance. The Somme offensive had begun.

Normal routine became a frantic programme of patrols, interceptions and balloon burstings, all with the deadly addition of anti-aircraft barrages from the Germans, who were trying desperately to hold ground against an equally desperate attempt to take it. Sheridan's Skuas, as the squadron was soon nicknamed, lost men and machines on every flight. The Nieuport was good, but it could not work miracles.

Rex was suffering his own personal torment. His last day in England had affected him disastrously. Delight that Chris was improving had been overset by the distress of his non-recognition. Then there had been the concert. As he had watched Laura perform, had watched those watching her, he had known she was a star. Yet, he had allowed her to drag him out there, as she had done on their wedding night, and peel back the layers to expose his ruling passion for her for all to see. He wondered whether she had used him as part of her act.

Yet he had been angry over his thoughts almost immediately, when he found her in a corner of the garden, overcome by tears.

"They're all so wonderful, yet so physically broken, I can't bear it," she had cried, turning into his arms. "You didn't see their faces as I did. They were like children round a Christmas tree." She had looked up at him with immense sadness on her lovely face. "But I made them happy, didn't I? Just for a while?"

"Of course, darling," he had assured her, drying her tears.

They had strolled together along the shrubbery paths, arms entwined, each very conscious of their coming parting the following morning. She had whispered loving words to him and called him her king of beasts. Yet, that night at the hotel, he had been no lion, but a lamb.

The humiliation of that impotency had weighed him down all the way back to France, and in the following weeks. He grew bad-tempered and antisocial. And as the holocaust of the Somme continued, he began taking on impossible odds in the skies in the almost insane need to push his tally of "kills" higher than any other pilot on either side. He succeeded. His score crept up towards fifty, and he returned day after day with a wild look in his eyes, his aircraft riddled with holes and breaking up around him. He was now drinking heavily night after night.

September, and the Battle of the Somme had still not been won. The cream of British youth, who had volunteered with such patriotic fervour, were now much reduced in numbers, tired, and ill. Trench fever, shellshock, dysentery and foot rot were all too common among them. And more often than not, sick men stayed on duty because the field hospitals were full of wounded and dying.

The Somme offensive had deteriorated into a death toll too horrific for the mind to contemplate. There was no end to it in sight . . . and it had begun to rain, day after day, to turn the surface of France into a sea of mud once more.

As Roland sat hunched in his greatcoat in the back of the ambulance, gazing out at the long ribbon of mire across which they had already travelled and at the endless snake of plodding men, he thought his heart would break. On roads like this, in emergency dressing stations set up near the trenches, in field hospitals behind the lines, the evidence of the Empire's finest young men being systematically wiped out caused him such·anguish he wanted to shout it for all the world to hear. Who would be left to tend the factories and mills, the gentle productive farmland? France would suffer even more, with the land as well as the people being destroyed. And what of Russia with its starving millions, and the rural peasant states like Hungary, Poland and Serbia? Finally, before the war could be terminated, Germany would also have to be brought to industrial and pastoral ruin.

Roland had been made a lance corporal on leaving for France, and although there had been a two-year lapse in his medical studies, he found them fresh in his memory. He was now a full corporal with responsibility for drugs—when there were any—and the daily running of the small field-ambulance unit beneath the command of a French-Canadian doctor, Matthew Rideaux. The two had struck up a cautious friendship, having much in common. They were both unmarried landowners, who spoke French fluently and had a passionate love of country and heritage. And both men protected their emotions jealously.

They were moving on now in the rain towards a village called Croix des Anges. A push forward by a Canadian battalion had gained some ground, and the troops were reputedly fortifying the village, which was little more than a ruin. The British soldiers they were accompanying were to reinforce the Canadians in a desperate attempt to hold on to an area of devastated farmland, which the Germans seemed just as desperate to take back.

"Oh my God, Corp," said a voice behind Roland suddenly. "Here come the Fokkers!"

True enough, a glance at the sky to their rear showed a group of black specks approaching low and fast, sighting the column as their target. There was a mad scramble as the men of the unit dropped to the road to scatter in every direction. Flying so low the pilots' faces could be seen, the Fokkers raced the length of that road three or four times, turning the slow, silent plodding khaki line into a writhing, bleeding serpent. The stutter of machineguns, the crack of grenades exploding, the screams of wounded men, the shrieks of terrified beasts, and the din of diving aircraft made a discordant symphony of war.

The Fokkers were distant specks in the sky again when Roland, shaken, ran with his men to tug out the stretchers from the back of the ambulance. They did what they could. The bandaging and cleansing of wounds could not be done in the pouring rain in the middle of a mire, yet there was no room in the ambulance for the large number of casualties. There were broken limbs, loss of sight and stomach wounds. Roland worked quickly and expertly. After supervising the dispatch of the walking wounded and those fit to travel in trucks, he went to join Matt who was administering morphine to those so seriously ill that the pain was unbearable.

When they reached Croix des Anges, they discovered that the Canadians they were supposed to be joining had advanced further. But the British commander wisely settled where he was. He knew from experience that rapid advances were usually followed by equally rapid retreats to a fortified standpoint. The Canadians would be back, he was certain, so he set his men to digging in. In no time there were trenches, fortifications, subterranean cookhouses and stores, and an underground hospital ward in the cellar of what had been a village inn.

The makeshift hospital was necessary owing to a message that reached the new arrivals soon after they dragged in to Croix des Anges. The road along which they had travelled was now in the hands of advancing Germans. This meant that the sick and wounded could not be moved out to base hospitals, and the ambulance unit would have to do what they could for an impossible number of patients, until traffic could get through once more.

So Roland helped carry stretchers into the comparative warmth of the ruined cellar and, with Matt, saw that every patient was well settled. He stacked what medicines they had in the most protected corner he could find and sorted out with the cook what type of meal could be produced from the rations they had.

The Canadians returned to Croix des Anges three days later. Less than one third of the battalion had survived the advance and retreat. Together with the British reinforcements, they settled into the trench network and began the usual routine of sniping, dawn and dusk rushes to put machinegun posts out of action, and nighttime raids to cut the enemy's wire.

But there were a few brighter aspects to the subterranean life under a sky full of bullets. Supply trucks bringing food, clothing, medicines and cigarettes got through to the village. Roland and

Matt welcomed the medicines and supplies as well as the opportunity to send their bad cases back to the rear, since the numbers in the cellar had been increasing steadily with every raid and sneak assault.

Throughout those weeks at Croix des Anges, Roland kept going with thoughts of Tarrant Hall and his estate. Tessa wrote long letters to him twice each week, telling a success story that he had no reason to doubt. More and more, he thanked heaven she had turned up at exactly the right time. He wrote equally long letters in reply, but he mentioned little of his present life, concentrating instead on the home so dear to his heart. He also wrote to Chris, but there were never any replies. Still, he prayed for the day when there would be.

12

The continuous rain and low cloud had prevented any clashes for some days, and as Rex circled the airfield at Saint-Brioche, he gazed down dully at the waterlogged grass. Then he scowled. His face was gaunt and hollow-eyed, his frame bony, his complexion yellow. Taxiing up to the sheds, he climbed from the cockpit and dropped heavily to the spongy ground that squelched round his boots as he made his way to the squadron office. Inside the damp, chilly room he threw down gauntlets and goggles and pulled off his leather helmet. He poured a drink and downed it defiantly as he slumped into the wooden armchair, shivering in clothes and scarf that had been saturated in an open cockpit. It did not seem to matter whether he was wet or dry. Nothing seemed to matter any more.

On his desk he saw there was a letter addressed in Marion's handwriting. Pouring another drink, he reached for it resignedly. He must read it in case there was something of importance . . .

Please believe that I thought long and seriously about this before writing to you, Rex. Daddy says you have a right to know; Tessa believes you should be kept in ignorance. But I believe your unfaltering friendship deserves mine now.

His heartbeat thumped agonizingly as he read on.

407

Laura left it far too late . . . some terrible old woman in a back street . . . must have been agony and she could have bled to death . . . pure chance that Tessa was in London and called to see her . . . down to Dorset in an ambulance . . . truly think Daddy saved her life . . . still desperately ill . . . you get compassionate leave . . . I hope I've done the right thing.

The mechanics were putting the Nieuport away as Rex opened the door and began crossing the rainswept area leading to the sheds. He knew nothing of his curt orders or their astonished questioning of them. He knew nothing of the propeller being swung, the preliminary run across the field in deteriorating visibility, or the takeoff. He knew nothing of the ghostly sensation of flying through a grey downpour that saturated him even further.

He was dying slowly. Since that night three and a half months ago, he had tortured himself with the memory of his failure in Laura's bed. Yet during those five days he had sired a child of their love, perhaps with red-gold hair and tiny petal hands, and now she had destroyed it. The thought broke his mind.

He did not know how much time had elapsed when the cloud began to thin and sunshine dazzled him with brightness. Breaking out into clear skies, he looked over the edge of the cockpit at the glittering ribbon of water below. Still on course!

But he was so busy studying the river that would take him to the coast, he forgot that others hunted in those same skies, and the familiar death rattle of bullets ripping through fabric and wood came without warning. As he turned to look over his shoulder, an excruciating pain raced through his right arm and he folded forward. The movement saved his life. The next burst of fire travelled a mere inch over his head to splinter the struts supporting the upper wing.

Gasping with agony and conscious of a warm stickiness gathering in his sleeve, Rex flung the Nieuport into a steep turn as a Fokker, painted a defiant yellow, flashed past. Trying to hold the joystick with fast-numbing fingers, Rex fired into the side of the enemy machine as it tried to correct its overshoot and turn on a sixpence. The pilot jerked and fell back; the machine plunged to the fields below. Rex had scored his fiftieth kill.

But the death rattle came from behind again, and Rex realized his aircraft had emerged from cloud right into an entire formation of enemy machines. Blood was running from his arm now and, to make matters worse, Rex discovered his ammunition drum was empty. He remedied his extremely dangerous situation by going into an immediate steep dive that took him down to about fifty feet from the ground. He raced along the course of the river like a fox making a desperate bid to escape a howling pack of hounds. Luckily, he had flown over northern France for the best part of two years now, and knew the terrain well. A few miles ahead a canal branched from the river, cutting through woodland. Here the French held a strongly fortified castle, with a line of trenches equipped with ancient but effective heavy artillery. That was where the fox would go to earth!

Rex dropped even lower, and several bursts of fire from the dark shapes screaming down on him hit his tail and tore the fabric badly. The machine began to waver and wobble, but just then he spotted the canal ahead. Weak and giddy now, he dropped to a dangerous fifteen feet to pass through a narrow cutting between the trees: the mere width of the canal, plus a few feet on either side.

His ruse worked. Unprepared for such a move, the Fokkers had flown on. But the wobble of his machine was worsening, and Rex was finding it more and more difficult to maintain height and steadiness. The cold steel-grey water looked menacing below; the trees seemed to be crowding in on him. But all he could think of was Laura, and there was wetness on his cheeks as his anguish conquered weakness of mind and body and kept him going.

The German pilots found him and renewed their pursuit far too late. The French fortifications were in sight now and, beyond rational thought, Rex flew on across these lines at a height that had the French gunners ducking their heads. But they recognized Fokkers when they saw them, and the afternoon broke apart as the big guns opened on easy targets. Just below his wheels, Rex was vaguely conscious of upturned faces, arms waving, and the sound of cheering. But then one youngster with the face of a child pulled a trigger in his excitement, and machinegun bullets smacked into the underside of the Nieuport.

Rex let out a cry of agony as his thigh seemed to split open, the sky around him darkening to night. The impact as his machine hit the ground threw him forward hard, and he knew no more until tremendous heat brought him to semiconsciousness. Wood and fabric were being eaten quickly by ravenous flames as he lay, unable to move.

If I ever crash and get trapped in a burning cockpit, Mike, don't rush over and drag me out.

But they did, and at the first tug Rex lapsed into unconsciousness so total he knew nothing more until he came to in a French hospital. They adopted Sherry Sheridan as their own hero then, and he was told he was to be awarded the Croix de Guerre for his action that day. No one asked what he had been doing so far from his squadron base heading for England.

THEY FLEW HIM BACK to England as a passenger in a two-seater. The authorities, in their wisdom, decided a home posting would be a timely move for their hero. In that bleak winter of 1916-1917 the Somme offensive had finally ground to a halt as an acknowledged failure. The inspiration and pride Sherry Sheridan instilled could be put to better use visiting cities and schools on lecture tours than in leading further missions that endangered his life.

So it was, in the middle of November, that Rex arrived at the airfield at Brooklands with his arm firmly held in plaster and still limping from the thigh wound, to be met by a battery of cameras and newsmen. He did his best to answer their questions, forcing himself to do as his superiors demanded because they had promised an official car to drive him to Tarrant Hall if he played the hero for them. There was the added carrot of a month's leave before starting a tour of the country to line up recruits.

So he played the hero. He told propaganda lies. He smiled and waved. He wore his scarf, winked broadly, and suggested there was no greater proof of virility and manhood than to go to glorious war. But all through it his yearning for Laura grew greater and greater until he feared he would fall apart.

Finally, the time came to leave the crowd of reporters for the waiting car. But a young woman rushed from the group to stand in Rex's path, her pretty face flushed with emotion.

"How long are you going to go on killing?" she cried in a well-bred voice. "I challenge you to look me in the eye and deny that it's a mortal sin to take a man's life . . . and another to go out urging boys who are mere children to do the same."

There was only one way of dealing with her. Pulling her to him with his uninjured arm, Rex kissed her soundly before murmuring, "Unite the women of Germany, my dear, and we'll all willingly stay at home." Then he went to the car, leaving her with colour even

410

further heightened and a bemused expression, as she watched his departure with as much admiration as her colleagues. It was a long journey down to Tarrant Royal, and all he could think of was Laura. News had reached him through official sources that she was recovering from her illness and was no longer in a critical condition. But as he sat in the back of that car, the miles passing, he began dying slowly all over again. How was he to face this woman who held his love in her hands, and who had been prepared to destroy it along with the child he had given her?

It grew dark long before they reached Dorset, and by the time the car was travelling the lanes of Tarrant Royal Rex was practically in a fever. When it turned into the steep approach to his home he was deeply afraid, as he had never been before.

But first there was old Minks to face, more stooped and even greyer, to give him a silent emotional greeting. And Priddy, who laughed and cried at the same time as she kissed him. Then Tessa, looking as glowingly healthy as ever.

"Welcome home, Rex. Thank God you're safe." Giving a grave smile she added, "Laura's up in your old room, and looks every bit as terrified as you do."

He left the others there, forgotten as he walked slowly up the staircase to the landing. At the door he hesitated, his heart thudding so strongly against his ribs it made him feel faint. Then he turned the handle and went in.

She was standing by the bed. The soft amber wool dress glowed with the light from the fire as it clung to her thin frame; her beautiful hair now hung near her shoulders in red-gold waves that gave her a feminine frailty; and her face, even paler and more pointed, seemed dominated by eyes that had lost all wickedness and turned to desperation as they gazed at him across the room.

He found it impossible to move, to say anything. All that had ever happened between them hung suspended in that moment, as they searched each other for a sign, for a foothold on a bridge that would link them, a bastion to sustain their weakness.

Taking a step towards him, then one or two more, she stopped and began to cry silently as she looked up into his face. "Say . . . say you'll forgive me, or I'll die."

The silence that followed was broken only by the spitting of a log on the fire. "Why?" he asked in a cracked voice. "Why?"

In reply, her hands covered her face and her shoulders shook.

411

"I suppose it was the damned theatre. Well, you've destroyed your hopes with your own hand," he said, hating himself with every word he uttered. "Your career is over and finished with."

Still she stood a few feet from him, weak with sobs and the emaciation of illness.

The fire inside him was reaching explosion point as he went on. "I'm in England for nine months. You'll go with me to lectures, and everywhere else I go, is that understood? You'll forget Madame Sherry and be plain Laura Sheridan. You'll be my devoted wife, and we'll have a proper marriage. You'll . . . oh, dear Lord in heaven!" He broke down, took two steps towards her, and held her against him with his sound left arm. "Don't cry like that, my darling . . . it tears me apart," he murmured through his own gathering tears. "Don't you know that if you had been lost, then so would I? Life *is* you. I thought I had shown you that."

EVERY SEASON SEEMED to bring its own delights. October had been a glory of coloured leaves, with mornings of glittering frost, afternoons of wreathing mists, and short periods of clear-skied brilliance. Now Chris concentrated on the squirrels who buried nuts willy-nilly and ate their fill of berries until their furry bibs were stained red with the juice.

His condition had greatly improved. Although his leg was still trapped in the weighted apparatus, his torso was now free of the tight strapping and thick covering of foul-smelling jelly designed to ease the agony of the burns. His skin was still a vivid pink and covered in crinkles, but the pain it gave him was much less.

They had to do more to his body now, so his periods of peace and solitude became more valued. But he hated what they did, washing him, smoothing ointment over his skin, bending his limbs in gentle exercise, massaging his shoulders and thighs. Sometimes Marion helped with the washing and massage as part of her general duties, and he hated the ritual even more on those days, finding himself unable to meet her gaze. He missed her very much, and deeply regretted his outburst that had sent her away that day. He hoped constantly that she would come to talk to him as she had done before. She never did, though, except when she had been told to do so.

But he had other forms of comfort and companionship now. One afternoon he had taken up a leather-bound book that the man called

412

Rex had brought on his very first visit, and a new world had opened up within its covers. He found he could read French with total ease, and the lyrical beauty of the love verses filled him with intense excitement. Another day an ode in an entirely different language floated into his mind. Immediately, a memory of Laura Sheridan in a white draped garment, a wreath around her short flaming curls, matched up with the words, and a whole flood of Greek poetry then rushed in from the past. From then on, she became the goddess of temptation, of love, and of inspiration.

Soon he began writing verse himself, painstakingly translating it into Greek if the sentiments allowed it, or using French if the words and similes were too modern for the classical language. His drawing pad also came into full use, and there was always a goddess featured somewhere in his sketches. But although he knew the goddess was Laura, he could never put a face on the figure. The image of her vivid pointed one always blurred, and somehow Marion's features became superimposed on it. It brought him a sense of desolation so great that he felt like a prisoner in some strange limbo where he was being punished for something he could not remember doing.

Then, one afternoon towards the end of November, Marion walked down the length of the ward and smiled in her old way as she approached.

"Feel ready for a surprise?" she asked gaily.

"It depends," was his cautious reply.

Her eyes twinkled at him in a way that pleased him. "Your brother and his wife are here to see you."

Excitement raced through him so fast he felt almost sick with it. "Rex?" he asked. "I thought he was back in France."

"He was. But he was badly wounded, and they brought him home to rest. He's now one of the most decorated pilots in the RFC."

"She'll be pleased about that," he said, burning with jealousy, knowing Rex would have done it all for her.

"Laura? Yes, I suppose so." It was said in an odd tone, and Marion walked away without another word. He stared down the hall after her in surprise, until she came back with his visitors.

In the first seconds he was incredibly disappointed, for they seemed like two strangers. The man in uniform had his arm in a sling and looked like an ageing nonentity as he limped down the ward. The girl with him was much thinner than he remembered,

413

and clung to her husband as if for support. When they reached his bed, however, he saw the lines of experience and pain on his brother's still-young face and the warmth of a smile that could only be for someone dear to him.

Then Chris realized that Laura was even more beautiful than he remembered. Her hair was longer and put back into a riot of curls that left the narrow lines of her face beautifully outlined. The wicked promise in her green eyes had now softened into a glow of adoration when they were turned to her husband.

"Hello, Chris," said Laura gently.

"You're progressing by leaps and bounds, by the look of things," added Rex, by way of greeting.

"That book you gave me is splendid," Chris told him. "I don't think I really thanked you for it on the day you brought it." Then he grinned. "I'm awfully glad you came today. I was feeling a bit lonely."

"I've brought you something, but I'm afraid it's not some more French poetry," Laura said, and gave him a small folder. "I thought you'd find these interesting."

Inside the folder were two or three dozen pages in vibrant colours, scenes and costumes for a stage production of *Julius Caesar*. "It's an original set dating back seventy-odd years," she added casually. "A friend gave them to me, but I thought you'd appreciate them more. Rex says you're a brilliant Latin and Greek scholar—and *Julius Caesar* is sort of Latin, isn't it?"

Delight flooded through him. A brilliant scholar! Why had they not told him before? He leafed through the sketches, finding each as precious as a crock of gold. "Thanks awfully," he mumbled, too overcome to meet her glance.

They talked for a while, then Rex got to his feet and ruffled Chris's hair affectionately. "We'll leave you to have a quiet spell before they bring your tea. We'll come again soon."

"I'd like that. And . . . and thanks for the *Julius Caesar*."

"I'm glad you're pleased," said Laura, looking so marvellous he was overcome with sadness because she was going. "Goodbye, Chris."

She bent to kiss him very gently, and he wanted to put his head on her breast and cry all the sadness out of him. Instead, he turned his head away so that he would not see them go. Then he took off his spectacles so that he would not see anything.

414

FOR THE NEXT WEEK he was completely happy and absorbed in the present Laura had brought him. He redrew and elaborated on the scenes, writing Latin inscriptions and putting in figures of the great orators and statesmen throughout the ages . . . in addition to a Laura goddess, of course. And he wrote and wrote, in French, Greek and Latin, all the things he had ever known seeming to come into his mind like a ravening horde.

Some of the things he wrote made no sense at all. But, after puzzling over them for a while, he realized that they must be something to do with the Greek or Roman wars, because they were all about troop movements, the position of guns, the dates of battles and routes taken by ships.

He knew all this must be kept secret, so he hid all his drawings and writing beneath the pillow whenever anyone approached, and under the mattress at night. But he must have been careless one day towards the end of that week, because the elderly nurse who always took night duty gave him his medicine, then stooped to pick something up from the floor. It was one of his sheets of paper.

"Hello, what's this, Mr. Sheridan?" she asked, as of a child. "Secret messages, is it? 'Two battalions moving up on Wednesday, and cavalry to form a pincer on each flank.' Whatever does all that mean?"

He had always hated her, even more so now. "Give it to me!" he demanded furiously. "It's mine."

"Now, now, now," she admonished. "That's quite enough of that, young gentleman, or I'll give you more bromide."

He made a lunge for the paper, bombarding her with threats and wild demands to hand over what was his. Others came and held him restrainingly while they put the needle in his arm, and that was when the elderly nurse discovered the remainder of his precious pages.

The screens went round him, and they held him down when he fought for possession of the secret documents now being shown to those standing by the bed. Soon a man in khaki uniform appeared, listened to what had happened, took a look at the papers, then gave low-voiced instructions.

By now Chris was feeling leaden, fighting the compulsion to close his eyes. They began to wheel his bed towards the door, and he looked up at them, crying helplessly because none of them would look his way, give him another chance. Marion could have saved him except that she was never there during the night. Now she would never know where he had gone; neither would Laura and Rex. They would probably be upset . . . and Roland. He had had a family, and a friend called Marion . . . and he wanted them all desperately. But the leadenness had reached every part of him now, and his lashes closed on the wetness within them.

WHEN HE OPENED HIS EYES, he lay in quiet terror, knowing that the blur could be eternity. But his spectacles were immediately put on his nose, and he saw he was in a small room with bars over the window. He could see nothing of the grounds he loved, only a brick wall outside. A man was standing beside him.

They came, one after the other, asking him about what he had written on the papers. But he remained silent, staring at them blankly. He must not break, no matter what they did to him.

Time blurred. Then one day a new man came through the door, tall, prematurely grey, with a strange accent. Chris recoiled from him on sight. He thought his name was Neil Frencham, and he was not interested in his knowledge but his body.

It was unbearably hot. They had had no water to drink since they had landed, and the Turks were just at the top of the cliff. The noise of gunfire hurt his ears. There were blasts on a whistle, and they all had to run uphill. They knew he would die, but they made him go. Neil tried to save him. *Those eyes with the long lashes curling over them were more than I could stand.* But that was why he had to go. It was only when he was halfway across that murderous open stretch that he realized he might be left with half a head, like Rochford-Clarke. But it was too late then.

Captive in his bed, all Chris could do now was hide from this man who had made him want to die. He took off the spectacles and threw them, as hard as he could.

13

The Anglo-Canadian force retreated from Croix des Anges on Christmas Day, 1916. The Germans chose Christmas Eve to mount a desperate offensive, and the dispirited, heavily depleted companies that had held the position since September trudged away under cover of darkness rather than be overrun.

The tiny medical unit had decided to remain in the cellar until the last possible moment with those patients who could not be moved, and with the new casualties of the present attack. It was hopelessly overcrowded. Supplies were low, and the bitter December weather penetrated the sandbagged walls to add to the misery of the wounded men shivering under insufficient blankets. The medical staff would do all they could for the serious patients before they left with the rearguard, taking with them only those fit to travel in the one temperamental motor ambulance.

To protect this precious vehicle from attack, it had been backed down the slope into the cellar, giving the staff even less room in which to work. There was no guarantee it would be safe there, of course. The German bombardment was bitter and indiscriminate as Matt Rideaux and Roland Sheridan moved from patient to patient, feeling the urgency of time running out on their work.

"Compliments of the season," said a voice in Roland's ear. He looked up to meet Matt's glance. "It's just gone midnight. I guess the bells are ringing out at home."

Roland hardly saw what he was doing, hands working automatically as his mind winged to the Dorset village where he had spent every Christmas before this one. When they were boys, he and his brothers had raced downstairs on Christmas morning to find their presents at the foot of a tall tree by the staircase, decorated with lanterns and garlands. More recently, they had exchanged gifts in the morning room after breakfast, thanking each other with affectionate smiles. But clouds passed over the brightness of Roland's memories as he heard once more the thud of shells.

"D'yer fink they're comin' over the top, Corp?" wheezed the youngster enduring the rough-and-ready treatment Roland was forced to give him.

"Not yet. Our rearguard hasn't come in." He put the blanket back over an oozing chest wound. "There you are, you'll find that more comfortable now, son."

Next minute Roland's attention was taken by figures that were materializing from the darkness of the various gaps in the sandbagged walls, and he found himself staring at the grey uniforms and bucket-shaped helmets of German troops. One of the soldiers shouted to an officer somewhere, and a middle-aged lieutenant appeared almost immediately to look around at the sombre scene.

"*Gott im Himmel!*" he exclaimed wearily. "*Was Unglück!*"

417

Roland thought the misfortune was theirs rather than their captors', and said so in tense tones. Surprised to hear someone respond in the same language, the German stepped further into the cellar, peering across the dimness to see who it was.

"What has happened to our men?" Roland asked, in the limited phrases of his student days. "The ones in the trenches."

"They are all dead," was the toneless response. "How did you expect to hold the line with so few?"

Conscious of Matt resuming his work on one of their patients as if there had been no interruption, Roland ignored the remark. "Have you any medical supplies with you?" he asked.

The German laughed harshly. "Have *you* any food?"

"Haven't you?"

"We have not enough for ourselves, much less for prisoners. We thought you had all gone." The man's voice was blunt and tinged with exhaustion. "What are you doing here?"

"We were to have gone with the rearguard," Roland informed him through a tight throat. "In that ambulance."

"You have no rearguard. And we need this place for our own wounded. You must clear these men out right away."

"Clear them out!" cried Roland angrily. "There's nowhere else to put them—and some of them are too ill to be moved, anyway. These men are wounded prisoners of war. You are obliged to take responsibility for them."

With a sudden surprising switch to guttural English, the man said, "Go! In that—go!" He waved a hand at the ambulance. "Quickly go and I say nothing."

"What are you two talking about?" asked Matt laconically, now taking an interest in what had been an incomprehensible conversation until then. "Go where?"

"The lieutenant has decided not to take us prisoner as we are a medical unit," put in Roland quickly, having a terrible suspicion that the slightest hesitation by them would suggest only one other solution to a man obviously at the limit of his endurance. "He is allowing us to rejoin the main force."

"Yes, yes," came the urgent affirmative. "All go. Now!"

Matt folded his arms. "Now let's get this straight, lieutenant. There is no possibility of us all going. Some of these men . . ."

"Will take a while to shift," put in Roland with heavy emphasis, praying Matt would understand what he was trying to get across to him. "Once we catch up with our own troops *we* can ensure they take the road to recovery, can't we, Captain Rideaux? That course of treatment I once told you about wouldn't be the right one here. We had better take them with us."

Matt gave him a long look that took in the implications of his words. "Do you mean the treatment you give to horses?"

"Exactly," agreed Roland fervently. "I think we should accept the lieutenant's honourable and humane gesture and set off as soon as possible."

It was a heartrending business piling suffering men one on top of the other into an ambulance designed to take only one sixth of their number. Even so, Roland and Matt worked swiftly, conscious that the bulk of the German force would be entering Croix des Anges before long and might not be as lenient as the advance-party commander.

Overloaded as it was, the ancient ambulance eventually set off. They drove without stopping for a long period.

"Just where did you learn that lingo?" Matt asked finally. "It was all kinda private between you and him."

Keeping his voice low in the jolting noisy vehicle, Roland said, "He told me they needed that cellar for their own wounded. When he suddenly resorted to English, it struck me he didn't want his men to know he was letting us go to our own people. That's when I got really worried. He was one of the old Officer Corps Germans, who still believe in the gentlemanly code of warfare. *They wanted no prisoners!* You know what would have happened to our wounded if we hadn't brought them with us?"

Matt shook his head in the darkness. "This finally does it. If you hadn't understood that guy's language and passed me the tip about shooting animals to end their misery, I'd have made one hell of a stand for suffering humanity. And we'd all now be dead. After the way you handled that situation, I'm recommending that you be sent home to qualify as a doctor and officer."

SPRING 1917, a time when land offensives should be made. But no one any longer had confidence in breaking the deadlock that was now in its third year. Generals were bewildered and at their wits' end; armies were on the verge of mutiny. So, while the entrenched troops noted the passing of time only because the eternal mud began to harden beneath their feet, warfare took to the air in earnest, the cocksure German pilots intending to knock the RFC from the skies for good.

There was a dogfight overhead as Roland climbed from the sidecar of the motorcycle that had brought him to his new posting in the front-line sector near the Belgian town of Ypres, known to the British troops as Wipers. He had only been away two months, yet the return to the battle zone shocked him anew.

"Welcome to Gillyhook, sir," said the driver, using the British soldiers' usual cosy pronunciation of the name of the village of Guillehoek.

Returning the man's salute, Roland picked up his bags and began scrambling across the desolate rubble to where he had been told he would find Colonel Reeder. While he was doing so, one of the aircraft overhead fell like a spinning torch to the earth, the black crosses on its wings proclaiming it as one of the enemy. When it exploded on impact, Roland was startled to hear the stark earth around him ring with the sound of hundreds of cheering voices. Looking from side to side, he then became aware that what looked like areas of muddy devastation were alive. Whole regiments of men living underground were waving anything they could lay hands on to their comrades of the air.

Roland had not had to return to England to qualify, after all. Such was the need for doctors at this desperate stage of the war that the authorities had read Matt's report, then put Roland through a written and practical examination at one of the main hospitals in France. At the end, they had told him he was more knowledgeable and experienced than many men already serving as medical officers. They gave him the rank of lieutenant, and sent him out as regimental medical officer.

But Roland had no illusions. Medical officers in the field lasted no longer than infantrymen, when posted to an area like Ypres, which had been bombarded by the Germans since the end of 1914 in an effort to capture it from the British. If he survived for six months, it would be a miracle.

Reaching the flight of reinforced steps leading down into a bunker somewhat ostentatiously labelled REGIMENTAL HEADQUARTERS, Roland descended into the earth, telling himself there was no other smell in the world like that of a vile trench. After being welcomed by a haggard yellow-faced lieutenant colonel, he was introduced to several infantry subalterns with whom he would share quarters.

421

One was an eighteen-year-old named Hilary Bisset, who was silently drinking absinthe.

During that first month of duty Roland found day-to-day life predictable. At dawn and dusk there was an artillery bombardment from both sides in anticipation of an attack. And at night the men took watches while certain groups ventured out to mend the wire or bring in wounded who had been sniped at. After his work with Matt Rideaux's unit, Roland found the new life soul-destroying because of its stagnation. Each day's sick parade brought the usual maladies and malingerers; each bombardment meant broken bodies and others who were mentally broken by one shell too many. In the bunker, young Bisset was fast going to the dogs over a faithless fiancée no older than himself. Seeing the boy's suffering, Roland had cause to be thankful he had not tied himself to any girl before leaving England.

After four weeks between the claustrophobic high mud walls of the trenches, Roland felt he had lost his identity. His longing for Tarrant Royal had never been more acute. To ease it, he began writing long letters to Rex full of "do you remember?" and "can you recall?"; he also wrote reams to Chris and Tessa. None of the letters told anything of his present life; they were full of recollections of home. Then, realizing that the letters were merely pen pictures to salve his own heartache for what he had left behind, he tore them up. But a partial solution to his growing restlessness came within that week. Word had gone round to the soldiers that the *Gillyhook Gazette* was about to be created by a major who had run a small-town paper in civilian life, and entreaties for copy came hard on the heels of the announcement. So, at the end of three concentrated days of tending the sick and wounded who were as depressed and far from home as he, Roland sat in his bunker and wrote, by the light of his last candle, a detailed description of English country life in the month of April. He signed it "Waysider", and sent it along to the major-turned-editor.

He was unprepared for the thrill of pleasure it gave him to see his words in print, and even more unprepared for the reaction they brought. His unsentimental but sincere account of home had reached the souls of even the toughest among the men. They wanted more! An appeal was circulated for the mysterious "Waysider" to write another column for the next issue.

Roland's writing was halted by several days of concerted German attacks which kept him busy all hours of the twenty-four. Heavy shelling, gas attacks, and nocturnal hellfire preceded an infantry assault on the trenches of the west flank. It was the first time Roland had experienced such sustained attack firsthand, and he worked automatically, his brain dazed. He began by dealing with casualties as they were brought in, but so many routes became blocked that he and the orderlies went out searching for wounded. With a medical bag slung over his shoulder and a gas mask on his face he ran along duckboards as fast as the congestion of desperate crouching men would allow, scrambled over piles of mud, and flattened himself against the walls each time he heard the approaching whine of a shell. He dressed wounds, administered morphine, and did what he could to relieve the terror and loneliness of fatal injuries. During that time he forgot all else but what he had learned in a London medical school a lifetime ago.

SEVERAL DAYS LATER they heard they were being sent to the rear for rest while other regiments that had been in reserve took over in the trenches. The prospect of a few weeks in Guillehoek was pleasant enough to put everyone in an amiable mood. The village was comprised of a group of typical Flemish cottages lying beside a cobblestone road, a small church, and a château that was now gutted; several of the adjacent cottages had also been reduced to rubble, but the remainder of the village was intact. The peasants continued their normal day-to-day routine; and bustling life was provided by the British army, who enjoyed the local girls and British nurses stationed there, and a charitable forces canteen where food, drinks and entertainment were offered.

The officers were billeted in local cottages, two to a building, and the family hosting Roland and Hilary Bisset were quiet peasant folk who made the foreign guests as comfortable as possible. On the first evening they retired early to leave the two officers alone in the main room of the stone cottage.

All at once, sitting there in a room lit only by the flickering light of the fire, and with a lovesick youngster who was plainly looking to him for advice, Roland felt an intense longing to be with his brothers again and somehow show them he understood more than he had before. Had he been too hard? he asked himself. He had been ruled by unbending standards and principles, but now he was growing to recognize that principles often had to be tailored to suit the circumstances. War and trench life were showing him that. Human nature was vulnerable, men were all different . . . and life was too short. Before turning in for the night, Roland told Hilary to forget the faithless fiancée and to look for a girl in the village to cuddle. He would find that infinitely more satisfying than absinthe.

The next day Roland kept much to himself. The end of April had brought a brief flash of very warm weather, so he took advantage of the freedom to enjoy the outdoors. He walked for a long while alongside the river, conscious of the bubbling, splashing water, yet lost in the lanes and meadows of the Dorset he had loved for twenty-six years. Then, coming to a low bridge, he stood with one booted foot on the cornerstone and gazed into the past as tears welled from his eyes. Had he been so very wrong to want to preserve it? With Chris broken in mind as well as body at nineteen, and Rex facing death or mutilation every time he climbed into a cockpit, was it so incomprehensible to everyone else that he had wanted to keep *something* of their past life so that it could never be entirely destroyed? Only now that he had witnessed the sacrifice of war at firsthand did he realize that England would have to be saved by a whole generation for the next one, so that children like David Sheridan would know and value all its traditions and beliefs.

At the thought of Chris's son, Roland bowed his head in regret. The child's father did not know of his existence; his senior uncle had deplored it. Only Rex had made him welcome in the family to which he rightly belonged, despite the mistake of his conception. To this two-year-old boy and his like would fall the responsibility of preserving the spirit of England, and the spirit of those who had fought to save it.

With that thought strong in his mind, Roland sat there beside the river and began to write in the notebook he carried all he wanted to say to his young nephew. It took the form of a letter, telling him the things about England that meant so much to him and asking the boy to regard them, in years to come, as a legacy of love from all those who had died that he might have them.

When he had finished he realized he could never send it. David was too young to read, and Marion would find such words insincere from the man who had turned her out of Tarrant Hall. At that point it struck him that he had just written the next offering by "Waysider" for the *Gillyhook Gazette*. Although it had come spontaneously from his longings, it must surely echo the thoughts of many.

Roland stayed out for most of that day, sitting beside the river to eat the bread and cheese given him by the Flemish family. When he finally went back to the house, he found that Hilary had been out all day also, and had returned in a strangely excited mood. At first, Roland thought he had been drinking heavily, but after the Belgian family had left them alone before the fire, Hilary revealed the source of his excitement. The boy had taken his advice and found a girl to cuddle. But she was not a Belgian girl. Rosie was a volunteer helper in the canteen in Guillehoek.

THE FOLLOWING WEEK Roland's unit was ordered back to the front because a big offensive was under way. Hilary seemed anguished at the news, but he fell in line with the others to march back to the trenches they had left less than two weeks ago.

A different trench, a different bunker. But it was all the same: the smell, the high enclosing walls, the sudden death. They all knew it would not be long before they would be ordered to make another all-out attack, which would gain them a few hundred yards and lose them a few thousand comrades.

Roland had never been involved in a concerted assault before, and the tense mood caught him. He sat well into the night writing letters to Rex, Chris and Tessa; to Priddy and Minks and Dawkins; to the rector of Tarrant Royal; to his solicitor; and finally, to David Sheridan. The last two were only to be posted in the event of his death.

Hilary was very quiet and drinking absinthe again. Seeing Roland write yet another letter, he stared at him with a frightened look on his face. Then, turning to pick up something from his bed, the youngster studied it as it lay in his hands. "If I get killed, Doc, will you give this to my girl in Gillyhook?"

Roland leaned forward, considering the youthful face.

"It's my mother's cameo," the boy went on. "My parents were missionaries in China. They were killed in an attack, and this cameo was all that was found in the ruins of the mission." He looked up at Roland. "Promise me you'll give it to her in person, to make sure she gets it. You'll find her in the canteen. Her full name is Rosalind Tierney."

Roland's surprise at the boy's request now turned to shock. The last time he had seen Rosalind was in a nightclub in London, where she had thrown a glass of red wine in his face while calling him a coward, in front of Laura. The humiliation of that incident flooded over him anew as he looked at Hilary.

"Of course I'll give it to her," Roland assured him slowly. "But you'll be able to hand it over yourself the next time we go to Gillyhook for a rest period."

AFTER INITIAL ADVANCES the fighting deteriorated into slaughter, and the Allies were forced to face the fact that the Germans must have brought up fresh troops without their knowledge. The RFC was asked for more concentrated observation services, but they were pushed to their limit, with exhausted pilots and faulty machines. On the ground, the faltering offensive continued, token attacks as diversionary measures being ordered all along the line. The Guillehoek contingent were engaged in one barely a week after their return.

Roland was busy with casualties soon after the attack began in the hour before dawn. The growing number of men waiting for his attention did not throw him into a panic, and he worked steadily with hands that were skilful and sure. He chatted to some of the men as he applied field dressings or injected morphine to help their anguish. He knew that the sound of a calm, confident voice against the moans and background gunfire gave them a sense of normality in the midst of hell. It seemed that he had been on the go for hours when he heard the call of "Quick, over here, Doc" from outside. Two stretcher-bearers were moving forward.

Roland straightened up from applying a dressing. "What's the problem?" he asked, nodding to an orderly to finish what he was doing, and starting to walk across to the men.

"It's Mr. Bisset, sir. He's dead."

Roland felt sick at heart, and tears began to flood down his face.

14

Dr. Bill Chandler came in at his usual time, smiling a greeting. "Hello. Had a good night?"

"Yes. It was the first time I didn't wake up in a sweat of fear," Chris told him.

"Good-oh. That's one bloody big step forward."

"Your language gets worse."

The doctor grinned. "Put it down to my chequered career down under. We can't all be English country squires."

Chris tried to shift to a more comfortable position. No longer afraid of Chandler because of his resemblance to Neil Frencham, he had gradually established a wary relationship with the specialist and trusted him enough to cooperate in their daily sessions.

Christmas had come and gone without his knowing, and he was still frightened at the way entire months could be lost from his life without warning. Bill Chandler called it involuntary withdrawal, due to the returning memory of something Chris did not want to face. And although he still did not want to recall the hell of Gallipoli, two days ago he had finally confessed the disillusionment of discovering Neil Frencham's true feelings for him.

Speaking about his months in Gallipoli helped Chris to gain a feeling of identity. He could now remember the shock of seeing Rochford-Clarke's mortal wound, the desperation of climbing a cliff to get away from Neil, and wanting to die. Yet something told him there had been more behind his death wish, that lay further back than Gallipoli; back in the part of his life that was still a blank. He was avid to learn what lay in that blank, yet frightened of doing so. No one would tell him the details of his past—he had to tell *them*; and he could only do that by remembering.

Now Chris said, "You know, I wanted to die in Gallipoli. I tried to climb to the top of the cliff so I would be seen and machinegunned. I couldn't face the fact that a man's mind counted for nothing against the attraction of his body. Neil wasn't the first person to show me that. It had happened before."

"Oh? At school, perhaps?" came the question. "A senior boy?"

"Perhaps."

"Or maybe it was a girl?"

Thoughts of Laura filled him immediately. Did she find his body attractive?

"You like girls, don't you?" the doctor nudged.

"If they're intelligent," was his immediate reply. But then came the grey mist once more that blocked his view into the past.

Undaunted, the specialist went on, "Chris, why do you always retreat whenever I mention sexual attraction? You're so proud of your mind! Why aren't you as proud of your body?"

427

"It's always the same, this obsession with my body," Chris flamed, in sudden inexplicable anger.

"Is it any worse than your obsession with your brain? There are few people who possess a mind equal to yours, which will mean a lonely life if that's all you're going to look for in people."

"I can't look for anything, can I, shut in here like this with no other view than a brick wall?" he accused. "At least last year there were visits from my brothers, as well as Marion."

"You liked her, did you?"

"Yes," he shouted. "She didn't ask foolish questions."

"All right, Chris, I've put you through enough today. But you're leaving this room tomorrow morning. We've decided it's time to transfer you to another hospital where you won't feel so lonely."

SO CHRIS NEVER DID walk through the shrubbery he had studied for a year. With Bill Chandler he left the hospital in an ambulance. After a time the rear doors were opened and several white-coated orderlies were there, ready to move him. Through the open doors Chris could see grey stone walls covered with ivy, sunshine on a neat gravel drive, and an impressive front entrance with a heavily studded door that stood open to reveal a polished wood floor. They slid the stretcher out carefully, and the vista widened to reveal a large crenellated house surrounded by trees.

Inside, Chris saw a huge panelled hall with an open fireplace, a graceful staircase leading to the upper floors, and a recessed window nook that revealed a hint of colourful gardens.

He looked up at Bill Chandler. "I'd like a window that lets me see trees and flowers."

The doctor nodded. "I think you'll be happy with yours."

Chris concentrated on looking round as they carried him through a long panelled corridor, past the open doors of rooms turned into wards, until the end of the impressive passageway was reached and light burst in from all directions. His room was, in effect, a very large conservatory.

It would be like living in the middle of the garden, he thought joyously. He would have a panoramic view of graceful lawns, beds of roses and forget-me-nots, a distant sunken garden and, beyond that, green hills covered with grazing sheep. In addition, he could see through the inner glass to the men in the ward.

Bill Chandler asked if he approved of his new quarters.

"I'll say," he enthused. "But I don't understand it at all. First, you keep me shut up in a place where I can't see a thing. Now, I'm suddenly put here where there's so much going on. I don't know what to concentrate on first. Why?"

The doctor gave a faint smile. "We thought you were ready to go one stage further in your recovery. I hope we haven't anticipated too much."

Chris was mystified. "But I am ready. In this room I'll progress very quickly, you'll see. I love it here already."

"You should, Chris, you were born and brought up here. Tarrant Hall is your home."

The bubble of happiness inside him vanished as the implication sank in. He took off the spectacles and laid them on the starched cover. He no longer wanted to look at childhood scenes that meant nothing whatever to him.

ANOTHER BLASTED HOTEL room, thought Rex as they were conducted to the first floor of the Hare and Hounds. They seemed to have done nothing for the past three months but pack suitcases in one country inn to unpack them some hours later in another, so he could once again give his lectures and train new pilots to fly.

For the first month of his posting in England his and Laura's reunion had not been totally rapturous, largely due to his own incapacity with a half-healed thigh wound and an arm in plaster, and her lingering physical sensitivity. Now, they could love each other as freely as they always had. Yet since she had given up the theatre, the fire seemed to have gone out of her.

"I asked the girl to bring up some tea," Laura now said, unfastening her fox fur and throwing it onto the bed.

"I'd rather go down for it. It would be nicer than sitting in here, surely."

She came across the room to him, and he thought again that he would never tire of looking at her. Her illness had made her willowy; her beauty had taken on a fragility.

"Sorry, darling. I know you hate being shut in. It's just that the journey seemed so long, and I feel filthy. I don't think I'm up to facing the public."

"I'm not asking you to do a song-and-dance act down there, Laura. You don't have to face the public to drink tea and eat a buttered muffin."

With surprising bitterness she said, "I know only too well, you are the last person to ask me to do a song-and-dance act!"

It touched him on the raw. "I didn't put an end to your career. You did that yourself. How long is it going to take you to adjust?"

She swung away, then spun round again to face him. "Adjust to what? This nomadic life going from city to city, village to village, living in country inns that are all sickeningly rustic? I have never made a secret of how I feel about the theatre, Rex."

"No. But the reason you gave for continuing was that you couldn't bear to sit at home reading the daily casualty lists while I was away fighting. You would go to pieces, you said, if you couldn't lose yourself in acting. I'm here now, safe and well."

She looked trapped standing there, her beautiful eyes darkened by distress. "I lied. And you knew it! That wasn't the only reason!" She gazed at him with green fire in her eyes. "Rex, you said once that you know I'm not the normal wife and mother type. You're right, I'm not!"

"And?"

"And the advent of peace won't change that."

He sat on the edge of a chintz-covered chair while he sorted out in his tired mind what she was telling him. Then, as she sat down next to him, he took both her unwilling hands in his.

"Laura, for me there's something that won't ever change, and that's my love for you. I don't like this mode of life any more than you do—I was born to fly, not go round giving speeches to boys I have to persuade to go off and kill. I want to get back there and start doing my job towards ending the war and returning to normal living."

He knelt on the floor and touched her bright hair with possessive tenderness. "Don't fight your love for me; don't resent mine for you. What we have is one of the few good things to come out of all the horror and misery."

She pulled his hand down to hold against her cheek, and he was surprised to feel wetness there.

"What a fool I am," she murmured. "There are thousands of women across the world crying for the men they have lost, and I'm crying over the one I've found." She gazed up at him. "Do you think I'm totally wicked?"

"Oh, absolutely," he said with a swift surge of pleasure now that the storm had passed. "What would I want with you otherwise?"

430

They had their tea and muffins in their room, after all, and Laura made certain that he had no regrets about it.

Later, as Rex lay drowsily, Laura came across to the bed to drop two envelopes onto his chest.

"The mail has arrived, darling."

He sat up swiftly, guessing one letter would be from his bank. He was right. He was overdrawn to a staggering sum, and even next month's salary would make little difference to it. Rex was finding it a tremendous strain to live on a junior officer's pay. All he had done until last November was provide Laura with rent for the apartment, the luxuries she enjoyed had been bought with her own earnings. Now that those had stopped, his money did not stretch anywhere near far enough for them both.

Rex ran his hand through his hair several times. He hoped the family bank would be lenient for old times' sake. Picking up the other letter, his heart quickened as he read it. Then he looked up to tell Laura.

She, however, was reading a letter of her own, and her face was flushed with excitement. "Rex, listen! You'll never guess who this is from," she murmured, still reading the page.

"No, I won't. So tell me," he invited.

"Colonel John Winters."

Immediately jealous, he said, "And who is he?"

She smiled at him vividly. "Colonel Winters, my splendid husband, is a financier who backs all kinds of enterprises, including theatrical shows. He wants me to go to his London office for a chat." She put her arms round his neck and ruffled his hair with her fingers. "Darling, this could be a wonderful chance for me."

He drew his head back. "To do what?"

"You know very well," she retorted crisply.

"And you know very well what my opinion on that subject is."

"I've tried keeping to your rules . . . darling, I have tried, haven't I?" she pleaded. "But it doesn't work, you know it doesn't. This man has only asked to talk to me. Please, darling?"

"No."

She pulled away from him. "You'll be back in France by September and I'll be left all alone again."

"No, Laura!"

Looking at him with dark passion, she cried, "Have you any idea what it's like for women in this war? I hate aeroplanes because you fly them. You love every minute in those machines, but I hate being married to a man who risks his life every time he climbs into one. And you're not going to stop doing it when this war ends. It's in your blood, Rex." She paused to see his reaction, then went on. "And the theatre is in mine."

He knew she was right. But he wanted her beside him every minute until he had to go back and face the horrors once more. He needed her to help him through these present months of frustration, needed her love to make him complete.

He told her all that, holding her close and burying his face in her hair. Then he murmured, "I want you to come with me to Tarrant Hall to see Chris. I have a letter saying he has been transferred there, and is so much improved he's been asking to see us both. Then maybe I'll let you chat with Winters when we go back to London. How does that sound?"

She showed him, with a rapturous kiss.

WHEN TARRANT HALL came into view, the driver took them automatically to the front entrance, and Tessa was there to greet them.

"You look more luscious every time I see you," Rex told her. "That glow on your face is too good to be true."

Tessa laughed merrily. "For a married man you're still impossibly saucy, Rex." She embraced Laura. "No need to ask if married life suits you, my dear. You look marvellous."

But Rex had just caught sight of someone standing on the far side of the hall, and cut short any further complimentary exchanges by walking in with his hand outstretched.

"Mike! You old rascal. What are you doing here?"

Tessa's brother was grinning with delight at his surprise, and thumped Rex on the shoulder in rough greeting. "I'm here to keep an eye on you, old mate," was his Australian comeback. "You're not the only flaming hero around. The ones above proclaimed that I was as much in need of a rest as you."

"Do come inside," Tessa begged them all. "Priddy's made tea, and some of her special treacle tarts for you, Rex."

The next half hour was a mixture of gladness and sorrow as Rex gave Priddy a bearlike hug, heard all her news, then sympathized with her sadness on being allowed to take Chris a meal, only to be treated as a stranger.

432

"I know, Priddy, it's a blow that's difficult to describe. But he *is* getting better. That's the important thing."

She went off then, leaving Tessa to break the news that Minks had died only two days ago. Rex should have been immune to the loss of friends, yet this death hit him hard. On top of all else it seemed too much to take. Could nothing and no one survive?

Tessa went to him as he stood gazing from the window into the early spring sunshine. "I'm sorry, Rex. He had the best possible attention round the clock, but Roland's departure was more than he could face at his age. He couldn't bear the thought of the young man he revered crawling around in the mud and carrying stretchers." She sighed. "The funeral is tomorrow, in the church at Tarrant Maundle. After Roland left, Minks vowed he would never enter the village again as long as he lived. I thought we should respect his wish, even now."

Very moved, Rex turned to her. "What a wonderful person you are." Then he said to Laura, "Come on, young Chris has been asking for us."

REX HAD NOT SEEN his brother since November, when Laura had given him the pictures of the stage sets for *Julius Caesar*, so he was prepared for anything. But it was a delightful surprise to walk into the conservatory and find Chris sitting up with only pillows for support, his handsome face almost free of the pinkness of burns, his hair brushed and shining, talking animatedly to a doctor.

Then Chris caught sight of them, and a blush swept over his face. Oh lord, thought Rex in dismay, I do believe the silly fool has fallen for Laura! The blush did not go unnoticed by the doctor, who glanced in their direction before getting to his feet.

"Hello, young Chris," Rex greeted. "So you decided your family wasn't half bad, after all, and came home."

"Hello, Rex," came the shy response. "Thanks for coming. You look better than the last time I saw you. You had an arm in plaster, and a frightful limp."

"You didn't look so hot yourself," he answered flippantly, still finding it unnerving—even more so now the boy was so much more himself—to converse with a beloved brother who responded as no more than a recent acquaintance.

"Every time I visit you, you look more handsome," Laura told him with her disconcerting candour.

433

Chris's blush deepened. "I wanted to write to you about the Julius Caesar pictures, Laura, but they wouldn't let me contact anyone for a bit. I hope you didn't think me frightfully rude."

She put a hand on his shoulder and gave him one of her most stunning smiles. "I knew when I gave them to you that you were pleased, my dear. I didn't require a letter to tell me so."

"I'm the miserable devil who stopped him," put in the doctor, coming forward. "The name is Bill Chandler, Captain Sheridan, and I'm really glad to shake your hand." He turned to Laura. "Madame Sherry, I join the long line of your admirers."

"Have you done any sketching lately, Chris?" asked Laura, after smiling at Dr. Chandler and taking the seat offered her. "You have a most wonderful view of the gardens from here."

"I'm really not that good yet," he answered. "My fingers stiffen up sometimes."

She smiled again. "I hear that you have a wonderful brain, Chris. Not like me. I'm a real duffer."

"Brains aren't everything," he responded quickly. "You can make a whole crowd of people happy just by singing and dancing. That's *really* clever."

Rex was standing practically openmouthed with surprise when the doctor tapped him on the shoulder and nodded at the door to indicate they should leave Laura with Chris.

It was a warm scented evening that was too nostalgic for Rex. The perfume of flowers when they stepped out into the garden wafted across to him in the gathering dusk, and unreality closed in on him fast. He was home, yet he was not. He was free and safe, but for how long? Laura adored him, but would it last for ever?

"I'm sorry about all us doctors making free with your home," Bill Chandler said beside him.

Rex turned from contemplating Longbarrow Hill with all its memories. "You don't have to be sorry. My brother Roland could be doing the same with a French château before long."

The doctor lit a cigarette. "We hoped Chris would remember his home. He didn't. That's an area in his life he's still frightened to approach."

Rex thrust his hands in his pockets. "Don't you think it's time he was told he's a married man with a two-year-old son?"

"No, I don't, Captain Sheridan. Chris is a very unusual case. People of rare intelligence like him find it difficult to form

434

normal relationships. But I have made great progress with Chris by establishing contact amounting to friendship and trust. Now he has actually reached the stage of wanting and asking for the company of others, and that's a real step forward. But there is one last hurdle that he has to face of his own free will. To tell him he has a wife and child and that he hated them so much he went to war to escape them would almost certainly condemn him to immense distress, if not worse. Chris's intelligence tells him there is something special about Marion, but his memory won't let him in on the secret yet."

"One thing I am sure of," said Rex harshly, "is that he blames Marion for their forced marriage and his sacrificed academic career, every bit as much as she blames herself."

"Yes. I've spoken at length to her. She is an otherwise sensible girl who ridiculously holds herself responsible for everything— including the war, it strikes me. When Chris withdrew into himself last November, she left the hospital. She has been ill—a breakdown. I'm not surprised, after all she has been through. It takes a lot of guts to nurse a husband who hated you enough to volunteer, and who then returns like a mummified stranger."

"Don't you think it takes a lot of guts for a man to wake up one morning, as Chris did, and not remember who he is?" asked Rex quietly. "I can't begin to imagine what it must have been like for him, but I'm not sure I could cope with it as well as he has."

"He tried to kill himself in Gallipoli."

"Say that again." Rex could only think of his father's suicide.

"He admitted to me that he ran away from a would-be male lover and intended climbing up the cliff to commit battle suicide. The man stopped him. That was the day before they sent him to do the same thing under orders."

Rex found that hard to take, and stopped to look out into the velvety darkness of the garden where he had played with his young brother. His throat tightened as he thought of that same boy feeling so alone and desperate that he would rather face death than go on. Then, into his mind came the words Chris had spoken a little while ago: *You can make a whole crowd of people happy just by singing and dancing. That's really clever.*

When they returned to the conservatory to find Chris and Laura laughing together, Rex was glad she would be chatting with Colonel Winters in London next week.

CHRIS FELT IMMENSELY pleased with himself as he sat in bed, sorting through the things Rex and Laura had brought him that morning from his old room. He remembered none of them, but they were all fascinating. He searched for an identity among scraps of Latin and Greek, sketches, newspaper clippings about archeological finds, and verses scribbled in his own handwriting. There were books inscribed with fond messages from his brothers on various birthdays; others given by someone who had merely written: *To Christopher from Father*. He had been told that his parents were dead, and that they had paid very little attention to him. Now he suddenly wanted to know everything he could about his past.

He had spent a long time alone with Laura the previous evening, and every minute of it had been wonderful. She smelled of dark red roses, and her low husky laughter made him think of funny things to say that would promote it. It was wrong to feel as he did about his brother Rex's wife . . . but the feeling was too strong to banish. Dreaming of her had helped him through those months of physical helplessness.

Now the staff nurse had just revealed that his leg fractures had finally healed well enough to allow him to spend periods of time sitting in a chair, and the prospect of learning to walk again filled him with delight.

He picked up another small book. It was a leather-bound volume with gilt-edged pages, the kind people used for keeping a journal. On each page was a beautifully pressed wildflower, with details of where and when it had been found. On the flyleaf was written: *To Christopher Wesley Sheridan from Marion Ann Deacon. June 18, 1909.*

He sat staring at it. A thirteenth birthday present from a girl who had known him well enough to produce something that was almost a work of art. He now recalled that Marion lived near Tarrant Hall! There *was* a mystery about that girl—he had sensed it from the start. Did she hold the key to something he still did not want to remember? Where was she now? Why had she left the hospital so suddenly?

All those questions swam round in his head until his happiness of the earlier part of the day vanished under a blanket of helplessness. He put aside the things and took off his spectacles. Then he fell asleep, worn out with contemplating the unknown.

REX AND MIKE walked down to the Deacons' house soon after breakfast on that second morning. Tessa was busy with accounts; Laura was still in bed. There had been a heavy shower just before they set off, and all down the lane to the village the hedgerows shimmered with diamond drops illuminated by a pale sun, and spiders' webs hung like crystal veils between the branches of thorn bushes. It all went unnoticed, though, because they were deep in discussion. America had finally come into the war as an ally. But the two fliers were battle-hardened and did not believe, as many now did, that the war would be over in a matter of weeks.

"It will take the Americans some months to prepare and train the numbers of men needed to tip the balance enough to bring the Huns to their knees," said Mike, shaking his head. "The war has gone on too long for any kind of negotiated settlement. Too many men have died, and the hatred has gone too deep."

Rex nodded in agreement.

"By the way," Mike went on, "how are you getting along with your recruiting drive?"

"Oh, I inspire young boys with patriotic lectures on the gallant life of a pilot," Rex told him with bitterness, "and then I can't get their eager faces out of my mind unless I dull it with brandy. I wonder what those boys will call me as their flesh begins to char and their eyeballs are scorched from their sockets."

Mike's steps slowed, and he turned to face Rex as they reached a gate. "You never said things like that over there."

Rex leaned on the gate, which faced out over a meadow. "I'm ashamed of what I'm doing here, Mike. I have to make it sound good and clean and noble, but their shining eyes and stupid adoration twist my guts every time."

"Do you think telling the truth would be better?" countered Mike with a touch of anger. "They've all got to go to war. Rex, you stand for something they have to hold on to or they'd never get as far as France."

Rex turned to his friend. "You should be doing this tour instead of me, Mike. And why are you in England, anyway?"

"Got the shakes, old sport, hadn't you noticed?"

He had, but made no comment other than, "You haven't changed."

"But you have." Mike gave Rex a keen look. "How is Laura?"

"Marvellous. When are you going to get yourself a wife?"

437

"The girl I want is already married to your young brother."

Rex sighed. "And Chris only has eyes for Laura. I hope that doctor is right in not telling him he has a wife and son."

"Seems an eminently sane bloke to me. He's after Tessa."

Rex gave an exasperated laugh. "How on earth do we have time for emotional tangles in the midst of everything else?"

"It keeps us all sane."

"Does it?" Rex thought of his flight to England, halted by a French machinegunner's error. He sighed. "I hope Tessa finds happiness. She's a girl in a million, and Roland should have realized that. He's so incredibly controlled, I sometimes wonder if he knows what to do with a woman."

REX HAD A SHOCK when he and Mike entered the Deacons' house. Marion looked far older than her twenty years: thin, ill and tired. But her face lit up when she saw the visitors her father ushered into the parlour, where she sat with a patchwork quilt tucked round her legs. Her lack of surprise at seeing Mike told her he had already been at the house.

"It's far too long since we met," Rex told her warmly as they sat down. "How are you, Marion?"

"Oh, lots better," she assured him. "It's a great help having a doctor for a father."

"You're keeping a stern eye on my young nephew, too, I hope," he said lightly to Dr. Deacon.

"Our boy is fine," was the uncompromising reply from the man who still avoided acknowledging any link with the Sheridan family. He left the room.

"I've brought young David a present," Rex said, to cover the moment. "It's quite respectable, I promise."

She smiled somewhat mistily at him. "You are a dear, Rex."

"I'm not going to be left out of this," put in Mike. "Don't you both agree that I'm a real old love?"

"No," said Rex promptly. "Go away and amuse young David for a few minutes while I talk to this gorgeous girl."

Mike went off to find the little boy, taking the musical drum Rex had brought.

"Did you know Chris is up at the house?" he asked.

"Yes. They told me he was being moved. They also said he had emerged from his latest setback." She fixed him with an intent gaze.

438

"I tried, Rex, you know I tried to atone for all I had done to him. Then Chris told me he didn't want me always round him." Her eyes began to fill with tears. "So I left the hospital and came home to forget, but David was here to remind me, night and day. I began taking laudanum from Daddy's cupboard to keep myself calm, and the amounts got bigger. One day I took too much."

Full of concern Rex leaned forward in his chair and took her hands. He understood only too well what she was describing.

"I don't know how long I was ill," she went on in a broken voice, clutching his hands tighter, "but during that time I realized that Chris had wanted to die rather than face life with me. Two months ago I wanted to do the same." She loosed his hands and sank back against her cushions, looking at him with utter desperation. "But neither of us died, and we are still tied together."

Very moved and feeling totally inadequate, Rex said, "But he'll be different. When he remembers it all, he'll be different."

Her tears began again, faster this time. "But I shan't! I love my child and I just want to live here with him in peace. But now that I know Chris is at Tarrant Hall, I can't. I don't ever want to set eyes on him again," she sobbed. "I wish they'd take him away . . . miles from here. Oh, Rex, dear God forgive me, but I wish he'd go permanently insane and set me free!"

15

The offensive in the Ypres sector gathered momentum as the series of diversionary attacks was linked into a concerted bid to break the German grip once and for all. During the first days of June a massive British attack at Messines signalled the start of the Allies' intentions.

Messines was taken and held, and the Germans were driven back across the canal running through the district, too weakened and demoralized to attempt a counterattack. Then, unbelievably, a temporary halt was called while plans and tactics were reviewed, revised or revoked. All along the Ypres front line, men waited in the soul-destroying limbo of prebattle.

Roland found his resources strained as an increasing number of patients appeared with dangerously high temperatures, internal disorders and persistent sicknesses. Knowing what it would be like once the battle got seriously under way again, he worried over the generally poor health of the men.

Ironically, when a minor epidemic did hit them, it was Roland who was the first victim. A couple of days of feeling off-colour was followed by the discovery that his body was covered with scarlet spots, which he diagnosed as measles. Ordered by his CO into Guillehoek for isolation in one of the small rooms for officers at the village's casualty clearing station, he spent several days in a room with the curtains drawn. Lying there in the darkness, he felt a great need to speak to someone of his experiences, his fears and sorrows.

There was only one outlet. His second contribution to the *Gillyhook Gazette*, that he had written beside the river that day, had been very well received, and he had become aware that he could put into writing all those things he found so difficult to express verbally. Asking a nurse for paper and pencils, he began writing another series of letters to his young nephew, in which he expressed with unsparing honesty the pulse beat of war, the things it did to men and women, and the horrors of the trenches. He wrote of the German lieutenant who had let them escape rather than force wounded men to die helplessly. And, to his surprise, he wrote of girls like Marion, who could not hit back at a world gone black because their children demanded a life from them.

Again, he had no intention of sending the letters. In years to come, the right moment would present itself, and Roland hoped the writings might help the boy understand his own father.

As soon as he was freed from isolation, he wrote a note to Rosalind Tierney asking her to visit him on a personal matter. There was no reply, and she failed to turn up. He was angry. It would be simple to send Hilary Bisset's cameo up to the canteen by one of the orderlies, but the boy had asked him to give it to her in person. So he had to wait a few weeks until he was fully recovered and could go himself.

He strolled up to the canteen on a late June evening that highlighted his sense of loneliness by its seductive heaviness. Once again his spirit travelled back to Tarrant Royal and past summers, and longing was added to loneliness.

It was unbearably hot and smoky inside the canteen, and someone was playing "If You Were the Only Girl in the World" on the gramophone. Roland glanced across the counter to see Rosalind enjoying the flirtatious attentions of two officers. He stood for a moment unobserved by her, wishing he had never been burdened with this mission. Looking at her now, it was hard to believe she had once been so proud and dignified. She had always been popular with the London and county set, with a coterie of admirers whether in the saddle or on the dance floor.

The laughter faded from her face as he went forward and she spotted him. Sensing that she was about to move away, his tone was sharper than he intended. "Don't walk off! I have had to come here, since you wouldn't respond to my note."

Her lip curled. "I don't respond to anything of yours, especially that imperious attitude."

"Is there somewhere private we could go for a moment?" he asked, trying to remain controlled. "Young Hilary Bisset asked me to deliver a gift to you—that's the only reason I'm here. He was killed in action last month."

"He's in good company, then."

"Is that all you can say?" he challenged.

"What did you have to say for two years while you played squire at Tarrant Hall?" she retaliated.

He left the canteen then in such a state of anger he could not bring himself to return to the hospital immediately. What was his duty to the young boy? Every instinct urged him not to hand over the cameo to a girl who would regard the gift with ingratitude. Yet Hilary had wanted her to have it.

Roland returned to the hospital after a solitary walk along the river. There, with sleep evading him and his loneliness now so strong it had become a torment, he wrote another letter to David Sheridan. It was unlike all the others he had written: full of bitterness, pain, and a sense of abandonment by the whole of mankind. Above all, it illustrated vividly the isolation of the soldier in a foreign land when he has reached the point of no longer believing in himself or what he is fighting for.

THE FOLLOWING DAY was hotter than ever. Roland ate breakfast and later went out for a walk. Halfway through the village he heard the sounds of an altercation ahead. Then he saw soldiers grouped round an ambulance, which had halted a short distance from the clearing station. He might have passed without further interest if the raised voices had not been interrupted by the frightened whinnies of a horse and a girl's imperious tone demanding action. Roland knew

441

the voice, but it was not for Rosalind Tierney that he interceded. It was for the horse.

One of a pair dragging the ambulance had succumbed to exhaustion and terror. Half collapsed between the shafts, the horse was unable to get up again because the traces were hopelessly twisted round its legs. The driver was plainly at the end of his tether. From inside the ambulance came demands to get on with it, and faint moans of men needing urgent attention.

Everyone was hot and irrational, and Rosalind was in a temper, cheeks flaming and eyes full of contemptuous anger as she faced the driver. "If you hit that poor animal once more, I'll have you tied to a gun," she cried. "The creature is half dead."

With that, the driver swung at the horse with his whip, more in defiance of the girl than any desire to punish the animal.

Rosalind snatched the whip from the unsuspecting man's hand and set about him with it so that he had to protect his head with his raised arms.

Several of the troops standing by started to laugh at the spectacle of the soldier being subdued by a canteen girl, when Roland said in a voice like thunder, "Stop this charade and get that horse up immediately!"

Rosalind was halted by the command, and her victim lowered his arms. Then the man stiffened to attention.

"God help us all in battle if you are an example of the British soldier's quick thinking," snapped Roland. "That horse is going to break a leg if it's not released soon."

So saying, he snatched the bayonet from the belt of one of the bystanders and began cutting through the traces holding the horse in its dangerous position. "Hold its head, Rosalind," he instructed over his shoulder. "It's so terror-stricken by now, it could bolt the moment it gets up."

As he worked on the leather, he was conscious of her taking the cheek straps in her hands and calming the animal with soft confident words. Finally Roland had the last trace severed, and he moved quickly to hold the cheek straps as the animal heaved to its feet with an energy inspired by fear. Together he and Rosalind struggled to hold it steady while it was still in close proximity to its partner. For a few minutes the horse remained restive, its eyes wild, its hooves stamping. But the original exhaustion triumphed and its head bowed and its whinnying ceased. Roland then spoke lovingly and

442

encouragingly to it as he led it gently from between the shafts and over to the side of the street.

"Roz, take this horse on up to the clearing station," he said. "The stables are at the rear. Go slowly and talk to it all the way."

She took over, to allow him to go back to the others still clustered round the ambulance. Roland confronted the driver with anger. "You're not fit to be in charge of horses."

The man's face was sullen. "I'm tired, sir. I've come a long way with this ambulance."

"So has the horse! But he has been pulling it, not sitting on his backside in the cab. What's your name?"

"Hancock, sir."

"Right, Hancock. There are about five hundred yards to go to the clearing station. Get in the shafts with that other tired horse and start pulling so that you get some idea of what it's like!"

Hancock was aghast. "I'm not strong enough to do that, sir."

Roland smiled grimly at the troops standing round. "I'm sure your chums will share the experience with you. Fall in, all of you! There are wounded men inside needing treatment."

The stunned soldiers recognized an order from an officer who also happened to be a doctor, and did as they were told. With Roland leading the remaining horse, they progressed up the bumpy road, overtaking Rosalind when they were nearly at the clearing station. Once there, the medical staff took over. Roland went straight to the stables with his horse and handed it over to a stable hand with advice to give it a long rest.

When Rosalind appeared with the other one, he gave similar advice and then turned to her. "Thanks for your help."

She half nodded. "Thanks for coming to my rescue."

He studied her. "I had to, didn't I? Old habits die hard."

As he started to walk away, she came up beside him. "Roland, wait a minute. Please." Slowing, he turned his head. "Don't . . . don't just walk away like that."

"Why not?"

His abruptness seemed to disconcert her for a moment or two. Then she gave a strained smile. "Because old habits die hard."

To cover his longing to reach out to her in some way, he said out of the blue, "I'd buy you a cup of tea, but I'm afraid the canteen isn't open yet."

She shook her head. "Come to my quarters and I'll make one."

"Is that allowed?"

"Of course not, but you did say you wanted somewhere private to talk, while you told me about Hilary."

Her room was at one end of a long hut housing the other girls, and they tiptoed in. It was spartan, furnished in the typical army style that made a bedroom look like an office. Roland's gaze took in a folding chair and a filing cabinet. A bottle of scent and a lace-trimmed handkerchief sachet beside the bed looked alien, yet strangely exciting in such masculine surroundings.

"I thought you wanted tea," said a soft voice.

Roland drew his gaze away to meet hers as she now stood beside him with a cup and saucer. "Thanks." He took the cup and hastily reached into an inner pocket where he kept Hilary's cameo. "I was asked to give you this in person." He held out the little package of soft satin. "It's an antique cameo."

"I really don't want it," she told him wearily. "I hardly knew the boy."

"That's not what he told me."

She had removed the starched cap that hid most of her lovely dark hair and, sitting sideways on the bed as she sipped her tea, her shape was outlined against light from the window. "He was a fool, like all the others," she murmured.

"Roz," he said, "you used to have pride. What's happened to you?"

She put her cup and saucer down with a bang. "War, my dear Roland. War has happened to me. I've been in it a sight longer than you have, don't forget."

He put his own cup down with a bang. "If you're back on that subject, there seems no point in my staying. This was a mistake."

She scrambled from the bed to stand before him, her dark blue eyes candid. "I'm sorry about that night in the bar. I've since learned you volunteered before conscription. But you can't get away from the fact that it took you a long time to do it. I was suffering right from the beginning."

"Do you think I wasn't?" he cried, taking hold of her shoulders. "Both my brothers joined at the outset. One is an acknowledged hero, but he didn't become what he is without facing death every day. Do you think I didn't suffer knowing I might never see him again? And the other one was blown up at Gallipoli. For eighteen months he has been hovering between sanity and lunacy."

444

Worked up to top pitch now and gripping her shoulders with fingers that shook, he went on. "And do you think I didn't suffer when people sent me white feathers . . . or when girls I had known and admired flung wine in my face? I stayed at home because I truly believed I was doing my best duty for my country and my brothers. All right, I was wrong!" he shouted huskily. "But for heaven's sake stop reminding me how wrong I was!"

Rosalind had paled, and there was something astonishingly like tears on her lashes as she stood there pliant in his grip. "So you do have feelings, after all."

He stood there under bombardment. She was his past, a world he had been forced to leave but had never forgotten. She was something he had shut from his heart rather than let it bleed. She was a way of life he would never find again. He reached for her.

Her body was a haven for his intolerable loneliness; her generosity was a joy he had almost forgotten existed. It did not matter that there had been others before him. For now, she was his sanity, his means to continue for a little longer.

For THE NEXT FOUR DAYS Roland spent every possible minute with Rosalind, walking along the riverbank to quiet places where he could lie with his head in her lap as they talked of all those times before August 1914, when they had been so very young and full of optimism. They spoke of horses; they reminisced about racing; they argued the respective merits of famous hunt venues. Those four days were a bubble floating above reality, and Roland's natural reticence dropped away in the company of a girl who supplied all he needed.

When the weekend came, they said goodbye like civilized people. Roland was welcomed back in the trenches with the usual gusto accorded those who had been hospitalized for a while, then returned for further duty. The delay was over, and the third battle for total control of the Ypres sector was on again. For almost a fortnight the plain stretching before the Allied trenches was continuously bombarded by heavy guns with the intention of demoralizing the enemy before the infantry advance. In addition, a massive air attack was mounted, and the skies above Ypres were black with every conceivable type of aircraft.

Those waiting days in the trenches became nerve-racked hours of thundering guns, the scream and whistle of shells, the aerial stutter of machineguns, and the whining of plunging aircraft. Then the weather broke, and torrential rain turned the plateau they must cross into a quagmire of cratered destruction. The battle order came, but it turned them all into victims of their own bombardment as they scrambled over the top and entered a hell of mud and slime, with unexpected shell holes filled with water that looked no more than surface puddles. It was a windswept plain of desolation vanishing into the mists of distance where the enemy waited.

While the khaki horde inched its way forward, shells continued to scream overhead, and mines that had lain underground for months exploded to add to the graveyard of war. Then, silent, merging with the mist, spreading out to every part of the plain, came the creeping yellow killer cloud of mustard gas. This was a new gas that was even more terrible and agonizing than before. It was only an excess of national grit and the rigid training of one of the finest armies in the world that ensured the continued advance across the mud of Passchendaele.

In the rear, Roland's unit stayed on its feet night and day to save as many lives as possible. But drugs ran out, bandages were inadequate, and the medical men were sickened, and helpless to do much for the appalling number of casualties that flooded in.

The days passed, and the sun came out. So, too, did the Fokkers, Nieuports and BEs; machines began falling from the sky, ally and enemy alike, to add to the burden of the doctors.

The advance continued slowly until the order finally came to halt and dig in. But Roland found little relief. At twenty-six he felt old, a thousand years old. It seemed that nothing would ever touch his senses again. While soldiers chaffed at fear or went mad, Roland retired into a corner for several hours with pencil and paper. When he had completed the many sheets of writing, he just put them with the other letters to David Sheridan, then went to sleep feeling drained.

IT WAS SOME WEEKS later that all doctors were told to attend a medical lecture on the new mustard gas, to be given in Guillehoek. Though it was a tedious business getting to the village now, and involved crossing the miles of cratered barren battlefield, they all felt it would be worthwhile.

446

The canteen was crowded when Roland walked in an hour after arriving in Guillehoek. As he opened the door, he almost expected to hear "If You Were the Only Girl in the World", but a new batch of recordings must have arrived from England. A female voice was singing:

> *You called me baby doll a year ago,*
> *You told me I was very nice to know.*

Half a dozen men were joining in above the laughter and conversation, and Roland had to raise his voice so that the girl behind the counter could hear his request to see Miss Tierney. He explained that he and Rosalind were old friends.

"Rosie?" she queried, busily pouring tea from a huge metal pot. "She ought to be here by now. It's funny she hasn't turned up. You're sure to find her at her quarters, if you know where they are. Do tell her to hurry, will you? It's getting too much for one person already."

It was a sultry evening with the hint of a storm in the offing, and it seemed strangely hushed without the sound of distant gunfire as Roland reached the hut on the outskirts of Guillehoek. There was no response to his knock, or to his quiet call to identify himself. On the point of turning away, he stopped. It might have been the need to see the room where she had given him the fortitude to go back that made him go in uninvited.

Rosalind was lying on the bed, fully dressed and as still as death. He knew instinctively that he was too late, as he saw the two empty aspirin bottles beside the bed. Even so, he dashed to the door and ordered the nearest passing soldier to run like the wind for a stretcher party, then returned to the unconscious girl and began what emergency treatment he could.

After sinking into a coma, Rosalind Tierney died at two am. A postmortem examination revealed that she had been in the first stages of pregnancy.

Roland missed the lecture on gas warfare. He went for a solitary walk along the riverbank, for hours he sat leaning back against a tree, and all he could hear was that record playing "If You Were the Only Girl in the World". He walked slowly back to Guillehoek in the late afternoon, shaken by an overpowering thought. That embryo child might have been his!

447

16

The new show had opened in mid-July and was an instant success. What the British public needed in that summer of 1917 was something to make them forget the war. They wanted laughter, catchy tunes, a look back on better, more leisurely times, and girls who were dressed in the most beautiful clothes imaginable. So, given the title *Bows and Boaters*, the show had a turn-of-the-century theme, with scenes at the Henley regatta, Hyde Park and Horse Guards Parade. Laura Sheridan, leading lady, had an outrageously daring set of costumes, which revealed her beautiful body without suggesting vulgar burlesque. The songs that had been especially written for her suited the low husky pitch of her voice, and were seductive rather than suggestive. Her dances were intricate, graceful and tantalizing.

With the opening night, Rex and Laura's marriage entered a new phase. From that evening back in April when Rex had reluctantly told her she could go to London to meet Winters, Laura had been so brilliantly happy he was forced to realize just how much a shadow of her true self she had been over the past months. Loving Rex with a generosity beyond words, she made every hour they spent together a joy he could scarcely believe.

Unfortunately, the time they now spent together was very little. Laura lived in the London apartment, despite Rex's fears about the frequent German bombing of the capital, and he was obliged to move round the country, as before, promoting the RFC, boosting morale at fetes and garden parties, and trying to teach boys the skill and experience of a long-term pilot before they faced the enemy. He went home as often as he could, but Laura had performances each evening and needed to sleep for most of the morning. There was little time left for togetherness.

When away from her, in lonely country inns, he drank to chase away the nightmares about burning men in burning aircraft. But there were now other nightmares: those of jealousy. Bevies of admirers waited outside the stage door every night for Laura, and when Rex was away she went to supper parties in smart places. He knew she loved only him, but he still felt jealous of those who could be with her when he was not.

Rex was now conscious of emotions pulling him in opposite

directions. Much as he yearned for September when he would go back to his real job, it looked like a black cloud over his passion for Laura. His frustration deepened in August when a spell at an east coast flying school meant he saw even less of her than usual. One day, when the promenades along the coast were full of folk enjoying the seaside, Rex took a student up on his first flight. The lad was sick after two circuits of the airfield, yet he remained eager to listen and learn during every moment of the flight. Teaching the boy mechanically, Rex travelled mentally to France while his accumulated frustrations consumed him. He had been in England too long. The Huns would think Sherry Sheridan was finished. They would forget him, forget their fear of the man with the famous cerise scarf.

Then a terrible thought struck him. *Was* Sherry Sheridan finished? Had marriage swamped his courage? Worst of all, would news of his return rouse the old German eagerness for his blood, or would the famous ace, von Richthofen, and his friends merely shrug and continue drinking schnapps?

On the heels of his longing to prove himself came a vision that suggested his thoughts had become reality. Floating out of a small fluffy cloud about two thousand feet above him and rapidly losing height, came an aircraft bearing a black cross on its wings. Rex recognized it immediately as a Gotha bomber—a great long cumbersome biplane that had nevertheless been successful over France and Belgium, and had recently been launched against England from bases just across the Channel.

Rex was unarmed, flying an old Nieuport two-seater suitable only for training purposes, but he headed for the Gotha, everything forgotten at the sight of his first enemy for months. With the big aircraft obviously in trouble, probably coming from a bombing raid down the coast, and still losing height, Rex gained on it quickly and saw the rear gunner hanging lifeless over the side. That meant the tail of the machine would be undefended and the best area for attack. The pilot was staring at him with apprehension, and the navigator was lying back badly wounded. A captured Gotha, to say nothing of its crew, Rex knew, would be invaluable.

Shouting instructions to the boy in the rear to train his gun on the enemy, Rex embarked on the most dangerous piece of bluff he had ever devised. Working on the premise that the pilot would never imagine an enemy would approach so boldly aiming two empty machineguns on him, he flew as close as he could. Then he pointed his gun forcefully in the direction from which the Gotha had just come, and waited, heart thudding, to see what would happen.

For a minute or two the German stared back, apparently assessing his chances. His hand crept to the handle of his own gun, while he looked the Nieuport over, as it clung like a limpet to his side, and he must have decided that two uninjured men in an undamaged fighter with two guns pointing straight at him were uneven odds. His hand dropped. Rex swallowed in relief and pointed inland again, emphasizing the order by edging so close that the wing tips actually touched for a brief second. The German had to turn to avoid a collision.

Slowly but surely, Rex edged the larger aircraft round until they were on a course that would take them back to the flying school. When they were almost above the field, Rex pointed downwards, receiving a nod of understanding in return. The great bomber dropped steeply towards the grass. But the descending glide turned into a dive as the nose dropped too far and, as Rex was accompanying his captive in, he saw it plunge into the ground and burst into flames. Throttling back rapidly, Rex swung away to land fifty yards off. Then, with his own engine still running, he scrambled out and ran towards the burning Gotha. But he had only gone a few yards when an explosion put an end to any hope of saving the occupants.

"We did it, sir. We did it!" exclaimed a voice beside him.

Shaking and sick, Rex turned on his heel and began walking away over the grass, lost in a world of his own.

HE WENT HOME for the weekend and, in the train window, all he could see was that burning wreck mirrored there. The press had gone to town on an incident that was a wonderful morale-booster to a British public demanding better protection against German raiders; the RFC had cheered an exploit they thought was colourful and daring. And the authorities had severely reprimanded him for risking the life of a student pilot.

It had all gone over Rex's head, diluted by the shocking truth he had to face. He was an instinctive killer. The sight of a black cross on that machine had made him forget where he was and who he was with. If his guns had been loaded, Rex would have unhesitatingly shot it from the sky. In attempting to capture them he had killed them, anyway. What had become of the young man who had flown *Princess* so joyfully over Longbarrow Hill? What had happened to

450

the person he had been then, when life had been a playground for the kind of adventure that had harmed no one?

When he reached his apartment, he found that Laura had already gone to the theatre. He had not seen her for four weeks, and an evening without her now stretched ahead like another four weeks. Feeling unreasonably bereft, he poured himself a brandy, then prowled round the empty rooms with growing desperation.

He had drunk a considerable amount by the time Laura let herself into the apartment, and he muttered thickly, "At last! Come here and compensate your poor husband for his long wait!"

She remained where she was, occupied with removing her shawl and elaborate hair ornament. Then she walked to the kitchen. "I think I'll have some warm milk and go straight to bed."

Rex got heavily to his feet. "Forget the warm milk! Let's go straight to bed."

Without looking at him she said, "I'm tired, Rex."

"So am I . . . but I want my wife first."

Turning to him as she reached the kitchen door, she cried, "I don't care what you want, for once."

"For once!" he exclaimed. "I haven't seen you for four weeks, you might note! When I do I expect you to behave like a wife."

His words unleashed a tigress. "You expect! Have you ever considered what I expect? Well, I'll tell you. I expect a husband, not someone who risks throwing his life away in the skies over England!" She was on the edge of tears. "It wasn't heroic, it was sheer stupidity. Suppose the bluff hadn't worked? You'd have been the ones on the ground in a great burning pile . . . and . . . and I'd have died, too." She put her hands to her temples, and her voice almost broke as she continued. "You once accused me of risking all we had for the sake of my career. But you did the same thing up there two days ago . . . don't you see?"

"Oh, Laura. I didn't do it for the sake of my career." He was fighting to stay upright in a room that seemed to be spinning around him. "Do you want the truth? I did it because that black cross now tells me to kill. It's instinct." He stared at her. "The only difference between Chris and me is that I have you to keep me marginally sane . . . except that . . . except that sometimes I expect even you to smoulder and blacken beneath my touch."

In a moment she was there against him, stopping his words with her mouth, bathing his wet cheeks with her own tears.

"Don't, oh darling, don't," she whispered. "I didn't mean what I said. I was so afraid, so terrifyingly angry that even here you were risking your life. Why haven't you told me this before?"

Somehow she got him to the bed, and he sank onto it sick and giddy, thanking God she was there with him to banish that vision of searing death.

ON SUNDAY of that week there was to be a special event at Tarrant Royal. Several of the young cricketers from the two rival villages were home on leave, and the rector had the idea of reviving the annual match that had lapsed since the start of the war. The occasion was intended to raise funds for war widows and their children, and with the promise of seeing Laura Sheridan, star of *Bows and Boaters*, the rector knew huge crowds would turn out.

For Chris it was a red-letter day. He felt excitement bubble inside him the minute he awoke that morning. Laura was coming! Since the launching of her new show she had not been down to Tarrant Hall, so she had no idea how well he had progressed.

Learning to walk had been difficult, very painful, and more than frustrating. But the impetus to keep trying had been his overwhelming desire to surprise and impress Laura. And not only would he be walking today, he would be wearing, instead of the blue hospital garb, a subaltern's uniform for the first time. As a nurse helped him to dress in it, his sense of anticipation increased.

He had been invited to a luncheon for team players and local dignitaries, to be served in a marquee on the lawns of Tarrant Hall. Bill Chandler had also been invited by Tessa to join the party. Now, standing on crutches beside Bill in the marquee, Chris found it difficult to concentrate on what those around him were saying. He was watching for Laura to come from the house, and everything else was unimportant until then. Suddenly, excitement was almost a pain in his chest. Laura was at the entrance to the marquee in a stage costume, and she drew all eyes as she entered on Rex's arm. An Edwardian dress of white lace with a bustle and scarlet ribbons everywhere fitted her voluptuous figure like a skin, and the sensational picture was completed by a huge white lace hat, trimmed with black ostrich feathers, and a scarlet silk parasol.

Chris hung on his crutches as he fought the sudden acceleration of his heartbeat. "Isn't she absolutely marvellous!" he exclaimed.

"Absolutely . . . but she's also *his* wife," came Bill's pointed comment, as Laura looked up at Rex and smiled into his eyes as if there were no other person present. Chris was riven by a shaft of jealousy.

It was inevitable that the glamorous star of *Bows and Boaters* should be surrounded, and it was some time before Rex freed himself from the bevy of admirers to come over to his young brother. Chris had never seen this stranger-brother out of uniform before, and the cream cricket flannels looked so right on him. His greeting was unselfconsciously warm.

"Hello, Rex. You look so assured, the other team ought to be trembling with fear already."

Rex laughed. "Fat chance of that. My word, young Chris, I'd forgotten what you looked like the right way up. You really have made wonderful progress. It must feel good to get on the move again."

"Yes, but I feel a bit like a crab trying to win a race," Chris confessed ruefully, "and it's hard on the armpits to lean on these crutches for long."

"At least you are back in the race," said Tessa quietly, having just joined them. "Poor Roland appears to be stuck in the mud somewhere in the vicinity of Passchendaele. I had a long letter from him this week."

"Yes, I heard from him too," said Rex on a quieter note. "He's all right, thank God."

Remembering something that had slipped from his mind in the excitement, Chris spoke up. "Rex, I wanted to ask your advice about something. Family business."

"Fire away," he replied. Bill and Tessa tactfully moved off, leaving the brothers alone.

Shifting his weight, Chris explained what was troubling him. "Roland sent me a letter, too. It had something in it—an antique cameo. He wrote that it had belonged to the mother of someone who had shared a dugout with him back in the spring. The fellow was killed, and as there were no next of kin Roland said he wanted me to have it. What do you think I ought to do?"

"Exactly what he says," came the immediate reply. "Roland never does anything without good reason, take my word."

"Yes . . . but a brooch! It's a funny thing to send a chap."

"You can always give it to . . . er, to a girl, one of these days." Rex gave a sigh. "I do think you should write to him, Chris. He's out

453

there in hell, believe me, and he's done no end for you. Any kind of response will mean more to him than you can guess."

"I don't know him like I know you," Chris protested.

"You never will get to know him if you ignore his letters," pointed out Rex quietly. "You always were inclined to give very little of yourself to others. Now's your chance to make up for it."

That piece of advice coincided with the arrival of Laura, and Chris immediately felt choked with emotion as he responded to her warmth and sparkle.

"I had no idea you had recovered to this extent, Chris dear," she exclaimed in her low, provocative voice. "They told us it would take absolutely ages before you'd be able to get about on your own. You must have worked like a Trojan."

Her unconscious reference to classical history pleased Chris tremendously, and he could not take his gaze from her lovely pointed face, blush-tinted cheeks, wicked eyes, and the rich red tendrils of hair that lay against the white lace underbrim of her hat.

"Hello, Laura," he managed. "You look jolly splendid."

"And so do you," she said enthusiastically. "I'm so used to seeing you in bed, now you're vertical you seem like an entirely different person. So much so, I almost feel shy of you."

"Oh no," he replied immediately. "It's the other way round. Being able to move puts all kinds of obligations on a fellow."

"I hear he's been chasing nurses up and down the wards," put in Rex with a grin. "A lad after my own heart, I can see."

Laura smiled. "I'm sure he's much more respectable than you, darling. He's always been the soul of propriety with me."

"That's because you're different from all the others," said Chris with feeling. "You're not for ever getting hurt when I don't remember something that means a lot to you. When I'm with you, I can be myself without worrying."

She smiled right up into his eyes in understanding. "You have nothing whatever to worry about. But look, can't we sit down?"

"Oh yes," he agreed thankfully, having just moved his crutches yet again to ease his aching arms, "there are a couple of chairs just over there."

Once seated, Chris realized Rex had wandered off to talk to a nearby group. They were comparatively alone.

"Have you been doing any sketching lately?" she asked.

Reaching inside his jacket he brought out a rolled sheet of thick foolscap and gave it to her. "It's for you to keep. I thought it wouldn't mean anything to anyone else."

As he watched her unroll it and spread it out, the suspense was unbearable. An age seemed to pass while she studied the drawing, and he knew the next few minutes would make the day into a triumph or a disaster.

When she looked up at him, it was with a mysterious expression he could not fathom. "This goddess is me, isn't it . . . at the hospital concert? Except that you've transferred the scene to Greece. It is Greece, isn't it?"

He shook his head, knowing the day was a triumph. "Not exactly. It's one of the islands we could see from Gallipoli."

"I . . . I really don't know what to say," she told him.

"You don't have to say anything," he hastened to assure her. "I can tell you're pleased. Your face always shows what you feel."

"But I had no idea you had taken in so much of that concert. It was in the early days when you were . . . were . . ."

"Like a silent effigy in bed?" he suggested. "But I had feelings, you know, even then."

To his astonishment a glitter of tears touched her eyes, and she smiled at him. "Thank you, Chris. I think this is the most flattering present I have ever been given."

Leaning forward, she kissed him on his cheek. But his instinctive response was halted by a voice saying, "Unhand that woman."

Chris looked up rather guiltily. Bill Chandler was making a comical bow before Laura.

"I've been sent by your beleaguered husband to escort you to the head table, ma'am. Take my arm."

Seeing his beautiful moment about to be ruined, Chris said with a hammering heart, "No, take mine, Laura."

As Bill started to speak, Laura silenced him with a look, leaving Chris to get to his feet with the aid of the crutches and turn in the right direction. It now looked a long way to the white-covered tables where Rex was standing, but Laura slipped her arm through his and he had no choice but to set off.

Their progress was slow. He had never walked with a girl on his arm before, and it was an experience that made him feel strangely protective. Then he realized that people had parted to let them through, their interest fastened on the progress of the fabulous Laura Sheridan on the arm of her disabled brother-in-law. The walk now turned into a marathon for Chris. Ahead he could see Rex watching, and he prayed nothing awful would happen.

His arms felt weak with effort, his legs became dragging weights, and sweat began to bead his forehead. Then Laura began chatting to him about the forthcoming cricket match, saying that she hoped he would explain the rules to her, just as if she was not aware that he was breathing harder with every step. Undaunted by the silence in the marquee, she literally *talked* Chris along those last few yards to the head table, and he made the tremendous effort because he knew he could not let her down. But he was giddy and aching all over when Rex quickly pulled out a chair for Laura to sit down, then pulled out another for him.

"Sit down, you've earned a rest, old lad," Rex said softly.

But it was to Laura that Chris gave his smile of gratitude.

CHRIS HAD BEEN LOOKING forward to his first glimpse of the village where he had apparently lived all his life. From the outskirts, Tarrant Royal appeared to be a beautiful peaceful cluster of thatched buildings. But he was unprepared for the size of the crowd around the green.

Sitting in the shaded enclosure, he felt utterly content. There was a marvellous afternoon in the sunshine ahead of him, and he had been told Rex and Laura would be staying overnight at Tarrant Hall. He had also decided to give Laura the cameo brooch Roland had sent him. Rex had said he should give it to a girl one day. What better girl than one who was a Sheridan?

Chris knew all about cricket. He was certain Rex would be very good at cricket, and so he was. Coming in to bat at number three, a tall muscular figure with hair even more vivid beneath the August sun, he thumped the ball far and wide with daring strokes that had the spectators going wild with delight. Chris watched and applauded with enthusiasm, until Rex was finally and inevitably caught out after whacking unwisely at a spinning ball.

With his interest in the match now diminished, Chris reached beneath his deckchair for his book. But he was not in a deckchair, and there was no book. His heart lurched as he jumped a time span of three years in one second.

Then the other occasion faded completely, and he recognized present reality. But he was deeply afraid of that memory, and with rising panic he knew he had to get away. It was coming too close, that last secret he did not want to know. Sweating, he struggled to his feet with the aid of the crutches.

"Where do you think you're going?" asked Bill Chandler.

"For a cup of tea," Chris muttered. He made his laboured way to a small shed behind the enclosure, and leaned against the sun-warmed wood in thankful isolation. Everything round him looked unfamiliar again, and that excursion into the past now seemed so vague he could hardly remember it. But it had happened . . . and could happen again at any time!

Propped against the shed, his hands gripping the crutches, he tipped his head back to gaze up at the branches of a great oak outside the village inn until they blurred with the tears welling up in his eyes. *Dear God, please don't let me remember*, he prayed. Yet it was not the truth his mind did not want to face that terrified him now. It was retreating into those lost months. He did not want to leave the world again in case it was no longer there when he finally came back.

Chris took off his spectacles to wipe the lenses. When he put them back on, he saw a girl standing a short distance away, holding a small boy by the hand as she watched the cricket. He waited a moment or two, not sure what to do. Then he gripped his crutches and set off.

There were so many people moving about, he reached her side unnoticed by her. She looked a lot thinner, and very different in a dress of soft yellow. It was nicer, less severe than the pink nurse's outfit she used to wear.

"Hello, Marion," he said in subdued tones.

She turned, and for one astounding moment he thought she was going to faint. The colour drained from her face and she seemed to sway as she backed away from him.

"Chris!"

"I say, are you all right?" he asked in concern.

"What are you doing out of hospital?" It came out as a whiplash accusation, as she pushed the child behind her skirt. But she did not wait for his answer. Another wild glance at him, then she turned to run, gathering the child up as she went.

"Marion," he called after her. "What's wrong?"

Two steps, and he sprawled headlong on the grass. Any further sight of her was obscured by people surrounding him to help him to his feet.

17

The day of the cricket match was one that would live in people's memories for a long time. After the match, narrowly won by Rex's team, the traditional supper was eaten with great gusto, and the concert was the best ever heard at Tarrant Royal, owing to Laura. She dragged Rex onto the stage to sing a duet with her, and the sight of this gorgeous flame-haired girl singing "Hold Your Hand Out, Naughty Boy" to her equally flame-haired flirtatious husband, brought the house·down.

For Rex it was one of the happiest days of his life. He had never felt more in love with Laura than he did that day. Looking incredibly lovely, she was there at his home charming people he had known and liked all his life, and she was there to watch him excel in a pastime that did not involve risking his life.

He had breakfast next morning with Tessa, and with Mike who had arrived from London halfway through the cricket match to stay overnight. Laura remained in bed, of course. Mike was planning to return on the afternoon train with her. Rex had to give a talk at Sherborne on the following morning, so would have to travel in the opposite direction on the evening train.

After breakfast Rex and Tessa strolled across to the stables and took out two horses for a ride across Longbarrow Hill. Dressed in an old shirt and breeches, Rex found that the casual clothes and the ride augmented a feeling of having returned to the peace of the past.

Tessa appeared to be in the same mood, and they talked about the estate and village as if war did not exist. It was clear she was doing a very good job of running the complex farming routine, and Rex thought again that she would make his brother the perfect wife. But Bill Chandler looked like snapping her up first. They would probably go back to Australia together after the war, and out of the lives of the Sheridans as if they had never been so closely involved with them.

Chris came through from the hospital just as they walked into the house from the stables. He looked rather strained, Rex thought, but his face lit up when he saw them.

"Hello," he greeted. "You two look very happy."

Feeling so fit and invigorated after his ride made Rex more than ever conscious of how his brother must feel, having to hang over two crutches just to stand for any length of time. And then Rex realized all was not well. Tessa must have sensed it, too, for she walked towards the kitchen saying, "Why don't you two go and have a chat? I'll get Priddy to bring you some coffee."

Rex nodded. The two men headed for the terrace, where Chris immediately settled himself into a seat. Rex sighed with contentment as he gazed around him.

"I'm either growing more discerning with age, or else I only appreciate this place now I can't come here any time I like." He turned at the sound of footsteps. "Ah, Priddy, you deserve a kiss on both cheeks," he said, taking the tray from her.

Her plump face broke into a smile. "That's the first time you've been your old self for longer than I care to remember."

When she had gone, Rex decided it was time to take the bull by the horns. "What's up, old lad?"

"A funny thing happened to me yesterday," his brother replied.

"What kind of funny thing?"

"While I was watching the match I remembered something. It was another cricket match—I don't know how long ago." He became a little hesitant. "I'm sorry, Rex, I can't expect you to understand because I don't myself, but . . . well, until yesterday I had to take your word for the fact that we were pretty good chums. But now I know . . . in here." He put a clenched fist on his breast. "Rex, I still don't remember anything before Gallipoli. But something is beginning to penetrate, and it scares me to death."

"In that case, you'd better talk to Bill Chandler about it."

Chris turned away to gaze out front the terrace. The droop of his shoulders and the prolonged silence were more than Rex could stand. Gripping his brother's shoulder, he said quietly, "If you think I can help, go ahead."

Chris suddenly put his head in his hands. "I do most desperately need advice. After yesterday, I realize you are my only hope. You know about me. The real me. You know about those years my mind doesn't want to remember."

Deeply sorry for his brother, yet mindful of Bill Chandler's warning that he must be allowed to recall the past without help, Rex rubbed his forehead with a worried gesture.

"Something else funny happened yesterday," Chris went on. "I saw Marion at the cricket match."

Heartbeat quickening, Rex thought of a girl telling him she hoped

Chris would go permanently insane and set her free. "Marion?" he echoed in pretended surprise.

Chris's head shot up. "Yes, Marion!" he said aggressively. "She took one look at me, nearly fainted, then ran away. You can drop the pretence that you hardly know the girl, Rex. She gave me a present on my thirteenth birthday, so she must have been a pretty good friend of ours. Is there something terrible connected with her?"

Rex sighed heavily. "It isn't terrible, Chris. I swear it isn't."

"But there is something connected with Marion?"

"Why don't you ask her?" he hedged.

"If she runs away when she sees me, I'll never catch her on these crutches," came the response. Reaching for them then, Chris got laboriously to his feet to stand eye to eye with Rex in one last appeal. "I want to be part of the Sheridan family. I want to be a person without secrets. But I'm so afraid, I don't know what to do. They say I must be ready to remember of my own free will, but every time I do I relapse and go away somewhere with no control over when I return. Can you imagine it, Rex?"

It was such a desperate plea for understanding, Rex was moved beyond words. Getting to his feet, he urged his brother across the terrace to the edge of the sunken garden.

"The unknown is always frightening, Chris. The only way I can survive as a pilot is to go looking for the enemy. Then I know what I'm facing and can get on with my job. Perhaps that's what you should do."

"Go in search of my past?"

Rex nodded. "Maybe you only retreat into this other world when recollection takes you unawares—like Fokkers coming fast out of the sun. Maybe, if you went determinedly to meet it, it wouldn't seem half as frightening." He turned to give his brother a steady look. "You've come so far in triumph, Chris, you're certain to go the rest of the way now."

Chris thought that over for a moment or two. "It's a good theory, but suppose I only hasten that limbo that frightens me?"

Rex could not retreat now, so he summoned a smile. "You'll also hasten your return . . . and I'll do my damnedest to be here."

THINGS SEEMED TO DETERIORATE for Rex after that. Saying good-bye to Laura was part of the anticlimax. They had both felt it was the ending of their brief episode of bliss, and Rex had kissed her

460

lingeringly at the station. Then he had spent half an hour with Chris before catching his own train. When he rose to go, his brother had smiled and said, "Don't leave it too long before you come again, will you? I might even be fit enough to gallop across Longbarrow Hill with you. I take it I do ride?"

Rex had grinned. "Not according to Roland. He used to clutch his locks in despair when you climbed onto a horse. But I could bear the experience, lad, if you're game."

The country inn he had been booked into seemed very lonely that night, and Rex drank too much in order to while away the time before going to bed. On the following afternoon he presented prizes at a charity garden party, then caught a train to Swindon, where he was due the next morning to address a rally designed to drum up financial donations for the production of more aircraft.

The morning dawned hot and airless, and in his thick uniform Rex found the rally an ordeal. The day passed tediously, and it was evening by the time he reached London. As he entered the apartment he knew Laura would have already left for the theatre, so he poured himself a liberal measure of brandy and settled down to sort through the letters on the table.

There was one from his bank manager, which he threw unopened into the wastepaper basket; one from Roland; and the last one, which was official would be his itinerary for the month.

Opening Roland's letter first, he found his brother had written at length, and the letter was mostly about Tarrant Hall and the village, as usual. But there was a surprising paragraph at the end.

I have written to Cummings about my will. You may remember I originally decided to ensure that Marion would not be mistress of the hall if Chris were ruled unfit to inherit on my death. I have reversed my decision. She is our brother's legal wife, and mother of his son. We three had such wonderful times growing up there, it would be sad if David could not do the same.

Rex downed another brandy thoughtfully. What had prompted dear old dyed-in-the-wool Roland to forgive and forget? What a good thing he did not know that Marion wished Chris permanently insane and divorced from her.

He sipped more brandy and reached for the official letter. The contents were a complete surprise! He was ordered back on active service, with the new rank of major, to command an elite squadron equipped with the new Sopwith Camel single-seat fighters that were the match of any German fighter aircraft. There were only forty-eight hours to prepare for departure. He would fly back to Belgium with Mike and the other returning pilots in the brand new machines on Sunday afternoon.

18

It took Chris some days to solve his problem of how to find Marion Deacon again. His main assets were good looks and Priddy, so he set about using them both. Just for telling a young nurse she looked nice that morning, he was brought an extra helping of treacle tart. When he remarked how shiny her hair was, she let him stay out in the garden during the matron's inspection. Delighted, he played his trump card on the third day. With very little effort he discovered from her that there was a doctor called Deacon who lived in the village, with a house almost opposite the green. Chris did not make the mistake of asking if there was a daughter living there!

Several days passed as he worked out the means of getting to his destination, and this was where his other asset was put to use. Priddy doted on him, and he went through the hospital to the house one day when the coast was clear, cornering the old soul while she was polishing the banisters. Within ten minutes he had her collusion in a plot to go for a drive with Dawkins in the pony and trap to see the village.

It was the first day of September and the hedgerows were thick with blackberries, as the trap headed down the hill and turned into the lane leading through the village. Chris felt a sense of triumph. Although he was not supposed to go anywhere alone, he had escaped unseen from his room and was out on his own. It was a marvellous feeling.

But as they neared the centre of Tarrant Royal, a chill began to wrap itself around his heart. Did he have enough courage to see this through to the end, whatever it might turn out to be? Then fate took a hand. As the trap rounded a corner by the village green and bowled along towards a small but attractive country house, Marion appeared in the garden with a basket over her arm and began cutting late roses.

462

Almost as if it were not part of himself, he heard his voice saying, "Stop here a minute, Dawkins!"

The old coachman turned a scared face towards him. "Here, sir? No, I don't think that's advisable."

"Just do as I say," Chris ordered calmly. "I wish to speak to Miss Deacon for a moment."

However, Marion's expression when she caught sight of him did not suggest it was going to be easy. She watched as he reached for his crutches and began the hazardous business of getting to the ground from the unsteady two-wheeled vehicle. He would rather have done it without her looking on, but Dawkins hobbled round to give him a helping hand. Then he crab-walked to the gate and stopped by the arch covered with honeysuckle.

"Hello," he began, then cleared his throat nervously. "Now I've gone to all this trouble to find you, may I come in?"

After a long moment she nodded, but made no attempt to help him negotiate the gate. He bungled the job badly, and Dawkins had to extricate him from a tangle of gate and crutches so that he could start up the path towards her. Before he reached her, however, two black labradors raced from the side of the house and flung themselves on him in ecstatic greeting, nearly knocking him off balance.

"Bandit . . . Hunter, get down!" cried Marion, coming swiftly forward. "Down! Oh, you disobedient dogs!"

Hanging over his crutches, Chris fondled the dogs' sleek heads, calming them with gentle hands and gentle words.

"I'm sorry about them," said Marion.

She looked different, thinner and not quite as pretty. As he sensed hostile resistance to what he had done, his mind teemed with confusing facts. This girl had helped him survive during those early days when he had not even known who he was, but how did that account for the way she was regarding him now, with fear and something approaching hatred? He stumbled over his words. "I shouldn't have come. It must be . . . I mean, you ran away that . . . that day at the match. I'd better go."

But he did not turn away, and neither did she.

"I won't hurt you, truly I won't," he ventured hesitantly. "Please don't be afraid of me."

She moved only a few paces to stand with shoulders bowed, as if helpless beneath some burden.

"Marion, if I ever hurt you in some way, I'm sorry," he offered in continuing awkwardness, only now realizing how very much he had missed her company. "I've asked many times to see you, and tried to find out where you'd gone, but all they would tell me was that you had left the hospital." She was biting her lip, and he noticed her hands holding the sides of her blue skirt were shaking. A rush of remorse made him say, "I owe a great deal to you."

Swinging round to face him, she cried emotionally, "Oh, Chris, don't. I can't take any more."

His heart sank. "Oh Lord, did I do something absolutely dreadful to you?"

Her answer to that was to hurry indoors, slamming the door. Hardly knowing what he was doing, Chris turned too quickly and overbalanced, falling headlong on the uneven path and jarring his leg so badly he felt sick with pain.

There followed a crisp altercation above him between Dawkins and another man who had just appeared.

"You should have known better than to bring him here."

"I didn't know he was a'going to do this, Doctor, or I never would've done."

"Well, there's nothing for it but to get him up on his feet and pray he's done no damage to himself. I'm not having him inside the house, mind!"

"Oh, Daddy, we'll have to," came Marion's agitated voice. "That leg has had multiple fractures, and the bones had to be reset a second time when he fell out of bed. You're a doctor, first and foremost, and Chris is someone in need of medical help."

"Very well," snapped the doctor.

They put hands on him, and Chris simulated unconsciousness while they lifted him carefully and began to carry him along. Not only did it give him time to think, it would surely boost Marion's concern for him, which seemed to have miraculously returned.

When Chris opened his eyes, he found he was in a doctor's surgery, lying on the examination couch. There were only Marion and her father. Dawkins had been sent to Tarrant Hall for an ambulance. Dr. Deacon was examining the injured leg, but Marion was studying Chris's face in a manner he found encouraging.

"Are you in much pain?" she asked.

"If I'm honest and say no, you won't go off, will you? Ouch!" he cried as her father moved his ankle experimentally. "I am now."

464

"Mmm. Nothing serious. A slight sprain, that's all," came the curt verdict. "But I'll give you a draught of something to help you cope with the transfer back to the hospital."

"I can do that, Daddy," Marion told him. "It'll be all right."

Dr. Deacon glared at Chris. "You should have stayed up at the Hall." Then the door shut noisily behind him.

"I hope the ambulance takes a long time in coming," Chris said softly. "I do very much want to talk to you."

"They'll be down right away," came her uncompromising answer, as she poured green liquid into a measure. "You've taken a risk, and they're going to be furious because you sneaked out."

Gingerly he struggled to a sitting position, wincing at the throbbing in his ankle. "I wouldn't have had to sneak out if you hadn't run away from me at the cricket match. I was so glad to see you that day," he explained, taking the measure from her and drinking the contents in one gulp. "Ugh! My insides must be bright green by now with the amount of that stuff I've swallowed."

She nodded silently as he handed the little metal cup back.

Sighing, he said into the silence, "Whatever I did to make you so afraid of me, I'm deeply sorry for. But if you came to that hospital to look after me, you must know I'm not really a violent person." As she seemed on the verge of tears, he found himself growing more urgent with the minutes ticking past. "Oh lord, Marion, what I'm trying to say is, I'm very upset that I've lost a friendship that must have been very close for you to have gone to such trouble over that beautiful book of pressed flowers. I found it in a box of my boyhood possessions."

Her face went down into her hands, and she mumbled, "Chris, stop! How cruel of you to do this! Why did you come here?"

He swallowed painfully. "To meet my fears halfway. But I've only increased them . . . and yours. Look, if you'll give me my crutches I'll wait outside for the ambulance."

She visibly pulled herself together as she glanced through the window. "It's all right. It's here now."

They came in with a stretcher, and when Chris reached the ambulance he was so struck by something he had seen while being carried from the house, he heard no word of Bill Chandler's angry remonstrance. He spent the rest of the short journey to Tarrant Hall trying to develop his theory.

The dogs had welcomed him with the hysterical canine delight reserved for people they adore and trust. So he must have been a frequent visitor at this house. But most astonishing, he had seen that same little boy Marion had had with her at the cricket match. The child had been running about in the garden, playing with a pet rabbit. At such close quarters he looked unmistakably like photographs of himself and his brothers as children. There was little doubt the child had Sheridan blood in him.

ROLAND WAS LONGING for home leave. He had been away for eighteen months now, and rumour had it there would be a ten day trip to England after the next big push to take Passchendaele. Preparations for it were already under way. A fierce battle for the Menin Road Bridge had been followed by two others within days of each other. Each had succeeded despite the additional torment of dust storms that had raced across the open ground.

But by mid-October the rain was back, the nonstop drenching cold rain of approaching winter, that turned the trenches into narrow canals where men stood waist-deep in water day and night. If despair and desperation had been on their faces before, now it was etched so deeply into their features, it would never entirely disappear again.

Roland's battalion was ordered to the front line on the same day they received the news that the threatened revolution in Russia had begun. These people who had been their allies were now too busy slaughtering each other to bother about fighting the Germans. It was a terrible blow, and they all marched up to their battle positions on a night when rain fell in almost solid curtains and a bitter wind blew back the skirts of their greatcoats. Roland felt as heavyhearted as anyone as he trudged through the nocturnal deluge to the muddy-walled trenches where they settled in to wait for the dawn.

With the coming of daylight came the order to stand to and prepare to advance. Then they heard planes coming low and fast right overhead, a whole squadron of Albatroses, the Germans' new aircraft. They had one obvious target: the ordered ranks in the trenches waiting to go up and over.

The planes had come so suddenly, everyone was taken by surprise. Soldiers fell in dozens. Then the second wave came. It was complete massacre and mayhem from the skies, and Roland was caught in it. All round him men were screaming in agony or trying desperately to run. But there was nowhere to run to. They were trapped in corridors in the ground that only led to other corridors.

The zooming aircraft came once again, and Roland threw himself against a side wall, pressing into the mud to escape the rain of bullets coming from the stuttering machineguns. Then came the bombing section, and the wall of earth was blown up by more explosions. Just as the trench disintegrated, leaving a great chasm that was filling with yellow-brown water, a screaming roaring shape flashed overhead, bringing a hail of lead. Solid fire thuddered into Roland's shoulder, knocking him backwards. He cried out with pain as he landed with a splash in the rushing water that started to close over his head.

Fear lent him strength and wits to struggle up out of danger from drowning and, clutching his upper arm, Roland scrambled up a pile of debris until he was well clear of the water. He half lay there for a moment while he assessed his situation. There was blood on his trousers round what looked like a superficial thigh wound, but the one in his shoulder was more serious. The bullet was still in there and would have to be extracted.

Suddenly such considerations were driven away by the sound of aircraft returning once more, and he was about to slide to the bottom of the trench when, from the mounds of earth as far as the eye could see, came the faint but growing roar of men cheering.

It was soon apparent why. A formation of RFC Camels had come onto the scene, and the distinctive green stripe on their under-bellies identified them as the renowned Arrow Squadron. Laughing somewhat shakily, Roland heard himself say, "Rex, who else but you would turn up at a time like this?"

There Rex was, easily recognizable by the famous cerise scarf that streamed out in the wind behind him. But he was too busy to notice one man on the ground as he and his pilots tangled with the German machines and began sending them out of the sky.

As Roland lay there, he realized he was watching his own brother face death and could do nothing to help him. The contest seemed much more deadly from then on; each time an aircraft fell he caught himself praying. Then one came suddenly from the clouds, twisting round and round, with black smoke pouring from it. It was a Camel with half a wing hanging broken. For a nightmare second Roland thought his heart would stop until he saw the pilot clearly. He wore no scarf.

The machine hit the ground about a hundred yards off in the

467

middle of no-man's-land, but the pilot was thrown clear in a somersault action. The aircraft burst into fire and began to burn fiercely. Then another Camel zoomed from the cloud, racing low over the area. This time it was Rex in the cockpit, hanging over the side to see the fate of the pilot. Hotly pursued by an Albatros that had dived after him, he was quickly up and away, zigzagging to avoid the stream of bullets coming from his enemy.

Looking back at the wreck, Roland had a shock. The pilot was moving, trying to crawl further away from his burning machine. But an Albatros was back, and directed a spurt of gunfire at the man. That was when Roland struggled to his feet and squelched over the mud into no-man's-land with just one thought in his mind. That wounded man could have been his brother, and he must be brought safely in.

Crouching low, he ran in a zigzag pattern, but his heart sank when he discovered that the pilot had passed out from the effort of moving with two broken legs. Roland knew he had to work fast. He bent to pick up the boy and sling him over his shoulder, very nearly passing out himself with the effort. But he had seen some physically impossible feats performed by men who had carried wounded comrades for miles, while losing blood themselves. Now he told himself he could do the same. There was a dark shape overhead again: more firing. But these bullets were directed at the aircraft, not the ground he was crossing. So he plodded on, feeling the boy's weight on his uninjured shoulder and sinking further into the mire with every step.

Yet the trench was gradually growing nearer, and he was conscious of the sound of cheering again. His vision began to blur as sweat ran into his eyes, and he had no free hand to wipe it away. He shook his head in an attempt to get rid of it, but that made him so giddy he staggered and almost fell.

Two men loomed in front of him. Taking the pilot, they placed him on a stretcher, asking Roland, "Are you all right, sir?"

"Oh, yes. Be careful, he has both legs broken."

They all walked the few yards to an underground ruin that had been a trench, where men lay groaning, and people said things to him as he passed.

"Well done, Doc. . . . Splendid effort! . . . If you Sheridans want to fight the war by yourselves, it's all right by me."

On the point of going with an orderly to the waiting ambulance,

Roland turned painfully and managed to ask, "By the way, does anyone happen to know if my brother got away safely?"

The sergeant's grin was roaming all over his face. "Oh yes, sir. Major Sheridan waggled his wings like mad before he took off with the rest of the Arrows. I'd give a fiver to see his face when he finds out it was you he was protecting out there."

Roland's nod was nearly his undoing. "Yes, I think I'd give a fiver, too, Sergeant."

THE TINY VILLAGE of Passchendaele was finally taken by Canadian troops in pouring rain on the sixth of November. But disasters in the other theatres of war, such as the Russian front, the Balkans and Italy, forced the Allies to abandon their plans to push on with a major campaign on the western front. The troops round Ypres were told to dig in for the winter. There was little else for them to do but go underground, because the entire area for miles around was a plain of cratered mud: a graveyard for men, horses and machines. They stayed because they had been through too much to give up.

Roland was given ten days' leave that November. He had looked forward to going home for so long, yet now the opportunity was there it almost seemed a hurdle he was reluctant to tackle. Those last days of the third great Battle of Ypres had left him, like those around him, in a hiatus that made it difficult to relate to the past, or contemplate the future. How could he adjust to such things as eating a decent dinner in a restaurant or driving in a pony and trap through green country lanes bright with holly berries? What if he went home and all those things he had always valued turned out to have no value at all?

So, in that state of mind, he gladly delayed his departure one more day in order to accept an invitation from the Arrow Squadron. For his rescue of the young pilot he was to be awarded the Military Cross, and the famous squadron had sent their thanks, with an invitation to dinner and total inebriation. Accompanying it had been congratulations from Rex.

With his kit all packed Roland climbed into the sidecar of a motorcycle. It was raining, as usual, and it was slow going, but Roland was lost in thoughts of Rex. At times he had felt a gap existed between them. Now, he understood so much that he had never comprehended before. Living as he had during the past eight months at Ypres had given him an insight into human behaviour that easily knocked down personality barriers. The tragedies of Hilary Bisset and Rosalind Tierney had left him infinitely more perceptive and far more tolerant. He would tell Rex this, show him that the gap between them had never really been there.

The motorcycle pulled up. There was congestion ahead. A supply cart had slipped off the road into the mud and was stuck. The ancient skinny horse pulling it was struggling in the slime due to the lashing it was being given by a driver maddened by delay. Roland was reminded of the horses so fiercely defended by Rosalind in Guillehoek, and he climbed to the road, filled with the same anger he had experienced that day.

Pushing his way past the line of traffic, he advanced on the scene. "Stop that at once," he roared, reaching the tilting cart. "If you have that much energy to spare, it might be more sensible to use it in attempting to pull the cart out." He looked round at all the waiting vehicles. "Get off your backsides and get over here, pronto!" he shouted at the occupants.

Roland then went round to release the horse from the shafts until the cart had been righted. The animal was not as exhausted as he feared, and once free of the traces, it lunged before Roland had a firm hold of the leathers. Unable to go forwards or backwards on the road, it veered straight into the quagmire, where it bucked and struggled in the sucking mud, whinnying with fright.

Roland knew exactly what to do. Stepping off the road into the mud, he fought his way towards the trapped horse, speaking to it as a friend. Responding to that instinct that tells an animal there is a bond to be had with man, the horse stopped whinnying and blew through its nostrils in a message of friendship.

Roland had just come up to it and taken hold of the bridle when someone on the road shouted, "Watch what you're doing, sir, that's an old minefield."

But his hand was on the long velvety nose, and he was renewing a never-forgotten brotherhood when the world ended.

19

The news of his brother's death reached Chris via Rex. He found it difficult to handle, as he confessed to Bill Chandler.

"I ought to feel as shattered as Rex plainly does, yet somehow I feel cheated. I've had no chance to get to know Roland and like him, as I've had with Rex. I think we quarrelled over something once, and now I've lost the chance to put it right."

Chandler said quietly, "There's not a man, woman or child who hasn't regrets over something that can't be unsaid or undone."

Chris turned on him. "But I don't even know which of us was to blame. Was it over some unimportant thing that grew out of all proportion, or had one or other of us done something almost unforgivable? For heaven's sake tell me."

The doctor shook his head. "You have to find out for yourself."

"You're always the same! I think you want me to withdraw again. It would give you a holiday."

"No, it wouldn't. I'd be given another patient, who wouldn't be half as interesting as you," the older man said, with his usual calm.

Chris's wrath left him, and he got up to walk haltingly to the end of his conservatory room with the aid of a cane, which was all he needed now. If his family was going to be taken from him, he wished he had never acquired them. Rex was back flying. What would he do if he lost his red-haired brother, too?

CHRIS COULD NOT SLEEP that night. Lying there hour after hour in the ghostly green light of the hospital night system, he found himself thinking more and more about Marion.

By morning he could deny his resolution no longer. Waiting for the busy period when the nurses were occupied with taking tea trays round, he took his greatcoat from the locker and left by the door to the garden. Skirting the house, he made his way through the shrubbery to break through into the lane leading down to the village. It was a cold bright day, and he felt invigorated just to be outside.

A strong urge drove him on. When he had been helpless, terrified and in need of an anchor, Marion had come to his bedside to be that anchor. Whatever part she had played in his past life, he must try to discover it. It was the very least he could do.

As he was nearing the gate to the Deacons' house, he saw Marion walking along the lane towards him carrying a shopping basket. The little boy was plodding at her side, his sturdy body warmly clad in a fawn coat and buttoned gaiters, his flaxen hair covered by a woollen cap of the same colour. She saw Chris and stopped in her tracks. It seemed to him that she drew the boy almost protectively behind the

471

skirt of her blue overcoat. A pinprick of hurt jabbed him at this sign that she feared him still. His steps slowed as he limped up to where she stood.

She spoke first, and sounded full of apprehension. "What are you doing in the village?"

"I was coming to see you."

"What about?" It was very sharp, and the little boy appeared to be pushed even further behind her coat.

Floundering, feeling inadequate to the task he had set himself, he said, "I know what it's like to feel lost and alone. Whatever I did that you find unforgivable, we were close friends once. I just wanted to say that if there's anything I can do for you, or the little boy, please tell me. What's his name, by the way?"

She stared at him with wild eyes. "You *still* don't remember?"

"No."

She seemed very upset as tears began glassing her eyes. But on the verge of trying again to touch her arm, Chris was spotted by the two labradors in the nearby yard. They rushed to him in delight, leaping up to put muddy paws all over his greatcoat, and upsetting his balance. Next minute, his spectacles were knocked to the ground and then all he could see was a moving blur of black against the brown lane as the dogs milled around him. Stooping, he groped on the ground at his feet, to no avail.

He looked up at Marion. "I say, can you see my spectacles . . . any . . . where?" He finished slowly as he saw the blurred vision of a girl who appeared to be wearing a bluebell.

The trip fell through due to this Balkans scare. . . . You don't have much faith in my ability, do you? . . . No one achieves anything with a negative attitude like that, Marion.

They were by the stream, and she was standing in it with a blue dress held up clear of the water. It was a hot day, and he was walking home because he had forgotten to let them know he was coming. It was the long summer holiday of 1914.

The spectacles were pushed into his hand, and he was shaking as he replaced them, fastening the shanks over his ears. November had vanished, and it was high summer. The girl before him stood with her arms behind her, sheltering a child, but then they were somewhere dark together. *I say, Marion, have you seen my spectacles? Come and get them!* This was the most exciting, irresistible experience of his life. They were both crying.

473

"Chris. Chris! Are you all right?"

He tried to move, but one leg was cumbersome. There was a cane in his hand that helped him to walk. November returned with a rush that caused vertigo.

"I . . . I didn't let them know I was coming. I'd better . . . I must go before . . ." He began to limp away.

"Can I get someone to help you?"

"No. I . . . I can manage. It's not . . . far. It's not far."

Have you ever been alone with Marion in her father's house in compromising circumstances? Chris, I wouldn't have said anything, but I had to.

"Please wait there. I'll get Daddy."

"There's no need. If it's going to happen . . . I have to get back!"

"Chris, please!"

He was walking, but no number of miles would give him escape now. The voices were speaking fast and furiously, breaking him apart.

My girl is carrying your child, and it's going to have a legal father if I have to force you to the church at the end of a rifle.

I can't marry her. I'm going up to Cambridge tomorrow.

You little fool. You threw away your whole life when you let your body rule your head. They won't take married men at the university, and I won't have any bastards bearing our name.

Oh Lord, Rex, it's so unfair. I just don't know how I'm going to face the next sixty years.

It was there for all the world to see—a small red-faced symbol of his lost life that screamed night and day so that he could hear it wherever he went. Because of that child, he had to talk of milk yield, lambing, manure and fertilizers; growing as dull and moronic as the sheep he herded. She was all right. She had got what she wanted. But she had taken everything from him, and would continue to do so for as long as he lived.

He found himself leaning on that same bridge, and he felt terribly ill. His arm holding the cane ached. He was much too hot, and waves of giddiness washed over him. Taking off the spectacles to wipe the lenses, he saw again that blur of a girl wading in the stream. But it kept changing into a man in uniform with a friendly smile.

You look awfully different without your spectacles, Chris. You have the most wonderful eyes of any boy I've ever seen.

The voices in his head went on and on, until he also heard his own, harsh and accusing, full of emotion.

I hate you, Marion.

I gave you my eager friendship. You destroyed all I had left!

He felt that same despair of nearly three years ago. They had turned him down at the recruiting office because of his eyes. Always his eyes! But he had fooled them; fooled them for days. Except that he had been continually afraid they would find out and send him back to Marion. That was why he had not written to Roland, because she was at Tarrant Hall.

Then, penetrating the past, came present grief. Roland was dead! The loyal, steadfast man with impossibly high standards, the good-looking horseman, the squire of Tarrant Royal who dedicated himself to the village, had gone for ever. A beloved brother who had sacrificed his medical studies and his treasured horses in order to pay for an academic future that had been thrown away for a school-boy's lust; that same beloved brother who had visited the hospital in the hope of being recognized, and who had written so many letters that had earned just one reply.

Chris's shoulders began to heave as he cried for all those times he had sat in a bed, silently staring at a blond-haired man in tweeds, denying brotherhood; for remembering it all too late!

In his grief he slithered and slipped down the bank to the stream where, sobbing, he leaned against a bridge support. An ambulance passed overhead without his being aware of it. Neither was he aware of voices calling his name from the road.

Exhausted and cold, Chris knew he had to seek refuge before they found him and took him back to Tarrant Hall. It was difficult to climb up the bank to the road. Each step was an effort, and he was shaking from head to foot. He was drenched with sweat. Or was it rain? He could not possibly go back now . . . now he knew that he had a wife, and a baby that screamed night and day.

Is there a terrible thing connected with Marion?

It isn't terrible, Chris. I swear it isn't.

But it was! It was terrible enough to send him to war; to make him, when added to an overture of love from a man he had thought of as a substitute for Rex, want to climb up a cliff to his death.

Chris felt so tired that he wanted to drift into sleep and wake up as an old, old man. It seemed he was walking and walking for ever. Then a face rose up before him. A face with whiskers.

"No money for a train ticket, Mr. Christopher? You'm always the same, sir. Since a little lad."

He sat in the moving carriage for a long while and dreamed of a beautiful redhead. She was standing out on a terrace dressed like a goddess, and he thought she looked like the most beautiful creature he had ever seen. He must tell her before it was too late. Before she died, like Roland.

A face loomed up in front of him again, but it had no whiskers. "Laura Sheridan? She's halfway through the show. You can't see her now. Are you feeling all right, sir?"

"Must . . . must see her. Say it's . . . it's . . ."

"Say it's who, sir?"

"Sheri . . . Sheridan."

"Sherry Sheridan? Blimey, Jock, is this gent Miss Sheridan's husband?"

"Nah . . . but 'ee looks a bit like 'im. What's it all about?"

"Seems ill, if you ask me."

"Well, better tell her. Just in case."

Laura was standing there, her lovely face frightened, asking him all kinds of questions. But Chris was so tired he could no longer speak. Then Laura took him off somewhere in a car. The streets were crowded with people. The driver helped him up a number of steps to a set of rooms. Laura gave the man money, then shut the door.

She was smiling at him. "Here, drink this, my dear."

"What is it?" He was always suspicious of glasses.

"Uncle Rex's medicine for times like these."

To his horror he began to cry. She took the glass away from him again and slipped her hand through his arm.

"Is it Roland, my dear?"

He was unable to answer.

"Does Dr. Chandler know you're here?"

He shook his head.

"Would you like me to tell him?"

He shook his head again.

"All right, let's talk about it in the morning. Come to bed. You look exhausted and drenched through." She led him into an adjoining room. "Heaven knows how you ever got as far as London. You must have been pretty desperate."

She took off his overcoat, jacket and tie. Then she eased him gently onto the bed while she removed his boots. It was wonderful lying there beneath an amber-coloured eiderdown, with the warmth and glow of a fire in the blue-tiled hearth. She was so lovely, and he loved her so much.

He knew he could sleep now and wake to find it was no more than the next day. All the time she was there with him, he could not withdraw into that dreaded limbo.

HER FACE WAS the first thing he saw when he opened his eyes. It was a blur until she put the spectacles over his nose.

"I'm filled with admiration, my dear. You can outsleep even me. It's midafternoon." She put down the small tray she was holding and sat on the edge of the bed. "Are you hungry?"

He shook his head on the pillow.

"At least drink some tea. I made it with my own fair hand."

"I'm most dreadfully in love with you," he told her, knowing it had to be confessed.

She smiled gravely. "I rather thought you might be. Is that why you came to see me last night?"

"Yes."

"Why last night?"

He lay gazing at her while he thought out the answer. "Because it was too late to say all the things I should have said to Roland. Because Rex might never return for me to say them to him."

She stared at him with those marvellous green eyes. "It's a mystery how you found me. You were in a state of physical collapse."

"Yesterday I started to remember," he told her. "There were too many things coming at me all at once. I couldn't cope with them. That . . . that black limbo began to beckon to me. I think I almost went there, Laura, but you beckoned me even more."

She regarded him for a moment or two, then said, "You're shivering! Come on, drink some of this tea. I'll poke up the fire."

He watched her as she moved across to the hearth to take up the poker. The dark green velvet of her dress gleamed in the light of the flames that leaped high as she stirred the logs. Then she walked to the window to draw aside the damask curtains, and he was surprised to see the hard bright light of snow, with huge twirling flakes brushing the panes.

He sat up slowly and reached for the tea. She made no comment

477

on the fact that his cup was rattling in the saucer between sips. She returned to sit on the side of the bed.

"Are you feeling better now, Chris?"

He nodded. "Yes, thanks." He put the teacup down. "You are the most wonderful person I've ever met."

She picked up his mutilated hand from where it lay on the eiderdown. "If that's the case, can't you tell me the real reason you made that incredible bid to reach me last night?"

It did not seem to matter that she saw the injuries he had always tried to hide from her before. He had come to her out of terror, and now he must confess the cause of it.

"There was nowhere else to go. At Tarrant Hall there would be that limbo waiting for me. Rex told me to go out and meet my fears, but I'd gone far enough and balked at the last hurdle." He looked down at her hand holding his. "He'd be disappointed in me."

"No, he wouldn't, my dear. Rex thinks you have the most tremendous courage of any person he knows. And so do I. Tell me everything that happened yesterday."

Because he loved her, because she was somehow part of his dreams of long-ago goddesses and temples, because she was sitting there holding his hand in a warm room that was safe from the chill reality beyond the window, he began to speak to her as he had never been able to speak to any other person in his life. Soon, words were pouring from him as he described all he had yearned for as a boy, how a girl he had known all his life had suddenly touched some chord in him that had led to the ruin of his hopes and aspirations. He told of the total despair that had led him to go to war as his only means of escape; he described the man he had sought as an anchor in his sea of fears, who had shocked him with an affection that had exacerbated the loathing of physical ravishment he then had.

Once or twice he broke down, but nothing could dam his flood of words. Then, in the silence that lasted long after he had run out of things to say, he realized something had happened in the telling. The five minutes in Dr. Deacon's examination room showed itself as an adolescent experiment practised on the wrong girl, not a cardinal sin for which he must pay with his life. Neil Frencham now appeared as a man as desperate and lonely as he had been, not a fiend. Life had changed beyond recall.

"Now you have to go back to Tarrant Hall and face them," said Laura gently, breaking into his profound revelations.

478

He nodded, realizing she meant Marion, his wife . . . and that little boy, who of course was his own son.

"I don't know how," he confessed. "It's too sudden, too much of a shock. I hated her so much then."

"Do you hate her still?"

He frowned. "I don't know. I liked her very much when I didn't know who she was. I've got used to liking her, I suppose."

"But you think she ruined your life. It was because of Marion that you were ever at Gallipoli. She blames herself for everything that's happened."

He shook his head slowly. "It's too long ago to blame anyone. Now she hates me."

Laura got up from the bed, took a piece of bread from the tray beside it, and walked across the room to pick up the toasting fork by the hearth. Sitting on the rug, she held the bread out towards the flames.

"It must have taken tremendous courage for Marion to do what she did at the hospital. She didn't have a brilliant brain and a promising academic career ahead of her, but she had a warm heart and a vast capacity for life and love. You robbed her of all that, Chris. Even so, she went willingly when she thought her presence and caring would help you through. She stuck it out for over a year, then broke down and was very ill."

Put that way it made him feel selfish and tremendously guilty. "My lord, no wonder she hates me now."

Laura turned, the firelight making her skin golden. "I don't think she hates you, my dear, it's just that at the moment she's empty of all feeling."

He scrambled from the bed, walked across to where she was, and sat on the edge of a low chair. "I haven't the first idea what to do now I know the truth. My son is almost three years old. While he's been growing up, I've been standing still."

Her smile was warm and wonderful. "No, you haven't, Chris. You've spent the past three years learning to be human."

THEY SPENT THE REST of the day in cosy companionship round the fire, watching the snow pile up outside the window. They talked nonstop. With growing clarity Chris was able to recount boyhood days at Tarrant Hall, and if he suspected she listened so intently because there was so much about Rex, he tried not to feel disappointed. Once or twice he had to stop because grief over Roland grew too sharp, but she helped him over his silences.

"Don't let regret haunt you, Chris," she advised gently. "He had been out there for months during some of the worst battles and must have come to understand what it was like for you not being able to recognize him. He was a doctor, don't forget."

"He sent me a cameo brooch," Chris told her. "I didn't really understand why—and then Rex told me I should give it to a girl someday. I see now he must have meant Marion."

To his consternation he suddenly noticed she was close to tears. "I say, have I upset you?" he asked.

She shook her head. "No, it's just me being silly. I miss Rex so dreadfully since he went back this time."

"He'll be all right," Chris said in clumsy reassurance. "Rex has got a charmed life. The Huns will never get him."

"That's what he believes. But . . . he's survived so much. I can't help feeling afraid." She curled her legs up on her chair. "Without him, I'm nothing. I wait for him to appear without warning—which is what he usually does—so that I can come alive again. When that happens, we live a hundred years in a few days. Then he vanishes again . . . and I never know if I'm going to die because he'll never come back." She angled her face away to gaze into the fire, then turned back. "Oh Chris, give me some of your courage. Tell me how to survive."

He was overwhelmed. "I . . . I don't think courage is the right word," he said hesitantly. "It's more that there's no alternative but to go on. I think that's how I survived."

"Is that what you're going to do now—go on towards Marion?"

He nodded bleakly. "I don't have much choice, do I?"

"No, Chris, no more choice than I have." She smiled with a suggestion of closeness. "But I'm sure you'll cope with it. Now you've come to terms with yourself, you're strong—and rather wonderful, like all the Sheridans."

LIFE SHOULD HAVE BEEN much easier for Chris after he was totally cured, but in one respect it was not. He didn't have the first idea how to tackle the problem of his marriage. Refusing any help from Bill Chandler, who still had not forgiven him for vanishing for two days and causing great anxiety, Chris spent a week going over the problem. He knew Marion had been told that he had recalled every

480

part of his past, but he felt it was pointless attempting to see her until he had some kind of proposal to put to her.

There was also Tessa to think of. Taking the news of Roland's death stoically, she had agreed to remain as bailiff until Chris had sorted out his affairs. He had moved into Tarrant Hall himself, only going through to the hospital for treatment on his leg, which was still causing a few problems. Bill Chandler came to him for discussions on the past, all of which he remembered with total clarity now. A decision was to be made on his future by the Army Medical Board by Christmas. Meanwhile, he had to give his word that he would not leave the house without telling the Australian doctor where he was going. However, snow made even a trip to the village out of the question for him, and he was too occupied with personal problems to want to go anywhere.

He had written a long letter to Rex full of gratitude for his excellent advice on going to meet his fears, and the wonderful outcome. It was a letter full of affection and pride in having such a hero as his lifelong friend. Then, inevitably, he had written of his deep sadness that recollection had come too late to enable him to write a similar letter to Roland.

Soon afterwards, Chris received from Rex a package containing Roland's personal effects. Among them were a vast number of letters, all of which appeared to have been written to David Sheridan. "I believe you should read them all very carefully," Rex had written, "because they are meant for your son."

So Chris sat for a whole afternoon reading a moving, vivid, brutal account of the war that had reached out to touch everyone, without exception and in many different ways. Chris knew that what he had in his hands in the form of letters from a soldier in the trenches to his young nephew was chillingly brilliant. He also sensed that Roland had repented his lack of caring for his nephew. So that it would not be too late, Chris must ensure that he did what his oldest brother would have done if he had lived. He sat for the rest of that day, his sensitive mind going beyond the mere words of those letters into the heart of their meaning. By the time he went to bed, he had found the resolution that had evaded him before.

AS SOON AS THE SNOW cleared, he sent a letter to Marion asking her to the Hall. It was a formal approach, explaining that he was now fully recovered and anxious to discuss the fact with her. She agreed

481

to come and chose the following Monday morning at eleven. He rehearsed all he was going to say, so there was no reason for nervousness. Nevertheless, he was consumed by it as he waited in the parlour by the cheerful blaze of a log fire. She arrived exactly on time and waited to hear his first words.

But his rehearsed speeches fled. All he did was ask her to take off her coat and sit down.

"No, thank you. I shan't be staying long," she told him quietly.

That threw him. "It was good of you to come, Marion, especially after the way I walked off in the village that day. It was the shock of . . . well, of too many things coming back to me at once."

"She apparently coped with the situation admirably."

"She?"

"Laura . . . the girl you ran to for help."

"Oh yes, she did. And now I remember everything very clearly. That's why I have allowed a while to pass before seeing you. I had a lot to think over and I tried to make the best decisions."

"Yes."

It was evident she had no intention of helping him, so he plunged ahead. "What happened three years ago is past, Marion, and we have both become different people. The war has changed everything. For some reason poor Roland left Tarrant Hall and all that goes with it to me, not Rex. But it is willed to you for David should I not be considered fit to run the estate."

A flood of vivid colour passed over her face, then left her rather pale. "Roland did that?"

Chris nodded.

She walked to the small casement window, and stood looking out at the lingering snow. He limped across the room to stand beside her. She looked round swiftly, and her eyes were bright with tears.

"Roland and I had been friends all our lives, yet we said terrible things to each other. I felt badly enough when I heard of his death. Now this. I wish he hadn't. It's all too late."

"What do you mean?"

"Oh Chris, you surely haven't asked me here to suggest we try to revive something that never really lived?"

Completely taken aback, he muttered, "It would be different now. I promise you I'm completely recovered—ask Chandler—and I'd try to be a good husband to you now."

"But we're both in love with someone else!"

482

He stared at her. "I don't understand."

"No, I don't suppose you do," she retaliated in broken tones. "You've been away in a world of your own for two and a half years while I've been waiting to see whether you'd go insane or not. Now the issue is settled. I'm glad for you, Chris, deeply glad. But I know I can take no more. I only accepted your invitation so that I could tell you I want a divorce. I'm sure any court will understand why, and grant it."

20

As 1918 dawned, the Allies were facing their worst and direst emergency yet. The fighting troops now comprised mostly inexperienced new recruits. Those of the old regulars who had miraculously not fallen were ill or severely shellshocked. There were no reserves. As soon as boys were conscripted, they were shipped out to the war zones in France, Belgium, Italy, the Middle East and the Balkans. The desperately needed Americans were still only trickling through to areas where ten times their number was needed if the war was to reach a decisive stage.

The Allied air power was frantically being increased, and the severe challenge to the skill and endurance of those who repaired the aircraft as well as those who flew them, was met with great courage. The Germans might not have battle superiority any longer, but they did have enviable supplies of aircraft, which enabled them to launch surprise attacks on Allied airfields, bombing machines as they stood on the ground, or bringing them down as pilots tried to take them airborne.

When Rex's squadron had twice suffered such on-the-ground attacks, he knew something would have to be done.

Though air warfare had become more organized while he spent the summer in England, Rex decided to ignore an order circulated by the officer in ground command of his sector, forbidding unauthorized flights by single pilots or a pair working together.

"I've heard the reasoning behind the order, and it only makes sense from where people sit at headquarters," he told Mike one morning when rain had grounded ally and enemy alike.

"It makes sense from where *I'm* sitting, too, old mate," said Mike, putting his booted feet up on Rex's desk near to where his squadron commander perched on its corner, drinking brandy. "The Huns no longer send up solo aircraft, so any fool on our side who decides on a solitary excursion is going to meet up with ten times his number."

"Only if he goes up when they're up." Rex waved his glass at his friend. "I cannot and will not have my squadron decimated on the ground. We're trained to fight in the air." He leaned forward to look Mike straight in the eyes. "Surprise is essential. That means taking off in the dark so that our arrival over their airfield is just as dawn is coming up. Or it means going up in weather conditions that usually stop all flying."

Mike assumed an unconcerned expression. "Like today?"

"That's right," Rex agreed in pleasant tones. "Just like today."

The mechanics tried to look as though they thought nothing odd about being told to prepare two machines for flight one morning in February when even the birds preferred a branch in a tree. The other squadron members pressed astonished faces to their windows to watch their commanding officer and senior pilot climb into rain-washed cockpits with a basketful of grenades apiece. They looked even more astonished an hour or so later when the pair returned, grinning and climbing from their machines with the empty baskets over their heads as protection against the rain. Of course the whole squadron knew that Sherry Sheridan was crazy—in the most attractive possible way, but crazy all the same.

But these days there was a demon driving Rex. Roland's death had hit him hard. His older brother had represented all that was good about the British way of life. Rex now recognized the joys and privileges of youth he had always taken for granted, and would sit for long periods with a bottle of brandy, lost in recollections of those sunny days when he would wheel *Princess* from the shed and float above the rolling hills of Dorset and Somerset, filled with the power and exuberance of youth.

Apart from grief and anger over Roland's death, and the concern over Chris's future now that he had recovered his sanity and lost his wife, Rex felt a burning urge to arrange his own future. Those letters forwarded with Roland's personal effects haunted him. They had painted such a vivid picture of lost ideals, lost chances, lost ambitions and lost men, he felt an overwhelming burden of responsibility to use his gift of life. While in England he had come to know many of the leading aircraft designers well enough to approach them by letter, asking to join their company after the war.

484

He had received enthusiastic replies, which had sparked off a regular correspondence concerning aircraft design allied to the needs of the men who flew them. He longed for the time when he could cast off his khaki and embark on this new phase of his life. And there was his passion for Laura.

It was six months since he had said farewell to her—the longest they had yet been apart—and the jealousy he had kept under control in England now ran riot. His wife had apparently been achieving all she had dreamed possible in her theatrical career, and Rex found it difficult to stay silent when new conscripts arrived raving about *Bows and Boaters*, with its star who was fast becoming the darling of the troops on leave. Where would it all lead? His longing to end the war and get back to sort it out, plus a compulsion to prove he was a better man than all the rest, augmented the almost superhuman drive that propelled him these days and sent his personal tally of enemy kills towards sixty.

He soon had need of that drive. On the thirteenth of March the Russians signed a separate peace with Germany, releasing hundreds of thousands of German troops from the Russian front to reinforce the depleted regiments on the western front. Within a week, the RFC was warned to stand by for a massive German attack, which intelligence reports believed would be launched in Flanders as the start of that year's spring offensive. Rex had the mechanics working night and day to get planes repaired and airworthy, while aircrews waited for the battle order to come through.

The men of Rex's squadron were gathered in his office listening to the latest information on the state of the battle, when the sound of approaching aircraft was heard by them all. It took but a moment for them to realize what was about to happen as Rex shouted, "Those Huns are after us again! Get into the air as fast as you can!"

Sure enough, out of the thin cloud of a grey March day came a formation of enemy aircraft, and as Rex ran with the others towards the Camels lined up on the field, the Germans flew over low, dropping bombs and tossing grenades. Then their observers in the rear cockpits used their machineguns to advantage as their pilots climbed after the attack.

All those on the ground were sitting ducks. The field seemed to be exploding all round them, sending showers of earth over their heads. Rex raced over the grass towards the leading Camel, shouting orders to clear a path. Some men were fanning out to climb into the aircraft, and an extra roar rent the air as engines were started for takeoff.

From then on it was a question of fighting for survival as bullets continued to rain down and grenades were dropped from no more than fifty feet up. The fabric of his wings grew full of holes as Rex taxied forward and then zigzagged across the field, unable to get up enough speed to take to the air. All round him he was aware of the members of his squadron doing the same. Yet when Rex desperately dragged his machine up from the ground at the very last minute, he noticed others taking to the skies beside him in defiance of the buzzing Germans above.

But Rex's own flight was of short duration. As he pulled up over the tops of trees, a spar snapped and half his lower wing tore away, weakened by the tattered fabric. His climb turned into a sideslip. The ground rushed up, and he used all his strength and flying skill to land again. He succeeded, although the impact jolted him badly, and the wheels sank into the muddy field, sending the Camel straight onto its nose.

Rex passed out momentarily, and that saved his life because the departing Germans must have taken his immobility as a sign that he was finished. As it was, he came to his senses to see them heading off into the cloud now that their advantage of surprise had been outlived. Climbing out and dropping to the ground after releasing his belt, Rex scrambled to his feet and looked heavenwards to see how many of his squadron had survived to chase their attackers.

But the others turned into blurred dots as his scrutiny fastened on just one Camel heading straight for him in a steep glide, engine spluttering and flames already licking round the cockpit.

"Oh, my God," he cried in a rasping breath, and felt his blood freeze as the machine hit the ploughed field no more than a few yards from him. His legs were already running; his breath was laboured when he unsteadily neared the wreck that was crackling and roaring with fire. But his laboured breathing turned to sobs of anguish when he saw, through the orange tongues of flame, that Mike was still alive. His friend was staring at him, his mouth wide open. The screams were drowned by the roar of flames and the crackle of wood, but Rex heard them inside his head and knew he would hear them for the rest of his life.

Tugging off his leather coat, Rex began beating at the fire, but he had no power against a flame that had a good hold on inflammable material. Next minute, the whole machine collapsed and lost any form of identity in one huge conflagration.

Rex backed away, staring with eyes that were almost blinded by brightness. Then he turned and staggered about aimlessly until he fetched up hard against something. He held on to it with a grip of iron until it asked him if he was all right.

They led him to an ambulance on the perimeter of the airfield, but he refused to get in it. Someone walked beside him back across the field to his office. He sat at his desk, noting the damage that had been done and organizing burial parties for the dead. He visited the wounded in sick quarters. That evening he wrote to the relatives of those who had been lost. But when he reached the last letter, the page remained blank save for the words: My dear Tessa. It stayed blank for the rest of that night.

THE REALIZATION THAT AIR POWER was going to be a significant element in future defence strategy had culminated in a decision to take the Royal Flying Corps away from the army, and the Royal Naval Air Service away from the navy, to combine the two in a separate service to be called the Royal Air Force. It was born on the first of April, but it was not a painless birth. Bitter opposition and jealousy accompanied it, to remain for a long time afterwards. But the men in the new service had to accept the inevitable and make the best of it.

Rex had always possessed the kind of nature that allowed him to do this. So when he was told to return to England for three days at the end of March to lend the glamour of his reputation to the inauguration of the RAF, he went, stifling his feelings over something he had no power to prevent. He was given complete freedom to do as he pleased during the times between official duties. It was not much, but Rex planned to make the most of it.

Reaching London after an all-night journey, he had no chance of letting Laura know he was in England. She refused to have a telephone in case it disturbed her sleep, and he decided against sending her a telegram for fear of frightening her. So the day dragged past, and all the while he thought of nothing else but the blessed peace of being with her and holding her in his arms to chase away the demons with which he now lived.

When he was finally free, he set off on foot with the idea of buying flowers at a florist. He noted that London was shabbier than when he had last seen it, with its rubble from air raids and sad-faced people wrapped against the March fog in drab coats. The florist closed when he was ten yards from it, the sour-faced woman resolutely pulling the roller blind over the glass door as he made frantic signs to her to let him in. Angry, he turned to a newspaper and confectionery shop next door, which was enjoying a roaring trade. It would have to be chocolates instead of flowers.

He never bought them. Just inside the door he was halted by something he could not initially believe. In a glass-fronted case were the picture postcards of film and stage stars that were extremely popular with the public, and among them were some of Laura. She smiled out at Rex from over her shoulder, which was bare along with her back down to well below her waist, and her wicked eyes invited him to study the rest of her body encased in a dark glittery clinging skirt that was slit from toe to thigh, exposing the whole of one shapely leg as she posed provocatively. It was the costume she wore for the finale of her show, but it seemed to be cut a lot lower than when Rex had seen it . . . and the vibrant sexuality she had always reserved just for him now fizzed from the picture like a star shell.

It was the last burden on his overladen soul. Because he had to hit out at something, he smashed his fist through the glass of that case, and left, feeling nothing of the cuts on his hand that had started to bleed profusely. At the corner he jumped into a taxi and gave the driver the address of his flat.

Rex left a trail of blood all the way up the flights of stairs he had to climb to reach his front door, and he was breathing heavily as he reached the last set of six. Then, from the half landing, he saw Laura come from the flat dressed for the theatre in a sable-trimmed evening coat. She turned, saw him, and seemed to freeze with shock that drained the colour from her cheeks. Then her face flooded with incredulous delight to make her more beautiful than he ever remembered. It broke him apart.

Wanting to destroy her as she was destroying him, he heard words pour from his lips in a ceaseless stream of accusation. "How could you do it? How could you agree to such a thing when you knew what it would do to me? Those postcards of you on public sale show almost the whole of your body!" His voice had risen and echoed around the hollow staircase. "How could you degrade yourself to such an extent?"

488

"Degrade myself?" she repeated in bewilderment. "I wear that costume in the show. You know I do."

"On stage you're acting a part," he shouted. "Those pictures are different."

"How different?" she cried. "They're only photographs."

"Photographs that are going to be guffawed over by troops and sailors everywhere!" The words began to run into each other as the volcano inside him reached the point of erupting. "You think they will bring you public veneration? All you are doing is selling yourself for tuppence to any man who wants you!"

In a fury she stepped forward and brought up her arm to strike him. But he anticipated the blow and jerked his head back out of her reach. The movement sent him off balance, his boot slipped on the edge of the step, and he fell backwards, dropping down the flight of steps to the landing below where he caught his forehead a mighty crack on the newel post.

When he came to, Laura was bending over him with fear darkening her face, and she seemed to have been crying.

"Are you badly hurt?" she asked him in a voice that trembled. "Have you broken anything? There's blood everywhere. I've sent for a doctor."

"I don't need a doctor," he mumbled. "Just let me lie here a while."

So Rex lay on the floor while Laura took off her velvet coat to fold beneath his head, and fussing neighbours offered advice. The volcano that had been within his breast seemed to have moved up into his head. But Laura was holding his hand and speaking softly, and her perfume wafted to him, adding to his sense of confusion over where he was.

The doctor arrived and examined him with experienced hands. Pronouncing that nothing was broken, he enlisted the help of the neighbours to get Rex to his feet and up to the apartment, and once there he studied the extent of the damage to his forehead.

"No abrasion, but a massive bruise coming already. You'll have a nasty headache from that," was his hearty opinion. "Still, that'll be nothing to a young man like you." He proceeded to remove splinters of glass from Rex's hand, then bandage the cuts.

Rex swallowed a powder the doctor mixed in a glass of water fetched by Laura, but it was all automatic. Oblivion seemed irresistibly attractive.

HE AWOKE TO BRILLIANT SUNSHINE and a blinding headache. It was a few seconds before he realized where he was. Then Laura was beside him, holding out a hand containing some pills and a glass of water. "Thank heavens! I've been on the verge of calling the doctor again," she said in a voice that was very subdued, for her. "I couldn't wake you, no matter what I did. It's already afternoon."

He stared at her, trying to marshal his thoughts. "I'm supposed to be at a conference. No, that was this morning. I think . . . Oh lord, I was one of the speakers at a luncheon. It's too late now."

She sat on the edge of the bed and put a cool hand against his cheek. In a burnt-orange dress, with her hair put up in a mass of bright curls, she looked like the girl he had first seen enter Tessa's lodgings with her arms full of boxes.

"Darling, the doctor has demanded that you rest for the next forty-eight hours, and I asked him to contact the appropriate people at the War Office. Stop worrying and take these."

He did as she directed, then studied her wet cheeks. "Why are you crying?"

She took his unbandaged hand in hers and held it tightly. "Because I love you so much, my dearest one, I can't contain it."

He considered that for a while, as his head continued to thud with every heartbeat. "Don't go away?"

"No. I'll sit here while you sleep."

"I shan't sleep."

"All right. Just lie there and dream of Tarrant Hall. I've arranged for us to go down the day after tomorrow and see Chris."

But when the dream began it turned into a nightmare almost at once. Tessa was at Tarrant Hall. How could he tell her about her brother? He tried to explain to Laura that he could not do it, could not go home. But she soothed him with soft words and her lips on his until he drifted away into deep sleep again.

CHRIS COULD SCARCELY CONTAIN his delight at the prospect of seeing Rex. It would add some warmth to the chill brought by his pending divorce. He was still struggling to understand that the nurse he had come to like and trust superseded the girl he had blamed for the ruin of his life. He liked Marion. He was sure he could like the little boy to whom Roland had written those brilliantly evocative letters. And that boy was *his* son. Surely he had a right to watch him grow and learn?

490

At Christmas Chris had been examined by an army medical board and was declared sane, although they gave him an immediate discharge on the grounds of disability due to his mutilated hand and the leg that would always be slightly inflexible. His eyesight alone would have brought the decision, anyway. As a result, he was now employed, in a civilian capacity, as a code breaker, translator and cipher expert, by those same people who had unthinkingly sent him to Gallipoli. But because Marion loved someone else, he had lost her and David, and that left him with nothing but his work. It no longer seemed to be enough.

Due to one of the strange quirks of war, the Tarrant Hall estate had made a great deal of money over the past few years by supplying grain, meat and timber under government contracts. Tessa had managed the business affairs better than many a man, and had brought the Sheridan bank balance appreciably nearer its old standard. Mike's death coming so soon after Roland's had almost extinguished her spirit, but she had refused Chris's suggestion that she return to Australia for a break. She was losing herself in work, and Bill Chandler continued his courtship.

The reunion between Chris and Rex was emotional, since it was the first time the two brothers had met on a normal footing since Chris's wedding day. But Chris was disturbed by Rex's appearance. There was a prodigious bruise on his forehead, where he had apparently fallen, and he looked pale and heavy-eyed. But it was the way he flinched from the fire burning in the hearth, and the absence of a smile, that made it seem as if the merry cavalier brother had been a figment of his imagination. Still, Chris realized that Rex had been facing almost four years of what he himself had experienced only briefly at Gallipoli. Was it any wonder that laughter was so hard to find for a man who had seen and suffered so much?

"I have you to thank for my progress," Chris told his brother warmly. "You persuaded me to take my future by the scruff of the neck."

"I just wish Roland had known you had pulled through all right," was all Rex replied. "I think he bitterly regretted his lack of understanding during those months following your marriage."

"I bitterly regret doing all I did to bring such fearful results," said Chris. "But I have to go on living with it."

They were strolling together after dinner, and an earlier shower had sharpened the scent of rich earth and massed rhododendrons.

491

"I'm glad you've come home just now," Chris continued as they passed the stables, their footsteps crunching the damp gravel path. "There's something I'd like to discuss with you. Rex, are you listening?"

"Mmm?" He pulled his gaze away from the stables.

"I've read those letters of Roland's over and over again. They are haunting, brutal, and full of quite astonishing insight into human nature. As an account of war, they're masterly; as an indictment against it, they are a brilliant cry to the next generation never to let this happen again. I want your agreement to go ahead and get them published."

Rex came to a halt and studied him shrewdly. "Some of it is pretty strong meat."

"So is this war."

"You'll face official opposition."

"I'll fight it."

"Then . . . go ahead."

"Where do you think we should send the proceeds?"

Rex thought about it a while. "To any organization that will use the money to buy a motor-driven vehicle to replace a horse-drawn one. Roland died trying to save one of the poor beasts, so I think it's appropriate, don't you?"

It was only as they had completed their walk and were heading back to the house that Chris looked at him with concern that was growing by the minute. "You ought to stay here for longer than a few days, Rex."

He shook his head. "I just want to get back there and finish it off with the others."

"What'll you do when it's all over?"

"Become a test pilot with Sopwith," was the immediate reply. "I've already been offered the job and accepted."

"You mean to go on flying?"

The green eyes looked back at him almost blankly. "That's all I've ever wanted to do. You know that."

Chris nodded. "People change, though. I'm very happy doing what I do now."

"What about the rest of your life?" Rex asked, pushing open the door.

He answered impulsively. "I'm going to try to obtain some kind of jurisdiction about David so that I can teach him some things." He

492

stepped inside the panelled hall and shut the door behind them both. "He's my son, so he probably has a decent enough brain. Marion told me she's in love with someone, so she might marry again. I don't want this man . . ."

"No, she won't. He's dead," put in Rex tonelessly. "Burned to ashes. Mike Manning is scattered all over the Ypres sector."

Chris stood still. "She's in love with Mike Manning? Oh, my lord, poor Marion!"

21

Rex and Laura planned to catch the afternoon train to London, because he had to fly back to Belgium the following day—twenty-four hours later than expected. He had to pinch himself every so often to prove he had really been at Tarrant Hall with Laura for the past three days.

His fall down the steps had shocked her to such an extent, she had abandoned her part in *Bows and Boaters* to her understudy, and was devoting every moment to making him happy with quiet, deep love. As for the picture postcards, she swore she would prevent any more from being manufactured.

Laura had helped him through the difficult meeting with Tessa, who looked thin and ill despite her determination to face up to her loss of both Roland and Mike. He was spared a meeting with Marion, because Dr. Deacon had taken his daughter and grandson to his sister in Bath.

Now, on the morning before Rex left, Laura was actually going for a walk along Longbarrow Hill with him. They went slowly, hand in hand, enjoying the tranquillity around them.

"Why did Roland leave everything to Chris, and not to you?" she asked.

"I get a percentage of the income. But I always told him I didn't want it."

"It wasn't because of me?"

He looked down at her anxious face. "No, darling. I was destined to fly, and flying and being a squire are incompatible."

"But you love Tarrant Hall?"

He nodded. "Now, more than I ever did. No, that's wrong. I always have loved it . . . but I took it for granted before." He put his arms round her and drew her towards him. "We should never take anything for granted."

She put up her hands to cover his arms as they held her. "That's why I always seize everything with both hands. I don't want to repent lost chances."

He tightened his hold on her as he whispered, "You're really a very wonderful girl."

"No, I'm not," she returned quietly. "There are some things I've said to you that I wish you'd forget."

He turned her within the crook of his arm and began walking her along the hill again. "Laura, in the past we've both said things we haven't meant. But I think our marriage is a bit like flying. Our love soars high and sometimes comes down with a crash, but we always take off again. The hurtful things are the crashes. They can't be forgotten, because they are the moments that teach us the most. Come on, just up here is the barn where I used to keep *Princess*. She was the most wonderful piece of construction ever put together."

They reached the barn, and he drew her inside the old familiar place, now empty save for some hay left from last summer. They stood in the shaft of sunlight that streamed in through the open door, and he described *Princess* in every detail.

Finally Laura squeezed his arm. "Darling, I'm sure she was a wonderful machine, but you've just described an aircraft that could have won the war for us long ago, if we'd had enough of them."

He looked at her earnestly. "We're going to build one like that at Sopwith, a design pilots will love to fly."

She smiled at him mistily. "Then I suggest you call it the *Sopwith Princess*."

She looked so beautiful standing there in the sunlight, he dedicated himself to her all over again. "I love you for ever, Laura."

Her fingers rested momentarily against his mouth. "Of all the things there are in the world, that's one I truly believe . . . and I always will."

He kissed her, and they both sensed there was something magical between them at that moment. The hay was warm beneath that great band of sunshine, and Rex made love to her almost reverently. Then they lay in each other's arms, listening to the song of the skylark high and free in the bluest of skies.

Laura sighed. "If I were to die at this very moment, I'd know I could never be more completely happy, however long I lived."

He turned his head to her. "What . . . what about my kind of four weeks?"

"What about them?"

"No regrets?"

She shook her head against the hay, and little pieces stuck to her curls. "They were inevitable, weren't they? We belong together, Rex, and always will. We both know that."

He drew her closer, knowing it was going to be all right. However high they soared, however bumpy the flight, they would always land safely.

THE SQUADRON WELCOMED their leader back, chaffed him about how he came to have such a bruise on his. head, then settled into routine once more.

Events moved quickly and dramatically in the next three weeks, as hundreds of thousands more lives were lost in grim frenzied battle with the Germans. The squadron was pressed to the limit during those April weeks, providing air cover for their own defending troops, attacking moving columns of enemy supplies, and destroying observation balloons.

Their exhausted spirits were cheered by the news that "the Red Baron" von Richthofen had been finally killed by a Canadian pilot, because they knew his legendary career had been a source of inspiration to German pilots. But von Richthofen's loss would also bring about the burning desire to retaliate. Sherry Sheridan's name was at the top of the list of every German aviator when he went hunting.

It did not worry Rex. But he was worried about the exhaustion that was beginning to master him. He caught himself falling asleep at all times of the day, yet no amount of rest seemed to refresh him. After several instances of dozing in the cockpit, he decided to give up his drinking, which had increased since Mike's death. One day in the second week of May he told the mess corporal to take all the brandy away from his office and quarters and put it under lock and key. The bewildered man had to remind him of his instructions when Rex returned two days later from a flight in which he had lost five men, and stormed over the fact that there was no brandy available.

"It was your own order, sir," the corporal told him.

"My order!" Rex repeated furiously. "I don't give stupid orders like that."

"You told me to take it away and lock it up," persisted the long-suffering man. "Said it made you fall asleep."

Rex looked at him with a frown. "Oh yes, perhaps I did. Sorry, I'd forgotten. Look, fetch me something for this dreadful headache, will you? I've had it all week."

In spite of the remedy brought by the mess corporal, Rex could not seem to get rid of the pounding in his head. It was still there when the base's commanding officer summoned him to his quarters later that afternoon. He got to the point quickly.

"Sit down, Sheridan." He pulled down a large-scale roller map, then picked up a pointer. "Within the next few days, the Germans are planning to move supplies of tank fuel and ammunition to their force that is pinned down right here, in this village. As you know, the roads into the village are impassable." He then ran the pointer along a narrow line of blue. "But this canal here is part of a large system of waterways stretching back into occupied Belgium, and thence to Germany itself. Army intelligence has been following the progress of a fleet of barges purporting to contain a cargo of fruit, but a Belgian spy has discovered the real cargo and its destination."

Rex knew there would be valid reasons why he was being told this classified information.

"It will be obvious to you, by now, that the fleet has managed to get to within two days' journey of its destination. As you see, the canal runs through woodland until just before the village in question. In the village and along the German positions to the west are artillery emplacements that would make concerted aerial attack very costly."

Rex then asked, "How wide is the canal?"

"Only just wide enough." His commanding officer gave a tight smile. "As someone who dabbled with explosives before taking up flying, can I offer a useful tip?"

Rex nodded. "Go ahead."

"Leaving aside the problem of flying through there without coming to grief on the trees, I'd concentrate on the leading barge. Get that alight and exploding, and a chain reaction will set off the other four."

"Are they all armed?"

"Machineguns, bow and stern."

Rex stared at him. "Lord, what a prospect!"

"It seems, on paper at least, to be a case of doing it at the first attempt or not at all. It'll have to be done tomorrow. You're free to decide at what hour you'll go. But by sundown tomorrow, the convoy will be rounding this bend, and by dawn the day after, it will be too near its destination, which would halve your chances."

Rex gave him a straight look. "How do you halve anything that small?"

His commanding officer sat down and laid the pointer carefully on his desk. "I should tell you we are asking only for a volunteer on this job."

"That went without saying," said Rex. "But when an old dog stops doing his tricks, he's finished, isn't he?"

HE DECIDED TO GO late in the afternoon, after working out the convoy's probable position at that time. It was leaving things to the last minute, but it would give him the most advantage because the sun would be going down and he would be approaching out of it. He stayed in his office all that morning, studying maps and details. Finally he sent an orderly for a strong pill to disperse the headache that had been increasing since morning.

He ate lunch at his desk, and drank cup after cup of black coffee to stave off the sleepiness creeping over him. To wake himself up, he walked over to check that his machine was ready, tested the guns, and watched the fixing of the bombs into the racks beneath the fuselage. Then he went to his quarters to take a cold bath.

By four thirty he was ready to leave, and the entire squadron turned out to watch him go. After takeoff he circled and waved to them all, before turning onto the course that would lead him towards the canal. He felt very calm and confident, as he always did once in the air. But he cursed the pain that still thudded through his head despite the MO's pill.

He gazed over the side at the green countryside beneath. It looked very peaceful. Thank heaven it was a clear day, for the sun would be his ally. But his headache seemed to be getting worse and his vision kept blurring. It was the worst thing that could happen just now when he needed perfect judgment. Blinking several times and shaking his head cleared it, and he breathed a sigh of relief.

A railway was in sight now, with bridges blown to block the tracks here and there. The canal would be about six miles ahead. If he hit

497

it west of the bend, he could turn to overfly it with the glow of the setting sun behind and slightly to the right of him. The men on the barges would have it full in their eyes as they rounded the bend.

Losing height when his objective came into sight he circled, looking for the break in the trees where the narrow canal ran. Yes, there it was. But only when he had dropped lower and lower until his wheels were almost brushing the tops of the trees did he realize the appalling difficulty of what he had been asked to do.

Gradually, carefully, he manoeuvred his aircraft until it was filling the width of the cutting with only a few feet to spare on either side. Now he flew the length of it without touching the trees, realizing only a superb aviator could successfully achieve what he was doing. The thrill of flight ran through him as he roared above that quiet waterway that was glittering silver and gold in the dying sunshine.

The curve ahead seemed to rush towards him fast, and his hand went to the bomb-release cord. Immediately the Camel wobbled, racing his heartbeat. The barges should be appearing round the bend now, according to his calculations. There would only be one chance, one right moment. He must not miss it; those supplies must not be allowed to reach their destination because he had failed in the greatest challenge of his life.

The bend was there now. Tension was making him sweat just as it dawned on him that something was wrong. The water ahead of him was empty, with no sign of any kind of boat.

He tried to think; racked his brains. What had gone wrong? Calling all manner of curses down on military intelligence, he tried to decide what to do. Confusion teemed through his head, preventing constructive thought. What was wrong with him? He felt curiously light-headed and unconcerned, and was no longer sure what he was doing there. His eyelids began to droop, but through the narrowing slits he then saw something like a blob on the water ahead.

Blinking himself awake, he almost came to grief as the plane's nose dipped. Recollection rushed back. This was a vital patrol to bomb some barges. They were the blob ahead. The sun behind him was low enough to put a glare on the water that partially blinded him, and he accepted his job was going to be more difficult than he had thought.

He now realized how loud the roar of his engine sounded in the stillness of that waterway. They would have heard him coming a

498

long way off. If they had any sense they would be manning the guns. It would have to be the first run or nothing.

Closer now, he saw that the barges had stopped and were drawn up alongside the right bank, one behind the other. The gunners were at their posts, looking straight at his approaching aircraft. The true hazards of this job became crystal clear. His bombs would be ineffective, since he could not now fly overhead to drop them. It would have to be the grenades that lay in a basket at his feet. But they were much more chancy. He could not fly that perilous corridor, pull the pins from the grenades, and throw them accurately over the side all at the same time.

Swiftly revising his plans, he sped on towards the barges as the first stutter of gunfire began. Praying that the setting sun was practically blinding them, he concentrated on the closing distance between them and judged the exact moment. It had to be very quick, or he would be lost. The moment came. Pulling the pin from one of the grenades with his teeth, he dropped it back into the basket a second before pulling the bomb-release cord. Then he snatched up the basket, hung over the side of the cockpit, and tossed the basket accurately onto the deck of the leading barge, hoping desperately that the timing of the fuse would allow him to get past before it went up.

The business of climbing up into the open and executing a left turn took his attention for a minute or two until the sound of a gigantic explosion rent the air. He levelled and gazed over the side at the gratifying scene below. It brought a chuckle. The single live grenade had set off the chain reaction he had wanted. Aided by the bombs that had exploded in the canal, the grenade had rocked the barges and sent washes of water to knock over the barrels of fuel and split open boxes of ammunition, spreading the subsequent fire that set off the rest of it.

The chuckle turned into an exultant laugh as he circled a hundred feet or so above the cut in the trees. Then, as he gazed down, an almighty roar signalled total success. Pieces of barge, boxes and barrels were flung into the air on tall spouts of water as the whole consignment exploded with a sound that would be heard by the Germans waiting desperately for the barges. It would also be heard back at base. He had done it! He had done it!

He felt immensely tired now—more tired than he had ever felt in his life. Sitting back in the total contentment of flying, he watched the sun going down in a blaze of red. It seemed very beautiful—not a bit like fire and destruction any more. As he sat there, the sound of the engine began to fade and the mysterious music of the heavens rose up around him to lull his weary brain. The headache that had been with him for so long had gone now. A wonderful lightness replaced it.

He glanced over the side. Down below was Longbarrow Hill, and Tarrant Hall stood out clearly on its crest, as it always did. It looked so very peaceful down there, with sheep dotting the hillsides, and the women waving their laundry at him in greeting. He grinned and waved back, at peace with the world. Roland would be home tomorrow; Chris at the end of the month. The long summer holidays lay ahead of them all, and *Princess* was his for every day of them. What more could a man want? He smiled to himself as he wandered in the realms of yesterday, tomorrow and beyond. His eyes slowly closed.

He did not see the arrival of companions of the sky bearing black crosses on their wings; was not aware of the astonished disbelief on the faces of men who saw their most sought-after quarry, with his celebrated cerise scarf, flying alone and defenceless over German lines. The German leader fired an experimental round, ripping the wing from centre to tip. The men of the squadron all exchanged looks as the British aircraft weaved and floated through the heavens where the first stars were beginning to twinkle. Then they closed in on their prey.

Beneath the onslaught the Camel gradually disintegrated as fabric and woodwork were blasted apart. The wreckage began to fall, and as it did, it burst into flames, plunging like a torch to the ground well inside the German sector and exploding in a shower of sparks and flames.

For some while the Albatros squadron circled the spot looking down at it. Yet no man signalled in triumph to the other, and they finally returned to base in instinctive unison, each one inexplicably ill at ease over what had happened.

The wreckage burned for a long time as a bright glow in the darkness. But Sherry Sheridan remained undefeated. The blood that had been slowly oozing through his brain since he had hit his head on the newel outside his apartment six weeks before, had killed him several minutes before the Albatros squadron had come on the scene.

22

Early the next day, Chris paced up and down the office of his solicitor. "But, dash it all, she's still my wife until the divorce is granted," he said heatedly. "I have a right to know where she is."

"You know where Mrs. Sheridan is, sir. In Bath, with her aunt."

"Where in Bath?"

"I cannot tell you that. Dr. Deacon's solicitor will pass on any further communications from you, but he is not obliged to reveal the address. Dr. Deacon has stated that his daughter is in need of peace and quiet."

"What about my son?" cried Chris belligerently.

"He is safe and well with his mother—as he has been since you relinquished responsibility for them both in 1915." Cummings, the family solicitor, rarely smiled at the best of times, but now he frowned at Chris. "Mr. Sheridan, your wife is determined to bring this marriage to an end. Her petition is entirely based on the conviction that further union with you would be impossible on the grounds of incompatibility."

Chris was angrier than ever. "How the devil does she know that, when she won't even try it? I'm a different person, I tell you, and the man she wanted to marry is dead. And what about the distress of my son?"

"He will feel no distress at losing a father, sir. He is unaware that he has one."

As Chris left the solicitor's office and walked through the streets of London, he thought of those last words. David Sheridan had managed for three years without a father. Why was he attaching such importance to the relationship? His own father had been no more than an occasional impersonal visitor, and had even killed himself. But Chris grew hot with shame as he realized he had been about to abandon his own son too until Neil Frencham stopped him. Small wonder Marion was not prepared to give him another chance.

Finally, he decided not to contest Marion's divorce petition after all. He owed her and the boy their freedom. Maybe one day there would be another son, another girl that he could truly love. A girl like Laura.

The loneliness filling him instigated the desire to hold on to those who still belonged to him. After all, there was Rex and his beautiful wife, who both cared about him. He was not all alone in a world that had been snatched from him one day in 1915, spun round in a black frightening no-man's-land, then flung back into his lap last November.

He climbed the steps to Laura's flat slowly. A maid answered the door, saying her mistress was at the theatre for the matinée and would he care to wait. He had forgotten the matinée. Feeling tired and frustrated, Chris said he would wait. But he had only been sitting in the elegant room for ten minutes when the maid appeared again. Her face was white and scared. In her hand was a telegram.

"Oh, sir, this has just come for Mrs. Sheridan."

As Chris stared at it, the world turned momentarily back into a black frightening no-man's-land, and his whole life cried a protest that rang around his head like the scream of a shell. *No, not Rex! No, no,* not Rex, who had seemed immortal!

But the words he read were irrefutable. DEEPLY REGRET MAJOR R. A. SHERIDAN, DSO, MC, CROIX DE GUERRE, RAF, KILLED IN ACTION MAY 18. THE AIR MINISTRY EXPRESSES SYMPATHY. The pain now within him was greater than all the physical anguish he had suffered during the past few years. With the destruction of Rex came the destruction of hope.

Then it hit him. Laura! How would she sustain the loss? How would she find the strength to go on alone? In control of himself now, he knew she would be as desperately in need of help as he had been when he had made that impossible stunned journey to reach her last November.

He took a taxi to the theatre and went round to the stage door. They let him in, knowing who he was, and he went straight to the small partitioned office of the producer. It was hot and dark backstage, and the sound of a full chorus out front echoed in the dim ghostly bareness. It was a severe test to tell the producer why he had come, because speaking the words meant declaring Rex indisputably gone from the world.

"Damn," swore the man softly. "It'll finish her."

"No, it won't," Chris told him with difficulty. "I'll stay with her and make sure it doesn't."

Through the wings he could see Laura doing her finale. She looked superb in a shimmering black dress, her vivid happiness radiating to all those beyond the footlights who had forgotten sadness and despair for a while. The music was growing louder and faster as the climax approached, and Chris found a lump blocking his throat. How could he say the words that would end that happiness; put out the bright star?

There was a sudden thump, near enough to shake the ground beneath his feet, but the next one came before he had time to act on the shocked message that had reached his brain. It was in the street just outside, and the blast blew in the wall containing the huge doors through which they brought the scenery. He was already running towards Laura when the third bomb landed.

It had all happened before at Gallipoli—the screams, the agony, people falling, the smell of burning, fear and terror, destruction. But here, it was dark. The lights had gone out, and he fought with all his strength to scramble over bricks, beams, and broken scenery to get to the spot where he had last seen her standing. Then he saw the first flicker of flames.

Out among the broken plush seats people were screaming, fighting their way to the exits. On stage and behind it heavy arc lights, beams, and lumps of masonry were plunging down on the torn bleeding players trying to crawl to safety, their costumes made garish by the harsh daylight that was beginning to penetrate as more and more of the roof collapsed.

Chris climbed over bodies, coughing from the dust in the air, praying he would find her. As savage as any other person there, he pulled aside anything in his way to get to that spot centre stage, where Laura had been standing.

Cries for help were floating up all round him; shouts from rescuers who had come in from the street. But Chris went on with determination, finding superhuman strength. The stage was covered with masonry, wood and broken lights, but he attacked them like a man possessed, knowing she must be under there somewhere. He dug furiously in his urgency to reach her before it was too late. But he was too late, and he knelt there as tears drenched his cheeks, knowing this had been the only way for her.

Her face was cut and bruised, streaked with greasepaint and dust. Those magnificent eyes were closed as if in sleep, and her mouth was slightly parted in a final sigh. The vivid hair had fragments of brick and wood caught in the curls, but it glowed in the light of the fire spreading on the far side of the theatre. Chris tore more debris away, sobbing with the effort, until she was free of it. Then he bent and picked her up in his arms.

504

She felt so light and supple as he stumbled with her towards the place where rescuers and rescued were congregating by an opening onto the street. Out there, the sun was shining, and people were picking up the pieces of their lives. But Chris knew he was nobody from nowhere once more.

He saw the beam falling the instant before it hit him. Swinging round so that Laura's beautiful body would be unharmed, he took the whole weight of it on his back and shoulders. Even as he fell, he kept her in his arms.

HE AWOKE to a familiar scene. There was an ache across his shoulders and a burning sensation in his back. But this hospital was not peaceful, as the others had been. There were at least twenty men in the ward with him, and the windows showed a view of dirty chimneys in long rows on grey slate roofs.

As he reached for the glass of water on the locker, a nurse noticed the movement and gave him a brief smile as she hurried up the ward. A few moments later, a man he knew appeared beside his bed, studied him silently, and then said, "There's not much of a view from these windows."

"Better than that room with the brick wall."

The lean face looked relieved. "You know who you are, then."

"Yes. I'm not sure where I am."

"London. All the air-raid casualties were brought here. It's the nearest hospital to the theatre. Are you ready to talk about it?"

"What is there to say? Everyone's dead."

"You're not."

"I wish I were."

Bill Chandler shook his head. "No, Chris. That wouldn't be worthy of them. You have to carry on or their sacrifice will have been in vain."

He shook his head. "I'm so terribly tired . . . and I feel a hundred years old."

"So do we all. But when all this ends, which it soon will, the world will need men like you to set it to rights. It's the men of learning who keep the world turning. Think back on your Greeks and Romans for proof."

Chris gazed at him. "Roland and Rex were both more worthwhile people."

"Only because they had already proved their worth. You've been too busy trying to hang on to life to do that yet. They were also very courageous. Roland earned the Military Cross, and Rex has now been awarded a Victoria Cross to add to his other array of medals for gallantry. It's today's headlines."

Angling his head to look at the row of chimneypots, Chris said, "Rex was someone very special, and the VC honours him as such. But it can't bring him back . . . or Roland."

"No, but look at it this way. Roland qualified as a doctor, and in the process he came to terms with his fellows and set free a remarkable ability to see into the heart of human understanding. Those letters of his will speak for him in decades to come.

"As for Rex, he has already become a legend. In the history of aviation his name will glitter like one of the stars in the skies he graced. He died achieving the ultimate in flying skill, which will be an inspiration for the generations to come. For him, life only began when he climbed up into the skies. Now he will stay up there . . . and she'll be there with him."

Chris had to look back then at the man who had helped him through so much. "Where is Laura?" he asked huskily.

"Here at the hospital. The press is calling for a big public funeral for the two of them."

"No!" Chris felt anger sweep over him. "That must be stopped."

"Maybe they would want it that way."

"Rex was never that kind of man, and even Laura would find it outrageous. It must be held quietly, at Tarrant Royal. Rex would have liked that."

"Of course." Bill Chandler got to his feet, touching Chris's arm as he did so. "See what I meant about a man to set things to rights when the rest of us have gone mad?"

"No one can do that," he said heavily.

"But you can have a good try, Chris. That's all any one of them would ask of you."

THE FOLLOWING DAY Chris had another visitor. She wore a costume of a shade that reminded him of early bluebells.

"The only time I ever see you is when I'm flat on my back," he greeted her quietly. "How did you know I was here?"

"Several people told me, and it's in all the newspapers." She took the seat beside the bed. "I was worried that this might start up your old trouble again."

"I'm perfectly sane," he told her quickly.

"I didn't mean that. It was your leg and stomach wounds. But the nurse says it's mostly cuts and bruises." She put a bunch of carnations on the locker. "I couldn't bring the kind of flowers I knew you'd prefer, because this is London, not Somerset."

He remembered those snowdrops she had once brought him. "Did you come because I was a patient again and you felt you should nurse me?"

She shook her head. "You'll be out of here in a day or two."

"So why, then?"

"I suppose it was that . . . that I've lost people, too, and it seemed to me that we are both going to need someone to help us through for a while. Why not each other?"

He studied her pale features, trying to read what lay behind their grave expression.

"Perhaps it's too soon to mention the subject," she said quietly, "but how would you feel about abandoning the divorce?"

A week ago he would have known the answer to that. Now, he felt nothing; was drained and empty of emotion. "I don't really know," he said with honesty. "Perhaps it is too soon."

She got to her feet. "I shouldn't have rushed up here like this."

"No, don't go!" He took hold of her hand. "I really am glad to see you, and you should know by now that I have few social graces."

She sat down again, leaving her hand in his. Her face looked very drawn with the harsh light from the window on it, and he found he was not as empty of emotion as he had thought. "Marion, I'm truly sorry about Mike. I liked him."

She looked down at their linked hands. "It was difficult not to like him. He came along when I was lost and very frightened."

Marion seemed close to tears, and he gripped her hand tightly. "I understand. It's all right."

"And there's Rex . . . and Roland," she whispered. "So many have gone. I thought . . . those of us . . . who are left . . ."

"Bill Chandler said something like that yesterday," he reflected. "Something about their sacrifice not being in vain." For a moment or two Chris tried to put from his mind the thought of all those he would never see again, then looked up at her. "If we decide to abandon the divorce, could you forget all I did to you?"

"Not forget. But I could put it aside, Chris, if you could do the same about what I did to you."

"It was taken from my memory against my will," he reminded her. "When it returned two years later, it didn't seem half as bad."

Her brow wrinkled in a slight frown. "What do you feel about David now?"

"I want to get to know him, to teach him things, make sure he gets the chances he deserves."

"That's a very good start," she told him, then hesitantly broached another point. "I know and understand how you felt about Laura. I . . . I couldn't be a substitute for her."

For a second he saw again that joyous flame-haired girl as she had been the moment before she had died; then the vision faded.

"No one could be a substitute for Laura," he told her simply. "She was out on her own, and always out of my reach up there with Rex. But you and I have been friends for a very long time, and survived everything the world has thrown at us. There must be something we like about each other that we can build on."

She got to her feet then, almost as if frightened by what she had brought about. "Think it over, Chris. I'll come back this evening when you've had a little longer to sort out your feelings."

"All right," he nodded, feeling very tired. "Wear that same costume, will you? It's pretty. Reminds me of the bluebells in the copse at home."

She turned away up the ward, and he closed his eyes, still thinking of the bluebells. They would be over now, but they would come again next year.

Epilogue

It was a bright blustery day on the second anniversary of the end of the Great War, as it was known throughout the world. The war to end all wars! It had also ended many other things. Social structures had collapsed, governments had fallen, women had become emancipated, nations had changed their frontiers and allegiance; the soldiers who had survived had gone home.

Everyone had had enough of death. They wanted to *live*. But the reminders of the war were there, just the same. The maimed victims had to be cared for; many wounded died; and shellshocked creatures went violently mad long after the armistice on the eleventh hour of the eleventh day of the eleventh month of 1918.

The heroes who survived made a new start with what was left. They became doctors, lawyers, carpenters or bricklayers once again, and their names were forgotten. The heroes who had died had served their purpose, and the people were grateful. In case they, too, were forgotten, memorials were going up all over England.

Tarrant Royal had its own memorial, on the edge of the village green, where those it honoured had played as boys, and the whole village turned out for the unveiling service on that eleventh day of November in the year of 1920.

Chris looked round at those clustered in a semicircle before the memorial covered, at the moment, with a Union Jack. His glance took in Tessa as she stood nearby with Bill Chandler, who had finally persuaded her to marry him. The wedding was to be at Christmas, but they were not returning to Australia. Bill had decided to stay in the army and work with the many sad cases still wandering in the realms of fear. Tessa, a wealthy woman with Mike's money as well as her own, had bought a small farm at Tarrant Maundle and planned to raise pedigree sheep.

Chris's gaze then lowered to his own young son, David. He would soon be six years old, and it was already clear where his sights were set. Up in the skies! He had a very good brain, but Chris acknowledged that the boy would not use it in academic studies. A robust, extrovert child, David was keen on anything mechanical. Inheriting his father's artistic talent, he used it for drawing aircraft. For now, he copied them methodically from pictures, but soon he would be making his own modifications.

Next, Chris's glance moved to Marion, beside him. Their second child was due at any time. He hoped it would be another boy, who might discover the thrill of academic achievement and go on to those heights that he had once sought. But life was very fulfilling now. After the war had ended, his talents had been put to the additional use peacetime created. Working first on a committee to resettle boundaries, he had travelled back to Gallipoli and the Balkans as a linguist and cultural adviser. Now, he was occupying much the same role on a subcommittee of the League of Nations. It meant he was away a lot, but Marion was happy and contented in the kind of life she had always known. The times they spent together were satisfying and peaceful, charmed by complete understanding of each other's needs and interests.

As he looked at her, he thought how well pregnancy suited her. She was wearing blue again, and he noticed that the cameo brooch had been pinned into her scarf for this special occasion. It was typical of her to make such a thoughtful gesture, and he loved her for it. Then the rector was concluding his address.

"So we have all come here today to honour these brave men. But we shall continue to honour them in our daily work, in our family lives, and in our pledge to the future, so that their sacrifice will not have been in vain." He indicated the flag-covered monument. "The names on this memorial are all those of men from our village. We humbly salute them."

He nodded to Chris, who stepped forward to unveil a memorial bearing the names of both his brothers. His throat constricted as the flag fell away to immortalize their names for ever, and he felt immeasurably close to them in that moment.

Then he rejoined his wife and son for the singing of a hymn. With his hand in Marion's he gazed down on the blond head of their son. Thank God he would never know war!

Elizabeth Darrell

Elizabeth Darrell is one of several pen names used by Edna Dawes, a prolific writer whose subjects range from the Crimean War to the Bolshevik uprising. The military interest of her novels is hardly surprising, since her forebears have a long record of army service, and she herself served in the WRAC before she married; but *At the Going Down of the Sun*, she says, is an "especially important" book for her because it was inspired by her own family.

"My father was one of five brothers in khaki during World War I," she relates, "and the character of Rex is based on my father's older brother, who was killed in Belgium in 1917. I never met this uncle, but as a young girl I fell in love with him—just by seeing his photograph. He looked very romantic to me, and apparently he was a wonderful pal to everyone he knew, including his brothers, whom he always helped out when needed. My father was quieter and more introverted, and I based the character of Chris on him. Roland is similar to yet another uncle."

And the inspiration for Laura?

"I have sung on the stage and at concerts," explains the author, "and I'm very interested in the music-hall era. So I suppose that Laura is a manifestation of what I might have been. And inevitably some of my own traits have crept into her personality. Like Laura, I am fiercely defensive of loved ones and anything I hold dear. I am also hopelessly emotional and romantic!"

If the descriptions of aerial warfare seem particularly authentic, it is because the author researched the subject in great depth. This included meeting a former Royal Flying Corps ace. "Now eighty-seven years old, he shot down many German pilots during the war and actually attended the funeral of the Red Baron. His comments about flying and fighting were fascinating and very helpful."

Edna Dawes lives in Bournemouth with her husband, Ken, who recently resigned from the Ministry of Defence to run the business side of her career. The couple have been married for twenty-seven years, and Mrs. Dawes says her success has depended on his "encouragement and total support". Readers will be glad to hear that she is currently working on a sequel to *At the Going Down of the Sun*, which will follow the lives of Chris Sheridan's children during World War II.

GOLDENROD. Original full-length version © 1972 by Herbert Harker. Canadian condensed version copyright © The Reader's Digest Association (Canada) Ltd. 1984. British condensed version © The Reader's Digest Association Limited 1985.

SURPRISE PARTY. Original full-length version © 1984 by William Katz Enterprises Inc. US condensed version © The Reader's Digest Association Inc. 1984. British condensed version © The Reader's Digest Association Limited 1985.

THIS TIME NEXT WEEK. Original full-length version © 1964 by Leslie Thomas. British condensed version © The Reader's Digest Association Limited 1985.

AT THE GOING DOWN OF THE SUN. Original full-length version © 1984 by E.D. Partnerships Ltd. US condensed version © The Reader's Digest Association Inc. 1985. British condensed version © The Reader's Digest Association Limited 1985.